Shaun Hutson is a bestselling ~~author who~~ has written novels under nine different pseudonyms. He was one of eight bestselling authors taking part in the BBC's *End of Story* competition and has appeared in his first film. He lives and writes in Buckinghamshire with his wife and daughter and two pairs of Michelle Pfeiffer's shoes.

For more details on Shaun Hutson and his books visit www.shaunhutson.com

Find out more about Shaun Hutson and other Orbit authors by registering for the free monthly newsletter at www.orbitbooks.net

By Shaun Hutson

SHAUN HUTSON

OMNIBUS 1

SHADOWS

AND

NEMESIS

orbit

www.orbitbooks.net

ORBIT

First published in Great Britain in 2007 by Orbit
This omnibus edition @ Shaun Hutson 2007

Shadows
First published in Great Britain in 1985 by Star Books,
a Division of W.H. Allen & Co. plc
Copyright @ Shaun Hutson 1985

Nemesis
First published in Great Britain by W.H. Allen & Co. plc, 1989
Copyright @ Shaun Hutson 1989

The moral right of the author has been asserted.

A CIP catalogue record for this book
is available from the British Library.

ISBN 978-1-84149-644-3

Papers used by Orbit are natural, recyclable products
made from wood grown in sustainable forests and certified
in accordance with the rules of the Forest Stewardship Council.

Typeset in Times by Hewer Text UK Ltd, Edinburgh
Printed and bound in Great Britain by Mackays of Chatham Ltd, Chatham, Kent
Paper supplied by Hellefoss AS, Norway

Orbit
An imprint of
Little, Brown Book Group
Brettenham House
Lancaster Place
London WC2E 7EN

A Member of the Hachette Livre Group of Companies

www.orbitbooks.net

SHADOWS

For Niki with thanks
I'll slow down after the next *one*
maybe . . .

Acknowledgements

I would particularly like to thank Miss Eleanor O'Keefe of the Society for Psychical Research, whose help and kindness were invaluable during the research for this book. I am greatly indebted to her. Also, thanks, as ever, to everyone at W.H. Allen. Special thanks to Mike Bailey ('If there had been an Institute in Germany, the director's name would have been Beckenbauer'). To Bob Tanner ('Blood, guts and Rock and Roll, what a combination'). To Ray, Peter and Tony ('Enjoy your breakfast'). Indirect thanks to Iron Maiden, Liverpool F.C., John Carpenter, Tobe Hooper and Sam Peckinpah. And, finally, thank you to my Mum and Dad, for everything. And to Belinda who really saw this one through from beginning to end. For listening to me blow up buildings, murder babies and slaughter people, this one is for you, with love.

Shaun Hutson

'Hence, horrible shadow,
Unreal mockery, hence.'
— *Macbeth, Act III, Scene IV*

PART ONE

'Dreams are true while they last, and do
we not live in dreams?
— *Alfred Lord Tennyson*

'We're running with the Shadows of
the night . . .'
— *Pat Benatar*

1

New York

She had never seen eyes like his before.

She shuddered slightly as the piercing orbs bore into her like lasers. As if they were staring at her soul, searching for something elusive.

His eyes sparkled like chips of sapphire, the whites surrounding them unblemished but for the tiniest red veins which dared to intrude from his eye corners.

His gaze was unbroken even by the movement of his eyelids and, as he extended a hand to guide her backwards, she felt as if she were drowning in those eyes. As she lay on the couch she finally closed her own eyes, aware now only of his presence beside her.

The room was dark.

There was little sound.

An occasional cough, muted and self-conscious. And there was his breathing. It became more laboured as he stood over her and he spoke something softly to her.

Without opening her eyes, she raised her hands and began unbuttoning her dress, exposing her stomach. As she touched the flesh of her abdomen she winced and sucked in a painful breath. She almost screamed aloud as she felt his hands touch her flesh. His fingers stroked and probed the area around her navel, pausing every so often over one particular place.

Lucy West lay perfectly still, aware only of the hands which roamed her lower body with swift urgent movements but conscious of the three large intestinal growths which nestled like bloated parasites within her.

The first doctor had suspected ulcers. Nothing more. Tests had shown them to be steadily growing abscesses but a second opinion had revealed what she herself had always suspected.

The growths were tumours. Malignant and deadly.

7

She had been told that they were too far advanced for surgery to make any difference. At the most she might gain a six month reprieve. But of that there was no guarantee.

She felt the hands on her stomach, moving gently.

This man was her last hope.

Jonathan Mathias looked down at the woman on the couch, his brow furrowed. She was, he guessed, forty-five – five years older than himself but the ravages of pain and her disease had carved lines into her face which had no right to be there. She looked twice her age.

Mathias wore a dark shirt, the sleeves of which were rolled up displaying thick, hairy forearms. As he continued to play his fingers over the woman's abdomen, the muscles of his arms began to bulge, as if he were holding some great weight. His eyes rolled upward slightly so that she was only in the periphery of his vision. He began to breathe more deeply, less regularly. A bead of perspiration popped onto his forehead and trickled slowly past his left eye.

He sucked in a long breath and held it, raising his hands over the woman.

For what seemed like an eternity, neither moved nor made a sound.

Mathias' eyes twisted in the sockets, then he suddenly plunged his hands down, as if to drive them through Lucy West's body.

He grunted loudly, his palms pressed flat to her stomach. His fingers were splayed, quivering wildly. Then, with infinite slowness, he raised his hands an inch or two.

Beneath his palms, the flesh of her abdomen began to undulate in small, almost imperceptible, movements at first but then stronger, more urgent motions.

A bulge appeared just below her navel, the skin stretching to accommodate the pressure from within.

Mathias was shaking now, his hands still positioned mere inches from the woman's stomach. Perspiration sheathed his forehead and face, glistening in clear droplets on the light hair of his arms.

There was another movement, another undulation, this time an inch or two above her pubic mound.

Lucy West made no sound. No movement.

Mathias grunted something unintelligible, his fingers curling inward slightly as the third bulge began to stretch the flesh until it was shiny.

8

And finally, his eyes swivelled in the sockets until they were glaring down at his own hands.

At the movement beneath those hands.

His entire body jerked spasmodically, as if someone were pumping thousands of volts of electricity through him. His eyes narrowed to steely slits, his teeth clenched together until his jaw began to ache.

The skin just below Lucy West's navel began to split open.

Like tearing fabric, it began as a tiny hole then gradually lengthened into a rent about five inches long.

Mathias began to breathe rapidly, his cheeks puffing with each sharp exhalation. He noticed a pungent odour as a second tear began to form beneath the first.

There was no blood. Only the smell. A rancid stench of pus which rose like an invisible cloud to envelop him.

He watched as the third razor-thin cut began to open.

Still Lucy West did not move.

Mathias drew in a deep, almost agonised breath and held it, his face contorted unnaturally for interminable seconds. The sensation of heat which he felt in his fingertips began to spread until it seemed to fill his entire body. He felt as if he were on fire. More sweat dripped in salty beads from his face. He glared down at his hands.

At her stomach.

At the three long thin splits in her flesh.

'Yes,' he grunted, his fingers twisting inward like hooked claws.

Something began to move in the cut above her pelvis. Something thick and solid. It was ovoid in shape, a reeking egg-shaped lump which nudged through the cleft of flesh as if coaxed by Mathias. His eyes bulged madly in their sockets as he saw the growth and his body began to shake with increased intensity.

From the cut below her navel another bloodied clot of dark brown matter began to rise.

The three narrow tears drew back like obscene lips, expelling their foul contents, and Mathias reached feverishly for the three rotting growths, scooping them into his hands like so many putrescent eggs.

His fingers closed around the lumps and a single droplet of pus dribbled through and ran down his arm as he raised both hands into the air above the unmoving body of Lucy West.

9

Mathias kept his eyes fastened on the trio of wounds, now slightly reddened at the edges. He closed his eyes tightly, body still shaking, the growths held aloft like grisly trophies. A vile stench surrounded him, almost palpable in its intensity, yet he seemed not to notice it. As he snapped his eyes open once more he looked down to see that the three rents had closed. The skin looked as smooth and unblemished as before he had begun.

For a moment he stood sentinel over her motionless form.

Another man, younger than Mathias, came forward carrying a shallow stainless steel bowl. He held it before Mathias who slowly lowered his arms, opening his hands to allow the growths to tumble into the bowl with a liquid plop. The man handed Mathias a towel, then retreated back into the shadows.

'Sit up,' Mathias said to the woman, his voice a low whisper.

Lucy West struggled upright, aided by Mathias' outstretched hand, and once more she found herself gazing into those hypnotic twin orbs of blazing blue.

'It is done,' he told her.

Lucy coloured slightly, aware that her dress was still open. With shaking fingers she began to button it once more. Mathias noticed her slight hesitation as she reached her stomach, the flicker of anxiety behind her eyes as she reached her navel.

He beckoned to his assistant and the younger man returned, carrying the bowl. Mathias took it from him and held it before Lucy.

She looked in at the growths. They reminded her of rotten plums but for their pale colour. The dark tinge which they'd had earlier seemed to have drained from them, creating the small amount of blood which was puddled in the bottom of the bowl.

She touched her stomach tentatively, both relieved and surprised to find that there was no pain. She pressed harder.

No pain.

It was at that point she broke down.

Tears flooded down her cheeks and she gripped Mathias' hand, as if threatening to wrench it off. He smiled thinly at her, those brilliant blue eyes twinkling with an almost blinding iridescence.

Another man, also dressed in a dark suit, approached from the other side and placed his hands on Lucy's shoulders, guiding her away from

10

Mathias who walked forward towards the swelling cacophony of shouts and applause which filled the hall. As the lights inside the building were flicked on once more he gazed out at the dozens of people who stood watching him. Dozens? Hundreds? He wasn't sure how many. Some could not stand because they were in wheelchairs. Some could not clap because they had withered limbs. Some could not see him because they were blind.

He raised his arms once more, a gesture designed to encompass them all.

The applause and shouting did not diminish for some time, not in fact, until Mathias turned and walked off the stage, the cries still ringing in his ears.

And some of them were cries of pain.

2

Mathias entered his dressing room and slammed the door behind him, as if eager to be away from any more prying eyes. He leant against the door, wiping the sweat from his face with one blood-smeared hand.

He crossed to the washbasin on the far side of the small room and turned the cold tap, splashing his face with water. As he straightened up he gazed at his own reflection in the mirror above.

Jonathan Mathias was a powerfully built man, his jaw square and heavy. Clean shaven and carefully groomed, he looked younger than his forty years, particularly when his eyes sparkled as they did now. Nevertheless, his forehead was heavily lined and his thick eyebrows, which strained to meet above the bridge of his nose, gave him a perpetual frown. He dried his face and sat down at his dressing table. Even now he could hear the persistent applause generated by those who had yet to leave the hall.

It was like this every time. At every meeting.

He held three a week. The one today had been conducted in a large red-brick building on New York's West Side. Next time it might be in Manhattan, Queens or the Bronx. Or maybe somewhere in one of the city's more affluent areas. Over the years he had found that the rich needed his attentions as badly as anyone else.

Those he didn't reach in person could see him twice a week on CBS, his hour-long television show attracting an audience in excess of 58,000,000. He was known throughout the country and most of Europe for his abilities as a psychic but, of the man himself, little had ever been revealed. He spoke with a New York accent but the harder edges had been smoothed off and he came across as a cultured man, though he was respected and ridiculed in roughly equal proportions. There were those who still branded him a fraud and a charlatan. With an annual income of 20,000,000 dollars, the barbs seemed to cut less deeply than they might otherwise have done.

He smiled at his own reflection and began wiping his face with a paper cloth.

There was a light rap on the door and Mathias turned in his seat as if he were expecting to see through the partition.

'Who is it?' he asked.

'Blake,' a distinctively English voice told him.

'Come in,' he called, his smile broadening.

As David Blake entered the room, Mathias studied the newcomer warmly.

He was twenty-eight, about five-ten, dressed in a pair of faded jeans and a sweatshirt which, despite the folds of material, could not disguise the powerful frame beneath it. A packet of cigarettes bulged from one of his pockets and, as the young man sat down, he took one out and lit it up.

'Very impressive,' he said, re-adjusting the tinted glasses on his nose.

'It isn't intended to create an impression, David,' said the psychic. 'You know that.'

'Well,' Blake told him, smiling, 'That's exactly what it does. Like it or not. I should know, I was in that audience tonight. It's remarkable.' He drew hard on his cigarette. 'I've seen scores of faith-healers, most are just elaborate con men. But not you. There's something more.'

'Thanks for the compliment.'

'I saw you cure a terminally ill woman tonight, without even touching her, without using any tools or implements.'

12

'Is it really that important to you, David?' the psychic asked. 'Must you discover how I perform my . . .'

'Miracles?' Blake interrupted.

Mathias smiled.

'I was going to say "work".'

'Yes, it is important. I don't like mysteries,' the Englishman admitted. 'Besides, if I do find out, there's a lot of potential there.'

'For a new book you mean?'

Blake was almost reluctant to admit it.

'Yes,' he said, shrugging his shoulders. He took a last puff on his cigarette and ground out the butt in an empty matchbox.

'Have you ever heard of a man called José Arrigo?' the psychic asked.

Blake nodded.

'He was killed in a car crash in Brazil in 1971. He was a psychic too. They called him the Phantom Surgeon. He performed nearly half a million operations between 1950 and 1960, all done with scissors and penknives and without anaesthetic. He removed a vaginal tumour the size of a grapefruit from a woman using only a kitchen knife. He was locked up a couple of times for practising medicine unlawfully.

'But people always went back to him. They went to him for the same reasons they come to me. Desperation and fear. When conventional methods won't work, people seek help elsewhere.'

'Arrigo claimed his powers came from Christ,' Blake protested. 'I've never heard you mention religion. You're a faith healer without any faith.'

'Power,' said Mathias, flatly. 'A strange choice of word, David.'

'Why? The abilities which you possess are a power of some description,' Blake said. 'I'd like to know where that power comes from.'

'It comes from here,' said Mathias, jabbing his own chest. 'From inside *me*.'

The two men regarded one another in silence for a while. Blake rubbed his chin thoughtfully. In the past five years he had written five world-wide best-sellers, all concerned with different aspects of the paranormal (supernatural was a word he disliked for it implied something which defied logical or reasoned explanation and Blake was concerned only with facts). But, in that time, he had never encountered anyone like Mathias. The man was an enigma, exuding a mixture of menace and benevolence.

Then there was his power.

Blake had seen it at close quarters during the five days he had been with the psychic and so far had collected reams and reams of questions but no answers – a wealth of research material with no discernible potential. He felt frustrated, almost angry with himself and he harboured the nagging conviction that the key to Mathias' power was something simple, so simple it could be easily overlooked. Mass hypnosis? Thought projection? He wondered if such tricks of the mind could work on the massive scale required for Mathias to retain credibility. Was it possible for someone to hypnotise an audience of 58,000,000 viewers so that they believed everything they saw? Blake doubted it.

He took a paper tissue from his pocket and began cleaning his glasses.

'Inside all of us there is another person,' Mathias continued, quietly. 'An inner being. Some psychics and probably you yourself know it as the Astral body. Jung called it "the other within". In ancient times it was thought to be the soul.'

Blake listened intently as the other man continued.

'To someone with the knowledge, the power, the Astral body can be projected and manipulated.'

'But lots of people are able to project themselves astrally,' Blake insisted. 'The sensation of leaving your own body is a skill which can be learned.'

'I agree.'

'Then I don't see what this has to do with your *powers*.'

'I can control other people's Astral bodies.'

Blake frowned, taken aback by the psychic's words.

Mathias returned his gaze, unblinking. There was a twinkle in his blue eyes which Blake mistrusted. He studied the American as if he were an exhibit in a museum, trying to muster his own thoughts.

'It's impossible,' he said, softly.

'Nothing is impossible, David,' the psychic told him.

14

Blake shook his head.

'Look, I know plenty about Out of the Body experiences,' he countered. 'I've met dozens of people who've had them but the idea of being able to manipulate someone else's Astral body . . .' The sentence trailed off as he felt his body stiffen. It was as if every muscle in his body had suddenly contracted and the sensation forced a gasp from him.

Overwhelming, numbing cold enveloped him until he felt as if his blood were freezing in his veins. He shuddered, the flesh on his forearms rising into goose-pimples. He caught sight of his own reflection in Mathias' dressing room mirror and his skin was white. As if the colour had been sucked from him.

Mathias sat unmoved, his eyes never leaving the writer who was quivering violently.

He felt light-headed, a curiously unpleasant sensation of vagueness which made him grip the chair as if anxious to assure himself he were not going to faint.

Mathias lowered his gaze and Blake felt the feeling subside as quickly as it had come. He sucked in a deep breath, the warmth returning to his body. He shook his head and blinked hard.

'Are you OK?' Mathias asked.

The writer nodded.

'Very clever, Jonathan,' he said, rubbing his arms briskly.

'*Now* do you believe me?' the psychic wanted to know. 'Can you deny what you felt?'

'If you have this ability, how does it tie-in with the faith-healing?'

'I can reach inside people. Inside their minds. Their bodies.'

'Then it would have to be a form of hypnosis, to make the subject believe you could cure them.'

'I can't give you all the answers, David,' Mathias answered. 'It doesn't matter. You can't alter the facts, you can't deny what you saw on that stage tonight or what you yourself felt here in this room.'

Blake chewed his bottom lip contemplatively.

'Think about what I've said,' the psychic added.

Blake got to his feet and announced that he had to get back to his hotel. The two men shook hands and the writer left the building via a side entrance. The sun outside was hot and the pavement felt warm

15

beneath his shoes in a marked contrast to the coolness of Mathias' dressing room.

He spotted a cab and sprinted across the street, clambering into the vehicle. As the cab pulled away, Blake glanced over his shoulder at the red brick building, watching as it gradually disappeared from view.

Jonathan Mathias sat before the mirror in his dressing room contemplating his own features. He rubbed his cheeks and blinked hard. His eyes felt as if they had grit in them but, as he sat there, he allowed his hands to drop to his thighs, one hand curling into a loose fist. He inhaled and looked down, his fist opening as he did so.

Cradled there, now shrunken and withered like rotten, foul smelling prunes, were the three growths he'd taken from the body of Lucy West.

3

As the yellow cab threaded its way through the tapestry of traffic which clogged the streets Blake looked abstractedly out of the side window. On all sides of him buildings poked upward at the sky like accusatory fingers, probing towards the occasional banks of white cloud which passed overhead. Apart from the odd smattering of cloud and the vapour trails of aircraft, the sky was a deep blue and the sun continued to bathe the city in its warm rays. But, for David Blake, there was nothing pleasant about the warmth because with it came humidity. He could feel the perspiration on his back and face despite the fact that the air conditioning was on. The driver was a fat negro who looked as if he'd been wedged behind the steering column. As he drove his chubby fingers tapped out an accompaniment on the wheel to the music which screamed from the radio. It partially covered the insistent roar of engines, the blare of hooters and the shouts and curses of other motorists.

16

Blake allowed his head to loll back onto the seat. He could feel the beginnings of a headache gnawing at the base of his skull. A condition which wasn't helped when the driver slammed on his brakes to avoid colliding with a bus which had stopped abruptly in front of him.

'Motherfucker,' growled the driver and swung the cab out and around the bus, giving the other driver the finger as he drove by.

Up ahead, Blake saw his hotel and he fumbled in his pocket for his wallet, pulling out a ten dollar bill. The taxi came to a halt and Blake got out.

'How much?' he asked.

'Call it an even five,' said the driver, pushing down the arm on the meter.

'I haven't got anything smaller,' Blake said, offering the ten. 'Keep it.'

The hotel doorman nodded politely as he passed but Blake didn't return the gesture. He walked across to the reception desk and got his key.

He rode the lift to the thirty-second floor, casting a cursory glance at his fellow passenger – a porter who was cleaning his ears out with the corner of a tissue.

On reaching his room he closed the door and locked it, glad to be away from things for a few hours. The room was large, comfortable without being extravagant. The writer crossed to the window and stood gazing out for a moment or two, looking over the vast expanse of greenery which was Central Park. It looked particularly inviting amidst the grey concrete and glass of the city.

He turned and walked into the bathroom where he turned both taps. As the water splattered noisily against the enamel he undressed and lay on the bed, eyes closed. He lay there for a moment or two, massaging the back of his neck in an effort to dispel some of the tightness there, then he got to his feet and wandered back into the bathroom where he switched off the taps. Steam swirled around the room like hot fog and Blake retreated, deciding to allow the water to cool off slowly. He remembered that he hadn't eaten since breakfast so he called room service.

As he sat waiting for the snack to arrive he thought back to the incident with Mathias earlier on. Had the psychic actually managed to summon Blake's own Astral body? Was it some form of mind control? He pulled a pad towards him and scribbled:

1. Hypnosis
2. Mind control
3. Astral Body

Beside the last of the three he drew a large question mark and underlined it. Mathias obviously had more weapons in his psychological arsenal than Blake had first thought. But, manipulation of someone else's Astral body? He shook his head, his thoughts interrupted by a rap on the door. Blake got to his feet and was about to open it when he realized he was still naked. He grabbed a towel and hurriedly wrapped it around his lower body. The maid swept in, deposited the order on the table near the window then swept out again.

Blake devoured two of the sandwiches then headed towards the bathroom once more.

The steam still swirled around and Blake almost slipped over on the tiles. He lifted the toilet seat and urinated noisily; then, discarding the towel, he turned towards the bath.

There was a body floating in the water.

Blake took a step back, nearly overbalancing, his eyes glued to the naked body before him. The entire corpse was bloated, the skin tinged a vivid blue, mottled from what appeared to be a long time in the water. The mouth was open, lips wrinkled and cracked. A swollen tongue protruded from one corner.

Blake shook his head, studying the face more closely.

He may as well have been looking in a mirror.

The corpse in the bath was identical, in every detail, to himself. He felt as if he were staring at his own dead body.

The writer clamped his eyes shut, screwing up the lids until white stars danced in the blackness. He raised both hands to his head and sucked in a deep breath.

'No,' he rasped.

When he opened his eyes again the corpse was gone. Nothing remained in the bath but the water. No bloated body. No deceased look-alike. Just water.

Blake swallowed hard and reached out a hand tentatively towards

18

the surface of the water, staring intently at it as if he expected the apparition to appear again.

He heard soft chuckling and snapped his head around.

It was coming from the bedroom.

The writer felt peculiarly vulnerable and he found his breath coming in low, irregular gasps. He edged towards the bathroom door gripped by a hand of fear which tightened its hold as he drew closer.

Again he heard chuckling.

By this time, his fear had gradually become anger and he stepped into the room without hesitation.

It was empty.

He walked across to the bed. Checked the wardrobes. Passed through into the other part of the room which served as a sitting room.

Empty.

Blake looked around him, wiping perspiration from his face. He was alone in the apartment. He headed back towards the bathroom but, as he reached the door he slowed his pace, his eyes scanning the bath anxiously.

There was no corpse floating there.

The writer licked his lips, finding that his mouth was dry and chalky. He crossed to the sink and spun the tap swallowing large gulps of cold water, then he turned towards the steaming tub once more.

The water looked inviting enough but it was a long time before he would step into it.

4

Oxford

'There was so much blood. It was everywhere. All over the floor and the bed. There was even some on the wall. It wasn't at all like you see on films or the television. When I shot her in the face her head just seemed to cave in and then the blood started spurting everywhere. I suppose that's how it got on the wall over the bed, it was like a fountain, especially from her neck. I suppose that's where the pellets hit her jugular vein. That is the big vein isn't it? The jugular? You see when you fire a shotgun at someone from close range there isn't time for the shot to spread. A shotgun cartridge is full of thousands of little lead pellets but, when you fire from close range, well, it all comes out in one lump. And I was standing very close to her. I had the barrel about an inch from her face.

'There was some thick, sticky looking stuff on the pillow. It was sort of greyish pink. I think it must have been her brain. I'd seen sheeps' brains in butchers' shops and it looked a bit like that so I suppose it must have been her brain. Anyway, when I went to move the body this sticky stuff got on my hands. It felt like . . . like porridge. I left her on the bed in the end.

'The baby had woken up, I suppose it was the noise of the gun. It was crying, not loudly, just the way it does when it wants feeding. I went into the nursery and picked him up but he wouldn't stop crying. Perhaps he was frightened of the blood and the smell. That's another thing they never tell you on the TV. Blood smells. It smells like copper. When there's lots of it.

'Well, I just dropped the baby on its head. It didn't move after that so I thought it was dead. I picked it up again and took it back to the bedroom and put it on the bed beside my wife.

'I'd left the hacksaw under the bed earlier so I . . . I only had to decide which one to start with. I cut up the baby first. The left arm to start with. I cut it off just below the shoulder but as I started cutting it screamed. I think the bang on the head only stunned it. The arm was almost off when it started to scream but it didn't move again after that. I cut off its right leg at the hip. It was easy, I suppose it's because the bones are still soft with babies. It wasn't even a year old you see. There was more blood, more than I'd expected. Especially when I cut the head off. It's funny isn't it? You wouldn't think a body that small could hold that much blood.

'I left the pieces on the bed then I started on my wife. It was harder cutting her leg off, sawing through the bone was like cutting wood but the noise was different, a kind of squeaking and all this brown stuff dribbled out of the bone. Was that the marrow? I suppose it was. Well, it took me nearly an hour to cut them both up and I was sweating when I'd finished. Butchers must be really fit, I mean, they cut up meat every day don't they? I was tired when I'd finished and I noticed that there was some . . . mess . . . well excrement. You know . . . faeces on the bed. I didn't know that happened when someone died. That they sh— that they messed themselves.

'I cut one of my wife's breasts off. I don't know why. Just to see what it was like I suppose. I expected it to puncture like a balloon, you would wouldn't you? But it didn't. I just cut most of it away and left it with the other pieces. So much blood though. So much blood. Funny really.'

Kelly Hunt reached forward and switched off the tape recorder.

She had heard that particular tape half a dozen times in the last week. This had been the first time she'd managed to sit through it without feeling sick. She pressed the 'rewind' button and the recorder squealed as the spools spun in reverse. She stopped it, pressed 'play'.

'. . . So much blood. Funny really.'

She heard her own voice.

'And the dream is always the same?'

'Always. It never varies. Every detail's the same.'

She switched it off again and ran a hand through her shoulder length brown hair.

Beside the tape recorder on the desk in front of her there was a manilla file and Kelly flicked it open. It contained details of the voice which she'd been hearing on the recording, facts and figures which made that voice a human being. To be precise, Maurice Grant, aged thirty-two. An unemployed lathe operator by trade. Married for ten years to a woman four years younger than himself named Julie. They had a ten-month-old baby, Mark.

Kelly had been working with Grant, or rather studying him, for the last seven days. The recording was one of many which she and her colleagues had made.

She scanned the rest of the file which contained further personal details about Grant.

He'd been unemployed for the last six months and, during that time, relations both with Julie and their baby had become somewhat strained. Kelly tapped the file with the end of her pencil. And now the dreams. Grant always described them as dreams – never

21

nightmares – though God alone knew that what he experienced during sleep was the stuff of nightmares. His detached attitude was unnerving. The tape recordings were made while Grant slept. By a combination of drugs, he could be unconscious and yet able to speak and to relay what he saw in his dreams. Dreams had been studied and monitored in the past, Kelly was well aware of that, but never before had the subject actually been able to speak whilst in that dream state, to describe the events as dispassionately as if he had been a mere observer.

In order to achieve this state, Grant was given a shot of Tubarine, a muscle relaxant usually used in medicine with a general anaesthetic, which would induce sleep. Prior to that, he would receive 45mg of methylphenidate orally. The drug was a derivative of amphetamine, designed to stimulate the brain. By this combination, Grant could be *forced* to dream. His observations would then be recorded as *he* saw them in his mind's eye.

Kelly knew, from what she had read in the file, that Grant and his wife had rowed constantly during the months leading up to his arrival at the Institute. Their marriage was virtually in ruins and Grant sometimes spoke of her with ill-disguised anger. An attitude mirrored, subconsciously, in his dreams.

Kelly looked at the tape recorder once more, wondering whether to run the tape again. Instead she got to her feet and crossed to one of the filing cabinets propped against the far wall. Above it was a photograph of her and several of her colleagues. It had been taken just after she joined the Institute fifteen months ago, two weeks after her twenty-fourth birthday.

The Institute of Psychical Study was a Victorian building set in six acres of its own grounds. The weather-beaten walls were the colour of dried blood, crumbling in places. The entire structure, covered by a clinging network of ivy, looked as though it would collapse but for the tangled tendrils which snaked over it like so much flexible scaffolding. Repair work had been done to the west wing of the building, the renovated brickwork and the large plate glass windows looking strangely innocuous set against the latticed panes which dotted the remainder of the structure. The building was being dragged, albeit reluctantly, into the twentieth century. Telephone wires ran from the pole on the roof, suspended above what had once

22

been belching chimney stacks but were now sealed holes. The gravel driveway snaked away through the grounds until it joined the main road which led into Oxford itself. Cedars and poplars lined the drive like sentinels.

However, if the outside of the building belonged to a more sedate age then the interior was modern, almost futuristic.

The old rooms had, over the years, been converted into fully equipped offices and laboratories, the latter providing every means possible for Kelly and her companions to pursue their very specialized work.

Since its inception in 1861, the Institute had devoted itself to the investigation and recording of all manner of psychic phenomena ranging from hauntings to telekinesis. Within the vast library beneath the building was housed the accumulated knowledge of over a century. But, during that time, progress had intervened and investigators now used word processors in place of quill pens and electronic surveillance equipment instead of eye-witness accounts and hear-say.

Kelly had plenty of eye-witness information about Maurice Grant including the file which she now slid from the drawer and glanced at.

It held an EEG read-out, one of the many taken from Grant while he slept. She studied it and shook her head. The puzzle was there before her.

The reading comprised five lines, four of which were flat, each representing an area of the brain.

It was the fifth line which interested her.

The tracer had drawn huge, irregular strokes across the read-out, indicating an incredible amount of activity in one particular part of the brain.

Kelly was convinced that it was the portion which controlled the dream response.

And yet she knew that there should have been movement shown on *all* the lines.

But for that one area of activity, the reading may as well have been taken from a corpse.

The office door opened.

'Excuse me barging in, Kelly,' the familiar voice apologised. The man smiled curtly, almost as an afterthought. 'I wanted to speak to you.'

Dr Stephen Vernon smiled again; a twitchy, perfunctory smile which never touched his eyes. He was what people euphemistically call portly. In other words he was fat. The buttons of his grey suit strained against his belly as if threatening to fly off at any moment. He kept his jacket fastened but, like his trousers, it was immaculately pressed. His trousers bore creases sharp enough to cut your hand on, even if the legs of the garment were two inches too short. For a man of fifty-five, Vernon had thick, almost lustrous hair which glistened beneath the fluorescent lights. His moustache, by comparison, resembled the type sprayed on advertising posters by paint-happy kids. He had narrow, hawkish features and eyes the colour of slate nestled between his puffy eyelids. Grey suit. Grey hair. Grey eyes. Vernon resembled an overcast day. But, there was a darting energy in those eyes and in that overweight frame. Vernon was as thirsty for knowledge now as he had been when he'd first joined the Institute nearly twenty-five years ago. He'd spent the last twelve years as its President. He was respected by all his investigators, both for his knowledge and also for his dedication. He would sit, most nights, in his office on the second floor, reading reports. Staying there until the small hours sometimes, when he would wander the empty corridors and deserted labs, enjoying the silence. He felt secure within the confines of the Institute walls.

He lived eight or nine miles away but it was almost with reluctance that he returned home at the end of the day.

Home.

Could he still call it a home when he was afraid to return there?

As Kelly passed him she caught the familiar smell which seemed to follow Vernon everywhere. It surrounded him like an invisible cloud. The scent of menthol. He was forever sucking cough sweets although Kelly had never known him to have so much as a cold. He carried a packet in his breast pocket as if it were a pen. As she sat down he popped another one into his mouth.

'Have you made any progress with this fellow Grant?' Vernon asked her.

Kelly told him about the tape recordings, the recurring nightmares.

'Yes, yes, I know about those,' he said, tersely. 'I heard something about an EEG.'

Kelly's green eyes met his slate grey ones and they held each other's stare for a moment.

'May I see it?' he asked.

Kelly handed the read-out to Vernon who shifted the menthol sweet to the other side of his mouth and ran an expert eye over the series of lines.

'His brain was stimulated?' Vernon asked.

'Yes,' Kelly told him. 'We're still using amphetamines.'

Vernon nodded slowly. As a qualified doctor he realized that the read-out should show much more activity. He was one of four physicians at the Institute. At least one had to be present to administer the drugs to subjects and to check that there were no adverse effects on them.

'Then why is only one area of the brain affected?' he mused aloud.

'It certainly looks as if it's the area which controls unconscious thought,' said Kelly. 'The reading taken when Grant was awake showed only minimal movement in that region.' She pointed to the jagged line.

The older man sucked hard on his sweet then folded the read-out and laid it on her desk.

'Run another EEG while he's awake,' Vernon instructed. 'Then another while he's asleep – but not a drug induced sleep. I want to see the normal readings.'

Kelly nodded.

Vernon crossed to the window and peered out at the rapidly falling rain.

'This is very important to me, Kelly,' he said, clasping his hands behind his back. He reminded her of a headmaster about to admonish an unruly pupil.

'The reading from the EEG would certainly seem to indicate that the subconscious mind is capable of functioning independently,' he said. 'We have to find a way to unlock that hidden area.'

She detected a note of something akin to desperation in his voice. It seemed only a matter of time before they discovered what they sought but time was one thing Vernon didn't seem to have. Not a day passed without him visiting Kelly in the lab or her office, and it had been that way ever since the research began. There was an urgency

25

about his interest which eclipsed his usual involvement. He was becoming obsessive. And Kelly couldn't help but wonder why.

She studied his broad back as he stood by the window, his fingers knotted together like fleshy hemp.

'I'll see about running the EEG now,' she said.

Vernon turned, nodded and swept towards the door.

'I'll be in my office,' he told her. 'Let me know as soon as you have the results.'

She smelt the menthol as he passed her, closing the door behind him. Kelly heard his footsteps echo away down the corridor.

She slipped the file back into its drawer, then she herself left the room, walking briskly towards the stairs which would take her down to the laboratories.

Stephen Vernon slumped into the leather chair behind his oak desk and closed his eyes, massaging the bridge of his nose between thumb and forefinger. In the outer office he could hear the clacking of his secretary's typewriter. An accompaniment to the tattoo which the rain was beating on his window.

His office was large, as befitted a man of his seniority. It was one of the few rooms in the building which acknowledged a debt to the past. The wood panelling of the wall smelt as if it had been newly waxed, as did his desk. Opposite him, above the empty fireplace, was a very passable copy of Gericault's '*Brigadier Gerard*'. Vernon regarded the painting blankly, his mind occupied with other thoughts.

Could the EEG of Grant's brain truly have exposed an area of the mind previously hidden? The key to the subconscious. After all these years, could he dare to hope for a breakthrough?

He sat forward in his chair and glanced at the phone.

The call might come in five minutes. Five hours. Five weeks.

But he knew it would come and he had been waiting a long time for it.

26

5

Paris

'Keep your eye on the watch.'

Jean Décard focused on the gently twisting gold object, watching as it spun gently around. His breathing had slowed to low rasping inhalations punctuated by small gasps as the air escaped his lungs once more. His right arm was propped up on the arm of the chair, his left lay across his lap.

'Clear your mind of all other thoughts,' the voice told him. 'See nothing but the watch. Think about nothing other than what I tell you.'

The voice seemed to be coming from a hundred miles away.

It was, in fact, coming from Alain Joubert who was kneeling less than a foot or two from him. It was he who was holding the watch, allowing it to turn gently back and forth at the end of its chain.

Beside him, Michel Lasalle watched the proceedings with a pen gripped firmly in his hand, prepared to write down whatever might happen. At thirty-eight, Lasalle was two years older than Joubert but his full features and ruddied complexion did not testify to that fact. They had worked together for the past two years and, during that time, had become close friends. Now Lasalle watched intently as Joubert leaned closer to Décard whose eyelids were beginning to sag.

'You are asleep but you will still hear my voice, you will still answer my questions,' said Joubert. 'Do you understand?'

Décard nodded slowly.

'Do you understand? Say so.'

'Yes.'

'What is your name?'

'Jean Décard.'

'Where do you live?'

'Sixteen Rue St Germain.'

'How old are you?'

'Forty-one.'

Lasalle scribbled something on his pad then watched as Joubert pulled a pen light from his breast pocket and shone it into Décard's eyes.

'He's well under,' Joubert said, noting the vastly dilated pupils of his subject. 'But, let's just make sure.' He reached back to the table nearby and retrieved two long, thick needles each one about six inches in length. Then, he pinched the skin together on the back of Décard's right hand and, slowly, pushed the first needle through.

There was no reaction from the subject.

'Can you feel any pain, Jean?' asked Joubert.

'No.'

He took the second needle and, opening the loose fist which Décard had made, Joubert pushed the second needle under the nail of the man's index finger until only the eye showed. There was no blood.

'Do you feel anything?'

'No.'

Joubert nodded to his companion then hastily tugged the wicked points free.

Lasalle pulled a pack of playing cards from his pocket and handed them to Joubert, standing behind his friend so that he himself could see the slim plastic sheets. The first one was the seven of spades.

'Which card am I holding, Jean?' Joubert wanted to know.

Décard told him.

'And this one?'

'Queen of Diamonds.'

Correct.

'Next?'

'Ten of Clubs.'

Correct.

They went through thirty cards and Décard was accurate every time.

'Amazing,' said Lasalle. 'Are you going to bring him out of it now?'

'In a moment,' Joubert assured him. Then to Décard;

'Jean, I am going to think of some words, I want you to tell me what they are. Do you understand?'

'Yes.'

Joubert scribbled them down on a piece of paper and showed it to his companion. Décard recited the words almost rhythmically.

Joubert smiled. Lasalle could only shake his head in amazement.

'There will be a bus crash in the Rue De Bologne.'

The words came from Décard with the same monosyllabic drone as before. Both Joubert and Lasalle looked at him aghast.

'Repeat what you said,' Joubert urged.

Décard obliged.

'When? How do you know?'

'I can see the . . . the dead.' He was staring blankly ahead as if looking beyond the walls to something which neither of the other men could see.

'When is this crash going to happen?' Joubert asked.

'At 3.49 today.'

Lasalle shot an anxious glance at his watch.

'It's 3.46,' he told Joubert.

'How do you know this is going to happen?' demanded Joubert.

'I can see it now.'

'How many will die?'

'Four.'

'Is it possible?' Lasalle said, his brow furrowed. 'Can he really be seeing it?'

Joubert didn't answer, he merely looked at his own watch and saw that it was 3.48.

Jean Décard was silent for a moment then his mouth opened wide in a soundless scream, his face contorted into an attitude of fear and pain so profound that Lasalle took a step back. Then, with a low grunt, Décard blacked out.

It took the two men ten minutes to revive him and, when he finally regained consciousness, he still seemed to be in a trance. He tried to rise but fell, knocking a table over in his wake. After another thirty minutes he was coherent. His face was ashen with dark smudges beneath his eyes.

Joubert gripped his arm.

29

'Jean, can you remember anything of what you said earlier?'

Décard shook his head.

'I feel sick,' was all he could say.

Lasalle fetched him a glass of water.

As the three men sat in the room there was a loud knock on the door and, a moment later, a thick-set man in the uniform of a gendarme entered.

'Which one of you is Jean Décard?' the uniformed man asked.

'I am,' Décard told him.

'And you two?' the gendarme wanted to know.

'We both work here at the Metapsychic Centre,' said Lasalle.

'Step outside, please,' the gendarme said.

'No,' said Décard. 'It's all right, what have I done wrong?'

'Nothing, Monsieur,' said the gendarme almost apologetically. 'I must tell you that I have some bad news.'

Lasalle and Joubert exchanged glances then directed their gaze back at the uniformed man. He had lowered his voice slightly, an air of expectant solemnity having fallen over the room.

At approximately 3.49 that afternoon, Jean Décard's twelve-year-old daughter had been killed when a lorry smashed into the bus which was carrying her and her schoolfriends home. There had been three other deaths besides hers.

'Where did it happen?' Décard wanted to know, tears filling his eyes.

The gendarme cleared his throat.

'The Rue De Bologne.'

6

Michel Lasalle scooped some cool water into his hand and then swallowed it. He felt the tranquilizer stick in his throat for a moment so he swallowed more water, finally wiping his hands on the towel beneath the sink. He exhaled deeply and replaced the bottle of pills in his trouser pocket. He probably didn't need them any longer but, over the past eighteen months since the death of his wife, the pills had become more than a mere psychological crutch for him. Lasalle was dependent on them, not daring to see what life was like without the temporary relief which they brought him. He did not look like a man who had suffered a nervous breakdown, but then again his wife had not looked like the kind of woman who would die suddenly of heart failure aged thirty-five. Lasalle had retreated within himself after her death. Like a snail inside its shell he refused to be coaxed out again by work or friends. He became hermit-like in his existence.

He and his wife had been childless. She had been infertile – her Fallopian tubes blocked. Lasalle's parents had been dead for five years so he had no one to turn to for help. His breakdown had begun slowly, gradually building up like some festering growth within his mind until, finally, his sense of reason seemed to collapse in on itself like a crumbling house.

He turned away from the sink and looked across the room at Joubert who was sitting with his eyes closed, a cigarette held delicately between his fingers. The ash looked as if it were about to drop off and Lasalle watched as smoke rose lazily from the butt. When Joubert finally moved his hand, the ash dropped on to the carpet. Lasalle quickly trod it in.

Lasalle had worked at the Metapsychic Centre for the past twelve years. The building itself stood on the outskirts of Paris, a large modern looking edifice constructed in the shape of a gigantic 'E'. Its smooth unbroken lines gave it the appearance of having been hewn from one single lump of rock instead of constructed piece by piece. Lasalle lived less than a mile from the building, near the church yard where his wife was buried.

As he stood looking absently around the room he tried to drive thoughts of her from his mind but every time he heard of more death, as he had with Jean Décard's daughter, the memories came flooding back.

His companion, Joubert, had no such ties. He was single once more after the break-up of his marriage but then again he had always found the attractions of work infinitely more exciting than those of domesticity. Despite being two years younger than Lasalle, he was possibly better informed on the subject of the paranormal, having worked at the Laboratory of Parapsychology in Utrecht for six years where he completed his Ph.D in Human Science. He had then moved on to the University of Frieburg in West Germany prior to joining the Centre in Paris.

Joubert was every bit as different psychologically from his colleague as he was physically. There was a certain detached coldness about Joubert. He saw everyone and everything as potential sources of information and study. The human volunteers with whom he worked might as well have been laboratory rats. He showed as much feeling towards them. To Joubert, work was everything and knowledge was the pinnacle. He would never rest until he had solved a problem. And, at the moment, he and Lasalle had a problem.

'Precognition.'

Lasalle looked at his companion.

'The business with Décard,' he continued. 'The telepathy and then seeing the accident. It had to be precognition.'

'Do you think he was able to see the vision because it involved his own daughter?' Lasalle asked.

'Décard didn't know that his daughter was going to be one of the victoms, only that there was going to be a crash and that four people would die. The fact that he was close to one of the victims isn't necessarily relevant.'

'What are you getting at, Michel?'

'We've tested three people, the same way we tested Décard. The results were the same in each case. Each one showed varying forms of telepathy while hypnotised but, with the other subjects, we brought them out of their trances earlier, quicker. If they had been under longer then they too may have been able to predict future events.'

Joubert got to his feet, crossed to the pot of coffee on the table nearby and poured himself a cup. He took a sip, wincing slightly as it burned the end of his tongue.

'Depending upon the susceptibility of the subject,' he continued, 'there's no limit to what future events we can learn of.' A brief smile flickered across his face. Not only could disasters be averted but foreknowledge of events could have its more lucrative side as well. Could a subject foresee the outcome when a roulette wheel was spun? Joubert took another sip of his coffee, this time ignoring the fact that it was so hot.

'But Décard was only able to foresee the future while in a hypnotic trance,' Lasalle interjected.

'Which points to the fact that there is an area of the mind which *only* responds when the subject is unconscious. An area previously unexplored, with the capacity for prophecy.'

There was a long silence finally broken by Lasalle.

'I'd better phone the Institute in England,' he said. 'They should know about this.'

'No,' said Joubert. 'I'll do it.'

He stepped in front of his colleague and closed the door behind him, leaving Lasalle somewhat bemused. Joubert went to his office and sat down behind his desk, pulling the phone towards him. He lifted the receiver but hesitated before dialling.

'An area of the brain previously unexplored,' he thought. His features hardened slightly. The discovery, once announced, would undoubtedly bring fame to himself.

It was not a secret he wanted to share.

He tapped agitatedly on the desk top, cradling the receiver in his hand a moment longer before finally dialling.

Kelly picked up the phone and pressed it to her ear.

'Kelly Hunt speaking,' she said.

'Miss Hunt, this is the Metapsychic Centre.'

She did not recognise the voice.

'Lasalle?' she asked.

'No. My name is Joubert. Alain Joubert. We have not spoken before.'

Kelly disliked the coldness in his voice. She was, however, relieved that he spoke excellent English, just as Lasalle did. Her French was no more than passable.

'Did you receive the copy of the tape recording I sent?' Kelly asked.

'We did,' he told her.

'Have you made any progress with your subjects?'

There was a hiss of static. A moment's hesitation.

'None,' Joubert said, flatly. 'That is why I am phoning. I feel that it is unproductive for our two Institutes to continue exchanging information on this subject.'

Kelly frowned.

'But it was agreed from the beginning that the research would be undertaken jointly,' she protested. 'You would use hypnosis, we would use drugs.'

There was a long silence.

'The subject we tested today was unreceptive,' the Frenchman lied.

Kelly sensed the hostility in the man's voice and it puzzled her.

'Lasalle told me that your use of hypnosis seemed to be showing results,' she said, irritably. 'He was very happy with the way the research was going.'

'My colleague has a tendency to exaggerate,' Joubert said, stiffly.

'Where is Lasalle? May I speak to him?'

'He is working. I don't want to interrupt him.'

'So you have nothing at all for me?'

'No.' The answer came back rapidly. A little too rapidly. Kelly moved the receiver an inch or two from her ear, looking at it as if she expected to see Joubert magically appear from the mouthpiece. His abrupt tone was a marked contrast to that of Lasalle who she was used to conversing with.

Kelly thought about mentioning the EEG on Maurice Grant but, before she could speak, Joubert continued.

'I have nothing to tell you, Miss Hunt,' he said, his tone unequivocal.

'I'll have to tell Dr Vernon . . .'

Joubert cut her short.

'Do as you wish, Miss Hunt.'

He hung up.

Kelly found herself gazing once again at the receiver. She slowly replaced it, her initial bewilderment at the Frenchman's unco-operative attitude subsiding into anger. Joubert had come close to being downright rude. Why, she wondered?

Was he hiding something?

If so, what reasons would he have?

She shook her head, annoyed both with Joubert and also with her own over-active imagination. Nevertheless, he had no right to sever contacts between the two Institutes. Perhaps she should speak to Lasalle, she had his home phone number.

Maybe *he* would contact her tomorrow.

She sighed and sat back in her chair, listening to the rain beating against the window behind her. On the desk before her lay the newest EEG read-out taken only an hour earlier from Maurice Grant. It looked normal, in marked contrast to the one taken when he'd been in the drug-induced state. She ran an appraising eye over the lines but could see nothing out of the ordinary. There was another polygraph scheduled for later, while Grant was asleep. Perhaps there would be discrepancies on that one, some kind of clue to the tricks his mind was playing.

She thought about his description of the nightmare. The ritualistic slaughter of his wife and child.

She wondered what it all meant.

7

Oxford

It was well past midnight when the powerful lights of the Audi cut through the gloom of the driveway which led up to Stephen Vernon's house. The rain which had been falling all day had stopped, to be replaced by an icy wind which battered at the windows of the car as if trying to gain access. Vernon brought the vehicle to a halt and switched off the engine, sitting for a moment in the darkness.

The moon was fighting in vain to escape from behind a bank of thick cloud and what little light it gave turned Vernon's house into some kind of dark cameo, silhouetted against the mottled sky. He sat there for a few more seconds then pushed open his door and clambered out. The wind dug freezing points into him, nipping at his face and hands. He ran towards the front door and fumbled for his key, his breath clouding around him as he exhaled. He finally found the key and opened the door, snapping on a light as he did so. The hall and porch were suddenly illuminated, driving back the shadows from the front of the house.

The building was surrounded by a high wooden fence which creaked menacingly in the high wind, so Vernon was effectively shut off from his closest neighbours. The house was tastefully decorated throughout, walls and carpets in soft pastel colours combining to form a welcoming warmth as he stepped inside and shut the door behind him, forcing out the wind.

There was a large envelope on the doormat. Vernon saw the postmark and hesitated a second before stooping to retrieve it. He carried it into the sitting room and dropped it on the antique writing bureau which nestled in one corner of the spacious room. Then he crossed to the walnut drinks cabinet, took out a tumbler and a bottle of Haig and poured himself a generous measure. As he drank he looked across at the letter on the bureau. When he put his glass down he found that his hand was shaking.

He passed into the kitchen, the fluorescents buzzing into life as he touched the switch. He hunted through the freezer and found a frozen chicken casserole. It took fifteen minutes according to the packet. Vernon decided that that was all he wanted to eat. He hadn't much of an appetite. He left the polythene-wrapped casserole in a pan of water and wandered back into the living room, ignoring the letter on the bureau which he still had not opened.

The stairs creaked mournfully as he made his way to the first floor. From the window on the landing he could see the two houses on either side. Both were in darkness, the occupants obviously having retired to bed. Vernon resolved to do the same thing as soon as he'd eaten.

Five doors led off from the landing: the door to his own bedroom, that of the spare room, then the bathroom and another bedroom which had once belonged to his son who had long since departed.

The fifth door remained firmly locked.

Vernon paused before it for a moment, swallowing hard.

He extended a hand towards the knob.

A window rattled loudly in its frame, startling him. He glanced at the door one last time then walked across the landing to his bedroom. Once inside he removed his suit, hung it up carefully and changed into a sweater and a pair of grey slacks. Without the restraint of a shirt, his stomach was even more prominent and it sagged sorrowfully over his waist-band. He tried to draw it in but lost the battle and allowed the fat to flow forward once more. Vernon glanced at the clock on the bedside table and decided that his supper would soon be ready so he flicked off the bedroom light and headed back across the landing once again.

As he approached the locked door he slowed his pace.

His breathing subsided into low, almost pained exhalations as he stood staring at the white partition. He felt his heart beating that little bit faster.

There was a loud crack and Vernon gasped aloud.

He spun round in the gloom, searching for the source of the noise.

The wind howled frenziedly for a second, its banshee wail drowning out his own laboured breathing.

The sound came again and he realized it came from inside the locked room. But it was muffled.

He took a step towards the door, freezing momentarily as he heard the sound once more – harsh scratching, like fingernails on glass.

On glass.

He realized that there was a tree directly beside the window of the locked room, it must be the wind blowing the branches against it. Nothing more.

Vernon felt angry with himself for having reacted the way he did. He glared at the door for a moment longer then turned and padded down the stairs. He walked through the sitting room, unable to avoid looking at the envelope which still lay on the bureau like an accusation. He would open it after supper he promised himself.

He sat in the kitchen and ate his supper, discovering that he wasn't as hungry as he thought. He prodded the food indifferently, left the plate on the table and went into the sitting room. There he poured himself another scotch and slumped in one of the high-backed armchairs near the fire. It was cold in the room and Vernon pulled his chair closer to the heat, watching as the mock flames danced before him. He downed most of the whisky, cradling the glass in his hand, gazing into its depths.

Above him, a floorboard creaked.

Merely the house settling down, he thought, smiling humourlessly.

He got to his feet and filled his glass once again, finally finding the courage to retrieve the letter. He slid his index finger beneath the flap of the envelope and started to open it.

The strident ringing of the phone pierced the silence and nearly caused him to drop the letter.

He picked up the receiver hurriedly.

'Stephen Vernon speaking,' he said.

'I tried to ring earlier but there was no answer.' The voice had a strong accent and Vernon recognized it immediately.

'What have you got for me, Joubert?' he said. The Frenchman told him about Décard's prophecy.

'Does anyone else know?' Vernon asked.

'Only Lasalle,' the Frenchman told him.

'You haven't told Kelly?'

'No, you told me not to give her any information other than that which you authorised.'

'What about Lasalle?'

'He knows nothing of what is going on, he . . .'

Vernon cut him short.

'I mean, what has he told Kelly?'

'She doesn't know anything about what happened today and from now on *I* will deal with her.'

Vernon nodded.

'Vernon? Vernon, are you there?'

He seemed to recover his senses.

'Yes, I'm sorry. Look, Joubert, when will you know for sure if the experiments have been successful?'

The Frenchman hesitated.

'That's difficult to say. I feel we *are* very close to a breakthrough though.'

'How long before you know?'

'You are asking for too much, Vernon. I cannot say for certain.'

'Then guess. I have waited too long for this.'

'You are not the only one.'

There was a long silence finally broken by Joubert.

'Two days, perhaps a little longer, but I can't promise.'

Vernon sighed.

'Remember, Kelly is to know nothing.'

'And if she becomes suspicious?'

'I'll take care of that.'

Joubert seemed satisfied by the answer. The two men exchanged cursory farewells then the Frenchman hung up. Vernon stood motionless for a moment then replaced the receiver, returning to his fireside chair. And his drink.

And the letter.

He opened it and pulled out the piece of paper inside. Vernon took another gulp from his glass before unfolding it.

Before he started reading he glanced, as he always did, at the heading on the paper:

FAIRHAM SANATORIUM

8

New York

Blake studied his reflection in the bathroom mirror. He shook his head. It was no use. The bloody bow-tie wasn't straight. As if he were grappling with some kind of angry moth, he pulled it from his throat and tried to fix it once again. He'd been trying for the best part of fifteen minutes but, so far, the bow-tie had resisted all attempts to remain in place and Blake was beginning to lose his temper. He looked at his watch and saw that it was 8.00 p.m., a fact confirmed by the announcer on the TV in his room who was in the process of introducing another re-run of *Magnum*.

Mathias had said he would pick the writer up at his hotel at 8.15. The drive to Toni Landers' house would take twenty or thirty minutes depending on New York's night time traffic.

Toni Landers was well known, by reputation anyway, to Blake. A stunningly beautiful woman who had, two nights ago, been presented with an Emmy for her performance in one of the year's biggest television spectaculars. At present, she was packing them in on Broadway in a production of Joe Orton's *Entertaining Mr Sloane*. Tonight she was giving a party to celebrate her triumph. Mathias had been invited and had cajoled Blake into joining him. The writer had been to showbusiness parties before and they usually bored him stiff, self-congratulatory affairs with clashes of ego which ranked alongside the collision of Mack trucks. In Los Angeles they were intolerable, the acting fraternity turning out in force to every one. Parties in L.A. were given for any reason, usually not good ones. Has-beens, no hopers, and would-be starlets thronged these almost masochistic gatherings where egos were flayed unmercifully. He had met writers who had yet to find a publisher but spoke as if they were the natural successor to Hemingway, encountered actors and actresses who spoke of the promised part they had in some forthcoming epic but who would more than likely end their days doing what they did between bit parts – either waitressing or cleaning cars.

New York parties were a little different. They had their share of bores, as did any party, but Blake found he could tolerate them slightly more easily because there didn't seem to be quite such a wealth of pretension in New York as there was on the West Coast. Nevertheless, he still did not relish the prospect of the party but Mathias had asked him, so what the hell?

He was still struggling with his bow-tie when his phone rang. Blake left the recalcitrant thing in its slightly lop-sided position and picked up the receiver.

'Yes.'

'There's someone for you in reception, Mr. Blake,' the voice told him.

He looked at his watch. It was 8.15, on the nose.

'I'll be straight down,' he said and, flicking off the lights in his room, he closed the door behind him and made for the elevator.

Blake recognised Mathias' chauffeur standing by the reception desk. He was taking a few hurried puffs on a cigarette which he reluctantly extinguished when he saw the Englishman step out of the lift. Blake approached him, by-passing a red faced man who was complaining about the soap in his room being dirty. The chauffeur smiled.

'Mr Blake,' he said, 'Mr Mathias is waiting for you in the car.'

The two of them headed out of the hotel lobby with its uncreasing drone of Muzak, into the symphony of car hooters, shouts and roaring engines which was 59th Street. A police car, its sirens blaring, swept past adding its own noise to the cacophony which already filled the air.

The chauffeur motioned Blake towards a waiting black Cadillac and, as he drew close, the door was pushed open for him. The writer felt like some kind of cheap gangster about to be taken for a ride. The grinning face of the chauffeur behind him and the inscrutable look of Mathias, who was seated in the back, added to that feeling.

The psychic was dressed completely in white. White suit. White shoes. White shirt. The only thing which broke up the pure expanse was a red tie. It looked as though Mathias was bleeding.

'Good evening, David,' Mathias said.

Blake returned the greeting. He wondered whether he should mention what had happened the previous afternoon. The voice in his room. The body floating in his bath. He eventually decided against it. He glanced across at Mathias, affording himself a swift appraising glance. The white suit seemed to make the psychic's feature's even darker, the areas around his eyes and neck almost invisible. His hands were clasped gently on his lap and Blake saw that he wore two rings, each one gold set with a large pearl.

'What sort of day have you had?' Mathias asked him.

'Considering I spent most of it in a library, not very inspiring,' the writer told him.

'More research?'

Blake nodded.

'Still trying to unlock the secrets of the mind?' the psychic chuckled.

Blake ignored the remark.

'Why did you ask me to come to this party with you tonight?' he enquired.

Mathias shrugged.

'You and I have become friends over the past six days and I thought you might enjoy it.' He smiled. 'You might, you know.'

'Are any of the guests clients of yours?' Blake wanted to know.

'Some of them have, from time to time, sought my help if that's what you mean.'

'In what ways?'

41

'Is it important?'

'I'm just curious.'

'You're curious about a lot of things, David,' the psychic said and looked out of the side window. Blake studied his profile for a moment then he too turned his attention to the busy street. On either side of them skyscrapers rose like concrete geysers spewed forth from the ground, black shapes surrounded by the dark sky. Many were invisible but for the odd lights which shone in some of their windows. It looked as if someone had taken hundreds of stars and hurled them at the gloomy monoliths. Multi-coloured neon signs burned above shops and cinemas, theatres and clubs, as if millions of glow worms had been sealed inside the glass prison of a bulb. The city that never slept was preparing for another night of insomnia.

'I asked you before why it was so important to you to discover the extent of my powers,' Mathias said, interrupting the relative silence which had descended.

'And I told you it was because I don't like mysteries,' Blake told him. 'I've never yet run into anything that's beaten me.' There was a firm, almost harsh, resolution in the writer's voice.

Even in the gloom of the Cadillac's interior the psychic's icy blue eyes sparkled challengingly.

'There are some things . . .'

Blake cut him short.

'. . . which it's better *not* to know.'

Both men laughed.

'Well, reeling off the world's worst clichés isn't going to stop me either,' the Englishman chuckled. A minute or two passed, then, his tone more sombre, Blake continued:

'This power, this manipulation of another person's Astral personality, if you do possess such abilities would you ever consider using them as a weapon?'

Mathias looked genuinely puzzled.

'I don't follow,' he said.

'If you can control someone else's mind and actions then there's no limit to what you can do. To what *you* can make others do.'

The cadillac was beginning to slow up. Ahead Toni Landers' house was a blaze of light.

42

'Do you think I haven't thought of that?' said Mathias, smiling.

The chauffeur brought the Cadillac to a halt behind a bright red Porsche then clambered out and held open the door for Mathias. Blake didn't wait for the same treatment, he stepped out of the other side, tugging once again at his bowtie as he did so.

The tarmac driveway which swung in a crescent before Toni Landers' house looked more like a car showroom. Blake counted five cadillacs, a couple of Transams, the Porsche and a silver Plymouth Fury as he and the psychic walked towards the porch.

The house itself was a three storey affair, flanked on two sides by trees, beneath which were carefully tended flower beds. Strings of light bulbs had been hung from the house to the tree branches and it seemed as if a light glowed in every single window of the building. The house looked like a beacon amidst the darkness. It was set slightly on a hill, the nearest neighbour being about five hundred yards away. Even from outside Blake could hear music and, as the door was opened, it seemed to sweep over him like a wave, mingling with the sea of conversation.

A maid took Mathias and Blake through into a spacious sitting room which looked slightly smaller than a ballroom. A staircase rose in a spiral from the centre of the room, leading up to the first floor landing where Blake could see people standing in groups or in couples chatting amiably. Two huge chandeliers hung from the ceiling like clusters of diamonds. But, for all the apparent pomp and grandeur, the house had a homely feel to it. There was a piano in one corner of the room and five or six people were gathered around it. Blake noticed that one of them, a man about his own age, was playing softly, quite oblivious to the sound coming from the Hi-Fi. The writer recognized him as the lead singer with the band currently topping the American charts. He spotted three or four well-known actors and actresses, and a film director he'd seen once or twice on TV.

Toni Landers was standing by the large open fireplace, a glass of champagne cradled in her hand. She was talking to a distinguished looking grey-haired man in his fifties who was perpetually pulling at the end of his nose, doubtless in an effort to disguise the fact he was trying to see even further down the front of her dress than the plunging neckline allowed.

43

Blake had seen her before but never this close and she was even more beautiful than he had first thought. She was not a tall woman, barely five-six with the benefit of long stiletto heels. She wore a black dress slashed to the thigh which, each time she moved, allowed him a glimpse of her smoothly curved legs. A shock of red hair cascaded over her shoulders, catching the light every so often to glisten like rust-coloured silk. She wore a black choker around her throat, a single diamond set in its centre.

'Our hostess,' said Mathias, nodding in her direction. He took a glass of champagne from the tray offered to him by a tubby waitress and Blake did likewise.

It was as he sipped his drink that Blake noticed eyes were beginning to turn in the direction of Mathias. In his white suit, the psychic was even more prominent, but Blake had the feeling that if he'd turned up in a worn-out sports jacket the effect would have been the same. A young woman approached him.

'You're Jonathan Mathias aren't you?' she said, the words sounding more like a statement than a question.

'Yes,' he answered, shaking her hand gently.

He introduced Blake who noticed that the girl seemed somewhat preoccupied. She smiled perfunctorily at the writer then turned back to Mathias, pausing to look at him as if he were a piece of precious metal before returning to the group from which she had emerged.

A man approached and shook hands with the psychic. Blake observed that same look of reverence on his face as had been on the girl's. He too smiled thinly at the writer then wandered away as if in some kind of daze. Blake looked on with mild amusement as this happened half a dozen times. With people constantly approaching Mathias, Blake felt rather like a dog waiting at its master's table for any scraps to fall. When a girl in a royal blue trouser suit spoke to him he was so surprised he hadn't time to answer before she walked away.

Blake took another glass of champagne when the tray came round. It wasn't that he particularly liked the bloody stuff, but at least it was better than standing there with his hands in his pockets looking like Mathias' bodyguard instead of a guest.

'They obviously know you,' he said to the psychic as the last of

44

his admirers left them. Blake drained what was left in his glass and put the empty receptacle down on a nearby table. God, what he wouldn't give for a pint. Even a can of luke-warm larger would have been respite enough from the endless flow of champagne.

'I've never met any of those people before, David,' said Mathias, sipping at his own drink.

'They know you by reputation then,' Blake insisted.

'People are fascinated by what they don't understand.' Those ice-blue eyes sparkled. 'And they can never hope to understand me.'

'Is that the way you want it?' Blake asked.

'That's *exactly* the way I want it.'

The two men regarded one another coolly for a second, eyes locked together like magnets.

'Jonathan.'

Both of them turned to see Toni Landers standing there. She was smiling broadly, displaying a set of teeth which testified to her dentist's expertise.

'I'm so glad you could come,' she said and kissed the psychic on the cheek.

'You look beautiful, Toni,' Mathias told her. 'It's a long time since we spoke.'

She turned to face Blake who returned her smile when he was introduced.

'Congratulations on winning the Emmy, Miss Landers,' he said, motioning to the statuette behind them on the mantelpiece.

'Thank you, please call me Toni,' she said. There was a soft lilt to her voice which made Blake feel immediately at ease. She was, indeed, a very beautiful woman combining a radiant innocence with that of uncultivated sexuality.

'What do you do, David?' she asked him.

'I'm a writer.'

'What sort of books?'

'Non-fiction, about the paranormal, the occult. That kind of thing.'

'No wonder Jonathan brought you along,' she said, slipping her arm through that of the psychic. 'Are you writing about him?'

'I'm trying.'

Toni chuckled and reached for her drink which was still on the

45

mantelpiece. A ten by eight colour photo in a gilt frame perched there. It was of a young boy, no older than eight, Blake guessed. The lad was smiling, his blond hair brushed back behind ears which were a little too large. Freckles dotted his nose and cheeks in an irregular pattern and, even beneath the glass of the frame, his eyes seemed to twinkle with some kind of untold mischief.

'That's my son, Rick,' she told him. 'He's staying with a friend for the night.'

Blake cast a quick glance at Toni's hands and saw no wedding ring. He wondered who the father of the child was.

'Do you have any family, David?' she wanted to know.

'I can hardly look after myself let alone anyone else,' Blake said, smiling.

'Rick means everything to me. If you had a child of your own you'd understand that,' Toni said, her tone changing slightly. She looked longingly at the picture. At her son. It had been an unwanted pregnancy and she had been through a difficult delivery. She still saw Rick's father now and again. He was one of the top publicity men at Twentieth Century Fox. He still lived in the house they had bought together those nine years earlier. It had been his idea that they live together. He was nearly ten years older than Toni so she listened to what he said. In those early days she would have done anything for him. She had worshipped him and he had adored her. The young, in-demand actress who had played two leading rôles within six months of moving to L.A. from her home in Virginia. She was already commanding fees of half a million a picture and things seemed to be running smoothly until she became pregnant. At first he had accused her of sleeping with other men but, when he finally came to his senses, the decision he made had been swift and, she realized with the benefit of hindsight, almost inevitable.

Get an abortion or get out of the house.

A child, he had told her, would wreck her career. Besides, *he* wasn't ready to be a father. For the first time in their relationship, Toni had followed her own instincts. There would be no abortion and if it meant the end of the relationship then so be it. She had gone to stay with a friend, working for as long as she could, finally doing voice-overs for commercials when she was too far advanced.

46

The combination of the break-up and the difficult birth, (a Caesarean delivery after sixteen agonising hours of labour) had brought her close to a breakdown. For three months she languished in the throes of such deep post-natal depression that her close family sometimes feared for her sanity but slowly she began to drag herself out of it. She decided that she had to go on for her baby's sake. It had been a monumental effort but somehow she had managed it. She began work five months later, helping out an old friend who was with the script department of MGM. Another month and she had, after rigorous exercise and dieting, regained her shapely figure and, another two months after that, she was offered a leading role in a highly successful ABC series. It had been a small step from there back to films and now, to the stage.

'How is Rick?' Mathias asked her, also studying the photo.

'He's fine,' she beamed, the very mention of the boy's name causing her to perk up. 'Jonathan was a great help to me when I started work again after having Rick,' she explained to Blake.

The writer nodded.

'So, what are you working on next?' he asked her.

Her smile faded slightly.

'Well, I have a slight problem there.'

'I'm sorry,' Blake said.

'No, what I mean is, I have a decision to make and it's difficult.'

'What kind of decision?' Mathias asked.

She drained what was left in her glass and placed it alongside the Emmy on the mantelpiece.

'I've been offered a part in the next *Star Wars* movie but it means being away from home for three or four months. I don't think I want that. I don't want to be away from Rick that long.'

'But you've been on location before and left him,' said Mathias.

Toni shook her head.

'Only for days at a time, like I said, here we're talking about months.'

'So what are you going to do?' Blake asked.

'I guess I'll have to refuse the part.' She sighed. 'Shit, my agent won't be very pleased, he busted his ass to get it for me.'

'But your son won't be alone. He'll have people to look after him won't he?' said the writer.

47

Toni turned to Mathias.

'Will he be OK, Jonathan? You can tell me. You can . . . *see*.'

Mathias sighed.

'I hope you didn't invite me here tonight to perform some kind of fairground trick,' said the psychic.

'Please, Jonathan.' There was a note of pleading in her voice.

'What do you want to know?' he said, quietly.

A look of relief passed across her face.

'I want to know if Rick will be all right if I decide to leave him for a few months,' she said.

Mathias nodded. He sat down in one of the chairs beside the fireplace while Toni turned and scuttled off towards a door on the far side of the room. Blake watched with interest. He had an idea what Mathias was going to do, his suspicions confirmed when he saw Toni return moments later with a pack of cards. He could see immediately from their size that this wasn't an ordinary pack and, as she placed them on the coffee table before the psychic, he saw that they were Tarot cards.

An expectant hush seemed to fall over the room. The Hi-Fi was silent, only the steady click-click of the needle in the run-off grooves came from the speakers. Someone eventually removed it.

The group gathered around the piano stopped singing and turned towards Mathias who was gazing down at the cards, his brow knitted into deep furrows.

Blake took a step backward, his eyes straying alternately from Mathias to the cards and then across the table to Toni Landers. She, for her own part, settled in the chair opposite the psychic. He reached for the pack and shuffled it thoroughly.

'Now you,' he said to her, passing over the cards.

She followed his example and handed them back. Some of the other guests moved closer, anxious to see what was happening.

A large breasted girl with straw-coloured hair giggled.

Mathias shot her a withering glance, his eyes homing in on her like radar-guided rapiers. The colour drained from her face and she clutched the arm of the man she was with, as if seeking protection from those piercing orbs.

Satisfied that he would not be forced to endure any further

interruptions, Mathias proceeded to divide the cards into ten packs of seven. This done, he held the first pack, face down, before him.

'Pack one,' he said, his voice low and resonant in the silent room. 'That which is divine.' He laid it on the table.

'Pack two. Fatherhood.' That too he placed on the table, above and to the right of the first. 'Three. Motherhood.'

Blake and the others watched as he laid that one above the first pack, this time to the left.

'Four. Compassion. Five. Strength. Six. Sacrifice.'

Blake felt a slight tingle run up his spine and wondered if he were the only one.

'Seven. Love,' Mathias continued. 'Eight. The Arts. Nine. Health.'

Toni Landers shifted uncomfortably in her chair.

'Ten. Worldly matters.' Mathias sat back slightly. 'The Tree is complete,' he announced.

'Tree?' said someone behind him.

'The Tree of the Cabala,' Mathias answered without taking his eyes from the cards. He reached for the first pack and turned the card, repeating the process until all ten showed their faces.

Blake watched with interest; he had seen numerous Tarot readings over the years, all symbols usually carrying variant interpretations. He wondered how Mathias would read them? The psychic held one up.

'Number eight,' he said. 'A decision.'

Toni Landers kept her eyes on the cards, hands clasped on her knees.

The psychic reached for another card.

'Number seven. Travel.'

Blake noticed that Mathias' hand was shaking slightly as he reached for the next card. The older man swallowed hard and flipped it over for all to see.

'Sixteen. Change.'

'What kind of change?' Toni wanted to know.

Mathias fixed her in those powerful blue twin-points and shook his head almost imperceptibly.

'I don't know yet,' he said, turning over another card. It was a card of the Minor Arcana. The dagger.

There were eight cards lying away from the cabbalistic pattern made up by the remainder of the pack. Mathias chose one of these but he hesitated before he turned it over, his hand shaking more violently now.

'What's wrong?' Toni asked, her voice full of concern. 'What can you see? Tell me what you see.'

Blake, like most other people in the room was watching the psychic's quivering hand. He felt the chill begin to wrap itself around him more tightly, as if someone had clamped him in a freezing vice and was slowly turning the screw.

On the mantelpiece, the photograph of Rick Landers began to shudder, as if blown by some invisible breeze. 'Turn it over,' said Toni Landers, exasperatedly. Her breath was coming in short gasps now. 'I want to see the card. Tell me what *you* can see.'

The picture of Rick continued to vibrate, its movement unnoticed by all except the girl with the straw-coloured hair. She could not speak, all she could do was raise one finger in the direction of the photo.

'Jesus Christ,' said the man beside her, noticing the movement.

Mathias turned over the final card.

'Danger,' he said, breathlessly.

'What kind of danger?' Toni demanded, staring down at the card. 'Tell me.'

'Your son . . .' Mathias began, falteringly.

There was a loud crash as the glass in the photo frame exploded outward as if there were a charge behind it. Slivers of crystal showered the guests nearby and Blake found himself stepping back to avoid the cascade.

A girl near him screamed.

The photo toppled from the mantelpiece and clattered to the ground. Toni Landers tore her gaze from the Tarot cards and saw the remains of the picture lying close by.

As she reached out to pick it up something red and shiny appeared on the photo, welling up from a cut in the paper.

It was blood.

Toni froze, watching as more of the crimson fluid dribbled over the slashed picture.

Blake looked on, mesmerised by the incident.

It was Mathias who finally snatched up the frame and its contents. He laid it gently on the table before him.

There was no more blood. The photo was unmarked.

Blake glanced at the psychic and then at the pieces of broken glass which littered the carpet beneath the mantelpiece.

'What happened?' Toni Landers wanted to know. 'What does this mean?'

Mathias hesitated.

'Is something going to happen to my son?' Toni asked. 'Jonathan, tell me, please.'

He nodded.

'Is he going to die?' she demanded.

'I saw danger, I didn't say he was going to die,' the psychic said in an effort at consolation but it didn't work.

Toni cradled the picture frame in her hands and stared down at the face of her son. Tears formed at her eye corners but she fought them back.

'I'm not leaving him,' she said. 'Not now.'

Mathias swallowed hard then looked up to see that Blake was watching him. The writer seemed relatively unmoved by what had happened. The other guests slowly began to disperse, their conversation now kept to a discreet whisper. The psychic got to his feet and put a hand on Toni Landers' shoulder.

'Perhaps it would have been better if I hadn't done the reading,' he said.

'No,' she whispered, shaking her head. 'I'm pleased you did. Thank you.'

'Will you be all right?' Blake asked her.

Another woman joined them, slightly older than Toni. She smelt of expensive perfume. The woman crouched beside her and gripped her hand. Blake and Mathias wandered across the room towards the open French windows, leading out into the garden. A cool breeze had sprung up and it washed over the two men as they walked out on to the patio.

'What *did* you see?' asked Blake, when they were out of earshot of the other guests.

'You know how to read Tarot cards, David,' said Mathias. 'You saw what I saw.'

51

'You know what I mean,' the Englishman challenged.

'Her son is going to die,' said Mathias, flatly. 'Is that what you wanted to hear?' He walked across the lawn towards a large ornamental fish pond which lay beneath the drooping arms of a willow. Leaves had fallen from the branches and were floating on the surface of the water. The liquid gleam caught the bright lights of the house in the background.

'You didn't read that in the cards did you?' said Blake, not sure whether it was intended as a question or a statement.

'No.'

'Then how did you know the boy was going to die?'

'You want to know all the secrets, David.'

'Yes I do.'

'I can't give you the answers.'

'You mean you *won't*.' Blake said, challengingly. 'What made the photo frame break? That glass looked as if it had been hit with a hammer.'

'The windows were open,' Mathias suggested. 'The breeze could have blown it off.'

'Come on, Jonathan,' said the writer, wearily. 'What the hell do you take me for?'

'What do *you* think made it break?' Mathias snarled, his brilliant blue eyes looking luminous in the darkness. 'This . . . *power* of mine?' The psychic turned and headed back towards the house, leaving Blake alone beside the pond. The writer walked slowly around the pool, catching sight of a fish once in a while. He let out a tired breath. The broken frame. The prophecy. Were they more of Mathias' tricks? A mindfuck – as he'd heard it put by an American psychologist? He was beginning to doubt if tricks was the right word. He had seen too much of the man over the past five or six days to dismiss him as a charlatan or fraud.

Blake shook his head and gazed into the pond, as if seeking his answers there. He caught sight of his own reflection.

Blake froze momentarily, gaping at the vision which stared back at him from the water.

It was his reflection but the features were contorted into a mask of sheer terror. The mouth open in a soundless scream, eyes bulging wide in the sockets.

He took a step back, eyes still riveted to the image, his feet crunching on the hundreds of tiny stones which surrounded the pool. One of them bounced into the water, breaking the surface as it sent out endless ripples.

The reflection disappeared and, as the water slowly regained its stillness, Blake found that his image had also returned to normal. For long moments he looked down, as if expecting that terror-stricken visage to appear once more, but it didn't. A particularly cold breeze ruffled his hair and he shivered slightly, deciding that it was time he returned to the house.

Whistling through the branches of the nearby tree, the wind sounded like soft, malevolent laughter.

9

3.04 a.m.

Blake pushed back the covers and clambered out of bed. He had been tossing and turning for the past hour and still sleep eluded him.

Mathias' chauffeur had dropped him back at his hotel just after 1.30. By the time they had left Toni Landers' house only a handful of people remained and the atmosphere retained the air of solemnity which seemed to have descended after the incident with the cards.

Upon returning to the hotel, Blake had downed a couple of much-needed bottles of beer in the bar then retreated to his room but he had found the oblivion of sleep elusive. Now he stood at his window looking out on the dark mass that was Central Park. Trees bowed and shuddered silently in the wake of the wind and the writer thought how forbidding the place looked once the cloak of night had fallen over it.

He switched on the TV, flicking from channel to channel until he found an old black and white film. Audie Murphy was busy winning the war single-handed for the USA. Blake gazed at the screen for a while then changed channels once more. There was a programme about Chinese cookery so he left it on, turning the sound down. After five minutes he tired of that as well and switched the set off altogether, seeking comfort from the radio instead. He twisted the dial until he found the rock station, adjusting the volume as Y & T thundered out the opening chords of 'Mean Streak'.

Outside, the wind crept around the building as if seeking some means of entry, wailing mournfully every so often.

Blake padded into the bathroom and filled one of the tumblers with water which he gulped down thirstily. Then he returned to the bedroom, seating himself at the writing table where his notes were spread out. He had already filled three large pads with information, random jottings, hard facts and a lot of speculation. All that would have to be filtered and sifted through before he could begin preparing his next book. Blake disliked research at the best of times but, in this case, the dislike had intensified. The subject of Astral travel, Astral projection and its related phenomena, he had discovered, was even vaster than he had first thought. The paradox being that the more he learned the less he knew. He had the pieces but could not fit the jigsaw together.

As the author of five world-wide bestsellers he could afford to live comfortably, one of the few writers who ever succeeded in making a decent living from such a precarious profession. The money and the attention had been welcome if somewhat unexpected. Blake had never intended to earn his living from writing books about the paranormal, it had all come about rather suddenly.

He'd left home at twenty, hoping to make his mark as a journalist but working for the local paper covering events like school fetes, or interviewing people who were complaining because their sewers were bunged up, did not hold his interest for long. He began writing fiction in his spare time. Tucked away in his minuscule bed-sit above a laundrette in Bayswater he would return from the office and set to work at his own typewriter. He had left the paper for a job in a West End cinema but the financial rewards were small. He eked out his meagre earnings by supplying pornographic stories to a magazine called *Exclusive* who paid him fifty pounds for each 5000 word opus he delivered. He had a couple of articles published by *Cosmopolitan* then he decided to write a novel. It took him just three weeks and was subsequently rejected by eight publishers before finally gaining acceptance from a small, independent house. It went the way of most first novels, sinking into obscurity within a month. But, he had never been one to give up easily. He turned to non-fiction and, after six months of careful research and another two actually writing, he produced his first book about the paranormal.

After four rejections it finally found favour with a prominent hard-back publisher.

A Light in the Black had been published two weeks before his twenty-second birthday.

Blake had used the advance to take a holiday. A luxury he had not been able to afford for three years. He returned to find that his book had not only been bought by Nova, a large paperback house, but the American rights had also been sold for a substantial sum. Blake suddenly found that he could afford to leave his bed-sit and rent a flat in Holland Park.

Two years and two more books later he bought the place and now, with five world-wide successes behind him, he had, only five months earlier, bought a large house off Sloane Square.

He no longer needed to rush his work either. He now took up to eight or nine months on research and the rest of the time completing the mechanics of the book – the actual typing. Blake was at his happiest shut away in his study working. He was not a solitary man however, quite the contrary in fact. He was well liked by most people. An easy smile always at the ready, he was comfortable around people and yet at times still preferred his own company. Someone had once told him that the key to popularity was hypocrisy. If it was possible to be all things to all men at all times – do it. Blake had cultivated an easy-going image over the years which even those closest to him found hard to penetrate. He *was* all things to all men. Those he hated he spoke to with the same apparent warmth which he reserved for those who *were* allowed to pierce his facade.

Women were drawn to his practised charm, each one made to feel that *she* was the only girl in his life. The numerous encounters he had enjoyed since leaving home (that number increased once he became well-known) had only ever been superficial. To Blake at any rate. He smiled as he remembered something he'd read, attributed to Saul Bellow. He couldn't remember the words exactly but the gist of it was there.

'Telling a woman you're a writer is like an aphrodisiac. She can't wait to go to bed with you.'

He chuckled now as he flipped open his pad and reached for a pen.

Outside the hotel bedroom window the wind continued to blow strongly, hammering soundlessly at the panes as if threatening to break in. On the radio The Scorpions were roaring through 'Coming Home' and Blake decided he'd better turn the radio down.

That done he returned to his chair and scribbled a brief account of what had happened at Toni Landers' house that evening, including the incident with the picture frame and also of seeing his own twisted reflection in the pond.

As he wrote he found that his eyelids were growing heavy, as if someone had attached minute lead weights to them. He yawned and sat back for a moment, stretching. It was good that he felt tired, perhaps at last he'd be able to sleep. He scanned what he'd written and sat forward once more, allowing his eyes to close tightly.

The lamp flickered.

It was probably the wind disturbing the power lines, he thought but then remembered that he was in New York where cables ran underground, and not in the English countryside where they were suspended from pylons.

It flickered again, this time plunging the room into darkness for a second or two.

Blake muttered something to himself and peered at the bulb. The bloody thing was loose, no wonder it kept going on and off. He picked up his pen once more, now scarcely able to keep his eyes open. He turned to a fresh page but, before he could start writing, he had slumped forward in his seat and, within seconds, he was sound asleep. The bathroom was full of steam.

Like a swirling white fog it curled and twisted in the air, condensation covering the mirror like a shroud so that when Blake looked into it, his reflection was smudged and unclear. He could still hear taps running, water splashing noisily into what was obviously an overfilled tub. Rivulets of water were running down the side of the bath which, for some reason, was hidden by the shower curtain which had been pulled around it. Blake shrugged, he didn't remember doing that.

He reached over and turned off the hot tap, cursing when he felt the heat in the metal. The condensation was on the shower curtain too, pouring down to puddle on the tiles beneath his feet.

Blake pulled back the flimsy plastic.

He shrieked aloud at the sight which met him.

Sitting up in the scalding water, skin covered by hideous welts from the blistering temperature, was a man.

The man was smiling broadly, his lips little more than ragged puffed up sores still leaking clear fluid. His head had obviously been immersed in the searing water because his face was red like a boiled lobster, the skin having risen to form innumerable liquescent blisters, some of which had burst and were spilling their contents down his cheeks. His entire body was scarlet and, such was the intensity of the water's heat, Blake noticed that three of the man's fingernails had been scalded free. They hung by thin tendrils of skin from the ends of the raw digits.

Blake stood rooted to the spot, his eyes gaping wide. But, it was not the appearance of the man which terrified him. It was his features.

Scalded and burnt though they were, they were unmistakably those of Blake himself.

He screamed again.

The scream woke him.

Blake sat bolt upright in his seat, perspiration beaded on his forehead. The lamp had stopped flickering, the room was bathed in a comforting yellowish glow. The sound of heavy rock music had been replaced by the sound of voices as the DJ interviewed his guest.

It took the writer a moment to realize that he'd been dreaming.

He swallowed hard and looked behind him to where the bathroom door was ajar. It was dark in there. No running water. No light. No steam.

Blake wiped his forehead with the back of his hand and released a sigh of relief.

'That's what you get for trying to work at this time in the morning,' he told himself, reaching forward to close the notepad.

The page which had been blank before he dozed off had several sentences written on it.

The letters were large and untidy but the handwriting was unmistakably his.

Blake rubbed his eyes and turned back a page. He must have written

57

the words before dozing off. But, as he re-read them, he realized that the words were new. He scanned the spidery writing:

*The power does exist I have seen it
I have seen the secrets*

The writer swallowed hard as he scanned the words. His own words. Blake had heard of this kind of thing before, of so-called 'automatic writing' but it usually only occurred when the subject was in a trance. Was what he saw before him an example of automatic writing?

He sucked in a deep breath and held the paper before him. This time, he did *not* intend keeping things to himself. He would tell Mathias about what had happened and about the nightmare. Blake tore the piece of paper from the pad, wincing suddenly as he did so. He felt pain in his right hand and, as he turned it over he saw that his palm and wrist were bright red and swollen slightly.

As if they'd been scalded in very hot water.

10

Oxford

'How many days is it since you last slept?' Kelly asked Maurice Grant who was drumming agitatedly on the table at which they sat. Between them was a tape recorder, its twin spools turning slowly, the microphone pointed towards Grant.

'Two,' Grant snapped. 'Why the hell are you asking? You ought to know, you're the ones who keep pumping me full of fucking drugs.' He got to his feet and walked away from the table towards the large plate glass window in the far wall. Outside the sun was shining.

'Look out there,' said Grant. 'It's a beautiful day and I'm stuck in here with you two bastards asking me stupid questions.'

The man seated to Kelly's right leant closer.

'What are you giving him?' asked John Fraser, quietly.

'Thirty mg of Methadrine,' said Kelly. 'But without the Tubarine to put him out at nights.'

Fraser nodded and scribbled something down on the note pad before him.

The room they were in was light and airy, mainly due to the large window at the far end. Two or three bright paintings decorated the white walls, adding a touch of colour, but the room was dominated by the bulk of an EEG machine. The Eléma Schonander Mingograf was the most up to date of its kind and was one of four which the Institute owned. Readings had already been taken earlier that morning from Maurice Grant, over an hour ago according to the large wall clock which hung over the machine. But, at present, Kelly and her colleague were more concerned with Grant's verbal reactions than those culled from an electroencephalogrammatic scan of his brain. He had been deliberately deprived of sleep for the last two nights, unable to live out, subconsciously, the nightmare which he usually experienced.

Both investigators watched him as he paced agitatedly back and forth before the window.

'Why don't you come and sit down again?' said Fraser.

Kelly had worked with John Fraser on a number of occasions. He was ten years older than her but looked closer to fifty than thirty-five. His face had a mottled appearance to it as if he'd been out in the sun too long. His bulbous nose was shiny and reminded Kelly of a bald head. His eyes were rheumy and heavy-lidded like those of a man about to doze off. But he had a lean muscular body which looked as though it had somehow acquired the wrong head. The youthful frame and the haggard features seemed at odds.

'I said, why don't you . . .'

Grant cut him short.

'Yeah, I heard you,' he rasped, hesitating a moment before stomping back to the table where he sat down heavily. 'Why the hell do you have to keep asking me so many questions? I just want to sleep.'

'Why do you want to sleep?' Fraser asked.

'Because I'm fucking shattered,' snapped Grant. 'Do I need a better reason?'

He glared at the two investigators with eyes full of rage. A razor hadn't touched his face for three or four days now and his cheeks and chin were carpeted by coarse bristles which rasped as he rubbed them.

'You knew that things might get a little uncomfortable when you first agreed to help us,' Kelly reminded him.

Maurice Grant didn't answer. He merely looked from Kelly to Fraser then back again.

'Are you ready to answer some questions?' she asked him.

'If I do, does that mean I can get some sleep?' he demanded.

She nodded.

'All right, ask your questions,' he said, picking at the skin around his fingernails, chewing it occasionally.

'When you can't dream, what do you think about?' she wanted to know, pushing the microphone closer to him.

'Things, I . . .'

'What kind of things?' Fraser interrupted.

'Things,' Grant hissed. 'All kinds of things, thoughts.'

'Can you remember any of them?' Kelly enquired.

'No,' he said, flatly.

'Then try,' Fraser insisted.

Grant clenched his, teeth, his malevolent gaze swinging round to focus on the investigator.

'I told you, I can't remember,' he said, the anger seething in his voice.

'Are any of the thoughts to do with your wife and son?' Kelly enquired.

Grant looked momentarily puzzled.

'Why should they be?'

'Look, if you keep answering a question with a question,' said Fraser, 'we're going to be here all day.'

Kelly shot her colleague an irritable glance while Grant rounded on him once more.

'What is this, some kind of fucking interrogation?' he snapped. 'You asked me to answer some questions, I'm trying to do that but you keep interrupting me.' His voice had risen in volume.

'Are any of the thoughts to do with your family?' Kelly asked him again.

Grant shook his head.

60

'Do you ever think about your wife and son when you can't sleep?' Kelly persisted.

'I just told you, no.'

'Come on, that's not natural. You mean to say you've wiped them from your memory?' said Fraser, a hint of sarcasm in his voice.

Grant brought his fist crashing down on the table top, his voice rising to a shout.

'I DON'T THINK ABOUT THEM.'

Fraser regarded the man warily. He was becoming a little nervous of Grant's aggression.

'Have you ever wanted to kill your wife and son?' Kelly asked.

'Kill them? Why?' Grant demanded.

'That's what we'd like to know,' said Fraser.

'Why should I want to kill them?'

'Because there may be a part of your mind which wants you to,' Kelly informed him. 'You've had a series of nightmares, in each one you kill your wife and son.'

'So what?' Grant snapped. 'What's so fucking important about a nightmare? Everyone has them.'

'You and your wife had experienced some problems hadn't you?' Kelly said. 'Marital problems.'

'What if we had? What's that got to do with this shit about nightmares?' demanded Grant, angrily.

'Would you like to kill your wife and son?' Fraser wanted to know.

Grant got to his feet.

'This is some kind of fucking game you're playing with me,' he growled, pointing an accusing finger at the investigators, both of whom moved back slightly from the table.

'Tell us the truth,' said Fraser. 'You want to kill them, don't you?'

'No, you bastard.'

'You've told us.'

'No.'

'You want to murder them,' Fraser said, a little too forcefully.

'No, NO.' The shout became a scream of rage and Grant suddenly grabbed the heavy tape-recorder, lifting it from the desk, raising it above his head. The plug was torn from the wall, the spools falling uselessly from the machine. Kelly and Fraser jumped back hurriedly as Grant spun round and, with demonic strength, hurled the recorder at the large window. There was an ear-splitting crash as the glass exploded, huge thick shards flying out like crystal javelins.

'Get help, quick,' Fraser snapped as Grant turned on him.

As Kelly bolted for the door, Grant flung himself at Fraser. He hit the table on the way and the two men crashed to the ground amidst the shriek of snapping wood. Fraser tried to roll to one side but Grant fastened both hands around his neck and began throttling him. Fraser felt his assailant's finger-tips gouging into his flesh and he struck out with one hand, catching Grant a stinging blow across the temple. This only seemed to inflame him more for he straddled the investigator and began slamming his head against the floor.

Fraser looked up into the face of his attacker, the eyes blazing wildly, spittle dotted on his lips as he continued to bang his victim's head against the ground with gleeful force. Fraser gripped Grant's wrists and tried to prise open the vice-like grip but the relief was only momentary. He felt himself losing consciousness.

Then suddenly, the pressure on his throat eased and through pain-clouded eyes he saw two men grab Grant and pull him to his feet. Kelly was there too, so was Dr Vernon. He held a hypodermic needle in his hand.

Things seemed to swim before him as he rolled to one side, massaging his throat, the hot bile clawing its way up from his stomach.

'Strap him down,' Vernon urged, watching as the other two men dragged Grant towards the EEG. They forced him on to the trolley and swiftly fastened thick leather bonds around his wrists and ankles securing them. Grant had, however, begun to calm down somewhat and as the electrodes were attached to his head he seemed to stop thrashing about, content instead to eye his opponents with fury. His teeth were clenched, a thin, silvery trail of saliva dribbling from one corner of his mouth.

Kelly crossed to Fraser who was lying amongst the wreckage of the broken table, trying to clamber upright. She knelt beside him and offered a hand but he refused her help, struggling precariously to his feet, one hand still on his throat. He coughed and tasted blood. Vernon gave him a cursory glance then turned his attention back to Grant.

The electrodes were in place on his forehead and temples, he was motionless but for the heaving of his chest.

One of the other investigators, a man with a button missing from one shirt cuff, stood beside the machine waiting. Kelly recognized him as Frank Anderson, a powerfully built man in his early forties.

Vernon nodded and Anderson flicked a switch which set the EEG in motion.

The five pencils swept back and forth across the paper as it left the machine, each one an indication of the brain waves picked up from Grant.

The fifth pencil, however, barely moved. Anderson noticed this and directed Vernon's attention to it. The older man looked puzzled.

'What the hell does that mean?' said Anderson but Vernon did not answer.

Kelly joined them, leaving Fraser to stagger over to the broken window where he gulped down lungfuls of air, still wincing in pain each time he swallowed.

'Could it be the area controlled by the subconscious?' Kelly said, directing her question towards Vernon but gazing at the virtually dormant line on the read-out.

Vernon didn't answer.

'Surely it must be,' she insisted. 'Theoretically, there should only be activity in that part of the brain when he's asleep. Put him out. This could be our chance to find out.'

Vernon did not hesitate. He rolled up Grant's sleeve, found a vein and ran the needle into it, keeping his thumb on the plunger until the last drop of Tubarine had left the slender receptacle.

Then, they waited.

They waited.

For ten minutes they waited. The only sounds in the room were the ticking of the wall clock and Grant's increasingly laboured breathing. Kelly stood over his immobile form and lifted one eye-lid, noticing how the pupil was dilated.

'He's asleep,' she said, softly, as if standing over a child she did not wish to wake.

Another five minutes and she noticed movement beneath the closed lids. The unmistakable motions of REM.

63

'He's dreaming,' she said, almost excitedly.

Vernon seemed not to hear, his eyes were riveted to the EEG read-out.

Four of the tracer lines were barely moving but the fifth was hurtling across the paper with frightening speed. He called Kelly to look at it.

'It certainly looks as if that fifth line denotes the area of the brain which controls the subconscious mind,' she said. 'It only registers activity when the subject is dreaming.'

All eyes turned to Grant.

'If only we knew *what* he was dreaming,' said Vernon. 'My God, this is incredible.' He was still watching the wildly swinging tracer. 'It looks as if the area is in the occipital lobe.' He lowered his voice slightly. 'The area of the brain concerned with vision.'

'Then he *is* seeing something,' said Frank Anderson.

Vernon nodded.

The knock on the lab door startled all of them.

At first no one moved but the knock came again, harder and more insistent.

Vernon muttered something under his breath and opened the door, surprised to find his secretary standing there.

'There's a phone call for you, Dr Vernon,' she said. 'It's . . .'

He cut her short.

'Can't it wait? I'm very busy here.' he snapped.

'It's the police.'

Vernon nodded, aware of the interest now generated by his colleagues.

'I'll take it here,' he announced, indicating the wall phone. He crossed to it and lifted the receiver to his ear.

'Dr Vernon speaking. Yes, that's correct.'

Kelly watched him, noticing that his forehead was slowly beginning to crease into a frown.

'When did this happen?' he asked. There was a moment's silence. 'I see. Yes, I understand.'

'Look,' said Anderson, tugging on Kelly's sleeve.

She glanced down.

The fifth tracer had ceased its frenzied movement and was now drawing lazy parabolas on the read-out.

Kelly crossed to Grant and felt for his pulse, noticing how cold his flesh was to the touch.

Vernon, meanwhile, had replaced the receiver and rejoined his companions.

He sighed, scraping one thumb across his forehead.

'What's wrong?' Kelly asked.

'The police wanted to know if Maurice Grant had left the Institute during the last hour or so,' he told her.

Kelly looked puzzled.

'A neighbour called round to his house,' Vernon continued. 'She swears that she saw Grant there.'

'But that's impossible,' Anderson interjected.

'The neighbour was adamant.'

'I don't see why the police are so concerned about where Grant was or is,' Kelly said.

Vernon sucked in a deep breath.

'Less than twenty minutes ago his wife and child were attacked and killed in their house. Dismembered the police said.'

'Jesus,' murmured Anderson.

Kelly did not speak, her eyes were fixed on the restraining straps which secured Grant firmly to the table.

11

To Kelly, passing through the door of Dr Vernon's office was like crossing the threshold into a bygone age. The room, with its panelled walls and huge bookcases bearing endless leather bound volumes, was like something from a museum. It was a room to be looked at and appraised, one to be treated with reverence, much the same as an aged person. It did not seem like a room where anything constructive could be accomplished. It reminded her of the reading room in some gentleman's club, a place where cigars were smoked and glasses of port sipped. She even felt slightly out of place in it, dressed as she was in a khaki blouse, beige skirt and tan shoes. She felt as if she were intruding on the solemnity of the place, that she would have looked more at home in a crinoline.

Beside her, John Fraser was still massaging his neck, complaining about the pain despite having refused the attentions of a doctor. Vernon himself stood facing the window, looking out over the sun-drenched lawns, enjoying the heat on his face. Despite the warmth in the room he had not undone a single button of his jacket. He popped another cough sweet into his mouth and the smell of menthol seemed to intensify.

Fraser sipped at the cup of tea which Vernon's secretary had brought five minutes earlier and found that it was cold. He replaced the cup and returned to the more urgent task of rubbing his throat. His head was beginning to ache as well where Grant had slammed it against the floor. All in all he looked, and felt, fed up with the whole situation. Since he had joined the Institute five years earlier, Fraser had gained something of a reputation as a moaner but today he felt he was justified in his complaints.

His grumblings, however, were not reserved for his work. He'd been married for twelve years and, during that time, his wife had been forced to endure a continual barrage of bleating and criticism. Indeed, Fraser only seemed to be truly content when he had a drink in his hand.

He was a heavy drinker and had been since he was eighteen. Fraser was walking the tightrope between social drinking and alchoholism and, just lately, he seemed to be losing his footing.

'I don't see that you have any choice, Dr Vernon,' he said. 'Stop the research before any more accidents happen like the one today.'

Kelly looked at him angrily.

'We can't stop the research now,' she said. 'There's still too much we have to learn.'

'That man could have killed me. It would be madness to continue. He's dangerous.'

'For God's sake, John. He was in that state for a reason. He attacked you for a reason,' Vernon interjected. 'And Kelly's right, there's no question of stopping the research.'

'You didn't exactly help matters, John,' Kelly said. 'You provoked him to a certain extent.'

66

'Provoked him?' Fraser gaped, incredulously. 'Jesus Christ. I asked him some questions that was all.'

Vernon turned to face the investigators.

'If you don't like the risks, John, there is an alternative,' he said, his voice low but full of authority. 'If you don't wish to work on the project any longer you can be re-assigned.'

Fraser shook his head.

'No, I don't want that,' he said. 'I just think we should move away from the drugs if we can . . .'

Vernon cut him short.

'It was agreed between the Investigators at the Metapsychic Centre and ourselves that *we* would use drugs, *they* would use hypnosis. It is important that we continue with our own methods. Today's incident was an isolated one.'

'How can you be so sure it won't happen again?'

Vernon fixed Fraser in an angry stare.

'It's a chance we will have to take,' he rasped. 'The work we are doing is very necessary. It will benefit a lot of people if we can find some of the answers we seek.'

'And it will benefit one person in particular won't it, Dr Vernon?' Fraser said.

The older man glared at him, his jaw set, the knot of muscles at the side pulsing angrily. His eyes looked like wet concrete.

Kelly looked puzzled.

'That's enough, Fraser,' the Institute Director said and Kelly heard the anger in his voice, well-disguised but nevertheless potent. 'The research will continue. If you don't wish to be a part of it then get out of my office now and stop wasting my time.'

Kelly was surprised at the vehemence in Vernon's tone, at the naked fury burning in his eyes. She saw Fraser visibly blench beneath the verbal onslaught. He slumped back in his chair, trying to hold the Director's stare but finding himself unable to do so. He lowered his head slightly and began picking at his nails.

Vernon sat down and folded his hands across his stomach, his eyes never leaving Fraser.

'It will benefit one person in particular.' Kelly looked at her fellow investigator, wondering what he had meant by the statement.

67

'I think it would be best if you left now, John,' Vernon said, quietly. 'There's nothing more to discuss.'

Fraser let out a deep breath and got to his feet. He glanced at Kelly then at Vernon before turning and heading for the door.

'And the next time?' said Fraser, challengingly. 'Will you take responsibility for what happens, Dr Vernon?'

The older man didn't look up.

'Get out, John,' he said, quietly.

As Fraser slammed the door behind him, Kelly, too, rose. She was anxious to speak with Fraser.

'Wait a moment, Kelly,' Vernon said.

She sat down again, brushing an imaginary speck of dust from her skirt.

'Do you want me to replace Fraser?' Vernon asked.

'I don't think it's up to me,' Kelly told him.

'You're the one who has to work with him.'

She opened her mouth to speak but the words remained locked inside and it was Vernon who broke the silence again.

'This project is too important to be jeopardised by one man.'

Kelly saw that the steel had returned to his eyes.

'I hope you agree with me?'

She nodded.

'Dr Vernon, don't you think that the murder of his wife and child might have some effect on Grant?'

'In what way?'

She shrugged, not sure whether or not what she was about to say would sound ridiculous.

'The catalyst, the object of his subconscious fantasies no longer exists,' she said. 'We assumed that his nightmares were unconscious manifestations of actual desires, but now his wife and son are dead he has nothing to direct that hostility towards.'

Vernon stroked his chin thoughtfully.

'You mean his wife was the object of his fury, the cause of the nightmares?' he suggested. 'So, theoretically, the nightmares should stop.'

Kelly nodded.

'It's strange though,' she said. 'She was murdered while Grant was under a drug-induced trance, in more or less the same manner as he had previously described. Almost as if the dreams had been warnings.

68

Perhaps that's the key we're looking for. Maybe Grant's nightmares weren't unconscious desires, they were visions of the future.'

Vernon shifted the cough sweet around inside his cheek where it bulged like a gum boil.

'Possibly,' he murmured.

Kelly sat a moment longer then got to her feet.

'If there's nothing else, Dr Vernon.'

He shook his head.

Kelly walked to the door, watched by the Institute Director. He coughed and, as Kelly turned the handle, Vernon spoke once more.

'Remember what I said, Kelly. This project means too much. There's a lot at stake. If Fraser causes any trouble I want to know about it.'

She nodded and left him alone in the office.

Vernon dropped his pen, his fingers bunching into a fist.

Fraser.

The last thing they needed now was opposition.

Fraser.

Vernon's breath came in short, angry gasps. No, Fraser must not be allowed to disrupt the research programme.

No matter what it took to stop him.

Kelly checked in John Fraser's office, in the labs, in the library.

He was nowhere to be found.

As she made her way back across the polished wooden floor of the Institute's reception area she spotted him outside, clambering into his familiar red Datsun.

Kelly ran out on to the gravel drive-way and across to the other investigator who had already started his engine and was in the process of pulling out.

He saw Kelly but did not slow up until she had reached the side of the car and banged on the window. He rolled it down.

'What do you want?' he said, sharply.

'Where are you going?' she wanted to know.

'I'm taking the rest of the day off,' Fraser said, sarcastically. 'I'm going to find the nearest pub and have a few beers. Maybe some shorts to wash them down.' He jammed the car into first, the gearbox groaned in protest.

'What you said in Vernon's office,' said Kelly. 'What did you mean?'

The roar of the revving engine almost drowned out her words.

'I don't know what you're talking about,' said Fraser.

'About the research,' she said. 'You said it would benefit one person in particular. Who did you mean?'

Fraser stepped on the accelerator, the back wheels spiining madly. A flurry of pebbles from the driveway flew into the air.

'Did you mean Vernon?' she persisted.

'Ask him,' hissed Fraser and drove off.

Kelly watched as the Datsun disappeared from view along the tree-lined drive. She stood silently for a moment then made her way back towards the main building.

She was not the only one who saw Fraser drive away.

From the solitude of his office on the second floor, Vernon had watched the entire tableau.

He stepped back out of sight.

12

Dr Stephen Vernon poured himself another scotch and returned to his chair beside the fire-place. The gentle strains of the New World Symphony issued forth from the record player and Vernon closed his eyes for a moment, allowing the soothing sound to wash over him. It did little to relax him and he jerked his eyes open almost immediately, seeking comfort instead in the whisky which he downed almost in one gulp, allowing the amber liquid to burn its way to his stomach.

Outside, the wind stirred the branches of the trees and clouds gathered menacingly in the night sky, like dense formations of black clad soldiers.

Inside the house the fire was warm, the room bathed in the comforting glow from the flames and the two lamps which burned, one behind him and the other on the table nearby. But, despite the warmth, Vernon felt uncomfortable. As if the heat refused to penetrate his pores. He swallowed some more of the scotch, regarding warily the A4 size envelope which lay on the table nearby. Only when he had downed the last dregs of the fiery liquid did he find the courage to open the envelope.

Inside was a file, a ring binder, and there was a letter paper-clipped to it.

Vernon read it hastily then balled it up and tossed it into the waste-bin beside him. His grey eyes narrowed to steely slits as he opened the file. The first page, neatly typed, had the familiar notepaper headed:

FAIRHAM SANATORIUM

It also bore a photo. A ten by eight, glossy black and white of a woman in her middle forties, a warm smile etched across her face. Even given the monochrome of the photo there was a welcoming radiance about the eyes and Vernon found himself gazing deep into them. The photo had been taken six years earlier.

He turned the page and there was another picture, smaller this time, more recent.

If he hadn't known he would have sworn it was a different woman.

The welcoming glow in her eyes and the warm smile had been replaced by a vision from a mortuary. A gaze devoid of understanding stared back at him from sockets which looked as though they'd been hollowed out of the skull with a trowel. The mouth was thin-lipped, little more than a gash across the face. Hair which had once been lustrous and shiny now hung in unkept hunks, unbrushed and lifeless like kelp. Set side by side the most recent picture seemed to exist almost as a mockery to remind him of what once had been.

Vernon swallowed hard and read the report:

SUBJECT NAME: VERNON. JANET
KATHERINE. NEÉ HAMPTON.
AGE: 50
MARITAL STATUS: MARRIED.
DATE OF COMMITTAL: 14/5/78
TRUSTEE: VERNON, STEPHEN PHILLIP.
RELATIONSHIP TO SUBJECT: HUSBAND.
DIAGNOSIS: DEMENTIA, PARAESTHESIA.
CHRONIC PARANOID DEMENTIA, SERIOUS

IMPAIRMENT OF SENSORY-MOTOR
FUNCTION.
CAUSE:

Vernon closed the file and slammed it down onto the table, almost knocking over his glass. He snatched it up but found, to his annoyance, that it was empty. He looked across at the half-empty bottle of Haig and contemplated re-filling his glass once more but, eventually, decided against it. The file lay where he'd put it, a memory as painful as a needle in soft flesh.

Six years.

Dear God was it that long since he had been forced to commit his wife? That long since . . .

The thought trailed away but he knew that he could never erase the memory of what had happened.

What had sent her to the verge of insanity.

Vernon got to his feet, turned off the fire and extinguished the lights, then, carrying the file, he trudged upstairs not bothering to put on the landing light. He moved slowly but easily through the darkness until he came to the locked door.

The wind had increased in strength and was howling now, like a dog in pain.

Vernon paused before the door, a cold chill enveloping him like some icy invisible glove which squeezed tighter the longer he stood there.

From the pocket of his cardigan he produced a key and, steadying his hand, inserted it in the lock.

There was a sharp crack from beyond the door, like bony fingers on glass, skeletal digits playing a symphony of torment in the gloom.

He turned the key.

The lock was well-oiled and opened without difficulty.

Vernon stepped into the room, shuddering as he did so. He felt like an intruder in this room. Like a thief in a church.

He heard the harsh clacking of the tree branch against the window and it startled him momentarily but, recovering his composure, he reached over and turned on the light.

The room smelt slightly of neglect, a faint odour of damp mingling

72

with the more pungent smell of mothballs. There was a thin film of dust on everything. On the bedspread, the side-board, the chairs, even the photos. He crossed to the wardrobe and opened it. Her clothes still hung there, the smell of naptha more powerful now.

He had kept her in this room for three months before finally committing her. For three months after it happened he had brought her food and tried to feed her as a parent would feed a helpless child. For that was what she had become.

His Janet. His wife. The woman he had loved so much.

The woman who had been reduced to the mental status of a cabbage by what she had witnessed those six years ago.

He had tried to cope as best he could, he had tried to help her but she had withdrawn deeper inside herself until Vernon had felt as through he were nursing a corpse. Only the movement of her eyes, bulging wide constantly, gave any indication that she was even alive. He had used all his expertise to try and salvage what was left of her sanity but finally he had lost the battle and had her committed to Fairham. The doctors there had made no progress though perhaps it was not surprising when he considered the events which had sent her into this death-like state of catatonia. It would, he decided, have been enough to send anyone insane.

So far, he had been able to keep his secret.

In the beginning he had thought that he could handle the problem. But, word had spread around the neighbourhood – rumours, speculation and guess-work until finally, he had found that there was no other solution but to lock her up. No one knew why Janet Vernon was in a sanatorium and he knew that, for all their do-it-yourself detective work, none of the neighbours could ever imagine anything as horrific as that which had caused her to lose her mind.

Now he stood in the room, looking around, listening to the wind outside.

He had left the room just as it had always been. For six years, only he had been inside. It contained too many memories, too much pain.

Vernon flicked off the light and retreated back on to the landing, locking the door behind him. He stood looking at it for long seconds then turned and headed for his own bedroom.

Six years.

73

He had searched for answers for so long and now, he felt that he might be close. The research was furnishing him with what he'd always sought. A way to cure his wife. A way to unlock her thoughts. No one must be allowed to stand in his way.

But, as he undressed, a thought passed through his mind.

What effect would it have on her? The horror of what she had witnessed that day had festered in her thoughts for so long.

Dare he release those memories?

13

New York

'It sure beats the shit out of *E.T.*,' said Rick Landers, gleefully.

Beside him, Andy Wallace was similarly impressed.

'You bet,' he murmured, watching as *The Thing* devoured another victim, ripping off both his arms below the elbow before exploding from his stomach cavity. The two boys watched mesmerised as the alien head detached itself and then dragged itself across the floor using a tentacle.

'Rewind it,' said Andy. 'Let's see it again.'

Rick nodded and scuttled across to the video, his finger seeking out the appropriate button.

'Yeah, *E.T.* was OK for kids,' Andy continued.

'My mum met the guy who made this picture,' said Rick, smugly.

'John Carpenter? Wow, when was that?'

'At some party I think.'

He pressed the 'play' button on the video recorder and pictures once more began to fill the wide screen. The two boys settled down again.

They were both nine years old, Andy perhaps a month or two senior. Both attended the same school about three blocks away. Rick knew that his mother didn't like him watching too many horror movies. She'd turned the video off halfway through his fifth viewing of *The Evil Dead* but, today, she was out filming a commercial until six o'clock so that gave him and Andy another two hours.

Andy lived about three houses down from the Landers place. His father, Gordon, wrote scripts for one of ABC's most successful comedy series and his mother, Nina, was a theatrical agent, so Andy was no stranger to the crazy world of showbusiness.

The Thing had just sprouted spider's legs and was about to scuttle away when the picture on the TV broke up into a network of lines and dots.

The two boys groaned and Rick leapt towards the video.

From the kitchen, the sound of the vacuum mingled with that of the waste-disposal unit in the sink.

The noise stopped, at any rate the grinding of the disposal unit did, the vacuum seemed to roar even louder.

'Mrs Garcia,' yelled Rick.

No answer.

'Mrs Garcia,' he bellowed louder and the vacuum was switched off.

'What you want, Rick?' Elita Garcia asked, appearing from the kitchen like a blimp emerging from a hangar. She was a huge Mexican woman who always reminded Rick of an extra in a spaghetti western.

'The vacuum is screwing up the picture on the video,' Rick told her. 'Couldn't you do it later?'

'Your mother ask me to have this finish before she come home,' Mrs Garcia informed him.

'Yeah, but the video . . .'

'I no help that. I do my job, Rick. Sorry.' And the vacuum started up again.

The two boys exchanged disconsolate glances and surrendered to Mrs Garcia and her cleaner. Rick switched off the video and the TV and suggested they go into the garden for a while.

'You no be long,' Mrs Garcia called above the roar of the vacuum. 'Your dinner ready soon.'

The two boys had been outside only minutes when Rick heard the approaching tones of an ice-cream van. He guessed it was less than a block away.

Lee Jacobs spun the wheel of the station-wagon, the tyres screaming as they tried to grip the road. The vehicle's back end skidded and slammed into a parked Ford.

'Jesus Christ, man,' snapped Tony Sollozzo, who was kneeling on the station-wagon's passenger seat. 'Look where you're fucking going will you.'

'You wanna drive, motherfucker?' shouted Jacobs, sweat pouring down his black face. It beaded in his short frizzy hair like dew. 'Are the cops still behind us?'

The sound of a siren answered his question for him and he glanced in the rear-view mirror to see the black and white speeding along in pursuit, lights flashing.

'Step on it, will you,' Sollozzo urged. 'The bastards are gaining.'

'If you'd stolen a car with somethin' under the hood maybe we could outrun those lousy fucks,' Jacobs protested. 'Why the hell did you have to steal a fucking station-wagon?'

'Maybe I shoulda' walked around some showroom first, picked out somethin' you liked, huh?' Sollozzo countered.

'We shoulda' just turned ourselves in like I said,' Jacobs said, swerving to miss a bus.

'With nearly a kilo of smack in the glove compartment? Are you kiddin' me?'

'Stealing a station-wagon,' Jacobs grunted, trying to coax more speed from the vehicle. 'Dumb fuckin' wop.'

'Who're you callin' a wop you nigger son of a bitch. Now drive, man, they're gettin' closer.'

The blaring of horns greeted them as they sped through a red light.

The police car followed.

'What time does Mrs Garcia leave?' Andy Wallace asked, picking up the frisbee and throwing it back.

Rick Landers watched it carefully, jumping to catch it with one hand.

'She stays until my mum gets home,' he said.

'How come? She never used to did she?'

'Mum's been acting kind of weird for the last couple of days,' Rick disclosed. 'She says she doesn't like to leave me on my own too much.' He threw the frisbee back.

'*My* parents are as bad,' Andy confided. 'I mean, they must think we're kids.'

Rick nodded then he cocked his head on one side as he heard the chimes of the ice-cream van once more. It was closer now. Just turning into the street he guessed.

'You want to get an ice-cream?' he asked Andy, noticing the look of delight on his friend's face.

'You bet,' he said.

The frisbee was forgotten as they both hurried around to the front of the house.

Lee Jacobs banged his hooter as the station-wagon narrowly missed a woman crossing the road. He yelled something and turned the vehicle into another street. Beside him, Tony Sollozzo slid a Smith and Wesson .38 from his jacket pocket. He flipped out the cylinder, checking that each chamber carried a round.

'What you doin', man?' asked Jacobs, glancing down at the gun.

'Just in case,' murmured Sollozzo, hefting the pistol before him.

'You crazy fuck. I didn't know you was packed,' Jacobs gaped. 'What you gonna' do?'

The police car drew closer, its bonnet little more than ten feet from the rear of the station wagon. Sollozzo could see the two uniformed men inside as he turned. He wound down his window, pulling back the hammer on the .38.

Up ahead, Jacobs caught sight of an ice-cream van parked in their way. It was blocking the route. To by-pass it he would have to drive up on to the wide pavement.

Sollozzo steadied himself, bringing the gun up to a firing position.

Rick Landers and Andy Wallace ran towards the ice-cream van, unaware of the two speeding cars hurtling down the road. Andy suddenly stopped as his money spilled out on to the ground. He had a hole in his trouser pocket. Rick chuckled and watched as Andy stooped in the driveway of the house to retrieve his coins. He, himself, reached the waiting white van and asked for a chocolate sundae with lots of nuts. He hoped Mrs Garcia wasn't watching.

As he turned to see where Andy had got to, Rick saw the two speeding cars.

* * *

77

Sollozzo took aim and fired twice, the pistol bucking in his fist. The first shot blasted off the wing mirror of the police car, the second punched a hole in its windscreen.

The station-wagon swerved violently as Jacobs momentarily took his eye off the road and glared at his companion.

'Stop it,' he shouted, reaching for the gun.

'Fuck you,' roared Sollozzo, firing again, a twisted grin across his face.

Jacobs looked ahead of him and screamed aloud as the white bulk of the ice-cream van loomed before him.

The station-wagon hit it doing about sixty, the impact catapulting Sollozzo through the windscreen. The steering column came back at Jacobs as if fired from a cannon, the wheel cracking, the column itself shattering his sternum and tearing through him as the two vehicles were pulped by the crash. Almost instantaneously, the petrol tank of the white van exploded with an ear-splitting shriek and both vehicles disappeared beneath a blinding ball of red and white flame.

Rick Landers, standing less than ten feet from the van, was lifted into the air as if by an invisible hand, his body catapulted a full twenty feet on to the pavement by the force of the explosion. His mangled body crashed to the ground, his clothes ablaze.

The patrolman driving the police car twisted the wheel to avoid the blazing inferno, the black and white mounting the sidewalk.

Too late the driver saw Rick's body lying ahead of him.

He slammed on his brakes but the car was travelling much too fast.

The front offside wheel ran across the boy's neck, crushing his spine and nearly severing his head. Blood burst from the shattered corpse, spreading out in a wide pool around it.

Watching from the driveway, Andy Wallace felt something warm and soft in the seat of his pants as he gazed at the carnage before him. A second later he fainted.

Tony Sollozzo lay on the grass nearby, his face and neck shredded by the glass of the windscreen. Flames from the wreckage licked hungrily at his outstretched hand. Above it all a black pall of smoke hung like a shroud.

The two policemen stumbled from their car, the first of them running towards the burning vehicles but unable to get close because of the blistering heat from the leaping flames. The driver knelt and saw the body of Rick Landers lying beneath the car.

'Oh Jesus God,' he murmured and straightened up, reaching inside the car for his radio.

He called for an ambulance and some back-up, trying to explain briefly what had happened.

As he walked away he saw that he left sticky footprints behind him where he'd been standing in the pool of Rick's blood. He dropped to his knees on the grass verge and threw up.

14

David Blake dropped his pen and yawned. He blinked myopically and scanned the pages which lay before him.

He'd been working flat out since ten that morning, pausing briefly at one o'clock to devour half a cheeseburger and some fries. Most of that now lay neglected on the table behind him.

His stomach growled noisily and he patted it gently. It was time he ate something more substantial.

Blake got to his feet and walked to the bathroom, turning the television on as he passed. A glance at his watch told him it was 5.58 p.m. The news would be on in a minute or two. He smiled to himself. It was time to find out what had been going on in the 'real' world. He'd been so immersed in his work for the past eight hours that New York could have disappeared and he wouldn't have noticed. Once safely locked away, pen in hand, Blake was oblivious to all else.

He entered the bathroom, crossing to the wash basin where he splashed his face with cold water. As he wandered back into his room, a towel pressed to his face, the news was just beginning. Blake decided to hear the headlines then get something to eat. He dried his face off, the water mingling with the perspiration on his forehead.

'. . . has promised a crackdown on some of the city's illegal gambling establishments . . .'

The voice of the newsreader droned on as Blake opened his wardrobe and took out a clean shirt.

'. . . and, as reported in our earlier bulletin, the son of Toni Landers, the actress who plays . . .'

Blake spun round to face the set.

'. . . whose son, Rick, was tragically killed today when he was involved in a car accident.'

'Jesus Christ,' muttered Blake as a photo of first Rick and then Toni Landers was flashed on to the screen. The writer sat down on the edge of the bed, eyes riveted to the set as the newsreader continued.

'Miss Landers, who was filming elsewhere in the city was unavailable for comment and it is believed that she is now at her home under sedation. Her son, Rick, is believed to have been killed at approximately 4.15 this afternoon after a stolen car crashed into an ice cream van outside his home. Both passengers in the car and also the van driver were killed but, as yet, the other three victims have not been named. Police . . .'

Blake shook his head slowly, his eyes and ears focused on the TV but his mind back-tracking to the party at Toni Landers' house.

To Mathias.

To the prophecy.

'Her son is going to die.' The psychic's words echoed inside his mind.

'Her son is going to die.'

Blake sat for a moment longer, then pulled on his shirt and hastily buttoned it up, tucking it into his jeans. He pulled on a pair of boots and, leaving the television set on, he left the room and scuttled across to the elevator at the end of the corridor. He rode it to the ground floor and ran through reception, out of the main doors and past the doorman who was enjoying a sly drag on a Marlboro.

The writer turned to his left and headed for the newsstand on the corner of the street. He fumbled in his pocket for change with one hand as he retrieved a late edition with the other. Half-way down the page was a photo of Rick Landers and, above it:

SON OF ACTRESS DIES IN ACCIDENT

Blake handed the vendor some coins, not waiting for his change, then he turned and made his way back to the hotel.

Once inside his room, Blake read the full story. The details didn't matter. The child was dead. That was enough. The writer folded the paper and dropped it on to the bed. He suddenly didn't feel so hungry. For what seemed like an eternity he sat there, gazing at the TV screen and then at the photo of Rick Landers.

'Her son is going to die.' He spoke the words aloud.

Blake got to his feet and switched off the TV. He snatched up the leather jacket which was draped over the back of a nearby chair, pulling it on as he made for the door of his room.

Outside, the storm clouds which had been gathering for the past hour or so were split by the first soundless flash of lightning.

Blake paid the taxi driver, peered out through the rain splashed window then pushed open the door of the cab.

The deluge hit him like a palpable wave, the heavens continuing to dump their load without hint of a respite. The storm was raging, whiplash cracks of lightning punctuating the almost continual growl of thunder. It sounded as if somewhere, deep below the surface of the earth, a gigantic creature was clawing its way up. Rain hammered against the roads and buildings, bouncing off like tiny explosions. Even as Blake left the cab he felt the hair being plastered to the side of his face, the hot droplets penetrating the material of his shirt. He knew that the storm would not clear the air, it would merely make the humidity more acute. Beads of perspiration formed on the writer's forehead, only to be washed away instantly by the driving rain.

The house of Jonathan Mathias stood before him, a large forbidding three storey building fronted by well-kept lawn and ringed by a high stone wall. Blake noticed as he approached the wrought iron gates that there were closed-circuit television cameras mounted on each side of the gates. They watched him with their Cyclopean eyes as he walked up the short driveway towards the house itself.

The building was a curious mixture of the old and new. The main structure looked as if it had been built in mock Edwardian style whilst an extension made up of glass and concrete seemed to have been grafted on to the wrong house.

The windows were unlit and the glass reflected the lightning back at Blake, they lowered over him like some kind of malevolent spectre.

There were more closed-circuit cameras above the front door. He rang the bell, pressing it twice and, a moment later, the door was opened by a man who Blake immediately recognised as Mathias' chauffeur.

'Mr Blake isn't it?' said the man, eyeing the writer who looked a sorry state with his brown hair dripping and his clothes soaked.

'I'd like to see Mr Mathias if that's possible,' the writer said.

'He doesn't like to be disturbed when he's at home,' the chauffeur began. 'I'll . . .'

'Let him in, Harvey.'

Blake recognised the voice immediately and, a moment later, Mathias himself stepped into view.

'Come in, David,' he said, smiling. 'You look as if you swam here.'

Blake stepped into the hallway.

'Come through into the study,' said the psychic.

Once inside the room, he poured himself a brandy and offered one to Blake who gratefully accepted, his eyes roving around the spacious room. He noted with bewilderment that there were no windows. The only light came from a desk lamp and two floor-standing spotlamps near the drink cabinet. On one wall there was a framed original sketch by Aleister Crowley depicting the Whore of Babylon. Blake looked closely at it.

'You knew Crowley?' he asked.

'We met once or twice,' said Mathias.

'The Great Beast himself eh?' murmured Blake, sipping his brandy. 'A self-confessed Black Magician.' Mathias didn't answer.

Blake allowed his gaze to shift to a photograph. It showed Mathias and another man who looked familiar to him.

'Anton Le Vey,' said the psychic.

'Another friend?' asked Blake.

Mathias nodded.

'Another Black Magician,' the writer commented.

The psychic seated himself behind his desk and cradled his brandy glass in one hand, warming the dark fluid.

'What can I do for you, David?' he wanted to know. 'It must be important to bring you out in weather like this.' He downed most of his brandy in one swallow.

Blake seated himself on the closest chair.

'It is,' he informed Mathias. 'Have you seen a newspaper today, or watched television?'

'No, why?'

Mathias finished his brandy and got to his feet, walking past the writer who turned until he was gazing at the psychic's back.

'Toni Landers' son was killed earlier today,' he said.

Mathias filled his glass once again then turned round, the bottle still in his hand.

'He was killed in an accident,' the writer persisted.

'Do you want another drink?' Mathias asked, apparently uninterested in what Blake had to say.

'Did you hear what I said?' the writer asked, irritably. 'Toni Landers' son is dead. Haven't you got anything to say?'

Mathias regarded him indifferently then shrugged his shoulders.

'I'm very sorry,' he said, softly. 'He was only a young boy.'

'You knew he was going to die,' Blake said, flatly. 'You told me at the party the other night, after the Tarot reading. Only you didn't learn of his death through the cards did you?'

'The cards act as a guide,' said Mathias, sipping his drink. 'They point me toward the truth.'

'Come on, Jonathan,' Blake muttered, exasperatedly. 'You're not talking to one of your bloody "flock" now.'

The two men regarded one another coolly for a moment, a heavy silence descending upon them. It was broken by Mathias.

'I told you that the Astral body can be controlled,' he said. 'Well, it can also be projected forward in time. I "saw" that Toni Landers' son was going to die because I felt no Astral presence from him.' He sipped at his brandy once again. 'The Astral body is like the life-line on a hand, someone with the knowledge can "see" it.'

'Tell *my* future,' said Blake, reaching for a pack of Tarot cards which lay on the desk near to Mathias. 'Do it now.'

He had already begun shuffling the cards.

'No,' said Mathias.

Blake divided the cards into ten packs and laid them out in the correct pattern.

'Do it, Jonathan,' he urged.

'I told you, I'm not a fairground showman,' muttered the psychic, irritably. He regarded the cards without emotion, his gaze slowly rising until his brilliant blue eyes were fixed on Blake. 'I'd appreciate it if you would leave now, David,' he said, quietly.

The two men locked stares for a moment then Blake took a step backward, brushing one strand of hair from his face.

'Are you afraid of what you might see?' he asked.

Mathias didn't answer. His face was impassive, registering no emotion at all. Finally, he exhaled, his features softening slightly.

'You asked me about my power,' he said. 'This force inside me, it's the power of the shadow.'

Blake looked puzzled.

'Not the shadow cast by sunlight or reflected in a mirror,' Mathias continued. 'The shadow of the inner self. The alter ego if you like. The Ancients called it the shadow because it represented the darker side of man, the side which only appeared in times of anger or fear. The side which could drive a man to commit acts of which he was not normally capable. Acts which went against his nature. Human nature.'

'Like a split personality?' said Blake.

'No,' Mathias corrected him. 'In cases of split personality the victim retains *some* traces of good within himself. The shadow is wholly evil.'

'Then your power is evil,' Blake said.

'Who is to say what is good and what is evil, David?'

There was another long pause then Blake turned and headed towards the door.

'I've told you as much as I can,' Mathias said. 'What more do you need to know?'

'A lot more,' he said, opening the door. Then, he was gone.

The psychic sat alone in his study, the Tarot cards still laid out in their cabbalistic pattern before him. He paused for a moment then reached towards the seventh pack. To Love. He turned the card slowly.

Thirteen.

La Mort.

Death.

Mathias stared at the sythe-carrying skeleton depicted on the card

84

for a moment then he reached for the top card on the ninth pack. To Health.

Fifteen.

Le Diable.

The Devil.

But he knew that the cards carried much more than their face value. The card marked XV also meant The Great Secret. Mathias smiled to himself. It seemed most appropriate in Blake's case.

He turned the card on the final pack, the breath catching in his throat as he did so.

Twelve.

Le Pendu.

The Hanged Man.

Mathias dropped the card as if it had been red hot; he swallowed hard and studied the image on the card.

The Hanged Man.

Catastrophe.

He wiped his brow, finding that he was perspiring slightly. It had another interpretation.

Saint or Sinner?

Outside the thunder rumbled loudly and Mathias sat still in his seat for a moment. He finally gathered up the cards, sorting them into some kind of uniformity.

As he reached for the one which bore The Hanged Man he wondered why his hand was shaking.

15

Oxford

As she approached the door which led into Maurice Grant's quarters, Kelly looked at her watch.

It was approaching 5.09 p.m.

She slowed her pace, conscious of the sound which her heels made in the solitude of the corridor. She felt strangely ill-at-ease, like a child who has performed, or is about to perform, an act for which it knows it will be punished. Kelly brushed one hand through her brown hair and attempted to control her accelerated breathing. This was ridiculous, she told herself. She had no reason to be nervous.

Over her skirt and blouse she wore a lab coat and in one of the pockets nestled a hypodermic syringe.

She had taken it, along with its contents, from the pharmacy on the first floor. Ordinarily, it was a place only frequented by the four doctors who worked for the Institute, although the other investigators were free to come and go as they wished amongst the rows and rows of bottles and medical equipment. Kelly had found what she sought without difficulty, then she had recovered a disposable syringe from the drawer which was so carefully marked. Everything in the pharmacy was maintained by a woman in her forties known to Kelly only as Mrs King. She was responsible for ensuring that everything was in its correct place and it was a job which she did very efficiently.

Kelly knew that Mrs King usually left for home at around 4.30 so she had waited until nearly 4.50 before venturing into the pharmacy.

To her relief it had been deserted but still she had felt the compulsion to hurry, wondering what explanation she was going to use if someone should discover her poring over the chemicals which were the domain of the physicians.

She had drawn off 10ml of atropine sulphate and then placed the syringe in her pocket.

Now, as she approached Maurice Grant's quarters thoughts began to tumble through her mind with increased rapidity. But one in particular seemed to flash like neon in her consciousness. The incident the day before last when Grant had finally persuaded her to undertake this new experiment without either the knowledge or authorization of Dr Vernon. Deprived of sleep for forty-eight hours, Grant had become violent and Kelly remembered how the subsequent tests on him had revealed activity in an area of the brain normally dormant. The question of what would happen to him if he were not allowed to sleep and dream for longer than two days had tortured her ever since. She had wondered what he'd be like after a week but Kelly didn't have a week. She would not, could not, wait that long.

The injection of atropine would have more or less the same results.

She knew that, given in overdose, the drug caused stimulation of the brain and autonomic nervous system. The usual dosage was 2ml.

She planned to give Grant three times that amount.

Kelly knocked on the door and waited, casting one furtive glance up the corridor as she did so. The Institute was silent.

'Come in,' Grant called and Kelly did so.

He was sitting at a table finishing a plate of fish and chips which had been brought to him ten minutes earlier.

'Sorry if I'm interrupting your tea, Mr Grant,' Kelly said.

He smiled and shook his head.

'I was just finishing,' he told her. 'That's one good thing about this place, the food's terrific.' He belched loudly, excused himself and pushed the plate away.

Kelly thought how different he looked from the last time she'd seen him. In place of the demonic, violent and unkempt would-be killer there was a calm, clean-shaven even handsome man. Grant wore only a white shirt and grey trousers, both of which looked neat and fresh.

'What can I do for you now?' he asked.

'I'm afraid we need your help with something else,' Kelly told him.

'Which is your polite way of saying "Excuse me Mr Human Guinea Pig, we want you back on the slab," right?'

Kelly smiled thinly.

'Yes it is,' she said.

Grant chuckled.

'No need to sound so apologetic. After all, I was the bloody fool who volunteered for all this,' he remarked, good-humouredly.

Kelly had one hand dug deep in the pocket of her lab coat, fingers toying with the syringe.

'What exactly is it that you want me to do?' Grant enquired.

'Do you remember anything about the incident the day before last?' she wanted to know. 'When you attacked one of my colleagues?'

He shrugged.

'Not much. I remember trying to . . .' The words trailed off, almost as if he were ashamed of the recollection. 'I didn't hurt anyone badly did I?'

Kelly shook her head.

'You'd been kept awake for over forty-eight hours,' she told him. 'People become aggressive when they're forced to go without sleep for too long.'

'Why?' Grant wanted to know.

'If we knew that for sure, Mr Grant, you wouldn't still be here.' She thought about mentioning the dream theory then decided not to. There was a long silence broken eventually by Kelly. 'For the last two nights have you dreamed?'

'Yes,' he said.

'The dream about killing your wife and son?'

He nodded.

'But it wasn't as vivid. In fact, last night it was different. I woke up before I killed them.'

'That was probably because you weren't given any drugs,' Kelly told him. 'The amphetamines we'd been giving you had been intensifying the dreams up until that point.'

'So, what happens now?' he asked.

Kelly felt the hypodermic in her pocket.

'We try a different approach,' she said.

On the table beside Grant's bed was a new tape-recorder and Kelly checked that it was working properly. Satisfied, she asked Grant to lie down. There were restraining straps which could be fastened around his wrists and ankles but, as yet, Kelly did not touch them. She ensured that Grant was comfortable then asked him to roll up the sleeve of his shirt which he did. The vein bulged invitingly in the crook of his arm and Kelly carefully pushed the needle into it, one thumb on the plunger of the syringe.

She began to push, the atropine flooding into Grant's bloodstream.

She watched the markers on the syringe as she forced the liquid into his vein.

0.25ml.

0.75ml.

1ml.

Grant still had his eyes open, wincing slightly as Kelly pushed a little too hard on the syringe. She could see the needle-point beneath his flesh as she pressed on the plunger again.

1.5ml.

2ml.

2.5ml.

She was trying to stop herself from shaking, worried that too much movement would tear the vein open. Grant sucked in a painful breath and Kelly apologised but kept the pressure on the plunger, watching as more of the liquid was transferred to the man's body.

3ml.

3.5ml.

4ml.

Grant closed his eyes, his chest beginning to heave as his respiration became more laboured. Kelly looked at his face then at the needle embedded in his arm and finally at the markers on the slim receptacle itself.

4.5ml.

5ml.

5.5ml.

Kelly knew that the atropine would not take long to work and, with the increased dosage she was administering, that time should be curtailed further.

6ml.

She hesitated. Grant had closed his eyes tightly now. His mouth also was clamped shut, his lips bloodless.

Kelly, the needle still clutched in her hand, the point buried in Grant's vein, looked at the man. He was visibly turning pale. Had she given him enough?

'Mr Grant,' she said.

He didn't answer.

'Mr Grant.'

A weary grunt was the only reply she received this time.

Kelly pushed harder on the plunger.

6.5ml.

7ml.

Perspiration formed in salty droplets on his face, some running together to trickle in rivulets across his flesh. On his arms too there was moisture, glistening like beads. The skin around the needle was beginning to turn a dark crimson, the blue veins pulsing more strongly.

89

7.5ml.

8ml.

Grant moaned, his mouth dropping open. Thick sputum oozed over his lips and onto the sheet beneath. His tongue lolled uselessly from one corner and he grunted again, coughed. Particles of spittle flew into the air and, as he moved slightly, the needle came free.

Cursing, Kelly pushed it back into the vein, ignoring the single tiny droplet of blood which had welled up through the first minuscule hole. She looked at his face which was now grey, streaked with perspiration. She knew she was taking a chance but this had to work.

9ml.

9.5ml.

10ml.

Kelly withdrew the needle and stepped back, dropping the syringe into her pocket once more. She switched on the tape recorder and moved the microphone as close as she dared to Grant. His body began to undergo almost imperceptible movements, tiny muscle contractions which made it look as if he were being pumped full of mild electrical current.

'Mr Grant,' she said. 'Can you hear me?'

He muttered something which she couldn't hear so she took a step closer, bringing the microphone nearer to his mouth.

'Mr Grant.'

His eyes were shut, the lids sealed as tightly as if they'd been stitched.

'Can you hear what I'm saying?'

Grant suddenly grabbed her wrist in a grip which threatened to snap the bones.

Simultaneously, his eyes shot open like shutters and she found herself looking down into two glazed, rheumy orbs which seemed to be staring right through her.

Kelly suppressed a scream and tried to pull away from the vice-like grip but it was useless.

'Help me,' murmured Grant, refusing to release Kelly. 'Oh God they're everywhere.'

He suddenly let her go, his hands clutching at his face.

'What can you see?' she demanded.

Grant suddenly sat up, his face contorted in a mask of rage and hatred.

'Fucking bastard,' he snarled, his blank eyes turning to face her. 'You stinking cunt.' His lips slid back in a vulpine grin and more saliva dribbled down his chin. 'She betrayed me. She thought I didn't know. *She* thought she could fool *me*.'

Kelly edged away slightly.

'Who thought she could fool you?' asked the investigator, moving to the end of the bed.

'*Her*. My wife,' Grant rasped. 'Fucking whore. She made me think the child was mine when it was *his* all along.'

'Is that why you wanted to kill her?' asked Kelly, moving towards the restraining straps, waiting for her chance to slip them over Grant's ankles although she didn't give much for her chances.

And what if she failed . . . ?

'Yes, I wanted to kill her. Her and the child. *His* fucking child,' Grant raved.

But, his anger seemed to subside with alarming speed and he was cowering once more from some unseen menace. Shielding his face and eyes with shaking hands.

'Get them off me,' he shrieked.

'What can you see?' demanded Kelly, deciding that it was time to fasten the straps.

'Spiders,' he told her. 'Thousands of them. All over me. Oh God, no.'

Kelly managed to fasten the two ankle straps, securing Grant to the bed, at least for the time being. The leather looked thick and stout. She hoped that it would hold.

Maurice Grant wondered why she could not see the eight-legged horrors seething over the floor of the room and onto the bed. Over his body, inside his clothes. He could feel their hairy legs on his flesh as they crawled onto his stomach, up his trouser legs, across his chest, up his neck to his face. And there they tried to force their way into his mouth. He felt one on his tongue and he plunged two fingers into his mouth to pull the creature out. The probing digits touched the back of his throat and he heaved violently.

Above him, the spiders were coming through the ceiling. They were

91

emerging from the stone-work itself and they were getting bigger. One the size of his fist dropped from the ceiling on to his face, its thick legs probing at his eyes and nose. One of the smaller creatures scuttled up his left nostril, trying to pull the swollen bulk of its abdomen inside the orifice.

From the wall beside him, a spider the size of a football emerged and clamped itself on his arm, pinning it to the bed. Another did the same with his right arm.

Kelly watched mesmerised as Grant wriggled beneath the imaginary host of arachnids but she was not too engrossed to by-pass the opportunity to secure his wrists to the bed.

'They're inside my head,' screamed Grant as he felt more and more of the spiders dragging themselves up his nostrils, into his ears.

'I know where they're coming from,' he screeched. '*She* sent them.'

'Your wife?' asked Kelly, watching as Grant continued to squirm.

'Fucking cunt. Fucking slut.'

His fear had been replaced once more by rage.

'I'm glad I killed her,' he roared. 'She deserved to die.'

The veins on his forehead bulged angrily as he strained against the straps. 'I don't care if anyone saw me. I had no choice. I saw them together,' he said, his body jerking wildly. 'I saw her with him. He stuck it between her legs, in her mouth. AND SHE FUCKING WANTED IT. I don't want to see it anymore.'

'Can you see it now?' Kelly asked.

'Yes.'

'What can you see? Tell me exactly.'

Grant was using all his strength to tug himself free and Kelly noticed with horror that one of the wrist straps was beginning to creak under the pressure.

'I can see her on the floor of the bedroom. *Our* bedroom. She's naked and so is he,' Grant snarled.

'Who is *he*?' Kelly wanted to know.

'She's sucking his cock. He's using his tongue on her.'

The right hand strap creaked ominously as Grant continued to thrash around.

'I don't want to see it anymore. Never again.'

Kelly wondered if she should get help. Grant was hallucinating madly it appeared but he was largely coherent. And, at last, she knew why he had wanted to kill his wife and son.

'She's rolled over on to her stomach and he's putting his cock into her. The filthy fucking whore. She wants him.'

'Who is he?' Kelly demanded.

'My brother,' roared Grant and, with that, made one last monumental effort to break free.

The right hand strap split first, then came free.

'I don't want to see it. I DON'T WANT TO SEE IT,' Grant bellowed, tugging himself out of the ankle restraints and the other wrist strap. He staggered to his feet, his chest expanding until it threatened to rip his shirt. 'I don't want to see it,' he said again and lurched towards the table in the middle of the room. There, his searching hands found the greasy fork.

'I NEVER WANT TO SEE IT AGAIN,' he shrieked and raised the pronged implement.

Kelly knew that she could never reach the door. Grant blocked her way but, as she looked at him anxiously, she saw that his anger was not directed at her.

'I won't watch,' he said, quietly, studying the fork which he held only inches from his face.

With quivering hand, he pushed the fork through his lower lid and into his eye. With infinite slowness he moved it in a digging action, the prongs gouging muscle and flesh as Grant shoved it further until the eye itself began to thrust forward. The prongs raked his skull as he prised the bursting orb from its socket. Blood gushed down his cheek, mingling with the vitreous liquid as the eye itself punctured. It did not come free but hung, suspended by the shredded remains of the optic nerve.

Mind numbing pain enveloped him but he managed to remain upright, guiding the fork towards his other eye.

Kelly gagged as she saw the prongs burrow through the upper lid this time, the curve of the fork enabling Grant to reach the retina itself. With a final despairing scream he managed to scoop the bloodied eye free of his skull.

There was a muffled, liquid plop as the orb left the socket, a vile sucking sound which was soon drowned out by Grant's agonised shriek.

The eye itself dropped to the floor and lay there intact until Grant dropped to his knees, squashing it beneath him as if it had been an oversized grape.

Kelly found herself transfixed by those oozing sockets from which crimson was pumping in thick spurts, dribbling into the man's open mouth.

She finally tore her gaze away and bolted for the door, wrenching it open and dashing out into the corridor.

The room was soundproofed. Until Kelly opened the door, the building had remained quiet but now the agonised shrieks of the blinded Grant echoed along every inch of the building. So great was the dose of atropine he'd received, so powerful the boost to his nervous system, Grant was even denied the merciful oblivion of unconsciousness. He merely slumped to the floor of the room moaning, the remains of one eye still dangling uselessly by a strand of nerve.

Inside the room, the tape recorder obediently captured the sounds of agony. Preserving them forever.

16

'How much did you say you gave him?' Dr Vernon asked Kelly, reaching for the syringe.

'10ml, perhaps a little more,' she said, quietly.

Vernon nodded and held the hypodermic between his fingers for a moment before setting it down on the table again. He laid it beside the bloodstained fork, allowing his gaze to ponder on the implement for a few seconds. He exhaled and looked around the room. The floor was spattered with blood, droplets of it had splashed a wide area, puddling into bigger pools in one or two places. There was a purplish smudge close to his foot where the eye had been squashed and Vernon moved to one side.

The remains of the restraining straps lay on or near the bed and, he noticed that there were even a few speckles of crimson on the sheets.

Maurice Grant had been removed about fifteen minutes earlier.

Now Vernon stood amidst the carnage, flanked by Kelly and John Fraser.

Fraser looked distinctly queasy and could not seem to tear his gaze from the blood-stained fork on the table. The mere thought of what it had been used for made him feel sick.

'Is he going to die?' asked Kelly, anxiously.

'The ambulancemen didn't seem to know one way or the other,' Vernon told her. 'Once the effects of the atropine wear off he'll go into shock. After that . . .' He allowed the sentence to trail off.

'So, first he nearly kills me,' said Fraser. 'Now he more or less succeeds in killing himself. Surely this is enough for you, doctor?'

'What do you mean?' Vernon wanted to know.

'There will have to be a full-scale enquiry into what happened today. There's no way that you can continue with this research now.'

'As Director of the Institute *I* will decide if an enquiry is necessary or not,' Vernon told him.

'Do you seriously think that the outside authorities are going to let something like this drop without investigating it?'

'I couldn't give a damn about the outside authorities,' snapped Vernon. 'What goes on inside these walls in *my* concern.'

'And the fact that a man could have died today doesn't bother you?' Fraser said, challengingly.

'Grant knew that he might be taking risks when he agreed to participate in the experiments.'

'Acceptable risks, yes, but . . .'

Vernon cut him short.

'Risks,' he said, forcefully.

Fraser now turned his attention to Kelly.

'With all due respect, Kelly, you are responsible for this,' he said.

'I realize that,' she said. Then, to Vernon:

'I'm prepared to resign.'

'No,' he said, without hesitation. 'That wouldn't solve anything.'

Kelly could not conceal the look of surprise which flickered across her face.

'She broke every rule of this bloody Institution,' growled Fraser. 'She nearly killed a man as well and you . . .'

It was Kelly's turn to interrupt.

'Don't talk about me as if I'm not here,' she snarled. 'I know I was in the wrong. God knows I wish I could repair the damage I've done.'

'The research had to be taken to its logical conclusion,' Vernon said, supportively.

'That conclusion presumably being the death of the subject,' said Fraser, sarcastically.

'There was no way of knowing exactly how the atropine would affect Mr Grant,' said Vernon, as if he were defending himself instead of Kelly. She looked on dumbfounded as he came to her rescue.

'A dose of 5ml is considered dangerous. We all know the effects of the drugs we use. Kelly should have known that injecting Grant with twice that amount would have serious side-effects.'

'Did Grant actually say anything of use while he was drugged?' Vernon wanted to know.

'Is that important now?' Fraser said, angrily.

Vernon turned on him, his grey eyes blazing.

'Yes, it is important. The only thing that matters is that this project is successful. If certain sacrifices have to be made then that's unfortunate but unavoidable.'

'You're insane,' said Fraser, his tone a little more controlled now. 'This isn't research to you anymore, it's an obsession. How many more people are going to be injured or killed before you're satisfied? Before you have the answers you want?'

'That's enough, Fraser,' Vernon warned him.

'Do you honestly think that any of this is going to help *you*?' the investigator said, cryptically.

Kelly looked at him, wondering what he meant.

'Fraser.' There was more than a hint of anger in Vernon's voice.

'What *are* you looking for, doctor?' the investigator demanded. 'Or more importantly, why are you looking?'

'This isn't the time or the place to . . .'

'Perhaps if we knew about whatever it is you've managed to hide for so long then . . .'

Fraser's words were choked back as Vernon lunged forward and grabbed him by the lapels. The older man's face was flushed and there was a thin film of perspiration on his forehead. He fixed the investigator in his steely grey stare and held him there. Kelly looked on with concern and interest, wondering whether or not she should intervene.

'This time, Fraser, you've gone too far,' hissed the doctor. He pushed the investigator away, watching as he fell against the table. 'Now get out of here. Out of this room. Out of this Institute. You're finished here.'

Fraser dragged himself upright and steadied himself against the table.

'Perhaps the police might be interested in what happened here today,' he said, threateningly.

'The police will be informed, when I think it's necessary,' Vernon told him. 'Now, get out.'

Fraser looked at Vernon a moment longer, then at Kelly.

'I'm sorry, Kelly,' he said apologetically and made for the door. They both heard his footsteps echo away down the corridor.

Vernon pulled a handkerchief from his trouser pocket and wiped his face. He pulled a chair out from beneath the table and sat down, ignoring the bloodied fork which lay before him. Kelly watched as he popped a menthol sweet into his mouth and sucked it. His face was still tinged red with anger and he shuffled his fingers impatiently before him.

Kelly licked her lips, finding them dry, like her mouth. She wanted to ask Vernon what Fraser had meant, just as she had when he'd made the other cryptic remark two days before.

'. . . whatever it is you've managed to hide for so long.' Fraser's words stood out clearly in her mind. Why had Vernon reacted so angrily?

'Dr Vernon, Grant said that he'd killed his wife. It was like a confession,' she said. 'It's all on the tape, every word.'

Vernon didn't speak.

'What could he have meant?' she persisted.

'It must have been the effects of the drug, you said he was hallucinating.'

'Yes, but no one mentioned to him that a neighbour had identified a man like him the day his wife and son were butchered. Why should he say that?'

'Look, Kelly, I think we have enough to worry about with what

97

happened today,' Vernon said, evasively. 'And it would be best if you left here. I'll call you in a fortnight or so, the research can't continue until after the enquiry anyway.'

'Can the authorities close the Institute?' she wanted to know.

Vernon shook his head.

'No. And don't worry, your job will still be here when you come back.'

'Why didn't you accept my resignation?' she asked.

'Because what you did was based on sound theory. It was a chance which had to be taken eventually.'

Kelly nodded although it was not an explanation which wholly satisfied her. Vernon appeared to have more than a scientific interest in the outcome of the research. The question was, why?

Finally, she slipped off her lab coat and decided it was time to leave. She and Vernon exchanged brief farewells and he repeated his promise to contact her in two weeks.

Vernon waited until she had left the room then he walked slowly around it, his eyes drawn occasionally to the spots and splashes of congealing blood, now slowly turning rusty as it solidified. There was a slight smell of copper in the air. He eventually reached the tape recorder. He pressed the re-wind button and watched as the twin spools spun in reverse. When the process was completed he took the full one and dropped it into his pocket, deciding to listen to it in the privacy of his office. As he made his way out of the room, two cleaners were entering armed with mops and dusters. They set about removing all traces of the horrors which had occurred in there.

Vernon crunched his cough sweet up and replaced it with another as he walked up the stairs towards his office. His secretary had gone home an hour earlier so he had the place to himself.

Nonetheless, he locked his office door before settling down to listen to the tape.

Twice he played it through, his face impassive, even when Maurice Grant's shrieks of agony began to erupt from the speaker. Half-way through the third play Vernon switched it off. He sat for what seemed like an eternity, his chair facing the window, then he swung round and reached for the phone. He hurriedly dialled the number he wanted and tapped agitatedly on the desk top with his stubby fingers as he waited for the receiver to be picked up. He heard the click as it finally was.

'The Metapsychic Centre?' he asked. 'This is Dr Stephen Vernon. I want to speak to Alain Joubert. Tell him it's important.'

10.06 p.m.

Kelly folded the last of her clothes and laid the skirt gently on top of the other things. The only light in the bedroom came from a bedside lamp which cast a warm golden glow over the room. Kelly decided that she had packed enough clothes and lifted the case from the bed onto the floor. She felt stiff all over, her neck and shoulders in particular ached. She resolved to take a shower and have an early night.

She intended leaving early in the morning.

The day had been an exhausting one both metally and physically and she felt the need to relax more than she usually did upon returning home in the evenings. She'd only half-eaten her dinner, washing it down with two or three Martinis. The effect of the drink was beginning to make her feel pleasantly drowsy. She unbuttoned her blouse, laying it over a chair before slipping out of her jeans and folding them carefully. Standing before the full length mirror on the wardrobe she unhooked her bra, her breasts remaining taut even when the garment was removed. Kelly skimmed off her panties and tossed them to one side, glancing at herself in the mirror. The reflection which stared back at her was a pleasing one.

Despite the fact that she was only five feet two inches tall, her slender frame gave her an appearance of striking elegance which was normally reserved for taller women. She had small but plump breasts, her lower body tapering in to form a tiny waist and smooth lean hips. Her legs were slim, usually appearing longer when she wore the high heels she favoured.

Kelly walked through into the bathroom and turned on the shower, stepping beneath its cleansing jets when it was at a suitable temperature. She stood motionless, allowing the water to run over her face, washing away what little make-up she used. She began soaping herself.

As she stood beneath the spray she allowed her mind to back-track to the events of earlier in the day. To Vernon.

Why was he protecting her? It didn't make sense. Unless, as Fraser had intimated, he *did* have something to hide. Vernon obviously saw Kelly as a useful tool.

As she closed her eyes, the vision of Maurice Grant, his eyes ripped from the sockets, flashed before her and she jerked her eyes open again.

She thought of his confession.

Had it been the drugs which had caused his outburst, she wondered? Instinct told her that there was more to it than that. And yet, how could he have killed his wife and son? She and three other people had seen him strapped down at the time the killings supposedly took place.

She stood beneath the shower a moment longer then flicked it off, dried herself and padded back into the bedroom. She sat on the edge of the bed and reached for the phone.

It was a recorded message, which suited her because she didn't feel much like talking. She scribbled down a few details as the metallic voice droned on then, finally, she replaced the receiver, glancing down at what she had written.

She would catch the 9.30 flight to Paris in the morning.

17

Paris

The restaurant in the Place de Wagram was crowded, more so than usual because many had sought shelter inside from the rain which was pelting down. Waiters threaded their way through the maze of tables balancing trays and plates precariously on their arms. A wine glass was dropped and shattered loudly on the wooden floor.

Lasalle spun round in his seat, startled by the sound. He saw a waiter picking up the pieces of broken glass while a customer complained loudly.

'Did you hear me?'

The voice brought Lasalle back to his senses.

'What did you say?' he asked, blankly, turning back to face Joubert who was chewing hungrily on a piece of meat.

'I said, I don't like the idea of her working with us,' Joubert repeated.

'Come now, Alain, when these experiments first began it was agreed that there would be co-operation between the two Institutes. I don't understand your objections.'

'The experiments carried out in England have not been as successful as ours,' Joubert complained.

'How do you know that?' Lasalle asked, sipping at his wine.

His companion paused for a moment, swallowing the piece of food he'd been chewing.

'Because we'd have heard more,' he said, quickly.

Lasalle looked up and saw a familiar figure making her way back towards the table. He tapped Joubert's arm and motioned for him to be quiet but the other Frenchman merely muttered something under his breath.

Kelly sat down and smiled across the table at Lasalle. Joubert did not look up from his meal. She picked up her knife and fork and set about her salad once more.

She had arrived in Paris over three hours earlier and, after booking into a hotel, she had taken a taxi to the Metapsychic Centre. Once there she had introduced herself to the Director and asked if she could see Lasalle. The two investigators had been friends for some time and he was happy to allow her to work with him.

The reaction of Joubert could not have been more different. Upon hearing that Kelly was to assist them in their experiments he had barely been able to restrain his anger, managing only by a monumental effort of will to disguise his open dislike of her presence.

She had explained, briefly, what had happened with Maurice Grant and why she had been forced to come to France. Joubert had been unimpressed and, when she had asked to look at the notes which the two men had compiled, he had been openly hostile, guarding the files jealously. She wondered why he should have taken such a dislike to her.

'If you'd let me know you were coming,' said Lasalle, 'I could have made up the bed in my spare room. It would have saved you paying for a hotel.'

'I'm fine where I am thankyou,' Kelly assured him, smiling.

'When were you thinking of going back?' Joubert asked without looking up.

'Not for a while yet,' Kelly told him.

'What exactly do you think you can learn here?' Joubert continued, still not paying her the courtesy of a glance.

'It's not so much a case of learning,' Kelly began. 'I . . .'

He cut her short, his dark eyes finally pinning her in a malevolent stare.

'Then what do you want here?' he hissed.

Kelly met his stare, her own anger now boiling up. Who the hell did Joubert think he was anyway? she thought.

'I told you why I came here,' she said. 'I couldn't carry on working at the Institute in England, not while the enquiry was being conducted. I thought I might be of some help to you.'

'Don't you think we're capable then?' he said, challengingly.

'Are you this rude to everyone or have *I* been singled out for that honour?' she said, angrily.

Joubert stopped eating and looked at her warily.

'Can't we all just finish our food in peace?' said Lasalle, looking at his two companions.

Joubert put down his knife and fork and wiped his mouth with a napkin.

'I've finished anyway,' he said. 'It's about time I went back to the Centre. There's a lot to do this afternoon.' He balled up his napkin and dropped it on to the table, getting to his feet. He looked down at Lasalle. 'I trust I'll see you later?'

Lasalle nodded.

'And no doubt you too, Miss Hunt,' Joubert added, scornfully. With that he pushed past some people who were waiting for a table and headed for the door. Lasalle watched him go.

'I must apologise for my colleague,' he said.

'I'm sorry if I've caused any trouble between the two of you,' said Kelly.

'Joubert is a good man but, sometimes, he lets our work get to him.'

'I noticed,' Kelly told him, spearing a piece of tomato with her fork. 'Speaking of work, have you made much progress?'

'There is so much to discover,' said Lasalle. 'The unconscious mind is a vast area.' He took a sip of his wine. 'We did have some success

102

three or four days ago. A subject named Décard. Whilst in a trance he was able to see the future.'

'Precognition?' she said, excitedly.

'But only while hypnotised. When he was brought out of the trance he could remember nothing of what he had seen.' The Frenchman paused. 'It was all rather unfortunate. He foretold the death of his own daughter.'

Kelly sat bolt upright, as if she had just been nudged with a cattle prod.

'I wasn't told about this,' she said.

Lasalle frowned.

'Joubert was supposed to have relayed the information to you.'

'I heard nothing,' Kelly assured him.

The Frenchman looked puzzled and a heavy silence descended momentarily.

Kelly wondered if she should mention the murder of Maurice Grant's family but she decided against it, content to let the thoughts and ideas tumble over inside her head.

'What I said about you staying with me,' Lasalle said. 'I hope you weren't offended by it.'

Kelly smiled.

'Of course not,' she said.

'I didn't mean anything by it but, since Madelaine died, the house has seemed . . . bigger than it used to.' He smiled humourlessly.

'I understand,' Kelly told him. 'How are you managing on your own?'

'I get by,' he said, reaching inside his jacket for the bottle of tranquilizers. 'With a little help.' He held one of the capsules before him, swallowing it with some water.

Kelly studied his face, noticing how much he had changed since the last time she had seen him. His dark hair was streaked with patches of grey, particularly around his temples. Deep lines cut swathes across his forehead and around his eyes and his cheeks appeared bloodless. He had lost weight too she suspected. But, for all that his eyes retained a glint of passion and energy which seemed to have deserted the rest of his body.

'Probably if we had had children then it wouldn't have been so

103

bad,' he said. 'As it is, there is no one else left for me.' He gazed at his wine glass for a moment longer then seemed to shake off the cloak of melancholy. A smile spread across his face. 'Enough of this,' he said. 'How are you, Kelly? Have you any plans to marry?'

'She looked at him aghast.

'Definitely not,' she said.

'You mean there is no man waiting to sweep you off your feet?' He chuckled.

'If there is he's keeping himself well hidden,' Kelly replied.

Lasalle laughed, an infectious sound which cut through the babble in the restaurant and caused a couple of heads to turn.

Her tone changed slightly.

'Michel, about this man who had the precognitive vision. Décard you say his name was?'

Lasalle nodded.

'What exactly did he see?'

The Frenchman told her.

'And was Joubert present when this happened?' Kelly asked.

'Yes, he seemed quite excited by it all.'

Kelly brushed a hand through her hair, stroking the back of it with her palm. Why hadn't Joubert told her about the incident? Why the secrecy? When the two Institutes were supposed to be working together it seemed only natural that information as important as that should be available.

She wondered what else the Frenchman had neglected to tell her.

Lasalle looked at his watch.

'I suppose we should be getting back,' he said.

Kelly got to her feet and the two of them made their way towards the exit. Outside it was still raining, the banks of dark cloud overhead showing no promise of respite.

As they ran towards Lasalle's car, Kelly wondered if Joubert's attitude might change as the afternoon wore on.

Somehow she doubted it.

18

Using a small wooden spatula Lasalle gently applied the sticky conductant to three places on Joubert's face. One at each temple and another just above the bridge of his nose.

Kelly attached the electrodes carefully and Joubert himself readjusted them, lifting his head slightly as Lasalle pressed the last two against the back of his head.

That done, Joubert lay back on the couch, hands clasped across his chest. The Frenchman lay motionless, his eyes peering at some point on the ceiling. Lasalle reached for his hand. He fumbled along the wrist and located the pulse which he took and noted on a clipboard. Then, like a doctor examining a patient, he took a penlight from his pocket and shone it in his companion's eyes, checking the pupillary reactions.

'Ready?' he asked.

Joubert nodded gently.

Lasalle turned to Kelly who flicked a switch on the EEG and, immediately, the five tracers began to move back and forth gently across the paper.

The Frenchman reached into his pocket and pulled out the pocket watch. He dangled it before Joubert, the golden time-piece twisting round slowly.

'Now, keep your eyes on the watch,' he said, seeing that his colleague's gaze had drifted to the spinning object. Lasalle began rolling the chain between his thumb and index finger.

'You can hear only my voice,' he said. Then, to Kelly:

'Turn off the lights will you?'

She left the EEG and scuttled across to the light switch, flicking it off. The room was immersed in darkness, lit only by a spot-lamp near the foot of the couch. The single beam occasionally glinted on the watch making it look as if it were glowing.

'You can see nothing but the watch,' said Lasalle. 'You can hear nothing but my voice. Do you understand?'

'Yes,' said Joubert, throatily.

'I am going to count to five and, as I do, you will become increasingly more tired. Do you understand?'

'Yes.'

'By the time I reach five you will be asleep but you will still be able to hear me. Do you understand?'

'Yes.'

Kelly moved slowly and quietly back towards the EEG, glancing down at the read-out. The lines made by the tracers were still relatively level. None showed too much movement. Just a gentle sweep back and forth.

Lasalle began counting.

He saw his companion's eyelids begin to droop but he kept spinning the watch even after Joubert had finally closed his eyes.

Kelly looked on with interest.

'You are now in a deep sleep,' said Lasalle. 'But, you are able to hear everything I say. Do you understand?'

'Yes.'

'What is your name?'

'Alain Joubert.'

'How old are you?'

'Thirty-six.'

Kelly glanced at the EEG read-out once again, noticing that the five tracers had begun to slow their movements until they were practically running in straight lines, only the occasional movement interrupting their unerring course.

'What is *my* name?' Lasalle asked.

Joubert told him.

'Can you tell me if there is anyone else present in the toom?'

'A woman. I can see her.'

Lasalle frowned and inspected his colleague's eyelids more closely. They were firmly shut. He reached back to the trolley behind him and picked up a stack of cards, each bearing a word.

'Tell me what this word is,' he said, running his eyes over the card marked DOG.

Joubert told him.

'And this one?'

'Cat.'

'Again.'

'Pig.'

Kelly noticed some slight movement from the fifth of the tracers.

Lasalle went through another ten cards and each time Joubert was correct.

'I feel cold,' Joubert said, unasked. Indeed, his body was quivering slightly and, when Lasalle gripped his hand the flesh was ice cold.

The movement from the fifth tracer became more pronounced. The other four, however, did not deviate from their almost arrow-straight course. Kelly swallowed hard. There was something distinctly familiar about this type of read-out. The vision of Maurice Grant flashed into her mind as the fifth tracer began to trace a jerky, erratic path on the paper. Whilst in a drugged, subdued state, it had been the same area of Grant's brain which had shown activity. Now it was happening with Joubert.

'I can see . . .' Joubert words trailed away.

'What can you see?' Lasalle asked him, urgently.

'A room. Like this one but there is a woman working in it. She's sitting at a typewriter with her back to me,' Joubert said. 'She doesn't know I'm behind her, she didn't hear me open the door.'

Kelly saw that the fifth tracer was now hurtling back and forth with such speed it threatened to carve a hole in the paper.

'Who is this woman?' Lasalle asked. 'Do you know her?'

'Yes, I've seen her many times before.'

'What is her name?'

'Danielle Bouchard.'

Lasalle swallowed hard.

'Describe her,' he snapped. 'Now.'

'She is in her thirties, long, curly hair. It's auburn, dyed I think. Her skin is dark, not negroid but coffee-coloured. She's wearing blue eye make-up, some lipstick.'

'Do you know her?' whispered Kelly to Lasalle.

The Frenchman nodded.

'She's part Algerian, a beautiful girl, she works in an office just

107

down the corridor,' he said, quietly, one eye on Joubert who was now flexing his fingers spasmodically. In fact, his whole body was jerking involuntarily.

'What sort of response is showing on the EEG?' asked Lasalle.

'There's no activity in any part of the brain except for the area around the occipital lobe,' she told him. 'Exactly the same as the subject we had.' She paused, mesmerised by the rapid movements of the tracer.

Joubert spoke again.

'She is wearing jeans, a red top. There is a slight tear near the seam of the top, beneath her arm.'

'Is she still typing?' asked Lasalle.

'Yes, she hasn't noticed me yet.'

Lasalle chewed his bottom lip contemplatively.

'This doesn't prove anything,' he said to Kelly. 'Joubert could have seen this woman earlier today.'

Kelly looked once more at the EEG read-out. The fifth tracer continued its rapid movement.

'I'm walking towards her,' Joubert said. 'She has stopped typing now, she is taking the paper from the machine. She still has her back to me.' He was silent for a moment then the tone of his voice seemed to change, it became harsher, as if his mouth were full of phlegm. 'I want her.'

'Tell me what is happening,' Lasalle ordered.

'I grab her hair with one hand and put my other hand over her mouth to stop her screaming. She falls off the chair and I climb on top of her, I must hold her arms down. She is stunned by the fall, she has banged her head. I think she is dazed. I pull up her top to reach her breasts and I am squeezing them, making red marks on them.'

Kelly looked in awe at the fifth tracer which was moving so fast it was little more than a blur.

'I try to keep my hand over her mouth to stop her screaming but she seems to be recovering. I must stop her. I am putting my hands around her throat. It feels so good, my thumbs are on her windpipe, pressing harder. Her eyes are bulging. I am going to kill her. I want to kill her.'

Kelly looked at Lasalle then back at the EEG with its wildly careering tracer.

'I WANT TO KILL HER,' bellowed Joubert.

There was a loud scream from outside the room, long and piercing. A moment's silence and it was followed by another.

'Bring him out of it,' snapped Kelly.

'Listen to me,' said Lasalle. 'When I count to one from five you will wake up. Do you understand?'

No answer.

From down the corridor there was the sound of a slamming door then another scream.

'Do you understand?' Lasalle said, loudly.

'Hurry,' Kelly urged.

Joubert did not respond.

'I can't bring him out of it,' Lasalle said, frantically.

He thought about shaking his colleague but he knew it would do no good. He swallowed hard and looked at Kelly who was already moving towards the door. 'See what's happening,' Lasalle told her.

Kelly hurried out into the corridor and saw that, about thirty yards further down, there were four or five people standing outside one of the doors. A tall man with blond hair was banging on it, twisting the handle impotently. He put his shoulder to it as he heard another scream from inside.

'Joubert, listen to me,' said Lasalle. 'I'm going to begin counting. Five . . .'

'There's something happening,' Kelly told him.

'Four . . .'

The tall blond man was taking a step back to gain more impetus as he tried to shoulder charge the door of the other room.

'Three . . .'

Joubert stirred slightly.

'Two . . .'

Down the corridor, the blond man gritted his teeth and prepared for one final assault on the locked door.

'One . . .'

Joubert opened his eyes and blinked myopically.

He too looked round as he heard the shriek of splintering wood.

109

The blond man crashed into the door, nearly ripping it from its hinges. It slammed back against the wall and he stumbled into the room, followed by the others who had waited.

'What's happening?' asked Joubert, pulling the electrodes from his head.

Kelly walked back into the room, a look of concern on her face. She switched off the EEG and pulled the read-out clear.

'What's going on?' Joubert demanded, getting to his feet. He crossed to the door and looked out in time to see the blond man supporting a dusky skinned girl in jeans and a red top from a room further down the corridor. Even from where he stood, Joubert could see that her top was torn, part of one breast exposed. The girl was bleeding from a gash on her bottom lip and there were several angry red marks around her throat.

Lasalle and Kelly joined him in the corridor as the others approached them.

'What happened?' asked Lasalle.

'Danielle was attacked,' the blond man told him.

'Who by?' Lasalle wanted to know.

As he spoke, the dark-skinned girl lifted her head, brushing her auburn hair from her eyes. She looked at Joubert and screamed, one accusing finger pointing at him. With her other hand she touched her throat.

The girl babbled something in French which Kelly did not understand. She asked Lasalle to translate.

'She said that it was Joubert who attacked her,' the Frenchman said.

'That's impossible,' Joubert snorted, indignantly. 'Anyway, why would I do such a thing?' He looked at Danielle. 'She's hysterical.'

'Well,' said the blond man. 'Someone attacked her. She didn't make these marks herself.' He indicated the angry welts on the girl's neck. 'But I don't see how he got out. The door was locked from the inside.'

Lasalle and Kelly exchanged puzzled glances as the little procession moved past them, heading for the infirmary on the second floor. Danielle looked around, her eyes filled with fear as she gazed at Joubert.

'How could I have attacked her?' he said, irritably, walking back into the room and sitting on the couch.

Kelly and Lasalle followed him.

'Can you remember anything of the last five or ten minutes?' Lasalle asked him.

Joubert shook his head, wiping his forehead with the back of his hand.

Kelly was the first to spot it.

'Joubert,' she said, quietly. 'Look at your nails.'

Beneath the finger nails of both hands were numerous tiny pieces of red cloth.

Exactly the same colour as the blouse worn by Danielle Bouchard. There were also several auburn hairs.

19

'Astral travel.'

Kelly's words echoed around the laboratory.

She looked at the pieces of cloth and hair which Joubert had scraped from beneath his fingernails and deposited in a Petri dish.

'You said you felt cold, just before it all began to happen,' she continued. 'That feeling of coldness is usually associated with Astral projection.'

'An Out of the Body Experience?' said Joubert, incredulously.

'Danielle Bouchard said she was attacked by you. I think she was right. You described her, you described how you tried to strangle her.' She held up the EEG read-out. 'There was a tremendous amount of activity in the occipital area of your brain at that time. That's exactly what happened with Maurice Grant.'

'But it isn't usual for the Astral body, once projected, to appear in tangible form,' Joubert countered. 'Danielle Bouchard doesn't just say she saw me, she says I touched her. Injured her.'

'Have you ever felt any feelings of anger or antagonism towards her?' Kelly asked.

'Not that I've been aware of,' Joubert told her.

'But, *subconsciously*, you may harbour some feelings such as those, for her. The hypnosis released those feelings, just as the drugs unlocked the violent side of Maurice Grant.'

'I don't understand what this has to do with the Astral body,' Lasalle interjected.

'The EEG read-outs seem to point to the fact that the area which controls the subconscious is housed in the occipital lobe,' Kelly said. 'The Astral body is controlled by the subconscious. It functions independently of the rest of the mind. That hidden area we've been looking for, this is it.' She jabbed the read-out with her index finger, indicating the fifth line.

'The subconscious mind controls the Astral body,' Joubert repeated, quietly.

'It looks that way,' Kelly said. 'You performed an act, while in the Astral state, which you could not have carried out while conscious.'

'Are you saying that the Astral body is the evil side of man?' said Lasalle. 'The violent, cruel part of us.'

'It's possible. And hypnosis or drugs can release that other identity,' she told him.

'The other identity knows nothing of right or wrong,' Joubert said. 'It's identical in appearance but not hampered by conscience, remorse or delusions of morality. A being which is completely free of the ethical restraints imposed upon it by society.'

Kelly caught the slight gleam in his eye.

'The Mr Hyde in all of us,' he said.

'What?' Lasalle asked, puzzled.

'Jekyll and Hyde. One side good, one side evil. The conscious mind is Jekyll, the unconscious is Hyde only it may be possible for that evil side to function independently of its host.'

'Think how this discovery will help the treatment of schizophrenia and other mental disorders,' Kelly said.

'But no one is to know of it yet,' Joubert snapped.

'Why?' Lasalle wanted to know. 'It is important, as Kelly says. People . . .'

Joubert cut him short.

'It's too early to reveal our findings,' he rasped.

112

There was a long silence, finally broken by Lasalle.

'Kelly,' he began. 'How do we know that everyone, every man, woman and child, doesn't possess this inner force of evil?'

'I think it's safe to assume they do,' she said, cryptically. 'Only as far as we know, it can only be released by using drugs or hypnosis.'

'As far as we know,' he repeated, his words hanging ominously in the air.

Kelly looked at the dish full of hair and fabric and shuddered.

20

The clock on the wall above him struck one and Lasalle sat back, rubbing his eyes. He checked the time against his own watch and yawned.

He'd been hard at work since seven o'clock that evening, since returning from the Metapsychic Centre. Before him on the polished wood desk lay a 6000 word article which he had been slaving over for the past six hours. He'd stopped only once for a cup of coffee and a sandwich at about 9.30 but most of the sandwich lay uneaten on the plate beside the typewriter. He looked up and found himself caught in the gaze of a woman with flowing blonde hair whose crisp green eyes he seemed to drown in.

The photo of his wife stood in its familiar place on his desk at home. Each time he looked at it he felt the contradictory feelings which had plagued him ever since her death. To look at her brought back all the agony which he had suffered when she'd been taken from him so suddenly, but he also found comfort in those green eyes – as if a part of her lived on and remained with him. He reached for the photo and studied her finely-shaped features. He, himself had taken the picture three years earlier. It was all that remained of her. That and the memories.

He replaced the photo and shook his head, trying to dispel the drowsiness which was creeping over him like a blanket. He knew that he must go to bed soon but there was just one more thing left to do.

He picked up his pen, pulled the writing paper towards him and began writing:

To the Editor,

You will find enclosed an article which contains details of a discovery as important as it is fascinating. Having worked at the Metapsychic Centre in Paris for the past twelve years I have encountered many strange phenomena but nothing of this nature has ever presented itself to me until now.

I realize that the subject of Astral Travel/Projection etc. is one which has fascinated people for many years but never before have facts been so far reaching in their importance as in the case I have recounted in my article.

I hope that you will see fit to publish this article as I feel it has far-reaching implications for all of us.

Yours sincerely,

Lasalle signed it, re-read it then pushed it into the envelope with the article. He sealed it and left it on the desk, deciding to post it in the morning on his way to the centre.

He wandered into the kitchen and poured himself a glass of milk, standing at the sink while he drank it.

What they had discovered that afternoon was far too important to withhold. Besides, Lasalle felt unaccountably ill at ease. The incident with Danielle Bouchard had worried him. Even as he thought about it he felt the hairs on the back of his neck rise slightly.

Others had a right to know the truth.

Whether Joubert liked it or not.

21

New York

Blake picked up a copy of *Time* then decided to wander across to the paperbacks to see if there was anything to pass the time on the flight home. He ran his eyes swiftly over the magazine shelves once more before turning to the books.

He could have been forgiven for not noticing the slim volume.

The cover bore the title: *Journal of Parapsychology*.

Blake reached for it, one of the cover stories catching his eye: *Astral Projection: The Truth*. He flipped open the magazine, found the table of contents and traced the article he sought.

He read the first three paragraphs standing there then he paid for the magazine and left the airport newsstand.

The voice of the flight controller told him that he should go through to the departure gate. Blake hurried to the washroom.

He had flown many times before but he still felt the same twinge of nerves each time. Nerves? Who was he trying to kid? Flying scared him shitless, it was as simple as that. Already his stomach was beginning to turn gentle somersaults. He found that he was alone in the room. He crossed to a sink and filled it with cold water, laying his magazines on one side.

He splashed his face with water, wiping off the excess with his hands when he could find no towel. Blake straightened up and gazed at his reflection in the mirror. He looked pale, his eyes red-rimmed and as he glanced at his watch he saw that his hand was shaking slightly. He had ten minutes before his flight left. He scooped more water into his hands and onto his face, blinking as it stung his eyes. Blake peered into the mirror again.

The image of Mathias stared back at him.

Blake retreated a step, his eyes fixed on the vision in the mirror.

The face of the psychic was immobile, only the eyes moved, those brilliant blue orbs pinning him in that hypnotic stare.

The writer tried to swallow but found that his throat was constricted. He raised both hands to cover his eyes.

He lowered them again slowly, peering into the mirror once more.

The image of Mathias was gone, only his own distraught face was reflected in the glass. Blake let out a relieved gasp and wiped the excess moisture from his face as he moved back to the sink. He peered down into the water.

This time it was his own reflection but the mouth was open in a silent scream, the eyes bulging wide in their sockets. The entire countenance was appallingly bloated and tinged blue.

'No,' rasped Blake and plunged his hands into the sink.

The apparition vanished and he stood there, immersed up to his elbows in water.

Indeed, the two men who walked into the washroom looked at him in bewilderment as he stood motionless, gazing into the sink, as if waiting for the screaming vision to re-appear.

'Hey, fella, are you OK?' one of the men asked, moving cautiously towards Blake.

He tapped the writer on the shoulder.

'I said . . .'

Blake spun round suddenly, his expression blank. He looked like a man who had been woken from a nightmare.

'Are you feeling OK?' the man asked him again.

Blake closed his eyes tightly for a moment and nodded.

'Yes,' he said. 'I'm all right.' Then, fumbling for his dark glasses he put them on, snatched up his magazines and left the washroom.

'Probably freaked out,' said the first man.

'Yeah, he looks like a goddam pot-head.'

'And would you believe that?' the first man said, pointing at the mirror above the sink where Blake had been standing.

Five jagged cracks criss-crossed the glass.

22

Paris

It sounded as if someone were trying to pound a hole in the door.

Lasalle hurried from the kitchen, leaving his dinner on the table. The banging continued, loud and insistent. He turned the handle and opened it.

Joubert barged past him, his features set in an attitude of anger.

For a moment Lasalle was bewildered but he closed the door and followed his colleague through into the sitting room where he stood, splay-legged, in front of the open fire-place. He was gripping something in his right first. A thin film of perspiration sheathed his face, the veins at his temples throbbing angrily.

'What's wrong?' asked Lasalle. 'It must be important for you to come barging into my house like this.'

'It *is* important,' rasped Joubert.

'Couldn't it have waited until tomorrow?' Lasalle said, a note of irritation in his own voice. He glanced at his watch. 'It is seven o'clock.'

'I know what time it is,' Joubert snapped.

'So what do you want?'

'I want to talk about *this*.' Joubert brandished the object in his right hand like a weapon for a moment before slamming it down on the coffee table nearby. 'What the hell do you mean by it?'

The copy of the *Journal of Parapsychology* lay before him on the table, bent open at the article written by Lasalle.

'What the hell did you hope to achieve by writing this . . . garbage?' Joubert demanded.

'I felt that the discovery was too important to be hidden away,' Lasalle explained.

'It was my . . .' He quickly qualified his words. 'It was *our* discovery.

117 ·

We agreed not to share it with anyone until the research was fully completed.'

'No we didn't. *You* decided that you wanted it kept secret,' Lasalle reminded him. 'I felt that other people had a right to know what happened.'

'So you took it upon yourself to write this article? And your . . . friend. Does she know about it?'

'Kelly? No. She didn't know that I intended writing the article.' He paused for a moment. 'And even if she did, I don't see that any of this is your business. I am not answerable to you, Alain.'

'If news of this spreads we'll have the press swarming all over the Centre. Is that what you want?'

'Our discoveries on Astral projection are some of the most important ever made. Not just for our own profession but for others too. Many will benefit from our work. Hospitals, psychiatric institutions . . .'

Joubert cut him short.

'And who will be credited with the discovery?' he asked, eyeing his colleague malevolently.

'Both of us of course. We . . .'

Joubert interrupted again.

'No. Not both of us. *You.*' He pointed at Lasalle. 'You wrote the article.'

'But I mentioned your name, how we worked together.'

'That doesn't matter, it's you who will take the credit.' He picked up the magazine. 'What did they pay you for this?' he asked, scornfully.

'Ten thousand francs. Why?'

Joubert shook his head.

'They bought weeks of work for ten thousand francs!'

'The money isn't important,' said Lasalle.

'And the recognition?' Joubert wanted to know. 'Will you want that? Will you be able to cope with that?' His voice took on a sneering, superior tone. 'Still, you have your little tablets to help you.'

'Get out of here, Alain,' Lasalle snapped. 'Get out of my house.'

Joubert stuffed the magazine into his pocket and, with one last scornful glance at his colleague, he headed for the front door. Lasalle heard it slam behind him as he left.

* * *

118

Joubert brought the Fiat to a halt outside his house and switched off the engine. He closed his eyes for a moment, sitting in the shell-like confines of the vehicle, almost reluctant to leave it. He let out a long, almost painful breath and banged the steering wheel angrily. Damn Lasalle, he thought. He glanced down at the magazine which was on the passenger seat. It lay there as if taunting him and he snatched it up and pushed open the car door, locking it behind him.

As he reached the bottom of his path he heard the phone ringing inside his house. The Frenchman didn't hurry himself. He found his front door key and unlocked the door, glancing down at the phone on the hall table as he entered. It continued to ring but he hung up his jacket before finally lifting the receiver.

'Hello,' he said, wearily.

'Joubert? About time.'

He recognised the voice immediately.

'Dr Vernon, what do you want?' he asked.

'I want to know what's going on.'

'I don't know what you're talking about.'

'Let me read you something then.' There was a slight pause and Joubert heard the rustling of paper at the other end of the phone:

' *"The discovery of this form of Astral projection is the culmination of many weeks of work and many years of study,"* ' Vernon quoted.

'Lasalle's article,' said Joubert.

'You were supposed to report any findings directly to me and now I read this plastered all over the magazine. What do you think you're playing at?'

'Don't lecture me, Vernon. That article was nothing to do with me. Perhaps you should ask the girl who works for you what she knows about it,' the Frenchman hissed.

'Who are you talking about?' Vernon wanted to know.

'Kelly Hunt. She's here. She's been with us for a week or more.'

There was a shocked silence, interrupted only by the occasional hiss of static.

'Vernon.'

'Yes.'

'I said she's been with us for more than a week,' Joubert hissed.

119

'I had no idea where she was,' Vernon said, irritably. 'I gave her some time off while the enquiry took place here. I didn't know she was going to work with you.'

'Well, she knows everything. You won't be able to hide anything from her any longer, Vernon.'

The Institute Director sighed.

'Anyway, that's your problem. I have my own with Lasalle,' Joubert continued.

'We cannot afford any more disclosures similar to the one in this magazine,' Vernon said, cryptically. 'As it is, this might alter our plans slightly.'

'You take care of the girl. I'll handle Lasalle. And I tell you this, Vernon, there will be no more disclosures. I will see to that.' He hung up and wiped his hands on his trousers. 'No more.'

There was a malevolent determination in his voice.

23

London

As the 747 touched down, Blake breathed his customary sigh of relief. The plane slowed down and he allowed himself a glance out of the window. Heathrow was covered by a film of drizzle which undulated and writhed like a living thing. The writer had tried to sleep on the flight back but had been constantly interrupted by the woman next to him who insisted that he should 'look at the wonderful view'. Blake had made the fatal error of telling her that he wrote books about the paranormal and had been regaled by her tales of tea-leaf reading and contacts with the spirit world. She had, she assured him, been blessed with this gift of second sight as compensation for the death of her smallest child five years earlier and the subsequent departure of her husband with another woman. Blake had nodded politely and smiled a lot during the verbal barrage, as was his habit. She had apologised for not having read any of his books but promised she would. Blake had smiled even more broadly at that point. He wondered if it was a general thing with writers, that anyone they spoke to immediately swore they would rush out and buy every book that writer had written.

Despite the distractions he had managed to snatch an hour or so of sleep but it had been troubled and he had woken, it seemed, every ten minutes.

At one point he had jerked bolt upright in his seat, his body bathed in sweat, the last vestiges of a nightmare fading from his mind. The plane had crashed into the sea but he had survived the impact only to be drowned in the wreckage.

Now, as the plane came to a halt he got to his feet and stretched, trying to banish some of the stiffness from his joints. He checked his watch and noticed that he'd forgotten to adjust it according to the time difference. The clock on the plane showed 6.07 p.m.

After Blake had recovered his baggage he made his way through the terminal to the waiting taxis outside.

The drive took longer than he'd expected but, as the vehicle drew closer to his home he shook off some of his tiredness.

'Where do you want to get out?' the driver asked.

Blake directed him.

'Nice gaff,' said the driver, admiring Blake's house. 'Must have cost a fair old screw, eh?'

The man was obviously fishing for a tip and Blake didn't disappoint him. He gave him fifteen pounds and told him to keep the change.

'A reasonable screw,' he said as he walked away from the cab, suit-case in hand.

His house was set back from the road and was surrounded by a sufficient expanse of garden to protect him from the neighbours on either side. A privet hedge, which needed trimming, fronted the property and waist-high wooden fencing formed a perimeter elsewhere. There was also a garage built onto one side of the building. It housed a second-hand Jaguar XJS which he'd bought from a friend three years earlier.

As Blake made his way up the short path he fumbled for his front door key and inserted it in the lock. The door opened, and the familiar cloying scent of paint greeted him. He'd had the place redecorated prior to leaving for the States and the aroma hung thickly in the air. Blake flicked on the hall light and the porch light. He smiled to himself. When his porch light was on it always reminded him of running up the Standard at Buckingham Palace. It was his mark that *he* was now in residence.

He stepped over two weeks worth of mail which lay on the mat, closed the front door behind him then scooped it up. There were circulars, four or five letters (most of which he could identify by their postmarks) and a couple of bills. The writer dropped his suitcase in the hall deciding that he would unpack later. Right now all he wanted was to pour himself a drink and flop down in a chair.

He passed into the sitting room, pulling off his shirt as he did so. It was warm in the room despite the fact that it had been empty for a fortnight. He drew back the curtains and the dull twilight dragged itself into the room. Blake switched on the lamp which perched on top of the TV. He poured himself a large measure of brandy, topped it up with soda and took a hefty gulp, then he selected a record from his massive collection, dropped it on to the turntable and switched on the Hi-Fi. While Elton John warbled away in the background, Blake skimmed through his mail. The bills he noted and then stuck in a bulldog clip on the shelf near the fire-place, the circulars he balled up and tossed into the nearby bin. Then he opened his letters. There was one from his accountant, one from a group calling itself 'The Literary Co-operative' (a bunch of struggling local writers to whom Blake had spoken before) and what looked like a couple of fan letters. Blake was always happy to receive mail from the public and he read them both with delight.

He finished his drink, re-filled his glass and wandered into the kitchen. Peering out of the back window he saw several lumps of dark matter on his patio.

'Cat shit,' he muttered, irritably. 'I'll buy a cork for that bloody thing.' He was referring to the overfed Manx cat which belonged to the family next door. It had taken to using his garden as a toilet whenever it could and, obviously, while he'd been away, had taken full advantage and dotted its calling cards about in abundance.

The writer opened his freezer and took out a pizza which he stuck under the grill. He didn't feel particularly hungry and, being basically lazy anyway, frozen food was heaven sent for his purposes. He left the pizza beneath the glow of the grill and returned to the sitting room.

It was large but comfortable and 'lived in' like the rest of the house. On the walls, framed carefully, were a number of film posters. *Taxi Driver* hung near the hall door whilst the wall nearest the kitchen bore an American print of *The Wild Bunch*. Beside it was *Halloween*.

But, pride of place went to a yellowed poster which hung over the fire-place. It was *Psycho*, and it bore Hitchcock's signature. Blake had been given it as a gift from a friend in the film business last time he had visited L. A.

The writer was not a man to overindulge in luxuries but, when he did, three things occupied him more than most. Films, books and music. His bookcase bulged, not with learned tomes and priceless first editions but with pulp creations. He read for entertainment, nothing more. Alongside the books, each one in its individual case, were video cassettes of his favourite films. Up to 300 in all.

His study, however, was a different matter.

Blake had been pleased, when he had bought the house, to discover that it not only possessed an attic but also a double cellar which ran beneath the entire building. He had converted the subterranean room into his study. Every day he retreated down the steps to work, free of the noises and distractions of everyday life.

Buried beneath the ground as it was, it reminded him of working in a giant coffin.

He kept the door locked at all times. The cellar was his private domain and his alone.

The smell of pizza began to waft from the kitchen. He ate it from the foil wrapper, saving himself any washing up. Then, still clutching his glass, he headed through the sitting room into the hall where he unlocked his case.

His notes were on top and Blake lifted them out carefully, hefting them before him. They had a satisfying heavy feel. The fruits of so much research. The hard part was almost over. Another week or so of note-taking and preparation and he could get down to the serious business of writing.

As it was, there was one more thing he had to do.

Blake opened the cellar door, peering down into the blackness below. He smiled broadly to himself and flicked on the light.

'Welcome home,' he murmured and walked in.

Before he descended the steps he was careful to lock the cellar door behind him.

The silence greeted him like an old friend.

24

New York

Across the untarnished brilliance of the azure blue sky the only blemish was the thin vapour trail left by a solitary aircraft.

There wasn't a cloud in the sky. The sun, even so early in the morning, was a shimmering core of radiance throwing out its burning rays to blanket the city in a cocoon of heat.

The heavens did not weep for Rick Landers but there were others who did.

There were a handful of people at the graveside as the small coffin was lowered into the hole. Toni Landers herself stood immobile, eyes fixed on the wooden casket as it slowly disappeared from view. The only part of her which moved was her eyes and, from those red-rimmed, blood-shot orbs, tears pumped freely, coursing down her cheeks and occasionally dripping on to her black gloved hands. There was a photograph of Rick on the marble headstone but she could not bring herself to look at it. Every now and then, the rays of sunlight would glint on the marble and Toni would squeeze her eyes tightly together but, each time she did so, the vision of Rick flashed into her mind – memories of that day a week or more earlier when she had been forced to identify his remains. She had gazed on the mangled body of her child, stared at the face so badly pulped that the bottom jaw had been ground to splinters. The skull had been shattered in four or five places so that portions of the brain actually bulged through the

124

rents. One eye had been almost forced from its socket. The head was almost severed.

It would have taken a magician not a mortician to restore some semblance of normality to a body so badly smashed.

Toni sucked in a breath, the memory still too painful for her. She shuffled uncomfortably where she stood and the two people on either side of her moved closer, fearing that she was going to faint. But the moment passed and she returned her attention to the gaping grave which had just swallowed up her dead child. The priest was speaking but Toni did not hear what he said. She had a handkerchief in her handbag yet she refused to wipe the tears away, allowing the salty droplets to soak her face and gloves.

Against the explosion of colours formed by countless wreaths and bouquets the dozen or so mourners looked curiously out of place in their sombre apparel.

Toni had deliberately kept the number of mourners to a minimum. She had phoned Rick's father in L.A. and told him but he had not condescended to put in an appearance. Amidst her grief, Toni had found room for a little hatred too. But now as she watched the ribbons which supported the coffin being pulled clear she felt a cold hand clutch her heart, as if the appalling finality of what she was witnessing had suddenly registered. Her son was gone forever and that thought brought fresh floods of tears from the seemingly inexhaustible reservoir of her pain.

This time her knees buckled slightly and her two companions moved to support her.

One of them, Maggie Straker, her co-star in her last film, slipped an arm around Toni's waist and held her upright. She could hear the other woman whimpering softly, repeating Rick's name over and over again as if it were a litany.

It was Maggie who first noticed that there was a newcomer amongst them.

The grave stood on a slight rise so his approach had been masked by the mourners on the far side of the grave.

Jonathan Mathias stood alone, a gigantic wreath of white roses held in his hand. He looked down at the final resting place of Rick Landers then across at Toni.

She saw him and abruptly stopped sobbing.

Mathias laid the floral tribute near the headstone, glancing at the photograph of Rick as he did so. He straightened up, listening as the priest finished what he was saying. He paused for a moment then asked those gathered to join him in reciting the Lord's Prayer.

Mathias stood by silently.

When the ritual was complete the mourners slowly moved away, back down the slight slope towards the black limousines which stood glinting in the sunlight like so many predatory insects. They too looked alien and intrusive amidst the green grass of the cemetery.

Mathias did not move, he stood at the head of the grave, gazing down into its depths at the small wooden casket. And it was towards him that Toni Landers now made her way, shaking loose of Maggie's supportive arm.

'I hope I'm not intruding,' the psychic said, softly.

'I'm glad you came,' Toni told him. She glanced down at the wreath he'd brought. 'Thank you.'

Maggie Straker approached cautiously.

'Toni, do you want me to wait I . . .'

'It's OK, Maggie.'

The other woman nodded, smiled politely at Mathias then made her way down the slope behind the other mourners. Toni and the psychic stood alone by the grave.

'What will you do now?' he asked her. 'What are your plans?'

She sniffed.

'I'm going to spend some time in England with friends,' Toni informed him. 'I can't bear to be around here. Not now.' She wiped some of the moisture from her cheeks with a handkerchief which Mathias handed her. Toni turned the linen square over in her hands.

'You knew he was going to die didn't you?' she said, without looking at him.

'Yes,' Mathias told her.

'Why didn't you tell me?'

'It wouldn't have made any difference. There was nothing you could have done about it.'

'Was there anything *you* could have done about it?'

'I wish there had been.'

126

He took her hand and, together, they made their way down the slope towards the waiting cars. But Toni hesitated momentarily, looking back over her shoulder towards the grave.

Towards her son.

It was over.

He was gone.

All that remained now were the memories.

She felt more tears streaming down her cheeks and Mathias put his arm around her shoulder, leading her away. She felt a strength and power in that arm and, as she looked up at him, a thought entered her mind. She looked back once more towards the grave of her son but this time there were no more tears.

A slight smile flickered briefly at the corners of her mouth.

Again she looked at Mathias.

25

Oxford

The smell of menthol was strong in the air.

Dr Vernon made loud sucking sounds as he devoured another of the cough sweets. The office smelt more like a pharmacy now.

Kelly crossed her legs, slipping one shoe off, dangling it by her toes as she waited for Vernon to finish reading the report.

It was her first day back at the Institute since she had returned from France barely thirty-six hours ago. In many ways she had been happy to return. The relationship between Joubert and Lasalle had deteriorated seriously since the appearance of the latter's article. The atmosphere had not been a pleasant one to work in and Kelly had decided that it was time to leave them to it. Armed with what she had learnt in France she was more confident about her own research, enjoying a newly-found enthusiasm which came only with a measure of success. However, she was worried about Lasalle. During the past week she had seen him wilt visibly beneath the open hostility displayed by

Joubert. Loathe to intervene, Kelly had been a helpless spectator at their confrontations, each more vehement than before. She found it difficult to understand how so many years of friendship could, for Joubert, have been ruined so quickly and for what seemed a relatively minor aberration on Lasalle's part.

But, the question had plagued her for a while.

Kelly could still not understand why he had reacted so violently to Lasalle's article. People *did* have a right to know the facts, there was no disputing that. Joubert seemed not to agree. Despite her desire to return to England, Kelly had been somewhat reluctant about leaving Lasalle having seen his psychological deterioration over the past seven or eight days. The tranquilizers seemed to be of little help to him, despite the fact that he had upped the dosage from 45mg to 75mg a day. He was in a perpetual daze, a condition doubtless helped by the effect of the drugs. Kelly had felt something akin to pity for him. She hoped he wasn't becoming unbalanced again.

Nevertheless, she had decided to leave the Metapsychic Centre and had arrived home at around noon nearly two days ago.

Vernon's call had come within one hour of her return.

It was as if somehow he had been watching her, waiting for the right moment before calling.

She had not been surprised by the call itself, only by the urgency in the Institute Director's voice as he had asked her to return to work as soon as possible and to present him with a full report on what she had witnessed while working at the Metapsychic Centre.

Not until she had replaced the receiver did she begin to wonder how Vernon had known of her whereabouts.

She had certainly not mentioned her intentions when she left the Institute two weeks earlier.

Now, she sat impatiently, watching him as he leafed through her report. Kelly wondered if she should say something to him. Ask him how he knew where she had been? She bit her tongue for the time being.

There was probably a perfectly reasonable explanation, she told herself, although she wasn't altogether convinced.

She administered a swift mental rebuke. She was allowing her imagination to run away with her. She was becoming paranoid.

128

Wasn't she?

'Presumably you've noted everything which took place at the Metapsychic Centre during your time there?' Vernon asked, waving the report before him. 'There's nothing you could have left out or forgotten?'

'I wrote down everything which I felt was relevant to the investigation,' she told him, a slight trace of anger in her voice. She was becoming annoyed at his patronising tone.

Vernon shifted the menthol sweet to the other side of his mouth and tapped the report with his index finger. He was gazing into empty air.

'The area of the brain which controls the Astral body also controls emotions and desires,' he said, abstractedly.

'Yes,' Kelly said. 'But emotions and desires not present in the conscious mind. The Astral body appears to be the alter-ego and, from the material I collected on Grant and Joubert, it *can* become a tangible force.'

Vernon nodded.

'It sounded like a form of bi-location at first,' said Kelly. 'But I've never heard of a bi-locative presence becoming tangible before.'

'There was an American named Paul Twitchell,' Vernon explained. 'In the early sixties he began to teach what he called the Eckankar doctrine. A number of his pupils claimed to have seen him, in solid Astral form, while he was actually miles away.' Vernon sighed. 'But, Twitchell was one on his own. This . . .' he picked up the report. 'This is more unusual.' He paused once again. 'It would explain many of the problems we have concerning the inner self, even some mental disorders.' He chewed his bottom lip contemplatively. 'Are you absolutely sure you've left nothing out?'

'I'm positive,' Kelly said in exasperation.

'Kelly, you don't need me to tell you how important this information is to our work, to . . .'

She cut him short, infuriated by his treatment of her.

'I'm not a fool, Doctor Vernon,' she said. 'Everything that I saw is noted down in my report, some of the conversations are verbatim.'

He nodded, placatingly, as if trying to calm her down.

'But there is one thing *I'd* like to know,' she told him.

Vernon eyed her warily.

'How did you know I was at the Metapsychic Centre?'

'I was in contact with them,' Vernon said. 'One of the investigators told me.'

Kelly wasn't altogether satisfied but she didn't press the matter. A heavy silence descended, finally broken by the woman.

'Have you seen anything of John Fraser since he left here?' she asked.

Vernon shrugged.

'He came back about a week ago to collect some things.' His tone abruptly changed, his eyes narrowing. 'Why do you ask?'

She detected the defensive note in his voice.

'I was just curious,' Kelly told him.

'Fraser has no more business here,' Vernon said, acidly.

Another long silence punctuated the conversation, the only sound being made by the Institute Director as he crunched up his cough sweet. Kelly eyed him suspiciously. Vernon was usually a calm, unflappable man but, in the last twenty minutes or so, he had revealed another side of his character – one which she had not seen before. His calmness had been replaced by a tetchy impatience, the unflappability giving away to an anxious and defensive demeanour. When he finally spoke again, however, some of the urgency had left his voice.

'Could what happened to Joubert be duplicated outside laboratory conditions?' he asked. 'I mean the Astral projection which he underwent.'

'I don't see why not,' Kelly told him. 'He was hypnotised, it was as simple as that. It should be perfectly possible to recreate the condition in another subject.'

Vernon nodded slowly, his grey eyes fixed on a point to one side of Kelly. She did not move. He didn't speak.

Finally, she rose.

'If that's all, Doctor . . .' She allowed the sentence to trail off.

'Yes,' he said. 'There's nothing else.'

'Could I have my report please?'

Vernon put his hand on the file.

'I'll keep it for now,' he said, his eyes fixing her in an uncompromising stare.

She hesitated a moment then nodded, turned and headed for the office door.

Vernon watched her leave.

He slumped back in his seat as she closed the door, his eyes falling to the report which lay before him. Long moments passed then he picked it up and dropped it into the black attaché case which stood beside his desk.

Before replacing it, he locked the case.

Kelly nodded politely to Dr Vernon's secretary as she walked out but she barely succeeded in masking her anger.

What the hell was Vernon playing at? she wondered. Since she'd returned he'd been like some kind of Grand Inquisitor, wanting to know every last detail of what happened in France. And why should he want to keep the report she'd made? He'd already perused it half a dozen times while she'd sat before him. That, apparently, was not sufficient for him.

She walked briskly down the corridor towards the stairs, her heels clicking loudly on the polished tile floor. Down one flight of steps to the first floor then along another corridor she walked until she came to Frank Anderson's office. Kelly tapped lightly on the door then walked in.

The room was empty.

She cursed silently and turned to leave but, before she did, she crossed to his desk and found a piece of paper and a pen. Kelly scrawled a quick note and left it where Anderson would see it.

A thought crossed her mind.

If Anderson could find it easily then so too could Vernon.

The Institute Director had a habit of wandering, uninvited, into his investigators' offices and this was one note which she did not want him to read. She stood still for a moment, wondering what she should do.

'Need any help?'

The voice startled her but she spun round to see Anderson in the doorway. A smile of relief creased her lips.

'Frank. I was looking for you,' she said, balling up the note and stuffing it into the pocket of her shirt.

131

'I gathered that,' he said, pulling at one frayed shirt cuff. 'What can I do for you, Kelly?'

'You were a friend of John Fraser's weren't you?' she said, lowering her voice.

Anderson looked puzzled.

'Yes.'

'I need to speak to him.'

'I haven't seen him since he left here. He hasn't been in touch.' Kelly frowned.

'But you know where he lives?' she asked.

Anderson nodded.

'And where he spends most of his time,' he said, smiling. 'The first is his home address, the second one is the pub he uses most often.'

Kelly turned to leave, scanning the piece of paper.

'Is something wrong?' Anderson called after her.

'That's what I want to find out,' Kelly told him and left him alone.

Anderson heard her footsteps echoing away and frowned.

What did she want with John Fraser?

26

The hands of the dashboard clock glowed green in the gloom.

9.36 p.m.

Kelly parked the Mini in the gravelled area beside the pub and sat behind the wheel for a moment. High above her, rain clouds spat erratic droplets on to the land. It was warm inside the car – muggy and uncomfortable. Kelly felt her tee-shirt sticking to her back as she leant forward and she squirmed. It felt as if someone had wrapped her upper body in a damp towel. She clambered out of the car, relieved to find that there was a slight breeze. Rain spots momentarily stained her jeans as she walked towards the building, ignoring the dirty water from puddles which splashed her ankle boots.

'The Huntsman' was a large pub about a mile outside Oxford. It wasn't pretty and it wasn't quaint but it was functional. There was a cheap and, consequently, popular restaurant attached to it which did not, on this particular night, appear to be too busy, hence her ease of parking. Normally the area was jammed with vehicles. Not so tonight. Kelly tried to see Fraser's car but, in the darkness, identification was almost impossible.

She decided to try the Lounge bar first.

It was crowded with people. In groups, in couples, on their own. One corner was occupied by seven or eight men who were playing cards around a large oblong table. Kelly scanned their faces, accidentally catching the eye of a ginger-haired youth in his late teens. He winked at her then directed his companion's attention to this slim newcomer. A chorus of subdued whistling and cheering rose from the men. Kelly turned away from them, searching the bustling bar for Fraser.

There was no sign of him.

She decided to try the Public bar.

If the noise inside the Lounge bar had been loud then in the Public bar it bordered on seismic proportions. A juke-box which was obviously set at full volume spewed forth an endless stream of the latest chart hits as if trying to drown out the clack of pool balls or the thud of darts as they hit the board. To add to the unholy cacophony, in one corner of the large room an electronic motor-racing game occasionally punctuated the din with the simulated explosion of a crashed car. Whilst, beside it, the ever hungry Pac-Man noisily devoured everything before it.

Kelly scanned the bar but could not see Fraser. She decided to sit and wait for him. There was a table near the door but it was occupied by a young couple who looked as though they were about to breach the Indecent Exposure act. The youth had his hand buried beneath his girlfriend's minuscule skirt while she was rubbing his crotch with a speed which looked likely to cause friction burns.

The bar seemed to be populated almost exclusively by youngsters, most of whom were teenagers. She drew several admiring glances as she perched on a bar stool. When she'd finally managed to attract the barman's attention, she ordered a shandy and fumbled in her purse for some money. As he set her drink down she deliberately took her time counting out the change.

133

'Do you know John Fraser?' she asked him.

The barman nodded, wiping perspiration from his face.

'Yeah, why?'

'Has he been in here tonight?'

'Not yet, but he will.' The barman smiled.

'You sound very sure,' Kelly said.

'He hasn't missed a night since I've worked here and that's two years.' A call from the other end of the bar took the man away.

Kelly sipped at her drink and turned slightly on the stool so that she could see the door through which Fraser must enter.

'Hello, stranger.'

She spun round again to see that the voice came from a tall, black-haired youth who was leaning on the bar beside her. He was dressed in a grey sweater and maroon slacks. His companion, like himself, was in his early twenties, his hair cut short and shaped so that it appeared as if his head was flat. Spots and blackheads dotted his face liberally. He smiled, his gaze drawn to Kelly's breasts.

'Do I know you?' she said, trying to suppress a grin.

'No,' said the black-haired youth. 'But we can soon put that right, can't we?'

He introduced himself as Neville. His friend as Baz.

Kelly nodded politely, forced to sip at her drink again to prevent herself laughing. This was the last thing she needed.

'I haven't seen you in here before,' said Neville. 'I would have remembered if I had.'

Kelly smiled, aware that Baz was still gazing at her breasts as if he'd never seen a woman at close-quarters before. She had little trouble convincing herself that might well be the case.

'It's a bit noisy in here,' Neville said, as if telling her something she didn't know. 'Fancy a walk?'

'I'm waiting for someone,' she told him. 'Thanks all the same.'

'What's his name?' asked Neville, looking quite hurt.

'I'm waiting for a girlfriend actually,' Kelly lied.

Neville seemed to perk up. He nudged Baz in the ribs, momentarily interrupting his appraisal of Kelly's shapely body.

'That's even better. We can make it a foursome when she gets here.'

Kelly smiled again.

134

'You don't understand,' she said, flashing her green eyes at him. 'She's more than just a friend.'

Neville looked blank.

Baz looked even blanker.

'We're *very* close,' Kelly continued, barely able to keep a straight face.

It was Baz who spoke the revelatory words.

'She's a fucking lesbian,' he gaped, already pulling his colleague away as if Kelly had just announced she had bubonic plague. She chuckled as she saw them leave, casting anxious glances at her as if they thought she was going to follow them. Kelly took another sip of her drink and checked her watch.

9.58.

Where the hell was Fraser?

Another ten minutes, she decided, and she would drive to his house.

She finished her shandy and ordered an orange juice instead.

She had her back to the door when Fraser walked in.

He strode to the far end of the bar where he was engulfed by his usual drinking companions. Kelly turned her attention back to the door, occasionally checking the faces in the bar.

Almost by accident she spotted who she sought.

She slid down off the stool and walked across to him, tugging at his arm.

'Fraser.'

He turned and saw her, a mixture of surprise and distaste in his expression.

'Who's your friend, John?' one of the other men asked, admiringly.

Fraser ignored the remark, addressing himself to Kelly.

'How did you know where to find me?' he wanted to know.

Kelly told him.

'I need to talk to you,' she added. 'It's important.'

'I'm not sure I've got anything to say to you, Kelly. You or anyone else concerned with the bloody Institute.'

'I need your help.'

'How can *I* help you? Is Vernon looking for more human guinea pigs?'

'It's Vernon I want to talk to you about.'

135

Fraser relaxed slightly, more intrigued now than annoyed. He picked up his glass and motioned to an empty table close by. They sat down, watched by the group of men standing at the bar.

'So what's suddenly important about the good doctor?' he said, sarcastically.

'Listen,' said Kelly, leaning close to him to make herself heard over the blare of the juke-box. 'When Vernon dismissed you, it wasn't because you protested about the research was it?'

Fraser sipped at his drink.

'You tell me.'

'I'm not playing games, Fraser,' snapped Kelly, angrily. 'I came here tonight because I thought you could help me.'

He raised a hand in supplication.

'OK, what are you talking about?' he asked.

'You mentioned something to Vernon about the research, about it being of benefit to one person in particular.'

Fraser shook his head slowly.

'Did you mean Vernon himself?' she continued.

He didn't answer.

'And there was something else,' she persisted. 'About what Vernon was hiding that he'd been hiding for a time. What did you mean?'

Fraser downed what was left in his glass.

'Have you ever heard Vernon talk about his wife?' he asked.

'I didn't even know he was married.'

'It's not something he likes to broadcast, at least not any more.'

Kelly leaned closer as the juke-box launched another high decibel assault.

'For all I know, his wife could be dead now,' Fraser continued. 'Something happened to her about six years ago. No one knows what it was and, so far, no one's found out. Vernon's too clever for that. But, whatever it was his wife disappeared and nobody knows where she is now.'

'How do you know this?' Kelly demanded.

'Vernon's quite a respected figure in our little community. When the wife of a prominent man goes missing there's always the odd rumour floating about.'

'Could he have killed her?' asked Kelly, warily.

136

'I doubt it. Perhaps she left him. Upped and walked out. The intriguing thing is, what made her leave? Whatever happened to her he's certainly managed to keep it quiet.'

Kelly ran her index finger around the rim of her glass, gazing reflectively into the orange fluid.

'And you think he's using the research to help his wife. Indirectly?' she said, finally.

'It's a possibility.'

'But how is our work on the unconscious mind going to help his wife?' she mused aloud.

'You won't know that until you know what's wrong with *her*. Or what happened to her anyway.'

Kelly sipped at her drink, thoughts tumbling through her mind. The sounds of the juke-box, the pool table and the electronic games seemed to diminish as she considered what she had heard.

'What could have happened that was so bad Vernon would keep it secret for six years?' she pondered.

Fraser could only shrug his shoulders. He started to rise.

'Where are you going?' she wanted to know.

'To get another,' he said, indicating his empty glass. 'What about you?'

'No thanks. I'd better get going. Look, thanks for the help. I appreciate it.'

He nodded.

'You can contact me at home if you want to,' he began. 'My address . . .'

She smiled.

'Anderson gave me that too,' she confessed.

'Frank always was thorough.'

They exchanged brief farewells and Kelly left.

As she emerged from the pub she found that the rain which had merely been spotting earlier had now been transformed into a fully-fledged downpour. She ran to her car fumbling for her keys as the warm rain drenched her. She slid behind the wheel and sat there, gazing out through the rivulets of water which coursed down the windscreen. Kelly ran a hand through her hair and then wiped her palm on her jeans. Through the cascade of rain she could see Fraser's Datsun.

Fraser.

Could he be right about Vernon's wife? Kelly wondered.

She started her engine and guided the Mini out onto the road.

High above her, a soundless flash of lightning split the clouds, reaching earthward as it lit the heavens with cold white light.

Kelly felt an unexpected chill creeping around her.

It was almost 11.05 by the time John Fraser left the Public bar of 'The Huntsman'.

He had not consumed as much booze as he normally did and he felt almost abnormally clear-headed. Fraser rarely got drunk no matter how much he had and tonight, especially, he felt only a pleasing calmness. He climbed into his car and, at the third attempt, started the engine. He made a mental note to get his battery checked.

The rain continued to pelt down and the storm which had been building all night had finally broken. Thunder shook the sky while the lightning etched erratic lines across the tenebrous heavens.

As he pulled out of the pub car park, a lorry roared past and Fraser stepped on his brakes.

The pedal sank mournfully to the floor beneath the pressure of his foot.

The car continued to roll.

The lorry swerved slightly to avoid the Datsun and Fraser gripped the wheel in terror, as if awaiting the impact, but the larger vehicle swept on, disappearing around a bend in the road.

'Jesus,' murmured Fraser, stamping on the brake pedal. This time the car stopped dead.

He tried it once more.

No problems.

He shook his head and drove on. Bloody brakes. He'd only had them checked the day before.

27

She had not slept much the previous night. Her mind had been too active, all too ready to present her with snap answers to questions for which she so badly sought concrete solutions.

Kelly glanced down at the piece of paper on the parcel shelf and re-checked Fraser's address. A sign post at the corner of the street confirmed that she had found the right place. She turned the Mini into the street and slowed down, scanning the doors for the number she sought.

The storm of the night before had cleared the air and the sun shone brightly over the carefully maintained houses with their neat gardens. Kelly saw an old man mowing his front lawn. On the other side of the street a youth was busy washing his car.

'Number fifty-nine,' she murmured to herself, squinting at the houses. 'Number fifty-nine.'

She saw it and pulled the Mini into a convenient parking space, switching off the engine. Kelly sat behind the wheel for a moment gazing at the house. She was reasonably sure that Fraser had told her everything he knew about Vernon but she had spent half the night wondering if there might just be something else which he might have neglected to mention. Perhaps in his own home, away from the noisy distractions of the pub, he might be able to give her some more information. Exactly what she was going to do with it she wasn't yet sure.

Confront Vernon?

Why should she need to confront him?

Kelly shook her head, as if trying to force the thoughts to one side, then she pushed open the door and climbed out.

There was a pleasing smell of blossom in the air, as if someone had opened a gigantic air freshener. The sun, broken up by the branches of the trees which flanked the road, forced its way through the canopy of leaves and blossom to brush warming rays against her skin. The blossom itself, stirred by a gentle breeze, fell from the trees like pink tears.

Kelly walked up the path to the front door of number fifty-nine and rang the bell. As she stood there she noticed that the garage door was closed. There was no sign of Fraser's Datsun. She hoped that he was at home.

A minute passed and no one answered the door. Kelly rang again, this time keeping her finger on the bell button for a time.

At last she heard movement from inside.

The door swung open and she found herself confronted by a rotund, middle-aged woman in a dark blue dress. Her greying hair was swept back from her forehead, giving her round face a severity which it perhaps did not merit.

'Mrs Fraser?' Kelly asked.

'No. I'm her sister,' the woman said, eyeing Kelly up and down. 'Who are you?'

Kelly introduced herself.

'I used to work with John Fraser,' she explained. 'It was him that I wanted to see really.'

The woman didn't speak at first then, slowly, she lowered her gaze and her voice softened.

'My sister is upstairs sleeping,' she said, quietly.

Kelly didn't have to be a detective to realize that something was wrong.

'And Mr Fraser?' she asked.

'He was killed in an accident last night. His car hit a tree. He was dead before they got him to hospital.'

28

New York

There were two of them waiting outside the house.

One was smoking a cigarette and pacing agitatedly up and down while the other squatted on the pavement and adjusted his camera. Both of them would occasionally stop what they were doing and peer in the direction of the building.

Toni Landers replaced the curtain, wondering if the newsmen had seen her.

She had not seen these two before although, since her son's death, so many had thrust themselves at her with notepads and microphones that she doubted if she would remember faces. The actress walked across the room to the drinks cabinet and poured herself a large measure of J & B which she downed virtually in one swallow, coughing as the fiery liquid burned its way to her stomach.

The house was deathly silent. She had given Mrs Garcia some time off, promising to ring her when her services were required again. Exactly how long that would be even Toni herself was uncertain of. On the sofa before her the copy of *Variety* was folded open at an appointed spot and she glanced at it briefly before returning to her vigil at the window.

As she stood gazing out at the two newsmen, she thought how odd it had been that she should discover the story in such a journal. She had read with interest that Jonathan Mathias was to visit England to appear on a TV special. She had seen him as her last hope. The only one she knew who possessed the kind of abilities she had need of. Toni didn't intend to allow him to slip away.

She had need of his services.

There was a loud beeping sound and she looked out to see that the

Ford Sedan had pulled up outside her house. The driver was banging the horn.

Toni drained what was left in her glass then scuttled for the front door, re-adjusting the dark glasses as she did so. She waited a second then walked out.

Immediately, the two newsmen approached her and she winced as the flash bulb momentarily hurt her eyes.

'I have nothing to say,' she told them.

'How soon will you be returning to the stage?' the first man asked, ignoring her declaration.

She swept on towards the waiting car.

'How will your son's death affect your career?'

The flash bulb exploded again, closer to her this time.

Toni struck out angrily, knocking the camera from the photographer's hands. It crashed to the ground, the lens splintering.

'Hey lady,' he shouted. 'That's an expensive fucking camera.'

She pulled open the rear door of the Ford and glanced at the driver.

'It ain't my fault your fucking kid is dead,' the photographer roared as the car pulled away.

'Where to, Miss Landers?' the driver asked.

She checked her watch. She had enough time.

'Kennedy,' she told him.

29

Paris

The occasional gusts of wind stirred the bells in the church tower, whistling through and around them to form a discordant, ghostly melody.

Michel Lasalle stood by the grave-side and read the inscription on the headstone.

Madelaine Lasalle; 1947—1982

Loved More Than Life Itself.

The wind stirred the flowers which adorned the grave, their white petals standing out in dark contrast to the darkness of the night. Lasalle bent and removed them, laying them on one side.

He reached for the shovel.

Putting all his weight behind it he drove the pointed implement into the ground, pressing down on it with his foot, levering a huge clod of dark earth from the top of the grave. He tossed it to one side and continued digging. He could feel the perspiration soaking through his shirt as he toiled, gradually creating a mound of mud beside the grave. When he had excavated half of the plot he paused and pulled his shirt off, fastening it around his waist by the sleeves as if it were some kind of apron. Then he continued digging.

It took him nearly thirty minutes to reach the coffin.

He heard the sound of metal on wood and stood back triumphantly, jamming the shovel into the damp earth at the bottom of the hole. Lasalle dropped to his knees and began clawing the final covering of dirt from the casket. He split two finger nails as he did so, scrabbling there like a dog trying to find a bone. Blood oozed from the torn digits but Lasalle paid it no heed. Only when the last fragments of earth had been pulled free did he straighten up, reaching once more for the shovel. He slid the pointed end beneath one corner of the coffin and weighed down on it.

The screw which held it in place was rusted and he had little difficulty removing it. In fact, none of them presented too much of an obstacle and, with a grunt of satisfaction, he succeeded in prising the lid free. It came away with a shriek of splintering wood and he flung it aside.

A cloying stench of decay rose from the body of his dead wife.

Lasalle stared down at the corpse, his gaze travelling inquisitively up and down it. The skin on the face and neck was dry, drawn taut over the bones. The eye sockets were gaping, empty caverns filled only with a gelatinous substance which, from the left eye, had dribbled down the remains of the cheek. A thick yellowish fluid resembling pus was seeping from both nostrils. The mouth was open to reveal several missing teeth. The gums had dissolved and the tongue resembled little more than a strand of withered brown string. One hand lay across the chest, the skin having split and peeled back to reveal brittle bone

143

beneath. The bottom of the coffin was stained with a rusty substance which looked black in the darkness.

Lasalle stepped into the coffin and knelt on the legs of his dead wife, wondering if the bones would snap beneath him. He was sweating profusely and his breath came in short gasps. As he wiped a hand across his forehead, blood from his torn fingers left a crimson smudge on his skin.

Madelaine had been buried in a black dress and Lasalle now bent forward and lifted it, pushing the fusty material up until it covered her putrescing features and exposed her festering pelvic region. Lasalle felt the erection bulging in his trousers and he tugged them down. He fell upon the body and spoke her name as he thrust, the stink of his own perspiration mingling with the vile stench which rose from her corpse.

A shadow fell across him.

Lasalle looked up and his grunts turned to screams.

Joubert stood at the grave-side, looking down at the obscenity before him, a smile etched on his face.

Lasalle screamed again and again.

Joubert continued to smile.

As he was catapulted from the nightmare, Lasalle gripped his head as if he were afraid it was about to explode. He could still hear screams and it was a second or two before he realized they were his own.

He sat up in bed, his body drenched and aching. As he swung himself round he discovered that he was shaking madly. His eyes bulged wildly in the sockets, the images from the dream still vivid in his mind.

He suddenly got to his feet and rushed to the bathroom, barely making it as the cascade of hot bile fought its way up from his stomach, gushing into his mouth. He bent double over the toilet and retched.

He staggered back, head spinning, and swilled out his mouth with water. Then, he staggered slowly back into the bedroom and sat down in the chair beside the window.

He did not sleep for the remainder of that night.

30

Oxford

It was a familiar drive for Blake. Although he hadn't visited the Institute of Psychical Study for over a year he had not needed to consult a map in order to find the place. He'd left London early, avoiding much of the worst traffic. The sun was shining with just enough power to make driving pleasant. Dressed in a pair of jeans and an open-necked white shirt, Blake felt comfortable and he whistled happily in accompaniment to the cassette as he swung the XJS into the driveway which led up to the Institute.

He found a parking space and turned off the engine, waiting until the track he'd been listening to had finished before getting out of the car. He slipped on a light jacket and made his way towards the main entrance of the building. There was a notepad stuffed into his pocket and the usual array of pens too. Blake chuckled to himself, remembering back to his days as a journalist when he'd dashed enthusiastically to each pissant little assignment armed with his trusty pad.

The entrance hall of the Institute was pleasantly cool and Blake paused, slowing his pace, trying to remember where he had to go.

He spotted someone emerging from a room ahead of him.

The writer was immediately struck by her shapely figure, the way her lab coat hugged her taut buttocks, the small slit at the back allowing him brief, tantalising glimpses of her slim calves. She walked easily and elegantly on her high heels and he realized that she hadn't noticed him.

'Excuse me,' he called, approaching her.

She turned and Blake found himself looking deep into her welcoming eyes. She smiled and the gesture seemed to light up her whole face. He chanced an approving glance at her upper body, her breasts pertly pressing against the material of her electric blue blouse.

'You're David Blake aren't you?' she said but it was more of a statement than a question.

He smiled broadly.

'Fame at last,' he beamed. 'How do you know me?'

'We have your books in our library, I recognize you from your photo on the jacket. It's the dark glasses,' she told him. 'They're quite distinctive.'

'Well, they hide the bags under my eyes,' he said, pleased when she chuckled. 'You seem to have me at a disadvantage, you know me but I don't know you.'

'Kelly Hunt,' she told him. 'I work here.'

Blake shook her small hand gently.

'You don't fit the image,' he said. 'I thought all investigators were crusty middle-aged men.'

'Not *all* of them,' Kelly said.

'So I see.'

They looked at each other for long moments, both liking what they saw.

'Is Dr Vernon in his office?' Blake said, finally breaking the silence.

Kelly frowned slightly.

'Are you here to see him then?' she asked.

Blake explained that he was. Kelly told him how to reach the Institute Director.

'Well, it's nice to have met you, Miss Hunt,' he said, heading for the stairs which led up to Vernon's office.

'You too,' Kelly said, watching as he disappeared out of sight.

She wondered exactly how friendly he was with Vernon.

Vernon was already on his feet, right hand extended, when Blake entered the office.

The men exchanged pleasant greetings and the writer sat down, accepting the drink he was offered.

'Sorry to call on you at such short notice,' he apologised. 'But I've written about two-thirds of the book and I need to check some details before I can finish it.'

Vernon produced Blake's letter from his desk drawer.

'I got it yesterday,' he said, smiling. 'So, how are things in the book business?'

Blake shrugged.

'It could be better I suppose but then again, it always could.'

'And how's your new book coming along?'

146

'Fine, as far as I can tell. But then who am I to judge?' He smiled.

Vernon's mood darkened slightly. He looked at Blake and then at the letter he'd received from the writer.

'You say your new book is about the unconscious mind?' he asked.

'The unconscious, dreams, Astral travel, that kind of thing. I've just got back from America, I spent some time with a man called Jonathan Mathias. You might have heard of him.'

Vernon nodded.

'He's a remarkable man,' Blake said. 'Powerful.' The writer's voice took on a reflective note.

'How do you mean, powerful?' Vernon wanted to know.

'It's difficult to explain. He performs acts of faith-healing and yet he's an atheist.' Blake paused. 'But, most important of all, he claims he can control the subconscious minds of other people. Their Astral bodies.'

'How?' Vernon demanded, sitting forward in his chair.

Blake regarded the older man over the top of his glass.

'It's some form of hypnosis,' he said. 'I'm sure of that.'

Vernon eyed the writer suspiciously.

'It's an extravagant claim,' he said.

Blake shrugged.

'Like I said, he's a remarkable man.'

The Institute Director reached forward and flicked a switch on his intercom.

'Could you send Miss Hunt up, please,' he said, then sat back in his chair once more.

'Do you believe what Mathias says about being able to control other people's subconscious minds?' he wanted to know.

Blake was about to answer when there was a knock on the door, and, a moment later, Kelly entered.

She looked at Blake but, this time, he was surprised to find that she didn't smile. He got to his feet.

'David Blake,' began Vernon. 'This is Kelly Hunt, one of our . . .'

Kelly cut him short.

'We've met,' she said, curtly. 'Hello again, Mr Blake.'

The writer was puzzled by the coldness of her voice. All the earlier warmth seemed to have been drained from it.

147

'Mr Blake will be conducting some research here for his new book, I'd like you to help him with whatever he needs.'

'But my work . . .' she protested.

'His work ties in with your own,' Vernon said, sharply.

'I hope I'm not causing anyone any inconvenience,' the writer said, aware of a newly found hostility in the air.

'It's no trouble,' Kelly said, sounding none too convincing.

He smiled thinly.

'Well, I suppose I'd better get started.' He thanked Vernon, then followed Kelly out of the office.

The Institute Director sat down at his desk and re-read the letter which Blake had posted two days earlier. He held it before him a moment longer then carefully, almost gleefully, tore it up.

'Did I do something to annoy you?' Blake asked Kelly as they headed down the stairs towards her office.

'What gives you that impression, Mr Blake?' she said.

'Your attitude,' he told her. 'And stop calling me *Mr* Blake will you? My name's David.'

'What sort of research are you interested in?' Kelly asked him, dutifully.

He repeated what he'd told Vernon.

'The old boy seemed very interested,' Blake said.

'How long have you been friends?' asked Kelly.

'Well, I wouldn't exactly call us friends. Acquaintances might be more to the point. I've been to the Institute a few times in the past while I've been working on other books.'

'How close are you?' she asked.

Blake stopped walking.

'What is this? Twenty questions?' he asked, irritably.

Kelly also stood where she was.

'Dr Vernon and I have met several times on what you might call a professional basis,' Blake told her. 'Although with all due respect, I don't really see that it's any of your business, Miss Hunt.'

'No, you're right, it isn't,' Kelly confessed, some of the coldness having left her voice. 'I'm sorry, Mr Blake.'

He sighed.

148

'David,' he told her. 'Look, we have to work together for a day or two, we might as well make the time pass pleasantly.'

'David,' she agreed, smiling thinly.

They began walking again but more slowly this time.

'Why is it so important to you to know whether Vernon and I are friends?' he enquired.

'I was curious.'

'I'm *still* curious. When I arrived here, when we first spoke, everything was fine. Since I spoke to Vernon you don't want to know me.'

'It's difficult to explain,' she said, evasively.

'Then don't try,' Blake said, smiling.

Kelly looked at him, aware that she felt more than a passing attraction for this man.

Blake was not handsome but his finely chiselled features and sinewy frame, coupled with the easy-going personality he exuded, served their purpose well.

'Vernon said you'd been doing work on dreams,' he said.

'That's what I'm still working on,' Kelly explained as they reached her office. She ushered him inside and motioned for him to sit down but, instead, the writer wandered over to the window and looked out across the rolling lawns which surrounded the Institute. Kelly seated herself behind her desk, studying Blake's profile as he gazed out into the sunlit morning.

'The weather's too nice to work,' he said, quietly.

She smiled.

'Standing there isn't going to get your book written is it?'

Blake turned and nodded.

'Quite right, Miss Hunt,' he said.

'Kelly,' she reminded him.

It was his turn to smile.

'How exactly *can* I help you?' she asked as he seated himself opposite her.

'I'd like to see the labs where you've been doing your research, ask you a few questions if that's all right but, otherwise, just give me free run of the library and I'll be happy. I'm not a difficult man to please.' He smiled that engaging smile once more and Kelly found herself drawn to him, to his eyes even though they were

149

shielded behind his dark glasses. She felt a peculiar tingle run through her.

'Shall we start in the labs?' she said, getting to her feet again.

He nodded.

'Why not?'

Kelly led him out of her office.

The library at the Institute never failed to fascinate Blake. Built up, as it had been, over a hundred years, it had books which dated back as far as the sixteenth century. Before him on the table he had an original copy of Collin de Planncey's 'Dictionaire Infernale'. The pages creaked as he turned them, scanning the ancient tome, pleasantly surprised at how much of the French he could actually understand.

He'd been in the library for over four hours, ever since he'd left Kelly back in her office. Now, with the time approaching 5.15 p.m., he heard his stomach rumbling and realized that he hadn't eaten since early morning. The writer scanned what notes he'd written, realizing that he must check one or two discrepancies against his manuscript at the first opportunity. As it was, he replaced the old books in their correct position on the shelves, scooped up his pad and made for the stairs.

Kelly was on her way down.

'I was coming to see if you needed any help,' she said, the warmth having returned to her voice.

They had found it remarkably easy to talk to each other that morning. Their conversation had flowed unfalteringly and Kelly had felt her attraction for Blake growing stronger. She felt at ease in his company and she was sure the feeling was reciprocated.

'Did you find what you were looking for?' she asked him.

He smiled and ran appraising eyes over her.

'I think I found exactly what I was looking for,' he said.

She coloured slightly and waited on the stairs while he made his way up. They both walked out into the hall which was now much colder than when Blake had first arrived.

'Will you be back tomorrow?' she asked him.

'I got the information I needed,' he told her, 'with your help. But if I ever have a haunting you'll be the first one I get in touch with. You've really been very kind. Thanks.'

'Are you driving back to London now?'

'Not yet. I'm going to have something to eat first and then I thought I might take you out for a drink this evening if you're not doing anything else.'

Kelly chuckled, unable to speak for a moment, taken by surprise by the unexpectedness of his invitation.

'If I'm in a good mood, I might even let you buy a round,' Blake added.

'What if I am doing something else?' she asked.

'Then I'll have to wait for another evening won't I?'

She shook her head, still laughing.

'Can I pick you up about eight?' he asked.

'Eight will be fine,' she told him. 'But it might help if you knew where to pick me up *from*.' She scribbled her address and phone number on a piece of paper and gave it to him.

'Tell Dr Vernon I'll be in touch,' Blake said, and, for a moment, he saw a flicker of doubt cross Kelly's face. 'I'll phone him and thank him for letting me use the library.'

She nodded.

Blake turned and headed for the door.

'Eight o'clock,' he reminded her.

She watched him go, stood alone in the hallway listening as he revved up his engine. He turned the XJS full circle and guided it back down the driveway towards the road which led into Oxford itself.

Kelly smiled to herself and returned to her office.

From his office window, Dr Vernon watched as the writer drove away. He paused a moment then reached for the phone and dialled.

31

'Cheers,' said Blake, smiling. He raised his glass then took a hefty swallow from the foaming beer.

Across the table from him, Kelly did likewise, sipping her Martini and meeting the writer's gaze.

They were seated in the garden of 'The Jester', a small pub about a mile or so outside Oxford. There were three or four other people enjoying the evening air as well. It was still agreeably warm despite the fact that the sun was sinking, gushing crimson into the sky. When it got too chilly they could easily retire into the comfort of the lounge bar. Blake looked at his companion, pleased with what he saw. She was clad in a dress of pale lemon cheese-cloth, her breasts unfettered by the restraints of a bra. The writer noticed how invitingly her dark nipples pressed against the flimsy material. With the sinking sun casting a halo around her, drawing golden streaks in her brown hair she looked beautiful. He felt something akin to pride merely being seated there with her.

Kelly noticed how intently he was looking at her and smiled impishly.

'What are you looking at?' she asked him.

'A very beautiful young woman,' he told her. 'But, I was thinking too.'

'About what?'

He raised his eyebrows.

'No,' she said. 'Perhaps I'm better off not knowing.'

Blake laughed.

'I was wondering actually,' he began, 'how you came to be in the line of work you're in. It is unusual for a woman, especially of your age.'

'It was what I wanted to do when I left University,' she told him.

'How did your parents feel about it?' he wanted to know.

'They didn't say much one way or the other. I'd worked in a library for a few months before I joined the Institute. They'd probably have been just as happy if I'd stayed on there. Security is the be-all and end-all in our family I'm afraid.'

Blake nodded.

'What about you?' Kelly asked. 'Writing's a precarious business isn't it? What made you want to write?'

'Well, it wasn't because I needed to share my knowledge with others,' he said, tongue-in-cheek. 'Not in the beginning anyway. I wrote a couple of novels to start with.'

'Did you have any luck with them?'

He shook his head.

'Writing fiction successfully needs more luck than talent. You need the breaks. I didn't get them.'

'So you turned to non-fiction? The stuff you write now?'

'The ratio's different. It's fifty per cent talent and fifty per cent luck.'

'You sell yourself short, David.'

'No. I understand my own limitations that's all.'

'What about your parents. How do they feel about having a famous author for a son?'

'Both my parents are dead. My father died of a stroke five years ago, my mother had a heart attack six months after him.'

'Oh God, I'm sorry, David.'

He smiled thinly.

'You weren't to know,' he said. 'I just wish they could have lived to see my success that's all.'

A heavy silence descended, rapidly broken by Blake.

'Well, now we've got the morbid stuff out of the way,' he said, with a reasonable degree of cheerfulness. 'Perhaps we can carry on with this conversation.'

She sipped her drink and looked at him over the rim of the glass. Losing his parents within six months of each other must have been a crushing blow and obviously he didn't want to dwell on the memory.

'I suppose you must be reasonably secure as a writer now,' she said, attempting to guide the conversation in another direction.

'You can never be secure in my business,' he said. 'One flop and it's back to square one. It's like walking a tightrope in a pair of wellies.'

Kelly chuckled.

'Does it bother you living alone?' Blake asked.

'Not anymore,' she told him. 'It did to begin with but I'm used to it now.'

'And you've never felt like getting married?'

'No.' She dismissed the suggestion as if he'd just asked her to commit suicide. 'I'm not the setting down type, I don't think.'

'I know what you mean,' he confessed.

'You're not telling me *you* haven't been tempted. There must have been girls who you've been close too,' Kelly said.

'A couple. But none that I'd want to spend the rest of my life with.' He smiled. 'I'm a selfish devil. Sharing isn't one of my strong points.'

'Too much give and take, is that it?'

'You ask a lot of questions, Kelly,' he grinned.

'That's because I'm interested in you,' she told him.

'Now that *is* a compliment.'

They sat in silence for a time, looking at each other, enjoying the warmth of the dying sun, the smell of freshly cut grass and the gentle breeze. It stirred the trees which flanked the pub garden on one side. Birds nesting in the branches watched over the activity below them. Near to where Kelly and Blake sat, three sparrows were busily picking at a piece of bread thrown down by a young couple who were eating sandwiches. Somewhere in the distance Kelly could hear a cuckoo. She sat back in her seat feeling more relaxed than she had done for many months. The combination of the surroundings and Blake's company had a calming influence on her. She wondered if he felt the same way.

The writer downed what was left in his glass and looked at Kelly. She still had most of her Martini left.

'I'll have to bring you out more often,' he said, peering at the glass. 'If one drink lasts you this long you're going to save me pounds.'

They both laughed.

'You have another,' she said.

'Very generous,' Blake replied.

'Let me get it,' she offered, fumbling for her purse.

Blake looked indignant.

'Let a woman buy drink for me?' He winked at her. 'Good idea.'

She balled up a pound note and tossed it at him, watching as he retreated back into the bar to fetch another pint. It was a matter of moments before he returned, holding the glass in one hand and her change in the other. He sat down and supped a third of it immediately, wiping the froth from his lip with his thumb.

'Did Vernon say anything when you told him I'd left this afternoon?' the writer asked.

'No,' Kelly said, suspiciously. 'Should he have?'

Blake smiled, wryly.

'You know, Kelly,' he said. 'I could be forgiven for thinking you're a tiny bit paranoid about Dr Vernon.'

Kelly didn't answer.

'Every time I mention his name you go cold on me,' Blake continued. 'Why? Or is it my imagination?'

She took a sip of her drink.

'Perhaps it's *my* imagination,' she told him, wondering if that was the answer. Maybe she *was* becoming paranoid.

'What do you mean?'

She thought about mentioning what had been going on, her suspicions and suppositions but then decided against it.

'Forget it, David,' she asked. 'Please?'

He nodded.

Kelly finished her drink and pushed the glass away from her.

'Do you want another one?' the writer asked.

She smiled and shook her head.

'No thanks.'

There was another long silence between them then finally Kelly spoke.

'To tell you the truth, David,' she began, wearily, 'I'm a little bit concerned at the amount of interest Dr Vernon is showing in my research.'

Blake frowned.

'I don't understand,' he said. 'Surely he's got every right to be interested. He is Director of the Institute after all. It's only natural.'

155

'But he seems obsessed with my work.'

She told him about the incident with Maurice Grant, her trip to France and how Vernon had insisted on keeping her report.

Blake didn't speak, he merely finished the rest of his beer and put down the empty glass.

'Well,' she said, challengingly. 'Do you think I'm being paranoid now?'

'There's probably a perfectly reasonable explanation for it, Kelly,' he said.

'Don't try and humour me, David.' He was surprised at the vehemence in her words. 'There are other factors too. Things which don't make sense, which have no logical explanation.' She emphasised the last two words with scorn.

'Like what?' he wanted to know.

Kelly shivered as the slight breeze seemed to turn cold. She looked up and saw that the crimson of the setting sun had been replaced by a layered sky of purple. Kelly felt goose-pimples rise on her flesh and she rubbed her forearms.

'I don't feel comfortable talking about them here,' she told him, as if she feared some kind of surveillance in the peaceful garden.

'I'll take you home,' Blake said without hesitation.

They got to their feet and walked to the car park where the writer opened the passenger door of the XJS, allowing Kelly to slide in. He clambered in behind the wheel and started the engine, guiding the Jaguar out into the road.

'Are you all right?' he asked, glancing across at her, a little puzzled by her silence.

She nodded, feeling more at ease within the confines of the car. She even managed to smile at the writer who reached across and squeezed her hand gently. Kelly felt the coldness draining from her, as if Blake's touch had somehow restored her composure. She gripped his hand in return, reassured by his presence.

After a fifteen minute drive they reached her flat.

Kelly no longer felt the cold seeping through her and she looked at the writer almost gratefully.

'Home,' he said, smiling, and once more she found herself captivated by that smile of his. No, more than that. She was ensnared by it, drawn

156

to him unlike any man before. He exuded a magnetism which she found irresistible, almost in spite of herself.

'How do you feel now?' he asked.

'I'm OK,' she told him. 'Thanks, David.'

'For what?' he wanted to know.

'Just thanks.' She reached across and touched his hand with her slender fingers. If any emotion registered in his eyes she couldn't see it because his dark glasses now hid them even more completely. 'Would you like to come in for a coffee?'

Blake needed no second bidding. He climbed out of the Jag and locked his door then walked around and let Kelly out, watching appreciatively as she walked ahead of him, searching through her bag for her key. The writer enjoyed the gentle sway of her hips as she walked, the muscles in her calves tensing slightly with each step she took, perched on her backless high heels.

He followed her.

Her flat was, as he'd expected it to be both spotlessly clean and impeccably neat. At her bidding he seated himself in one of the big armchairs which flanked the electric fire. Kelly passed through into the kitchen and Blake heard water running as she filled a kettle.

She returned a moment later, crossing to the window to close the curtains. Then she flicked on the record player, dropping a disc onto the turntable.

'Do you mind some music?' she asked.

'Not at all,' he said.

The sound of Simon and Garfunkel flowed softly from the speakers.

'Coffee won't be a minute,' she told him, seating herself in the armchair opposite and, as she did so, she found once again that her gaze was drawn to the writer.

'Is this your own place?' Blake asked.

'It will be eventually,' Kelly told him. 'In another twenty years time probably.' She shrugged. 'By the time I'm an old, withered spinster at least I'll own my own flat.'

Blake smiled.

'I don't think there's much chance of you becoming an old withered spinster, Kelly,' he said.

'My mother keeps asking me why I'm not married yet. Why I'm

157

not knee deep in wet nappies and babies.' Kelly smiled. 'Parents love the idea of grandchildren until they actually have them. Then they complain because it makes them feel old.' Kelly felt a warm thrill run through her as she relaxed in the chair, feeling quite happy to let Blake look at her, to examine her with his eyes. Every so often she would see them flicker behind the dark screen of his glasses.

'Are you sensitive to light, David?' she asked him. 'I mean, the dark glasses.' She pointed to them.

'Slightly,' he said. 'I suppose that's what comes of squinting over a typewriter for five years.'

The kettle began to whistle. Kelly got to her feet and walked back into the kitchen, returning a moment later with two steaming mugs of coffee, one of which she handed to Blake. Then, she kicked off her shoes and, this time, sat on the floor in front of him, legs drawn up to one side of her.

'Kelly, I don't want to pry,' Blake began. 'But you said there were things about Vernon which you didn't understand. What did you mean?'

She sucked in a weary breath and lowered her gaze momentarily.

'From what you told me at the pub, I can't see any reason to suspect that Dr Vernon's up to something, especially not anything as sinister as you seem to think,' said Blake. 'What reasons would he have?'

'David,' she said, trying to keep her voice calm. 'I was responsible for what happened to Maurice Grant. What I did was wrong. It broke the rules of the Institute. The authorities could have closed the place. That Institute is Vernon's pride and joy. He could have lost it because of me and yet he didn't so much as give me a warning or suspend me.' She decided to put down her mug. 'Instead, he protected me when he had every right to dismiss me on the spot. Then, when I got back from France, he wanted to know everything that happened and he kept my report.'

Blake sat forward in his chair.

'You make Vernon sound like a monster when all he tried to do was help you,' he said.

'He's hiding something, David,' she said, angrily. 'John Fraser knew what it was. That's why he was killed.'

'Who's Fraser?'

158

She explained as much as she knew about the events of the last two days.

'But if Fraser was killed in a car crash, how could Vernon be involved?' the writer wanted to know. 'It was an accident, surely?'

'He knew about Vernon's secret.'

Another heavy silence descended, finally broken by Blake.

'I don't see how you can suspect Vernon of being involved in Fraser's death,' he said.

'David, he won't let *anyone* come between him and this research.'

'Does that include you?' Blake asked, cryptically.

It was at that point that the phone rang.

32

For long moments neither of them moved as the strident ringing filled the room. Then, finally, Kelly got to her feet and walked across to the phone, lifting the receiver tentatively, wondering why she felt so apprehensive. Blake watched her, noticing the hesitancy in her movements.

'Hello,' she said.

No answer.

'Hello,' she repeated, looking across at Blake as if seeking reassurance.

Words suddenly came gushing forth from the caller at the other end, some of which she didn't understand. Not merely due to the speed with which they were uttered but because they were in French.

'Who is this?' she asked, holding the phone away from her for a second as a particularly loud crackle of static broke up the line. 'Hello. Can you hear me? Who's speaking?'

'Kelly. It's Michel Lasalle.'

She relaxed slightly.

'Listen to me, you must listen,' he blurted, and Kelly was more than aware of the high-pitched desperation in his voice. His breathing was harsh and irregular, as if he'd been running for a long time. 'I saw Madelaine,' he told her, his voice cracking. 'I saw her.'

159

'You had a nightmare, Michel, it's understandable . . .'

He interrupted.

'No, I touched her, felt her,' he insisted.

'It was a nightmare,' she repeated.

'No. Joubert saw her too.'

Kelly frowned.

'What do you mean? How was he involved?' she wanted to know. She felt the tension returning to her muscles.

'He was there, with me,' the Frenchman continued, panting loudly. He babbled something in French then laughed dryly. A sound which sent a shiver down Kelly's spine. 'He watched me making love to her. She felt cold in my arms but it didn't matter, she is still mine. I still want her.'

Kelly tried to speak but couldn't.

'Joubert has not forgiven me,' the Frenchman said, softly. 'I don't think he ever will.'

'Forgiven you for what?' Kelly wanted to know.

'Writing that article.'

'Did he speak to you?' she asked, wondering whether or not she should humour the distraught man.

'He is always there, Kelly. Always. Watching.'

An uneasy silence fell, broken only by the gentle hiss of static burbling in the lines.

'Michel, are you still there?' Kelly finally said.

Silence.

'Michel, answer me.'

She heard a click and realized that he'd hung up. For long seconds she stared at the receiver then slowly replaced it.

'What was it?' Blake asked, seeing the concern on her face.

She walked slowly back towards him and seated herself on the floor once again, reaching for her coffee. It was cold.

'Kelly, who *was* that?' the writer persisted.

'Lasalle. One of the men from the Metapsychic Centre,' she told him, then proceeded to relay what the Frenchman had said to her.

'He's convinced that it was real,' she said.

Blake shrugged.

'Nightmares are usually vivid,' he said.

160

Kelly shook her head.

'But Lasalle won't accept that he had a nightmare,' she protested. 'He's convinced that what he experienced actually happened.' She sighed. 'I hope to God he's not heading for another breakdown. He had one when his wife died.' She looked up at Blake. 'And Joubert, he mentioned that Joubert was present in the nightmare. He sounded frightened of him.' She lowered her gaze once more. 'First Fraser, now Lasalle. One man's dead, another is close to a nervous breakdown and all because of the research I'm engaged in.'

'You can't blame yourself, Kelly,' Blake said, reaching out and gently lifting her head with his right hand.

She gripped that hand, aware of the combination of gentleness and strength in it but more conscious of the warmth which seemed to flow from it, from his entire being. She looked up at him, trying to see his eyes, searching for a glimmer behind the tinted screens which masked them. Kelly kissed his hand and moved closer to him, resting her own right hand on his knee as he slowly stroked the back of her neck beneath her hair. She squirmed beneath his subtle caresses, moving nearer, anxious to touch him fully. His other hand began gently kneading the smooth flesh of her shoulder and she closed her eyes.

'What if Vernon *is* responsible for Fraser's death?' she said, quietly, enjoying the sensations which were coursing through her.

'Then he's a dangerous man,' Blake said. 'You should stay away from him.'

'And Joubert?'

'Kelly. If there is any possibility that either of them have some kind of psychic power then you'd do best not to let them know you suspect.'

'But I must know the truth, David,' she protested, turning to face him.

As she did so, Blake leant forward and kissed her. Their lips brushed gently for a moment then, unhesitatingly, Kelly pressed her mouth to his. Blake responded fiercely, matching her passion with his own desire.

Kelly snaked her hand up around his neck, as if reluctant to break the kiss. When she finally did, she was panting softly, her eyes riveted to Blake. Her body was burning, as if fire were pouring through her veins. She felt her nipples, now stiff and erect, straining almost painfully against her dress and between her slender legs she felt a glowing moistness. Blake sensed her excitement and she could see that he felt similarly aroused by the contact they had enjoyed. Her hand strayed to the beginnings of bulge in his trousers, massaging and rubbing until Blake himself grunted under his breath.

Kelly moved away from him slightly, lying back on the carpet before him, inviting his attentions. The writer was not slow to respond and he joined her, his hands moving over the thin material of her dress until they came to her breasts. He rubbed gently, feeling the hardened points beneath his palms as she arched her back. Kelly felt as if she were floating, the warm glow between her legs becoming an all-consuming desire which filled every part of her. She took Blake's left hand and guided it up inside her dress, moaning as his fingers stroked the smooth flesh of her inner thighs, pausing there for agonisingly exquisite seconds before moving higher. She felt his probing digits reach her panties, his forefinger hooked, pulling down the flimsy garment. She lifted her buttocks to allow him to remove them, watching as he first kissed the sodden material before laying it on one side.

She pulled him close to her, their mouths locking once more as she thrust her pelvis towards his searching hand, almost crying aloud as his finger touched the hardened bud of her clitoris and began rubbing gently. She fumbled for his zip and freed his bulging erection, encircling it with her slender fingers, working up a gentle rhythm as she teased his stiff shaft. For three or four minutes they remained like that and then she suggested they undress.

It took them mere moments then, naked, they were free to explore every inch of the other's body. Blake lowered his head to her breasts and took first one nipple then the other between his teeth, rolling it gently as he flicked it with his tongue. Kelly felt his other hand trace a pattern across her belly before gliding through her soft pubic hair once more to search for her most sensitive area and she rolled onto her side, allowing him to push his heavily muscled thigh against her. She ground hard against him, eventually manoeuvering herself so that he was beneath her. She straddled his stomach.

'Take these off,' she said, quietly, reaching for his dark glasses. 'I want to see your eyes.'

Blake himself removed them and then turned to look at her.

162

Kelly felt as if the breath had been torn from her, as if someone had punched her hard and winded her.

Blake's eyes were the colour of a June sky. A deep blue which she found overwhelming in their intensity. She felt as if she were a puppet, suspended by wires which came from those eyes, her movements and feelings controlled by them. A renewed and much more powerful surge of emotion shook her and she bent forward to kiss him. But, he gripped her waist and almost lifted her up on to his chest, smiling as she rubbed herself against him. He felt the wetness spilling from her, dampening his chest. She moved a little further so that he could reach her with his tongue.

Kelly gasped as she felt it flicking over her distended lips, reaming her swollen cleft before fastening on her clitoris. She spoke his name, her head thrown back as she surrendered to the feelings which were sweeping over her. Kelly felt a tightening around her thighs, the first unmistakable sign of approaching orgasm. His hands reached up and found her swollen nipples, adding to her overall pleasure which was now building up like an impending explosion.

She twisted around so that she could reach his penis, lying on him in order to allow it to reach her mouth. She studied the bulbous head for a moment then took it into her mouth, wrapping her tongue around it, her free hand working away at the root, fondling his testicles. She felt him stiffen, realized that his excitement was a great as hers. But she needed him more fully. Kelly rolled to one side, kissing him briefly as she did so then she knelt over his groin, cradling his throbbing member in one hand, lowering herself slowly until it nudged her aching vagina. They both gasped as the union was completed. She sank down onto him, his shaft swallowed by her liquescent cleft.

Kelly knew that she would not be able to hold back any longer. She stared into Blake's eyes and began moving up and down. The sensations began almost at once. She was aware only of the throbbing pleasure between her legs and his welcoming blue eyes which seemed to fill her entire field of vision. She could not look away from him and, as she speeded up her movements, she felt as though she were being joined with him, melting into him to form one entity.

The power of the orgasm made her cry out loudly. She bounced up and down on him, each wave of pleasure more intense than the one before. She had never felt anything so overwhelmingly wonderful in her life and that pleasure, almost impossibly, suddenly re-doubled as she felt him writhe beneath her as his own climax washed over him. Kelly moaned loudly as she felt his hot liquid spurt into her and she ground herself hard against him, coaxing every last drop from him. Shaking and bathed in perspiration, she slumped forward, kissing him gently, unable to look anywhere else but at his eyes.

They lay still, coupled together as he softened within her.

It was a long time before either of them spoke. The record player was silent, the record having finished long ago. Only the sound of the wind outside was audible.

'You don't have to drive back to London tonight do you?' Kelly asked him.

'You try getting rid of me,' he said, smiling.

They both laughed.

Kelly ran a finger across his lips then kissed him softly.

Her gaze never left his deep blue eyes and, once more, she felt that glorious sensation of floating. As if she had no control over her own body.

Blake smiled broadly.

PART TWO

'All human beings, as we meet them, are
   commingled out of good and evil . . .'
                    — *Robert Louis Stevenson*

'He who shall teach the child to doubt,
   Shall ne'er the rotting grave get out.'
                    — *William Blake*

33

London

The Waterloo Club, in the heart of London's Mayfair, was a magnificent anachronism.

Founded a year after the battle of Waterloo by a group of Wellington's infantry officers, the building was more like a museum. There was a subdued reverence about the place, much like that usually reserved for a church. It languished in cultivated peacefulness and had defied all but the most necessary architectural changes since its construction in 1816. But, for all that, it retained an archaic splendour which was fascinating.

David Blake sipped his drink and scanned the panelled walls. The room seemed dark, despite the lamps which burned in profusion, complimented by the huge crystal chandelier which hung from the ceiling. There were a number of paintings on view including excellent copies of Denis Dighton's 'Sergeant Ewart capturing the Eagle of the 45th', a picture which Blake remembered from a history book. Behind the bar was Sir William Allen's panoramic view of Waterloo, a full fifteen feet in length. It hung in a gilt frame, as imposing a piece of art as Blake had seen. On another wall were two polished cuirasses, the breast plates still carrying musket ball holes. Above them were the brass helmets of Carabiniers, the long swords of the Scots Greys and various original muskets and pistols.

Blake was suitably impressed with the surroundings despite being somewhat perplexed as to why the BBC should have chosen such a setting for the party to welcome Jonathan Mathias to England. Other guests chatted amiably, some, like himself, gazing at the paintings and other paraphernalia. He guessed that there must be about two dozen people there, most of whom he recognized from one or other branch of the entertainment industry.

He spotted Jim O'Neil sitting in one corner. He was on the British leg of a European tour which had, so far, taken him and his band to ten different countries encompassing over eighty gigs. He was a tall, wiry man in his late twenties, dressed completely in black leather. The rock star was nodding intently as two young women chatted animatedly to him.

The writer was aware of other well-known faces too. He caught sight of Sir George Howe, the new head of the BBC, speaking to a group of men which included Gerald Braddock.

Braddock was the present Government's Minister for the Arts, a plump, red-faced man whose shirt collar was much too tight for him, a condition not aided by his tie which appeared to have been fastened by a member of the thugee cult. Every time he swallowed he looked as though he was going to choke.

Next to him stood Roger Carr, host of the chat show on which Mathias was to appear.

Elsewhere, Blake spotted actors and actresses from TV, an agent or two but, as far as he could see, he was the only writer who had been invited.

He'd been a little surprised by the invitation although he had written for the BBC in the past, most notably, a six part series on the paranormal. When he learned that Mathias was to be the guest of honour he'd accepted the invitation readily.

At the moment, however, there was no sign of the American.

'Do you get invited to many dos like this?' Kelly asked him, looking around at the array of talent in the room.

Blake had been seeing her for just over a week now, driving back and forth to Oxford, staying at her flat most nights and returning to his home to work during the day. When he'd told her about the invitation, initially she'd been apprehensive but now, as she scanned the other guests, she did not regret her decision to accompany him.

'There *aren't* many dos like this,' he told her, looking around, wondering where Mathias had disappeared to.

The psychic arrived as if on cue, emerging from the club cloakroom like something from a Bram Stoker novel. He wore a black three-piece suit and white shirt, a black bow-tie at his throat. Cufflinks bearing large diamonds sparkled in the light like millions of insect eyes. The psychic was introduced to Sir George Howe and his group. All eyes turned towards the little tableau and the previously subdued conversation seemed to drop to a hush. It was as if a powerful magnet had been brought into the room, drawing everything to it.

'He looks very imposing in the flesh,' said Kelly, almost in awe. 'I've only ever seen him in photographs.'

Blake didn't answer her. His eye had been caught by more belated movement from the direction of the cloakroom as a late-comer arrived.

'Christ,' murmured the writer, nudging Kelly. 'Look.'

He nodded in the appropriate direction and she managed to tear her gaze from Mathias.

The late-comer slipped into the room and over to the group surrounding the psychic. Kelly looked at him and then at Blake.

'What's *he* doing here?' she said, in bewilderment.

Dr Stephen Vernon ran a nervous hand through his hair and sidled up beside Sir George Howe.

Blake and Kelly watched as the Institute Director was introduced. Words were exchanged but, no matter how hard she tried, Kelly could not hear what was being said. Gradually, the babble of conversation began to fill the room again.

Kelly hesitated, watching Vernon as he stood listening to the psychic.

'Kelly,' Blake said, forcefully, gripping her arm. 'Come on. Let's get another drink.'

Almost reluctantly, she followed him to the bar where Jim O'Neil now sat, perched on one of the tall stools. He was still listening to one of the girls but his interest seemed to have waned. As Blake and Kelly approached he ran an appreciative eye over Kelly whose full breasts were prominent due to the plunging neck-line of her dress. A tiny gold crucifix hung invitingly between them. O'Neil smiled at her and Kelly returned the gesture.

'Hello,' said O'Neil, nodding at them both but keeping his eyes on Kelly.

The writer turned and smiled, shaking the other man's outstretched hand.

Introductions were swiftly made. O'Neil took Kelly's hand and kissed it delicately.

'Would you like a drink?' asked Blake.

'Make it a pint of bitter will you,' the singer asked. 'I'm sick of these bleeding cocktails.' He pushed the glass away from him.

The barman gave him a disdainful look, watching as the other man downed half of the foaming pint.

'Christ, that's better,' he said.

Kelly caught the sound of a cockney accent in his voice.

'No gig tonight?' Blake asked.

O'Neil shook his head.

'The rest of the band have got the night off,' he said, scratching bristles on his chin which looked as if you could strike a match on them. 'My manager said I ought to come here. God knows why.' He supped some more of his pint. 'I'm surprised they invited me in the first place. I mean, they never play any of my fucking records on Radio One.' He chuckled.

Kelly pulled Blake's arm and nodded in the direction of a nearby table. The two of them said they'd speak to O'Neil again later then left him at the bar ordering another pint.

The writer was in the process of pulling out a chair for Kelly when he saw Mathias and his little entourage approaching. The psychic smiled broadly when he saw Blake. Kelly turned and found herself looking straight at Dr Vernon. They exchanged awkward glances then Kelly looked at Mathias who was already shaking hands with Blake.

'It's good to see you again, David,' said the American. 'How's the book coming along?'

'I'm getting there,' the writer said. 'You look well, Jonathan.'

'I see there are no need for introductions where you two are concerned,' said Sir George Howe, smiling.

'We're not exactly strangers,' Mathias told him. Then he looked at Kelly. 'But I don't know you. And I feel that I should.'

The psychic smiled and Kelly saw a glint in his eye.

She introduced herself then stepped back, one eye on Vernon, as Sir George completed the introductions.

Blake shook hands with Gerald Braddock, wincing slightly as he felt the pudgy clamminess of the politician's hand.

Then came Vernon.

'This is Dr Stephen Vernon, an old friend of mine, he . . .'

'We've met,' Blake told Sir George. 'How are you, Dr Vernon?'

'I'm very well,' said the older man. He looked at Kelly. 'I didn't expect to see you here tonight, Kelly.'

She didn't answer.

'Well, it seems as if everyone knows everyone else,' said Sir George, aware of the iciness in the air. His stilted laugh died away rapidly.

'How long are you here for, Jonathan?' Blake asked the psychic.

'Three or four days. Long enough to do the show with Mr Carr, and a couple of newspaper interviews, radio pieces. You know the kind of thing,' Mathias told him.

'I saw in the paper that you were coming to England,' Blake said. 'When are you doing the TV show?'

'It's being broadcast the day after tomorrow,' Roger Carr said, stepping forward. 'You should watch it, Mr Blake, I mean you deal in the same kind of tricks don't you? Only you write about them instead.' The interviewer smiled.

Blake returned the smile.

'You know, Mr Carr, there's something I've never been able to figure out about you,' the writer said. 'You're either stupid, in which case I'm sorry for you, or you're pig-ignorant. But I haven't been able to figure out which it is yet.'

Carr shot him an angry glance and opened his mouth to speak but, before he could, all eyes turned in the direction of the cloakroom.

There was an unholy din coming from there, a cacophony of shouts through which the high-pitched voice of a woman could be heard.

Seconds later, a figure dressed in a grey coat, spattered with rain, burst into the peaceful confines of the Waterloo Club. Her hair was wind-blown, her make-up streaked by the rain. She stood panting in the doorway, her eyes fixed on Mathias.

'My God,' muttered Sir George. Then, to a green-coated doorman who had tried to stop the woman entering:

'Could you please eject this lady.'

'No,' Mathias said, raising a hand. 'Leave her.'

'David, who is she?' asked Kelly, noticing the look of recognition on Blake's face as he gazed at the woman.

'Toni Landers,' he said. 'She's an actress.' But the woman whom he had met in New York had been a radiant, sensuous creature. The

171

woman who now stood in the doorway was pale and unkempt, her features haggard. She looked as though she'd aged ten years.

'Do you know this woman?' asked Sir George, looking first at Toni, then at Mathias who had not taken his eyes from her.

'Yes, I know her,' the psychic said.

'Could someone explain what the hell is going on?' Sir George demanded.

'Jonathan, I have to speak to you,' Toni said, her voice cracking. She leant against the bar for support.

Jim O'Neil was on his feet, ready to intervene. Toni looked ready to keel over. She sat down on a bar stool, her gaze still on the psychic.

'How did you find me?' he asked, moving towards her.

'I knew you were coming to England. I've been waiting for you. I found out which hotel you were staying in. They told me where you'd be tonight,' she admitted.

'She's bloody mad,' snapped Roger Carr, dismissively. 'Get her out of here.'

'Shut up,' Mathias rasped. 'Leave her.'

The doorman took a step away from Toni.

'Is this one of your theatrical tricks, Mathias?' Carr demanded.

Blake turned on him.

'Just for once, keep your bloody mouth shut,' he snapped. He motioned to the barman. 'Give her a brandy.'

The man hesitated, looking at Sir George.

'Come on, man, for Christ's sake,' Blake insisted.

'Give her the fucking drink. You heard him,' snarled Jim O'Neil, watching as the barman poured a large measure and handed it to Toni. She downed most of it, coughing as the fiery liquid burned its way to her stomach.

'Toni, what do you want?' Mathias asked her, quietly.

'I need your help, Jonathan,' she told him, tears glistening in her eyes. 'You're the only one who can help me now.'

'Why didn't you come to me before? What were you afraid of?'

She swallowed what was left in the glass.

'That you'd turn me away.'

He shook his head.

'Jonathan, I haven't been able to stop thinking about Rick. Every

172

time I see a child I think about him.' The tears were coursing down her cheeks now. 'Please help me.' Her self-control finally dissolved in a paroxysm of sobs.

Mathias supported her and she clung to him, her body trembling violently.

'What do you want me to do?' he asked.

'Reach him,' she said, flatly. 'Now.'

Mathias didn't speak.

'Please, do I have to beg you?' Some of the despair in her voice had turned to anger. 'Contact my son.'

34

'This is a London club, not a fairground tent,' protested Sir George Ward as the massive oak table was dragged into the centre of the room by Blake, O'Neil and a third man.

'What I intend to do is no fairground trick,' Mathias told him, watching as a number of chairs were placed around the table.

The other guests looked on in stunned, anticipatory silence, Kelly amongst them. Every so often she cast a glance in Dr Vernon's direction, noticing that he was smiling thinly as he observed the proceedings.

Gerald Braddock plucked at the folds of fat beneath his jaw and shifted nervously from one foot to the other.

Toni Landers sat at the bar, the glass of brandy cradled in her shaking hand.

'What are you trying to prove by doing this, Mathias?' Roger Carr wanted to know.

'I don't have to prove anything, Mr Carr,' the psychic said, turning away from him. He held out a hand for Toni Landers to join him. She downed what was left in her glass and wandered across the room. 'Sit there,' the psychic told her, motioning to the chair on his right.

Blake watched with interest, aware that Kelly was gripping his arm tightly. He took her hand and held it, reassuringly.

'I cannot do this alone,' Mathias said, addressing the other guests. 'I must ask for the help of some of you. Not for my own sake but for this lady.' He motioned towards Toni. 'There's nothing to be afraid of. Nothing can hurt you.'

Jim O'Neil was the first to step forward.

'What the hell,' he said, sitting beside Toni then turning in his seat to look at the others.

Roger Carr joined him, sitting on the other side of the table.

Blake looked at Kelly and she nodded almost imperceptibly. They both stepped forward, the writer seating himself directly opposite where Mathias would be.

'Thank you, David,' said the psychic.

As if prompted by Kelly's action, Dr Vernon pulled up a chair and sat down next to her. She eyed him suspiciously for a moment then looked at Blake who had his eyes closed slightly.

'Sir George?' Mathias said, looking at the head of the BBC.

'No, I want no part of this,' said the bald man, defiantly.

Gerald Braddock, who had been rubbing his hands together nervously finally moved towards the table.

'What are you doing, Gerald?' Sir George asked him.

'It can't do any harm,' Braddock said, wiping his palms on his trousers. He looked at the others seated around the table and swallowed hard.

No one else in the room moved. Mathias walked to his seat between Toni Landers and Roger Carr. Opposite him was Blake. To *his* right, Kelly. At the writer's left hand sat Braddock then O'Neil.

'Could we have the lights turned off please?' Mathias asked. 'All but the one over the table.'

Sir George surveyed the group seated before him for a moment then with a sigh he nodded to the club's doorman who flicked off the lights one by one until the table was illuminated by a solitary lamp. Shadows were thick all around it, the other guests swallowed up by them.

'Could you all place your hands, palms down, on the table,' Mathias asked. 'So that your finger-tips are touching the hands of the person on either side of you.'

'I thought we were supposed to hold hands,' muttered Carr, sarcastically.

174

'Just do as I ask, please,' Mathias said.

Kelly looked up. In the half light, the psychic's face looked milk-white, his eyes standing out in stark contrast. She felt a strange tingle flow through her, a feeling not unlike a small electric shock. She glanced at Blake, who was looking at the psychic, then at Vernon, who had his head lowered.

'Empty your minds,' said Mathias. 'Think of nothing. Hear nothing but my voice. Be aware of nothing but the touch of the people beside you.' His voice had fallen to a low whisper.

The room was silent, only the low, guttural breathing of the psychic audible in the stillness.

Kelly shivered involuntarily and turned her head slightly looking at the others seated with her. All of them had their heads bowed as if in prayer. She too dropped her gaze, noticing as she did that Blake's fingers were shaking slightly. But then so were her own. Indeed, everyone around the table seemed to be undergoing minute, reflexive muscular contractions which jerked their bodies almost imperceptibly every few seconds.

Mathias grunted something inaudible then coughed. His eyes closed and his head began to tilt backward. His chest was heaving as if he were finding it difficult to breathe.

'Don't break the circle,' he muttered, throatily. 'Don't . . . break . . .'

He clenched his teeth together, as if in pain and a long, wheezing sound escaped him. It was as if someone had punctured a set of bellows. His body began to shake more violently, perspiration beading on his forehead, glistening in the dull light. His eyes suddenly shot open, bulging wide in the sockets, his head still tilted backward.

He groaned again, more loudly this time.

The light above the table flickered, went out then glowed with unnatural brilliance once more.

'The child,' croaked Mathias. 'The . . . child . . .'

His groans became shouts.

Kelly tried to raise her head but it was as if there was a heavy weight secured to her chin. Only by monumental effort did she manage to raise it an inch or so.

Somewhere behind her one of the swords fell from the wall with a loud clatter but none of those seated at the table could move to find the source of the noise. They were all held as if by some invisible hand, aware only of the increasing warmth in the room. A warmth which seemed to be radiating from the very centre of the table itself.

'The child,' Mathias gasped once more.

This time Kelly recoiled as a vile stench assaulted her nostrils. A sickly sweet odour which reminded her of bad meat. She coughed, her stomach churning.

The feeling of heat was growing stronger until it seemed that the table must be ablaze. But, at last, she found that she could raise her head.

If she had been able to, she would have screamed.

Toni Landers beat her to it.

Standing in the centre of the table was the image of her son.

His clothes, what remained of them, were blackened and scorched, hanging in places like burned tassles. Beneath the fabric his skin was red raw, mottled green in places. The left arm had been completely stripped of flesh and what musculature remained was wasted and scorched. Bone shone with dazzling whiteness through the charred mess. The chest and lower body was a mass of suppurating sores which were weeping stickly clear pus like so many diseased eyes. But it was the head and neck which bore the most horrific injury. The boy's head was twisted at an impossible angle, a portion of spinal column visible through the pulped mess at the base of the skull. The head itself seemed to have been cracked open like an egg shell and a lump of jellied brain matter bulged obscenely from one of the rents. The bottom lip had been torn off, taking most of the left cheek with it, to expose ligaments and tendons which still twitched spasmodically. Blood had soaked the boy's upper body, its coppery odour mingling with the overpowering stink of burned skin and hair.

Toni Landers tried to raise her hands to shield her eyes from this abomination which had once been her son but it was as if someone had nailed her fingers to the table. She could only sit helplessly and watch as the apparition turned full circle in the middle of the table, meeting the horrified, gaze of all those present before bringing its milky orbs to bear on her. One of the eyes had been punctured by a piece of broken skull and it nestled uselessly in the bloodied socket like a burst balloon.

The apparition took a step towards her.

It was smiling.

Kelly looked across at Mathias and saw that there was perspiration pouring down his face as he gazed at the sight before him. She then turned slightly and looked at Blake. He was not looking at the child but at the psychic, the writer's own body trembling convulsively.

The figure of the boy moved closer to Toni Landers, one charred hand rising before it as it reached the edge of the table.

Finally, by a monumental effort of will, Toni managed to lift her hands from the table.

As she covered her face she let out a scream which threatened to shake the building.

'Look,' urged Jim O'Neil.

Like the image on a TV set, the apparition of Rick Landers began to fade. Not slowly but with almost breathtaking suddenness until the table was empty once more. Above them, the light dimmed again.

'My God,' burbled Gerald Braddock. 'What *was* that?'

Even if anyone heard him, no one seemed capable of furnishing him with an answer.

Sir George Howe strode to the panel of switches behind the bar and snapped on the lights himself.

Mathias sat unmoved at the table, his eyes locked with those of Blake. The writer was breathing heavily, as if he'd just run up a flight of long steps. The two men regarded one another a moment longer then Mathias turned to Toni Landers who was sobbing uncontrollably beside him.

'Fuck me,' was all Jim O'Neil could say. His voice a low whisper.

Dr Vernon stroked his chin thoughtfully, looking at the spot on the table top where the apparition had first materialized. It still shone as if newly polished. He inhaled. There was no smell of burned flesh any longer, no cloying odour of blood. Only the acrid smell of perspiration.

Beside him, Kelly touched Blake's hand, seeing that the writer looked a little pale.

'Are you all right, David?' she asked, aware that her own heart was beating wildly.

Blake nodded.

177

'And you?' he wanted to know.

She was shaking badly and Blake put one arm around her shoulder, drawing her close to him.

Roger Carr sat where he was for a moment, looking at the others around the table, then he got to his feet and stalked across to the bar where he downed a large scotch in two huge swallows. Only then did he begin to calm down. He looked back over his shoulder at Mathias.

Not only was this man very good at what he did, the bastard was convincing too. Carr ordered another scotch.

Jonathan Mathias finally managed to quieten Toni Landers, wiping away some of her tears with his handkerchief. He helped her to her feet and led her outside into the rain soaked night. He told his chauffeur to take her home and then return.

As the psychic stood alone on the pavement watching the car disappear from view he looked down at his hands.

Both palms were red raw, as if he'd been holding something very hot. His entire body was sheathed in sweat but he felt colder than he'd ever felt in his life.

35

Blake hit the last full stop, pulled the paper from the typewriter and laid it on top of the pile beside him:

Without the clacking of typewriter keys, the cellar was once more silent.

The writer picked up the pages next to him and skimmed through them. Another day or so and the book would be finished, he guessed. He had submitted the bulk of it to his publisher shortly after returning from the States. Now he was nearing the end. He sat back in his chair and yawned. It was almost 8 a.m. He'd been working for two hours. Blake always rose early, completing the greater part of his work during the morning. It was a routine which he'd followed for the last four years. Down in the cellar it was peaceful. He didn't even hear the comings and goings of his neighbours. But, on this particular morning, his mind had been elsewhere.

As hard as he tried, he could not shake the image of Toni Landers' dead child from his mind. In fact, the entire episode of the previous night still burned as clearly in his consciousness as if it had been branded there. He remembered the terror etched on the faces of those who had sat at the table with him, the horrified reactions of those who had looked on from the relative safety beyond the circle.

The gathering had begun to break up almost immediately after the seance. Blake himself, rather than drive back to Oxford, had persuaded Kelly to stay at his house for the night. She had readily agreed. She was upstairs dressing. He had woken her before he'd climbed out of bed, they had made love and she had decided to take a long hot bath before he drove her home.

He put the cover back on the typewriter and made his way up the stone steps from the subterranean work room, locking the door behind him as he emerged into the hall.

'What are you hiding down there? The Crown Jewels?'

The voice startled him momentarily and he spun round to see Kelly descending the stairs.

Blake smiled and pocketed the key to the cellar.

'Force of habit,' he said. 'I don't like to be disturbed.'

They walked through into the kitchen where she put the kettle on while he jammed some bread into the toaster. Kelly spooned coffee into a couple of mugs.

'Are you all right, Kelly?' he asked, noticing that she looked pale. She nodded.

'I'm a little tired, I didn't sleep too well last night,' she told him.

'That's understandable.'

'Understandable, but not forgivable.'

He looked puzzled.

'David, I'm a psychic investigator. My reactions to the paranormal, anything out of the ordinary, should be . . . well, scientific. But what I saw last night at that seance terrified me. I couldn't even think straight.'

'If it's any consolation,' he said. 'I don't think you were the only one.' He caught the toast as it popped up.

179

Kelly watched him as he buttered it, finally handing her a slice.

'I'd still like to know how Vernon managed to get an invitation,' she said.

'He's a friend of Sir George Howe, the old boy told us that.'

Kelly nodded slowly.

'I still don't trust him,' she said.

Blake leant forward and kissed her on the forehead.

'I don't trust anyone.'

The kettle began to boil.

It was 2.15 when Blake parked the XJS back in his driveway: The journey back from Oxford had taken longer than he'd expected due to a traffic hold up on the way back into the town. Now he clambered out of the Jag and headed for his front door, waving a greeting to one of his neighbours as she passed by with her two children.

Blake walked in and discovered that the postman had been during his absence. There was a slim envelope which bore a familiar type-face. He tore it open and unfolded the letter, heading towards the sitting room as he did so. The writer perched on the edge of a chair and read aloud.

'Dear David, I'm sorry to have kept you waiting but I have only recently managed to read the manuscript of "From Within". I'm even sorrier to tell you that I do not feel that it matches the quality of your earlier work, which was based on solid facts and research. This latest effort seems comprised mostly of speculation and theorising, particularly on the subject of Astral travel and mind control. I realize that these subjects are open to question but the book does not convince me as to the validity of your statements. So how can we expect the public to believe it?

Despite the fact that you are well established and a proven top-seller, I feel that I cannot, as yet offer you a contract based on the manuscript in its present state.'

Blake got to his feet, still glaring angrily at the letter.

It was signed with the sweeping hand of Phillip Campbell, his publisher.

'I cannot offer you a contract ...' Blake muttered, angrily. He crossed to the phone and picked up the receiver, punching buttons irritably.

'Good morning ...'

He gave the receptionist no time to complete the formalities.

'Phillip Campbell, please,' he said, impatiently.

There was a click at the other line then another woman's voice.

'Phillip Campbell's office, good afternoon.'

'Is Phillip there?'

'Yes, who's calling?'

'David Blake.'

Another click. A hiss of static.

'Good afternoon, David.'

He recognized Campbell's Glaswegian accent immediately.

'Hello, Phil. I'd like a word if you can spare me the time.'

'Sure. What's on your mind?'

' "I cannot offer you a contract", that's what's on my mind,' Blake snapped. 'What the hell is going on, Phil? What's wrong with the bloody book?'

'I thought I told you that in the letter,' the Scot said.

' "Speculation and theorising" is that it?'

'Look, Dave, don't start getting uptight about it. If you can't stand a bit of criticism from a friend then maybe you're in the wrong game. What I wrote was meant to help.'

'You haven't seen the completed manuscript yet,' Blake reminded him.

'Fair enough. Maybe I'll change my mind once I have but, like I said, you need more concrete facts in it. Especially this business about someone being able to control another person's Astral Body. You're going to have trouble making the readers believe that.'

'Phil, I'm telling you, I know it can be done,' said Blake.

'Facts, Dave,' the publisher reminded him. 'Once I've seen the finished manuscript then maybe we can sort something out.'

There was a moment's pause then the Scot continued.

'David, I want this book in print as much as you do. We both stand to make a lot of money out of it but, in its present form, we'll be laughed out of court if we publish. You realize that.'

Blake sighed.

'Facts,' he said. 'All right, Phil, I'll get back to you.' He hung up. The writer stood there for a moment then he balled up the letter and threw it into a nearby waste-basket.

He headed back towards the cellar.

36

Oxford

The book fell from his hand and hit the bedroom carpet with a thud.

Dr Stephen Vernon sat up, disturbed from his light sleep. He yawned, retrieved the book and placed it on his bedside table. Then he reached across and flicked off the light. The hands of his watch glowed dully, showing him that it was almost 1.05 a.m. He pulled the sheet up to his neck and closed his eyes but the sleep which had come to him earlier now seemed to desert him. He rolled onto his side, then his back, then the other side but the more he moved the more he seemed to shed any desire to sleep.

He sat up again, reaching for the book.

He read three or four pages without remembering a single word and, with a sigh, replaced the thick tome. He decided that his best strategy was to get out of bed. He'd make himself a hot drink, that usually did the trick. Vernon clambered out of bed and pulled on his dressing gown. He left the bedside lamp burning and padded across the landing.

He was at the top of the stairs when he heard the faint knocking.

Almost instinctively he turned and looked at the door of the locked room but it took him but an instant to realize that the sound had originated downstairs.

He hesitated.

The knocking came again.

Vernon swallowed hard and moved cautiously down the first three or four steps.

Outside, in the darkness, he heard the sound of movement, the crunching of gravel beneath heavy feet.

Vernon peered over the bannister, down into the pit of blackness which was his hallway. The light switch was at the bottom, beside the large window which looked out onto the gravel drive and the front garden.

He glanced down, his heart quickening slightly.

He had neglected to draw the curtain across that window.

The movement seemed to have stopped so Vernon scuttled down the stairs, gripping the bannister with one hand in case he overbalanced in the gloom.

He was level with the window when he saw a dark shape three or four feet from the glass.

It moved rapidly back into the gloom and seemed to disappear.

Vernon felt himself perspiring as he reached the light switch, not sure whether to turn it on or not. If he did then *he* would be visible to anyone outside. His hand hovered over the switch but, eventually, he decided against it and moved cautiously into the sitting room, ears ever alert for the slightest sound.

From the brass bucket beside the fire-place he retrieved a poker then he turned and walked back into the hall, pausing at the front door, listening.

There was more movement outside.

Footsteps.

Should he call the police, he wondered? If it was burglars then there might be more than one of them. What if they should attack him?

What if he called the police but they didn't arrive in time?

What if . . .

The sound was right outside the front door now.

Vernon, with excruciating care, slipped the bolt then the chain and fastened his hand around the door handle, raising the poker high above his head in readiness to strike. His heart was thudding madly against his ribs, his mouth as dry as parchment.

He pulled open the door.

Nothing.

Only the wind greeted him, a cool breeze which made him shiver.

He exhaled almost gratefully and lowered the poker, squinting into the blackness in search of that elusive shape.

He saw nothing.

Vernon waited a moment longer then turned.

He almost screamed as the hand gripped his shoulder.

It appeared as if from nowhere and the older man tried to raise the poker once more but his co-ordination seemed to have deserted him. It fell from his grasp with a dull clang.

He turned to see the figure standing before him.

'You?' he gasped, one hand clutched to his chest. 'What do you think you're doing creeping about in the dark? I could have hit you with this.' He retrieved the poker. 'I wasn't expecting you so soon.'

Alain Joubert walked past Vernon into the house.

37

London

Toni Landers held the small bottle before her and read the label.

Mogadon.

She unscrewed the cap of the bottle and upended it, coaxing the contents into one hand. There were twelve of the white tablets, all that remained since she had begun taking them soon after Rick's death.

Rick.

The thought of his name brought a tear to her eye and she sat down on the side of the bath, still clutching the tablets, remembering the monstrous image which had appeared before her the night before, called by Mathias. That abomination, that disfigured, mutilated monstrosity had been her son.

She opened her hand and looked at the tablets again.

Would twelve be enough?

She had contemplated suicide only once since he'd been killed but, after what had happened the previous night, the prospect of ending her own life now seemed positively inviting. She wiped a tear from her eye and spread the tablets out on the ledge beside the sink.

It was after three in the morning but the house was not silent.

Across the landing she could hear the muted, muffled sounds of cautious lovemaking. An occasional stifled moan of pleasure, a whispered word. It only served to remind her of her own loneliness.

She had been staying with friends ever since Rick's death but she realized that she must go back to the States eventually. Back to her own home. The home she had shared with Rick.

She looked at the sleeping tablets once more and realized that there was no way she could return. Toni picked one up and held it between her fingers for a moment. It wouldn't be difficult. She'd take the tablets then wander back to bed and fall asleep. It was that simple. All she had to do was take the first tablet. Then the second. Then . . .

She filled a beaker with water and got to her feet.

As she did so, she realized that the sounds of lovemaking had stopped. The house was silent again.

Toni heard footsteps, soft and light crossing the landing. She scooped up the Mogadon and pushed them back into the bottle, slipping it into the pocket of her housecoat. But, the footsteps receded momentarily and she guessed that whoever it was had gone into the nursery.

The baby was asleep in there, in the room close to her own.

The baby.

She felt tears welling up once more and, this time, they spilled down her cheeks. Her body was racked by a series of uncontrollable sobs which, no matter how hard she tried, she could not disguise. A second later there was a light tap on the bathroom door.

'Toni,' the voice asked. 'Are you all right?'

She choked back her sobs with a monumental effort and wiped her face with a flannel.

'Toni.' The voice was low but more insistent.

She crossed to the door and slid back the bolt, opening it slightly.

Vicki Barnes stood before her, her long, thick blonde hair uncombed, her eyes puffy from tiredness.

Even models could look ordinary at three in the morning.

'I was just checking on the baby,' Vicki whispered. 'I heard you crying.'

Toni shook her head.

'I'm OK now,' she lied, sniffing.

'Come on,' Vicki urged, taking her hand. 'Let's go downstairs. I'll make us both a cup of coffee. I can't sleep either.'

'I know,' Toni said, managing a slight smile. 'I heard you.'

Vicki raised her eyebrows and shrugged.

'Sorry,' she smiled. 'Paul says I should wear a gag when we have guests.'

The two women made their way across the landing, past the baby's room and down the stairs to the kitchen. Once there Vicki filled the electric kettle and plugged it in. In the cold white light of the fluorescents she could see how pale Toni looked, how dark her eyes were, the whites streaked with veins.

Vicki was two years younger than her friend. They'd met back in the mid-seventies when Vicki had been on a modelling assignment in New York. The bond between them had grown steadily since then and Toni had been Matron of Honour when Vicki had married a record producer three years earlier. The actress was also Godmother to their child, Dean, now almost fourteen months old.

'Vicki, do you ever think about dying?' asked Toni, staring straight ahead.

The model looked shocked.

'No,' she said, softly. 'Why do you ask?'

'I never used to, not until . . .' The sentence trailed off as she bowed her head. Vicki got up and stood beside her friend, snaking an arm around her shoulder.

'Don't talk about it,' she said.

Toni reached for a tissue in her housecoat pocket and, as she did, the bottle of Mogadon fell to the floor. Vicki spotted it first and picked it up.

She understood immediately.

'Is this your answer, Toni?' she asked quietly, replacing the bottle on the table in front of the actress.

'I'm not sure I want to go on without Rick,' said the American, her voice cracking. She clenched her fists. 'He was all I had. He meant everything to me. Vicki, if you'd seen that . . . thing the other night.'

'You mean at the seance?'

Toni nodded.

'He was there,' she paused for a moment, trying to compose herself. 'I know it was Rick. He looked the way he did when I had to identify him, just after it happened. After the accident. That was my son,' she said, tears running down her cheeks.

'No one's saying you haven't got a right to feel the way you do. But this isn't the answer.' Vicki held up the bottle of tablets. 'And before you beat me to it, I know it's easy for *me* to say.'

Toni didn't speak.

'Please Toni, for Rick's sake, think about it.'

The American nodded.

'I'm frightened, Vicki,' she admitted. 'When I get back to the States, I don't know how I'm going to be able to go inside that house again. There are too many memories there.'

'You'll do it. If I have to come with you, you'll do it.'

Toni smiled thinly. The other girl got to her feet and kissed her gently on the cheek. They held each other for long moments.

'Thank you,' Toni whispered.

'I wish there was more I could do,' Vicki said. She stepped back. 'Do you want to go back to bed now? If not I'll sit up with you.'

'You go, I'll be OK,' Toni assured her.

'And these?' Vicki held up the bottle of tablets.

'Take them with you.'

The model slipped them into her hand and made for the kitchen door.

'See you in the morning, Toni.'

The actress heard footfalls on the stairs as her friend made her way up the steps. For what seemed like an eternity, Toni sat in silence, sipping at her coffee then, finally, she got to her feet, rinsed the cup and wandered out of the kitchen, flicking the light off behind her.

As she reached the landing she trod more softly, not wanting to disturb her hosts. The house was silent. The only thing which she heard was her own low breathing.

Toni paused outside the nursery, looking at the door as if she expected to see through it. She reached for the handle, hesitated a second then turned it. She stepped inside and closed it gently behind her.

187

The cot stood in the far corner of the room. On a table close to her was a small lamp which bathed the room in a warm golden glow. The walls were painted light blue, the lower half decorated with a kind of mural showing teddy bears riding bikes, flying aircraft and climbing trees. It had, she guessed, been painted by Vicki's husband.

A profusion of soft toys littered the floor near to the cot. A huge stuffed penguin in particular fixed her in the unblinking stare of its glass eyes and she saw her own distorted reflection in them as she approached the cot.

The child was awake but made no sound, he merely lay on his back gazing wonderingly up at her with eyes as big as saucers.

Toni smiled down at him, chuckling softly as he returned the gesture. She took one tiny hand in hers and shook it gently, feeling the little fingers clutching at her.

The baby gurgled happily and Toni reached down and ran her finger-tips over the smooth skin of his chubby face, stroking the gossamer strands of his hair before moving her fingers to his mouth. She traced the outline of his lips with her nail, smiling at the little boy as he flailed playfully at the probing digit. His mouth opened wider and he gurgled.

Suddenly, with a combination of lightning speed and demonic force, Toni rammed two fingers into the child's mouth, pressing down hard as her nails raked the back of its throat.

The baby squirmed and tried to scream but the sound was lost, gurgling away into a liquid croak as blood began to fill the soft cavity.

With her free hand she clutched the child's head, holding it steady as she forced another finger into its mouth, hooking them inside its throat until it gagged on its own blood and the intruding fingers.

As Toni pushed a fourth finger into the blood-filled orifice, the soft skin at each side of the baby's mouth began to rip. Toni was pressing down so hard it seemed that she would push the child through the bottom of the cot.

Blood splashed her hand and flooded on to the sheet, staining it crimson and still she exerted yet more pressure, grunting loudly at the effort. The baby had long since ceased to move.

Toni lifted it from its cot, her fingers covered in blood, some of

188

which ran up her arm to stain her housecoat. She held the child before her, gazing into its sightless eyes.

She was still holding the child when the door of the nursery was thrown open.

Toni turned slowly to face Vicki Barnes and her husband, both of whom stood transfixed by the sight before them.

Toni heard screams echoing in her ears but could not seem to comprehend that they were coming from Vicki who had dropped to her knees and was staring at the monstrous scene before her.

Then, as if someone had pulled a veil from her mind she was able to see herself just what she'd done. She held the bloodied bundle at arm's length, her expression a mixture of horror and bewilderment.

The next screams she heard were her own.

38

Oxford

The dining room table must have been fully eight feet long, perhaps half that in width and yet every single carefully polished inch of the surface seemed to be covered with pieces of paper. Some were still in the files they had originated in, others were scattered about like the pieces of some huge, unsolvable puzzle.

And to Dr Stephen Vernon, that was exactly what all these notes were. A puzzle. Yet somehow it had to be solved.

He looked across the table at Joubert who was making notes, scribbling down words and phrases, sifting through the mud in an effort to find those elusive nuggets of information. Since his arrival at Vernon's house the previous night, he had done little else. Now, as the clock ticked around to 6 p.m., he dropped his pen and sat back in the chair.

'There's something missing,' said the Frenchman, surveying the piles of paper, the type-written sheets, the crammed notepads, the EEG read-outs.

'But I thought you brought *all* your findings,' Vernon said.

'Lasalle must have some of the research material with him,' Joubert said, irritably.

'Then all of this is useless?' Vernon suggested.

'No, it isn't useless but there are other factors too,' the Frenchman said, getting to his feet and crossing to the phone.

Vernon watched him as he dialled, sucking enthusiastically on his cough sweet, enjoying the smell of menthol which filled the air around him.

Joubert drummed agitatedly on the side-board as he waited for the receiver to be picked up. Eventually it was and Vernon listened as the investigator rattled out some questions in French. In the middle of it all he caught the name Lasalle. Joubert muttered something and pressed the cradle down, dialling again. He waited for an answer.

'Lasalle,' he said, quickly, as the receiver was picked up. 'This is Joubert.'

'Alain, where are you? Why weren't you at the Centre, I . . .'

'Listen to me, Lasalle,' he interrupted. 'Our notes on Astral projection, I need them. Do you have any?'

'That's what I wanted to tell you,' Lasalle said. 'All the files have gone from the Centre. Everything relating to that one project.'

'I know, I *have* them,' Joubert told him. 'But there are some missing.'

'You took them from the Centre?' he asked. 'But why?'

Joubert finally lost his temper.

'For God's sake. How many times do I have to say it? Shut up and listen to me,' he barked. 'Do you have any of the notes relating to that project?'

'Yes I have.'

'I'm going to give you an address, I want you to send everything you have to me. No matter how unimportant it may seem, I want the files. Do you understand?'

'Yes,' he answered, vaguely. His voice was almost subservient.

Joubert gave him the address of Vernon's house, his irritation growing when he was forced to repeat it.

'Why are you in England?' Lasalle wanted to know.

'Send me those notes,' his companion snapped.

'Alain, you are needed here,' Lasalle said, weakly. 'There are

190

newspaper and television people at the Centre every day. I can't cope with their questions. They want to know so much. I cannot work *and* answer them. I need help . . . I feel overpowered . . . trapped. Alain, please.'

'This fiasco is of your own making, Lasalle,' Joubert hissed. 'If you hadn't written that damned article none of this would be happening.'

'I need help here . . .'

'And I need those notes,' he rasped and slammed down the phone. He stood motionless for a moment, the knot of muscles at the side of his jaw throbbing angrily. Vernon watched him in silence.

'He has what I need. I should have been more thorough,' the Frenchman said. He went on to tell Vernon what Lasalle has said about the press. As he did so, his face grew darker and finally, he slammed his fist down on the table top. '*I* should be the one being interviewed not him,' he snarled.

'Is the recognition *that* important to you?' Vernon asked.

Joubert sucked in a weary breath and nodded.

'Eight years ago I was working for the Metapsychic Centre investigating a series of hauntings in a hotel in the Hauts-de-Seine area of Paris.' He reached for a cigarette and lit it, drawing the smoke into his lungs. 'I was working with another man, named Moreau.' The Frenchman frowned, his eyes narrowing. 'We had been at the hotel for over two months, making recordings, taking statements from the people who stayed there. It seemed as if there was an entity of some kind present in the building. Eventually we managed to get a clear recording of its movements. The next night we even photographed it. A *true* haunting. As you know, most of those reported are either imagined or psychologically rooted but not this one. We had visual evidence.'

'What happened?' Vernon asked.

Joubert stubbed out what was left of his cigarette in the saucer and sat back in his chair.

'Moreau took the photographs and the tape recordings to the Director of the Metapsychic Centre. He claimed that *he* had discovered the entity. Despite my protestations, he was credited with it. Now he's one of the Directors of the Parapsychology Laboratory in Milan. One of the most respected men in his field in Italy. After that happened, I

191

swore that I would never share any such finding with anyone. What I worked on, what I discovered would be mine. No one else's. But look what has happened. The single most important breakthrough in the study of the paranormal for twenty years and Lasalle is being credited with it. When this is over, who will remember Alain Joubert?' He glared at Vernon. 'No one. Well, this time it will be different. I had kept things quiet until the time was right to reveal the discoveries. The only reason I agreed to help you was because I knew that you offered no threat, you wanted the secret for your own reasons. You would not take away the recognition which was rightfully mine.' His tone turned reflective. 'I underestimated Lasalle.'

'I don't see that there's much you can do,' Vernon said. 'If the press have the story then . . .' He shrugged, allowing the sentence to trail off. 'What *can* you do?'

Joubert did not answer, he merely gazed past Vernon to the overcast sky outside.

Clouds were gathering.

39

Paris

He awoke screaming.

Lasalle sat up, as if trying to shake the last vestiges of the nightmare from his mind. He gulped in huge lungfuls of air, one hand pressed to his chest as his heart thudded madly against his ribs.

He had seen her once more.

His wife.

His Madelaine.

Or what had once been her.

He had been bending over the grave laying fresh flowers on it when a hand had erupted from the earth and gripped his wrist, pulling him down as she hauled herself free of the dirt. She had sought his lips with hers, only hers were little more than liquescent pustules. She had

192

embraced him with those rotting arms, pulling him close in an obscene attempt to push her decaying body against him, writhing at the contact. He had felt pieces of putrescent flesh peeling off in his hands like leprous growths as he fought to push her away.

Lasalle got to his feet, holding his stomach. He scurried to the kitchen and stood over the sink feeling his nausea building. He splashed his face with cold water and the feeling passed slowly. The Frenchman found that he was shaking uncontrollably so he gripped the edge of the sink in an effort to stop the quivering. Perspiration beaded on his forehead and ran in salty rivulets down his face.

He remembered falling asleep at the table in the sitting room. He'd been slumped across it when he'd woken. Lasalle closed his eyes, but the image of his dead wife came hurtling into his consciousness. He filled a glass with water then walked back into the sitting room, fumbling in the pocket of his jacket for the tranquilizers. He swallowed one. Two. Three. The Frenchman washed them down with the water and sat motionless at the table, his hands clenched into fists.

On the sideboard opposite, the photo of his wife smiled back at him and Lasalle, unaccountably, felt tears brimming in his eyes. He blinked and one trickled down his cheek.

'Madelaine,' he whispered, softly.

He closed his eyes once more, trying to remember how he had come to fall asleep so early in the evening. It was not yet 9 p.m.

It must have been after the phone call, he guessed.

The phone call.

He swallowed hard. He had spoken to Joubert. That much he *did* remember.

Lasalle raised both hands to his head as if he feared it might explode. He could not seem to think straight. Thoughts and images tumbled through his mind with dizzying speed.

The phone call. The nightmare. Madelaine.

He exhaled deeply, wiping more sweat from his face.

The nightmare still stood out with unwelcome clarity. That monstrous vision filled his mind again and he shook his head but, this time, there was something else. Something which he only now remembered.

As the decomposing corpse of his wife had embraced him, he had

193

heard soft malevolent laughter and he knew what had propelled him, shrieking, from the nightmare.

The laughter had been coming from the graveside.

From Joubert.

40

London

The young make-up girl smiled as she applied the last few touches of foundation to the face of Mathias. She then took what looked like a small paint brush and flicked away the residue. The layer of make-up was sufficiently thick to protect his face from the bright studio lights he would soon be facing.

Mathias returned her smile, watching as she gathered her brushes, powder pots and small bottles and slipped them back into a leather bag she carried. He thanked her then got to his feet and opened the door for her. She smiled and left.

As the psychic was about to close the door again he saw a tubby man approaching along the corridor. The man was dressed in jeans and a grey sweatshirt and he had a set of earphones around his neck.

'Are you ready, Mr Mathias?' he asked. 'There's two minutes before you go on.'

The psychic nodded and stepped back inside the dressing room for a moment to inspect his reflection in the large mirror, then he followed the tubby man along the corridor towards a door marked: STUDIO ONE.

As they drew closer he could hear the muted sounds of many voices coming from inside. An occasional laugh which signalled that the audience were settling down. There was a red light above the door and a sign which read: ON AIR.

The tubby man opened the door carefully and ushered Mathias through.

The sound of the audience was very loud now but Mathias paid it little heed as he was led to a chair behind the main set.

* * *

From where he sat he could see numerous spotlights suspended over the set but, other than that, he could see only crew members dashing furtively about, obeying the orders of the floor manager whose instructions they received via their headphones. High up above the studio was the room where the director and his assistants sat, watching everything on banks of screens, relaying information to the floor.

Mathias could hear Roger Carr's voice. He was speaking about the supernatural, dropping in the odd joke where he felt it necessary. The audience laughed happily. Mathias sipped at the glass of water on the table before him and shook his head.

The tubby man turned to him and held up one finger.

The psychic got to his feet.

Roger Carr turned towards the camera on his right hand side, noticing that a red light had just blinked into life on top of it. He smiled thinly at it, getting himself more comfortable in his leather chair.

'My last guest tonight,' he began. 'Many of you may already have heard of. Certainly in America, he's what you might call an institution. Some might even say he should be *in* an institution.'

The audience laughed.

'He's revered by millions as a healer, an expert on the supernatural. Someone even dubbed him "The Messiah in the Tuxedo".'

Another ripple of laughter.

'Whether his powers are genuine or not remains to be seen but there are countless Americans who claim that he is truly a miracle worker. Perhaps after this interview, you can form your own opinions. Saviour or charlatan? Messiah or magician? Judge for yourselves.' Carr got to his feet. 'Please welcome Jonathan Mathias.'

There was a sustained round of applause as the American walked onto the set. He glanced at the audience and smiled as he made his way towards Carr. The host shook hands with him and motioned for him to sit. The applause gradually died away.

' "The Messiah in a Tuxedo" ' said Carr, smiling. 'How do you react to comments like that?'

'I don't take much notice of criticism,' Mathias began. 'I . . .'

Carr cut him short.

'But surely, some of the things you claim to have done do leave you open to it?'

'If I could finish what I was saying,' Mathias continued, quietly. 'Yes, I do receive criticism but mostly from people who don't understand what I do. Didn't someone once say that any fool can criticise and most do.'

There was a chorus of chuckles from the audience.

'You mentioned what you do,' Carr continued. 'You claim to be a faith-healer and . . .'

'I've never claimed to be a *faith*-healer,' Mathias corrected him.

'But you do perform acts of healing? Non-medical acts.'

'Yes.'

'If that isn't faith-healing then what is it?'

'People come to me because they know I will help them. I have never claimed . . .'

'You charge money for this "healing"?' Carr said.

'A small fee. Usually people donate money. I don't ask for much from them. They give because they want to. As a token of appreciation.'

Carr nodded.

'You also appear on American television, do you not?' he said. 'Presumably you are well paid for that?'

'I don't have a pay cheque on me right now,' Mathias said, smiling. 'But, yes, the pay is good. As no doubt yours is, Mr Carr.'

'You wouldn't deny then that your basic interests are commercial.'

'I have a talent, a gift. I use it to help others.'

'But you wouldn't perform for nothing?'

'Would *you*?'

There was a ripple of laughter from the audience.

'No,' Carr told him. 'I wouldn't. But then I don't exploit the fears and gullibility of sick people.'

'I wasn't aware that *I* did, Mr Carr.'

The interviewer shifted uncomfortably in his seat, angry that Mathias was taking his verbal assault so calmly.

'Then what do you class yourself as?' he asked. 'Surely not an ordinary psychic? The fact that you're a multi-millionaire seems to lift you out of the category of ordinary.'

'My powers are greater than an ordinary psychic . . .'

Carr interrupted.

'Can you give me an example of your *power*?' he said. 'Read my mind.' He smiled.

'Would it be worth it?' Mathias japed.

The audience joined him in his amusement. Carr did not appreciate the joke. The veins at his temple throbbed angrily.

'If we wheel in a couple of cripples could you make them walk?' the interviewer hissed.

'I don't perform to order, Mr Carr,' the psychic told him.

'Only if the price is right, yes?'

The floor manager looked anxiously at the two men, as if expecting them to leap at one another. Mathias remained calm.

'How would you answer the charge of charlatan?' Carr said.

'It's for each individual to decide whether or not they believe in my powers,' the American said. 'You may believe as you wish.'

The two men regarded one another for long seconds, the interviewer seeking some flicker of emotion in the piercing blue eyes of his guest. Haw saw none. Not even anger. Carr eventually turned away and looked directly into the camera.

'Well, as you have heard, Mr Mathias invites us to make up our own minds as to his . . . *powers*. Although, having seen and heard his answers tonight I, for one, will draw just one conclusion. And I think you know what that is. Goodnight.'

As the studio lights dimmed, Carr got to his feet and glared down at Mathias.

'Clever bastard aren't you?' he snarled. 'Trying to make me look like a prick in front of millions of viewers.'

'I don't think you needed my help on that score,' Mathias said. 'You were the one looking for the fight, not me.'

'Well, you can take your fucking powers and shove them up your arse,' he snapped.

As he stormed off the set, the floor manager shouted something about the director wanting to see him.

'Fuck him,' Carr retorted and disappeared through the exit door.

Mathias was getting to his feet when the floor manager approached him.

197

'The director told me to apologise to you for Mr Carr's remarks during the interview,' said the man.

Mathias smiled.

'No harm done,' he said.

The floor manager nodded and walked away.

Only then did the psychic's smile fade.

41

The bedroom window was open and the cool breeze caused the curtains to billow gently.

Roger Carr lay naked on his back, arms folded behind his head. He was gazing up at the ceiling, his eyes fixed on a fly which was crawling across the emulsioned surface. It eventually made its exit through the open window and Carr was left gazing at nothing but white paint. He lay there for a moment longer then rolled on to his side and reached for the bottle of beer which was propped on the bedside table. He tipped it up, discovering to his annoyance that it was empty. Carr tossed it away and it landed with a thud on the carpet, close to a pair of discarded knickers. The owner of the garment was out of the room at present. Carr thought about shouting to her to fetch him another bottle of beer. Instead he rolled over once more and returned to gazing at the ceiling.

With his hands behind his head, the ticking of his watch sounded thunderous in the silence. The hands had crawled round to 12.18 a.m.

He wondered what Mathias was doing.

Bastard.

Flash Yank bastard.

Carr had been surprised by the American's composure during the interview earlier in the evening. Most people usually crumbled beneath such a concerted verbal onslaught, but Mathias had managed to remain calm throughout.

Fucking bastard.

198

Carr realized that the psychic had bettered him during the argument. It could scarcely be called a discussion after all. In front of millions of viewers and the studio audience, Carr had met his match and that hurt him deeply. The image of Mathias flashed into his mind and he sat up, his breath coming in short, angry grunts. He swung himself off the bed and walked across to the window where he inhaled the cool night air and looked out into the darkness.

The street was quiet, but for the barking of a dog. The house was less than five minutes drive from the BBC and Carr had chosen it for its peaceful surroundings. He didn't like noise, he didn't like interference. He was a solitary person once he left the studio. He liked to pick and choose whose company he kept, therefore few people ever got close to him. Or wanted to for that matter.

Since his wife had walked out on him over three years earlier, Carr had become even more embittered and antagonistic in his dealings with others. At the time she had tried to force him into a reconciliation but Carr was not a man to be forced into anything. He'd even packed one suitcase for her before hurling her car keys at her and showing her the door. She had told him she would give him another chance if he could try to change his ways. Four affairs in as many years had been too much for her.

Carr hadn't wanted another chance.

He smiled as he remembered that night she left but the smile faded as he found himself thinking again about Mathias.

Once offended, Carr would stop at nothing to make things even. He bore grudges almost gleefully.

'Yank bastard,' he said, aloud.

'First sign of madness.'

The voice startled him, he hadn't heard her footfalls on the stairs. Carr spun round to see Suzanne Peters perched on the edge of the bed with a glass of milk in her hand.

'What did you say?' he asked, irritably.

'I said it's the first sign of madness,' she told him. 'Talking to your-self.'

Carr didn't answer her, he merely turned around and walked back to the bed, flopping on it lazily.

Suzanne muttered something to him as she almost spilt her milk.

She placed it on the table beside the bed and stretched out beside him pushing her naked body against his, allowing her ample breasts to press into his side while her left hand snaked across his chest.

At twenty-two, Suzanne was almost half his age. She worked as a receptionist at Broadcasting House and had done for the past ten months. During that time, she and Roger Carr had become lovers although it was a term Carr disliked because, to him, it implied that there was some emotion involved in the relationship. In his eyes that was certainly not the case.

She nuzzled his chest, kissing it as she allowed her hand to reach lower towards his penis. She took his organ between her fingers and began to rub gently. He stiffened slightly but then she felt his own hand close around her tiny wrist, pulling her away from him. Suzanne sat up, sweeping her thick blonde hair back and looking at her companion with bewilderment.

'What's wrong with you tonight?' she wanted to know.

Carr didn't even look at her.

'I've got something on my mind,' he said.

'That's obvious. Is it anything *I* can help with?'

Carr eyed her almost contemptuously.

'*You*, help me? Give it a rest.'

He returned to staring at the ceiling.

'I only asked,' she said, lying down beside him once more. She ran one finger through the thick hair on his chest, curling it into spirals.

'That bastard Mathias made me look like an idiot,' Carr said, angrily. 'He's a bloody con-man.' The interviewer's voice took on a reflective tone. 'I'll have him for what happened tonight. One way or another I'll fix that shitbag.'

Once more Suzanne allowed her hand to reach lower towards his groin. She enveloped his penis in her smooth grip and, this time she felt him respond. He stiffened in her hand and she kissed his chest, nipping the flesh of his stomach as she moved down onto his growing erection. Suzanne flicked at the bulbous head with her tongue, watching as a drop of clear liquid oozed from it. Her lips closed around his throbbing shaft and she felt him thrusting his hips upwards trying to force himself further into the velvet warmth

200

of her mouth. Her hand continued to move expertly on his root and she sensed an even greater swelling as his penis grew to full stiffness.

Carr gripped her by the back of the neck and pulled her off, dragging her across him, kissing her hard. His hands found her breasts and she almost cried out as he kneaded the soft mounds with furious vigour, but the discomfort was tempered by an overriding pleasure and her nipples grew into hard buds as he rubbed them with his thumbs.

She felt his knee rise to push against her pubic mound as he rolled her over first onto her back and then her stomach. She felt him grip her hips and she arched her back to allow him easier access. He thrust into her violently, a deep angry grunt accompanying his almost frenzied penetration of her. Suzanne gasped, both at the pleasure and the power of his movements. She knelt, feeling his heavy testicles against her buttocks as he moved inside her. Suzanne ground herself back to meet his every thrust and, as they formed a rhythm, she felt her own excitement growing.

Carr gripped her hips, clinging onto her soft flesh so hard that he left red welts where his fingers had been. He pulled her onto his throbbing shaft, grunting more loudly now.

She could not suppress a whimper of pain as he grabbed a large hunk of her hair and pulled, tugging her head back with a force which threatened to snap her neck. He held her like that, still spearing her unmercifully, only now her pleasure had given way to pain. Carr made a guttural sound, deep in his throat and pulled harder on her long hair. Some of it came away in his hand.

'No,' she managed to squeal, breathlessly.

He ignored her complaint, his own climax now drawing closer. The speed of his thrusts increased.

She could no longer bear his weight so she lowered herself until she was lying face down on the bed, her legs still splayed wide as Carr drove into her relentlessly.

Suzanne felt a sudden, unaccountable flicker of fear as he fastened first one, then two hands around her throat.

He began to squeeze.

She let out a wheezing gasp and tried to claw at his hands to release the increasing pressure but the more she tugged at those twin vices,

201

the harder he pressed. She felt his nails digging into her flesh as he crushed her windpipe and, all the time, he continued his violent movements which threatened to split her in two.

White light danced before her eyes and she flailed helplessly behind her, trying to scratch Carr. Anything to relieve the unbearable pressure on her throat. It felt as if her head were going to explode.

Roger Carr grinned crookedly, his face a mask of rage and triumph as he held her beneath him.

Suzanne felt herself growing weaker. It seemed only a matter of moments now before she blacked out.

With one last vigorous thrust he felt the pleasure build to a peak then, gasping loudly, he pumped his fluid into her. Carr shuddered as the sensations gradually subsided. He withdrew from her and lay on one side.

He wondered why she wasn't moving.

Suzanne coughed, horrified to see spots of blood mingling with the sputum which stained the pillow. Still lying on her stomach she raised one quivering hand to her throat and tentatively felt the deep indentations there. She felt Carr's hands on her shoulders, turning her over and, despite her pain she found the strength to push him away. He looked down at her ravaged neck and raised both hands to his head. In the semi-darkness his eyes looked sunken, only the whites standing out with any clarity.

She coughed again and tried to sit up, her head spinning. Carr reached out to touch the welts on her flesh, his gaze straying to those on her hips too. She slapped his hand away and staggered to her feet.

'You stay away from me,' she croaked, pointing at him with a shaking finger. 'I mean it.'

Carr got to his feet and moved towards her.

'Suzanne, I . . .'

'Get away you . . .' She coughed and more blood-flecked spittle dribbled over her lips. 'You're mad. You could have killed me.'

He hesitated, listening as she crossed the landing to the bathroom.

Carr sat down heavily on the edge of the bed, head bowed. He was drenched in perspiration but he felt almost unbearably cold. He found his dressing gown and pulled it on. His fingers, he noticed, had some blood on them so he hurriedly wiped it off with the corner

202

of a sheet. His initial bewilderment by now had turned to fear. Carr rubbed his face with both hands, aware that his chest was heaving from the effort of trying to slow his rapid breathing. He looked at his hands as if they were not his own, as if they had been guided by a will other than his.

Suzanne returned from the bathroom and gathered up her clothes.

'Look, I don't know what to say . . .' he began.

She interrupted.

'Don't say anything,' she told him.

'I don't know what came over me, I . . .'

'Just leave me alone,' she demanded, picking up the last of her clothes. He watched as she hurried from the room, listening as she made her way down to the ground floor.

Carr shuddered once more as a chill ran through him.

He found her pulling on her jeans, tears trickling down her cheeks to smudge her make-up.

'Suzanne,' he said, almost apologetically. 'Honest to God, I don't know what happened.'

'I do,' she snapped, fastening the button at the waist. 'You tried to kill me.'

'I didn't know what I was doing.'

She pointed to the angry red marks on her neck.

'How am I supposed to explain these away?' Suzanne asked.

She pulled on her coat and turned towards the door which led through to the kitchen. 'I'll go out the back way, I don't even want anyone to know I've been with you.'

He followed her, slapping on the light.

'Stay away from me, Roger,' she said, a note of concern in her voice. 'I mean it.'

'You have to believe me,' he said. 'I didn't know what I was doing.' Again he felt that cold chill sweeping through him.

He caught her by the arm, spinning her round.

'Let go,' she shrieked and struck out at him, raking his cheek with her nails, drawing blood.

Carr's nostrils flared and his face darkened. With a roar he hurled Suzanne across the kitchen.

She slammed into the cooker and lay motionless for a moment but, as she saw Carr advancing on her, she managed to claw her way upright. He overturned the table in his haste to reach her.

Suzanne made a lunge for the door but Carr grabbed her by the collar. The material of her blouse ripped, the buttons flying off. Her large breasts were exposed but she cared little for that. Her only thought was to get out of the house.

But Carr moved too quickly. He shot out a grasping hand and tugged her back by her hair, slamming her head against the fridge as he did so. A cut opened just above her hairline, crimson fluid running down her face and staining the white door of the fridge as she lay against it.

As he lunged for her once more she flung open the fridge door and rammed it against his legs, struggling to get to her feet.

Carr snarled angrily and almost fell but he recovered in time to see her pull a long serrated blade from the knife rack on the wall nearby. She turned on him, the vicious blade glinting wickedly. He did not hesitate, he grabbed for her, his hands aimed at her throat but Suzanne struck out with the knife.

The combined force of his momentum and her own upward thrust was devastating.

The blade punctured the palm of Carr's right hand and erupted from the back, sawing through several small bones as it did so. Blood burst from the wound and Suzanne tore the knife free, nearly severing his thumb as she did so. He roared in pain and held up the mutilated limb almost as an accusation, watching the tendons and muscles beneath the skin moving frantically. It felt as if his arm were on fire but, despite the severity of the wound. Carr did not hold back. He reached for a chair and lifted it above his head, bringing it down with bone-crushing force across Suzanne's outstretched arm.

The knife was knocked from her grasp and she fell backwards, blood now flowing more freely from the rent in her scalp.

Carr grinned maniacally and struck again.

So violent was the impact this time that the chair broke as he brought it down across her face and upper body. Her bottom lip exploded, her nose merely collapsed as the bones in it were obliterated. In one fleeting second, Suzanne's face was a bloody ruin.

Carr dropped to his knees, one hand groping for the discarded knife. He gripped it in his gashed hand, ignoring his own pain as he took hold of a hunk of Suzanne's hair and lifted her head.

She tried to scream but her bottom jaw had been splintered and the only sound she could make was a liquid gurgle.

Carr pressed the knife to her forehead, just below the hairline, using all his strength as he moved the serrated blade quickly back and forth, shearing through the flesh of her scalp. He slid it in expertly towards her ear, slicing off the top of the fleshy protruberance as he did so and, all the time, her body jerked violently as waves of pain tore through her.

The knife grated against bone as he sawed madly at her head, tugging on her hair as he did so until finally, with a loud grunt, he tore most of it free.

Like some bloodied wig, the hair came away in his hand, most of the scalp still attached.

Suzanne lay still.

Carr staggered upright, the grisly trophy held before him.

There was loud banging from the direction of the front door, growing louder by the second.

Carr closed his eyes tightly, suddenly aware of an unbearable pain in his right hand. The entire limb was going numb, he could hardly lift it. He staggered back, seeking support against the sink and, gradually, a vision plucked raw and bloody from a nightmare swam before him. Only he wasn't dreaming.

He looked down in horrified disbelief at the scalped body of Suzanne Peters, almost shouting aloud as he recognized the matted mass of hair and flesh which he held. He dropped it hurriedly.

'No,' he murmured, quietly. 'Oh God, no.' His voice began to crack and he edged away from the girl as if she were somehow going to disappear. He continued to shake his head, not able to comprehend what had happened. Or how.

The banging on the front door intensified but all Roger Carr was aware of was the agonising pain in his hand, the stench of blood which hung in the air like an invisible pall.

And the icy chill which had wrapped itself around him like a frozen shroud.

42

The restaurant was small, what the owners liked to refer to as intimate. But, due to the number of people crowded into it, the place looked more like a gigantic rugby scrum. Not at all intimate, thought David Blake as the waiter led him through the melee towards the appropriate table.

Amidst the sea of lunch-time faces, the writer spotted Phillip Campbell immediately.

The Scot was sitting near to the window, sipping a glass of red wine and poring over a thick pile of A4 sheets, scribbling pencilled notes on the pages every so often. He was dressed in a light grey suit which seemed to match the colour of his hair. A red rose adorned his button-hole as it did on every occasion that Blake saw him. He wondered, at times, if Campbell was propagating the flowers in the breast pocket of his jacket. As each new one came up. Snip. Into the button hole.

He looked up as Blake reached the table, rising to shake hands with the writer.

They exchanged pleasantries and the younger man sat down, loosening his tie as he did so. The waiter scuttled over and placed a large glass before him.

'Thank you,' said Blake, looking rather surprised.

'Vodka and lemonade,' Campbell told him, smiling. 'You haven't started drinking something else have you?'

The writer chuckled, shook his head and took a sip from the glass.

'I make a point of knowing all my author's requirements,' the Scot said, raising his glass. 'Cheers.'

Both men drank. The waiter arrived with the menus and left them to decide.

'What do you think of the completed manuscript now that you've read it?' Blake asked, indicating the A4 sheets.

'You're no closer, David,' Campbell told him. 'I'm still not convinced about half the things you claim in here.' He tapped the pile of typewritten pages.

The writer was about to speak when the waiter returned. The two men ordered and he hurried off through the throng to fetch their first course.

'It's too muddled,' Campbell continued. 'You don't name any sources for some of the theories you've put forward, especially the ones to do with Astral projection. *Control* of the Astral body.'

'I met a girl at the Institute of Psychical Study,' Blake said. 'She's conducted laboratory tests into this kind of thing.'

'Then why isn't she named as a source?'

'Her superior is keeping a pretty tight rein on the research they're doing. I don't think he'd be too pleased if her findings turned up in my book.'

'How well do you know this girl?'

'We're pretty close,' Blake told him.

Campbell nodded.

'The Astral body can be activated by artificial stimulus like drugs or hypnosis, she told me.'

'Then use her name for Christ's sake,' snapped Campbell. 'Can't you speak to her superior about this information? Maybe he'll release some details.'

The waiter returned with the first course and the two men began eating.

'I can't use her name or her findings and that's final,' Blake told him.

'Then you've still got nothing concrete and until you have, this manuscript is no good,' said Campbell, pushing a forkful of food into his mouth.

'I take it that means you're not ready to negotiate a contract?' Blake said.

Campbell nodded.

Blake smiled humourlessly.

'You could do with a demonstration, Phil,' he said.

The Scot took a sip of his wine.

'That I could,' he smiled. 'See if you can arrange it, eh?'

Blake chuckled. Behind the tinted screens of his dark glasses his eyes twinkled.

43

Gerald Braddock reached forward and wound up the window of the Granada. It was warm inside the car but he decided that the heat was preferable to the noxious fumes belching from so many exhaust pipes. The streets of London seemed even more clogged with traffic than usual. High above, in the cloudless sky, the sun blazed away mercilessly.

The politician fumbled for the handkerchief in his top pocket and fastidiously dabbed the perspiration from his face. He thought about removing his jacket but decided against it, realizing that they were close to their destination. The driver threaded the car skilfully through the traffic, hitting the horn every so often to clear offending vehicles out of the way.

Braddock sat back and closed his eyes but he found it difficult to relax. The events of two nights before were still uncomfortably fresh in his mind.

He had told no one of what he had witnessed at the seance, least of all his wife. For one thing she would probably never have believed him and, if she had, Braddock realized that mention of it may well have disturbed her. For his own part, the image of that maimed and burned child had surfaced, unwanted, in his mind on a number of occasions since. Albeit fleetingly. He wondered how long it would take to fully erase the image and the memory. He was thankful that nothing about the incident had appeared in any of the papers. Even the gutter press had so far remained blissfully ignorant of what would, for them, have been front page fodder. Braddock was grateful for that because he knew that the Prime Minister would not have looked kindly on his participation in such a fiasco.

He had held the post of Minister of the Arts in the last two Conservative administrations. Prior to that he had served as a spokesman on Finance in a career in the House of Commons which spanned over twenty years. Some had seen his appointment as Arts Minister as something of a demotion but Braddock was happy with his present position as it removed some of the pressure from him which had been prevalent when he'd been with the Exchequer.

As traffic began to thin he decided to roll down the window slightly. A cooling breeze wafted in, drying the perspiration on him. He glanced to his right and saw a sign which read: BRIXTON ½ MILE.

Another five minutes and the Granada began to slow up.

As Braddock looked out he saw that there was already a sizeable crowd gathered in the paved area which fronted the new Activity Centre. The building had been converted from four derelict shops, with the help of a two million pound Government grant. The minister scanned the rows of black faces and felt a twinge of distaste.

As the driver brought the car to a halt he saw two coloured men approaching. Both were dressed in suits, one looking all the more incongruous because, perched on his head, was a multi-coloured woollen bonnet. His dreadlocks had been carefully pushed inside. Braddock smiled his practised smile and waited for the driver to open the car door.

He stepped out, extending his hand to the first of the black men.

Braddock cringed inwardly as he felt his flesh make contact with the other man and he hastily shook hands with the Rastafarian, allowing himself to be led across the concret piazza towards a make-shift platform which had been erected in front of the entrance to the Activity Centre. As he made his way up the three steps the crowd broke into a chorus of applause.

Braddock scanned the faces before him, some white but mostly black. He continued to smile although it was becoming more of an effort. The first of the organisers, who had introduced himself as Julian Hayes, stepped forward towards a microphone and tapped it twice. There was a whine from the PA system and Hayes tapped it again. This time there was no interference.

'It's been more than two years since building first started on this Centre,' Hayes began. 'And I'm sure we're all happy to see that it's finally finished.'

There was some more clapping and the odd whistle.

Hayes smiled broadly.

'As from today,' he continued. 'We shall all be able to use the facilities. I would like to call on Mr Gerald Braddock to officially open the Centre.' He beckoned the politician forward. 'Mr Braddock.'

There was more applause as the minister reached the microphone. Beside it he noticed there was a small table and on it lay a pair of shears with which he was meant to cut the gaily coloured ribbon strung across the doors of the centre.

He paused before the microphone still smiling, scanning the rows of dark faces. Braddock felt the disgust rising within him. He coughed, suddenly aware of a slight shiver which ran down his spine. The sun continued to beat down relentlessly but, despite the heat, the politician felt inexplicably cold.

'Firstly,' he began, 'I would like to thank Mr Hayes for asking me to declare this new centre open. He must take credit for so much of the organisation which went into ensuring that the project was completed.'

There was more vigorous clapping.

Braddock smiled thinly and gripped the microphone stand.

'The cutting of the ribbon is symbolic,' he said, 'in as much as it marks the cutting of ties between you people and my Government. We have pumped over two million pounds into the development of this Centre. I hope that it will be put to good use.'

Hayes looked at his Rastafarian companion who merely shrugged.

'In the past we have tried to help this area but, up until now, that effort has been largely wasted,' Braddock continued. 'Our good faith has not been repaid. I sincerely hope that it will not be the case this time.' The politician's voice had taken on a dictatorial tone, one not unnoticed by the crowd.

There were one or two disapproving comments from the assembled throng. A babble of unrest which grew slowly as Braddock pressed on regardless.

'There are many deserving causes to which we could have given a grant such as the one received to convert these old shops into this fine new Centre,' he said, 'most of which would normally come higher on our list of priorities. Nevertheless, partly through pressure from leaders of your community, we decided to furnish your committee with the appropriate funds.'

Julian Hayes looked angrily at Braddock's broad back then at the crowd who were muttering amongst themselves, angered by the politician's remarks.

'You seem to think that you qualify as a special case,' Braddock said, vehemently, 'because you're black.'

'Steady, man,' the Rastafarian rumbled behind him.

Hayes raised a hand for him to be silent although his own temper was becoming somewhat frayed as the minister ploughed on.

'It will be interesting to see how long this Centre remains intact. How long before some of you decide to wreck it. As it is, one of the few advantages that I can see is that it will give some of you a place to go, instead of hanging idly around on street corners.'

The crowd, by this time, were now gesturing menacingly at Braddock. Someone shouted something from the rear of the crowd but the minister either didn't hear it or ignored it. His own face was flushed, perspiration running in rivulets over the puffy flesh, yet still he felt himself encased in that invisible grip which seemed to squeeze tighter, growing colder all the time.

'Perhaps now,' he hissed, 'with your own Centre, you will stop bothering the decent white people who are unfortunate enough to have to live in this filthy "ghetto" you have created in Brixton.' He was breathing heavily, rapidly. His eyes were bulging wide and, when he spoke it was through clenched teeth.

'That's it,' snapped the Rastafarian, stepping forward. 'Who the hell do you think you are, man?'

Braddock spun around, his eyes blazing.

'Get away from me you stinking nigger,' he roared, his voice amplified by the microphone.

The crowd raged back at him.

'Mr Braddock . . .' Julian Hayes began, moving in front of his colleague to face the politician. 'We've heard enough.'

'You black scum,' rasped the minister.

In one lightning movement, he snatched the shears from the table and drove them forward.

The twin blades punctured Hayes' stomach just below the navel and Braddock tore them upwards until they cracked noisily against the black man's sternum. Blood burst from the hideous rent and Hayes dropped to his knees as a tangled mess of purplish-blue intestines spilled from the gaping hole. Hayes clawed at them, feeling the blood and bile spilling on to his hands and splattering down the front of his trousers. He whimpered quietly as he attempted to retain his entrails, pushing at them with slippery hands.

In the crowd someone screamed. Two or three women fainted. Others seemed rooted to the spot, not sure whether to run or try to confront Braddock who stood on the platform facing the Rastafarian, the dripping sheers now held in both hands.

'Motherfucker,' rasped the black man and lunged forward.

Braddock sidestepped and brought the razor sharp blades together once more.

They closed with ease around his opponent's neck and, with a movement combining demonic force and seething anger, the politician snapped the blades together.

Two spurting crimson parabolas erupted from the Rastafarian's neck as the shears bit through his carotid arteries, slicing through the thick muscles of his neck until they crushed his larynx and met against his spine.

Braddock roared triumphantly, exerting more force on the handles until the black man's spinal column began to splinter and break. He was suspended in mid-air by the shears, held there by Braddock who seemed to have found reserves of strength he hadn't formerly been aware of. Blood gushed madly forth, much of it covering the politician himself, but he ignored the crimson cascade, grunting loudly as he finally succeeded in severing his opponent's head. It rose on a thick gout of blood as the body fell to the ground, twitching slightly.

The head rolled across the platform, sightless eyes gazing at the sky as torrents of red fluid poured from the stump of the neck.

Some of the crowd, by now, had scattered, others had surrounded the platform but, understandably, seemed reluctant to approach Braddock.

The politician had lowered the shears and his breathing seemed to have slowed. He stood motionless, like a child lost in a supermarket. Those watching saw him raise one bloodied hand to his forehead and squeeze his eyes tightly shut. When he opened them again his expression had changed from one of anger to utter horror. He looked at the

212

headless corpse at his feet, then at Julian Hayes who was rocking gently back and forth clutching at his torn belly.

Finally, Braddock lifted the shears before him, staring at the sticky red fluid which covered them. And him.

He dropped the weapon and staggered backward, his face pale and drained.

Somewhere in the distance he heard a police siren.

As the sun burned brightly in the sky, he shivered, his entire body enveloped by an icy chill, the like of which he had never experienced before.

Gerald Braddock took one more look at the carnage before him then vomited.

44

The dashboard clock showed 6.05 p.m. as Kelly pulled the Mini into Blake's driveway. She tapped the wheel agitatedly, wondering, when she didn't see his XJS, if he was out. She decided that he might have put it in the garage, hauled herself out of her own car and ran to his front door, clutching the two newspapers which she'd gathered from the back seat.

The sun was slowly sinking and the air was still warm from the daytime heatwave. Kelly felt her blouse sticking to her. The drive had been a long and tortuous one, especially once she'd reached inner London. Now she banged hard on Blake's front door, almost relieved that she'd completed the trip.

She waited a moment but there was no answer.

Kelly banged again, this time hearing sounds of movement from inside. The door swung open and she saw Blake standing there.

'Kelly,' he beamed. 'What a great surprise. Come in.' He ushered her inside, puzzled by her flustered appearance and look of anxiety.

'Is something wrong?' he asked. She had still not smiled.

'Have you seen the news today?' she asked. 'Or watched TV at all?'

213

Blake shook his head in bewilderment.

'No. I had lunch with my publisher. I've been working since I got back. I haven't had time to look at the papers. Why?'

She held two newspapers out before him, both were folded open to reveal headlines. He looked at one, then the other:

ACTRESS KILLS BABY

Blake read it then looked at Kelly.

'Read the other one,' she told him.

TELEVISION PERSONALITY CHARGED WITH MURDER

Below it was a photograph of Roger Carr.

The writer looked at the first article once more and noticed the name Toni Landers.

'Jesus Christ,' he murmured, sitting down on the edge of a chair. 'When did this happen?'

'Last night they found Roger Carr in his house with the body of a girl,' said Kelly. 'The night before, Toni Landers killed the baby. The article said it belonged to her friend.'

Blake frowned and skimmed the articles quickly.

'That's not all,' Kelly told him. 'When I was driving home from the Institute today, I had the radio on. Do you remember Gerald Braddock?'

Blake nodded.

'According to the radio he went crazy this afternoon and killed two people,' Kelly told him.

The writer hurriedly got to his feet and switched on the television.

'There might be something on here about it,' he said, punching buttons until he found the appropriate channel.

'. . . Mr Braddock today. The Arts Minister is now in the Westminster Hospital, under police guard, where he was treated for shock prior to being charged.' The newsreader droned on but Blake seemed not to hear the rest.

'Treated for shock?' said Kelly. 'That's a little unusual isn't it? Do murderers usually go into a state of shock after committing the crime?' She exhaled deeply.

'I wish I knew,' said Blake. 'I know less than you do.' He scanned the papers once more. 'As far as I can make out Toni Landers and Roger Carr can remember nothing about the murders they committed. Yet they were both found *with* their victims.'

214

'So was Gerald Braddock,' Kelly added. 'Only there were witnesses in his case.'

'Three respected people suddenly commit murder for no apparent reason,' Blake muttered. 'They can't remember doing it and nothing links them.'

'There *is* a link, David,' Kelly assured him. 'They were all at the seance the other night.'

The two of them regarded each other warily for a moment then Blake got to his feet once more and picked up the phone. He jabbed the buttons and got a dial tone.

'Can I speak to Phillip Campbell, please?' he asked when the phone was finally answered. He waited impatiently while the receptionist connected him.

'Hello, David,' the Scot said. 'You were lucky to catch me, I was just about to leave.'

'Phil, listen to me, this is important. Do the names Toni Landers, Roger Carr and Gerald Braddock mean anything to you?'

'Of course. Toni Landers is an actress, Carr's an interviewer and Braddock's a politician. Do I get a prize for getting them all right?'

'In the past two days, each one of them has committed a murder.'

There was silence from Campbell's end.

'Phil, are you still there?' Blake asked.

'Yes, look, what the hell are you talking about, David?'

'It's all over the papers, on the TV as well.'

'But I know Braddock,' Campbell said in surprise. 'He couldn't fart without help, let alone murder anyone.'

'Well, all that changed today,' Blake said. He went on to explain what had happened to Toni Landers and Roger Carr. 'None of them could remember what they'd done. It's almost as if they were in some kind of trance. In my book I've discussed the possibility of some kind of unconscious reaction to an external stimulus . . .'

Campbell interrupted.

'If you're trying to use three random killings to justify what *you've* written, David. Forget it,' snapped the Scot.

'But you'll admit it's a possibility?'

'No. Christ, that's even more bloody conjecture than you had before. Ring me when you've gathered some *real* evidence.'

215

Blake exhaled wearily and dropped the receiver back into place.

'What did he say?' Kelly asked, tentatively.

The writer didn't answer. He was staring past her, his eyes fixed on the twin headlines:

ACTRESS KILLS BABY

TELEVISION PERSONALITY CHARGED WITH MURDER

Outside, the dying sun had coloured the sky crimson.

Like cloth soaked in blood.

45

The smell of roast meat wafted invitingly through the air as Phillip Campbell stepped into the sitting room of his house.

The television was on and, through the open kitchen door, he could hear sounds of movement. As he drew closer, the smell grew stronger, tempting him toward the kitchen like a bee to nectar. He paused in the doorway and smiled. His daughter had her back to him, busily inspecting the dials on the cooker. Her black hair was long, spilling half-way down her back, almost to the waist band of her jeans. She looked a little too large for the pair she wore, possessing what were euphemistically known as 'child-bearing hips'. But her legs were long and relatively slender. She wore a baggy sweater, cut off at the elbows, which she'd knitted herself during her last break from University. She always came home during the holidays, only this time she had felt it as much out of duty as a desire to be with her parents.

Campbell's wife was in Scotland and had been for the past two weeks. Her mother was terminally ill with colonic cancer and was being nursed through her final few weeks by her family. Campbell himself had been up to see her twice but, after the second visit, he had been unable to bear the sight of the old girl wasting away. His wife phoned every other night and the presence of his daughter in some way compensated for her absence.

'Whatever it is it smells good,' the publisher said, smiling.

216

Melissa spun around, a look of surprise on her face.

'I didn't hear you come in, Dad,' she told him. 'You must be getting sneaky in your old age.' She grinned.

'You cheeky little tyke,' he chuckled. 'Less of the old age.'

Her mood changed slightly.

'Mum phoned earlier,' Melissa told him.

Campbell sat down at the carefully set table.

'What did she say?' he wanted to know.

'Not much. She sounded upset, she said something about being home next week.'

'Oh Christ,' Campbell said, wearily. 'Well, perhaps it's a kindness if her mother does pass on. At least it'll be the end of her suffering.'

There was a moment's silence between them then Campbell got to his feet.

'I'm going to get changed before dinner,' he said.

'You've got about five minutes,' Melissa told him. 'I don't want this to spoil.'

'You cooks are really temperamental aren't you?' he said, smiling.

The cuckoo clock on the wall of the kitchen burst into life as the hands reached 9 p.m.

Campbell set down the plates on the draining board and picked up a tea-towel as Melissa filled the sink with hot water.

'I'll do the washing up, Dad,' she told him. 'You go and sit down.'

He insisted on drying.

'Are we going to be seeing any more of this young fellow Andy or whatever his name was, next term?' Campbell asked, wiping the first saucepan.

'I don't know. He's gone grape-picking in France for the summer,' she chuckled.

'You were keen on him though?'

'You sound as if you're trying to get me hitched.'

'Am I the match-making type?' he said with mock indignation.

'Yes,' she told him, handing him a plate. 'Now, can we change the subject, please?'

Her father grinned.

'What sort of day have *you* had?' Melissa asked him.

217

They talked and joked while they cleared away the crockery, pots and pans and cutlery then Melissa decided to make coffee.

'I've got a few things to read before tomorrow,' he told her.

'I thought you didn't usually bring work home with you?'

'Sometimes it's unavoidable.'

'I'll bring your coffee in when it's ready,' she said.

He thanked her then wandered through into the sitting room, searching through his attaché case for the relevant material. Seated in front of the television, Campbell began scanning the synopses and odd chapters which he had not found time to get through at the office. There was work from established authors, as well as unsolicited efforts from those all too anxious to break into the world of publishing. The mystique which seemed to surround the publishing world never ceased to amaze the Scot.

Melissa joined him in the sitting room and reached for the book which she had been reading. They sat opposite one another, undisturbed by the television. Neither thought to get up and turn it off.

It was approaching 11.30 when Melissa finally put down her book and stretched. She rubbed her eyes and glanced at the clock on the mantlepiece.

'I think I'll go to bed, Dad,' she said, sleepily.

Campbell looked up at her and smiled.

'OK,' he said. 'I'll see you in the morning.'

He heard the door close behind her as she made her way upstairs. The Scot paused for a moment, his attention taken by a photograph of Gerald Braddock which had been flashed up on the TV screen. He quickly moved forward and turned up the volume, listening as the newscaster relayed information about the horrific incident in Brixton that afternoon. Campbell watched with interest, remembering his phone conversation with Blake. He shook his head. How could there possibly be any link between Blake's theories and Braddock's demented act? He dismissed the thought as quickly as it had come, returning to the work before him. Campbell yawned and rubbed his eyes, weariness creeping up on him unannounced. He decided to make himself a cup of coffee in an effort to stay awake. There wasn't much more to read and he wanted everything out of the way before he eventually retired to bed. He wandered into the kitchen and filled the kettle, returning to his chair in the sitting room. He slumped wearily into it and decided to watch the rest of the late news before continuing.

He yawned again.

Phillip Campbell made his way quietly up the stairs, pausing when he reached the landing. He heard no sounds from Melissa's room and was certain that he hadn't disturbed her. The Scot slowly turned the handle of her door and edged into the room. He smiled as he looked at her, sleeping soundly, her long black hair spread across the pillow like a silken smudge. She moved slightly but did not awake.

Campbell paused for a moment running his eyes over the numerous pen and ink, watercolour and pencil drawings which were displayed proudly in the room. Beside the bed was a plastic tumbler crammed with pieces of charcoal, pens and pencils and, propped against the bedside table was an open sketch-pad which bore the beginnings of a new drawing.

Campbell moved closer to the bed, his eyes fixed on his sleeping daughter. Even when he stood over her she did not stir.

He bent forward and, with infinite care, pulled down the sheets, exposing her body. She wore only a thin nightdress, the dark outline of her nipples and pubic mound visible through the diaphanous material. Campbell felt his erection growing, bulging urgently against his trousers. Without taking his eyes from Melissa, he unzipped his flies and pulled out his rampant organ.

It was then that she rolled on to her back, her eyes opening slightly.

Before she could react, the Scot was upon her, tearing frenziedly at the nightdress, ripping it from her, exposing her breasts. He grabbed one roughly, using his other hand to part her legs. She clawed at his face then attempted to push him off, using all her strength to keep her legs together but he knelt over her and struck her hard across the face. Still dazed from sleep, she was stunned by the blow and her body went momentarily limp. Campbell took his chance and pulled her legs apart, forcing his penis into her.

Melissa screamed in pain and fear and bit at the hand which he clamped over her mouth but he seemed undeterred by her feeble assaults and he struck her once more, harder this time. A vicious red mark appeared below her right eye.

219

With a grunt of triumph he began to thrust within her, using one forearm to hold her down, weighing heavily across her throat until she began to gasp for air. She flailed at him weakly and he slapped her hands away contemptuously as he speeded up his movements, thrusting harder into her.

With his free hand, Campbell reached for the bedside table and pulled a pencil from the pastic container. The point had been sharpened repeatedly to a needle-like lead tip and he gripped it in one powerful hand.

Melissa, who was already on the point of blacking out now seemed to find renewed strength as she saw him bringing the pencil closer, but the weight on top of her prevented her from squirming away from her father.

He guided the pencil inexorably towards her ear.

She tried to twist her head back and forth but he struck her again and she felt the pressure on her throat ease as he held her head steady.

With fastidious precision, Campbell began to push the needle sharp pencil into her ear, putting more weight behind it as the wooden shaft penetrated deeper.

He felt his daughter's body buck madly beneath him and her eyes bulged wide as he pushed the pencil further, driving it into the soft grey tissue of her brain, forcing it as far as it would go. Almost a full half of the length had disappeared before she stopped moving but still Campbell forced the object deeper, as if he wished to push it right through her skull, to see the bloodied point emerge from the other side.

The Scot grunted in satisfaction and continued to pound away at her corpse, a crooked smile of pleasure on his face.

Phillip Campbell awoke with a start, his body bathed in perspiration. He was panting like a carthorse, his heart thudding heavily against his ribs. He looked across at the empty chair opposite him.

'Melissa,' he breathed, a note of panic in his voice.

He hauled himself out of his chair and bolted for the stairs, taking them two at a time, stumbling as he reached the landing. He threw open the door of his daughter's room and looked in.

She was sleeping soundly but, as he stood there, breathless, she murmured something and opened her eyes, blinking myopically at the figure silhouetted in her doorway.

'Dad?' she said, puzzlement in her voice. 'What's wrong?'

He sucked in a deep, almost painful breath.

'Nothing,' he told her.

'Are you all right?'

The Scot wiped his forehead with the back of his hand.

'I must have dozed off in the chair,' he said, softly. 'I had a nightmare.' He dare not tell her about it. 'Are *you* OK?' he added, his voice full of concern.

She nodded.

'Yes, of course I am.'

Campbell exhaled.

'I'm sorry I woke you,' he croaked, and pulled the door shut behind him.

He walked slowly back across the landing, pausing as he reached the top step.

There was a sticky substance on his underpants, a dark stain on his trousers. For a moment he thought he'd wet himself.

It took but a second for him to realize that the substance was semen.

46

How long the phone had been ringing he wasn't sure but the discordant tone finally woke him and he thrust out a hand to grab the receiver. 'Hello,' Blake croaked, rubbing a hand through his hair. He glanced at the alarm clock as he did so.

It was 12.55 a.m.

'David, it's me.'

Blake shook his head, trying to dispel some of the dullness from his mind.

'Sorry, who is it?' he asked.

221

Beside him, Kelly stirred and moved closer to him, her body warm and soft.

'Phillip Campbell,' the voice said and finally Blake recognised the Scot's drawl.

'What do you want, Phil?' he said, with surprising calm.

'I had a dream . . . a nightmare. It was so vivid.'

'What about?'

Campbell told him.

'So now you believe what I've been telling you about the subconscious?' Blake said, almost mockingly.

'Look, we'll sort out the contract in a day or two. All right?'

'That's fine.'

Blake hung up.

Kelly, by now, was partially awake.

'What was that, David?' she purred. Her voice thick with sleep.

He told her of Campbell's insistence on going ahead with the book.

'I'm glad he's decided to publish the book, I wonder why he changed his mind?' she said.

Blake didn't speak. He merely kissed her gently on the forehead then lay down again.

Kelly snuggled up against him and he pulled her close.

In no time they had both drifted off to sleep again.

47

Paris

The full moon was like a huge flare in the cloudy sky, casting a cold white light over the land. The breeze which was developing rapidly into a strong wind, sent the dark banks scudding across the mottled heavens.

Michel Lasalle stopped the car and switched off the engine, sitting motionless behind the wheel. Despite the chill in the air he was sweating profusely and wiped his palms on his trousers before reaching over onto the back seat where the shovel lay. He pushed open his door and clambered out.

The gates of the cemetary, as he'd expected, were locked but Lasalle was undeterred by this minor inconvenience. He tossed the shovel over the wrought iron framework where it landed with a dull clang. He stood still, looking furtively around him in the darkness then, satisfied that no one was around, he jumped and managed to get a grip on one of the gates, hauling himself painfully upward until he was in a position to swing over the top.

The impact jarred him as he hit the ground but the Frenchman merely rubbed his calves, picked up the shovel and headed across the darkened cemetery towards the place he knew so well. Trees, stirred by the wind, shook their branches at him, as if warding him off, but Lasalle walked on purposefully, a glazed look in his eye.

The gendarme had heard the strange noise and decided that his imagination was playing tricks on him. But, as he rounded a corner of the high wall which guarded the cemetery, he saw Lasalle's car parked outside the main gates. The uniformed man quickened his pace, squinting at the vehicle through the gloom in an attempt to catch sight of anyone who might be inside. He moved slowly around the car, tapping on two of the windows, but received no response.

As the moon emerged from behind the clouds he peered through the gates of the graveyard.

Illuminated in the chilly white glow was a figure.

A man.

The gendarme could see that he was busy digging up the earth of a grave.

The uniformed man looked up and saw that the walls were covered by barbed wire, his only way in was over the metal gates. He leapt at them, gained a grip, and began to climb.

Lasalle had dug his way at least three feet down into the earth of his wife's grave when he looked up and saw the gendarme approaching. Lasalle murmured something to himself and froze for precious seconds, not sure what to do.

He bolted, still clutching the spade.

223

'Arrêtez!'

He heard the shout and looked over his shoulder to see that the gendarme was pursuing him.

Lasalle didn't know where he was going to run. The uniformed man had blocked his only way out of the cemetery. He had no chance of scaling the wall at the far side and, more to the point, the other man was gaining on him. Weakened by the exertions of his digging, Lasalle stumbled, peering round a second time to see that his pursuer was less than ten yards behind. The uniformed man shouted once more and Lasalle actually slowed his pace.

He spun round, the shovel aimed at the gendarme's head.

A blow which would have split his skull open missed by inches and cracked into a tree.

The uniformed man hurled himself at Lasalle and succeeded in bringing him down. They crashed to the ground, rolling over in the damp grass. The gendarme tired to grip his opponent's arms but, despite Lasalle's weakness, he found a reserve of strength born of desperation and, bringing his foot up, he flipped the other man over. The gendarme landed with a thud, the wind knocked from him as he hit a marble cross which stood over one of the graves.

Lasalle snatched up the shovel again and brought it crashing down.

There was a sickening clang as it caught the other man on the back, felling him as he tried to rise.

Lasalle hesitated a moment then sprinted back the way he had come, towards the grave of his wife.

The gendarme hauled himself to his feet and spat blood, trying to focus on his fleeing quarry. He tensed the muscles in his back, wincing from the pain where he'd been struck but there was a determined look on his face as he set off after Lasalle once more.

It only took him a moment to catch up with the running man.

Again, Lasalle swung the shovel, his blow shattering a marble angel, the head disintegrating to leave a jagged point of stone between the wings.

The swing set him off balance and the gendarme took full advantage, hitting the other man with a rugby tackle just above the knees.

Lasalle grunted. The sound turning to a scream as he toppled towards the broken angel.

The moon shone brightly on the jagged stone.

The point pierced Lasalle's chest below the heart, snapping ribs and tearing one lung. Wind hissed coldly in the gaping wound as he tried to suck in an agonised breath. Impaled on the marble angel, he tried to pull himself free but blood made the stone slippery. He tasted it in his mouth, felt it running from his nose as his struggles became weaker.

The gendarme rolled free and attempted to pull the other man clear, the odour of blood filling the air around them.

Lasalle finally freed himself and toppled backward, blood pumping madly from the gaping hole in his chest. His body shook once or twice but, even as the uniformed man knelt beside him, he heard a soft discharge which signalled that Lasalle's sphincter muscle had given out. A rancid stench of excrement made him recoil.

The moon shone briefly on the dead man's open eyes.

The gendarme shuddered as the wind hissed through the branches of a nearby tree.

It sounded like a disembodied voice.

A cold, invisible oration spoken for the man who lay before him.

The last rites.

48

Oxford

The sun shone brightly, pouring through the windows of her office and reflecting back off the white paper before her. She told herself that was the reason she found it so hard to concentrate. She had read the same two pages half-a-dozen times but still not a word had penetrated. It was the heat. It had to be the heat that was putting her off. Kelly sat back in her chair and dropped the wad of notes.

She sighed, knowing full well that her lack of concentration had nothing to do with present climatic conditions.

Since arriving at the Institute that morning she had been able to think of nothing but Blake. Even now, as the vision of him drifted into her mind she smiled. For a moment she rebuked herself, almost angry that she had become so strongly attached to him. She felt almost guilty, like a schoolgirl with a crush on a teacher but, the more she thought about it, the more she realized how close to love her feelings for Blake were becoming. Was it possible to fall in love with someone in such a short time? Kelly decided that it was. She was certain that he felt the same way about her. She felt it in his touch, in the way he spoke to her.

Kelly shook her head and chuckled to herself. She could hardly wait for the evening to see him again.

Once more she began reading the notes before her.

There was a light tap on the door and, before she could tell the visitor to enter, Dr Vernon walked in.

Kelly's eyes widened in unconcealed surprise.

Standing with the Institute Director was Alain Joubert.

He and Kelly locked stares as Vernon moved into the room.

'I believe you already know Alain Joubert,' he said, motioning to the Frenchman.

'Of course,' Kelly told him, shaking hands with Joubert curtly.

'How are you, Miss Hunt?' Joubert asked, his face impassive.

'I'm fine, I didn't expect to see you again so soon. Is Lasalle here too?'

Joubert opened his mouth to speak but Vernon stepped forward. His face was suddenly somehow softer and Kelly noticed the difference in his features.

'Kelly, you were a friend of Lasalle's weren't you?' he said, quietly.

'What do you mean "you were"? Why the past tense?' she asked.

'He was killed in an accident last night.'

'What kind of accident?' she demanded, her voice a mixture of shock and helplessness.

'We don't know all the details,' Vernon explained. 'The Director of the Metapsychic Centre informed me this morning. I thought you had a right to know.'

She nodded and brushed a hand through her hair wearily.

'He was dying anyway,' Joubert said.

'What do you mean?' Kelly snapped, looking at the Frenchman.

226

'He was cracking up. Taking more of those pills of his. He was dying and he didn't even realize it.'

Kelly detected something close to contempt in Joubert's voice and it angered her.

'Doesn't his death mean anything to you?' she snapped. 'The two of you *had* worked together for a long time.'

The Frenchman seemed unconcerned.

'It's a regrettable incident,' Vernon interjected. 'But, unfortunately, there's nothing we can do.' He smiled condescendingly at Kelly, the tone of his voice changing. 'That wasn't the real reason I came to speak to you, Kelly.'

She looked at him expectantly.

'You're probably wondering why Joubert is here?' he began.

'It had occurred to me,' Kelly said.

'I want you to work with him on the dream project.'

Kelly shot a wary glance at the Frenchman.

'Why?' she demanded. 'I can handle the work alone. I've been doing it since John Fraser . . . left,' she emphasised the last word with contempt.

'Joubert is more experienced than you are. I'm sure you appreciate that,' Vernon said. 'In fact, I felt it only fair to put him in charge of the project.'

'I've been involved with the work from the beginning. Why should Joubert be given seniority?'

'I explained that. He's more experienced.'

'Then you don't leave me much choice, Dr Vernon. If you put Joubert over me, I'll resign.'

Vernon studied Kelly's determined features for a moment.

'Very well,' he said, flatly. 'You may leave.'

Kelly tried to disguise her surprise but couldn't manage it.

'If that's the way you feel, then I won't try to stop you,' Vernon continued, unwrapping a fresh menthol sweet. He popped it into his mouth.

She got to her feet and, without speaking, picked up her leather attaché case and fumbled for the notes on the desk.

'Leave the notes,' said Vernon, forcefully.

She dropped them back on to the desk.

227

'I'm sorry you couldn't have accepted this situation,' Vernon told her. 'But, as you know, the work of the Institute comes first.'

'Yes, I understand,' she said, acidly. 'I hope you find what you're looking for.' She glanced at Joubert. 'Both of you.'

Kelly felt like slamming the door behind her as she left but she resisted the temptation. As she made her way up the corridor towards the entrance hall she felt the anger seething within her.

She stalked out into the bright sunshine but paused for a moment, narrowing her eyes against the blazing onslaught. She found that the palms of her hands were sweating, her breath coming in short, sharp gasps. She marched across to her waiting car and slid behind the wheel, sitting there in the cloying heat, not allowing herself to calm down. She thumped the steering wheel in frustration, looking to one side, towards the Institute.

How could Vernon let her walk out just like that? She inhaled and held the breath for a moment.

And Joubert.

The arrogant bastard. She wondered if his research was the only reason for being in England.

The reality of the situation suddenly seemed to hit her like a steam train and she felt tears welling in her eyes.

Tears of sadness for Lasalle.

Tears of frustration for herself. Of anger.

Her body shook as she felt the hot, salty droplets cascading down her cheeks and she reached for a tissue, hurriedly wiping them away.

She wondered if Joubert and Vernon were watching her.

The seed of doubt inside her mind had grown steadily over the past few weeks until now, it had become a spreading bloom of unquenchable conviction.

There was, she was sure, a conspiracy taking place between the Frenchman and the Institute Director. Nothing would dissuade her from that conclusion now.

First John Fraser, then Michel Lasalle. Both had been involved with the projects on Astral projection and both were now dead.

Coincidence?

She thought about what had happened over the past couple of days as she started the engine and drove off.

The seance.

Toni Landers. Roger Carr. Gerald Braddock.

She glanced over her shoulder at the gaunt edifice of the Institute. Even in the warm sunshine it looked peculiarly menacing.

She rang Blake as soon as she got in. She told him what had happened that morning. He listened patiently, speaking softly to her every now and then, calming her down. She felt like crying once more, such was her feeling of helplessness and rage.

He asked her if she was OK to drive and, puzzled, she said that she was.

'Will you come and stay with me?' he wanted to know.

Kelly smiled.

'You mean move in?'

'Stay as long as you like. Until this is sorted out or, you never know, you might even decide that you can put up with me for a few more weeks.'

There was a long silence between them finally broken by Blake.

'Best food in town,' he said, chuckling.

'I'll start packing,' she told him.

They said their goodbyes and Kelly replaced the receiver, suddenly anxious to be with him. She hurried through into the bedroom, hauled her suitcase down from the top of the wardrobe and began rummaging through her drawers for the items she would need.

She felt a slight chill but disregarded it and continued packing.

49

London

The crushed lager can landed with a scarcely audible thud on the stage in front of the drum riser. A roadie, clad in jeans and a white sweatshirt, scuttled to pick up the debris and remove it. On the far side of the stage two of his companions were dragging one of the huge Marshall amps into position alongside three others of the same size. Each was the height of a man.

Jim O'Neil picked up another can of drink and downed half in one huge swallow. He wiped his mouth with the back of his hand and wandered back and forth behind the curtain. From the other side he could hear the sound of almost 2,000 voices muttering, chatting expectantly. Whistles punctuated the gathering sea of sound.

He guessed that the theatre was full to capacity and the crowd were growing restless as the minutes ticked away until the curtain rose. The place smelled of sweat and leather.

O'Neil himself looked like something from a gladiatorial arena clad as he was in a pair of knee boots, leather trousers and a waist-coat decorated with hundreds of studs. On both arms he wore leather wrist-bands which covered his muscular forearms, the nickel-plated points glinting in the half-light.

There was a burst of sound from his left and he turned to see his lead guitarist, Kevin Taylor, adjusting his amps.

A loud cheer from the other side of the curtain greeted this involuntary action and when the drummer thundered out a brief roll there was even more frenzied shouting from the waiting crowd.

O'Neil wandered over towards Kevin Taylor and tapped the guitarist on the shoulder. He turned and smiled at the singer. At twenty-four, Taylor was almost five years younger than O'Neil but his long hair and craggy face gave him the appearance of a man much older. He wore a white tee-shirt and striped trousers.

'Go easy on the solos tonight,' O'Neil said to him, taking another swig from his can of lager. 'There are four of us in the band you know.'

'I don't know what you mean,' said the guitarist, a slight Irish lilt to his accent.

'At the last gig you nearly wore your fucking fingers out you played so many solos.'

'The audience seems to enjoy it.' Taylor protested.

'I don't give a fuck about the audience. I'm telling you, don't overdo it and keep it simple. Nothing fresh. Right?'

'You're the boss.'

'Yeah,' O'Neil grunted. 'I am.' He finished the lager, crushed the can in one powerful hand and dropped it at the Irishman's feet.

O'Neil walked away, wondering if he was the only one who felt cold.

'Two minutes,' someone shouted.

The singer moved towards the front of the stage and tapped the microphone then, satisfied, he retreated out of view and waited for the curtain to rise. The lights were lowered until the theatre was in darkness and, as the gloom descended, the shouts and whistles grew in intensity finally erupting into a shattering crescendo as the curtain began to rise and the coloured lights above the stage flashed on and off. As the band opened up with a series of power chords which would have registered on the Richter scale, even the swelling roar of the audience was eclipsed. The explosion of musical ferocity swept through the hall like a series of sonic blasts, the scream of guitars and the searing hammerstrokes forged by the drummer merged into a force which threatened to put cracks in the walls.

O'Neil took the stage, his powerful voice soaring like an air raid siren over the driving sound of his musicians.

As he sang he ran from one side of the stage to the other, grinning at the hordes of fans who clamoured to get closer to the stage, occasionally pausing to touch their upraised hands. Like some leather clad demi-God he strode the platform, his disciples before him, fists raised in salute and admiration.

The heat from the spotlights was almost unbearable but still O'Neil felt an icy chill nipping at his neck, spreading slowly through his entire body until it seemed to fill him. He gazed out at the crowd, their faces becoming momentary blurs to him as he spun round and moved towards Kevin Taylor.

O'Neil raised the microphone stand above his head, twirling it like a drum-major's baton, much to the delight of the crowd.

Even Taylor smiled at him.

He was still smiling when O'Neil drove the stand forward like a spear, putting all his weight behind it, forcing the metal tube into Taylor's stomach. The aluminium shaft tore through his midsection and, propelled by O'Neil, erupted from the guitarist's back just above the kidneys. Blood burst from both wounds and Taylor croaked in agony as he was forced back towards the stack of amps behind him. O'Neil let go of the mike stand as Taylor crashed into the speakers.

231

There was a bright flash as they shorted out and, the guitarist, still transfixed, began to jerk uncontrollably as thousands of volts of electricity ripped through him.

There was a blinding white explosion as the first amp went up.

The PA system began to crackle insanely as a combination of feedback and static accompanied the short circuit.

Another amp exploded.

Then another.

Rigged to the same system, it was like dropping a lighted match into a full box.

Flames began to lick from the first amp, devouring Taylor's twitching body hungrily, writhing in his long hair like yellow snakes. He looked like a fiery Gorgon. On the far side of the stage the other banks of speakers began to blow up, some showering the audience with pieces of blazing wood.

Those in the front few rows clambered back over their seats, anxious to be away from the terrifying destruction before them but those behind could not move fast enough and many were crushed in the mad stampede to escape. Anyone who fell was immediately trodden underfoot as fear overcame even the strongest and panic rapidly became blind terror. On the balcony, some stared mesmerised at the stage which was rapidly becoming an inferno.

Flames rose high, destroying everything they touched. The other musicians had already fled the stage and a roadie who dashed on to help was crushed beneath a falling amp, pinned helplessly as he burned alive, his shrieks drowned out by the deafening crackle coming from the PA and the horrified shouts of the crowd.

The curtain was lowered but flames caught it and it became little more than a canopy of fire, suspended over the stage like some kind of super-nova. Dozens of lights, unable to stand up to the heat, shattered, spraying glass on to those below. A large frame holding eight football-sized spotlights came free of its rigging and plummeted into the audience where it exploded. Dozens were crushed, others were burned or sliced open by flying glass which hurtled around like jagged crystal grapeshots.

Motionless on the stage, framed by fire, stood Jim O'Neil, his face pale and blank as he gazed uncomprehendingly around him at the

232

destruction. He saw people in the audience screaming as they ran, he saw others lying on the floor, across seats. Bloodied, burned or crushed.

A roadie ran shrieking across the stage, his clothes and hair ablaze. The acrid stench of burned flesh filled O'Neil's nostrils and he swayed as though he were going to faint.

Behind him, still impaled on the microphone stand, the body of Kevin Taylor was being reduced to charred pulp by the searing flames which leapt and danced all around the stage.

O'Neil could only stand alone and shake his head. Like some lost soul newly introduced to hell.

Sweat was pouring from him but, despite the blistering temperatures, he felt as if he were freezing to death.

50

As darkness crept across the sky, Blake got to his feet and crossed the room to draw the curtains. Kelly watched as he shut out the gloom, feeling somehow more secure, as if the night were comprised of millions of tiny eyes – each one watching her.

The writer paused by the drinks cabinet and re-filled his own glass. Kelly declined the offer of a top-up. She felt that she had already consumed a little too much liquor since arriving at Blake's house earlier in the day.

Throughout the journey to London she had felt an unexplained chill, an inexplicable sense of foreboding which only seemed to disappear once she saw Blake. She felt safe with him. But, more than that, she was now even more convinced that she was falling in love with him.

He returned to his chair and sat down, glancing across at Kelly.

Barefoot, clad only in a pair of skin tight faded jeans and a tee-shirt, she looked more vulnerable than he had ever seen her before. And also, perhaps because she was unaware of it, more alluring. Yet he knew, beneath that apparently anxious exterior, she still retained the courage and determination which had first drawn him to her.

'Are you feeling all right?' he asked, noticing how intently she stared into the bottom of her glass.

'I was just thinking,' she told him, finally gracing him with her attention. 'I know we've been over this dozens of times but I can't seem to get it out of my mind. I'm convinced that someone at that seance is responsible for what's been going on, for these murders.'

'Go on,' he prompted her.

'The only one who knew all five victims . . .'

Blake interrupted.

'How can you call Braddock and the other two, *victims* when they were the ones who committed the murders?'

'They did them against their will. They were used.' She looked intently at him. 'And I'm sure that the same person who influenced them was also responsible for the deaths of Fraser and Lasalle. It has to be Dr Vernon.'

Blake shook his head.

'Fraser was killed in a car crash, right? You've already told me that Lasalle was starting to crack up again. What proof is there that Vernon had anything to do with *their* deaths?' he said. 'Who's to say that both men didn't die in bona fide accidents?'

'Whose side are you on?' she snapped.

'It's nothing to do with sides, Kelly,' he said, angrily. 'It's a matter of practicality. You can't go accusing someone like Vernon without proof. Besides, if it were true, how the hell are you going to prove it? There isn't a policeman in the country who'd believe you. The whole idea of controlling someone else's Astral personality is difficult enough to understand, even for people like you and I, let alone for someone with no knowledge of the subject.'

'Are you saying we're beaten?' she muttered.

'No, I'm just trying to be practical,' Blake explained.

'Three of the people involved in that seance have already commited murder. What about the rest of us? How long before something happens to us?'

Blake picked up the phone.

'I'm going to call Mathias and Jim O'Neil,' he said. 'I want to know if they're aware of what's been happening. They could be in danger too.'

'And so could we,' Kelly added, cryptically.

Blake didn't answer.

'Grosvenor House Hotel. Can I help you?' said a female voice.

'I'd like to speak to Mr Jonathan Mathias,' said Blake. 'He has a suite at the hotel. My name is David Blake.'

There was a moment's silence and, from the other end of the line, Blake heard the sound of paper rustling.

Kelly kept her eyes on him as he stood waiting.

'I'm afraid Mr Mathias checked out this morning,' the voice told him.

'Damn,' muttered the writer; then to the receptionist, 'Have you any idea where he is? Where he went? It is important.'

'I'm sorry, I can't help you there, sir,' she said.

Blake thanked her and pressed his fingers down on the cradle.

'No luck?' Kelly asked.

'He's probably back in the States by now,' the writer said, reaching for a black notebook which lay close to the phone. He flipped through it, running his finger down the list of names and numbers. He found what he was looking for and tapped out the correct number, listening as the purring tones began.

'Come on,' he whispered, impatiently.

'Are you calling O'Neil?' Kelly wanted to know.

Blake nodded.

'He's probably on stage at the moment but perhaps if I can talk to one of his crew I can get him to ring me back.' The purring went on. Blake jabbed the cradle and pressed the numbers again.

Still no answer.

'What the hell are they playing at?' he muttered.

He flicked the cradle and tried yet again.

A minute passed and he was about to replace the receiver when he heard a familiar click from the other end.

'Hello, is that the Odeon?' he blurted.

The voice at the other end of the line sounded almost unsure.

'Yes. What do you want?'

Blake detected a note of unease in the voice. Fear perhaps?

'Is Jim O'Neil still on stage? If . . .'

The man at the other end cut him short.

'Are you from a newspaper?' he asked.

'No,' Blake told him, puzzled. 'Why?'

'I thought you might have heard about the accident. No press allowed. The police won't let any of them through.'

'What's happened there?' the writer demanded. 'I'm a friend of O'Neil's.'

'There was an accident, a fire. God knows how many people are dead.' The man's voice began to crack. 'O'Neil killed one of his band. It happened on the stage. I . . .'

'Where's O'Neil now?'

Kelly got up and walked across to the table. Blake picked up a pencil and scribbled a note on a piece of paper. She read it as he continued speaking: O'NEIL HAS KILLED. FIRE ON STAGE. PEOPLE IN AUDIENCE KILLED.

'Oh my God,' murmured Kelly.

'Where is O'Neil at the moment?' the writer repeated.

'The police took him away,' the other man said. 'I've never seen anything like it. He looked as if he didn't know what was going on, he . . .'

The phone went dead.

Blake flicked the cradle but could get no response. He gently replaced the receiver.

For long moments neither he nor Kelly spoke, the silence gathering round them like an ominous cloud.

'Toni Landers. Gerald Braddock. Roger Carr and now O'Neil,' Kelly said, finally. 'Who's going to be next?'

Her words hung, unanswered, in the air.

51

New York

Jonathan Mathias raised both arms above his head and stood for a moment, surveying the sea of faces before him. All ages. All nationalities. But with a single purpose.

To see him.

The hall in the Bronx was the largest that he used and as he ran an appraising eye over the throng he guessed that somewhere in the region of 2,000 people had packed into the converted warehouse. They stood in expectant silence, waiting for a sign from him.

'Come forward,' Mathias said, his powerful voice reverberating around the crowded meeting place.

Men working for the psychic, dressed in dark suits, cleared an aisle through the middle of the horde, allowing the procession of pain to begin. First came the wheelchairs, some of their occupants looking expectantly towards the stage where Mathias stood. He saw a young woman being brought forward by two men who had laid her on a stretcher. She lay motionless, sightless eyes gazing at the ceiling, her tongue lolling from one corner of her mouth.

Dozens hobbled towards the psychic on crutches, many struggling with the weight of the callipers which weighed them down. Others were supported by friends or relatives.

Mathias counted perhaps twenty or more figures moving slowly behind those on crutches. Most carried the white sticks which marked them out as blind, others were led forward by members of the crowd or by the dark-suited stewards. One of them, a man in his forties, stumbled and had to be helped up, but he continued on his way, anxious to reach the figure whom he could not see but who he knew would help him.

As the last of the sick passed through the midst of the crowd, the gap which had opened now closed. The people drifting back to their places. From where Mathias stood, it looked like one single amoebic entity repairing a self-inflicted rent in itself. The sea of faces waited as the lights in the hall dimmed slightly, one particularly bright spotlight focusing on the psychic, framing him in a brilliant white glow.

The psychic had still not lowered his arms. He closed his eyes for a moment and stood like some finely attired scarecrow, his head slightly bowed. In the almost palpable silence, even the odd involuntary cough or whimper seemed intrusive.

Without looking up, Mathias nodded imperceptibly.

From the right of the stage, a woman put her strength into pushing a wheelchair up the ramp which had been erected to facilitate the countless invalid chairs. A steward moved forward to help her but Mathias waved him back, watching as the woman strained against the weight contained in the chair. Eventually, she made it and, after a swift pause to catch her breath, she moved towards the psychic who fixed both her and the boy in the wheelchair in his piercing gaze.

The occupant of the chair was in his early twenties, his ruddy features and lustrous black hair somehow belying the fact that his body was relatively useless. The boy had large, alert eyes which glistened in the powerful light and he met Mathias' stare with something akin to pleading. He still wore a metal neck-brace which was fastened to his shattered spine by a succession of pins. Paralysed from the neck down the only thing which moved were his eyes.

'What is your name?' Mathias asked him.

'James Morrow,' the youngster told him.

'You're his mother?' the psychic asked, looking at the woman fleetingly.

She nodded vigorously.

'Please help him,' she babbled. 'He's been like this for a year and . . .'

Mathias looked at her again and, this time, his gaze seemed to bore through her. She stopped talking instantly and took a step back, watching as the psychic gently gripped her son's head, circling it with his long fingers, their tips almost meeting at the back of the boy's skull. He raised his head and looked upward, momentarily staring at the powerful spotlight which held him like a moth in a flame. His breathing began to degenerate into a series of low grunts and the first minute droplets of perspiration started to form on his forehead. The psychic gripped the boy's head and pressed his thumbs gently against his scalp for a moment or two, passing to his temples, then his cheeks.

James Morrow closed his eyes, a feeling of welcome serenity filling him. He even smiled slightly as he felt the psychic's thumbs brush his eyelids and rest there.

Mathias was quivering violently, his entire body shaking madly. He lowered his head and looked down at Morrow, his own teeth now clenched. A thin ribbon of saliva oozed from his mouth and dripped on to the blanket which covered the boy's lower body.

The psychic gasped, a sound which he might have made had all the wind suddenly been knocked from him. He felt his hands beginning to tingle but it wasn't the customary heat which he experienced. It was a searing cold, as if someone had plunged his hands into snow.

James Morrow tried to open his eyes but was unable to do so due to the fact that Mathias' thumbs held his lids closed. The boy felt a slight increase of pressure on the back of his head as the psychic gripped harder.

Mathias felt the muscles in his arms and shoulders throbbing as he exerted more force, pushing his thumbs against Morrow's closed eyes. He was aware of the youngster trying to pull his head back and, as if from a thousand miles away, Mathias heard him groan slightly as the fingers and thumbs dug into him.

The psychic looked down at him and smiled thinly, his face appearing horribly distorted by the blinding power of the spotlight.

Even if Morrow had been aware of what was happening, there was nothing he could have done to prevent it. All he felt was the steadily growing pain as Mathias gripped his head with even more force, a vice-like strength which threatened to crack the bones of his skull. But, as it was, all he could do was remain helpless in the wheelchair, unable to sqirm away from those powerful hands which felt as if they were intent on crushing his head.

The pressure on his eyes became unbearable as Mathias' thumbs drove forward.

Mathias felt some slight resistance at first but then he grunted triumphantly as he felt Morrow's eyes begin to retreat backward beneath the force he was exerting. Blood burst from the corner of the left one and cascaded down the younger man's cheek. Mathias felt the glistening orb move to one side, his thumb slipping into the crimson wetness which was the socket. His nail tore the lid of Morrow's right eye, scraping across the cornea before puncturing the entire structure. The psychic felt his other thumb tearing muscle and ligaments as he began to shake his paralysed victim.

With both thumbs embedded in Morrow's eyes, Mathias forced him backwards, aided by the motion of the wheelchair.

The watching crowd were stunned, not quite sure what was going on. They saw the blood, they saw Morrow's mother running forward but still they looked on in dumb-struck horror.

It was Morrow's keening wail of agony which seemed to galvanise them into action.

In the watching throng, a number of other people screamed. Shouts rose. Shouts of fear and revulsion.

One of the screams came from James Morrow's mother who ran at the psychic, anxious to drag him away from her son, who sat motionless in his wheelchair as the psychic continued to gouge his thumbs ever deeper into the riven cavities of his eye sockets. Blood was running freely down the boy's face now, staining his shirt and the blanket around him.

Mathias finally released his hold, turning swiftly to strike the approaching woman with one bloodied hand. The blow shattered her nose and sent her sprawling.

The body of James Morrow, sitting upright in the chair, rolled towards one side of the stage where it tipped precariously for a second before toppling over. The lifeless form fell out and the psychic watched as Mrs Morrow, her face a crimson ruin, crawled helplessly towards it, burbling incoherently.

Mathias blinked hard, aware that people were moving away from the stage. Away from *him*. He glanced down at the struggling form of Mrs Morrow, draped over her dead son like some kind of bloodied shroud. He took a step towards the carnage then faltered, his head spinning, his eyes drawn to the twin gore-filled holes which had once been James Morrow's eyes.

The psychic looked down at his own hands and saw that they were soaked with blood. A fragment of red muscle still clung to one thumb nail. The crimson fluid had run up his arms, staining the cuffs of his shirt.

He shook violently, struggling to breathe as he surveyed the grisly scene before him.

The spotlight pinned him in its unremitting glare but, despite the heat which it gave off, Mathias found that he was shivering.

52

London

Kelly slipped off her jeans and shivered momentarily before climbing into the large bed in Blake's room. She heard the sound of footfalls approaching across the landing.

Blake entered the room and pulled the door closed behind him. He began unbuttoning his shirt.

'I'll drive to the Institute tomorrow,' he said. 'Confront Vernon. I'll mention his wife. Anything I have to in order to get him to respond.'

He walked to the bedside cabinet and knelt down. The bottom drawer was locked but a quick turn of the ornate gold key and the writer opened it. He reached inside and lifted something out, hefting it before him.

It was a .357 Magnum. A snub-nose model. Blake flipped out the cylinder and carefully thumbed one of the heavy grain bullets into each chamber then he snapped it back into position. He laid the revolver on top of the cabinet.

Kelly regarded the gun warily.

'If Vernon does respond,' said Blake slipping into bed beside her, 'then, at least you'll know you were right. If he doesn't, then you can start looking for another suspect.'

'That narrows the field down quite a bit,' Kelly said, cryptically. She moved close to him, nuzzling against his body, kissing first his chest then his lips. 'Please be careful,' she whispered.

Blake nodded, glanced one last time at the Magnum then reached over and flicked off the lamp.

She was blind.

Kelly thrashed her head frantically back and forth, the terror growing within her.

She could see nothing.

She tried to scream but no sound would come forth.

It took her a second or two to realize that she had been gagged. A piece of cloth had been stuffed into her mouth, secured by a length of thick hemp which chafed against the soft flesh of her cheeks. Her eyes had been covered by more, tightly fastened, strands of knotted material, sealed shut as surely as if the lids had been sewn together.

She felt someone moving beside her, felt a hand gently stroking her flat stomach before first moving upwards to her breasts and then down to her pubic mound.

Kelly attempted to move but, as she did, red hot pain lanced through her wrists and ankles as the rope which held her to the bed rasped against her skin. She made a whimpering sound deep in her throat, aware that her legs had been forced apart. She lay spreadeagled, her body exposed to whatever prying eyes chose to inspect it. Her legs had been pulled apart to such an extent that the muscles at the backs of her thighs felt as if they were about to tear. Pain gnawed at the small of her back, intensifying as she struggled in vain to free herself. The rope which was wound so tightly around her wrists and ankles bit hungrily into her flesh until she felt a warm dribble of blood from her left ankle.

Kelly was aware of movement, of a heavy form positioning itself between her legs.

She felt fingers trickling up the inside of her thighs, seeking her exposed vagina.

In the darkness she felt even more helpless, unable to see her assailant because of the blindfold.

Something nudged against her cleft and she stiffened.

Whatever it was, it was excruciatingly cold on that most sensitive area. She lay still as the freezing object probed deeper and, again, she tried to scream.

Kelly heard soft chuckling then a guttural grunt of pleasure.

It was followed by a rapid, rhythmic slopping sound which seemed to keep time with the low grunts.

She realized that her invisible assailant was masturbating.

The cold object between her legs pushed deeper, now adding pain to the other sensation she was feeling.

Another second and Kelly felt warm fluid spilling onto her belly in an erratic fountain. The grunts of her captor grew louder as he coaxed the last droplets of thick liquid from his penis.

Light flashed into her eyes as the blindfold was torn free and, in that split second, she saw the face of her attacker.

His penis still gripped in one fist, the other hand holding the gun against her vagina, he grinned down at her.

She heard a noise which she knew to be the pulling back of the revolver's hammer but her senses were already reeling as she stared with bulging eyes at the man who hovered above her.

David Blake smiled down at her, his face twisted into an unearthly grimace.

Kelly awoke from the nightmare bathed in perspiration. She let out a moan of terror and sat up, looking around her, trying to convince herself that what she had experienced had been the work of her imagination.

The room was silent.

Blake slept soundly beside her, his chest rising and falling slowly.

She let out a long, almost painful breath and ran her hands through her sweat-soaked hair.

As she did so she became aware of a slight tingling in her hands and feet so she pulled the sheet back and glanced down.

Kelly stifled a scream.

On both her wrists and ankles, the flesh was puffy and swollen. Ugly, vivid red welts disfigured the skin.

They were very much like rope burns.

53

The sound of the alarm shattered the silence and shocked Blake from his slumber. He shot out a hand and silenced the insistent buzzing before lying back for a moment to rub his eyes. He took two or three deep breaths and blinked at the ceiling before easing himself slowly out of bed.

Beside him, Kelly did not stir.

The writer gathered up some clothes and crept out of the room in an effort not to wake her. He paused once more when he reached the bedroom door, satisfied that Kelly had not been disturbed.

He showered and dressed, returning to the bedroom once more to retrieve the Magnum. He then made his way downstairs where he slipped the revolver into his attaché case and clipped it shut.

Blake ate a light breakfast then he got to his feet and, case in hand, headed out to the waiting XJS.

The drive to Oxford should take him a couple of hours.

Kelly watched from the bedroom window as Blake climbed into the Jag and started the engine.

She remained hidden in case he looked round but she need not have worried. The sleek vehicle burst into life and the writer guided it out onto the road.

Kelly had heard the alarm clock earlier but had lain awake, eyes still closed, while he had slipped away. She had feigned sleep, aware of his presence in the room. She had heard him moving about downstairs and then, finally, she'd listened as he had walked out to the car. Only at that point had she clambered, naked, out of bed and crossed to the window to watch him leave. Now she returned to the bed and sat down on the edge.

First she inspected her ankles, then her wrists

They were unmarked.

She told herself that she should have woken Blake immediately after she'd had the nightmare but it had frightened her so much that she had decided to remain silent. Even now, in the light of day, she could not find the courage to speak to him about it. That was why she had chosen to give him the impression she was still sleeping when he left.

The dream had been so vivid. Too vivid. Parts of it still burned brightly in her mind like a brand. Ugly and unwanted.

Kelly dressed and made her way downstairs where she found a note propped up on the kitchen table.

SEE YOU LATER, SLEEPYHEAD.

It was signed with Blake's sweeping signature.

She smiled, folded up the note and slipped it into the pocket of her jeans. As she waited for the kettle to boil she put two pieces of bread in the toaster and propped herself against the draining board, waiting.

Should she tell Blake about the dream when he returned? She ran a hand through her hair and decided that she shouldn't. After all, it had been only a dream, hadn't it?

She looked at her wrists and remembered the rope burns which she'd seen the previous night.

Kelly sighed. She wasn't even sure she *had* seen them.

The toast popped up and she buttered the slices, chewing thoughtfully.

She heard a noise from the front of the house and wandered through the sitting room in time to see the postman retreating back up the path. Kelly walked through into the hall and picked up the mail he'd pushed through. As she straightened up she glanced across at the door which led to Blake's underground workroom.

The key was in the lock.

Kelly placed the mail on a nearby table and wandered across to the cellar door. She turned the handle and found that the door was unlocked anyway. She pushed it, reaching for the light switches inside. Kelly slapped them on and the cellar was bathed in the cold glow of fluorescents.

Apart from the steps which led down to the work area itself, the floor had been carpeted. She scurried down the stairs, the coldness of the concrete on her bare feet giving her added speed. Finally she stood at the bottom, glad of the warmth from the carpet. The cellar was large, stretching away from her in all four directions. A huge wooden desk occupied central position and she noticed that there was a typewriter on it. A small waste bin, overflowing with scraps of balled up paper stood nearby. There was a telephone too. The entire cellar had been decorated in white; it positively gleamed and, as she moved around, Kelly detected the scent of an air freshener. Bookcases lined two walls, huge, dark wood creations creaking with hundreds of volumes but, unlike those which Blake displayed on his shelves upstairs in the sitting room, these books were more in the manner of research material. A great many were bound in leather and, as Kelly drew closer, she realized that most were very old.

She reached up and took one.

The gold leaf title was cracked and barely readable so she opened the book and scanned the title page: *Inside the Mind*. She checked the publication date and saw that it was 1921. Replacing it she found another, this one even older: *Psychiatry and the Unknown*. It was dated 1906.

No wonder Blake kept these books hidden away, Kelly thought, scanning more titles. They must be worth a fortune. She ran her index finger along the shelf, mouthing each title silently as she went.

She came to a shelf which consisted entirely of ring binders, each one labelled on the spine. She recognised Blake's writing on the labels.

'*Dreams*,' she read on the first and took it down, flipping through quickly.

Some of the pages were typed, others hand-written. Here and there she spotted a photograph. There was one of Blake's house and, beside it, a rough drawing of the same building. It was almost childlike in its simplicity, drawn, as it was, with a thick pencil. However, the similarity was unmistakable. Kelly replaced the file and reached for another.

'*Hypnosis*,' she murmured.

There was a photo of Mathias inside.

Kelly turned the page and found one of Blake himself but apparently he was sleeping. It must, she reasoned, have been taken with an automatic timer. She was puzzled as to why he should have taken such a shot though. Kelly scanned what was written beneath the photo but saw only a date. The photo, it seemed, had been taken over a year ago. She wondered if Blake had, perhaps, asked someone else to take it but she still couldn't understand why he would need such a photograph.

She reached for another file marked 'Astral Projection' and skimmed through that.

There were more photos.

Of Mathias. Of Blake himself.

Of Toni Landers.

She turned a page.

There was a newspaper clipping which featured Roger Carr.

Kelly swallowed hard and perched on the edge of the desk as she read one of the typewritten sheets in the file.

'*December 6th*,' she read, keeping her voice low, as if she were in a library.

'*The Astral body is a separate entity. I am sure of that now. From what I have observed and read, but, more importantly, from experi-*

mentation upon myself, I know that it can be summoned in tangible form. By a long and tortuous process I have actually managed to separate my Astral body from my physical body at will. To unlock the part of the mind previously unexplored by scientists and psychologists. I now feel confident enough to use this process on others.'

Kelly swallowed hard and read on:

'In order to confirm that tangible Astral projection is possible, I conducted the following test. While in a self-induced trance, I inflicted injury upon my own Astral body and discovered that this injury was subsequently manifested on my physical body.'

There were two photographs beneath. One showed Blake looking at the camera, the other, identical in appearance, highlighted a small scar on his left shoulder. The photos were marked with dates and times. The unblemished one bore the legend: *December 4th 7.30 p.m.* The second: *December 5th 8.01 a.m.*

'This proved two important things, firstly that it is possible to possess two centres of consciousness simultaneously and also that any injury sustained in the Astral state will manifest itself on the host body. The proof is irrefutable. Tangible Astral projection is possible, so too is the manipulation of another person's subconscious mind.'

Kelly closed the file, got to her feet and replaced it. For long seconds she stood motionless in the silent cellar then she scurried back up the steps, aware of the icy chill which seemed to have enveloped her.

She closed the cellar door behind her, noticing that her hand was shaking.

54

It was almost 3.15 p.m. when the XJS came to a halt outside the house.

Kelly, watching from the sitting room, peered out and saw Blake lock the vehicle before gathering up his attaché case. He headed for the front door and, a moment later, she heard the key turn. As it did she moved across to the sofa and sat down, her eyes on the hall door.

Blake smiled at her as he entered.

She watched as he laid the attaché case on the coffee table and flipped it open, removing the Magnum which he placed beside it.

'Vernon didn't try anything?' she said, looking at the gun.

The writer shook his head.

'If he has acquired some kind of power then he knows how to control it,' he said, crossing to the drinks cabinet and pouring himself a large measure of Haig. He offered Kelly a drink and she accepted a Campari.

'Did he say anything at all?' she wanted to know.

'Nothing that I found incriminating if that's what you mean,' Blake told her. 'I mentioned his wife. You were right, he does get touchy about *that*. He wanted to know how I knew about her, what I knew about her. When I mentioned John Fraser he threatened to have me thrown out or arrested.' The writer downed a sizeable measure of the fiery liquid.

'You didn't accuse him of killing Fraser did you?'

'Not in so many words. I just told him what *you'd* told *me*. He didn't react very favourably.'

There was a long silence, finally broken by Blake.

'I don't know where we go from here,' he said.

Kelly didn't speak for a moment then she sucked in a long breath and looked at Blake.

'David, how much do *you* know about Astral projection?' she asked.

He sipped at his drink, his eyes glinting behind the dark screen of his glasses.

'Why do you ask?' he said, his voice low.

'I was just curious,' she told him. She opened her mouth to speak again but couldn't seem to find the words.

Blake sat beside her on the sofa and placed one arm around her, drawing her to him. He smiled reassuringly. She moved closer to him, aware of an icy chill which surrounded her.

He held her firmly and only when her head was resting on his shoulder did his smile disappear.

He looked across at the Magnum.

55

Oxford

The strains of 'God Save the Queen' died away gradually to be replaced by a rasping hiss of static, so loud that it jolted Dr Stephen Vernon from his uneasy dozing. He moved to get up, almost spilling the mug of cocoa which he held in one hand. He switched off the television and stood silently in the sitting room for a moment. He was alone in his house. Joubert was at the Institute and would be for the remainder of the night, going through reams of notes so far untouched.

Vernon gazed down into his mug of cold cocoa and winced as he saw the film of skin which had covered the surface. He put it down and headed for the sitting room door, turning off lights as he went.

He had reached the bottom of the staircase when he heard the noise.

Vernon froze, trying to pinpoint the direction from which it had come. He felt his heart begin to beat a little faster as he heard it once more.

A dull thud followed by what sounded like soft whispering.

He turned, realizing that it came from the study, behind him to the left. The white door was firmly shut however, hiding its secret securely.

Vernon hesitated, waiting for the sound to come again.

He heard nothing and prepared to climb the stairs once more. He'd left the window in the room open. A breeze might well have dislodged something in there, knocked it to the floor, caused . . .

He heard the sound like whispering again and, this time, turned and approached the door.

Vernon paused outside, his ear close to the wood in an effort to detect any sounds from within. His hand hovered nervously over the knob, finally closing on it, turning it gently.

He tried to control his rapid breathing, afraid that whoever was inside the study would hear his approach. Also, as he stood there waiting for the right moment to strike, he felt suddenly vulnerable. He released the door knob and looked around the darkened hallway for a weapon of some kind.

There was a thick wood walking stick propped up in the umbrella stand nearby; Vernon took it and, for the second time, prepared to enter the study.

Beyond the closed door all was silent once again, not the slightest sound of movement disturbed the solitude. A thought occurred to Vernon.

What if the intruder was aware of his presence and, at this moment, was waiting for *him*?

He swallowed hard and tried to force the thought from his mind.

He gripped the knob and twisted it, hurling open the door, his free hand slapping for the light switches just inside.

As the study was illuminated, Vernon scanned the area before him, the walking stick brandished like a club.

His mouth dropped open in surprise as he caught sight of the intruder.

Hunkered over the large table, one of the files open before him, was David Blake.

'You,' gasped Vernon, lowering his guard.

That lapse of concentration was all that Blake needed. He flung himself across the table, catapulted as if from some gigantic rubber band. He crashed into Vernon, knocking the walking stick from his hand, rolling to one side as the older man lashed out at him. Vernon managed to scramble to his feet, bolting from the room but Blake was younger and quicker and he rugby-tackled the doctor, bringing him down in the hallway. They grappled in the gloom and Vernon found that his fear gave him added strength. He gripped Blake's wrists and succeeded in throwing him to one side. The younger man crashed against a nearby wall but the impact seemed only to slow him up for a moment. He scrambled to his feet and set off after the older man again, following him into the kitchen this time.

Vernon tugged open a drawer, the contents spilling across the tiled floor. Knives, forks, spoons, a ladle – all rained down around his feet with a series of high pitched clangs. He snatched up a long carving knife and brandished it before him.

Blake hesitated as he saw the vicious blade winking at him and, for what seemed like an eternity, the two men faced one another, eyes locked. Like two gladiators, they both waited for the other to move first.

'What do you want?' asked Vernon, the knife quivering in his grip.

The younger man didn't answer, he merely edged forward slightly.

'I'll kill you, Blake, I swear to God I will,' Vernon assured him, making a sharp stabbing movement with the blade.

Blake was undeterred. He took another step forward, something on the worktop to his right catching his eye.

It was a sugar bowl.

With lightning speed, he picked it up and hurled the contents into Vernon's face. The tiny grains showered him, some finding their way into his eyes, and he yelped in pain, momentarily blinded by the stinging shower of particles. Blake took his chance. Dropping to one knee, he grabbed a corkscrew and hurled himself at Vernon who somehow managed one last despairing lunge before Blake reached him.

The blade sliced through the younger man's jacket and laid open his left forearm just above the wrist. Blood spurted from the cut and plashed on to the tiles. But Blake slammed into Vernon with the force of a pile-driver, knocking him back against the sink. He snaked one arm around the older man's neck and held him firmly, bringing the corkscrew forward with devastating power.

The sharp point pierced Vernon's skull at the crown and he screamed in agony as Blake twisted it, driving the curling metal prong deeper until it began to churn into the older man's brain. White hot pain seared through him and he felt himself blacking out but, just before he did, Blake tore the corkscrew free, ripping a sizeable lump of bone with it. Greyish red brain matter welled up through the hole and Vernon fell forward on to the tiles as Blake struck again. This time driving the corkscrew into the hollow at the base of his skull, ramming hard until it erupted from Vernon's throat. There was an explosion of crimson as blood spouted from both wounds and his body began to quiver uncontrollably as Blake tore the twisted weapon free once more

He stood there for a moment, gazing down at the lifeless body before him, now surrounded by a spreading pool of red liquid. Then, almost contemptuously, he tossed the corkscrew to one side, stepped over the body and headed back towards the study.

Kelly let out a strangled cry as she sat up, the last vestiges of the nightmare still clinging to her consciousness like graveyard mist.

She closed her eyes tightly for a moment, aware that her heart was thundering against her ribs. But, gradually, she slowed her breathing, aware that the dream was fading.

Blake was sleeping peacefully beside her. Apparently he had not heard her frightened outburst. She thought about waking him, telling him what she had dreamt but she thought better of it. Kelly could hear his gentle, rhythmic breathing beside her and she looked down at his still form.

The breath caught in her throat.

There was a small dark stain on the sheet.

She prodded it with her finger and found that it was still damp. Kelly noticed that whatever the substance was, it also coloured her finger. In the darkness of the bedroom it looked black but, as she sniffed it, she caught the unmistakable odour of blood.

Blake moved slightly, turning on to his side.

Kelly pulled the sheet back further and ran her gaze over his body.

On his left forearm, just above the wrist, there was a cut.

She stood in the bedroom doorway for a full five minutes, her eyes riveted to Blake's sleeping form then, certain that she had not disturbed him, she crept downstairs to the sitting room.

Kelly did not turn on the light, not even one of the table lamps. She found the phone and selected the appropriate number, waiting for the receiver to be picked up, hoping that she had remembered Dr Vernon's number correctly.

She didn't have to wait long for an answer.

'Yes.' The voice sounded harsh and she realized that it wasn't the doctor.

'Can I speak to Dr Vernon, please?' she whispered, casting a furtive glance towards the door behind her.

'Who is this?' the voice asked.

'I'm a friend of his,' she persisted. 'Could I speak to him please?'

'That isn't possible. Dr Vernon was murdered earlier tonight.'

Kelly hung up, banging the phone down with a little too much force. She wondered if Blake had heard her but the thought swiftly vanished. There was no sound of movement from upstairs. She stood alone in the dark sitting room, perspiration forming droplets on her face and forehead.

Vernon murdered.

She sat down on the edge of the sofa, her head cradled in her hands, still not fully comprehending what she had heard.

She thought of the blood on the sheet. Of her nightmare. The cut on Blake's wrist.

And of what she had read earlier in the day;

'An injury sustained in the Astral state will manifest itself on the host body.'

Kelly suddenly felt more frightened than she could ever remember.

56

Kelly brought the Mini to a halt and sat behind the wheel for a moment, scanning the area in front of Dr Vernon's house. In addition to the doctor's Audi, there was a dark brown Sierra in the driveway and, by the kerbside itself, a Granada. She could see two men seated in that particular car. One was eating a sandwich while the other, the driver, was busy cleaning his ears out with one index finger. Both men wore suits despite the warmth of the early morning sunshine.

She wound down the window a little further, allowing what little breeze there was to circulate inside the car. She was perspiring, but not all of it was due to the heat of the day.

The drive from London had taken over two hours. She'd told Blake that she wanted to pick up some more clothes from her flat. He'd seen her off like the dutiful lover he'd become, then retired to his workroom for the day. She had not mentioned anything to him about either her nightmare or the phone call to Vernon's house. She had not slept much the previous night, not after returning to bed. What was more, she'd been mildly disturbed to find that the bloodstains on the sheet had all but disappeared and, that morning, Blake's wrist appeared to be uninjured but for a minute red mark which looked like little more than a cat-scratch.

Now Kelly sat in the car staring across the road at the Granada and the house beyond it, realizing that, sooner or later she was going to be forced to make her move. Her palms felt sticky as she reached for the door handle and eased herself out of the Mini. She sucked in a deep breath then headed across the road towards the driveway.

She was a foot or two beyond the Granada when a voice called her back and she turned to see one of the men getting out, his cheeks bulging, hamster-like, with the last remnants of his sandwich.

'Excuse me, Miss,' he said, trying hurriedly to swallow what he was chewing.

Kelly turned to face him, noticing as she did that he was reaching inside his jacket. He produced a slim leather wallet and flipped it open to reveal an ID card which bore his picture. It was a bad likeness, making his thick brown hair appear ginger.

'I'm Detective-Sergeant Ross,' the man told her. 'May I ask what you're doing here?'

'Police?' she said, feigning surprise.

He nodded and succeeded in forcing down the last of his food.

'What are you doing here?'

Ross smiled thinly.

'*I* asked first, Miss,' he said.

The lie was ready on her tongue.

'I've come to see my father,' she told him.

Ross's smile faded suddenly and he almost took a step back.

'We weren't aware that Dr Vernon had any close family,' he told her.

Kelly felt her heart beating a little faster.

'Is something wrong?' she wanted to know, hoping that her little act was working.

'Could you come with me please, Miss?' the DS said and led her up the driveway towards the house. As they drew nearer, Kelly tried

254

frantically to slow her rapid breathing. She had suddenly begun to doubt the success of her little venture. The front door opened and a man dressed in a grey suit, carrying a black briefcase, emerged.

He exchanged brief words with Ross then climbed into the Sierra, reversed out of the driveway and sped off.

'You still haven't told me what's going on?' Kelly insisted, not trying to disguise the mock concern in her voice.

They were inside the house by now and Ross ushered her into a sitting room where she sat down on one of the chairs.

'I'll be back in a minute,' he told her and disappeared.

Kelly looked around the room, hands clasped on her knees. She swallowed hard and attempted to stop her body quivering. Her roving eyes scanned the shelves and tables for photos. If there was one of Vernon's daughter then she was finished. Although Ross had told her that the police were unaware he'd had a family, it did little to comfort her. She was still in the process of composing herself when Ross returned, accompanied by a taller, older man with a long face and chin which jutted forward with almost abnormal prominence. He introduced himself as Detective Inspector Allen.

'You're Dr Vernon's daughter?' he asked, eyeing her up and down.

'Yes,' she lied.

Allen looked at his companion then at Kelly. He cleared his throat self-consciously and proceeded to tell her what had happened the previous night. Kelly reacted with all the rehearsed shock and grief she could muster.

'As far as we know, nothing was stolen,' Allen continued. 'There was still money in one of the drawers upstairs and your father's wallet was in his jacket which is hanging in the hallway.'

'So why was he killed?' Kelly asked, reaching for a handkerchief which she clutched between her hands in mock despair, tugging at it most convincingly.

'We were hoping you might be able to shed some light on that,' Allen said. 'Did he have any enemies that you know of?'

Kelly shook her head.

'He kept himself to himself,' she said, lowering her eyes slightly.

'Did you know that there was someone living in the house with him?' the DI wanted to know. 'One of the guest rooms is occupied.'

255

'I didn't know that,' she said, with genuine surprise.

Allen frowned.

'How often did you see your father, Miss Vernon?'

Kelly licked her lips self-consciously. She was going to have to tread carefully.

'Not regularly. I live in London at the moment. But that's not my permanent address.'

'Alone?'

'What?'

'Do you live alone?'

She paused a second or two longer than she should have and, what was more, she was aware of that fact. Kelly realized that she was on the verge of blowing the entire facade wide open.

'You'll have to excuse me,' she said, pressing the handkerchief to her eyes. 'I can't seem to think straight. After what you've told me about my father I . . .' She allowed the sentence to trail off.

Allen nodded comfortingly.

'I realize it must be difficult,' he said, softly. 'Take your time.'

How many more questions, she wondered?

She was spared the trouble of answering by Ross who popped his head around the corner and called to his superior. Allen excused himself and left the room for a moment. Kelly let out an audible sigh of relief, grateful for the momentary respite. She heard voices in the hallway, one of which she was sure she recognised.

A moment later, Alain Joubert entered the sitting room, followed by Allen.

The Frenchman stopped in his tracks when he saw Kelly, who shot an anxious glance in the policeman's direction, thankful that he hadn't noticed her reaction. He did, however, glimpse the surprised expression of Joubert.

'Do you two know each other?' Allen asked.

'We . . .'

Kelly cut him short.

'My father introduced us about a month ago,' she said, stepping forward. 'How are you, Mr Joubert?'

The Frenchman managed to conceal his bewilderment and Kelly prayed that he wouldn't give the game away.

'I'm sorry to hear what happened,' Joubert said, flatly.

Kelly nodded.

'Were you aware that Mr Joubert had been staying at your father's house for the past two weeks?' asked the policeman.

'No,' Kelly said. 'But I knew that he was working on a new project with someone. I wasn't aware it was Mr Joubert though. My father likes to keep his work to himself.

'You claim that you've been at the Research Institute all night?' Allen said to the Frenchman.

'Yes I have,' Joubert told him. 'The night-watchman will verify that if you ask him.'

'As far as we can see, nothing of Dr Vernon's was taken, but you might like to check your own belongings,' the DI suggested.

Joubert nodded.

'It would be more convenient for all of us if you could leave the house for a day or two, sir,' Allen said. 'While the lads from forensic go over the place.'

Joubert nodded.

'I'll book into a hotel,' he said. 'I'll get some things from upstairs.' The Frenchman glanced once more at Kelly then left the room.

'How *was* my father killed?' Kelly asked.

'He was stabbed,' said Allen, hastily.

'Knifed?'

The policeman swallowed hard.

'No. He was stabbed with a corkscrew. I'm sorry.'

Kelly closed her eyes for a moment, the details of her dream suddenly flashing with neon brilliance in her mind. She felt a twinge of nausea but fought it back. Allen moved towards her as if he feared she would faint but she waved him away.

'I'm all right,' she assured him, smiling thinly.

Joubert returned a moment later carrying what looked like an overnight bag.

'There is one more thing I'd like to check on before I leave,' he said, entering the study.

Kelly and DI Allen followed him.

The Frenchman muttered something in his own tongue as he surveyed the empty table in the study.

'The files,' he said, wearily. 'They've been taken.'

'What files?' Allen demanded.

'The project that Dr Vernon and I were working on,' Joubert snapped. 'All the information was compiled in half a dozen files. They're gone.'

'What kind of information?' the policeman persisted.

'Just research notes, of no importance to anyone but us.' He cast a sly glance at Kelly.

'Are you sure they've been taken?' said Allen.

'They were here,' Joubert snapped, tapping the table top.

'Can you describe them?' asked Allen.

The Frenchman shrugged.

'Six plain manilla files, what more can I tell you?'

'Whoever took them knew what they were looking for,' Kelly interjected.

Joubert nodded and looked at her once more.

'Damn,' he said, under his breath.

'Well,' Allen told him. 'It's not much to go on but, we'll do our best to trace them.' He paused for a moment. 'I'd like the name of the hotel you're staying in, Mr Joubert, if you could phone me at the station as soon as you've booked in.' He handed the Frenchman a piece of paper with a phone number on it. 'And you, Miss Vernon, I'd appreciate an address where I can reach you.'

She gave him that of her flat in Oxford.

'I don't think we need keep you any longer,' the DI told them. 'But we'll be in touch.'

Joubert was the first to turn and head for the front door.

Kelly followed, catching up with him as he reached his car. She glanced round, making sure they were out of earshot.

'Did Lasalle know what was in those files?' she asked.

'What the hell has *he* got to do with all this?' Joubert barked. 'And you are taking a chance posing as Vernon's daughter aren't you?'

'Joubert, I have to speak to you. But not here.'

His expression softened somewhat.

'It's important,' she persisted.

'Very well. Perhaps you could recommend a hotel.' He smiled humourlessly.

'I've got my car,' she told him. 'Follow me into the town centre. We must talk. There's a lot that needs explanation.'

He regarded her impassively for a moment then nodded, climbed into his Fiat and started the engine. Kelly scuttled across the road to her own car and twisted the key in the ignition. She waited until Joubert had reversed out into the street, then she set off. He followed close behind. Kelly could see the trailing Fiat in her rear view mirror as she drove.

She wondered if finally she would learn the answers to the questions which had plagued her for so long.

57

There were only a handful of people in the bar of 'The Bull' hotel. It was not yet noon and the lunchtime drinkers had still to appear.

Kelly sat over her orange juice, waiting for Joubert to join her. When he finally sat down opposite her she noticed how dark and sunken his eyes looked, a testament to the fact that he had been working all night. He sipped his own drink and watched as Kelly did the same.

'You said you wanted to talk,' the Frenchman said. 'What had you in mind?'

'For one thing, I'd like to know what the hell you and Vernon had been up to for the past month or so,' she said, challengingly. 'Ever since the two institutes began work on Astral projection and dream interpretation it's been more like working for MI5 than a psychic research unit. What were you and Vernon working on?'

'What happened to the famous English quality of tact?' he said, smiling. 'What do you want to know?'

'If I asked all the questions that are on my mind we'd be here until this time next year. Right now I'll settle for knowing why you and Vernon were so secretive about the research findings.'

Joubert sipped his drink once more, gazing into the glass as if seeking inspiration.

'How much did you know about Vernon?' he asked.

'Personally, not a great deal. Professionally he seemed obsessed with the work on Astral projection and mind control,' Kelly said.

'He was. But with good cause, as I was. We both had reasons for wanting the findings kept quiet until a suitable time.'

'Reasons worth killing for?' she asked.

Joubert looked aghast.

'Certainly not,' he said, indignantly. 'Why do you say that?'

'The death of Lasalle didn't seem to make much of an impression on you.'

'You thought I was responsible for Lasalle's death?' he said, although it sounded more like a statement than a question.

She nodded.

'He was cracking up, close to insanity when he died,' said Joubert. 'No one could have helped him, least of all me. He was afraid of me.'

'You gave him cause to be. I noticed the hostility between you.'

'It was nothing personal. I was angry with him for revealing our findings so early. That was all.' The Frenchman lowered his voice slightly. 'Lasalle was a good friend of mine,' he said, reflectively. 'But he did a lot of damage to our research with that article he wrote. It brought too much media attention to a project which should have been fully completed before being put up for scrutiny. And, he ruined my chances of making a name for myself in our field.' He went on to recount the story he had told Vernon, about how the limelight had been snatched from him once before. 'So, perhaps you can understand *my* reasons for secrecy. That was why I was unco-operative with you. I didn't want anybody or anything to interfere with my chances of making the breakthrough. *I* wanted to be the one who was remembered for making one of parapsychology's greatest finds.'

Kelly exhaled.

'And Vernon?' she said. 'Why was he so fascinated by mind control?'

'His reasons were even more genuine than mine,' said the Frenchman.

'One of my colleagues said that he was hiding something about his wife. He . . .'

Joubert interrupted.

'Vernon's wife has been irretrievably and irreversibly insane for the past six years. When you masqueraded as his daughter this morning you took a bigger risk than you could have imagined. Vernon *has* a daughter. Admittedly, he hadn't seen her for six years and, as far as she is concerned, he had no place in her life but she exists nevertheless.'

Kelly raised her glass to her lips but she lowered it again, her full attention on Joubert as he continued.

'He had a grandson too. As he explained it to me, the child, who was less than a year old at the time, was being cared for by Mrs Vernon. She doted on the boy, worshipped him as if he were hers. Vernon himself has always been a nervous man, afraid of burglars and intruders. He and his wife owned two Dobermans. They were kept in a small compound during the day and released at night.' He sighed. 'This particular day, they escaped. The baby boy was crawling on the lawn. There was nothing Mrs Vernon could do. The dogs tore the child to pieces before her eyes.'

'Oh God,' murmured Kelly.

'She went into a state of shock and then slipped into a catatonic trance. Vernon thought that if he discovered a way to unlock the subconscious mind, he could use it to cure his wife. That was his *secret*. Nothing sinister.'

Kelly shook her head almost imperceptibly.

'If only he'd said something,' she whispered.

'He never intended the truth to be revealed,' Joubert said. 'But now it doesn't matter.'

'Who would want to kill him?' she asked, as if expecting the Frenchman to furnish her with an answer.

'The same person who would want to steal those files,' he said. 'I can't think what possible use they would be to anyone not acquainted with the paranormal. Besides, who else but Vernon and myself even knew they were at the house?' He shook his head.

'I saw Vernon murdered,' Kelly said, flatly.

Joubert looked at her aghast.

'In a dream,' she continued.

'Have you had precognitive dreams before?' he asked, somewhat excitedly.

'Never.'

261

'Did you see who killed him?'

Kelly took a long swig from her glass, wishing that it contained something stronger. She nodded.

'His name is David Blake,' she said. 'The man I'm living with.'

Joubert watched her across the table, aware that she was quivering slightly.

'Could there have been some mistake?' he asked.

She shrugged.

'I don't know what to believe any more.'

'Kelly, if it's true then you could be in a great deal of danger.'

'He doesn't know I suspect him,' she said, her voice cracking. 'Besides,' Kelly wiped a tear from her eye corner, 'I love him.' Her eyes filled with moisture which, a second later, began to spill down her cheeks. 'Oh God it can't be him. It can't.'

Joubert moved closer and curled one comforting arm around her shoulder.

'He wouldn't hurt me though, I know he wouldn't,' she murmured.

'How can you be sure?'

She had no answer.

58

London

It was late afternoon by the time Kelly drew into the driveway outside Blake's house. There was no sign of his XJS. He was either out for a while or the car was in the garage. She left her Mini where it was, locked it, then headed for the front door.

As she stepped inside the hall, the silence seemed to envelop her like an invisible blanket and she stood motionless for a moment as if reluctant to disturb the solitude. She glanced across at the cellar door.

It was open slightly.

Kelly approached it silently, listening for the noise of a clacking typewriter from below but there was none.

'David,' she called and her voice sounded hollow in the stillness.
No answer.

She walked back to the sitting room door, opened it slightly and peered in, calling his name as she did so.

Nothing.

Kelly wandered to the bottom of the staircase and looked up.

'David, are you up there?'

The silence reigned supreme.

She opened the cellar door wider and gazed down into the subterranean chamber.

Kelly began to descend.

Half way down the stairs she called his name once again, now satisfied that the house was empty. The extractor fan was on, a slight whirring sound filling the calmness. Kelly felt that all too familiar ripple of fear caress her neck and spine. The cellar looked vast, stretching out all around her, making her feel vulnerable and exposed. She moved towards his desk, her pace slowing, her jaw dropping open.

Perched on top of the typewriter were the six manilla files.

Kelly froze for a second then reached forward and picked one up, flipping it open. She recognised Lasalle's handwriting on the first page.

'Found what you're looking for?'

The voice sounded thunderous in the silence.

Kelly spun round, almost dropping the file, her eyes fixed on the figure at the top of the stairs.

Blake stood there motionless for a moment then slowly descended the steps.

His face was expressionless as he approached her, one hand extended. He motioned for her to give him the file which she did, not shifting her gaze from his eyes, trying to look through those twin dark screens which covered them.

'Why did you kill Dr Vernon?' she asked, falteringly.

'Kelly,' he said, softly. 'You shouldn't have come down here. What goes on in this room is my business.'

'You did kill him didn't you, David?' she persisted.

'Yes,' he said, unhesitatingly. 'I needed the files.'

'I've been to his house today. I've spoken to Joubert.'

Blake chuckled.

263

'Not so long ago you were convinced that Vernon and Joubert were responsible for these events,' he said.

'Tell me why you did it,' she said. 'Why you caused all those deaths.'

He didn't answer.

'Why?' she roared at him, her voice a mixture of fear and desperation.

He saw a single tear trickle from her eye corner. She wiped it away angrily.

'Ever since I can remember, even before I began writing about the paranormal, the idea of Astral projection has fascinated me,' he began, his tone measured and calm. 'Not just travelling through space on an ethereal level, but actual *physical* movement of the Astral body through time. The tangible realization of that movement which meant I could literally be in two places at once. In control of *two* centres of consciousness. I made it work. It took years to master but I learned how to do it and the more I learned, the more I realized that it was possible to manipulate the subconscious personalities of others as well. To use them.' He regarded her with no hint of emotion on his face.

'Like Toni Landers and the rest?' she said.

'I learned to control the Shadow inside them.'

'The Shadow?' Kelly said, looking vague.

'The alter-ego. What you know as the subconscious. That part of the mind which controls our darker side, that's the Shadow. I found a way to release it.'

'How?' she wanted to know. 'Is it by a form of hypnosis?'

'Yes, combined with my own ability to absorb the energy which the Shadow radiates. It's like an infra-red beacon to me. I can tap into it. Feed on it. It increases my own power. Everyone, no matter who they are, has this darker side to their nature. Most people are able to control it, and it's kept in check by their code of morals or by the law. But when the force is released, they act out thoughts and desires which had previously been hidden.'

Kelly shook her head.

'Why did you do it, David?' she asked, tears brimming in her eyes once again. 'What did you hope to achieve by having Toni Landers kill that baby, or Roger Carr murder that girl. Or Braddock or O'Neil.

Why did they have to kill?'

'I had to be sure of my own abilities. Now I am,' he said, impassively. 'The seance gave me a perfect opportunity to use that power, to prove once and for all that I could influence other people's alter-egos. Use them. Can't you appreciate what this means?' His voice had taken on a note of excitement. 'Politicians could be manipulated. Leaders of the Church, Heads of State.'

'You're mad,' she said, taking a step back.

'No, Kelly, I'm not mad,' he said. 'This power is too great to be wasted. Think about it. There need be no more wars, no more civil unrest, because those who provoke such incidents could be found and destroyed before they were able to create trouble. Any trace of evil inside their minds would be visible to someone like me who knew how to use the power of the Shadow.'

'And if you did discover some evil inside them?'

'I told you, they would be destroyed. Executed. This knowledge gives me the power of life and death over anyone I choose. It's a weapon too.'

'For selling?' she asked, cryptically.

'If necessary,' he told her. 'There's no weapons system on earth to match it.'

'But why use it to kill?'

'Every discovery has its sacrifices,' he said, smiling. 'You should know that.'

'No one will believe it.'

Blake smiled and crossed to his desk. He pulled open one of the drawers and took out a letter. Kelly watched him, warily.

'If you'd searched my office more thoroughly,' he said. 'You'd have found this.' He unfolded the letter. 'It arrived two days ago, from Thames TV. I've been invited onto a discussion programme. Myself and two other "experts" are supposed to discuss whether or not the supernatural is real or imaginary. Nice of them to include me don't you think?'

'What are you going to do?'

His smile faded.

'I'm going to prove, once and for all, exactly how powerful the Shadow is,' Blake told her.

Kelly took another step back.

'I loved you, David,' she said, softly, tears rolling down her cheeks.

'Then stay with me,' he said, moving towards her.

'You're a murderer. I saw you kill Vernon.'

'Ah, your dream,' he said, that chilling grin returning. 'I had already been probing your mind for a week or two prior to that little incident. Can't you see, Kelly, you and I are one. We belong together. You can share this power with me. Learn how to use it.'

'Learn how to kill, you mean?' she said, vehemently.

'All right then, leave. Go to the police. Tell them I killed Dr Vernon but who the hell is going to believe you? How could I have killed him?' he added, mockingly. 'I was in bed with you last night.'

She swallowed hard, realizing he was right.

'Go. Get out,' Blake roared. 'I offered you the chance and you refused. Leave here.'

He watched as she turned and hurriedly climbed the stairs, disappearing into the hall. A moment later he heard the front door slam behind her. His expression darkened as he gripped the file. He clutched it a second longer then, with a grunt, hurled it across the room.

Kelly knew Blake was right.

As she started the engine of the Mini she realized she would never convince the police of his guilt. She was helpless, something which made her feel angry as well as afraid.

She guided the car out into traffic, wiping more tears away with the back of her hand. Combined with that feeling of helplessness was also one of loss, for somewhere inside her, despite what she knew, she retained her affection for Blake. Kelly felt as if the world were collapsing around her.

She knew that she must tell Joubert what she had learned. There was a phone box on the corner of the street. Kelly slowed down and prepared to swing the car over. She checked her rear view mirror.

She could not supress a scream.

Reflected in the mirror, glaring at her from the back seat, was the face of Blake.

Kelly twisted the wheel, her eyes riveted to the visage in the mirror.

All she heard was the loud blast of the air horns as the lorry thundered towards her.

It was enough to shake her from her terror and now she looked through the windscreen to see the huge Scania bearing down on her. The driver was waving madly for her to get out of his way.

She pushed her foot down on the accelerator and the Mini shot forward, swerving violently, missing the nearest huge wheel by inches. Kelly yelped as the car hit the kerb with a bone jarring bump before skidding across the pavement and coming to rest against the hedge of the garden opposite.

A car behind her also came to a grinding halt and the lorry pulled up a few yards further on, the driver leaping from the cab.

Kelly shook herself and twisted in her seat.

The back seat was empty.

There was no sign of Blake.

She felt sick, the realization of what had just happened slowly dawning on her. She heard footsteps approaching the car then her door was wrenched open.

The lorry driver stood there, his face flushed.

'Are you all right?' he asked, anxiously.

She nodded.

'What the hell were you doing? You pulled straight in front of me. I could have killed you.'

Kelly closed her eyes tightly for a moment.

'I'm sorry,' she whispered.

The driver of the other car had arrived by now and he reached in to undo Kelly's seatbelt. The two men helped her from the car, standing beside her as she sucked in deep lungfuls of air.

'I'll phone for an ambulance,' said the truck driver.

'No.' Kelly caught his arm. 'I'll be OK. I wasn't hurt.'

'You look pretty shaken up,' he told her.

'Please. No ambulance.'

She wasn't sure what had disturbed her the most. Nearly being hit by the lorry or the sight of Blake's leering face.

'I'm fine, really,' she assured them both.

Other vehicles slowed down as they drove by, glancing at the road-side tableau.

Kelly eventually clambered back into the Mini and strapped herself in. The two men watched as she guided her car off the pavement back on to the road.

'Thanks for your help,' she said and drove off, leaving the two men shaking their heads as she disappeared into traffic.

After another mile or so and Kelly came to a second phone box. Glancing somewhat nervously into her rear-view mirror she signalled then pulled in, clambering out of the car and reaching the box moments before two young girls, who began muttering to each other and pacing up and down outside.

Kelly fumbled for some change and dialled the number of Joubert's hotel. She tapped agitatedly on one glass panel of the phone box as she waited to be connected. Finally she heard the Frenchman's voice.

Scarcely had he identified himself than she began babbling her story to him. About Blake. About Vernon's death. The murders committed by Toni Landers and the others. Blake's TV appearance.

The power of the Shadow.

The Frenchman listened in stunned silence, only his low breathing signalling his presence on the other end of the line.

The rapid pips sounded and she pushed in another coin.

'Kelly, you must get away from there,' Joubert said, finally.

'I can't leave now,' she told him.

'For God's sake, he could kill you too.'

'He must be stopped.'

'But Kelly . . .'

She hung up, paused a moment then walked back to her car. As she opened her hand she glanced at the bunch of keys resting on her palm.

One of them unlocked the front door of Blake's house.

The thought hit her like a thunderbolt. She scrambled behind the steering wheel and started the engine.

It was 5.56 p.m.

She had time but it was running out fast.

PART THREE

'We'll know for the first time,
If we're evil or divine . . .'
— *Ronnie James Dio*

'The evil that men do lives after them . . .'
— *Julius Caesar, Act III, Scene II*

59

At 6.35 David Blake walked from his house, climbed into the waiting XJS and started the engine. Despite the relative warmth of the evening, the sky was a patchwork of mottled grey and blue. Away to the north clouds were gathering in unyielding dark formations and Blake wondered how long it would be before the impending storm arrived. As if to reinforce his supicions, a distant rumble of thunder rolled across the sky.

He guided the Jag out into the street and swung it right.

He didn't see Kelly.

She had been standing about twenty yards further down the street for almost an hour, watching and waiting, the key to Blake's front door clutched in her hand.

Now she watched as the XJS pulled away, disappearing around the corner.

As if fearing that he might return, she paused for another five minutes then began walking briskly towards the house, not hesitating as she made her way up the path, attempting to hide the anxiousness in her stride. She reached the front door and pushed in the key.

'He's just gone out.'

She gasped aloud as she heard the voice, turning to discover its source.

Kelly saw the middle-aged man who lived next door to Blake. He was struggling to hold his Alsatian under control, the large dog pulling on its leash as if threatening to tug the man off his feet. He stood there, watching as Kelly turned the key in the lock.

'I don't know where he's gone,' the man persisted.

She smiled as politely as she could manage.

'It's all right, I'll wait,' she told him and stepped inside.

Through the bevelled glass of the front door, Kelly could see the distorted image of the man next door. He appeared to be standing staring at the house but, after a moment or two, he moved on. She sighed and moved quickly across the hall to the staircase, scuttling up the steps towards Blake's bedroom.

She paused outside the door, aware of a slight chill in the air but she ignored it and walked in. The silence swallowed her up and she was aware only of the sound of her own heart beating.

Kelly moved around the bed to the cabinet, her eyes fixed on the ornate gold key in the lock of the bottom drawer. She dropped to her knees and turned it.

It was almost seven o'clock by the time she left the house. As she clambered into the Mini she guessed that the drive across London would take her forty-five minutes if she was lucky. She prayed that the traffic wouldn't be too heavy. Her heart was still thumping hard against her ribs and she took a tissue from her handbag to wipe the moisture from the palms of her hands.

As she dropped the bag on to the passenger seat she noticed how heavy it was.

The .357 Magnum nestled safely inside.

Blake turned up the volume on the casette and drummed on the steering wheel as he waited for the lights to turn green. Traffic in the centre of London was beginning to clog the roads but the writer seemed unperturbed by the temporary hold-up. The show he was due to appear on was going out live but he looked at his watch and realized he'd make it in time. He smiled as he saw the traffic lights change colour.

Another fifteen minutes and he would be at the studio.

Another ominous rumble of thunder shook the heavens. The storm was getting closer.

Kelly looked first as the dashboard clock and then at her own watch. She drove as fast as she was able in the streams of traffic, slowing down slightly when she saw a police car cruise past in the lane next to her. Almost without thinking, she reached over and secured the clasp on her handbag, ensuring that the revolver didn't fall out. Kelly could feel the perspiration on her back and forehead, clinging to her like dew to the grass.

She guessed that Blake must have reached his destination by now.

Another glance at her watch and she estimated it would be over ten minutes before she caught up with him.

The first spots of rain began to spatter her windscreen.

60

By the time Kelly reached the Thames Television studios in Euston Road the rain was falling in torrents. Large droplets of it bounced off the car and she squinted to see through the drenched windscreen. Her wipers seemed quite inadequate for the task of sweeping away the water which poured down the glass.

She found a parking space then jumped out of the car, picking up her handbag. She sprinted towards the main entrance, slowing her pace as she saw a uniformed doorman barring the way. A thought crossed her mind.

What if he wanted to search her bag?

She held it close to her and looked at him warily but his only gesture was to smile happily at her. Kelly smiled back, as much in relief as anything else. The man opened the door for her and she walked inside the vast entry-way.

'Could you tell me which studio David Blake is in?' she asked.

'Who?' he said.

'David Blake,' she repeated. 'He's a writer. He's taking part in a discussion programme tonight at eight. I hope I'm not too late.'

'Oh yes, that's Studio One, they started about ten minutes ago. It's that way.' He hooked a thumb in the general direction.

Kelly walked past him.

'Just a minute, Miss,' he called.

She froze.

'Have you got a ticket?' he wanted to know.

She opened her mouth to speak but he continued.

'There's a few seats left. If you see that young lady behind the desk, I'm sure she'll be able to help you.' He smiled and indicated a woman who was sitting beneath a large framed photo of a well-known comedian.

Kelly asked for a ticket.

'I'm afraid that the programme in Studio One is being transmitted live,' said the other woman, apologetically. 'It's not normal policy to allow members of the audience in while the show is on.'

'Damn, my editor will kill me,' said Kelly, with mock exasperation. 'I'm supposed to cover this show for the paper, talk to the guests afterwards. We're doing a feature on one of them this week.'

'Do you have your press card with you?' asked the receptionist.

'No, I don't, I was in such a rush to get here I . . .' She shrugged, wondering if the ruse would work.

The woman ran an appraising eye over her.

'Which paper?' she asked.

'*The Standard*,' Kelly lied. 'It is very important.' She played her trump card. 'You can call my editor if you like.'

The woman thought for a moment then shook her head.

'No, that won't be necessary. I think we can get you in.' She called the doorman over. 'George, can you show this lady into Studio One. But they are on the air at the moment.'

The doorman nodded, smiled politely at Kelly and asked her to follow him. She swallowed hard, trying to control her breathing as they made their way up a long corridor. The walls on either side bore framed photographs of celebrities past and present. Kelly felt as if she were being watched, scrutinised by each pair of monochrome eyes, all of whom knew her secret. The .357 suddenly felt gigantic inside her handbag and she hugged it closer to her, watching as the doorman paused beneath a red light and a sign which proclaimed: STUDIO ONE. He opened the door a fraction and peered inside.

'Keep as quiet as you can,' he whispered and led Kelly into the studio.

Apart from the area which made up the studio floor, the entire cavernous room was in darkness. Kelly saw rows and rows of people before her, their attention directed towards the four men who sat in front of them.

She caught sight of Blake.

The doorman ushered her towards an empty seat near the back of the studio where she settled herself, mouthing a silent 'Thank you' to him as he slipped away. A man seated in front of her turned and looked at her briefly before returning his attention to the discussion being conducted by the four men.

Kelly glanced around the studio.

Cameras moved silently back and forth. She saw a man with head-phones hunched close to the interviewer, a clip-board clutched in his hand. He was counting off seconds with his fingers, motioning a camera forward as one of the four men seated amidst the modest set spoke.

Blake was seated between the interviewer and an elderly priest who was having trouble with a long strand of grey hair which kept falling over his forehead. He brushed it back each time he spoke but, within seconds, the gossamer tentacle had crept back to its original position.

Arc lights burned brightly, pinpointing the men in their powerful beams while sausage-shaped booms were lowered carefully by the sound engineers, all of whom were intent on staying out of camera shot. The sound was coming through loud and clear but Kelly seemed not to hear it. Her gaze was riveted to Blake who was in the process of pouring himself some water from the jug on top of the smoked-glass table before him. He smiled cordially at a remark made by the old priest and sipped his drink.

Kelly watched him, unable to take her eyes from the writer's slim frame. She heard his name spoken then his voice filled the studio.

'In the course of my work I've come across all manner of religions, each one as valid as the next,' he said.

'But you mentioned voodoo earlier,' the old priest reminded him. 'Surely you can't class that as a religion?'

'It's the worship of a God or a set of Gods. As far as I'm concerned that makes it a religion.'

'Then you could say the same about witchcraft?' the priest countered.

'Why not?' Blake said. 'The deities worshipped by witches were thought to be powerful in their own right. A God doesn't have to be benevolent to be worshipped.'

'Do you have any religious beliefs yourself, Mr Blake?' asked the interviewer.

'Not in God and the Devil as we know them, no,' the writer told him.

Kelly sat motionless, watching him, her eyes filling with tears once more. She touched the Magnum inside her handbag but, somewhere deep inside her, she knew that she could not use the weapon. What she should be feeling for Blake was hatred but, in fact, she felt feelings of love as strong for him now as she had ever known. Could this man really be evil? This man she felt so much for?

'What do you believe in then?' the interviewer asked Blake.

'I believe that there is a force which controls everyone's lives but I don't believe that it comes from a God of any description,' the writer said. 'It comes from here.' He prodded his own chest.

'Don't you, in fact, use this theory in your forthcoming book?' the interviewer said. 'This idea of each of us having two distinct sides to our nature. One good, one evil.'

'That's hardly an original concept,' said the psychiatrist, haughtily. 'Surely every religion in the world, in history, has revolved around the struggle between good and evil.'

'I agree,' said Blake. 'But never before has it been possible to isolate the evil side of man and make it a tangible force independent from the rest of the mind.'

Kelly shuddered, her mind suddenly clearing as if a veil had been drawn from it.

She slid one hand inside her handbag, her fist closing around the butt of the .357. She slowly eased back the hammer, glancing around furtively to see if anyone else had noticed the metallic click.

There was a man standing directly behind her.

He wore a short sleeved white shirt and dark trousers and, Kelly caught a quick glimpse of the badge pinned to his chest: SECURITY.

She took her hand off the Magnum and hurriedly turned to face the studio floor once again, her heart beating madly against her ribs. She glanced at Blake.

A camera was moving closer towards him.

She realized the time had come.

'What exactly are you suggesting?' the interviewer asked, smiling.

Blake looked into the camera.

'Everyone can be *made* to commit acts normally abhorrent to them,' he said.

The camera zoomed in on him.

Kelly allowed her hand to slip back inside the handbag, and, once more, she gripped the revolver. She could hear the low breathing of the security guard behind her but she realized that she had no choice.

She began to ease the gun slowly from its place of concealment.

Behind her, the security man moved and Kelly swallowed hard as she heard his footsteps gradually receding. The next time she saw him he was a good fifty feet away, to the left of the studio's set. Kelly watched him for a moment longer then turned her attention back to Blake.

He was staring into the camera, motionless in his chair.

The other three men looked at him in bewilderment and, after a minute or so of silence, some impatient mutterings began to ripple through the audience but Blake merely sat as he was, his eyes fixed on the camera as if it were a snake about to strike him.

The cameraman was not the only one in the studio to feel as if iced water had been pumped through his veins. He shivered.

Kelly too felt that freezing hand grip her tightly but the tears which ran down her cheeks were warm.

She could not take her eyes from Blake and now the cold seemed to be intensifying, growing within her until it was almost unbearable.

She slid the Magnum from her handbag and stood up, holding the gun at arm's length, fixing Blake hurriedly in the sights.

The man in front of her turned and opened his mouth to shout a warning.

From the studio floor, the security guard spotted her.

He raced towards her, his eyes fixed on the gleaming Magnum.

The noise was thunderous.

As Kelly squeezed the trigger, the .357 roared loudly. The savage recoil nearly knocked her over and she winced as the butt smashed against the heel of her hand. The Magnum bucked violently in her grip as it spat out the heavy grain bullet. The barrel flamed brilliant white for precious seconds and, in that blinding illumination, members of the audience dived for cover, most of them unaware of what had made the deafening blast.

The bullet hit the floor and drilled a hole the size of a fifty pence piece in the hard surface.

Kelly fired again.

The second shot shattered the smoked glass table in front of Blake who turned and looked up into the audience, the muzzle flash catching his eye. Shards of glass sprayed in all directions and the old priest yelped in pain as one laid open his cheek. He felt himself being pulled to one side by the psychiatrist.

Blake rose, his arms outstretched.

The writer presented a much bigger target and, this time, Kelly didn't miss.

Moving at a speed of over 1,430 feet a second, the heavy grain slug hit him squarely in the chest. It shattered his sternum and tore through his lung before erupting from his back, blasting an exit hole the size of a fist. Lumps of grey and red viscera splattered the flimsy set behind him and Blake was lifted off his feet by the impact. He crashed to the floor and rolled over once, trying to drag himself away, but Kelly fired once more.

The next bullet hit him in the side, splintering his pelvis, decimating the liver as it ripped through him.

He clapped one hand to the gaping wound as if trying to hold the blood in. His chest felt as if it were on fire and, when he coughed, blood spilled over his lips and ran down his chin, mingling with that which was already forming a pool around him.

Nevertheless, fighting back the waves of agony which tore through him, he managed to claw his way across the set and he was on his knees when the third bullet hit him. It smashed his left shoulder and spun him round, fragments of bone spraying from the exit wound, propelled by the eruption of blood which accompanied the blast.

He sagged forward across the chair, hardly feeling any pain as another round practically took his head off. It caught him at the base of the throat, the massive force throwing him onto his back where he lay motionless, a crimson fountain spurting from the large hole.

Kelly stood at the back of the studio, the gun hot in her hand, her palms stinging from the constant recoil. The smell of cordite stung her nostrils but she seemed not to notice it and, as the security man approached her, one eye on that yawning barrel, she merely dropped the Magnum and looked blankly at him.

He slowed his pace as he drew closer and she saw his lips moving as he spoke but she heard nothing. Only gradually did the sounds begin to filter back into her consciousness.

The screams. The shouts.

She shook her head then looked in bewilderment at the security man, her eyes wide and uncomprehending. She looked down at the gun which lay at her feet then back at the set.

Kelly saw two or three people gathered around a body and it took her a moment or two to realize it was the body of Blake.

She saw the blood. Smelled the cordite. Her ears were still ringing from the explosive sound of the gunshots.

First aid men scurried on to the set to tend to Blake but she saw one of them shake his head as he felt for a pulse and heartbeat. Another man removed his jacket and laid it over Blake's face.

She realized that David Blake was dead.

The security guard took her by the arm and she looked at him, her eyes wide and questing. She shook her head, glancing down once more at the gun.

In that instant, as she was being led away, Kelly felt as if her entire body had been wrapped in freezing rags.

61

The room inside Albany Street police station was small. Despite the dearth of furniture it still appeared minuscule. Less than twelve feet square, it contained two chairs, one on each side of a wooden table.

A cracked wash-basin was jammed into one corner near the door and there was a plastic bucket beneath it to catch the drips which dribbled through the chipped porcelain. The room smelt of perspiration and cigarette smoke, but the windows remained firmly closed. Powerful banks of fluorescents, quite disproportionately bright for the size of the room, blazed in the ceiling.

Inspector Malcolm Barton lit up another cigarette and tossed the empty packet onto the table in front of Kelly.

'How well did you know David Blake?' he asked.

'I've already told you,' Kelly protested.

'So tell me again.'

'We were lovers. I was living at his house. I had been for about a fortnight.'

'Then why did you kill him?'

'I've told you that too.'

Barton blew out a stream of smoke and shook his head.

'You can do better than that, Miss Hunt,' he said. 'First you told me you intended to kill Blake then you said you didn't remember pulling the trigger. Now, I'm just a thick copper. I like things plain and simple. Tell me why you shot him.'

Kelly cradled her head in her hands and tried to keep her voice calm. She had been at the police station for over an hour, taken directly there from the Euston Road studios.

'He was dangerous,' she said.

'He never seemed like a nut-case to me the odd times I saw him on the box. What gave you this special insight?' The policeman's voice was heavy with scorn.

'He told me about his powers,' said Kelly, wearily.

'Of course, his *powers*. I'd forgotten about them.'

'If you won't believe me then at least let someone else back up what I've told you. Blake had the ability to control people's minds, to make them act out their worst desires. That was his power.'

'And you know of someone who'll verify that do you?' Barton chided. 'I'd be interested to meet him.'

'Then let me make a bloody phone call,' Kelly snapped. 'Like you should have done when you first brought me here.'

Barton pointed an accusatory finger at her.

'Don't start giving me orders, Miss Hunt, you're not in a bargaining position,' he hissed. 'Jesus Christ you were seen by dozens of people. You told me yourself that you had to kill Blake.'

'Have I ever denied I shot him?' she said, challengingly.

'You said you didn't remember pulling the trigger.'

'I didn't. I wasn't even sure what had happened until I saw him lying there.'

There was a moment's silence then Barton crossed to the glass panelled door behind him.

'Tony, bring the phone in here will you,' he called, then turned back to face Kelly. 'All right, you make your phone call.'

A tall, slim man in a sergeant's uniform entered the room carrying a trimphone which he plugged into a socket in the wall near Kelly. He hesitated a moment then walked out.

'Go on,' urged the Inspector, nodding towards the phone.

Kelly picked up the receiver and dialled the number of the hotel where Joubert was staying. She wiped perspiration from her face with her free hand, looking up occasionally at Barton who was rummaging through his pockets in search of another packet of cigarettes. He found one and lit up.

On the other end of the line, Kelly heard the sound of Joubert's voice.

'Blake made the broadcast,' she told him. 'I couldn't stop him in time.'

He asked where she was.

'I killed Blake. The police are holding me here now. Please Joubert, you must come to London. It might already be too late.' She gave him instructions on how to reach the police station then hung up.

'Too late for what?' Barton wanted to know.

'Everyone who watched that programme,' she said.

'He might have been bluffing,' said Barton, disinterestedly.

'I wish to God he had been,' Kelly said, quietly.

There was a knock on the door and the tall, slim sergeant entered, carrying a piece of paper. He passed it to Barton. The Inspector read it, glancing occasionally at Kelly as he did so. He sucked hard on his cigarette.

'What do you make of it, guv?' said the sergeant.

'When did these reports come in?' Barton wanted to know.

281

'These were the first three, they came in less than an hour ago.'
Barton looked puzzled.

'What do you mean, the first three?' he asked.

'We've had five more reports since,' the sergeant told him.

'I suppose you'd take this as proof of your little story would you, Miss Hunt?' the Inspector said, tapping the piece of paper.

'What is it?' she asked.

'At 8.07 a pet shop owner in Kilburn slaughtered every single animal in his shop with a knife. One of our constables found him in the street outside the shop. He'd just gutted a couple of kittens. At 8.16 a woman in Bermondsey held her eight-week-old child against the bars of an electric fire until it died. At 8.29 a man in Hammersmith killed his wife and daughter with a chisel.'

Kelly closed her eyes.

'Oh God,' she murmured.

'Go on then, tell me it was your friend Blake who caused these killings.'

'It doesn't matter any more,' said Kelly, wearily. 'It's already begun and there's no way to stop it.'

This time Barton did not add a sarcastic remark.

He felt inexplicably afraid as he lit up another cigarette.

And he wondered if he was the only one who felt the peculiar chill in the room.

62

Manchester

8.36 p.m.

The scissors fell to the carpet with a dull ring as Laura Foster knocked them off the arm of the chair. She reached down and retrieved them, replacing them next to her. Her husband, Paul, got to his feet as she handed him the trousers she'd finished turning up. He pulled them on and strutted around the sitting room happily.

'They're OK aren't they?' he asked.

'They are now,' Laura told him. 'You'd have worn them without me turning them up. They looked like concertinas on your shoes.'

Paul slipped them off again and walked across to her chair, bending down to kiss her. She giggled as he slipped one hand inside her blouse and squeezed her unfettered breasts.

'Shall I bother putting my others back on?' he asked.

Laura chuckled again, pointing out how comical he looked in just his socks and underpants.

He moved closer, kissing her fiercely and she responded with equal fervour, one hand straying to the growing bulge in his pants. She slipped her hand beneath his testicles and fondled them, feeling his erection throbbing against her fingers.

Paul closed his eyes as she pulled his pants down, freeing his stiff organ.

The next thing he felt was an unbearable coldness as the scissor blades brushed his testicles. His eyes jerked open and, for interminable seconds he found himself gaping at Laura. Her own eyes were glazed, almost unseeing. Her face was expressionless.

The blades snapped together.

Laura sat impassively as he dropped to his knees, hands clutching his scrotum. Blood sprayed from the neatly severed veins and Paul found that his agony was mixed with nausea as he saw one egg-shaped purple object glistening on the carpet before him.

As he fell backward he heard laughter and, just before he blacked out, he realized that it was coming from the television.

Liverpool

8.52.

The child was small and it had been common sense to keep him in plain view at all times since his premature birth two weeks earlier. Now he gurgled happily in his carry-cot, his large brown eyes open and staring at the multi-coloured TV screen nearby.

Terry Pearson looked down at the child and smiled.

'Is he all right, love?' asked his wife, Denise, who was glancing through the paper to see what other delights the networks were offering for the remainder of the evening. She and Terry had been watching the screen since six that evening. Though Denise doubted if there'd be anything else to match the excitement of what had happened on the chat show they'd been watching.

'I suppose there'll be something on *News at Ten* about that fella getting shot,' she said, putting down the paper and crossing to the carry-cot.

Terry nodded, not taking his eyes from his son. Denise also gazed down at the baby, both of them mesmerised by it.

It looked so helpless. So tiny.

Terry reached into the cot and, with contemptuous ease, fastened the fingers of one powerful hand around the baby's neck, squeezing tighter until the child's face began to turn the colour of dark grapes. He held it before him for a moment longer, watched by Denise, then, with a grunt, he hurled the child across the room as if it had been a rag doll.

The baby hit the mirror which hung on the far wall, the impact bringing down the glass which promptly shattered, spraying the carpet with needle-sharp shards of crystal.

Terry crossed the room and prodded the tiny body. There was blood on the wall and a sickly grey substance on the carpet.

He reached for a particularly long piece of mirror, ignoring the pain in his hand as it cut into his palm. Blood dribbled down his arm, the flow increasing as he put his weight behind the rapier-like implement.

Denise chuckled as she watched her husband tear her child's flesh and raise it to his lips.

Then she held the tiny body still as Terry set about hacking the other leg off.

Norwich

9.03.

The book fell from her grasp and she awoke with a start, picking the paperback up, muttering to herself when she saw that she'd lost her page. Maureen Horton found her place and folded down the corner of the page, checking that Arthur wasn't looking. He hated to see books being mistreated and, as far as he was concerned, folding down the corner of a page was a particularly heinous crime. He'd reminded her time and again what bookmarks were for. Well, she didn't care. This was one of *her* books. A good old romance. Not that pompous Jeffrey Archer stuff that Arthur always had his nose in.

Arthur.

She looked across to his chair but he was gone.

Probably out making a cup of tea, she reasoned. He'd left the TV on as usual. She was always nagging him about wasting electricity. What was the point of having the television on if they were both reading she insisted? Arthur always tried to tell her he preferred what he called 'background sound'.

She smiled to herself and leant forward to turn up the volume. The news had just started.

She heard a slight whoosh then felt a numbing impact across the back of her head as her husband struck her with the petrol can.

Arthur Horton grabbed his semi-conscious wife by the hair and dragged her back into her seat.

She lay there, twitching slightly, watching him through pain-racked eyes. Maureen could feel something warm and wet running down her back, pouring freely from the cut on her skull.

He moved to one side of her and she heard the noisy squeaking of the cap as he unscrewed it. Arthur gazed down at her with glassy eyes, the aroma of petrol stinging his nostrils. He upended the can, emptying the golden fluid all over his wife and the chair, watching as she tried to move. Maureen opened her mouth to scream but some of the petrol gushed down her throat and she gagged violently.

He struck the match and dropped it on her.

Maureen Horton disappeared beneath a searing ball of flame which hungrily devoured her skin, hair and clothes. She tried to rise but, within seconds, the searing agony had caused her to black out. Her skin rose in blisters which burst, only to be replaced by fresh sores. Her skin seemed to be bubbling as the flames stripped it away, leaving only calcified bone.

Arthur Horton stood motionless as his wife burned to death, the leaping flames reflected in his blank eyes.

63

London

Kelly coughed as Inspector Barton stubbed out his half-smoked cigarette, the plume of grey smoke rising into the air. The entire room seemed to be full of fumes, so much so that she felt as if she were looking at the policeman through a fine gauze.

'Is there anything in this statement you want to amend?' he said, tapping the piece of paper before him with the end of his pen.

'What's the point?' she wanted to know.

'The point *is*, that you're looking at a twenty year stretch for murder, that's what the point is.'

'Perhaps I should plead insanity,' she said, cryptically.

'Looking at some of the things that are in this statement you'd probably get away with it too,' snorted Barton.

'Why can't you understand?' Kelly rasped. 'Blake had the ability to reach people on a massive scale. For him, this TV show provided the ultimate opportunity to display his ability to control the minds of those watching, to summon their evil sides. From the amount of reports you've been getting, it looks as if he succeeded.'

'It's coincidence,' said Barton, although he sounded none too convinced.

'No, Inspector,' Kelly sighed. 'It isn't coincidence and, so far, the reports have been restricted to a small area of London. That show was networked, nationwide.'

'So you're telling me there are people carving each other up from one end of Britain to the other?'

'Anyone who saw that programme is at risk,' Kelly said.

'That's bollocks,' snapped Barton, getting to his feet. He left the statement lying on the table in front of her. 'You read that over again,

I'll be back in a while, perhaps you'll have some more convincing answers for me then.' He closed the door behind him. Kelly heard the key turn in the lock.

She slumped back in her chair, eyes closed. Where the hell was Joubert? It had been over an hour since she'd phoned him. She opened her eyes and looked down at her hands. The hands which had held the gun. Kelly found that she was quivering.

She remembered reaching into her handbag for the pistol but, after that, her mind was a blank. Nothing remaining with any clarity until the point when she was grabbed by the security guard. She wondered if Toni Landers, Roger Carr, Gerald Braddock and Jim O'Neil had felt the same way after committing *their* crimes.

She glanced at her statement, aware of how ridiculous the whole affair must appear to someone like Barton.

Alone in that small room she felt a crushing sense of desolation.

Blake had released a wave of insanity which was now unstoppable.

64

Glasgow

9.23 p.m.

The shrill whistling of the kettle sounded like a siren inside the small flat.

Young Gordon Mackay got slowly to his feet and wandered through from the sitting room, glancing back at the television as he did so.

'Turn it off, Gordon,' shouted his younger sister, Claire. 'It'll wake the baby up.'

He nodded wearily and switched off the screaming kettle.

'Why couldn't you do it?' he asked Claire who was sitting at the kitchen table with three or four books spread out in front of her.

'Because I'm doing my homework,' she told him. 'Anyway, all you've been doing all night is sitting in front of the television.'

'Fuck you,' grunted Gordon, pouring hot water on to the tea bag in his mug. He stirred it around then scooped the bag out and dropped it into the waste-disposal unit of the sink. As he flicked it on it rumbled into life, the vicious blades churning noisily as they swallowed the solitary tea-bag. That was one of the perks of baby-sitting, Gordon thought. Normally his mother wouldn't let him near this lethal device but, when she and his father left him to mind the other three kids, it was like a new toy to him. He took some withered flowers from a vase on the window sill and watched as they were gobbled up by the hungry mouth of the machine.

'Mum said you weren't to use that,' Claire bleated.

Gordon ignored her, feeding more refuse into the gaping hole.

Claire got to her feet and crossed to the sink.

'Turn it off, Gordon,' she said, angrily.

He ignored her.

Claire reached across him for the button which controlled the machine.

Gordon grabbed her arm tightly.

'Let go,' she shouted, striking him with her free hand, trying to pull away.

As he turned to look at her, his eyes were glazed, as if he didn't see her at all. Claire was suddenly afraid.

With a strength that belied his size, Gordon wrenched her towards the sink, guiding her hand towards the churning blades of the waste-disposal unit.

Claire began to scream as her finger tips actually brushed the cold steel of the sink bottom. She clenched her hand into a fist but it only served to prolong the moment for precious seconds.

Gordon thrust her hand into the machine, forcing her arm in as far as the wrist.

Blood spurted up from the razor sharp blades, spewing up crimson fountains as the limb was first lacerated then crushed. He heard the noise of splintering bone as her arm was dragged deeper into the yawning hole, the skin being ripped away as far as the elbow. The stainless steel sink flooded with thick red fluid and, as Claire's shrieks of agony grew shrill, the noise of the machine seemed to be deafening. Her hand was torn off and she fell back, blood spurting from the

288

shredded stump that was her arm. Gordon looked down at her, at the pulped flesh and muscle and the spreading puddle of crimson which formed around the mutilated appendage.

He didn't realize that bone was so white. It gleamed amidst the crimson mess, fragments of it floating on the red puddle.

The sound of the waste-disposal unit filled his ears.

Southampton

9.46.

The garage door opened with a distressing creak and Doug Jenkins peered from beneath the bonnet of his car to see who had come in. He saw the door close and the sound of footsteps echoed throughout the garage as Bruce Murray approached the old Ford Anglia.

'Sorry, Doug,' Murray said. 'That all night spares place doesn't carry the parts for a car as old as this. I rang them before I came over.'

Jenkins cursed under his breath.

'Why the hell don't you buy a new car?' Murray wanted to know. 'This one's twenty years old at least.'

'I've had this since I was eighteen,' Jenkins protested. 'I've got a soft spot for it.'

'The best spot for it would be the bloody junk yard,' Murray chuckled as he stepped forward to inspect the engine. 'Have you been working on it all night?'

'No, only for the past hour or so, I've been watching TV.'

Jenkins stepped back, wiping his hands on an oil-covered rag. He shuddered, despite the warmth inside the garage.

'Pass me that wrench will you, Doug?' said Murray, holding out a hand.

His companion selected one from the dozens which hung on the wall and passed it to Murray. The wall was like something from a hardware store. Hammers, spanners, saws, wrenches, hatchets and even a small chainsaw were hung neatly from nails, all of them in the correct order. Doug Jenkins was nothing if not methodical. He rubbed his eyes with a dirty hand, leaving a dark smudge on his face. The cold seemed to be intensifying.

'I heard there was some trouble on TV earlier,' said Murray, his back to his friend. 'Somebody got shot in full view of the camera or something. Did you see it?'

Silence.

'Doug, I said did you see it?' he repeated.

Murray straightened up and turned to face his companion.

'Are you going deaf, I . . .'

The sentence trailed away as Murray's jaw dropped open, his eyes bulging wide in terror. A sound like a revving motorbike filled the garage.

'Oh Jesus,' Murray gasped.

Jenkins advanced on him with the chainsaw, holding the lethal blade at arm's length, its wicked barbs rotating at a speed of over 2,000 rpm.

'What are you doing?' shrieked Murray, gazing first at his friend's blank eyes and then at the murderous implement levelled at him.

Jenkins drove it forward.

Murray tried to knock the blade to one side with the wrench but fear affected his aim. The chainsaw sliced effortlessly through his arm just below the elbow. He shrieked as blood spouted from the stump and he held it up, showering both himself and Jenkins with the sticky red fluid.

Jenkins brought the spinning saw blade down in a carving action which caught Murray at the point of the shoulder. There was a high pitched scream as the chainsaw cut through his ribs, hacking its way deeper to rupture his lungs which burst like fleshy balloons, expelling a choking flux of blood and bile. The churning blade chewed easily through muscle and sinew, finally severing Murray's bulging intestines. Like the glutinous tentacles of some bloodied octopus, his entrails burst from the gaping rent in his stomach, spilling forth in a reeking mass.

As he fell forward into a pool of blood and viscera, his body jerked uncontrollably as the final muscular spasms racked it.

Jenkins switched off the chainsaw and, in the silence, looked down at the corpse of Murray.

He looked on disinterestedly as blood washed over his shoes.

London

9.58.

The diesel was picking up speed.

As the train hurtled through Finsbury Park station, people on the platforms appeared only as rapid blurs to Derek West. He had only been driving for about five or ten minutes, since picking up the diesel at the Bounds Green Depot earlier on. Up until then he and five or six of the other drivers and guards had been sitting idly around reading the papers or watching TV. Derek had consumed yet another mug of strong tea then clambered into the cab and started the powerful engine. The diesel was pulling eight tankers behind it. Each one containing almost 71,000 litres of liquid oxygen.

Now, Derek felt the massive engine throbbing around him as he glanced down at the speedometer.

As the train roared through the last tunnel it was travelling at well over ninety miles an hour.

Up ahead of him, Derek could see the massive edifice which was King's Cross, lights gleaming in the darkness.

He smiled thinly.

Out of his eye corner he caught sight of a red warning light but he paid it no heed.

The needle on the speedo touched ninety-five.

The diesel thundered on, travelling as if it had been fired from some gigantic cannon. It swept into the station, the air horn sounding one last defiant death-knell which echoed around the cavernous interior of the station.

It struck the buffers doing ninety-eight.

Concrete and metal seemed to dissolve under the crushing impact of the hundred ton train. The huge machine ploughed through the platform, sending lumps of stone and steel scything in all directions like shrapnel. Such was the power with which it hit, the engine buckled and split open, the top half of it somersaulting, blasting massive holes in the gigantic timetable a full fifty feet from the buffers. Screams of terror were drowned as the engine exploded, followed, a second later, by a series of devastating detonations as

291

the liquid oxygen tanks first skewed off the track and then blew up.

An eruption of seismic proportions ripped through the station as a screaming ball of fire filled the giant building, melting the glass in the roof and roaring upward into the night sky like a searing, monstrous flare which scorched everything around it. Concrete archways were simply brushed aside by the incredible blast and part of the great canopy above fell inward with a deafening crash. It was impossible to hear anything over the high-pitched shriek of the flames which shot up in a white wall. People not instantly incinerated by the fireball were crushed by falling rubble or flattened by the shock wave which ripped the station apart as if it had been made of paper. The searing temperatures ignited fuel in the engines of other trains and more explosions began to punctuate the persistent roar of the main fire. Wheels, buffers, sleepers and even lengths of rail flew through the air, those that hadn't already been transformed to molten metal by the fury of the temperatures.

The glass front of the station exploded outward, blown by the incredible shock wave, and the street beyond was showered with debris. Taxis waiting in the forecourt were overturned by the blast.

It was as if the station had been trodden on by some huge invisible foot. Huge tongues of flame still rose, snatching at the darkness, melting everything near them with the blistering heat. Platforms had been levelled, people inside the once proud building had been blasted to atoms, pulverised by the ferocity of the explosion. The entire building had become one massive ball of fire.

It looked as if a portion of Hell had forced its way up through the earth.

65

Mere seconds after she heard the loud bang, Kelly felt the floor move. She gripped the table and looked anxiously around her as if fearing that the roof were going to fall in on her. She heard the unmistakable sound of shattering glass and was thankful that the room had no windows. There were shouts and curses from the rooms beyond hers.

She guessed that the violent vibrations continued for a full fifteen seconds then the room seemed to settle once again. A couple of pieces of plaster fell onto the table and she cast an anxious glance at the ceiling once more.

Kelly was aware that there had been a massive explosion somewhere close but she could not have imagined it was as close as King's Cross.

Phones began to ring. It sounded like pandemonium beyond the locked door.

She closed her eyes, wondering what could have caused the blast, her mind tortured by the fact that the perpetrator was more than likely acting out some maniac scheme previously hidden deep within his subconscious.

Until tonight.

Until Blake had . . .

She got to her feet and paced up and down for a moment, still partially stunned by the bang and its subsequent tremor.

Even she had not fully believed that anyone could possess such an awesome power as Blake had claimed. Now, she had been given ample proof. Kelly wondered what would have happened if she had arrived at the studios earlier. If she had not walked out on him. If she had joined him.

If she had killed him earlier.

The questions were immaterial now. The final act had been completed. The horror unleashed.

She glanced up at the clock, then at her own watch.

Where was Joubert?

Had he been butchered by some demented victim of Blake's master plan? she wondered, but then hurriedly pushed the thought to the back of her mind. He would come. She knew he would come. How foolish she had been to doubt him. Those suspicions stung even more now as she remembered how she had confided in Blake, never suspecting the man she had trusted, lived with. Loved.

She sat down once more, her head cradled in her hands, eyes fixed on the statement before her – her admission of guilt, although she still did not remember pulling the trigger and blasting the writer into oblivion. All she remembered was the feeling of cold, a sensation she had experienced many years earlier whilst in a haunted house. The coldness which comes with absolute evil.

Kelly slumped forward on the desk, tears trickling down her face.

She didn't raise her head when she heard the footsteps from the direction of the door.

'What happened?' she asked. 'I heard an explosion.'

Silence greeted her enquiry.

'I asked you what happened,' Kelly said, wondering why her companion was silent. She looked up.

Had she been able to, Kelly would probably have screamed. As it was, she felt as if someone had fastened a cord around her throat and was slowly twisting it, tighter and tighter, preventing her from making any sound. She shook her head slowly from side to side.

Standing before her was David Blake.

66

For long seconds, Kelly could not speak. Her eyes bulged madly in their sockets as she gazed at Blake.

Or was it Blake? Was she too losing her grip on sanity?

He reached forward and touched her hand and she felt a shiver run through her. It seemed to penetrate her soul.

'How?' was all she could gasp, her voice a horrified whisper. 'I saw you die.' She screwed up her eyes until they hurt then looked again.

Blake remained opposite her.

'Tell me how,' she hissed.

'The power of the Shadow,' he told her, quietly. 'It enabled my Astral body to live on after death. Only total destruction of my physical form can cause my Astral body to disappear.'

She ran both hands through her hair.

'How will it end?' she asked him.

Blake didn't answer.

'Did you use hypnosis?' she said.

'A form of hypnosis, but the word is inadequate.'

'Stop it now, please,' she begged. 'Let it end.'

'It's only just beginning,' he whispered.

Kelly finally did manage a scream, a long wild ululation of despair. Tears were squeezed from her eyes as she closed the lids tightly. She slumped forward on the table, sobbing.

'Make it stop,' she whimpered. 'Please, make it stop.'

She raised her head.

Blake was gone. She was alone once more.

The door to the room was flung open and Barton dashed in.

'What's wrong?' he asked, seeing how distraught she looked. 'We heard you scream.'

Kelly could not answer him. Tears dripped from her face and stained the statement sheet below. She saw Barton motion to someone behind him and, a second later, Joubert entered the room.

'They told me what happened,' said the Frenchman, watching as she wiped the tears from her face. She looked at Barton.

'Where was Blake's body taken after he was shot?' she asked.

Barton looked bewildered.

'Great Portland Street Hospital,' he said. 'What the hell does that matter?'

'It has to be destroyed,' Kelly told him. 'Burned. Dismembered. Anything. But please, Inspector, you must destroy Blake's body.'

'You *are* off your head,' the policeman said.

She turned to Joubert.

'Blake was here. In this room. Not two minutes ago,' she babbled. 'He's found a way for his Astral body to survive beyond death. These atrocities will continue unless the physical form can be destroyed.'

'Hold up,' Barton interrupted. 'Are you trying to say that Blake isn't dead, because if he's not, who's the geezer laid out at Great Portland Street . . .'

'*I* understand what she means, Inspector,' Joubert interrupted.

'Well I fucking well don't,' snapped the policeman. 'Now one of you had better start making some sense, and fast, because I'm not known for my patience.'

'Just destroy the body,' Kelly said, imploringly.

'Forget it,' said Barton. 'Who the hell do you think I am? The body's at the hospital and it stays there until it's buried.'

He turned and left the room, slamming the door behind him.

Kelly and Joubert looked at each other and, if defeat had a physical face, then it was mirrored in their expressions.

67

The light flickered once then died.

'Sod it,' muttered Bill Howard getting to his feet. He put down his copy of *Weekend* and fumbled his way across to the cupboard set in the far wall. He banged his shin on one of the slabs and cursed again, rubbing the injured area.

There was some light flooding into the basement area but it was largely dissipated by the thick glass and wire mesh which covered the ground level window, the only window in the morgue of Great Portland Street Hospital.

Bill had worked there for the past thirty-eight years, ever since he'd been de-mobbed. He'd tried a spell as ward orderly but his real niche had been down below in the morgue. He felt curiously secure within its antiseptic confines. He knew it was a place where he would not be disturbed by the day-to-day running of the hospital. As long as he did his job then things went along fine. Clean up the stiffs, make sure they were ready for the post-mortems which were carried out in the room next door. Not once, in all his years at the hospital, had the task bothered him. Hardly surprisingly really, he reasoned, after having spent six years in the army medical corps treating all manner of wounds, gangrene, dysentery and other illnesses from Dunkirk to Burma. He'd seen sights which made his present job positively tame.

His wife had died three years earlier after a long battle with cancer but now Bill lived quite happily with his dog in a nice little flat not far from the hospital. Another half an hour and he'd be able to go home.

Bill found his way to the cupboard and opened it, peering through the gloom in search of the strip-light he required. In the dark confines of the morgue he had but one companion.

Bill had been informed that the body would be removed the following day by the police. It had been brought in at about 8.30 that evening, the man had been shot, so Bill had been told. He'd waited until the police and hospital officials had left then he'd lifted the plastic sheet which covered the body and glanced at it. They had left it clothed and the name tag pinned to the lapel of the man's bloodied jacket read 'David Blake.'

Now Bill took the light tube from its cardboard casing and went in search of a chair to stand on.

As he passed the body he shuddered involuntarily. The morgue was usually cold but tonight it seemed positively wintry. Bill saw his breath form gossamer clouds in the air as he exhaled. He wouldn't be sorry to get home in the warm. He would not have to return until nine the following morning.

Bill clambered up onto the chair and removed the old light and slotted in the replacement.

He heard a faint rustling sound.

Bill froze, trying to detect where the noise was coming from. He realized that it was coming from the direction of his desk. He paused a moment, ears alert.

Silence.

He stepped down off the chair.

The rustling came again.

Bill hurried across to the light switch, his hand poised over it but, as he was about to press it, he saw what was making the noise. A slight breeze coming from the half open door was turning the pages of his magazine. He smiled.

Getting jumpy in your old age, he told himself.

Bill almost gasped aloud as he felt a particularly numbing sensation on the back of his neck. It felt as if someone had placed a block of ice against his back. He felt his skin pucker into goose-pimples.

Bill switched on the light and turned.

He suddenly wished he hadn't.

68

The night was alive with the sound of sirens as dozens of accident and emergency vehicles raced towards the blazing inferno which was King's Cross. For miles around flames could still be seen leaping through the fractured roof, turning the clouds orange. A dense pall of smoke hung over the ruins raining cinders down on all those nearby.

Inside Albany Street Police station Sergeant Tony Dean was hurriedly, but efficiently, answering phone calls and barking instructions into the two-way radio on his desk. The tall sergeant was sweating profusely due to his exertions.

'How's it going?' asked Inspector Barton.

'I've called in the blokes who were off duty tonight,' Dean told him. 'And we've got every available man at the scene.'

'Don't spread us too thin, Tony,' Barton reminded him. 'With so many coppers in one place, the villains could have a field day.'

'Scotland Yard have been on the blower, they've sent an Anti-Terrorist squad to the station to check it out.'

'It must have been a bloody big bomb then,' said Barton, sceptically, remembering the devastating explosion. He looked warily at the sergeant. 'Have there been any more reports in like the ones we had earlier? You know, the murders.'

Dean nodded.

'Another six since nine o'clock,' he said. 'I checked with a couple of other stations as well. It's happening all over the city, guv.'

Barton didn't answer, he merely looked towards the door which hid Kelly and Joubert from his view. He decided he'd better check on them. As he turned he heard Dean's voice, loud in his ear:

'You took your bleeding time, didn't you?'

The Inspector saw PC Roy Fenner hurrying through the door towards the desk where he stood.

'Sorry, Sarge, I got held up, there was loads of traffic,' he babbled. 'Evening, Inspector,' he added.

'Get your uniform on and get back out here,' Dean told him.

'What's been going on anyway?' Fenner wanted to know. 'I've been watching telly all night. First this bloke got shot. In full view of the camera, I thought it was a gimmick but . . .'

'Move yourself,' bellowed Dean and the PC disappeared into the locker room to change.

Barton stroked his chin thoughtfully, a flicker of uncertainty passing across his eyes.

'Something wrong, guv?' the sergeant asked him.

He shook his head slowly.

'No,' he murmured then passed through the door which led him to Kelly and Joubert.

Dean snatched up the phone as it rang again and jammed it between his shoulder and ear as he scribbled down the information.

'Christ,' he muttered, as he wrote. 'What was that again? Some bloke's killed his wife by pressing a red hot iron into her face. Yes, I got it. Where was this?' He scrawled down the location. 'Gloucester Place. Right. Have you called an ambulance? OK.' He hung up. Dean stared down at what he'd written and shook his head, then he turned towards the door of the locker room.

'What are you doing, Fenner? Making the bloody uniform?'

The door remained closed.

'Fenner.'

There was still no answer.

Dean opened the door and poked his head in.

'For Christ's sake, what . . .'

His sentence was cut short as Fenner leapt forward, bringing his hard-wood truncheon up with bone-crushing force.

The impact lifted the sergeant off his feet and the strident sound of breaking bone filled his ears as he heard his lower jaw snap. White hot agony lanced through him and he felt consciousness slipping away from him. But, through a haze of pain, he saw the constable advancing. Dean tried to speak but as he did, blood from his smashed jaw ran down his face and neck and the sound came out as a throaty croak. He could see Fenner looking at him, but the constable's eyes did not seem to register his presence. He looked drunk.

Dean managed to scramble to his feet as Fenner brought the truncheon down again.

The sergeant succeeded in bringing his arm up and the solid truncheon cracked against his forearm but he managed to drive one fist into Fenner's face, knocking him backward. He fell with a crash, the truncheon still gripped in his fist.

All three of them heard the sounds from beyond the door but Kelly was the first to speak.

'What's happening out there?' she asked.

Barton hesitated a moment, looking first at Kelly, then at Joubert. They stood motionless for a moment then there was another loud crash, like breaking wood. Barton turned and scuttled through the door.

'We have to get out of here,' said Kelly.

'But how?' Joubert wanted to know.

'There has to be a way. We must find Blake's body and destroy it.' She was already moving towards the door which she found, to her relief, was unlocked.

'No,' said Joubert, stepping ahead of her. 'Let me go first.' He pulled the door open and both of them saw that a narrow corridor separated them from another, glass panelled door about twenty feet further away. Through the bevelled partition they could see the dark outlines of moving figures. Shouts and curses came from the room beyond and Kelly swallowed hard as they drew closer.

They could have been only a yard away when they heard a demonic shout.

A dark shape hurtled towards the glass-panelled door.

Inspector Barton crashed through the thick glass, his upper body slumping over the door which swung under the impact. Shards of glass flew towards Kelly and Joubert, one of them slicing open the Frenchman's left ear; he clapped a hand to the bleeding appendage, using his body to shield Kelly from the worst of the flying crystal. Barton lay across the broken shards, one particularly long piece having pierced his chest. The point had burst from his back and now held him there, blood running down it.

300

Joubert pulled the door open a fraction more, edging through.

Kelly followed.

She was almost through when she felt a bloodied hand close around her wrist.

Joubert spun round as she screamed and he saw that the dying Barton had grabbed her as she passed. Impaled on the broken glass, the policeman raised his head as if soliciting help. Crimson liquid spilled over his lips and he tried to lift himself off the jagged points but, with one final despairing moan, he fell forward again.

Kelly shook free of his hand and followed Joubert through the door.

Albany Street Police station resembled a bomb-site.

Filing cabinets had been overturned, their contents spilled across the floor. Furniture was smashed and lay in pieces everywhere. The windows were broken. Kelly saw blood splashed across the floor and on the far wall.

Close by lay the body of Sergeant Dean, his face pulped by repeated blows from the truncheon. A foot or so from him, the leg of a chair broken across his head, lay PC Fenner.

'Come on, let's get out of here,' said Joubert and the two of them bolted. They dashed out into the rainy night, pausing momentarily to gaze at the mushroom cloud of dark smoke and orange flame which still ballooned upward from the blazing wreckage of King's Cross. Then, Joubert pulled her arm, leading her towards his car.

They scrambled in and he started the engine.

'How far is Great Portland Street Hospital from here?' the Frenchman asked, guiding the Fiat into traffic.

'Not far,' she told him.

Joubert glanced at her but Kelly was looking out of the side window.

If they could get to Blake's body, perhaps they still had a chance to stop the horror he had released.

Perhaps.

301

69

'There,' Kelly shouted, pointing to the dimly lit sign over the hospital entrance.

Joubert waited for a break in the stream of traffic then swung the Fiat across the street and parked it outside the large building. Apart from the dozen or so lights which burned in the big windows, the hospital appeared to be in darkness. Kelly scrambled out of the car and hurried up the stone steps to the main entrance, Joubert following closely behind.

The entry-way was bright but the light was not welcoming. It reflected off the polished floors as if they were mirrors, causing Kelly to wince. There was a desk directly opposite, a steaming mug of coffee perched on it. Whoever it belonged to was nowhere in evidence. For fleeting seconds a terrifying thought crossed Kelly's mind.

What if one or more of the patients had seen the programme earlier in the evening? Even now, the wards could be full of butchered, helpless invalids. She shuddered and tried to push the thought to the back of her mind but it refused to budge.

'Kelly, here,' said Joubert, pointing to a blue sign which proclaimed: MORTUARY. A white arrow pointed down a flight of stone steps and, moving as quickly and quietly as they could, the two of them made their way towards the morgue.

As they descended, the darkness seemed to grow thicker until it swirled around them like a cloud, hardly broken by the low wattage lights set in the walls. As they reached the bottom of the stairs a long corridor faced them and, almost unconsciously, both slowed their pace, suddenly not so eager to reach their destination. The lights in the corridor flickered ominously for a second then glowed with their customary brilliance once more. Kelly swallowed hard as she advanced towards the door of the morgue, her heels clicking noisily in the cloying silence.

They drew closer.

It was Kelly who noticed that the door was ajar.

There were some spots of dark liquid on the polished floor which Joubert knelt and touched with his finger. He sniffed it.

'Blood,' he told Kelly, softly.

Inside the morgue itself, apart from the half-light coming through the street-level window, everything was in darkness. The door opened soundlessly and the two of them stepped inside, glancing to left and right for any sounds or movements.

There was a faint humming in the background which Kelly took to be the hospital generator. Other than that, the morgue was unbearably silent. She heard the blood singing in her ears, her heart thumping noisily as she tip-toed towards the one slab which bore a body.

Covered by a sheet, it looked shapeless in the gloom.

They both approached it slowly, their eyes not leaving the motionless body.

There was more blood on the floor beside the slab.

A dark shape suddenly passed over them and Kelly spun round in panic.

It was a second or two before she realized that it had merely been the shadow of a person walking by outside.

Joubert looked at her and she nodded slowly in answer to his unspoken question.

The Frenchman gripped one corner of the sheet which covered the body.

Kelly moved closer.

There was a soft click behind them and, this time, Joubert felt his heart skip a beat. He squinted through the gloom to see that a slight breeze had pushed the morgue door shut. The Frenchman used his free hand to wipe a bead of perspiration from his forehead.

He took hold of the sheet more firmly, aware of the biting chill which seemed to have filled the room.

Kelly nodded and, gritting his teeth, he whipped the sheet away.

Lying on the slab, glazed eyes bulging wide in terror, was the body of Bill Howard.

Kelly and Joubert exchanged anxious glances, the Frenchman touching the face of the dead man with the back of his hand.

'He hasn't been dead long,' he told Kelly, keeping his voice low.

She took a step back, allowing an almost painful breath to escape her lungs.

Bill Howard had obviously died in agony and it showed in his contorted features. A long metal probe had been rammed into his mouth, puncturing his tongue before being driven through the base of his skull above the hollow at the back of his neck.

A question burned brightly in her mind.

Where was Blake's body?

As the two of them emerged from the stairway into the hospital entry-way, they were surprised to find it still deserted. Once more Kelly wondered if the patients had been butchered in their beds, maybe the staff as well. She slowed her pace slightly, her eyes shifting to the solitary mug of tea which still stood on the desk. It was no longer steaming. Whoever had put it there had not returned to claim it.

'Kelly, come on,' Joubert urged, making for the main door. She hesitated a moment longer then followed him out to the car.

'Where to now?' he asked.

She gazed ahead of her, her voice soft but determined.

'There's only one place left where the body could be.'

Joubert understood.

70

The traffic was surprisingly light in the city centre. The drive to Blake's house took less than thirty minutes. Joubert brought the Fiat to a halt and switched off the engine, peering through the side window at the large building.

Rain coursed lazily down the windows of the car and, overhead, a loud rumble of thunder was instantly answered by a vivid but soundless flash of lightning.

Kelly brushed fingers through her hair, noticing that her hand was shaking. She clenched her fists together for a moment, drawing in a deep breath.

'What if the body *isn't* in the house?' asked Joubert, cryptically.

'It has to be there,' she said. 'Blake would feel safe hiding it there.'

They both clambered out of the Fiat, ignoring the rain as they stood facing the house. A single light burned in the porch. Far from looking forbidding, Blake's house seemed positively inviting. It beckoned to them and they responded, moving quickly but cautiously towards the dwelling, never taking their eyes from it. Once more Kelly felt a shiver run up her spine.

They paused at the end of the short driveway.

'It'd be better if we split up,' Kelly said. 'That way we'll have a better chance of finding the body. And it won't take so long.'

Joubert regarded her warily for a moment.

'I'll check inside the house,' she said, producing her key ring and showing him the key to Blake's front door which she still possessed. 'You search the garden and garage.'

The Frenchman nodded.

A particularly brilliant flash of lightning iashed across the rain-soaked heavens, bathing the two investigators in cold white light. For fleeting seconds they resembled ghosts, their faces distorted and white in the flash.

Kelly hesitated a moment longer then, with a final look at Joubert, she headed towards the front door.

He waited until she was inside then he moved cautiously forward, his sights set on a door at the side of the garage.

Kelly stepped into the hall and quickly looked around her, searching the darkness with uncertain eyes. She raised her hand, wondering whether or not she should put on the light, but she felt simultaneously exposed *and* safe in the glow. She eventually decided to switch it on.

Nothing moved in the hallway.

To her right, the sitting room door was slightly ajar.

Ahead of her, the stairs disappeared upward into the impenetrable darkness of the first floor.

On the left, the door of the cellar was closed and, this time, there was no key in it. She decided to leave it until last and moved towards

305

the sitting room, pushing the door wide open. Light from the hall offered her sufficient illumination to find the nearest table lamp. This she also switched on.

Standing in the sitting room, Kelly could feel the silence closing in around her as if it were a living thing.

Outside, the storm was reaching its height.

Joubert found that the door which led into the garage was unlocked but the catch was rusty and he needed to put all his weight behind it to shift the recalcitrant partition.

It swung open with a despairing shriek and the Frenchman practically fell into the dark abyss beyond. He stumbled but managed to keep his feet, looking round for a light switch. He found one close to the door and flicked it on. The fluorescents in the ceiling sputtered into life and Joubert scanned the inside of the garage. The floor was spotted with congealed patches of oil and slicks of petrol but, apart from a small toolbox shoved into one corner, the place was empty. There was certainly nowhere to hide a body.

He took one last look then retraced his steps, flicking off the light as he did so.

Outside in the rain again he wiped some of it from his face and decided which direction to follow next.

There was a narrow passageway beside the garage and the side of the house which, he suspected, led to the back garden. Joubert moved cautiously towards it, attempting to see through the short, but darkness-shrouded, passageway. It was less than four feet wide, perhaps three times that in length and it was as black as the grave in there. He put out one hand and fumbled his way along the stone wall, unable to see a hand in front of him.

There was a loud clap of thunder and Joubert prayed for a flash of lightning which would at least give him a few seconds of light. Enough to reach the end of the passage or perhaps alert him if he were not alone in the gloom.

He tried to force that particular thought to the back of his mind but it would not budge.

Inch by inch he edged onward, deeper into the blackness.

Something touched his leg.

Something solid.

Joubert jumped back, not knowing what he was going to do, fear overwhelming him.

In that split second there was an ear-shredding whiplash of lightning which lit up the entire passage.

A foot or so from the end of it, there was a wooden gate. He had walked into it in the blackness, unable to see the object.

Joubert closed his eyes for a second and smiled thinly, moving forward once again. He succeeded in slipping the catch on the gate and passed through and out of the passage. The Frenchman found himself in the back garden. The rain continued to pelt down, plastering his hair to his face, streaming into his eyes. Another crack of lightning lit the heavens and Joubert saw that, ten or twelve yards further on, nestling in some trees at the bottom of the garden, was what looked like a wooden shed. He trod quickly over the sodden grass towards the small hut and tugged on the handle.

It was locked.

He pulled on it again, finally using his foot to dislodge the timber door. It swung open, a pungent smell of damp and decay billowing out to greet him. He coughed and stepped inside.

There was no light in the hut.

The bulb was still in place but it was broken. He narrowed his eyes in an effort to see around the confines of the small structure, which seemed, to all intents and purposes, like a garden shed. He saw a lawn-mower, a roller and sundry other garden implements.

Joubert even spotted a large, double-handed axe. Blake had obviously intended chopping down some of the over-hanging branches which grew around the shed, Joubert assumed. He moved forward and picked up the axe, glad of a weapon though he wondered if it would be of any help if the need arose.

The rain was pounding the shed so violently now that it reminded the Frenchman of waves breaking continually on rocks. He shivered in his wet clothes and took one last look around the tiny hut.

Hidden behind a pile of boxes and encrusted with grime as it was, he almost failed to see the freezer.

It was long, perhaps six feet and at least half that in depth. Quite large enough . . .

307

Gripping the axe tighter, he moved towards it, pulling the boxes aside in his wake until he could reach the old freezer without any trouble. He hooked his fingers beneath the rim and prepared to fling it open.

There was a harsh crack as the wind blew the shed door shut, plunging Joubert into darkness.

He muttered something in French and hurried across to the door, pushing it open once again, allowing the rain to lash his face for a second, then he returned to the freezer. He dug his fingers under the filthy lid and lifted.

It was empty.

Only a large spider and some woodlice scuttled about inside.

Joubert slammed the lid down again, his heart still beating fast. He wiped his face with the back of his hand and leant back against the empty freezer to catch his breath.

The lights inside the house dimmed for a moment then glowed once more as thunder continued to roll across the heavens. Kelly stood quite still in the darkness, her eyes darting back and forth, ears alert for the slightest sound. But all she heard was the driving rain and the fury of the storm outside.

As the lamp in the sitting room came on she moved slowly towards the kitchen.

The door was open.

Kelly stopped for a second and glanced over her shoulder before entering the next room. She flicked on the lights and looked around. There were a couple of dirty mugs in the sink but, apart from that, everything seemed to be in its place.

The lights went out again.

She waited for the brightness to return, her heart thudding more rapidly in her chest.

She waited.

Outside the thunder roared loudly.

Waited.

'Come on, come on,' she whispered, trying to steady her breathing.

Waited.

The house remained in darkness.

* * *

308

From inside the garden shed, Joubert had seen Kelly turn on the kitchen lights and now, as he stood looking at the house, he too wondered how long it would be before the power supply was restored. The Frenchman decided that he would be better employed aiding Kelly in her search of the house. Carrying the axe with him, he headed for the door.

A gust of wind slammed it in his face.

He gripped the rusty knob irritably and tugged it open.

Joubert found himself face to face with David Blake.

Before the Frenchman could move, he felt powerful hands grabbing for his throat, hands which felt like blocks of ice as they squeezed. He struck out vainly at Blake who finally hurled the intruder to one side where he crashed into a pile of boxes. As he tried to rise he felt an incredible pressure on his skull as Blake gripped him in a vice-like grip, his fingers resembling talons as they threatened to plunge through the Frenchman's skull.

Joubert felt the cold filling his head, his torso. His entire body.

He screamed but the sound was lost as thunder tore open the dark clouds and the rain lashed the hut unmercifully.

He felt himself being hurled to the floor where he landed with a jarring impact. When he opened his eyes there was no sign of Blake. Joubert didn't know how long he'd been unconscious. A minute? An hour?

The Frenchman got to his feet, picking up the axe as he did so. He held it before him, studying the heavy, wickedly sharp blade. He looked towards the house and thought of Kelly. The axe felt as if it were a part of him, an extension of his arms.

He kicked open the door and trudged across the lawn towards the darkened house, the large, razor-sharp weapon held before him.

A smile creased his lips.

71

When the power inside the house went off, Kelly could hear nothing but the rumbling of thunder. The electric wall clock stopped ticking and she was deprived of even that welcome sound.

Now she stood alone in the darkness, praying for the light to return. The thought that the fuse box might have blown began to creep into her mind.

Or had someone in the house turned the power off?

She spun round, her imagination beginning to play tricks on her. Had she seen movement in the sitting room behind her?

The lights came back on so suddenly she almost shouted aloud in surprise and relief.

Kelly licked her lips but found that her tongue felt like old newspaper. She quickly checked in the pantry then turned, intent on heading back through the house to look upstairs.

In the light flooding from the kitchen windows, she saw Joubert approaching across the small lawn.

She breathed an audible sigh of relief and knelt to undo the bolt on the back door, preparing to turn the key in the lock to let him in. He obviously hadn't found anything, she reasoned, except for the axe which he carried. He had almost reached the back door.

She turned the key in the lock, her hand resting on the knob.

As he saw the door opening, Joubert uttered a high-pitched yell of fury and swung the axe with all his strength. It scythed through the wooden door, ripping it free of one hinge. Kelly's own scream mingled with the shriek of splintering wood. She turned and ran for the sitting room as Joubert stove in the remainder of the door and crashed into the kitchen.

Kelly slipped and fell as she reached the hall, looking over her shoulder in time to see him emerge from the kitchen.

He looked like something from a nightmare with his hair plastered down, his face scratched and bruised and his mouth spread in a kind of rictus. He hurdled a coffee table and hurried after her.

Kelly leapt to her feet, slamming the hall door behind her, darting towards the stairs.

She took them two at a time, stumbling once again at the top.

Below her, Joubert flung open the door and hurried across the hall, pausing on the bottom step before ascending slowly.

Kelly was faced by four doors.

She raced towards the first, hearing his heavy footfalls on the stairs as he climbed higher.

The door was locked.

Kelly hurried to the second one, praying that it was open.

She pulled open the door and ran inside, flinging herself beneath the bed.

Through the half-open door, she could see when Joubert reached the landing. He stood at the top of the stairs for what seemed like an eternity, only his feet visible to Kelly but she realized that he must be deciding which door to try first.

He moved towards the room on her left.

The locked one. She heard him twisting the handle then she heard the sound of shattering wood as he smashed off the knob and kicked the door open.

Kelly closed her eyes, wondering if this was all a nightmare. If she would wake up in a second. She tried to swallow but her throat was constricted.

She heard his footsteps, saw his feet as he stood in the doorway of the room in which she hid.

He took a step inside.

Kelly bit her fist to stifle a cry.

He moved closer towards the bed.

If only she could roll out on the other side, run for the door . . .

But what if she slipped? What if he reached the door before her? What if . . .?

He was standing beside her now, his feet together.

She imagined that axe poised over the bed.

With a strength born of terror, Kelly snaked her arms out, fastened

311

them around Joubert's ankles and tugged. She succeeded in pulling his legs away from him and he went down with a heavy thump, the axe falling from his grip.

She rolled over, scrambling clear of the bed, jumped to her feet and ran for the door.

Joubert was up in a second. He flung out a hand and managed to grab a handful of her hair. Kelly yelped as some of it came out at the roots and she felt herself overbalancing. She grabbed for the door frame and managed to retain her stance but he had slowed her up and, as she reached the landing, the Frenchman hurled himself at her, bringing her down in a pile-up which knocked the wind from them both.

Kelly struck out with her nails, raking his face. Joubert bellowed in pain and tried to pull her down again but Kelly got to her feet and kicked him hard in the side, bringing the heel of her shoe down on his outstretched hand so hard that it penetrated. Blood welled from the puncture and Joubert rolled to one side. But, he was still between Kelly and the stairs.

As the Frenchman struggled to his knees, Kelly ran at him and lashed out again with a kick which caught him firmly in the solar plexus. He fell backward, clutching at empty air for a second before tumbling down the stairs, thudding to a halt at the bottom with his head at an unnatural angle.

She gazed down at his motionless form realizing that his neck must be broken. Kelly ran into the bedroom and picked up the double-handed axe, moving quickly from bedroom to bedroom in search of Blake's body.

The rooms were empty.

Kelly began descending the stairs, the axe held firmly in her hands. She paused beside the body of Joubert, holding the razor sharp blade above his head as she felt for a pulse.

Nothing. As she'd thought, his neck had been broken in the fall.

She suddenly felt overwhelmed by sadness, not just for his death but for all the other people who had died that night and who would die if she did not complete her task. Her grief slowly became anger as she realized that all of the carnage, all of the suffering had been caused by Blake.

312

There were two more rooms in the house to be searched.

She went through the dining room quickly. That left the cellar.

The door was locked but that did not deter Kelly. She brought the axe down twice, shattering the lock, knocking the door wide open. She slapped on the lights and slowly descended into the subterranean room.

The silence crowded around her, an almost physical force. She stood still at the bottom of the steps, her eyes searching.

Next to one of the large bookcases, almost invisible on first glimpse, was a small door, no bigger than three feet square, its handle also painted white to make it even more inconspicuous. Kelly bent and tugged on the handle.

It opened effortlessly and she recoiled as a rancid smell of rotten wood and damp earth rose from the tiny compartment. But, if the door was small then what lay beyond it was not. The space behind the door looked as though it had been made many years earlier. It stretched back into darkness, she wasn't sure how far. The walls were soft and slimy and she had to duck low to avoid scraping her hair on the dripping ceiling. The stench was almost overpowering.

Lying undisturbed, covered by a blanket, amidst the muck and filth, was the body of Blake.

Kelly grabbed both ankles and, using all her strength, pulled. Inch by inch, the corpse came clear of its resting place until it lay in full view in the cellar. Kelly noticed that the eyes were still open. They seemed to fix her in a reproachful stare and, for a moment, she was rooted to the spot.

There was another deafening clap of thunder, audible even in the depths of the cellar.

The room was plunged into darkness as the lights flickered then died.

A second later they came back on again and Kelly finally managed to tear her gaze from the body of Blake.

She reached for the axe and raised it above her head, knowing what she must do, praying for the strength to perform this final act of destruction. Tears welled up in her eyes then trickled down her cheeks and the axe wavered in the air. Kelly squeezed her eyes tightly shut for a moment, anxious to avoid the reproachful stare of Blake's dead eyes.

313

The lights began to flash on and off, blinking wildly as the thunder now seemed to become one continual salvo of sound.

Kelly screamed as she brought the axe down.

The blade buried itself in the right shoulder of the corpse and she heard a loud cracking of bone as the scapula was shattered. Kelly wrenched it free and struck again, her aim slightly off but the weight of the weapon was enough. It severed the right arm. She lifted it again and, after two more powerful strokes, succeeded in hacking off the other arm. Tears were now pouring freely down her cheeks and the storm offered a macabre accompaniment to her own sobs and the thick, hollow sound the axe made as it sheared through dead flesh.

She changed position to attack the right leg, the axe skidding off the pelvic bone and shaving away a portion of thigh. Kelly recovered her balance and struck again, forced to stand on the torso to pull the blade free. Her next blow exposed the femur and, with a despairing grunt, she smashed the thick bone and managed to hack the leg off. The remains of the body shuddered beneath each fresh impact but Kelly continued with her grisly task, perspiration soaking through her clothes. It took five attempts to sever the left leg.

Panting like a carthorse, she took a step back, realizing that she had still not completed the monstrous task.

With a blow which combined horrified determination and angry despair, she struck off the head. It rolled for two or three feet across the floor, coming to rest on the stump. She noticed with relief that the sightless eyes were facing away from her.

Kelly stood amidst the pieces of dismembered corpse and dropped the axe, shaking her head gently. Her breath came in great choking gasps which seared her throat and lungs. She leant back against the nearest wall for support, closing her eyes for a moment.

The cellar door slammed shut and Kelly shot an anxious glance towards it.

At the top of the stairs stood David Blake.

Kelly shuddered as the room seemed to fill with icy air, as if someone were sucking all the warmth from the cellar and replacing it with the bone-chilling numbness she now felt.

Blake began to descend, his eyes fixed, not on her, but on the hewn corpse.

314

'It's over, Blake,' she said, her voice a harsh croak.

He didn't answer. He merely continued his purposeful stride, his face impassive until he reached the bottom of the stairs. Then, his nostrils flared. With a roar of rage he ran at her.

Tired from her exertions, Kelly could not move fast enough to avoid his fearsome lunge. He grabbed her by the throat, lifting her bodily from the ground.

Kelly found herself looking deep into his eyes – into bulging orbs which were pools of sheer hatred. But there was something else there too.

Fear?

She felt the cold seeping through her like gangrene through a rotting limb but Blake's powerful grip was beginning to weaken. With a grunt he lowered her to the floor where she sprawled before him, gazing up at his contorted features. He took a step back, almost tripping over the mutilated remains of the corpse. *His* corpse.

The Astral body of David Blake, the tangible embodiment of his evil, staggered drunkenly for a second, one hand held towards Kelly in a last act of defiance.

With a despairing groan, he dropped to his knees, his eyes still fixed on the girl who was cowering a few feet from him. Kelly saw him open his mouth to scream but the sound, when it came forth, was like nothing human. The thunderous utulation rattled around the cellar, causing Kelly to cover her ears for fear that they would be damaged. The lights in the room went out for a moment then came back on with an increased brilliance.

Blake's scream died away as his face began to split open. Huge, jagged fissures opened in his flesh, as if his mirror image had been broken. An evil-smelling, yellowish-white substance bubbled up from the rents which were now spreading all over his body. He clawed at his chest, pulling his shirt open, a large lump of skin coming with it, exposing the bloodied internal organs beneath. His fingers seemed to shrivel like dying flowers and Kelly saw more of the pus-like fluid oozing from the deep cuts which were spreading along his arms and legs like rips in fabric.

He fell forward, his head disintegrating as he hit the ground. It split open, pus and blood bursting from the ruptured skull. A tangle of intestines snaked upward, as if propelled by some inner force as his stomach burst.

Kelly looked away, feeling her stomach somersault. The odour of corruption, that rank and fetid stench which floated in the air like an invisible cloud, surrounded her. She coughed and thought she was going to be sick. But the feeling passed.

The room was plunged into darkness again as the lights dimmed for fleeting seconds and a massive thunderclap shook the house.

Kelly managed to look back at the decaying form of Blake. The last moments lit by the faintly glimmering lights which seemed to act like strobes as they flickered.

As the electrical power was restored, the cellar was bathed in the cold white light of the fluorescents.

Blake had vanished.

Nothing remained.

No blood. No pus.

Nothing.

Only the dismembered corpse lay before her.

Kelly got slowly to her feet, swaying uncertainly for a moment. She was soaked with sweat. Every single muscle in her body ached and it took a monumental effort for her to even walk. She was completely drained. As close to collapse as she could ever remember but, somewhere amidst that exhaustion, there was a feeling of triumph. She had succeeded in stopping Blake. Now she prayed that she had been able to end the reign of terror he'd unleashed. There was no way of knowing yet.

All she could do was wait.

And hope.

She knew that there was one more thing which had to be done.

Crossing to the phone on the nearby desk, she lifted the receiver and pressed out three nines. She had no choice but to tell the police. Kelly heard the purring at the other end of the line.

The lights flickered once more and she muttered under her breath as she heard the phone go dead.

She was about to try again when the hand closed on her shoulder.

She spun round, the scream catching in her throat.

316

The figure which faced her was identical in every respect. A mirror image of herself.

And it held the axe.

Her alter-ego smiled as it brought the vicious weapon down with incredible force. The blade aimed at Kelly's head.

It was the last thing she saw.

NEMESIS

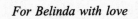

For Belinda with love

August 15, 1940

They were getting closer.

There was no doubt about it.

The rumbling which filled the subterranean corridor seemed to emanate from every brick, swelling around him like an approaching storm.

George Lawrenson knew that the tunnel which he now hurried along was at least seventy feet beneath the pavements of Whitehall, but still the reverberations rocked him as he walked. Flecks of dust floated from the ceiling every now and then, tiny pieces of plaster, dislodged by the incessant shaking detached themselves and fell like solid snow. Lawrenson wiped some of the dust from his jacket as he walked, looking up as the lights flickered once.

Below ground there was light. On the surface all was darkness.

The peculiar reversal of roles, the dislocation of normality which everyone had been living through for the last few weeks was illustrated perfectly by this particular example, Lawrenson thought. Where there should be blackness there was light. Where street lights should be burning there was gloom.

The only light on the surface was that which came from the fires.

From the incendiary bombs which the Luftwaffe dropped. From the blazing wreckage of houses and factories.

It had been like this every night for the past two weeks and no one knew how much longer it would go on. The skies above London were full of German planes, pouring bombs onto the capital, transforming it into a gigantic torch which flared with the flames of a thousand fires.

Lawrenson walked on, the file gripped firmly in his right hand. He turned a corner and proceeded down another long corridor. Above him the lights dimmed briefly then flared into life once more.

The bombs were falling on the embankment now.

Coming closer.

How many would emerge from the relative safety of the underground stations the following morning to discover that their houses no longer existed? That the places they had called homes had been reduced to piles of blackened brick.

Every night they poured down the steps and onto the platforms of the stations, there to spend the night sleeping or lying awake listening to the pounding from above. Then, the following morning they would emerge from below ground like a human tidal wave.

Like souls let loose from hell.

Only they were climbing the stairs *into* hell.

Into streets cratered by bombs, littered with human remains and obliterated vehicles.

But, for now, they were below ground like so many rabbits and all they could do was wait and hope. And pray.

Lawrenson thought briefly about his own wife as he strode along the corridor. His home was in the country, about forty miles from the capital. Unlike others, he was reasonably sure she was safe. He spoke to her by phone every evening and she had told him that she had seen the crimson glow which came from the city. She had told him she was frightened. Afraid for his safety. But, every night he told her not to worry then he retreated below ground like some kind of be-suited troglodyte, there to sit out the fury which Hitler's air force unleashed with the coming of night.

The rumbling grew louder and the lights dimmed once again but this time Lawrenson walked on without slowing his pace. He held the file close to his chest, as if protecting it from the tiny pieces of debris that fell from the ceiling.

As he turned the corner the two figures seemed to loom from the walls themselves and, despite himself, Lawrenson faltered.

He nodded a cursory greeting towards the first of the uniformed men then reached inside his jacket for his security pass. He held it up for inspection, allowing the senior of the two men to scrutinise the small photo which adorned the pass. He glanced at the picture then at Lawrenson as if to reassure himself that the man who stood before him was indeed who his pass declared him to be. Satisfied with that fact, the soldier turned towards the door, knocked once then stepped back, ushering Lawrenson through.

On the other side he was greeted by a third uniformed man. An officer.

The military man nodded affably and then returned to the table to his left where he and two other men were gathered around a map which was spread out before them.

Maps covered the wall too. The room was about twenty feet square and it seemed that every single inch of wall space was covered by maps and diagrams. Lawrenson spotted one which showed the British army's withdrawal to Dunkirk.

The room smelt of coffee and cigarette smoke and he waved a hand before him as if to dispel the odour. The men inside the room glanced quizzically at him, those who hadn't seen him before, others who knew him nodded greetings. No one smiled.

Lawrenson brushed a stray hair from his forehead and approached the large table which was set in the centre of the room. Two men stood behind it, looking down at yet another map. As Lawrenson approached they both looked up and the elder of the two nodded deferentially. He glanced at the file which Lawrenson held, watching as it was laid before him.

Others now gathered around the table, as if the file were acting as some kind of magnet, drawing them from all corners of the room. But only the older man sat, rubbing his eyes briefly then re-adjusting his glasses.

Outside, the earth shook as another shower of bombs fell.

Inside the subterranean Headquarters Winston Churchill began to read the contents of the file marked 'Genesis'.

1

The car came within inches of his motorbike and Gary Sinclair swerved violently to avoid being struck by the speeding vehicle.

'You stupid bastard!' he bellowed at the retreating tail lights but, in seconds, the car had disappeared around a bend in the road, swallowed up by the night.

Gary sucked in a deep breath, both shocked and angered by the near miss. Hadn't the driver seen him? Maybe the stupid sod was pissed. Either way it had been a close thing. Another couple of inches and he'd have been off. The bike juddered beneath him as if sharing his apprehension and, instinctively, he glanced down at the fuel gauge. The needle was almost touching red, the tank close to being empty. Gary muttered to himself and eased off slightly on the throttle. Perhaps, he thought, if he took it steadily, he'd get home before the bike packed up on him. When he'd taken it for a couple of test runs he'd been sure that the fuel tank was leaking but his brother, who'd sold him the bike, had assured him there was nothing to worry about.

Nothing to worry about, Gary thought irritably, glancing down once more at the gauge. He had another five miles to go before he reached Hinkston, he doubted if he'd make it.

As if to reinforce his doubts the bike slowed noticeably and refused to speed up even when he twisted the throttle violently. The engine spluttered dismally then died. Gary instinctively allowed his left foot to drop to the ground to steady himself as the Kawasaki came to a halt.

He grunted in annoyance and swung himself off the saddle. Then, propping the bike up against the hedge which ran along the roadside, he pulled his helmet off and glared at the bike. He drew his fingers through his shoulder length brown hair and squatted down beside the 750. Inspections, mechanical or otherwise, seemed somewhat pointless at this stage, he thought after a moment. He was stuck five miles from home. There was nothing else to do but wheel the bloody bike back into town. He pulled a packet of cigarettes from one of the side pockets of his leather jacket and lit one, allowing the smoke to burn its way to his lungs, then he took hold of the handlebars and guided the bike away from the hedge, the helmet hanging from the throttle.

A strong breeze had blown up in the last hour or so and it caused Gary's hair to flap around his face like so many writhing snakes. He pulled some strands from his mouth, cursing his brother once more for selling him the bike. It would take him more than an hour to walk into Hinkston from his present location and the weight of the bike

326

made that journey all the more uncomfortable. He stopped every few hundred yards and drew in a couple of deep breaths.

The wind was keen and he was glad he wore a sweatshirt beneath his jacket. However, pushing the bike kept him warm, it was just his face that felt cold.

On both sides of him trees bowed as the wind grew in strength. The moon had retreated behind a bank of thick cloud. The road was dark, flanked by tall hedges beyond which stood the trees that rattled their branches almost mockingly at him. Low hills rose to his right, masking the approaches to the town of Hinkston, hiding the glow of street lights and making it seem as if he were much further than five miles from the town. He glanced down at his watch and saw that it was almost 12.15 a.m. And he had to be up at six in the morning. He cursed his brother once more. He'd be lucky to reach home before 1.30 at this rate. Four hours sleep if he was lucky – Christ, he'd be wrecked by tomorrow. He thought about ringing in and saying he was ill but he decided against that. The job at the bakery was the first he'd had since leaving school two years earlier. Jobs weren't easy to come by and he couldn't afford to be choosy. An eighteen year old with two CSE's and negligible work experience wasn't exactly an employer's dream.

He guided the motorbike around a bend in the road, kicking several tree branches aside. The wind must have been stronger than he thought. It whistled through the tall hedges, a shrill banshee wail. Gary trudged on, now feeling quite warm from the effort of pushing the Kawasaki.

The car was parked about two hundred yards ahead of him.

There was a kind of makeshift lay-by, little more than a gap in the right hand hedge with a muddy verge before it but the vehicle was standing motionless there, lights on, smoke rising from its exhaust.

Gary smiled thinly to himself. Maybe the driver would give him a lift into Hinkston. He could wedge the 750 into the boot. Surely the bloke wouldn't mind. He increased his pace in an effort to reach the car before it pulled away.

There was something familiar about it.

Something . . .

He was about fifty yards away when he realised it was the same car that had almost forced him into the hedge further back on the road.

327

Gary felt the anger rise within him briefly but he fought it back. If the driver was willing to give him a lift then the previous aberration could be overlooked. He might mention it in passing, just as a joke. But, he reasoned, why make an issue out of it?

He drew closer to the car and heard the engine idling in the stillness of the night.

Maybe the driver wasn't alone. He might have his girlfriend in there with him. Maybe he'd pulled over for a quick one. Gary chuckled then shook his head. If they were romping about on the back seat the driver wasn't likely to have left his engine running and all his lights on.

The dull purring of the car engine continued to fill the otherwise noiseless night.

The wind had slackened slightly although the tree branches still swayed as if pulled by invisible strings.

Gary rolled his bike up to within twenty feet of the car and peered into the vehicle.

It was empty.

The bloke must have nipped behind the hedge for a slash, he thought, moving closer. He'd just wait until he came back then ask for a lift.

Gary leant the bike against the hedge and walked closer to the car, admiring the sleek bodywork, deciding that he would start saving up for driving lessons. He liked the bike but a car had more class. He walked around it, patting the bonnet as if he were inspecting the car with a view to purchase.

The engine continued to purr.

Gary glanced behind him towards the hedge, wondering where the driver could have got to. He sighed and continued with his tour of inspection of the vehicle, sliding his hand almost unconsciously to one of the handles.

The door opened as he pulled.

He frowned.

This was weird, he thought. It was bad enough leaving all the lights on and the engine running but to leave the car unlocked too? The driver was either very trusting or very stupid. Gary tried the rear door.

That too was unlocked.

He walked around to the driver's side and tried that door as well. Not surprisingly he found it unlocked.

The car moved.

Only a matter of inches but the motion was enough to startle Gary who took a step back, realising that the handbrake must be off. The car came to a halt a couple of inches further on, engine still ticking over. Gary stepped forward again, reaching for the handle, deciding he'd at least reach inside and pull up the handbrake, stop the car rolling down the slight hill which sloped away ahead of it. He reached for the door.

Hands gripped the back of his head.

He felt uncontrollable force and strength at the base of his skull as two strong hands fixed themselves around his neck, fingers digging into his throat.

Taken by surprise he was helpless, unable to stop himself as the hands forced him forward with incredible speed, slamming his head into the driver's side window of the car.

The impact opened a hairline cut across his forehead and a thin trickle of blood oozed down his face.

As he shouted in pain and surprise, he felt himself being propelled forward a second time, with even more force.

His face was driven into the top of the car door and he felt searing agony fill his head as two of his front teeth were shattered, one of them forced backwards into his tongue. Blood filled his mouth and spilled down his chin as he tried to twist, to fight off his attacker.

But his hidden assailant was taking full advantage of Gary's helplessness and another sickening contact with the car roof splintered two more of the youth's teeth and chipped the bone of his lower jaw. He tried to scream but the pain had already driven him to the edge of consciousness. As the hands relaxed their grip on the back of his neck, Gary Sinclair fell across the bonnet of the car then slid to the ground, his vision clouded by agony. He rolled onto his back on the muddy verge, looking up at his attacker who stood over him for brief seconds then knelt beside him, grabbing a handful of his hair, lifting his bloodied face as if to inspect the damage.

It was then that Gary saw the knife.

The blade was about ten inches long. Slightly thicker than a knitting needle.

Gary opened his mouth, moaning as he felt fresh waves of pain from his smashed jaw. He tried to squirm away from the hand which held him so firmly but it was useless.

The point of the knife actually brushed his upper eyelid and he felt his bowels loosen as fear overcame him.

The wickedly sharp point of the knife punctured the bulging orb of his right eye effortlessly.

It was pushed with no haste. It wasn't driven into the writhing boy's eye, it was *inserted* with a kind of sadistic precision.

And now he did find the breath to scream but the frantic bellow was cut off abruptly as two more inches of the blade disappeared into his eye socket, pushed with an even pressure.

Two inches.

Three.

Four.

Vitreous liquid spurted onto his cheek, mingling with the blood which already covered his skin.

The eye seemed to burst like a water-filled balloon. The white turned red and the orb seemed to collapse in upon itself as the blade was pushed deeper. One final surge of pressure and it punctured the frontal lobe of the brain.

Gary Sinclair shuddered then lay still.

The knife was pulled free then the driver of the car calmly unlocked the boot and pushed it open.

It took only a moment to lift Gary's body and push it unceremoniously into the rear compartment of the vehicle. The lid was slammed down and the driver walked unhurriedly around to the door, slid behind the wheel and guided the vehicle back out onto the road.

Once again, the tail lights were swallowed by the blackness.

2

It looked as if someone had been shading beneath her eyes with charcoal.

Susan Hacket looked at the reflection which stared back at her from the mirror and sighed. She picked up the brush which lay on the dressing table and swept it through her hair, listening to the static electricity crackling. She fluffed up her shaggy locks with her fingertips then reached for her make-up. She plucked a brush from the hand-shaped container on her left and began applying foundation to the pale visage which confronted her. The brushes and the make-up had been a present for her twenty-fifth birthday, just seven months earlier. But, at the moment, she felt a hundred and twenty-five.

Susan sighed again, tiring of her own efforts to brighten her appearance. She got to her feet, crossed the landing to the bathroom and washed the foundation off, towelling her face dry, glancing at herself in the bathroom mirror this time.

She was grateful that she didn't feel as rough as she looked.

Even the ravages of so much worry, so many sleepless nights, could not hide her natural attractiveness. She rarely wore heavy make-up. People were always telling her she didn't need it. But, in the last couple of months she had taken to wearing it on these nightly visits. Taken to making an effort. He had always liked her in make-up before, had always complimented her on her appearance. What reason was there to stop? Just because . . .

She splashed her face with more water, dried it a second time then returned to the bedroom where she hastily but expertly applied some mascara and eye-liner. The dark smudges beneath her eyes didn't look too bad she told herself. A few good nights' sleep and they would vanish. Exactly when those nights would come she had no idea.

She pulled on a sweatshirt and jeans, stepped into a pair of short suede boots and headed back out onto the landing once more. The door directly opposite her was slightly ajar. Sue crossed to it and moved silently into the room, careful not to collide with the half-a-dozen mobiles which hung from the ceiling. Snow White and the Seven Dwarfs. Dumbo. Postman Pat. All swayed gently in the slight breeze which wafted through the window. Sue rubbed her hands together, thinking how cold it was turning. She crossed to the window and closed it, pressing a hand to the radiator as she stepped away.

She moved close to the bed and crouched down beside it, pulling the sheet back from the tiny sleeping form cocooned within it.

Lisa Hacket lay still as her mother gently brushed some strands of fine, silver-blonde hair from her face. Then Sue leant across and kissed her four-year-old daughter on the cheek.

'I love you,' she whispered, then slowly straightened up and crept out of the room.

At the foot of the stairs she picked up her handbag and jacket then popped her head round the door of the sitting room.

'I'm off now, Caroline,' she said, smiling. 'I'll be back in a couple of hours.'

From the sofa, Caroline Fearns turned and smiled. A bright, pretty, sixteen-year-old with uncomfortably large breasts, she nodded and smiled broadly at Sue.

'I really am sorry I had to call you at such short notice,' Sue said. 'But John's got a meeting at the school and I'm not sure what time he'll be back. If he gets back before me could you tell him I've left some food in the oven for him, please?'

Caroline nodded briskly, smiled again then turned her attention back to the TV screen. She enjoyed baby-sitting for the Hacket's. They paid her well and they had a colour TV as well as a video. Her own father refused to buy a colour TV despite the fact that, during snooker matches, he spent the entire time complaining about not being able to figure out which balls the players were trying to pot. But besides the money and the TV there was an added bonus. Mr Hacket always insisted on taking her home in his car after the baby-sitting was over. Caroline found him unbearably sexy (even though he *was* pushing thirty). She wished *her* English teacher looked like him.

She heard the front door close and glanced at her watch.

6.35 p.m.

She'd wait until the soap opera she was watching had finished then she'd make a cup of tea. She stretched out contentedly on the sofa.

As Sue stepped out into the night she shivered. The wind whistled around her and she pulled up the collar of her jacket as she headed for her car, fumbling in her handbag for the keys. She slid behind the wheel of the Metro and started the engine, checking her reflection briefly in the rear-view mirror. Cheerful enough? No cracks in the mask?

She pulled away, making a note to stop off at the garage and get some flowers.

Flowers were so important.

They saw her leave.

Hidden by the darkness, sitting in the car parked about fifty yards down the street, they watched her as she pulled away.

6.38 p.m.

One of them glanced at the house, at the light burning in the front room.

They would wait a little longer.

3

He heard the thud from above and squinted at the ceiling, as if expecting it to cave in. But no cracks appeared, there was no rending of beams or crashing of concrete. The ceiling remained as unblemished now as it had been ten minutes ago when he'd first fixed his eyes on the spot above his head.

John Hacket draped one arm across his forehead, catching sight of his watch in the process. The ticking sounded thunderous in the relative silence of the bedroom. As even as his own low breathing.

'Penny for your thoughts.'

The voice came from beside him, a slight Irish lilt to it.

Hacket turned his head slowly to look at Nikki Reeves. She was looking at him with those large brown eyes, fixing him in the kind of gaze which had first drawn him to her. There were a thousand clichés for those eyes, for that look. *Come to bed eyes. Hypnotic glances.*

Hacket almost laughed.

How about, *Screw me and to hell with your wife eyes?*

She asked him again, brushing hair from her face.

'What are you thinking about?'

Hacket shook his head dismissively, watching as she raised herself up onto one elbow to look down on him. Her right hand rested on his chest, her index finger tracing patterns across his skin. He could smell her perfume. He knew the smell well. He should do, he'd bought it for her. The delicate aroma mingled with the stronger musky scent of their own post-coital exertions.

'What makes you think I've got something on my mind?' Hacket asked her, raising one finger and gently running it along her bottom lip.

She flicked out her tongue and licked the tip of the probing digit.

'Because you're quiet,' she said, smiling.

He shrugged.

'Be thankful for small mercies.'

Hacket lay still while she continued stroking his chest, only now his eyes were on her, taking in the details of her face and upper body. The sheet had slipped down to reveal her breasts, the nipples still erect. He looked at her face and, again, found himself lost in those eyes. His finger strayed from her lips and he took to stroking her cheek, enjoying the smoothness of her skin. And, all the time he could smell her perfume. It was one of the things which had first attracted him to her. The fact that she was good-looking had seemed almost secondary. Romance begins in many different ways and Hacket could think of a thousand more clichés to describe that particular peculiarity which men and women put so much faith in. But he knew that this was not romance. It was an affair. Pure and simple.

He almost smiled again at the irony of that phrase. There was nothing pure about it and simplicity was rapidly eroded when a man took a lover.

334

She was twenty-two, eight years younger than Hacket. The affair had been going on for the past three months. Ever since . . .

He tried to push the thought from his mind but it persisted.

Ever since Sue's father had become ill.

Hacket wondered if he was trying to justify his actions to himself. Even trying to shift the blame for his indiscretions onto his wife.

Her father was dying. She was worried. She hadn't enough time for Hacket so he'd found a lover. There, he thought, bitterly, it *was* simple when you thought it through.

Nikki leant across him and pressed her lips to his. He felt her tongue flicking urgently against his teeth then it slipped inside his mouth, stirring the warm wetness. Hacket responded fiercely and when they finally separated both were breathing heavily. He could feel her nipples pressing into his chest, his own erection now nudging her belly as she lay closer to him.

After a moment or two she pulled herself across him and sat on the side of the bed.

'Was it something I said?' he asked, watching as she got to her feet and reached for a baggy T-shirt on the chair nearby.

She smiled and slipped it on, the voluminous folds hiding her shapely figure as she padded towards the door. She paused there, silhouetted by the soft light which was spilling from the sitting room.

'I'm hungry,' she told him. 'Do you want something?'

He shook his head.

'No thanks I'll . . .' He coughed. 'I'm fine.'

I'll have something to eat when I get home. I'll eat the food that my wife has prepared for me, Hacket thought. He exhaled deeply, almost angrily, and sat up, reaching for his cigarettes, pulling the packet from the pocket of his trousers. He lit a Dunhill and sucked hard on it. Sue would be at the hospital by now, he thought, glancing at his watch. The nightly vigil. Christ, why did she torture herself like that? Every single bloody night she was at the hospital. He blew out a stream of smoke watching it dissipate slowly in the air. And how much longer was it going to last? No one knew, no one could tell her. The same way no one could tell *him* how long his affair with Nikki was going to continue. Nagging doubts at the back of his mind told him he should end it now. But the doubts only came when he

335

was at home, when he was away from her. When he was with her the desire to end the relationship wasn't so pressing. He didn't love her, that much he knew, but he felt for her more strongly than he should have done. She filled a gap in his life, a gap which should never have been there to begin with. Was he blaming Sue again? The role of neglected, misunderstood husband didn't suit him particularly well.

How about husband who's feeling sorry for himself?

Hacket took another drag on the cigarette.

How about unfeeling, selfish bastard? That seemed to suit him perfectly.

Hacket's philosophical musings were interrupted by Nikki's return. She was carrying a glass of milk and a plate with a couple of hastily-made sandwiches stacked on it.

She shivered, commented how cold it was in the kitchen then sat down on the bed beside him and took a bite from one of the sandwiches.

'Pig,' he said, watching her as she ate.

'Oink, oink,' she replied, giggling.

He snaked an arm around her waist and drew her closer to him, kissing her ear. She put down the sandwich, kissed him lightly on the tip of the nose then reached for the glass of milk. She took a mouthful but didn't swallow it. Instead she leant closer to him, the white liquid staining her lips. As she kissed him he opened his mouth and allowed her to pass some of the milk to him. When they parted she was smiling broadly. She allowed one hand to drop to his thigh, stroking the hair which grew so thickly there. Then her fingers were exploring higher, her nails gently raking his scrotum before gliding around his stiffening penis.

'I'll have to go soon,' he whispered as she gripped his shaft more tightly, working up a rhythm, coaxing him to full hardness.

'Soon,' she breathed in his ear.

They lay back across the bed, bodies entwined.

4

The houses in this particular part of Clapham all looked similar. Terraced and semi-detached, inhabited by unremarkable people with unremarkable lives.

People like John and Susan Hacket.

It was their home which the men in the grey Ford Escort had been watching for the last twenty minutes.

As if some kind of silent signal had been given both of them swung themselves out of the car and walked unhurriedly up the path towards the passageway which led towards the back garden of the Hacket's house. The street lamp outside the house was off, and it afforded the two men the cover they needed. The curtains of the houses on either side were drawn. It was too late in the day for people to be peering out checking on callers. A couple of doors down a dog barked but the two men paid it no heed. The first of them, a tall man with what seemed like abnormally long arms, gently lifted the catch on the passage door and opened it.

His companion followed him into the enveloping gloom.

The passage was about fifteen feet long, the floor of chipped concrete. The two men moved cautiously along the narrow walkway, careful not to create any noise as they made their way to the back of the house.

The garden was in darkness.

A rusted tricycle stood close by and the first man pushed it with his foot, ignoring the protesting squeal from its wheels. He smiled broadly and looked at his companion but the other man was already trying the back door, finding, not surprisingly, that it was locked.

The knife he took from his belt was about eight inches long, double-edged and wickedly sharp.

He stuck it into the frame of the window, working the blade expertly up and down until the window lock finally came loose. He nudged it gently and the window opened a fraction.

Peter Walton smiled and nodded to his companion who squatted down, clasping his hands together to form a stirrup. Walton put his foot on the helping hands and allowed himself to be hoisted up onto the window-sill. He paused there for a moment then swung himself inside, the sound of the TV reaching his ears as he eased himself down onto the tiles. He stood in the darkened room, watching as the tall man followed him inside.

Ronald Mills moved with remarkable dexterity for a man of over six feet. He clambered through the window and joined Walton in the kitchen, taking a step towards the closed door. He too could hear the sounds coming from the lounge.

Walton chewed his bottom lip contemplatively. He hadn't expected anyone to be at home. His expression of bewilderment gradually melted into a grin of satisfaction. This was an added bonus.

He looked at Mills and nodded, reaching for the handle of the door.

It opened soundlessly.

Both men stepped into the hall, the staircase to their right.

The sound of the TV was louder now.

Caroline watched the end credits of the soap opera. She even watched the adverts after it had finished. It was like seeing them for the first time watching them in colour. But finally she decided to make herself a cup of tea then check on Lisa. She hadn't heard any noise from the girl's bedroom, she never had any trouble with her, but she thought it part of her duty as baby-sitter, to actually check her temporary charge. Caroline stretched then got to her feet, glancing back at the television, as if reluctant to leave it for too long. She pushed open the door and walked out into the hall, slowing her pace.

It was dark.

And yet, hadn't Mrs Hacket left the hall light on when she'd gone out?

Caroline was actually reaching for the switch when the hand grabbed her by the throat, stifling any attempt at a scream. She was yanked backwards, almost lifted off her feet by the hand which held her.

She felt something cold against her cheek and realised that it was a knife.

Ronald Mills pressed the razor sharp blade against her flesh and whispered in her ear, his voice low and rasping.

'You make one sound and I'll cut your fucking head off!'

August 26, 1940

She wouldn't stop screaming.

Lawrenson had tried to calm the woman, tried to reassure her, but his efforts had been useless.

They couldn't stop her screaming.

'Give her an epidural for God's sake,' snapped Maurice Fraser. 'She's in agony.' He bent close to the woman's face, seeing the pain in her bulging eyes, as if he needed further proof that she was indeed suffering.

'No pain killers,' Lawrenson said, quietly, his eyes never leaving the woman. She was in her mid-twenties but the pain etched on her face gave her the appearance of someone ten years older. Her feet were secured in the metal stirrups by thick straps, her arms also held firmly. Despite the restraining straps though, she jerked and shuddered incessantly as wave upon wave of pain tore through her.

The white gown which she wore had slipped away from her lower body, exposing her swollen belly and, as Lawrenson watched, he could see the sometimes violent undulations from inside her abdomen.

It looked as though the baby was trying to tear its way free.

A particularly violent contraction tore through her and she unleashed a scream which reverberated around the room. Lawrenson felt the hairs at the nape of his neck rise.

'She's losing a lot of blood, doctor,' Nurse Kiley told him, watching the steady flow from the woman's vagina. Several swabs had already been used, unsuccessfully, to stem the outpouring of crimson fluid, they now lay discarded in a metal receiver like thick placental fragments. Another pint of blood was attached to the drip which fed blood into the prone woman by way of a twisted tube to her left, the needle jammed securely into the crook of her arm.

'Remove the baby, for God's sake, Lawrenson,' Fraser said. 'Perform a Caesarian before it's too late. We'll lose them both.'

Lawrenson shook his head.

'It'll be all right,' he said.

Another piercing scream filled the room and drummed off the walls.

Nurse Kiley, who was standing between the woman's legs, peered towards the weeping vagina then glanced at Lawrenson.

'It's starting,' she said.

Lawrenson moved closer, anxious to see the birth.

Fraser gripped the woman's shoulder, trying to offer some comfort but she continued to scream in pain as the contractions became more violent. She felt something inside her tearing, as if part of her insides were detaching themselves then, incredibly, the pain seemed to intensify.

Lawrenson saw the top of the baby's head, the lips of the woman's vagina sliding back like fleshy curtains to expose the first couple of inches of the child. The bloodied lips reminded him of a mouth, trying to expel something bloated and foul tasting. The labia swelled until it seemed it must tear, until it appeared that the woman would begin to split in half. Blood pumped from the widening cleft which was now opening ever wider to release its precious load.

The woman began thrashing madly on the bed, so ravaged by pain that she actually managed to pull her left arm free of the restraining strap. As she waved it before her, the drip came free and blood spurted madly from her arm and also from the end of the tube. Nurse Kiley hurried to re-attach it.

'Come on,' shouted Lawrenson, watching as more of the baby's head came free. 'Push. It's nearly over.'

There was a soft, liquescent spurt as the woman defecated, the waste mingling on the reeking bedclothes with the blood which still streamed from her vagina.

The head was free now, the child itself twisting from side to side, as if anxious to escape its crimson prison. The woman's labial lips spread ever wider as the child slithered into view. Lawrenson reached for it, ignoring the blood which drenched his hands.

340

He lifted the child, the umbilical cord hanging from its belly like a bloated snake, still attached to the placenta which, seconds later, was expelled in a reeking lump.

The woman's head lolled back, sweat covering her face and body, her hair matted to her forehead.

Fraser turned to look at the child which Lawrenson held aloft, gripping it like some kind of trophy.

'Oh Jesus,' murmured the doctor, his eyes bulging wide.

Nurse Kiley saw the child and could say nothing. She turned away and vomited violently.

'Lawrenson, you can't . . .' Fraser gasped, one hand clapped to his mouth.

'The child is all right, as I said it would be,' Lawrenson beamed, holding it up, not allowing it to squirm out of his grip. The umbilical cord still pulsed like a thick worm. It looked as if a putrescent parasite was burrowing into the child's stomach.

He held it towards the mother who had recovered sufficiently to look up. Her eyes were blurred with pain but as she blinked the clarity quickly returned and she saw her child.

'Your son,' said Lawrenson, proudly.

And she screamed again.

5

Walton guessed that the girl was seventeen, maybe older. He didn't care.

She stood before him, hands clasped, shuffling her fingers like fleshy playing cards. There were tears in her eyes as she looked back and forth at the two men who stared so raptly at her. One of them, the taller one, kept wiping the back of his hand across his mouth and Caroline was sure he was dribbling. His breath was a low rasping wheeze, like an asthmatic gasping for air.

'You're pretty,' said Walton, touching her cheek with the point of the knife.

Caroline tried to swallow but her throat was dry. She closed her eyes and, this time, the tears did flow, running down her cheeks.

Walton pressed the knife against her flesh, allowing one of the salty droplets to dribble onto the metal. He withdrew the blade and licked the moisture with his tongue. Then he smiled at Caroline.

'Take your blouse off,' he said, softly, still smiling.

'Please don't hurt me,' she said, wiping the tears away with the back of her hand.

'Take the blouse off,' Walton urged, his voice now almost inaudible. He took a step closer to her, his face close to hers. He breathed stale cigarettes and tooth decay over her.

Still she hesitated.

'Take the fucking thing off or I'll take it off for you,' he hissed through clenched teeth.

Caroline reached for the top button, her hands shaking uncontrollably but, slowly, she managed to undo the fastener then repeated the procedure until the blouse hung open. Even through her fear she blushed.

'I said take it off,' Walton reminded her. 'Do it.'

'Please . . .'

'Do it,' he snarled.

She eased first one shoulder then the other out of the flimsy material, allowing it to drop to the floor in front of her. She sniffed, trying to fight back the tears but not succeeding.

'Please don't hurt me,' she whimpered, looking at both men as if expecting to find some trace of compassion. There was none.

'Why are you crying?'

It was Mills who asked the question this time.

He moved closer to her, and rested one hand on her left shoulder, peering at her breasts, which she attempted to cover.

He slapped her hands away and pulled at the strap of her bra.

'You've got lovely hair,' he told her, winding it around his hand, pulling her head to one side, towards his face. 'Kiss me.' He smiled broadly then looked at Walton, who nodded as if to urge his companion on.

'Well, go on, kiss him,' Walton said.

'Please . . .'

She got no further.

Mills pulled her round to face him, pushing his mouth against hers.

She gagged as she felt his thick tongue pushing against her lips, his spittle running down her chin.

'A virgin. Never been kissed before?' Mills asked, pressing the point of the knife under her chin, digging it into the flesh gently at first. He watched as tears mingled with his own sputum.

'Take your bra off,' Walton said. 'Show us your body.'

Caroline shook her head almost imperceptibly, sobbing now.

'You said you didn't want us to hurt you,' Mills reminded her, grabbing a handful of her hair once again. He pressed the razor sharp knife against her taut locks and sliced effortlessly through, pulling the handful of hair free. 'Hair today, gone tomorrow,' he chuckled, looking at Walton who merely nodded.

'Take off the bra,' he snapped. 'Now.'

She tried to plead, tried to beg but no words would come. Instead she reached behind her and unfastened the clasp of her bra, holding it for precious seconds before releasing it, pulling the garment free and exposing her breasts.

Walton rubbed his growing erection through his trousers.

'Now the jeans,' he said.

She was crying softly all the time now, tears pouring down her cheeks.

The two men stood a couple of feet back, watching the obscene strip-show with growing excitement.

'Don't kill me,' she sobbed, standing before them in just her knickers. 'I'll do what you say but don't kill me.'

'Take off your panties,' Mills told her. 'Slowly.'

She hooked her thumbs into the elastic and eased them down over her hips and thighs, shrugging them off to finally stand naked before her tormentors. She raised a hand to cover her sandy pubic hair but Mills gripped her wrist, lifting her hand instead to his own crotch, forcing her to touch the throbbing erection he now sported.

'Have you got a boyfriend?' Walton asked, pressing himself against her.

She didn't answer.

'Have you?' he snarled, jerking her head around so that she was looking directly into his staring eyes.

She shook her head, her eyes now clouded with tears, her whole body shaking.

343

'So you don't know what it's like to be touched by a man?' Walton said, softly. 'You don't know what you're missing.' He chuckled and gazed at her breasts for a second. 'Now if you're good we won't hurt you. Are you going to be good?'

She tried to nod but it was as if her body was paralysed. She thought she was going to faint.

'Dance for us,' said Mills, smiling.

'I can't,' she wailed, close to breaking point.

'Come on,' he said, childingly, pressing the knife to her left cheek. 'Every young girl can dance.'

'You said you wouldn't hurt me. Please . . .'

Walton bent down and picked up her bra on the end of his knife. He dangled it before her like some kind of trophy.

'Dance,' he said.

'Mummy.'

All three of them heard the word.

Mills spun round, a faint smile on his thick lips.

'Who else is in the house?' snarled Walton, grabbing Caroline by the hair.

'It's a child,' said Mills, his eyes blazing.

'Where is she?' Walton rasped.

'Upstairs,' sobbed Caroline.

Again the plaintive call.

Mills moved towards the door.

'Don't hurt her,' Caroline shouted but the exhortation was cut short as Walton clamped his hand over her mouth and forced her down onto the sofa, the knife held against her throat.

'I'll see to her,' Mills said, softly, heading out of the room and towards the stairs.

'He's very good with little children,' Walton informed her, fumbling with the zip of his trousers. 'Now, you just stay quiet for me, all right?'

Mills reached the bottom of the stairs and paused, listening to the calls from upstairs then, slowly, he began to ascend.

He reached the landing and moved towards the door which was slightly ajar.

He saw the child sitting up in bed as he opened the door, his frame silhouetted against the light.

The child was silent as he walked into the bedroom.

'Hello,' he said, gaily.

Lisa looked puzzled by this newcomer. She'd never seen him before but she remained silent as he knelt beside her bed.

'You're a very pretty little girl,' Mills breathed. 'What's your name?'

She told him.

'What a pretty name.' He pushed her gently back into bed, looking down at her, smiling, wiping his mouth with the back of his hand.

Then he reached for the knife.

6

The ward sister nodded politely as Susan Hacket passed her. She managed a smile in return and walked on up the corridor.

A tall nurse also smiled at Sue. Most of the staff recognised her by now. After all, she'd been coming to the hospital every night for the last six weeks. If was as if she belonged there. As she pushed the door to room 562, she wondered how much longer she would be repeating this ritual.

She paused in the doorway for a moment, closing the door slowly behind her.

The air carried the familiar smell of stale urine and disinfectant, but tonight it was tinged with a more pungent odour. Sue recognised it as the stench of stagnant water. The flowers which stood by the bedside were wilting, some of them weeping their shrivelled petals onto the cabinet. The water was cloudy. It was three or four days since she'd changed it.

She walked towards the bed, aware of the chill in the air. She shuddered involuntarily and noticed that the window was open slightly.

She murmured something to herself then shut it, keeping back the cold breeze which had been hissing under the frame. Then she turned towards the bed.

'Hello Dad,' she said, softly, smiling as best she could.

He didn't hear her.

Over the past two weeks he'd been slipping in and out of consciousness more frequently. Sometimes it was the extra doses of morphine they gave him, at other times his body just seemed to give up, to surrender to the pain and seek release in the oblivion of sleep. Sue reached across and touched his hand. It felt like ice. He had only one blanket to cover him and this she hastily pulled up around his neck, easing both arms beneath it too.

As she leant over him she smelled the stale urine more strongly. As his condition had deteriorated they had fitted him with a catheter and now she glanced down to see that the bag was half full of dark urine. Sue swallowed hard, thinking how undignified they were. It was as if the bag was one of the final concrete illustrations that he was helpless, unable even to reach the toilet. He never left his bed now. When the illness had first struck he had been able to walk up and down the corridor, even take the odd trip into the hospital gardens but, as the cancer had taken a firmer hold, all he had been able to do was to lie there and let it devour him from the inside.

She stood by the bedside for a moment longer gazing at his face. The skin was tinged yellow, stretched so tightly over the bones it seemed they would tear through.

Tom Nolan had never been a big man even when he was in the best of health but now he looked like an escapee from Belsen. His eyes were little more than sunken pits, the lids slightly parted as if he were watching her. Watching but not seeing. She could hear his low rasping breaths, and only the almost imperceptible rise and fall of his chest, accompanied by those grating inhalations, told her he was still alive. His thinning white hair had been swept over to one side of his head, a couple of strands having fallen untidily onto his forehead.

Sue reached into the drawer in the bedside cabinet, took out a comb and carefully ran it through the flimsy hair. As she withdrew she found that her hands were shaking. She stood gazing at him for a moment longer then picked up the vase with the dead flowers and threw them into the waste bin nearby. She then washed the vase in the sink and arranged the flowers she'd bought on her way to the hospital.

As she was replacing the vase she noticed that there was an envelope on the top of the cabinet. Sue opened it and pulled out a card which bore the words 'HOPE YOU'RE SOON FIGHTING FIT'.

Underneath was a picture of a boxer. She flipped it open, her teeth clamped together as if to fight back the pain. Sue didn't recognise the name inside, didn't know who'd written 'Get well soon'.

She tore the card and the envelope up with almost angry jerks of her arm then tossed the remains into the bin with the dead flowers.

'Get well soon,' she repeated under her breath, her eyes fixed on the shrivelled, shrunken shape which was her father. She almost smiled at the irony. You didn't 'Get well soon' when you had lung cancer, she thought. You didn't get well at all. You did what her father was doing. You lay in bed and let the disease eat you away from the inside. You let it transform you into a human skeleton. You let it tear you apart with pain.

The tears came without her even realising.

Every night she saw him, sat by him and, every night she swore she wouldn't cry but, again, the sight of him lying there waiting for death proved too much. She sat on the edge of the bed and pulled a handkerchief from her pocket, wiping her eyes.

Her own subdued whimperings momentarily eclipsed the low rasping sound coming from her father. She clenched her teeth hard together, until her jaws ached, then she blew her nose and sighed wearily. How much longer was this going to go on? How many more nights of waiting? There had been times, especially during the last couple of weeks, when she had felt like praying for his death. At least it would mean the end of his suffering. But when she had thoughts like that she swiftly rebuked herself. Life was so precious that it was something to be grasped, to be retained no matter what the indignities, no matter what the suffering. Life with pain was better than no life at all.

She wondered if her father thought the same.

Sue squeezed his hand through the thin material of the blanket and felt again how thin he was. It was like clutching the hand of a skeleton, hidden beneath the cover she could easily have imagined that no flesh covered the bones and that to exert too much pressure would crush the hand. She held him a second longer then wiped her eyes again, the initial outpouring of emotion now passed. All that was left was the feeling of helplessness, the feeling which always came after the

347

tears. An awful weariness and, at the same time, bewilderment that, after so long watching him wither away before her, she still had tears to offer. Every night as she arrived at the hospital she told herself that she would not cry, that she had become used to his appearance, to the knowledge that she was marking time waiting for him to die. But, every night, when she saw those ravaged wasted features and realised again that he would soon be gone forever, the tears came.

She knew she was the only one who ever visited him. It had been the same when he'd been in his flat in Camden, prior to being struck down with the illness.

Sue had a sister a year older than herself who lived about forty miles outside London, less than an hour's drive but she had visited the hospital only twice, at the beginning. Before the cancer took a real hold. Sue didn't blame her for that. She knew that there were practical reasons which prevented more frequent visits. And, besides, over the last two or three weeks, she had come to feel that the nightly visits were almost a duty. She came out of love but also because she knew she had been the one her father had doted on when she'd been growing up. She was still his 'little girl'. She *had* to be there for him.

She sniffed back more tears and clutched his hand again. He felt so cold, even when she took to rubbing his hand with her own, he still seemed frozen. It was almost as if he were sucking in the chill air and storing it in his waxen skin.

There had been none of this interminable waiting when her mother died. A stroke had taken her nine years earlier. The swiftness of it had been devastating but now, as Sue sat with her father she was beginning to wonder which was preferable. Although she, like everyone else, knew that there was *no* preferable way. Death brought pain and suffering, whichever guise it chose to arrive in. After her mother's death, Sue had realised both the awful finality of it but also how empty it leaves the lives of those who remain. She had seen the devastating effect her mother's death had wrought on her own father. The flat where they had lived for thirty years, where they had raised a family, had become a prison for him. A cell full of memories, each one of which held not joy but pain because he had known that memories were all he had. There was no future to look forward to, only the past to dwell on.

Sue knew that feeling now. There had been good times with her father but, once he was dead, there would be just memories and memories sometimes faded. Even the good ones.

This thought brought a fresh trickle of tears which she hurriedly wiped away with the back of her hand.

She touched his cheek with the back of her hand, stroking gently, feeling the prominent cheekbones, tracing the hollows which had formed in his features. This time no tears came, and she remained like that for the next fifty minutes, stroking his face and hair, clutching his hand.

Sue finally glanced at her watch, saw that visiting hours were over, and heard others leaving, making their way down the corridor outside. Slowly she got to her feet then pulled up the blanket again, tucking it around him to keep out the cold. Then she leant forward and kissed his forehead.

'Goodnight, Dad,' she whispered. 'See you tomorrow.'

She turned and did not look back, pulling the door open and slipping out silently, as if not to disturb him.

7

He pulled on his shirt, tucking it into his jeans as he heard the sound of the shower from the bathroom. Through the open door he could make out the blurred silhouette of Nikki behind the frosted glass.

Hacket buttoned his shirt then pulled on his trainers and started tying them. He sat on the edge of the bed, glancing up as he heard the shower being turned off. A moment later, Nikki stepped from inside, her body glistening with water, and Hacket admired her figure for a few seconds before she wrapped herself in a towel. Her hair was hanging in long tendrils, dripping water onto her shoulders as she walked back into the bedroom. She crossed to Hacket and kissed him softly on the lips, some of the water from her wet hair dripping onto his shirt. She slid the bath towel from around herself and began drying her arms and legs. He watched her for a moment longer, still sitting on the edge of the bed.

His eyes were fixed on the gold chain which she wore around her neck and the small opal which dangled from it. Another of his gifts to her. *If you're going to have an affair then do it with style,* he reminded himself. Buy her things. Show her that you care. Hacket almost laughed aloud at his own thoughts. *Care.*

What the hell did he know about caring? If he cared for anyone he'd be at home now, not preparing to leave the flat where his lover lived.

The self-recrimination didn't strike home with quite the vehemence it was meant to. He exhaled deeply, reaching out to touch her leg as she raised it, placed her foot on the bed and started to pat away the water with the towel.

'Do you have to go now?' she asked him.

Hacket nodded.

'Sue will be back from the hospital soon,' he told Nikki. 'I'd better make a move.'

'Won't she wonder where you've been?'

'I told her I had a meeting.'

'Is she trusting or just naive?' There was a hint of sarcasm in Nikki's voice which Hacket didn't care for.

'Do you really want to know? I thought you didn't want to hear anything about my wife,' he said, irritably.

'I don't. You mentioned her first.' She finished drying herself and reached for her housecoat which she pulled on, then she began drying her hair. 'Do you think about her when you're with me?'

Hacket frowned.

'What is this? Twenty questions?' He rolled up the sleeves of his white shirt revealing thick forearms. They regarded each other silently for a moment then Nikki's tone softened slightly.

'Look, John, I didn't mean to sound so bitchy,' she said.

'Well you made a bloody good job of it,' he snapped.

'I want you. I don't want to know about your wife or your family and if that sounds callous then I'm sorry. You chose to have this affair, just like I did. If you've got second thoughts, if you feel guilty, then maybe you shouldn't be here.'

'Do you want me here?' he demanded.

She leant forward and kissed him.

'Of course I do. I want you whenever I can have you. But I'm no fool either. I know this affair won't last. It can't. And I'm not going to ask you to leave your wife for me. I just want to enjoy it while I can. There's nothing wrong with that is there?'

Hacket smiled and shook his head. He got to his feet, enfolded her in his arms and kissed her, his tongue pushing past her lips and teeth, seeking the moistness beyond. She responded fiercely, the towel falling to the floor, her breasts pressing against his chest. When they parted she was breathing heavily, her face flushed. She looked at him questioningly and Hacket was held by the intensity of her stare.

'What do you want, John?' she asked him. 'What do you get out of it? What am I? Just a quick fuck? A bit on the side?' Her Irish accent had become more pronounced, something he always noticed when she was upset or angry.

'You're more than a bit on the side,' he told her. 'Christ, I hate that expression.'

'What would you call me? A lover? Makes it sound more respectable doesn't it? What about a Mistress?'

'A mistress is an unpaid whore,' he said, flatly. 'What do names matter, Nikki? You ask too many questions.' He stroked her gently beneath the chin with his index finger.

She caught the finger, raised it to her mouth and kissed it, flicking the tip with her tongue.

'You spend your money on me,' she said, touching the opal necklace. 'Don't hurt me, John, that's all I ask.'

He frowned.

'I'd never hurt you. Why do you say that?'

'Because I'm scared. Scared of becoming involved, of starting to think too much of you. You might hurt me without even knowing it.'

'It cuts both ways. I can't turn my emotions on and off Nikki. I'm at as much risk as you. And I've got more to lose. If I fall in love with you I've got . . .' He allowed the sentence to trail off.

'Your wife and daughter,' she continued.

'Yeah, wife, daughter and mortgage to support,' he said, smiling humourlessly.

'So we carry on,' she said, pulling him closer. 'Like I said, I want you whenever I can have you. I just have to be careful.' She kissed him.

Hacket looked at his watch then headed for the door. She wrapped the towel around her again and followed him out to the hall.

'When will I see you?' she asked.

He paused, one hand on the door knob.

'Tomorrow at the school. We can walk past each other and pretend we've never met just like we always do,' he said with a trace of bitterness in his voice.

'You know what I mean. Will you call me?'

He nodded, smiled at her, then he was gone.

Hacket took the lift to the ground floor then walked across to his car. He slid behind the wheel of the Renault and sat there for long moments in the darkness then, he glanced behind him, towards the window of Nikki's flat where the light still burned. He exhaled, banging the steering wheel angrily. He cursed under his breath then, with a vicious twist of his wrist, he started the car, stuck it in gear and drove off.

If the traffic was light he should be home in less than forty minutes.

8

The first police car was parked up on the pavement close to the street entrance.

Susan Hacket drove past it, noticing the uniformed men inside it as she drew closer to her house. However, she was almost blinded by the profusion of red and blue lights which seemed to fill the night. On top of ambulances and police cars they turned silently and, with the men around them moving about in relative calm it looked like a scene from a silent film. Sue frowned, suddenly disturbed by the sight of so many official vehicles.

It took her only a second to realise that they were parked outside her own house.

'Oh God,' she whispered under her breath and brought the car to a halt. She clambered out from behind the wheel and hurried across to the pavement where a number of uniformed policemen were standing around in well ordered groups, most, it appeared, guarding the gates of the other houses. Sue could see lights on in the front rooms of the other houses, could see faces or at least silhouettes peering out into the night, anxious to see what was happening.

Uncontrollable panic seized her as she saw two ambulancemen entering her house.

She broke into a run, pushing past a policeman who tried to bar her way.

Two more men moved to intercept her as she reached the front door.

'What's going on,' she blurted, her passage blocked by a burly sergeant. 'Please let me in. I live here. My daughter is inside.'

It was another man, a man in his mid-thirties, dressed in a brown jacket and grey trousers, who finally spoke. He appeared behind the sergeant, eyeing Sue up and down appraisingly as if trying to recognise her.

'Mrs Hacket?' he finally said.

'Yes. What's happening, please tell me?'

The sergeant stepped aside and Sue rushed into the hall.

The smell struck her immediately.

A pungent stench of excrement, mingling with a smell not unlike copper.

The man in the brown jacket now barred her way and, as she tried to push past him, he caught her arms and held her. His face was pale, his chin dark with stubble. Even in such a tense moment Sue noticed how piercing his eyes were. A flawless blue which seemed to bore into her very soul. They were sad eyes.

'Please tell me what's happening,' she pleaded, trying to shake loose of his grip.

'You are Mrs Susan Hacket?' he asked.

'Yes, please tell me what's going on.' she practically screamed it at him. 'Where's my daughter?'

It was then that the ambulancemen emerged from the sitting room and Sue became aware of the smell once more, stronger now.

On the stretcher they carried was a sheet which, she assumed had once been white. It was soaked crimson and Sue realised that the thick red stain was blood. Her eyes bulged madly and she moved towards the stretcher.

The man in the brown jacket tried to hold her back but she wrenched one arm free and tugged at the sheet, pulling it back a few inches.

'No!' she shrieked.

As the ambulancemen hurried to cover the bloodied body of Caroline Fearns, Sue felt the bile clawing its way up from her stomach. In that split second she had time to see that Caroline's face had been slashed in a dozen different places, her lips clumsily hacked off so that only a hole remained where her mouth was. Her hair was matted with blood which had pumped from the wounds which had caused her death.

The man in the brown jacket tried to guide Sue into the kitchen away from the sight of Caroline's body but she seemed to resist his efforts until he practically had to lift her bodily from the hall.

'Where's Lisa?' she gasped, unable to swallow.

'Mrs Hacket, I'm Detective Sergeant Spencer, I . . .'

Sue wasn't interested in the policeman's identity.

'Where's my daughter?' she shrieked, tears beginning to form at her eye corners.

'Your daughter's dead,' Spencer said, flatly, trying to inject some compassion into his words but knowing it was impossible.

He held on to Sue for a moment then she shook loose and stumbled back against the table. For a moment he thought she was going to faint but she clawed at one of the chairs and flopped down on it.

'No,' she murmured.

'I'm so sorry, Mrs Hacket,' he said, gripping her hand.

She felt so cold.

'Where is she?' Sue demanded, her face drained of colour, her eyes searching Spencer's face imploringly for an answer.

'She's upstairs,' he told her then, quickly added, 'we've been trying to reach your husband . . .'

'I must see her,' she blurted. 'You must let me see her. Please.'

She got to her feet and tried to push past Spencer who, once again acted as a human barrier.

'Let me pass,' she shouted. 'I have to go to her.'

354

Spencer pushed the kitchen door shut behind him, penning her inside the room with him.

'There's nothing you can do,' he said. 'Your daughter is dead.'

Sue suddenly froze then, with a final despairing moan, she *did* pass out.

9

By the time Hacket arrived home there was just one police car parked outside the house. He gave it only a cursory glance as he walked towards the front door, fumbling for his keys, remembering he'd left them in his other jacket. He rang the doorbell and waited, blowing on his hands in an effort to warm them.

The door was opened by Spencer.

Hacket looked aghast at the policeman, standing on the doorstep even when he was ushered inside.

Across the road a curtain moved as the family opposite tried to see what was happening.

'Mr John Hacket?' Spencer asked.

The teacher nodded, finally finding the will to step over the threshold. The front door was closed behind him.

'Who are you?' he said, falteringly.

Spencer introduced himself.

'I don't understand. Why are you here?'

Hacket found himself manoeuvred into the kitchen where another plain-clothes man waited. The second man introduced himself as Detective Inspector Madden. He was older than his subordinate by five years, his hair greying at the temples, a stark contrast to his jet black moustache and eyebrows which knitted over his nose giving him the appearance of a perpetual frown. However, there was a warmth in his voice that seemed almost incongruous to his appearance. He asked Hacket to sit down and the teacher obeyed, finding a mug of tea pushed towards him.

'Will someone tell me what the hell is going on?' he said, irritably. 'Has there been an accident? My wife, is it my wife?'

355

'Your wife is with your next-door neighbours,' Madden told him, softly. 'She's been sedated, she's sleeping now.'

'Sedated? What the fuck are you talking about? What's happening?' His breath was coming in gasps now, his eyes darting back and forth between the two policemen.

'Your house was broken into tonight,' said Madden, his voice low and even. 'We found two bodies when we arrived. One we believe was a girl named Caroline Fearns, the other we think was your daughter. They're dead, Mr Hacket, I'm sorry.'

'Dead.' The word, the very act of speaking it seemed to drain all the anger and irritation from Hacket. His head bowed slightly. He tried to swallow but it felt as if his throat had filled with sand. When he spoke the word again it came out as a hoarse whisper.

'I'm sorry,' Madden repeated.

Hacket clasped his hands together before him on the table, his gaze directed at the cup of steaming tea. He chewed on one knuckle for a moment, the silence enveloping him.

Both policemen looked at each other, then at the teacher, who finally managed to croak another word.

'When?'

We think between seven and eight this evening,' he was told.

Hacket gritted his teeth.

'Oh God,' he murmured, feeling sick, wondering if he was going to be able to control himself. He closed his eyes, squeezing the lids together until white stars danced before him. Between seven and eight. *While he was with Nikki.*

He rubbed his face with both hands, still fighting to control his nausea. His mouth opened soundlessly but no words would come. He wanted to say so much, wanted to know so much but he could not speak. Only one word finally escaped.

'Why?' he asked, pathetically. 'Why were they killed?'

The question had an almost child-like innocence to it.

Madden seemed embarrassed by the question.

'It looks as if someone broke in with the intention of robbing the house,' he said. 'When they found your daughter and the young girl they ... ' He allowed the words to fade away.

'How was it done?' said Hacket, an unnerving steeliness in his tone,

356

despite the fact that he could not bring himself to look directly at either of the policemen.

'I don't think you need to know that yet, Mr Hacket,' Madden said.

'I asked how it was done,' he snarled, glaring at the DI. 'I have a right to know.'

Madden hesitated.

'With a knife,' he said, quietly.

Hacket nodded quickly, his gaze dropping once more.

In the resultant silence, the ticking of the wall clock sounded thunderous.

It was Spencer who finally coughed somewhat theatrically, looked at his superior then spoke.

'Mr Hacket, I'm afraid that your daughter will have to be formally identified.'

Hacket let out a painful breath.

'Oh Christ,' he murmured.

'It has to be done within twenty-four hours if possible,' Spencer continued almost apologetically.

'I'll do it,' Hacket said, his words almost inaudible. 'Please don't tell my wife. I don't want her to see Lisa like that.'

Spencer nodded.

'I'll pick you up tomorrow morning about eleven.'

'Would you like one of my men to stay outside the house tonight, Mr Hacket?' Madden asked. 'It'd be no trouble.'

Hacket shook his head and, once more, the three of them endured what felt like an interminable silence finally broken by Madden.

'We're going to have to ask you to leave the house too, Mr Hacket, until the forensic boys have finished. Is there somewhere you can stay? It'll only be for a day or two.'

Hacket nodded blankly.

'Just let me see it,' he murmured.

Madden looked puzzled.

'Where it happened,' the teacher said. 'I have to see.'

'Why torture yourself?'

He turned on Madden.

'I *have* to see.'

357

The policeman nodded, watching as Hacket walked out of the kitchen and through into the sitting room.

The sitting room had been wrecked.

The furniture had been overturned, ornaments smashed, television and video broken, but it was not the wanton destruction which shocked Hacket – it was the spots of blood on the carpet, so delicately covered with pieces of plastic sheeting. He pulled one of the armchairs upright and flopped down lifelessly in it, gazing around the room, his eyes bulging wide, looking but seeing nothing. He sat there as the minutes ticked by, surrounded by silence. Alone with his thoughts. Then, slowly, he hauled himself to his feet and walked towards the hall, pulling the sitting-room door closed behind him.

He hesitated again at the bottom of the stairs, as if the climb were too much for him or he feared what he might find at the top but then, gripping the bannister, he began to ascend.

He faltered again when he reached the landing, looking at the four doors which confronted him.

The door to Lisa's room was now firmly shut, but it was towards that one which he advanced, his hand shaking as it rested on the handle.

Hacket turned it and walked in.

More plastic sheeting.

More blood.

Especially on the bed.

He felt a tear form in the corner of one eye and roll slowly down his cheek. As he turned to step back out of the room his foot brushed against something and he looked down to see that it was one of his daughter's toys. Hacket stopped and picked up the teddy bear, holding it before him for a second before setting it on top of a chest of drawers. Again his gaze was drawn to the bed.

So much blood.

He felt more tears dribbling down his cheeks as he stared at the place where she had been killed.

How much pain had she suffered?

Had she screamed?

He clenched his fists together, each question burning its way into his mind like a branding iron.

How long had it taken her to die?

Does it matter? he asked himself. All that matters is that she's dead. *Perhaps if you'd been here . . .*

The thought stuck in his mind like a splinter in flesh. He turned and closed the door behind him, wiping the tears away with one hand, sucking in deep breaths.

He undressed swiftly and slid into bed beside her, feeling the warmth of her body against him. She murmured something in her sleep and he gently placed one arm around her neck, wanting to hold her more tightly. Wanting *her* to hold *him*.

She woke up suddenly, as if from a nightmare then, immediately, she saw him and Hacket could see that her face was unbearably pale and drawn. Even in the darkness he could see the moisture on her cheeks.

'John,' she whispered, her voice cracking and now he held her tightly, more tightly than he could ever remember. An embrace more intense than any born of love. She looked so vulnerable. And he felt her tears on his chest as he held her, his own grief swelling and rising once more.

'If only we'd been here,' she whimpered. 'If I hadn't been at the hospital and you hadn't been at that meeting she'd still be alive.'

Hacket nodded.

'We can't blame ourselves, Sue,' he said but the lie bit deep and he finally lost control. Hacket could, and did, blame himself. 'Oh Jesus,' he gasped and they both seemed to melt into one another, united in grief.

September 10, 1940

The voices outside the room grew louder.

One he recognised, the other he had not heard before.

Garbled, angry words then the door swung open as he rose.

'I tried to stop him, George,' said Lawrenson's wife, Margaret, looking helplessly at her husband who merely smiled and nodded at her.

'It's all right,' he said, eyeing the other newcomer with suspicion. 'You can leave us.'

She hesitated a moment then closed the door behind her. The veneer of civility which Lawrenson had managed to retain dropped sharply.

'Who are you?' he demanded. 'How dare you burst into my home like this?'

The man who faced him was tall but powerfully built, the thick material of his uniform unable to conceal the muscles beneath. He had a long face with pinched features and his cheeks looked hollow, giving him an under-nourished look which was quite incongruous when set against the rest of his physique. He strode across to Lawrenson's desk, a steely look in his eye and, even as the doctor noticed the man's rank, he introduced himself, albeit perfunctorily.

'Major David Catlin,' he announced, stiffly. 'Intelligence.'

Lawrenson didn't offer him a seat but Catlin sat down anyway.

'And to what do I owe this intrusion?' Lawrenson wanted to know.

'I'm here on official business, from the Home Office. It's about project Genesis.'

Lawrenson shot him a wary glance.

'Your work on the project is to stop as of now,' said Catlin, his eyes never leaving the doctor.

'Why?' Lawrenson demanded. 'The work has been going well, I've made great strides. Is someone else being put in charge?'

Catlin shook his head.

'The whole project is being shut down,' he said.

'You can't do that. You mustn't do that, I'm close to finding an answer. There are certain things which need perfecting, I know . . .'

The Major cut him short.

'The project is to cease immediately, Doctor,' he snapped. 'And I can understand why.'

'The Army, the Home Office, everyone was behind me at the beginning,' Lawrenson protested.

'That was until we saw the results,' Catlin said, quietly. 'Lawrenson, listen to me, if the public found out what this work involved there would be massive outcry. No one would stand for it, especially if the press got hold of it. Can you imagine the repercussions if a newspaper managed to get some photos of your work?' He shook his head. 'Work. God, I don't even know if that's the right word for it.'

'The Government encouraged me to perfect Genesis,' Lawrenson insisted, leaning on his desk and glaring at the officer. 'They funded me while I was researching.'

'That funding is also to be withdrawn,' Catlin informed him.

'Then I'll carry on alone.'

'Lawrenson, I didn't come forty miles to *advise* you to stop work on Genesis, I'm ordering you.'

The doctor smiled thinly.

'I'm not in your army Major, you can't give me orders,' he said.

The officer got to his feet.

'You are to stop work immediately, do you understand?'

'I've only been working under laboratory conditions for a month, less than that. You can't judge the results as early as this. It's unfair.'

'And what you're doing is inhuman,' snapped Catlin.

The two men regarded one another angrily for a moment then Lawrenson seemed to relax. He moved away from his desk towards the window which overlooked his spacious back garden. In the splendour and peacefulness of the countryside it was difficult to believe there was a war on, that, forty miles away in London, people would soon be preparing themselves for the Luftwaffe's nightly onslaught.

'What is more inhuman, Major,' Lawrenson began. 'The work that I'm involved in, work that could help mankind, or the senseless slaughter of millions in this bloody war we're fighting?'

'Very philosophical, Doctor but I didn't come here to discuss the rights and wrongs of war.'

Lawrenson turned and looked at the soldier.

'I will not stop my work, Major,' he said, flatly.

'Is it that you *cannot* or *will* not see why Genesis must stop now?' the officer asked.

'When I first began work on the project everyone backed me. I was hailed as a saviour.' He laughed bitterly. 'And now, I'm to suffer the same fate as the first saviour, metaphorically speaking.'

'Even you must realise the risks,' Catlin said. 'If details of your work were discovered there's no telling what would happen. That is why you must stop.'

Lawrenson shook his head.

'Tell the Home Office, tell your superiors, tell the Prime Minister himself that I will continue my work.'

Catlin shrugged.

'Then I can't be responsible for what may happen.'

Lawrenson heard the iciness in the soldier's voice.

'Are you threatening me, Catlin?' he snapped.

The Major turned and headed for the door, pursued by Lawrenson.

The officer strode towards the front door, past Margaret Lawrenson, who had emerged from one of the rooms leading off from the large hallway.

Lawrenson caught up with him as he reached the front door.

'Tell them to go to hell,' he roared as the soldier walked briskly across the gravel towards his waiting car. The driver started the engine and the officer slid into the passenger seat.

'You keep away from here, Catlin,' Lawrenson shouted as the car pulled away.

As he watched it disappear down the short driveway towards the road he wondered who the man in the back seat was.

The man who stared at him so intently.

10

Christ he needed a cigarette.

Hacket fumbled in his pocket for the fifth time and then glanced across the small waiting room at the sign which proclaimed, in large, red letters, 'NO SMOKING'.

Had it not been for the circumstances he may have found the irony somewhat amusing. Cigarette smoke was hardly likely to damage the residents of this particular building.

He sat outside the morgue, eyes straying to the door through which,

362

minutes earlier, DS Spencer had disappeared. It felt as if he'd been gone for hours. Hacket felt utterly alone despite, or because of, the smallness of the waiting room. It was painted a dull, passionless grey. Even the plastic chairs which lined the wall were grey. The lino was grey. The only thing that wasn't grey was the NO SMOKING sign which he glanced at again, shifting uncomfortably in his seat.

Outside he heard an ambulance siren and wondered, briefly, where it was going. To an accident? A road smash?

A murder?

Hacket tired of sitting and got to his feet, pacing steadily back and forth in the small room. There weren't any magazines to look at to pass the time, no three-year-old copies of *Readers Digest* or *Woman's Own*. For some absurd reason a joke sidled into his mind. A joke about a doctor's waiting room. *Two men talking, one said I was at the doctor's lately, I read one of the newspapers there. Terrible about the Titanic isn't it?*

Terrible.

Hacket fumbled for his cigarettes once more and, this time he ignored the sign and lit up, sucking deeply on the Dunhill. He blew out a stream of grey smoke which perfectly matched the colour of the walls.

He found, when he took the cigarette from his mouth, that his hand was shaking. Neither he nor Sue had slept much the previous night. She was at the house now, still sedated. A neighbour was sitting with her. Hacket wouldn't have wanted her here with him, he wasn't even sure how *he* was going to stand up to seeing his daughter laid out on a slab. For fleeting seconds he wondered if the Fearns family had identified Caroline yet. Had they felt like he felt now? Had they stood in this same waiting room wondering, fearing what they were going to see?

The thought faded, merging into thousands of others which seemed to be whirling around in his head. And yet despite all the apparent activity inside his mind there was a peculiar emptiness. A numbness. He sat down again and almost reached out to touch the chair beside him to reassure himself it was actually there. He was a million miles away, his mind sifting through details with a swiftness that created a vacuum. He took another drag on the cigarette then stubbed it out beneath his foot.

He felt sick and rubbed a hand across his forehead, feeling perspiration. He'd rung the school earlier that morning and said that he wouldn't be in for a few days. No details. A family bereavement he'd said, wanting to keep it simple. He didn't want too many questions asked. They'd find out soon enough when the story appeared in the papers. Then would come the questions, the enquiries, the consoling handshakes. He sighed and looked at the door again.

It opened and Simpson emerged, raising his eyebrows in a gesture designed to beckon Hacket forward.

He'd been waiting for this moment, wanting to get it over with, but now he would have given anything to sit for a while longer in that grey room in one of those grey chairs. He walked purposefully towards the door and entered.

The morgue was smaller than he'd imagined. There were no rows of lockers, no filing cabinets for sightless eyes. No white-coated assistants wandering back and forth with hearts and lungs ready to weigh.

And there was only one slab.

On it was a small shape, covered by a white sheet.

As he drew nearer to it, Hacket visibly faltered, he felt the colour drain from his face and his throat seemed to constrict.

Simpson moved towards him but he shook his head gently and advanced to within a couple of feet of the slab and its shrouded occupant.'

The coroner, a short man with heavy jowls and a balding head attempted a smile of sympathy but it looked more like a sneer. He looked at Spencer who nodded.

He pulled back the sheet.

'Is that your daughter, Mr Hacket?' the DS asked, softly.

Hacket let out a breath which sounded as if his lungs had suddenly deflated. He raised one hand to his mouth, his eyes rivetted to the small form on the slab.

'Mr Hacket.'

She was as white as milk, at least the parts of her which he could see through the patchwork of cuts and bruises. Her face and neck were tinged yellow by bruises and, across her throat was a deep gash which curved upwards at either side like some kind of blood-choked rictus.

'Why are her eyes still open?' he croaked.

'Rigor mortis,' the coroner said, quietly. 'The involuntary muscles sometimes stiffen first.' His voice trailed away into a whisper.

'Is it your daughter, Mr Hacket?' Simpson persisted.

'Yes.'

The detective nodded and the coroner prepared to pull the sheet back over Lisa but Hacket stopped him.

'No,' he said. 'I want to see her.'

The coroner hesitated then, slowly, he pulled the sheet right back, allowing Hacket to see the full extent of his daughter's injuries.

Her chest and stomach were also covered in dark blotches and deep gashes. The area between her legs was purple and he noticed that the inside of her thighs were almost black with bruising. The contusions continued right down her legs to her feet. Hacket looked on with lifeless eyes, there was no emotion there. It was as if the shock of seeing her had sucked every last ounce of feeling from him. He looked repeatedly up and down her tiny corpse.

'How was it done?' he asked, his eyes still on his daughter. 'Have you done the post-mortem?'

The coroner seemed reluctant to answer and looked at Simpson who merely shrugged.

'I asked you a question,' Hacket said, flatly. 'How was she killed?'

'No post-mortem has been done yet but, from external examination you can see ... well, I decided that death was caused by massive haemorrhage, most likely from the wound on her throat.'

'What about the bruising,' he pointed to the purplish area between her legs. 'There.'

The coroner didn't answer.

Hacket looked at him, then at Spencer.

'You have no right to keep information from me,' he said. 'She was my daughter.'

'We thought that it would save you any more suffering, Mr Hacket ...' Spencer said but the teacher interrupted him.

'You think it can get any worse?' he snapped, bitterly. 'Tell me.'

'There was evidence of sexual abuse,' said Spencer.

'Was she raped?' Hacket wanted to know.

'Yes,' the detective told him. 'There was evidence of penetration.'

'Before *and* after her death,' added the coroner by way of thoroughness.

Hacket gritted his teeth.

'Would she have felt much pain?' he wanted to know.

Simpson sighed wearily.

'Mr Hacket, why torture yourself like this?'

'I have to know,' he hissed. 'Would she have felt much pain?'

'It's difficult to say,' the coroner told him. 'During the rape, yes, probably, she may have been unconscious by that time though, she'd already lost a lot of blood before it happened. The cut across the throat would have sent her into traumatic shock. The rest would have been over quickly.'

Hacket nodded and finally turned away from the tiny body.

The coroner replaced the sheet and watched as Hacket strode out of the room, followed by Simpson.

The body was hidden from view once more.

11

The drive from the hospital back to the house seemed to take hours, though Hacket assumed that it was actually less than thirty minutes.

Spencer drove at a steady speed and Hacket gazed aimlessly out of the Granada's side window hearing only the odd phrase which the detective spoke.

'. . . Positive identification of the killers . . .'

Hacket noticed a woman and her two children trying to cross the road up ahead, waiting for a break in the traffic.

'. . . Criminal records as far as we know . . .'

One of the children was only about four. A little girl and she held her mother's hand as they waited for the cars to pass.

'. . . No doubt that two men were involved . . .'

Hacket seemed to see nothing but children during the drive back. It was as if the world had suddenly doubled its population of four-year-olds.

With one notable exception.

'. . . Let you know as soon as we have any information . . .'

'What kind of man rapes a four year old?'

The question took Spencer by surprise and Hacket repeated it.

'You'd be surprised,' he said. 'Men you'd never expect. Fathers like yourself . . .' The DS realised his mistake and let the sentence trail off. 'I'm sorry,' he added.

'What are the chances of catching him?'

'Well, we got good dabs from around the house, blood type we know, approximate height, weight and age. We'll get him.'

Hacket laughed humourlessly.

'And if you do? What then? A ten-year sentence? Out in five if he's a good boy,' he said, bitterly.

Spencer shook his head.

'It's not like that, Mr Hacket. He'll go down and he'll stay down.'

'Until the next time,' Hacket said, still looking out of the side window.

Hacket said a brief goodbye to the detective when they reached the house in Clapham and Spencer promised to be in touch as soon as he had any information, then he thanked the teacher for his co-operation, offered his sympathies once more and drove off. Hacket stood on the pavement for a moment then turned and headed towards the front door, letting himself in rather than ring the bell and risk disturbing Sue.

He found her sitting in the kitchen with the next-door neighbour, Helen Bentine. The two women, Sue a little younger, were sitting over a cup of tea talking, and Hacket thought how much brighter his wife looked. Granted she still had dark rings beneath her eyes and she looked as if she hadn't slept for a fortnight, but she actually managed a smile as he entered, rising to make him a cup of tea from the recently-boiled kettle.

Helen beat her to it, handed the teacher his drink then said she'd better go. They both thanked her, listening as the front door closed behind her.

'The doctor said you should rest, Sue,' he said, sipping his tea, loosening his tie with his free hand.

'I'll rest later,' she told him. 'I don't want to keep taking those pills he gave me, I'll get addicted.'

He sat down beside her, touching her cheek with his fingertips.

'You look so tired,' he said, looking at her.

She smiled weakly at him then took a sip of her tea.

Hacket knew she was about to say something but, when it came, he was still unprepared.

'What did she look like?' Sue wanted to know.

He shrugged, unable to think of a suitable answer.

Well, she was cut up badly, she'd been raped and the bastard had knocked her about so much there was hardly an inch of skin left unmarked, but apart from that she looked fine.

'John, tell me.'

'She looked peaceful,' he lied, attempting a smile.

'We'll have to tell the family, your parents, my family. They'll have to know, John.'

'Not just yet,' he said, softly, clasping her hand.

'Why did they pick on us?' she asked, as if expecting him to furnish her with an answer. 'Why kill Lisa?'

'Sue, I don't know. Would knowing the answer make it any more bearable? She's still dead, knowing why she was killed isn't going to bring her back.'

'But it isn't fair.' There were tears in her eyes now. 'My Dad's dying – that's hard enough to take – and now this.' She laughed bitterly and the sound caused the hair to rise on the back of Hacket's neck. 'Perhaps God is testing our faith.' She sniffed, wiped a tear from her cheek. 'Well if he is he's going to be unlucky.' Hacket gripped her hand more tightly, watching as the tears began to course more freely down her cheeks. 'God is a sadist.' She looked at Hacket, her eyes blazing. 'And I hate him for what he's done.'

Hacket nodded, got to his feet and put his arms around her. They stayed locked together for some time, Sue sobbing quietly.

'I just wish that I could have said goodbye to her,' she whispered. 'To have held her just one last time.' She looked up into his face and saw the tears in *his* eyes. 'Oh, John, what are we going to do?'

He had no answer.

*　　*　　*

At first he thought he was dreaming.

The ringing sounded as if it were inside his head, but, as he opened his eyes, Hacket realised that it wasn't make-believe.

The phone continued to ring.

He rubbed his eyes and eased himself from beneath Sue's head. She had taken two of her tablets and been asleep for the last hour or so. He had dozed off as well, the strain of the last twenty-four hours finally catching up with him.

Now he stumbled towards the hall and the phone, closing the sitting room door behind him. He picked up the receiver, blinking hard in an effort to clear his vision.

'Hello,' he croaked, clearing his throat.

'Hello, John, it's me, Nikki. Look, I'm sorry to ring your home.' Her voice was low and conspiratorial.

'What do you want?' he said, wearily.

'I needed to speak to you,' she said. 'Someone at school said you weren't going to be in for a few days.'

'That's right, why is there a problem? Are you keeping a check on my movements or something?' The acidity of his tone was unmistakeable.

'What's wrong?' she asked. 'Are you all right?'

'Look, is this important? Because if it's not will you get off the line now.'

'I said I was sorry for phoning you at home,' Nikki said, both surprised and irritated by his aggressiveness. 'Is your wife there, is that why you can't talk?'

'Yes she is but that's not the reason. You shouldn't have called me.'

'We were supposed to meet tonight, I was waiting . . .'

He cut her short.

'Don't call me here again, all right?'

'I cooked us a meal.'

'Eat it yourself,' he rasped and slammed the phone down. He stood in the hallway, his hand still on the receiver, the residue of that soft Irish accent of hers still lingering in his ears.

He couldn't tell her the truth. How could he?

From behind him in the sitting-room he heard Sue call his name and he turned to rejoin her.

As he did he cast one last glance at the telephone, as if expecting it to ring again.

12

The banks of black cloud which brought the rain also seemed to hasten the onset of night.

Like ink spreading over blotting paper the tenebrous gloom slowly seeped across the heavens above Hinkston. Icy rain came down in sheets, driven by a wind which cut into exposed skin as surely as a razor blade.

Bob Tucker pulled the scarf tighter around his chin in an attempt to protect himself from the elements and looked down into the grave.

The coffin was already hidden beneath a thin layer of muddy earth but the rain was rapidly washing it away, exposing the polished wood beneath. Bob shoveled a few more clods into the hole, paused to light a cigarette, then continued in earnest. The rain quickly extinguished the cigarette and he stuffed the sodden remains into the pocket of his overcoat, cursing the weather, his luck and anything else which came to mind as he toiled over the open grave. He knew he had to work fast. The rain falling on the excavated earth would rapidly transform it to mud. The soil in Hinkston was like clay at the best of times, but when it rained some parts of the town resembled Flanders in 1918.

Bob paused for a moment, straightening up, groaning as he felt the bones in his knees click. His back was beginning to ache as well. Occupational hazard, he told himself. He'd been grave-digger at Hinkston cemetery for the last twelve years. He liked the job too. Bob had never been much of a mixer, he enjoyed his own company and the job certainly gave him plenty of time alone. He had never married. Never wanted to. Approaching his fortieth birthday he was happy alone. He had a couple of friends who lived in the town, men he could share a drink with if he felt the need for company, but most of his time was spent in the small bungalow which overlooked the cemetery.

It came with the job. He'd converted one of the sheds in the back garden into a workshop and he did his most precious work there. Carving shapes from lumps of wood he picked up in the cemetery. The thick growths of trees which populated the graveyard offered him plenty of raw material. The walking sticks he made from fallen branches he'd often sold at Hinkston's twice-weekly market. Some had fetched upwards of fifty pounds each, but it wasn't the monetary rewards which interested Bob, it was the craft itself.

He stood at the graveside a moment longer, peering through the rain towards the lights of the town. The street lights looked like jewels twinkling on a sheet of black velvet.

The cemetery was about half a mile from the town centre, on a steep hill designed to help drainage, but some of the older graves had begun to break up and sink and Bob feared that there might be some subsidence. However, the damage to the graves was not all attributable to natural causes.

There had been a spate of vandalism during the last three weeks. Gravestones had been smashed, flowers scattered from new plots, paint sprayed on headstones and, in the worst case, a grave had been tampered with. About two feet of earth had been excavated but, fortunately, the vandals had not dug down as far as the coffin.

Bob wondered what kind of people found pleasure from disturbing the dead and where they rested. The consensus of opinion in Hinkston itself seemed to point to youngsters. Bob had caught a young couple about a fortnight ago, laid out naked on top of one of the older graves but vandalism had been the last thing on their minds. He smiled at the recollection. Of how the boy had tried to run with his trousers round his ankles while the girl screamed and scuttled along beside him waving her bra like some kind of white surrender flag. Bob hadn't reported that particular incident to the police but the vandalism itself worried him. Many nights he'd left his bungalow and walked the tree lined paths through the cemetery in an effort to catch the vandals but his vigils so far had proved fruitless.

He continued to shovel earth into the grave, anxious to finish his task and return to the warmth of his home, to get out of his wet clothes.

The flowers from the funeral lay in a heap to one side of the hole, he would replace those when he'd finished. The rain tapped out a steady rhythm on the cellophane which covered the blooms, running off the clear covering like tears.

Bob shovelled more earth, trying to ignore the growing ache in his back.

The noise came from behind him.

At first he wasn't sure whether or not it was merely the rain pattering through the thick branches which hung overhead but, when it came again he was sure that the sound was coming from beyond the cluster of bushes which gathered around the grave like camouflaged mourners.

Bob stopped immediately and looked round, shielding his eyes from the rain and attempting to see through the darkness to the source of the noise.

He stood and waited but heard nothing.

After a moment or two he continued with his task.

Another foot or so and he would be finished, he thought, thankfully.

The noise came from behind him again, this time slightly to the left.

Bob dropped the spade and spun round, almost slipping on the wet earth.

It could be an animal of some kind he reasoned, taking a step towards the bushes. He'd found squirrels, even a badger during some of his nocturnal strolls through the cemetery. But, it was too early to be a badger. Despite the darkness his watch told him that it was only just 7.30 p.m.

Vandals perhaps? No, surely they'd wait until late, until they were sure no one was around.

He parted the bushes and eased through the first clump, surprised at how high they grew.

No one hiding behind them.

The rain continued to pelt down.

He felt something touch his shoulder.

Bob almost shouted aloud, his hand falling instinctively to the Swiss Army knife in his coat pocket.

The branch which had slapped against him had been blown by the wind.

The lower, leafless, branches were flailing about like animated flagellums and Bob shielded his face from the stinging twigs which whacked into him as he turned back towards the grave.

The figure which stood before him was holding the spade he had dropped.

In the driving rain Bob could not make out the features, he merely strode towards the figure, calling that it was private property and, besides that, to put his spade down.

The figure swung the spade in a wide arc which caught Bob in the side of the face. The powerful impact splintered bone and his left cheekbone seemed to fold in upon itself. The strident crack of bone was clearly audible over his strangled cry of pain. The figure advanced and stood over him for a moment, watching as blood from his pulverised face poured down his coat. Then the figure brought the spade down a second time, this time on his legs.

Both shin bones were broken by the blow and Bob screamed in agony, feeling one of the shattered tibias tear through the flesh of his leg.

He fell back into the mud, the merciful oblivion of unconsciousness enfolding him, but seconds before he slipped away he felt his head being lifted almost tenderly.

Then he saw the long, thin, double-edged knife which, seconds later, was pushed slowly into his right eye.

The figure pushed on the blade until it felt the point scrape bone, then, as easily as a man lifts a child, the figure lifted Bob Tucker's body.

All that remained to show that a struggle had even taken place was the blood on the ground and, as the rain continued to fall, even that was soon washed away.

13

She looked at her watch and lit up a cigarette, puffing slowly on it, gazing at the phone as if it were a venomous snake sure to bite her the moment she extended her hand.

Nikki Reeves sat for five minutes until she finally picked up the receiver and jabbed out the digits. She waited, taking a last drag of her cigarette and stubbing it out in the ashtray. The tones sounded in her ear. She waited.

'Come on,' she whispered, ready to replace the receiver if necessary.

There was a click and she heard a familiar voice.

'Hello.'

She smiled.

'Hello, John, it's me, can you speak?' she said.

'If you mean is my wife here the answer is no,' Hacket said, irritably. 'I told you not to call me at home again, Nikki.'

'I had to speak to you. I have to know what's going on. You haven't been in to the school, I was worried.'

'I'm touched,' he muttered, sarcastically.

'John, what's wrong?' she wanted to know. 'I'm sorry for calling your home, I can understand you being angry about that.'

'When I told you not to call again I meant it. Not just here but anywhere.'

Nikki sat up, her brow creasing into a frown. She gripped the receiver more tightly.

'What are you saying? You don't want to see me again?'

There was silence at the other end then finally Hacket spoke again, his tone softer this time.

'You said you realised the affair couldn't go on indefinitely. I think it's time we stopped seeing one another.'

'Why the sudden change of heart?' she wanted to know.

'Things have happened that I can't discuss, that I don't want to discuss. It's over between us, Nikki. There wasn't much there to begin with, but I've been thinking and it's best ended now.'

'A sudden attack of conscience?' she snapped. 'It isn't quite as easy as that, John. We both knew what we were getting into. Why can't you talk to me, tell me what's bothering you?'

'For Christ's sake, Nikki, you're not my wife, you're just . . .' The sentence faded as a hiss of static broke up the line.

'Just a quick fuck,' she snapped. 'You don't have the right to just drop me like that. I'm not a tart you picked up in a bar. You didn't pay me. Unless that's what the perfume and the jewellery were.' She touched the onyx almost unconsciously.

'What do you want me to do, stick a cheque in the post?' Hacket said, angrily.

'You bastard.'

'Look Nikki, I made a mistake, right? End of story. My wife needs me now.'

'And what if *I* need you?' she said, challengingly.

'It's over,' he told her again.

'And what if I hadn't rung you. What were you going to do, hope that I'd forget what had happened in the last three months? Avoid me at work? You could have had the courage to tell me to my face, John.'

'Look, I can't talk any longer, Sue will be back any minute. It's finished.'

She was about to say something else when he hung up.

She gripped the receiver for a moment longer then slammed it down on the cradle, her breath coming in short gasps. Finished was it? Nikki lit up another cigarette and got to her feet, walking through to the sitting room where she poured herself a brandy, her hands shaking with anger.

Finished.

She fought back her tears of rage.

Finished.

Not yet, she thought.

September 23, 1940

George Lawrenson looked at the file marked 'Genesis' and nodded. The notes, the thoughts and theories contained within that manilla file were the sum of his work over the last ten or fifteen years. Only in the last few months had his ideas actually seen fruition.

And then, once those ideas had become facts, those who sought to control him had ordered him to stop the work which had been a greater part of his life. They had no right to stop him.

They had no understanding.

'Do you think they've changed their minds about the project?' Margaret Lawrenson asked, watching as her husband slipped the file into his small suitcase.

'I won't know until I get there,' he said.

The call from London had come late the previous evening. He had been told to come to the capital for 're-evaluation' (he hated their jargon) of his work. 'First they order me to stop and now they ask for more results.' He shrugged.

Margaret smiled and crossed to him, kissing him lightly on the cheek.

'You take care of yourself while I'm away,' he said, softly. 'Remember, there are two of you now.' He smiled and patted her stomach.

'What if they order you to stop, George?' she asked.

'Do you want me to stop?' he countered.

'I know you believe in what you're doing. *I* believe in what you're doing. Be careful, that's all I ask.'

He locked the suitcase.

'Where are the copies of my notes?' he asked finally.

'Hidden,' she assured him. 'If the originals are destroyed I've got the copies, don't worry.'

'They won't destroy them, they're not that stupid. Genesis is far too important for that and they realise it.' He picked up his suitcase and headed for the stairs. She descended with him, walking to the front door and out onto the drive. He slid the case onto the passenger seat of the car then walked around to the driver's side.

'Call me when you get to London,' she said, watching as he clambered behind the wheel and started the engine. Then she retreated to the front door and watched as he pulled away.

Lawrenson guided the car slowly down the driveway, turning to wave as he reached the end.

It was then that the car exploded.

The entire vehicle disappeared beneath a searing ball of yellow and white flame, pieces of the riven chassis flying in all directions. The concussion wave was so powerful that Margaret Lawrenson, standing more than fifty yards away, was thrown to the ground, her ears filled by the deafening roar as the car blew up.

376

A thick, noxious mushroom of smoke rose from the wreckage, billowing up towards the sky like a man-made storm cloud. Flames engulfed what little remained of the car, burning petrol spreading in a blazing pool around the debris. Cinders floated through the air like filthy snow and, as Margaret finally pulled herself upright and ran towards the flaming shell of the car she could smell burning rubber and a sickly, sweeter stench.

The odour of burning flesh.

The heat of the flames kept her back, away from the twisted remains of the car which were now glowing white from the incredible heat. But inside she could see what was left of her husband, burned so badly he resembled a spent match, still clutching what was left of the steering wheel with hands that had turned to charcoal.

She dropped to her knees in the driveway, sobbing.

Other eyes had seen the blast.

More professional eyes.

The two figures who sat in the jeep across the road, hidden by trees, watched appreciatively as the car first exploded then blazed.

The first of them smiled, the second reached for the field telephone.

'Give me the Prime Minister's personal aide,' he said, in clipped tones. There was a moment's silence then he continued. 'Tell Mr Churchill that, as of 10.46 a.m. today, Project Genesis ceased.'

Major David Catlin replaced the phone and gazed once more at the flames.

14

Hacket felt as if he'd been hit with an iron bar. His senses were dulled, his head aching. He moved as if in a trance, stopping to hold on to furniture every now and then as if afraid he was going to fall.

On the sofa, Sue sat quietly, her face pale, her eyes red and puffy from so many tears. She looked exhausted, as if the effort of so much sobbing had sucked every last ounce of strength from her.

She still wore the black skirt and jacket which she'd worn to Lisa's funeral.

Hacket had tried to coax her into changing after the last of the mourners had gone but she had merely shaken her head and remained on the sofa, her eyes vacant. He had wondered a couple of times if she had slipped into shock but, each time he'd touched her she'd managed a smile, even kissed his hand as he'd brushed her cheek.

Now he stood in the kitchen waiting for the kettle to boil, hands dug in the pockets of his trousers.

The day had passed so slowly. It seemed that each minute had somehow stretched into hours, each hour into an eternity. The pain of their loss had become almost physical. Hacket rubbed a hand across his forehead and watched the steam rise from the kettle, just as he had watched it first thing that morning when he'd risen, dreading what was to come.

The arrival of the flowers.

Then the guests. (They had limited those present to his own parents and Sue's sister and her husband.)

And finally the hearse.

Hacket swallowed hard, fighting back tears at the recollection.

The huge vehicle had completely dwarfed the tiny coffin. Hacket had thought how easily he could have carried the box himself, under one arm.

He made the coffee, reaching into the cupboard for an aspirin in an effort to relieve the pain which still gnawed at the base of his skull. He took a sip of coffee, scarcely noticing when the hot liquid burnt his tongue.

And at the cemetery they had watched as the box was lowered into the grave, again so pitifully small. He had feared that Sue would collapse. She had spent the entire service crushed against him, weeping uncontrollably, but he had tried to fight the tears, to be strong for both of them. It had been a fight he had no hope of winning. As the small box had come to rest on the floor of the grave he had surrendered to the pain inside him and broken down. And they had supported each other, oblivious to those around them, to the empty words the vicar spoke. Words like 'resurrection'.

Hacket now shook his head slowly and sighed.

The service had seemed to take an age and finally, when it was over, both he and Sue had been led like lost children back to the waiting car and driven back to the house. The mourners, feeling as though they were intruding, had stayed for less than an hour then left the Hackets alone with their grief.

Sue had slept for a couple of hours that afternoon but Hacket could find no such peace. He had paced the sitting room, smoking and drinking, wanting to get drunk, to drink himself into oblivion but knowing that he had to be there when Sue woke up. She needed him more now than ever before.

Even more than Nikki needed him.

He pushed the thought to one side angrily, picked up the mugs of coffee and headed back towards the sitting room.

Sue had her eyes closed and Hacket hesitated, thinking she was asleep but, as he sat down opposite her she opened her eyes and looked at him.

'I didn't mean to wake you,' he said, softly, smiling.

'I wasn't asleep. Just thinking.'

'About what?' he asked, handing her the coffee.

'About that stupid phrase people always use when someone's died. "Life must go on." Why must it?' Her face darkened.

'Sue, come on, don't talk like that. We have to go on, for Lisa's sake.'

'Why, John? She's dead. Our child is gone. We'll never see her again, never be able to hold her, kiss her.' Her eyes were moist but no tears came. Hacket wondered if tear ducts could drain dry as he watched Sue wipe her eyes. She shook her head, wearily.

So much pain.

'I should go and see my father tomorrow,' she said, quietly.

'No. Not yet. You're not ready.'

'And what if he dies too? What if he dies when I should have been with him?'

Hacket got up, crossed the room then sat down beside her, pulling her closer.

'Your sister could have stayed for a few days, she could have visited him.'

'She had to get back to Hinkston, her husband has to work and they have a child, John. It wouldn't be fair to leave him alone.'

'You do too much, Sue. If ever anything's needed to be done, you're the one who's done it. Never Julie. You take too much responsibility on yourself.'

'That's the way I am.'

'Well maybe it's time you started putting yourself first in order of priorities instead of coming second to everyone else's needs.' He gently held her chin, turned her head and kissed her on the lips. She gripped his hand and squeezed.

'I love you,' she whispered.

'Then prove it. Come to bed, get a good night's sleep.'

'In a while,' she said. 'You go up, I won't be long.' She glanced down at the coffee table and noticed a letter addressed to her lying beside a card offering 'Sincerest Sympathies'. 'What's this?' she asked him, reaching for the letter.

'It came this morning. I figured you'd read it when you felt like it.'

'I don't recognise the writing,' she said, turning the envelope over in her hands.

'Can't it wait until the morning?'

'Just give me a minute, John. Please,' she asked softly and kissed him.

Hacket rose and headed for the hall.

'One minute,' he reminded her then she heard his foot-falls on the stairs as he climbed.

Sue put down her coffee, let loose a weary breath then opened the letter. It was just one piece of paper, no address at the top and, as she glanced at the bottom, she noticed it wasn't signed either. She checked the envelope again, ensuring that it hadn't been delivered to the wrong house. Her name was there, the address was correct.

'Dear Mrs Hacket,' she read aloud, her eyes skimming over the neat lettering. 'I know what you will think of me for writing to you but I had a feeling you would want to know what has been going on between myself and your husband, John . . .' The words faded into silence as she read the remainder of the note, her mouth open slightly.

She read it again, more slowly this time. Then, she folded it, gripped it in her hand and got to her feet.

She paused at the bottom of the stairs, looking up towards the landing, then at the crumpled letter.

Sue began to ascend.

15

'I should have stayed with her for a couple of days,' said Julie Clayton, gazing out of the side window of the Sierra. 'I should have gone to see Dad too.'

'They're best left on their own, there's nothing you could do,' Mike Clayton said, glancing agitatedly at the car ahead of him. He indicated to overtake, saw that the car ahead was speeding up and dropped back again. 'Come on you bastard,' he hissed. 'Either put your foot down or get out the bloody way.'

He looked down at the dashboard clock.

10.42 p.m.

'We're not going to make it back in time at this rate,' he said, irritably. 'I said you should have come alone.'

'Sue *is* my sister, Mike,' Julie snapped. 'She needed me there.'

'Well your own son needs you now,' he reminded her, attempting to overtake the car in front once again. He stepped on the accelerator hard, easing the Sierra out into the centre of the road, ignoring the lights which he saw coming towards him.

'Mike, for God's sake,' Julie gasped, seeing the oncoming vehicle but her husband seemed oblivious to the approaching car. He pressed down harder, the needle on the speedometer touching eighty as he sped past the van ahead of him.

The car coming the other way swerved to miss the Sierra, the driver slamming on his brakes, simultaneously hitting the hooter. The car skidded and looked like crashing but the driver wrestled it back onto the road and drove on.

381

Mike Clayton, now clear of the van which had been blocking him put his foot down.

They passed a sign which read 'HINKSTON 25 MILES'.

Clayton shook his head, trying to coax more speed from the car.

Julie also glanced at the clock and saw that it was fast approaching 10.47. She guessed it would take another twenty minutes before they reached home, provided there were no more delays.

She swallowed hard and looked across at her husband who was gripping the wheel so tightly his knuckles were white.

She too was beginning to wonder if they would reach Hinkston in time.

She prayed that they did.

16

'Who is she, John?'

Sue stood in the bedroom doorway, the letter held before her like an accusation.

Hacket looked across from the bed and frowned, not quite sure what was happening. Sue crossed to the bed, standing beside it, looking down at him, a combination of anger and hurt in her eyes.

More pain.

The realisation slowly began to creep over him.

'I had a feeling you would want to know what has been going on between myself and your husband,' she read aloud.

Hacket exhaled deeply, wanting to say something but knowing that whatever words he found they would be inadequate.

'I do not care what you think of me,' Sue continued, reading from the crumpled letter. 'But I felt you had a right to know what has been happening between us.'

'Sue . . .'

She interrupted him.

'I do not like being used,' she read, her eyes still rivetted to the paper. Then, finally, she looked at him. 'Who is she?'

He knew that it was pointless to lie.

At least clear one part of your conscience, eh?

'Her name's Nikki Reeves,' he said, quietly. 'She works at the school.'

It was said. There was no turning back now.

'You had an affair with her?' Sue said and it was a statement rather than a question. 'How long did it last?'

'Three months.'

He watched as she sat down on the edge of the bed, the letter still held in her hand. She had her back to him as if to look at him caused her disgust. He wouldn't have blamed her if disgust was the emotion she was feeling but he guessed it was more painful than that.

'Is it over now?' she wanted to know.

'Would you believe me if I told you?'

'Is it over?'

'Yes. I finished it a couple of days ago.'

She looked at him finally, a bitter smile on her lips.

'All those meetings at school you went to, you were really with *her*.' Her eyes narrowed suddenly. 'You never brought her here did you?'

'No, never.'

'And where did your little *liaisons* take place, John?' she asked with something bordering on contempt. 'In the back of the car? In an empty classroom or office?'

'Sue, for Christ's sake it wasn't as sordid as that. She has a flat . . .'

'Oh, her own place, how convenient. Somewhere to wash away the dirt afterwards.' The last sentence was barbed and it cut deep. 'How old is she?'

'Twenty-two. Is that really important?'

'I thought teachers were meant to have flings with pubescent pupils, nymphomaniac sixth-formers. Still, you always liked to do things differently didn't you, John. Why someone so young? Re-affirming your attractiveness now you're reaching the dreaded thirtieth birthday?'

'Don't be ridiculous.'

'Me? You're the one who had a bloody affair with a secretary at your school, John. I would have thought *that* qualified as ridiculous, wouldn't you?' She glared at him, her eyes moist.

383

'Don't patronise me, Sue,' he said, irritably. 'I know it was wrong and I'm sorry. If it's any consolation I feel pretty bloody lousy about it as well.'

'It *isn't* any consolation,' she snapped.

They sat in uncomfortable silence until Sue spoke again.

'Why, John? At least tell me that,' she said, quietly.

He shrugged.

'I don't know. I really don't know. Whatever explanation I give you is going to sound inadequate, pointless.' He sucked in a deep breath. 'I can't explain it.'

'Can't or won't?' she demanded.

'I can't,' he replied with equal anger, trying not to raise his voice but frustrated in the knowledge that whatever she said she was right. What he had done was indefensible. 'Look, I'm not proud of what I did. It just happened.'

'Affairs don't just *happen*,' she chided. 'What was the attraction anyway? Is she pretty? Got a nice figure? Is she good in bed? Not that you'd have known that until you got her back to her flat though, would you? Well come on, tell me, I'm curious. Did this pretty young thing just fall into your arms?'

He shook his head but didn't answer.

'Tell me,' she snarled, vehemently. 'Is she pretty?'

'Yes,' he confessed.

'*And* good in bed?'

'Sue, for God's sake . . .'

'Is she good? Come on, I'm curious, I told you. Is she good in bed?'

He smiled humourlessly.

'What do you want me to do, rate her one to ten?'

'Just tell me if she was good,' Sue snarled.

'Yes,' he said, almost inaudibly. 'It was only ever a physical thing. I didn't feel anything for her. I never stopped loving *you*, Sue.'

'Am I supposed to be grateful, John? You'll be telling me next that I should understand why you did it. Well, perhaps I ought to try and understand. Tell me why, make me understand.'

'Since your father's been ill . . .'

'Don't blame it on my father, you bastard.'

'Let me finish,' he snapped, waiting until she was looking at him once again. 'Since he's been ill you've been obsessed with him, with what he's got. You've been distant. Perhaps I felt neglected, I know it sounds like a fucking lame excuse but it's all I can think of.'

'Oh I'm sorry, John,' she said, sarcastically. 'I should have realised you weren't getting enough attention, it's practically my fault you had this affair. It sounds as if I forced you into it.'

'That's not what I'm saying and you know it.'

'You're saying that you couldn't have what you wanted from me so you picked up some little tart and fucked her,' Sue spat the words.

'She's not a tart.'

'Why are you defending her, John? I thought you said it was only a physical thing. If you wanted sex that badly you might as well have found a whore, paid for it. I do apologise for having other things on my mind, if only you'd let me know how you were suffering perhaps I could have fitted you in a couple of nights a week.'

'Now you *are* being ridiculous.'

'What the hell do you expect?' she yelled at him. 'Rational conversation? On the day my daughter is buried I find out my husband's been having an affair.' He saw her expression darken, her eyes narrow. Hacket could almost see the thoughts forming inside her mind. That final piece of deduction which would damn him forever. 'You were with her the night Lisa was killed weren't you?'

He didn't answer.

'Weren't you?' she hissed.

He nodded.

'I can't get that out of my mind,' Hacket whispered. 'The thought that if I'd been here it probably wouldn't have happened. You don't have any idea what that's doing to me, Sue.'

'I don't care what it's doing to you,' she said, coldly. 'You killed our daughter.'

'Don't say that,' he snapped.

'You didn't hold the knife but you're as responsible for her death as the man who killed her. Our daughter died for the sake of your bloody affair.'

She lashed out at him, wildly, madly, the suddenness of the attack taking him by surprise. Her nails raked his cheek, drawing blood. Hacket tried to grab her wrists, seeing now that tears were coursing down her cheeks. She struck at him again but he caught her arm and held it, getting a good grip on the other wrist too. She struggled frantically to be free of his restraining hands, wanting also to be away from the touch of his skin against hers. It was as if he were something loathsome.

'Let go of me,' she shouted, glaring at him. 'Don't touch me.'

He released her and she pulled away, moving from the bed, almost falling as she reached the door. Hacket swung himself out of bed and moved towards her but she held up a hand to ward him off.

'Don't you come near me,' she hissed. 'Don't.'

He hesitated, knowing that whatever words or actions he chose were useless. The two of them remained frozen, like the still frame of a film, then, finally, Hacket took a step back. A gesture of defeat.

'Sue, please,' he said. 'Don't shut me out. Not *now*. We need each other.'

She almost laughed.

'Do we? Why do you need me? You can go back to your whore can't you?' She glanced at him a second longer then turned and left the bedroom.

He thought about following her as he heard her footfalls on the stairs but he knew it was useless. Instead, he spun round and, with a roar of rage and frustration, he brought his fist down with stunning force on the dressing table. Bottles of perfume and items of make-up toppled over with the impact. Hacket gripped the top of the dressing table, gazing at his own pale reflection in the mirror.

The face that looked back at him was despair personified.

17

The barking of the dog woke him.

In the stillness of the night it seemed to echo inside the room, inside his head and he sat up in bed immediately, glancing to one side, squinting at the clock.

1.46 a.m.

Brian Devlin thought about snapping on the bedside light but hesitated. He rubbed his eyes, the barking of the dog still reverberating through the darkness. The animal could be anywhere on the farm, perhaps even in one of the fields, noise carried a long way in the stillness of such a late hour.

Devlin hauled himself out of bed and padded across to the window which overlooked the main farmyard.

The porchlight which burned offered little by way of penetrative glow and Devlin could see no further than the land rover which was parked just outside his back door. Again he thought about putting on a light, but again he hesitated, reaching instead for the torch which stood on the floor beside the bed.

Then he slid a hand beneath the bed and pulled out the Franchi over-under shotgun. He broke the weapon, thumbed in two cartridges from the box in the bedside cabinet then moved quickly towards the stairs, the torch gripped in one hand, the shotgun cradled over the crook of his other arm.

At the back door he paused to step into his boots, pulling his dressing gown more tightly around him. It was cold and he cursed as his bare feet were enveloped by the freezing wellingtons.

Outside, the dog continued to bark.

Devlin unlocked the back door and slipped out into the night.

He stood still for a moment, squinting into the gloom, letting his eyes become accustomed to the darkness, then he headed off in the direction of the barking Alsatian.

Devlin was sure the sound was coming from the rear of the barn. From the chicken coop. He'd lost nearly a dozen chickens to foxes over the last month or so. This time he'd catch the bastard, blow it to pieces. The woods which grew so thickly on the eastern side of his land were perfect breeding ground for foxes and he had already searched part of them in an effort to track down the vermin, but so far with no success.

Other farmers, on the western side of Hinkston, had reported no such losses of poultry and that, in itself, irritated Devlin. He'd been running the farm for the past twenty years, ever since his twentieth birthday, he didn't have the resources that the farmers on the other side of the town had. His was a small concern built up over the years first by his father and now by himself. The farm was a consuming passion. So much so that his ex-wife had found it impossible to accept that the farm and farm business would always take precedence. Perhaps, Devlin had thought when she'd left him, she didn't like taking second place to a sty full of saddle-backs. He smiled at the recollection. Of how she had tried to play the farmer's wife, milking the cows, even mucking out the pigs but, after a year or so the novelty value had worn off and she'd seen it for what it really was. Bloody hard work. Devlin worked a sixteen-hour day sometimes to keep the farm ticking over. There was no time for a social life. It had been almost inevitable that the marriage should break up. There had been no children though, and consequently no complications. She was only too happy to leave and he was quite content to carry on devoting *all* his time to the farm. If he had one regret it was that they had been childless. The thought that, after his death, there would be no one to run the farm bothered him. But, he mused, when he was six feet under he wouldn't be worrying about anything anyway, would he?

Right now, all that worried him was the barking Alsatian.

He steadied the shotgun in his other hand, ready to drop the torch and fire should he see a fox, but as he drew closer to the barn and the chicken coop beyond a thought occurred to him. Surely the dog's insistent barking would have frightened the would-be predator away by now? Why was the animal still so agitated?

The barking stopped suddenly and Devlin found himself enveloped in the silence. He paused for a moment, waiting for the Alsatian to begin again.

It didn't.

The silence persisted.

Maybe frightened the bloody fox off, Devlin thought, chased it away and now it's going back to get some sleep which is what he himself ought to be doing. He was supposed to be up again in less than five hours.

Nevertheless he advanced towards the barn noticing that one of the doors was slightly open. He muttered to himself and moved towards it.

He was almost there when he tripped over something.

388

Cursing to himself he flicked on the torch, shining it over the ground around him.

The beam picked out the dead Alsatian.

Devlin frowned as he looked at the animal, leaning closer.

From the angle of its head he guessed that its neck had been broken. Its tongue lolled from one side of its mouth and he saw that blood was spreading in a wide pool around its head, spilling from its bottom jaw. The dog's mouth looked as if it had been forced apart, its bottom jaw almost torn off. Devlin prodded it with the toe of his boot, spinning round when he heard a rustling sound from inside the barn.

He was seized by a deep anger. Whoever had done this to his dog was probably still inside.

'Right, you bastard,' he hissed under his breath and blundered into the barn, shining the torch all around. Up to the second storey where hay and straw were kept. The light bounced off the row of tools which were lined up against one wall. The rakes, the spades, the cultivators, the sythes and the pitchforks.

Nothing moved.

'You've got ten seconds to come out,' he shouted, hearing a slight creak from above him.

There was someone up on the second storey.

It was accessible only by a ladder which led up through a trap-door and it was towards this ladder which Devlin now moved, anger at the killing of his dog overriding all other emotions. Whoever was up there was going to pay, one way or another he thought as he reached the ladder.

He paused, one foot on the bottom rung. Then he jammed the torch into the waistband of his dressing gown and gripped the shotgun in his free hand.

He began to climb.

'You're on private property,' he called as he ascended. 'What I do to you is *my* business. You're on my land.'

He was half-way up by now.

'You didn't have to kill my dog, you bastard.'

Devlin slowed down as he reached the trapdoor, pushing against it hard. It flew back and crashed to the floor with a bang that reverberated throughout the barn.

'I'll give you one more chance to come out,' he called, pulling himself through the narrow entrance. 'You can't get past me, this is the only way out.'

Silence.

'I've got a shotgun,' he called.

Nothing.

Devlin took a couple of paces towards where he thought he'd first heard the sound, holding the shotgun in one hand, playing the torch beam ahead of him, over the bales of hay and straw which were stacked like over-sized house bricks.

There were plenty of places to hide, he thought.

The beams creaked beneath his feet as he walked, stopping every few paces to shine the torch behind him, checking that the intruder hadn't tried to slip out through the trapdoor.

Below, the barn door banged shut.

Devlin spun round, running back to the trap door, peering through.

The door swung open again then crashed shut once more and he realized that it was the wind which had caused the movement.

He straightened up and continued with his search of the loft area.

Had his ears been playing tricks on him, he wondered? The loft seemed to be empty. No one hiding behind the bales. No sign of any disturbance. The barn appeared to be empty. Devlin shone the torch back and forth over the upper level once more then shook his head and turned, heading back towards the ladder.

He laid the torch and the shotgun on the rim of the trap door as he lowered himself onto the ladder.

The barn door creaked open again and remained open.

Devlin jammed the torch back into one of the pockets of his dressing gown and, holding the shotgun in one hand climbed down carefully.

He stood at the bottom of the ladder, listening.

Only silence greeted him.

Puzzled and a little disappointed, Devlin made for the door, closing it behind him. He turned, his torch shining ahead of him.

The body of the dog was gone.

There was just a puddle of crimson to show where it had been laying. The dead animal had vanished as if in to thin air.

Devlin sucked in an angry breath.

This had gone too far. If someone was pissing about with him then he didn't find it very funny. He stormed off back across the farm yard towards the house.

Behind him, the barn door opened a fraction.

Devlin pushed open the back door and stormed in, snapping on lights now, putting down the shotgun and cursing to himself.

The figure was standing in the kitchen

Devlin opened his mouth to say something but no words would come. He reached back for the shotgun but it was too late.

The figure lunged forward, driving the pitchfork before it like a bayonet.

The twin steel prongs punctured Devlin's chest, one of them skewering his heart, the other ripping through a lung, bursting it like a fleshy balloon. Blood erupted from the wounds, spraying the kitchen, and the farmer was propelled backwards with incredible force, driven by the sheer strength of the thrust.

He crashed back against the wall, blood spattering the plaster and leaving a red smear as he slid down to the ground, still transfixed by the pitchfork. He tried to scream but his throat was full of blood and, as he tried to move he could hear the air hissing through his ruptured lung, could feel the cold breeze gushing through the hideous rent. While, all the time, blood from his punctured heart fountained into the air as if expelled from a high pressure hose.

As unconsciousness began to overtake him he saw the figure standing over him.

Saw the long, stiletto blade being held before him.

Devlin found some lost reserve of strength and, even with the pitchfork still embedded in his chest, he tried to drag himself towards the open back door.

But the figure merely knelt beside him, like a priest administering the last rites.

Devlin felt his head being cradled almost lovingly in the intruder's hands and then, as he found the breath for one final scream of agony, he felt the knife being pushed slowly into his right eye.

18

In the days following Lisa's funeral Hacket found himself enveloped by a feeling similar to isolation. Despite his return to work (perhaps *because* of it – the endless chorus of condolence rapidly became tiresome) and the necessity to mix with people once more, he found that Sue was becoming even more distant. He felt like a lodger. She spoke to him as if he was a stranger for whom she existed solely to put food on the table and to offer perfunctory conversation.

Instead of returning to her own job as a secretary at a computer firm she had considered giving up work completely. Hacket had suggested that, under the circumstances, that might not be a very good idea. Something which had only served, it seemed, to push her into resignation more rapidly. The firm had given her four weeks' compassionate leave but Sue felt that wasn't enough.

And she had begun returning to the hospital on a nightly basis to visit her father.

His condition had deteriorated during the past week and it now seemed only a matter of days until the inevitable happened.

As Hacket sat staring blankly at the television screen he heard the door open and realised that Sue had returned from another of her nightly vigils. She closed the front door behind her and walked straight into the kitchen where she made two coffees, returning to the sitting room to set one of them in front of Hacket. He smiled gratefully but received no reciprocal gesture.

She sat down in one of the armchairs and looked, with equal indifference at the screen.

'Is there any change in your father's condition?' Hacket asked, watching as she kicked her shoes off.

Sue shook her head.

'Have they said how long?' he said, quietly.

392

'They can't be specific. Days, weeks. They don't know,' she told him, still gazing at the TV. She took a couple of sips of coffee then picked up her shoes. 'I feel tired. I'm going to bed.'

'It's only nine o'clock,' he said.

'I said I was tired.'

'Sue, wait. We have to talk.'

'About what?'

'You know what. About us. About what's happened. We can't go on like this.'

'Then perhaps we shouldn't go on,' she told him, flatly.

Hacket frowned, surprised by the vehemence of her words and disturbed by their implication.

'You mean you want us to split up?' he said.

She shrugged.

'I don't know, I haven't thought about it properly. I've got other things on my mind.'

'Listen to me,' he said, trying to control the tone of his voice. 'We've been married for almost seven years. I love you, I don't want to lose you. I want you back, Sue.'

'I want Lisa back but wishing for it isn't going to make it happen is it?' she countered, acidly.

'Lisa's dead,' he said, through clenched teeth and then finally, he raised his voice in frustration. 'Jesus Christ, Sue do you think you're the only one feeling that pain. You haven't got a monopoly on grief you know. I miss her as much as you do. She was my daughter too, in case you hadn't noticed.' His breath was coming in gasps.

Sue regarded him impassively.

'We've got to rebuild our own lives,' he continued, more calmly. 'I'm not saying we should forget Lisa, we should never do that, she was the most precious thing in both our lives. But now all we've got is each other.' He sighed. 'I know you still feel angry about what happened between me and Nikki but it's over now, Sue. I said I was sorry and I'll keep on saying it as many times as you want me to. For as long as it takes for things to go back to normal between us.'

'They can't ever be normal again, John,' she told him with an air of finality. 'We're not talking about just an affair. We're talking about

the death of our daughter. A death you *caused* because of your affair.'
She eyed him angrily.

'I have to live with that knowledge,' he rasped. 'I don't need you
to remind me all the fucking time. Do you have any idea what I'm
feeling? What it's like to carry that guilt with me all the time? Do you
care?'

'No John, I don't. All I care about, all I know is that our daughter
is dead. That you've wrecked our marriage. Don't mention love to me
again, you don't know the meaning of the word.'

'So what's the answer?' he wanted to know. 'Divorce? Is that going
to make things better? It certainly isn't going to bring Lisa back is it?
And if that sounds harsh it's because it hurts me to say it. Hurts me
more than you'll ever know.'

There was an uneasy silence, finally broken by Sue.

'I've been thinking it might be best if I go away for a while,' she
told him. 'To stay with Julie in Hinkston. We don't see much of each
other now. And I need the break.'

'What about your father? Who's going go visit him?'

'I can drive in from Hinkston, it only takes an hour.'

'How long will you go for?'

'As long as it takes.' She got to her feet, shoes in hand, and walked
to the door.

Hacket sank back on the sofa, drained. He heard her footfalls on
the stairs as she climbed. He stared at the TV screen for a moment
longer, listening to the endless catalogue of strikes, accidents, murders,
kidnappings and rapes that the newsreader was relaying, then finally
he got up and switched the set off.

He sat in silence for what seemed like an eternity then suddenly
got to his feet, walked through into the hall and picked up the phone.

'I'd like to speak to Detective Inspector Madden please,' Hacket said
when the phone was finally answered.

Madden wasn't available.

'What about Detective Sergeant Spencer?'

The man on the other end of the phone told him to wait a moment.

Hacket shifted the phone from one hand to the other agitatedly as
he waited.

DS Spencer was in the office, he was told, but the man wanted to know what the call was about.

'Is it important? I want to speak to Spencer. Just tell him it's John Hacket,' the teacher told him.

There was a moment's silence at the other end, a hiss of static then the other man agreed, announced he was connecting Hacket, and the teacher heard a series of crackles and blips. The Spencer's voice.

'Mr Hacket, what can I do for you?' the policeman asked.

'Is there any news on the men who murdered my daughter?' he wanted to know.

'We're following several leads. It's still early days . . .'

Hacket cut him short.

'Have you arrested anyone yet?' he snapped.

Spencer sounded somewhat perplexed.

'I told you, Mr Hacket, we have leads which we're following up but no arrests have been made yet. We'll inform you as soon as anything happens.'

Hacket nodded, thanked the DS then hung up. He stood staring down at the phone for a moment then looked up the stairs towards the landing, towards the room where his wife slept.

He clenched his fists until the nails dug into the palms of his hands.

No arrests yet.

And when they did catch the men, what then?

Hacket stalked back into the sitting room, reaching for his cigarettes. He lit one and sucked hard on it.

What then?

The thought had come to him only fleetingly to begin with, but now, as he stood alone in the deserted sitting room, that thought began to grow stronger. Building, spreading like some festering growth within his mind.

And he nurtured that thought.

Nurtured it and clung to it.

395

May 7, 1941

The contractions had begun almost an hour ago.

Margaret Lawrenson hauled herself out of the chair, her bloated belly almost causing her to topple over. She paced back and forth for a few moments, trying to relieve the awful cramping pains which came so rhythmically. Over the last sixty minutes the contractions had become more frequent and more intense. Each one almost took her breath away and, twice she reeled as if she were going to faint.

She was alone.

No doctor had been called to the house. No doctor *would* be called. Her husband had assured her that the birth would be a straightforward one and she had believed him.

The thought of George Lawrenson made her momentarily forget even the pains of labour.

Her husband had been dead almost nine months now, and since his murder (she had no doubt that he had been killed even though the autopsy and examination of the car had suggested a faulty petrol tank) she had lived in the large house on the outskirts of Hinkston alone. She had become reclusive, venturing into the town itself as little as possible. She had no friends there so no visitors ever came out to the house. But Margaret had preferred it that way. She had remained in the large building like some kind of guardian, her husband's papers, his notes on Project Genesis, safe in her care.

As she struggled towards the lab her legs buckled and she fell heavily, falling on her side. She felt a sudden gush of liquid from between her legs and looked down to see a flux of thin, blood-flecked discharge spreading across the carpet. Margaret grunted and tried to pull herself upright but it seemed the weight of the child she was carrying prevented that action and she was forced to drag herself along the floor, gasping for breath as she drew nearer the lab.

If only she could reach its sterile environment, its pain killers.

A contraction so savage it practically doubled her up caused her to cry out and, for a moment, she stopped crawling. It was difficult enough with the huge weight of the child in her belly, but now the pain was coursing through her as if it were liquid pumped into her veins by some insane transfusion.

Pain killers.

She moaned in agony and felt more warm liquid spilling onto the inside of her thighs. She looked down to see that it was blood.

She was less than ten feet from the door of the lab but it may as well have been ten miles. Every inch took a monumental effort both of will and endurance.

Margaret Lawrenson suddenly surrendered to the pain, rolling onto her back, knowing that she was not going to make it. Excruciating pain seemed to numb her lower body and she gripped the carpet in anguish as she felt the child move, beginning its slow emergence. She tried to breathe as her husband had taught her, tried to think about him standing beside her. Tried to think about anything other than the savage pain which followed her and caused her to cry out.

She screamed as she felt the child's head push clear of her vagina and now she was unsure whether it was being propelled by her own muscular contractions or using its own strength to escape the prison of the womb. Blood spattered onto the carpet and she felt the incredible pressure ease momentarily as the child's head showed. It nestled between her legs, stained with blood and pieces of placental waste. Margaret gripped the carpet in both fists, her jaws clamped together to prevent the escape of another scream. Perspiration beaded on her forehead and cheeks then ran in rivulets down her face.

She pushed harder, her muscles finally expelling the child which lay on the floor beneath her, still joined to her by the umbilical cord.

Margaret tried to sit up, to reach the child and, as she did she felt the remains of the placenta burst from her vagina in a swollen lump. She swivelled round, her body still enveloped by pain and reached for the child. It was coughing, its mouth filled with blood and saliva. She took it into her arms, using her index finger to scoop the thick mixture of crimson mucous from its tiny mouth. It began to cry immediately.

She raised herself up onto her knees, the baby held in her arms, the umbilicus dangling from its belly. It had to be severed.

She laid the child down again then took the slippery coil in both hands and raised it to her mouth.

Ignoring the taste of blood she bit through the cord, bright flecks of crimson filling her mouth and running down her chin. But she fought the need to vomit and swiftly tied the cord, wiping her mouth with the back of her hand.

The child continued to cry and she smiled as she heard the sound. It was a healthy yell to signal its arrival in the world. Margaret looked down at it. At her son. He was perfectly formed, and as she picked him up his sobs diminished slightly. She rocked him to and fro in that cold corridor, her hair matted with sweat, her clothes drenched with blood. The coppery odour of the crimson fluid was strong in her nostrils but she ignored it. All that mattered now was that her son was alive.

The second wave of contractions took her completely by surprise, both because of their intensity and the unexpectedness of their arrival.

She looked down at her belly to see that the flesh was undulating slowly, swelling then contracting.

As the pains grew more severe she realised what was happening.

She screamed in agony as the head of the second child nudged its way free.

19

The drive to Hinkston took her about an hour due to the heavy traffic leaving London, but as she guided the car down the main street of the town Sue Hacket noted that it was still barely noon.

The sunshine which had accompanied her on the first part of the drive had given way to a cold wind and the promise of rain. She glanced at the shoppers in the high street, noses red from the cold, some walking briskly, others standing and chatting.

Hinkston was a busy little town close enough to London to qualify as green-belt commuterland but also with enough distance to rightfully be called a country town. Its population, she guessed, was around eight thousand. At least that's what it had been three years ago when she and Hacket had last visited.

Sue drove through the town, past a library, and found herself surrounded by houses which were beginning to take on a solid uniformity. She knew she had entered the estate where her sister lived. She found the street then slowed up, looking for the number of the house. She counted them off as she drew nearer, smiling as she saw Julie standing on the front doorstep talking to the window-cleaner. As Sue parked the Metro outside the house, Julie waved and walked out to meet her. They embraced, watched by the window cleaner who nodded affably as Sue approached him, carrying a small suitcase. Julie introduced her and the window cleaner smiled, making some comment about how alike they were and both so sexy. Julie laughed and slapped him playfully on the shoulder. Sue could see his blue eyes lingering on her own breasts, his attention caught by the fact she wore no bra beneath her blouse. She slid past the window cleaner, leaving Julie to pay him.

Sue stood in the hallway of her sister's home and put down her suitcase, glancing around at the entryway.

There was a chain-store copy of 'The Haywain' hanging on one side of the hall, opposite a particularly large cuckoo-clock which looked as though it could have comfortably housed a vulture. Sue noticed that it was almost twelve o'clock and moved towards the sitting-room to avoid the appearance of the noisy bird. Sure enough, the mechanical occupant of the clock duly shot forth on the hour and proceeded to fill the hall with the most unholy din as the hour hand touched twelve.

Inside the sitting-room Sue again glanced around, noting the fixtures and fittings which filled her sister's house. The room was overflowing with ornaments. Perched on every available ledge. On top of the TV, the wall units, the bookcase. There was even a plastic model of the Eiffel Tower on top of the stereo.

'Mike brought that back from Paris for me,' Julie announced, entering the room. 'He was there on business the other week. He doesn't like ornaments himself but he collects them for me whenever he goes away.'

Sue smiled and held out her arms to embrace her sister. The two of them clung to each other for a moment then Julie kissed her lightly on the cheek.

'I'm pleased you came,' she said, softly.

They exchanged pleasantries, chatted about the weather and Julie told her sister about the window cleaner, what a randy sod he was. She chuckled as she poured tea for them both as they sat in the kitchen. Sue listened and smiled when she felt she should but her mind was elsewhere. Something Julie wasn't slow to notice.

'I'm not going to ask you what's on your mind,' she said, finally. 'You don't know how sorry we were to hear about Lisa. I thought what I'd have been like if anything had happened to Craig.'

Mention of her nephew seemed to coax a smile from Sue and she looked across the table at her sister.

'Where is he?' she asked.

'He's across the road playing with one of his friends. It keeps him from under my feet while the school half-term is on. He'll be pleased to see you. I'll fetch him in a little while.'

Sue nodded and sipped her tea.

'Mike's working late tonight, so . . .'

Sue chuckled at her sister's words and Julie looked puzzled.

'I'm sorry,' Sue explained, sighing. *Working late. Meetings.* She thought of John and his lover. The perennial excuse. *I've got to work late.* She finished her tea and began tracing a pattern around the edge of the cup with her index finger.

'What's going on, Sue?' Julie wanted to know. 'When you rang and asked to stop with us it was all *I* need to get away, and *I* can't stand to be in the house anymore. You never mentioned John. He could have come with you, you know.'

'John was one of the reasons I had to get away,' Sue said, raising her eyebrows.

'Why? What's wrong?'

Sue exhaled wearily wondering whether she ought to burden her sister with her worries but knowing that she had to tell someone. She couldn't carry on bottling up her feelings.

'He had an affair, Julie.' The words came out with ease. She went on to explain what had happened. The letter. The discovery. The row.

How she blamed him for Lisa's death.

Julie listened intently, her face impassive.

'That's why I had to get away,' Sue continued. 'To give myself time to think, to decide where I go from here.'

Julie still didn't speak.

'I don't know if I can ever forgive him,' said Sue. 'I don't even know if I *want* to.'

The two women regarded each other silently, across the table. Sue feeling slightly drained after relaying the revelations of the last few weeks, Julie not sure what to say.

The silence was broken by the sound of the back door being flung open.

Craig Clayton bounded in, spreading dirt over the kitchen carpet as he bounced his football. He was smiling happily, the football strip which he wore covered in mud, just like his face. He saw Sue and bounded towards her.

She held out her arms to grab him, lifting him up onto her knee and kissing his muddy cheek.

Julie could see the tears forming in her sister's eyes.

'How's my favourite nephew?' Sue asked, hugging him.

'I'm all right,' he beamed and slipped from her grasp, heading for the sitting room.

'Boots off, football kit off, and into the bath,' Julie said. 'Look at the state of you. I've told you not to come into the house with your boots on.'

'But Mum, Mark's just as dirty as I am,' he told her as if that information would somehow pacify her.

'Well it's a good job you didn't bring him over here with you then, isn't it. No dinner until you've had a bath.'

He shrugged and looked at Sue as if expecting her to offer assistance but when she only smiled he turned and stalked back outside to remove his football boots.'

'Kids,' said Julie, smiling. 'Sometimes . . .' She allowed the sentence to trail off, feeling suddenly awkward.

'I'm going to change,' Sue told her, getting to her feet. 'I know where the spare room is. You take care of Craig.' She smiled and walked through into the sitting room then beyond to the hall, where she picked up her case and climbed the stairs.

Julie sat at the kitchen table a moment longer then went to see how her son was managing with his football boots.

Outside, the first spots of rain were beginning to fall.

20

She woke with a start, propelled from the nightmare with a force that shook her and left her trembling.

Sue sat still in the darkness, trying to calm her laboured breathing, worried in case she'd woken anyone else in the house. The silence which greeted her seemed to indicate that she hadn't. She lay back down, her heart still beating fast, perspiration glistening on her forehead despite the chill in the room. She shivered then swung herself out of bed and closed the window.

The rain which had begun as a shower had turned into a full-scale downpour with the coming of night and Sue stared out into the gloom for a moment, noticing lights on in other bedrooms in other houses on the estate. Aware suddenly of her own naked-ness she reached for her dressing gown and pulled it on, realizing that she would not be able to find the comfort of sleep so easily now. Instead she walked, barefoot, from the bedroom and out onto the landing, passing Julie and Mike's room. She paused to listen for any sounds of movement, any indication that she'd disturbed them.

Silence.

She repeated the procedure outside Craig's room, pushing his door open slightly to look in on him.

Clad in pyjamas with pictures of motorbikes on them, he lay cocooned underneath his quilt, his mouth slightly open, his breathing even. Sue stood looking at him for a moment longer. He was just two years older then Lisa. A healthy, strong boy. Sue carefully pulled his door closed and made her way downstairs.

Craig's eyes snapped open, his mind instantly alert. He heard footsteps on the stairs which he knew didn't belong to his mother or father. He lay beneath the quilt, only his eyes moving.

Sue snapped on the light in the kitchen and sat at the table while she waited for the kettle to boil. When it finally did she made herself a cup of tea and drank it slowly, gazing into empty air, listening to the steady ticking of the clock on the wall behind her. As she got to her feet to return to bed she noticed that it was 3.11 a.m.

She drifted off to sleep after about ten minutes, the pattering of the rain on the window an accompaniment to her steady breathing.

The door to the bedroom opened soundlessly and Craig stepped inside, his gaze never leaving Sue.

He moved to within two feet of the bed, looking at her, watching as she moved restlessly. But even her movements did not prevent his silent vigil. He remained beside the bed.

Julie had heard the movement and eased herself out of bed, careful not to disturb Mike.

Now she made her way down to her son's bedroom and peered round the door.

She saw that the bed was empty.

'Oh God,' she whispered, swallowing hard.

She turned and headed for the spare room.

Craig was still standing beside Sue looking down at her, watching the steady rise and fall of her chest.

Julie crossed to him and gripped his shoulder firmly.

He turned round and looked at her, smiling. Then he looked back at Sue.

'No,' Julie whispered, shaking her head, trying to coax him out of the room.

He hesitated then allowed himself to be led away.

Julie glanced at her sister, ensuring that she was still asleep. Then she closed the door and ushered Craig back to his own room.

He climbed back into bed and slid down beneath the quilt.

Julie knelt close by him and once again shook her head.

'No,' she said, quietly. 'Not her.'

21

He would kill them.

That was the only answer.

He had lain awake thinking about it, even at work the idea was constantly with him.

Somehow Hacket was going to kill the men who had murdered his daughter. He didn't know how and he didn't know when. All he knew was he was going to kill them.

Of course there was the matter of practically. If the police didn't know who they were then how was he to find out alone? And, even if he succeeded, what then? What if he found them and actually managed to end their lives? It would mean arrest, imprisonment. No jury in the land, no matter how sympathetic they might feel to his predicament, would be allowed to bring in a verdict of not-guilty once he was tried. But Hacket didn't seem to care about that. The thought that by ending the lives of his daughter's killers he would effectively be ending his own life made little impression on him.

What had begun as a vague wish had begun to turn slowly but surely into an obsession. Scarcely an hour passed that he did not think about finding and killing the men. He considered how he would make them suffer. Plotting and planning ways to rid the world of them. He revelled in his own inventiveness. He rejoiced in his capacity to imagine what he might do to them. Castration.

God, how he would love to draw the knife so slowly around the scrotum of the one who had penetrated his daughter. To slice through that soft flesh and expose the reeking purple egg-shaped objects inside. He would cut them free one at a time then, while the bastard bled to death, Hacket would push the knife into his anus. Split his bowel. And finally he would take the penis, that vile member which had violated his little girl and he would insert the point of the knife into the slit in

404

the glans and he would push. Push until he sliced the organ in two, cutting slowly and carefully, finally severing it at the root.

Jesus, the thought was a good one and, as he lay in bed gazing at the ceiling he smiled to himself.

At first he had been horrified that such thoughts should have found a home within a supposedly educated and civilised mind like his own but then, as the thought of his dead daughter flashed back into his mind more vividly, the sight of her tiny body on that mortuary slab, he had actively pursued the thoughts. Each method of torture and death had been dredged from blacker regions of his mind until he felt as if he were pillaging the thoughts of some degenerate sadist.

He enjoyed the thoughts.

He would destroy their eyes.

The organs with which they had first looked upon his little girl.

Hacket thought how he would take the blade and cut across the glistening orbs, or else he would carve them from the sockets.

He would cut off each of their fingers in turn.

Cut off their ears.

Shatter their knees with an iron rod then methodically break every bone in their bodies.

Make them eat their own faeces.

The thoughts tumbled around inside his mind, each one to be savoured. Punishment for him would be meaningless. Nothing the law could do to him could make him suffer more than the death of his daughter.

And, perhaps, he thought, with vengeance would come forgiveness. When Susan saw what he had done to the killers of their child she would love him again. She would want him back.

He knew now, more than ever before, that his only hope of atonement lay in finding and killing the murderers of his child.

He swung himself out of bed, reaching for the bottle of whisky on the cabinet beside. He drank straight from the bottle, some of the fiery liquid spilling down his chest. The amber fluid burned its way to his stomach and he sucked in a deep breath, holding the bottle before him. He grinned, seeing his own distorted image in the glass.

If madness was a mirror then Hacket was indeed studying his own reflection.

22

It all had an appalling familiarity about it.

The flowers in their cellophane wrappers, the empty words of the priest. The tears.

And the grave.

The inevitability of Tom Nolan's death made the event no less traumatic and Hacket found that, even though he hadn't known the man that well, he was fighting back tears as he stood at the graveside beside Sue, Julie and Mike.

Sue stood motionless, gazing down into the grave as if trying to read the brass nameplate. Hacket thought how serene she looked but he realised that what he had mistaken for serenity was something bordering on shock. He felt like waving a hand before her to see whether or not she would blink.

Julie was crying softly, comforted by her husband who kept her in his arms throughout the ceremony.

Grey clouds rolled by overhead, spilling a thin curtain of drizzle onto the tiny band of mourners. There were others standing nearby although they seemed reluctant to move closer to the grave for fear of intruding. Hacket guessed they were friends of Tom's. One or two of them were crying also but their anguished utterances were carried away on the wind which whipped across the cemetery.

When the time came, Sue moved forward and gently tossed a handful of earth on top of the coffin then stepped back to stand beside her husband.

Julie did not move.

The vicar finished speaking, offered his usual perfunctory words of condolence then waddled off back towards the church to greet the next cortège which was just passing through the cemetery gates.

More pain, thought Hacket.

Even death had become like a production line.

'I'm going to take Julie back to the car, Sue,' Mike said, leading his sobbing wife away. He nodded to Hacket who managed a smile.

Sue continued looking down into the grave.

'I know this isn't the right time,' Hacket said, self-consciously. 'But can we talk?'

'Just give me a minute,' she said, without looking at him.

Hacket nodded and turned, walking slowly towards a seat beneath a tree away to his right. He brushed some fallen leaves from the seat and sat down, watching Sue who stood gazing down into the grave. Hacket could see her lips moving and wondered what she was saying. Her father's death didn't seem to have hit her as badly as Lisa's. Perhaps the end of his suffering had been something of a relief to her, he thought although he decided not to mention it. Instead he waited as she walked towards him.

He brushed the seat with his gloved hand and she finally sat down.

'Thanks for taking care of the funeral arrangements, John. I appreciate it,' she said, quietly.

'I knew you wouldn't be in any state to do it. I owed you that at least.'

'It doesn't earn you any gold stars,' she said, a slight smile on her lips but also he saw the tears in her eyes.

He moved towards her, wanting to hold her, she held up a hand as if to keep him at a distance. Hacket clenched his teeth.

'I'll be OK,' she said, quietly. 'What did you want to talk about?'

'I wanted to know when you're coming home.'

'I'm not.'

Hacket swallowed hard. Was that it, he wondered? The final pronouncement on their current state of affairs?

'You mean it's over between us?' he asked, almost incredulously.

'What I mean is I can't come back to that house, John. There are too many memories there.'

'So what will you do? What will *we* do?' he wanted to know.

'I'll stay with Julie for the time being. I know I can't do that indefinitely, but . . .' She sighed. 'Like you said, this isn't the right time to talk about it.' She moved to get up and Hacket reached for her arm, holding it for a moment.

407

She pulled free from his grip, glancing at him for a second. He saw something akin to hatred in her eyes and lowered his hand.

'Julie needs me,' she said. 'I'll have to go.'

'*I* need you,' he said, trying to control the anger in his voice. 'We have to talk, Sue.'

'But not now,' she repeated, walking away from him. He watched as she strode down the narrow path towards the tarmac area which served as a car park. He saw her climb into the back seat with her sister, then he looked on as the car turned and sped away.

Hacket stood alone for a moment, the wind whipping around him, then he too turned and headed back towards his car. There was so much he had wanted to say to her. To tell her that he would sell the house and move to Hinkston, that they could start afresh if she'd have him back. So much to say. But, more than words he had wanted to hold her, just to feel her in his arms for a moment.

He'd been denied even that simple pleasure and, as he climbed into the car and started the engine, he began to wonder if it was one which was to be denied him forever.

He'd lost her.

Hacket was convinced of it.

First he'd lost his daughter, and now his wife. There wasn't the appalling finality of loss with Sue that there had been with Lisa but he was still sure that their relationship was over. She might as well be dead.

He sat alone in the sitting room of their house, a glass of scotch in one hand, his head buzzing from the amount he already drunk. Half a bottle remained from the full one he'd opened just an hour earlier.

Hacket looked around the room suddenly realising how much he hated it. Sue was right, it held too many memories. But it held them for him too, couldn't she see that? But he couldn't run from them. He could never escape the memories no matter where he went because the thoughts which tortured him were *inside* him. Eating him away as surely as the cancer had eaten away at Sue's father. And yet still he clung to the hope that revenge would be his salvation.

He took a long swig from the glass, some of the fiery liquid running down his chin.

Hacket let out a roar of rage and frustration and, as he did, he squeezed with even greater force on the glass.

It shattered. Thick shards of crystal tearing into the palm of his hand. Others flew into the air along with a mixture of whisky and blood which spurted from the savage gashes. He dropped the remains of the glass and slowly turned his palm to look at it. Glass had lacerated the flesh in several places and thick crimson fluid pumped from the wounds. A piece of crystal the size of his thumb had punctured the palm and was still protruding from the flesh. Hacket reached slowly for it and pulled it free, holding it before him for a second before tossing it aside.

He studied his bloodied hand then slowly raised it to his face and, with measured movements, he drew the torn and bleeding appendage across each cheek until his face was smothered with the thick liquid.

He sat motionless, like some war-painted Indian brave, the throbbing pain in his hand growing worse but dulled by the amount of whisky he'd drunk. The smell of blood was strong in his nostrils. He could feel the life-fluid congealing on his cheeks, while, by his side, it dripped from his slashed palm.

Hacket smiled then laughed. Stupidly, drunkenly.

And slowly the tears of laughter became tears of despair.

23

To say that the dining room of The Bull was small would have been an understatement. It consisted of five tables and, as he pulled his chair out and sat down, Stephen Jennings tried to visualise the place full of diners. He doubted if that ever happened.

The Bull was what people like to refer to euphemistically as 'homely'. In other words it was cramped. A small, family run hotel (even the description seemed rather grand for somewhere as modest as The Bull) in the centre of Hinkston, it was cheap, immaculately clean and friendly. He had stayed in dozens like it and many much worse. Jennings had worked for the past three years as a rep for a company of jeans manufacturers. It wasn't the greatest job in the world but it got him around the country and he had a company car and a reasonable salary. However, now approaching his twenty-seventh birthday, he was wondering if the time had come to move on. Better himself, as his mother always liked to say. She was also fond of saying that he should settle down and marry, something which he had definitely *not* given any consideration to. He'd been in an on-off relationship for the last eighteen months, although his time on the road seemed to ensure that it was more 'off' than anything else. Still, he was too young to settle down, he kept telling himself. Too old to rock and roll, too young to die, he thought, and smiled to himself.

Casting aside his philosophical musings, Jennings picked up the menu and glanced at it for a moment before taking another look at the dining room of the hotel. Each table had a vase of flowers at its centre, every napkin and tablecloth was spotlessly clean. The lighting was subdued to the point of gloom. Perhaps to hide the state of the food when it finally arrived, he thought, returning his attention to the menu.

The choice was small but fairly adventurous for a place of The Bull's modest means. Steak in red wine and mushroom sauce. He glanced at the price. Expensive, but what the hell, it was going on his expense account. He checked the wine list.

'Hello.'

The voice startled him from his considerations and he looked up to see a young woman standing there. Woman was somewhat over-stating the fact, perhaps and a quick appraisal told Jennings this newcomer was in her late teens. She smiled at him and he noticed the pad in her hand and realised that she was the waitress.

She was slim, that fact accentuated by the tight fitting black skirt and top she wore. A thick mane of shaggy blonde hair cascaded over her shoulders, framing her thin face from which two eyes like chips of sapphire seemed to shine as if lit from within. She wore no make-up and the freshness of her complexion seemed almost unnatural for a girl in the throes of pubescence. She stood beside the table patiently and Jennings glanced down to see that she was wearing not the flat shoes of a waitress but a pair of high heels. The girl was little short of stunning.

She smiled at him again when she noticed his surprise.

'Did I startle you?' she said, happily. 'Sorry. My Dad's always telling me not to sneak up on customers.'

Jennings returned the smile.

'Your dad?'

'Yes, he owns the hotel. Him and Mum have been running it for about twenty years, since before I was born.'

She kept those sapphire eyes on him, also appraising.

'You're new here aren't you?' she said. 'Just arrive today?'

He nodded.

'So, you know all the guests?'

'That's not difficult,' she told him. 'We hardly have any at this time of the year.' She looked more deeply at him. 'At least none like you.' No blushing. No quick glance down at her pad. The remark hadn't slipped out by mistake.

Jennings could not resist a sly glance at her breasts, the nipples pressing gently against the cotton of her blouse.

'Thanks for the compliment,' he said. 'Is that included in the price of the room?' He smiled.

'I had a boyfriend who looked like you,' she said, her gaze unwavering.

He raised his eyebrows.

'*Had*?'

'We split up. I got tired of him.' She smiled. 'He couldn't keep up with me. Not many of them can.'

Jennings coughed, trying to disguise the laugh which threatened to escape him. She wasn't flirting with him, she was practically propositioning him. About as subtle as a sledgehammer. But then again, as he looked at her face once more, the laugh faded. No doubt about it. She was stunning.

'I'd better order something,' he said, looking at the menu.

'Am I making you nervous?' she asked, brushing a speck of dust from her skirt with exaggerated slowness, pulling the material tight at the top of her thigh to ensure he saw the outline of her suspenders through the skirt.

411

'No,' he told her, rather enjoying the game. 'But I don't think you Dad would like it if he walked in and heard the way you were talking to me. He'd probably ask me to leave the hotel.' He winked at her. 'Then what would I do for the night?'

'Dad doesn't care what I do,' she said, still gazing at him. 'Nor does Mum. So why should it bother *you*?'

He shrugged, again drawn to those blazing eyes. Jennings ordered then handed her the menu, watching as she walked away, unable to keep his eyes from her legs. She disappeared through into the kitchen leaving him alone in the dimly lit dining room.

'Would you like a drink while you're waiting, Mr Jennings?' Tony Kirkham called from behind the bar. 'I see Paula's taken your order.'

Another five minutes and she'd have taken my bloody trousers, Jennings thought with a smile.

He ordered a pint of bitter, retrieved it from the bar and returned to his table. Paula returned a moment later with his starter which she duly set down before him.

'Thanks. By the way,' he said, spearing a couple of prawns with his fork, 'is there any nightlife around here. I was planning on going out after I'd eaten.'

'There's a cinema down the street, a couple of discos,' she shrugged. 'Not much. We have to make our own entertainment.'

He smiled.

'I thought that's what you'd say. Maybe I'll wander down to the pictures. Thanks.' Jennings wasn't sure whether or not to continue the little game. A glance at her persuaded him. 'It's a pity you're working. You could have showed me around.'

'I still can,' she whispered. 'Later.'

He nodded.

'I'll keep that in mind.'

She turned and left him alone.

He finished his meal, drank a couple of brandies, then decided to venture out and sample Hinkston's somewhat limited nightlife.

As he stepped out of the hotel the wind whistled around him and he pulled up the collar of his jacket. Then, hands dug deep in his pockets, he set off down the street.

412

Hidden by the darkness of the bedroom, Paula Kirkham watched him disappear out of sight.

24

'No'.

'He has a right to be told.'

The two men faced each other across the small office, cigarette smoke floating lazily in the air like a grey shroud.

'I said no,' DI Madden snapped, stubbing out the Dunhill and pushing the overflowing ashtray towards the edge of his desk.

'Why can't we tell him?' Spencer wanted to know.

'Because we'd be breaking the rules.' There was a note of sarcasm in the senior officer's voice.

'To hell with the rules,' Spencer rasped. 'Hacket's daughter was butchered by this fucking maniac.' He held up the arrest sheet, brandishing it before him as if it were some kind of accusation.

'We can't prove that, yet,' Madden reminded him, getting to his feet. He lit up another cigarette.

'Then why did we even bother pulling him in? Was that *procedure*?' Spencer glared at his superior. 'We can hold him for twenty-four hours and then we have to charge him. Only we've got nothing to charge him *with*. So what happens?'

'He walks,' said Madden, flatly. He sucked hard on the cigarette then wearily blew out a stream of smoke.

'Call Hacket,' Spencer insisted.

'What good would it do?' Madden wanted to know.

Spencer continued to gaze at his companion, his expression challenging.

Madden shrugged then, slowly, pushed the phone towards Spencer.

25

The man was tall, powerfully built, larger than Hacket. Subduing him had been difficult. The wounds on the side of his face and his scalp testified to the number of blows from the hammer it had taken to finally batter him into unconsciousness.

Now Hacket stood over the man who was beginning to come round, his eyes rolling in their sockets like the reels of a fruit machine. He blinked hard, trying to clear his blurred vision and, finally, he looked up at Hacket.

The man tried to straighten up but found that his arms were secured by rope, tied so tightly that the hemp bit into his flesh when he squirmed to escape the bonds. His ankles too were similarly secured. He was spread-eagled on the floor of what looked like an abandoned warehouse.

And he was naked.

Hacket held the claw hammer in his right hand and took a step closer to the prone figure, then he twisted the tool so that the steel prongs of the claw were facing his captive. With a blow combining incredible power with uncontrollable rage, Hacket brought the hammer down onto the right knee-cap of the bound figure.

The claws shattered the patella, tearing through the cruciate ligaments at the back of the knee and almost ripping the knee cap itself off. Blood from the hideous injury ran freely from the site of the damage and the man on the ground screamed in agony as he felt Hacket trying to pull the hammer free. The claws had wedged behind the knee cap and, with each tug on the shaft, the flat piece of bone rose a few more millimetres until Hacket realised he was levering it free. The sound of tearing ligaments was almost audible above the man's insane screams. Hacket put more weight behind the hammer, determined to lift the patella free.

It came away with a vile, sucking sound, the shattered bone skittering across the floor, pieces of it dangling on the end of tendrils formed from ripped muscles and ligaments.

The man on the floor writhed in uncontrollable pain and Hacket looked at his face, wanting to see the agony register.

But the man *had* no face.

Where the features should have been there was just smooth skin. No eyes. No mouth.

The screams seemed to be coming from inside Hacket's head as he stood over the man, the hammer dripping blood.

No face.

Hacket began to laugh, the sound joined by the faceless man's terrible screams. And by a new noise.

By the strident ringing of the telephone.

Hacket sat up in his chair, his face bathed in perspiration, his cut hand still throbbing madly.

Momentarily disorientated, he looked around him, looking for the claw hammer. For the faceless man.

Neither was present and, as the phone continued its monotone screech, he realised that he'd been dreaming. All that *was* real was the pain in his hand. He winced as he dragged himself out of the chair, wrapping a handkerchief around the swollen appendage.

The phone continued to ring.

Hacket staggered across the room, towards the hall wondering why his face felt so stiff but then remembering the congealed blood which caked it. He scratched at one cheek with his index finger and saw some of the dried, mud coloured mess come away beneath his nail.

He blundered through the doorway to the hall and snatched up the phone.

'Yeah,' he panted. 'Who is it?'

'Mr Hacket?' the voice asked.

'Yeah.'

'It's Detective Sergeant Spencer. I'm sorry to disturb you but you did say you wanted to know if there were any developments in your daughter's case.'

Hacket gripped the phone more tightly.

'And?'

'We've got a suspect in custody. We think he might have been involved in your daughter's murder.'

26

It was almost 10.30 when Jennings returned to The Bull. He'd decided to by-pass the cinema in Hinkston. The idea of sitting through the umpteenth cinematic episode of 'Star Trek' hadn't appealed to him. He'd eventually ended up in a pub a couple of streets away called 'The Badger's Set.' There he'd spent a couple of reasonably diverting hours with a couple of the locals discussing topics ranging from the possibility that Margaret Thatcher was a man to Liverpool FC's latest trophy-winning exploits.

Now he pushed open the door which led into the reception area of The Bull and withdrew his hands from his pockets, feeling the welcoming warmth.

Irene Kirkham was behind the desk. A rotund woman in her early forties who still had a pretty face. Perhaps Paula inherited her looks from her mother, thought Jennings with a grin. He wondered who she'd inherited the sexual precocity from but decided it had been nurtured rather than inherited. He crossed to the desk and asked for his key and an alarm call for the morning.

'Is there any chance of something to eat?' he asked. 'Just a sandwich would be fine, thanks.'

'You go to your room and I'll take care of it,' Mrs Kirkham told him, handing over the key.

He thanked her and bounded up the stairs to the first floor, the boards creaking beneath his feet as he entered his room. He closed the door behind him and pulled off his coat, throwing it onto the bed, then he flicked on the TV and wandered into the bathroom to relieve himself.

He was half-way through draining his over-filled bladder when

416

there was a knock on his door. He finished then hastily zipped up his jeans, cursing as he caught a pubic hair in the metal teeth. Re-adjusting himself he crossed to the door and opened it.

Paula stood there holding a tray which bore a plate of sandwiches and a glass of milk.

She had changed from earlier. Now she wore a pair of faded jeans which bit into her crotch so deeply he could practically see the outline of her labia. It was obvious she wore no panties. Just as she still wore no bra, a fact arrested to by the prominence of her nipples which strained against her white T-shirt. She was barefoot.

'Room service I presume,' he said, smiling, stepping back to allow her entrance, his eyes flicking admiringly over her bottom as she wiggled past.

'Where do you want it?' she asked, raising her eyebrows.

Ha, bloody, ha, thought Jennings. More games.

He decided to play.

'On the bed?' he chuckled then shook his head and motioned to the dressing table. She set down the tray and looked at the various toiletries on show. There was some anti-perspirant, some after-shave. Paula unscrewed the lid of the bottle and sniffed it.

'Well,' she said. 'How did you enjoy Hinkston's nightlife?'

She sat down on the stool which faced the dressing table, one leg drawn up beneath her.

Jennings hesitated a moment then closed the door of the room. She smiled as he crossed to the dressing table and picked up a sandwich. As he stood before her she reached up and ran one hand gently across his thigh, allowing it slide higher towards his penis.

Game on. Your move, Jennings told himself.

He swallowed the remains of the sandwich and looked down at her. She didn't attempt to stop her firm stroking and, despite himself, Jennings felt a tightening in his groin. Paula smiled up at him, those chips of sapphire pinning him again in that electrifying gaze.

'What about your parents?' he said, quietly, his erection now painfully constricted by his jeans.

'I told them I was going to bed after I'd given you your food. They won't check on me.' She began to rub more firmly over the bulge in his jeans, outlining his stiffness with her thumb and index finger then she loosened the popper on his waistband and, slowly eased his zip down.

Jennings sighed as the pressure was relieved, that sigh of relief turning to one of pleasure as she eased his pants over his hips exposing his throbbing erection. She bent forward and closed her lips around the bulbous head. He moved closer as she flicked her tongue around the glans, allowing her fingers to trace a pattern across his tightened scrotum. He began to thrust gently in and out of her mouth as she covered his throbbing member with her saliva, still sucking greedily at it.

He slid his hands through her hair, amazed at the fineness of it. Then his hands slipped to her shoulders then down to seek her breasts which he kneaded through the material of her T-shirt, coaxing the nipples to even greater stiffness.

She pulled away suddenly, allowing his penis to slip from her mouth. Then, with a grin on her face she pulled the T-shirt off and moved swiftly across to the bed. Jennings stepped out of his jeans, tugged his socks off then removed his shirt, watching mesmerised as she shrugged off her own jeans, undulating and writhing on the bed, peeling them off like a snake sloughing its skin.

Naked, they were joined on the bed.

He cupped her left breast in his hand and squeezed, his tongue flicking over the stiff nipple, teasing it between his teeth before repeating the procedure on the other. Her hand found his shaft and she enveloped it in her fingers, beginning a rhythmic motion which brought him immense pleasure. He twisted round so that his face was between her legs, nuzzling his way through her tightly curled pubic hair until he found her swollen vaginal lips. He flicked his tongue along each in turn before seeking her clitoris, drawing back the fleshy hood with his teeth, feeling the firmness against his tongue.

Her cleft wept moisture into his mouth as he brought one hand around and began softly stroking the inside of her thighs. Her breathing became deeper.

Then she rolled over, pulling him onto his back, lowering herself onto his face, pressing her wet pubis against his mouth for a moment longer before sliding down his chest, leaving a moist trail. She straddled him taking his penis in one hand, guiding it towards her wetness, rubbing his swollen glans against her clitoris. Using him to stimulate her further. If this was still a game then he was playing by *her* rules now.

'Fuck me,' she gasped, insistently and lowered herself onto him, enveloping his penis with her cleft so that it felt as if he was being seized by a slippery glove which tightened more as he thrust up to meet her downward movement. She gasped and ground against him harder, moaning as he rubbed her swaying breasts, knowing that he was close to orgasm himself.

Paula leant forward and kissed him, her tongue pushing into his mouth, flicking across his lips as she rode him faster. She sucked his tongue into her mouth and he felt it against the hard edges of her teeth. Felt her own tongue retreat to allow *his* to probe deeper.

Felt her front teeth closing on his tongue.

Felt the uncontrollable agony as she bit through it.

Blood burst from the tumescent appendage, filling his mouth and hers, spilling over his chin to stain the sheets beneath.

She sat back, swallowing the tongue with one huge gulp then she bent towards him again, still riding his now shrinking penis, still feeling the uncontrollable pleasure building within her as he bucked beneath her.

Her orgasm came as she tore off his top lip.

She took it between her bloodied front teeth and bit deep, pulling. Shaking her head from side to side until it came away. She chewed once and swallowed that too.

Her pleasure was limitless now.

The shattering power of her climax sent what felt like an electric charge through her body and, as blood from his severed tongue spilled down her naked torso, she rocked back and forth on top of his writhing body, her arms holding him down with surprising strength.

He tried to scream but the blood flooded back into his throat.

She slid off him, reaching for the vase on the bedside table, bringing it down with terrifying force on his head.

The vase shattered, the blow opening another savage gash on his forehead.

His eyes rolled upwards in the socket as she clambered back onto him, like some unsatisfied lover in search of gratification.

She used the jagged, broken edges of the vase to open his stomach, the muscles and flesh splitting like an overripe peach.

She thrust one hand inside the reeking cavity, her fingers closing around a length of intestine. It felt like a throbbing worm, bloated and slimy but, undeterred, she pulled hard, ripping the bulging length free. Paula raised it to her mouth and bit into it ignoring the blood which poured down her arms and torso. It trickled through her pubic hair like crimson ejaculate and she slid back and forth in the reeking mess, her eyes closed in ecstasy. Her mouth bulging as she filled it with the dripping entrails, chewing happily.

Jennings had stopped moving. Even the muscular spasms which had racked his body having ceased.

He was dead by the time she began peeling pieces of skin from his face, pushing them into her mouth with a gourmet's fervour.

It was as she reached for his eye that the door opened.

27

'Who is he?'

Hacket's voice sounded like gravel as he sipped at the coffee, gazing through the two-way mirror into the interrogation room.

The room was bare but for a table, two chairs and three men.

A uniformed sergeant. Detective Inspector Madden and a third man.

'His name's Peter Walton,' said DS Spencer, looking down at a sheet of paper fastened to the clip-board which he held. 'Age thirty-two, no fixed abode. Eleven previous convictions. All small-time stuff though. Handling stolen goods, mugging, that kind of thing.'

'You call mugging small-time?' said Hacket, his eyes never leaving Walton. He studied every inch of the man's face as he sat toying with an empty packet of cigarettes. The lank hair, streaked with grey here and there. The sallow complexion, sunken eyes. Unshaven. His lips were thick and puffy, as if he'd been chewing the bottom one repeatedly until it swelled. He had a dark birthmark on the left side of his neck,

420

just below his jaw. Hacket noticed with disgust that there was some hardened mucous around one nostril. When he tired of playing with the cigarette packet, Walton began picking at that particular nostril, examining the hardened snot before wiping it on his trousers.

Spencer had not expected the school teacher to drive to the police station after the phone call. He was even more surprised by his appearance. Hacket's hand was crudely bandaged, the blood still seeping through. His hair was uncombed and the dark rings beneath his eyes made him look as though he hadn't slept for a week. Spencer noticed the smell of whisky on his breath but made no comment. Instead he had shown the dishevelled man straight through into the office which looked onto the interrogation room, watching as Hacket sat down, his eyes never leaving Walton. As if he were trying to remember every single detail about the man.

Hacket himself had washed his face when he'd finished speaking on the phone to Spencer, scrubbing the dried blood away. The he'd bandaged his hand, pulled on a jacket and driven to the police station. The cold night air combined with the news he had just heard had served to shock him out of his stupor even though he was still aware of the smell of drink on his breath.

Now the two men sat in the small room gazing through the two-way mirror as if they were watching fish inside an aquarium.

'We picked him up in Soho,' said Spencer. 'He was trying to sell some videos. Cassettes which had been stolen from your house.

'You said that there were lots of fingerprints in the house when Lisa was killed.'

'There were. Unfortunately, none of them match with Walton's.'

Hacket exhaled deeply.

'You must be able to hold him on something,' the teacher rasped.

'Apart from receiving stolen goods, there's nothing.'

'You mean you're going to let him go?' Hacket snarled, turning towards Spencer for the first time. The DS saw the fury on the teacher's face. 'He killed my daughter. You can't let him go.'

'We can't prove that, Mr Hacket. Not yet. And, until we can, we can only hold him for forty-eight hours. After that he's free.' Spencer shrugged. 'I don't like it any more than you do but it's the law. *He* has his rights, regardless of what you or I think.'

'And what about my daughter?' Hacket muttered through clenched teeth. 'What about *her* fucking rights?'

'Look, I told you that we thought two men were involved well, perhaps Walton can lead us to the other man. To the one who really murdered your daughter.'

'How do you know it wasn't him?'

'Because his blood group is different to that of the man who raped your daughter.'

Hacket swallowed hard and turned away, his attention returning to Walton. He could see the man nodding or shaking his head as Madden asked him questions. He didn't seem very concerned. At one point he even smiled. Hacket gripped the arms of the chair until his knuckles turned white. What he wouldn't give for ten minutes alone with the bastard.

Forty-eight hours and he would be free again.

Hacket closed his eyes tightly, as if hoping the rage would vanish but, when he opened them again Walton was still there. The rage was still there.

The pain.

And the guilt.

He got slowly to his feet, wiping one hand across his face.

'What did you do to your hand?' asked Spencer, nodding towards the bandaged appendage.

'Just an accident.' Hacket turned towards the door.

'One of my men could drive you home, Mr Hacket.'

The teacher shook his head, pausing with his hand on the door knob.

'You let me know what happens. Please,' he said, without looking at Spencer. 'If you manage to hold him. If he spills the beans on his . . . partner. You'll let me know?'

'Yes,' said Spencer, watching as Hacket left.

The schoolteacher paused a moment on the steps of the police station, sucking in deep lungfuls of night air. As he stood there a police car pulled up and two uniformed men got out, running past him into the building.

Another emergency?

Hacket walked to his car and climbed in, sitting there for a moment before starting the engine. As he twisted the key it purred into life.

'Peter Walton,' he said under his breath.

He had a name and he knew what the bastard looked like.

It wasn't much but at least it was a start.

He pulled away, guiding the car out into traffic.

28

Her fingernails were deep inside his eye socket.

Like hooks, ready to pull the orb free of his skull but, as she heard the door open, Paula Kirkham turned, her blood spattered hand falling to her side. She chewed slowly on a portion of Jennings small intestine, pieces of it sticking to her chin. Her torso was smothered in his blood. The room smelled like a slaughterhouse. Crimson had soaked the bed itself, elsewhere it had sprayed up the walls as if directed by a hose. Some of it had even spattered the sandwiches which Jennings had asked for.

Paula swallowed what was left of the intestine and looked blankly at her parents.

Tony Kirkham slipped inside the room, pulling the door shut behind him. Irene crossed towards the bed, towards Paula and the mutilated remains of Stephen Jennings. She smiled benignly at her daughter and held out a hand, watching as the young girl slid from Jennings' torn body. Irene wrapped a blanket around her then gathered up the clothes which lay in an untidy bundle on the floor, some flecked with blood.

Paula smiled lovingly at her parents and, as she passed him, she paused and kissed her father softly on the cheek.

He smiled and touched her hair. Hair that was matted with blood.

Irene led her from the room and Tony was left alone with the remains of Jennings.

He wasted little time.

First he wrapped the body in the sheets and covers from the bed, cocooning it. Then he reached into his jacket pocket and pulled out the string he carried, wrapping long lengths around the bloodied corpse to keep the covers in place. The stench was appalling but he continued with his task, fetching Jennings' small suitcase from the wardrobe. Into it he pushed the dead man's clothes, his shoes, and anything else he could find which gave the appearance that someone had stopped in the room. He moved through into the bathroom, scooping up the rep's toothbrush and razor. Those too he tossed into the suitcase.

The mattress was sodden with blood, Tony made a mental note to burn it later. The large wood-burning stove in the basement of the hotel would be more than adequate for that task.

He would dispose of Jennings' body in there too. And his clothes.

As for his car, that could wait. He would drive it out into the countryside in the small hours and dump it. Even when it was found there would be nothing to connect it to the hotel, to the Kirkham family.

To his beautiful daughter.

Tony smiled as he looked down at the blood-drenched parcel of bedclothes which formed a shroud for Stephen Jennings. Some blood was beginning to seep onto the carpet. He would have to move fast before it left too indelible a stain.

The crimson which had spattered the walls would also need to be washed off.

He left the room for a moment, hurrying along the corridor to a utility room from which he took a mop, bucket, several cloths and dusters. By the time he returned to the room, a puddle of thick red fluid was beginning to spread out around the corpse. Tony muttered to himself, knelt down and lifted the body. He was a strong man and the weight bothered him little. He carried Jennings into the bathroom and dumped the corpse unceremoniously in the bath, looking down at it for a moment before returning to the bedroom.

As he picked up one of the cloths to wipe down the dressing table, the door of the room opened and Irene walked in.

'How is she?' he asked.

'She's sleeping now. I cleaned her up first then put her to bed.' She surveyed the blood spattered room indifferently. 'How long will you be?' she wanted to know.

'Give me an hour,' he said.

Irene nodded and glanced at her watch.

11.57 p.m.

She turned and left Tony to his task, hurrying down to reception. She ran her finger down the guest register and found Jennings' name. Then, with infinite care she changed the date of which he was due to leave. If anyone came looking for him, which was doubtful, they would say that he didn't stop the night, that he had to leave suddenly. That he hadn't left an address where he could be contacted.

That task done she scuttled back upstairs to her husband who was washing down the walls.

'What about the body?' she asked.

'I'll take care of it in a minute,' he said, calmly. 'There's no rush.'

No rush. No fuss.

They were used to the ritual by now.

12.57 a.m.

He'd said an hour and he'd been right.

The body was gone, all of Jennings' belongings were gone.

Irene Kirkham looked at her husband, who nodded.

She reached for the phone and dialled.

29

The house was large. An imposing edifice with a mock-Georgian front, its stonework covered by a creeping blanket of ivy. The windows peered from beneath this canopy like questing eyes, gazing out into the darkness. During the hours of daylight it was possible to see over most of Hinkston from the main bedroom of the house. The building set, as it was, on one of the many hills which swelled around the town.

A gravel drive curved up towards the house from the main road which led down into the town. Hedges which had once been subject to the complex art of topiary had been allowed to merge into one and now formed a boundary along the bottom of the spacious lawn and also on either side of the curving drive.

There was a pond in the centre of the lawn but it was empty of fish. A couple of weatherbeaten gnomes stood sentinel.

The house boasted eight bedrooms but, at present, only one was used. Downstairs there was a sizeable library, a sitting-room which again looked out over Hinkston itself, and a kitchen.

The surgery had been installed over twenty-three years ago. It had been constructed from two other rooms, one turned into an office, the other a waiting room.

It was in the surgery that Doctor Edward Curtis sat, his jacket off, his sleeves rolled up.

He was cradling a glass of gin in one strong hand, massaging the skin above his eyebrows with the other.

Curtis was a tall, lean man in his late forties. His brown hair was cut short, his skin smooth apart from the moustache which covered his top lip. He turned the glass slowly in his hand, looking down into the clear liquid and telling himself that he would go to bed when he'd finished his drink.

He'd said that after the first two. Now, gazing at his fourth, he determined to keep to his word. He took a sip of the gin.

The house was particularly quiet at this time. Not even the creak of settling timbers disturbed the solitude. Curtis enjoyed silence. He was grateful that the house was set outside the town itself, more than half a mile. Of course a frequent bus service brought his patients to him during surgery, those who didn't drive. But, apart from his work, Curtis was rarely disturbed. He was on call, naturally, twenty-four hours a day, preferring not to employ a locum as the surgeries in town did. Many of his patients called him by his first name and he had found that his rapport, carefully cultivated over the years, helped them to relax. Perhaps, he reasoned, private practice offered more time than that available to his overworked colleagues working for the NHS but it was something which Curtis found both rewarding and necessary.

He had been practising in Hinkston for the last twenty-one years, ever since his return from medical school and he was now a well established member of the community, his skills sought by both old and young, not just in Hinkston but also further afield. There was one woman on his books who came from London to see him, such was her faith in him.

426

Curtis employed just two people, both on a part-time basis. A receptionist and a housekeeper, although it would be more appropriate to call her a cleaner. But he disliked the term, finding it demeaning to the woman who performed such a necessary task. She cleaned both the surgery and the house itself.

But not the cellar.

The subterranean part of the house was the private domain of the doctor. He had installed a simple but sophisticated store of machinery and equipment which allowed him to perform some fairly complex tests. His ability to test for diseases such as diabetes and various renal problems, to name but two, removed the need for patients to travel to hospital and so cut down the time they had to wait for results. He even had a small X-ray unit down there. Blood tests and urine tests could be analysed on the spot, the patient able to know the results before they left the surgery.

Most of the money to set up the surgery, and certainly to install the equipment, had come from his parents. Now both dead, they had left him not only the house but a sizeable amount of money which Curtis had invested wisely. His fees were more than reasonable and, living alone, he had minimal overheads. Just the wages of his two staff and his everyday living requirements.

He took another sip of the gin and glanced at his watch.

1.36 a.m.

He rubbed his eyes and yawned.

The door to the surgery opened and Curtis looked up as the newcomer walked across to the desk and sat down opposite him.

'Join me?' Curtis asked, pushing the bottle and a glass towards the other occupant of the room.

He filled the glass, watching as his companion drank.

'Sorry if I woke you,' he said.

The other merely shrugged.

'I had to go into Hinkston. An emergency,' he explained, finishing his drink.

The figure also drained the glass and pushed it towards Curtis, who promptly re-filled it.

'I'm going to bed,' Curtis announced, yawning again. He got to his

427

feet, picked up his jacket and headed for the door that led through the waiting room and beyond to the stairs.

The remaining occupant of the surgery sat drinking, only the sound of low, rhythmic breathing breaking the deathly silence.

30

She guessed she'd slept less than three hours all night.

Sue Hacket splashed her face with cold water, dried it then wandered back into the bedroom to apply some makeup. She inspected the dark rings beneath her eyes before adding eye-liner and a touch of lipstick. She rubbed her cheeks, noting the paleness of her skin and finally gave in to the temptation of touching on some rouge.

Downstairs she could hear the sound of the radio, the vacuous ramblings of the DJ periodically replaced by the even more vacuous music he played. She slipped out of her housecoat and pulled on jeans and a sweater, stepping into her shoes before she made her way downstairs.

'Well, come on then,' she said to Craig who was sitting at the kitchen table trying to fasten the laces on his shoes. 'You've got to show me the way and we don't want you being late do we?'

'I won't be late,' he assured her, jumping down from the chair and rushing into the sitting room to retrieve his satchel.

'Thanks for taking him to school, Sue,' said Julie who stood at the kitchen sink, her face looking distinctly haggard. 'Mike would have stayed off work but he says they've got a big contract to finish . . .'

Sue held up a hand to silence her.

'Leave the washing up, I'll do it when I come back,' she said.

'No. I'd rather keep myself occupied. It stops me thinking about Dad,' Julie told her.

'I know what you mean.'

'I'm ready, Auntie Sue,' announced Craig, appearing in the doorway like a soldier ready for inspection. Sue smiled and heard the front door open as he rushed out to the Metro to wait for her. She turned and looked at Julie then followed him out.

Craig sat in the passenger seat beside her, well strapped in, happily telling her directions to his school, pointing at friends he knew as they passed them on the journey.

Sue saw mothers with younger children and her expression hardened.

The emotion she was feeling was something close to resentment. That others should be enjoying the simple pleasure of walking their children to school while she would never know that joy. Was it resentment she asked herself? Envy or jealousy? It all amounted to the same thing.

'That's Trevor Ward,' Craig announced pointing to a tall, thin child with glasses who was crossing the road ahead of them. 'He picks his nose and eats it.'

'Does he really?' Sue answered, deciding that kind of personal detail didn't interest her too much.

'His Mum and Dad can't afford a car,' said Craig with glee.

'Not everyone is as lucky as *your* mum and dad, Craig,' she told him, the merest hint of rebuke in her voice. Some people aren't even lucky enough to have children she felt like adding, administering a swift mental slap for the feelings of self-pity she felt surfacing. But, surrounded by children as she was, it was difficult not to feel the resentment which Lisa's death had brought. Sue suddenly felt very weary.

She brought the car to a halt outside the main gates of the school and leant across to unlock the door for Craig.

He told her he'd get a lift home with a friend of his. His mum always picked him up. Sue told him to get a teacher to ring if there was any change of plan. He nodded happily, unfastening his seat belt and pushing open the door.

'See you later,' she said, smiling. 'Don't I get a kiss goodbye?'

He looked at her and chuckled, as if it were something he'd meant to do but it had just slipped his mind. She turned her face slightly to allow him to kiss her cheek.

Craig took hold of her chin, turning her face back towards him then, kneeling on the seat, he kissed her full on the lips, pressing his against her own for what seemed like an eternity.

429

Then he pulled away and jumped out of the car.

Sue watched him run off into the playground, still shocked at his response, still able to feel the pressure of his lips against her own.

She raised two fingers to her mouth and gently ran them across her lips.

As she did she saw that her hand was shaking.

31

Hacket stared down at the black marble stone and glanced at the inscription, feeling the tears begin to prick his eyes. He sniffed them back, holding the small bouquet of violets in his hands. The right one was still heavily bandaged and, even with the benefit of pain killers, he could feel a dull throbbing pain coming from it.

The sun was out but it was cold, the light breeze occasionally intensifying into a chill wind which caused him to shiver. The flowers which already stood in the small pot on Lisa's grave had wilted, some shedding their withered petals, and it was these petals that the wind scattered like discarded confetti.

Hacket stood for a moment longer looking down at his daughter's grave then he knelt and began removing the old flowers from the pot, laying them on the wet grass.

The sunshine and the Sabbath day had coaxed a number of people to the cemetery and he glanced around to see others performing tasks similar to his own. Replacing flowers, pulling unwanted weeds from plots. He saw an elderly woman cleaning a white headstone with a cloth. Not far from her a man in his early forties stood, hands clasped before him, gazing down at a grave. Hacket wondered who the man had lost. A wife? A mother or father? Perhaps even a son or daughter like himself. Death held no discrimination for age, sex or creed.

Hacket began placing the new flowers in the pot his mind full of thoughts. Of Lisa. Of Sue.

Of the phone call he'd received earlier that morning.

DS Spencer had phoned about ten a.m. with the news that, due to lack of evidence, Peter Walton had been released.

Hacket had barely given him time to finish speaking before angrily slamming the phone down.

Released.

The bastard had gone free, just as Spencer had warned.

So, now what?

Hacket continued pushing flowers into the pot, the question eating away at him.

Did he go looking for Walton? Try to trace him? Spencer had said that his address had been unknown so where did Hacket begin? He had no doubt of his own ability to kill Walton should he find him but his first, main problem, was actually hunting the bastard down. And Hacket was no detective. Where did he start? He exhaled wearily. In films it was so simple. The avenging angel always knew where to find his intended prey. Everything always went according to plan. Only this *wasn't* a film, this was real life with all its attendant complexities.

Hacket had no doubt he could kill Walton.

No doubt?

He had fantasised about it, dreamt of the most elaborate ways of inflicting pain on the killer of his child and yet, if the time came would he have time to make Walton suffer as he wished him to? Would Walton kill *him*?

And Spencer had also said that another man could be involved.

What then?

What? If? How? When?

Hacket turned and hurled the dead flowers into the nearby waste bin. He turned back and looked at the grave, massaging his forehead gently with one hand. He could feel the beginnings of a headache, the pressure building slowly but surely. Just as it was building within him until all he wanted to do was scream and shout. Anything to release the pent up emotion which swelled like a malignant tumour. Only *this* cancer was eating away his soul.

He looked down at the grave and thought of Lisa.

Of Sue.

Hacket had never felt so lonely in his life.

He turned and walked slowly back towards the car.

32

The crying awoke her.

Michelle Lewis sat up quickly, rubbing her eyes as she heard the howls from the bottom of the bed.

Beside her, Stuart Lewis grunted and swung himself out of bed.

'The joys of parenthood,' he said, smiling thinly.

Michelle also clambered out of bed and moved towards the cot which held their child.

Daniel Lewis was crying loudly, his face creased and red.

'He looks like a bloody dishcloth,' said Stuart, yawning, looking down at the screaming bundle which his wife carefully lifted into her arms.

'You probably looked like that at six weeks,' she told him, rocking the baby gently back and forth.

'Thanks,' he muttered, watching as she unfastened her nightdress and eased one swollen breast free, raising the child to the nipple it sought.

He had been a large baby, over nine pounds at birth, but Michelle had been fortunate. The delivery had been an easy one. She had always had what Stuart referred to as 'child bearing hips' which was his way of saying she needed to lose a little weight. But she had already begun her exercise classes to lose the pounds she'd gained while carrying Daniel and she was confident she'd soon have her figure back. After all, she was only just past her twentieth birthday, her body was still very flexible.

'I'm going to make a cup of tea,' said Stuart, running a hand through his hair. 'Do you want anything?'

She didn't answer, merely hissed in pain as Daniel chewed rather over-enthusiastically on her nipple, coaxing the milk from the large bud and gurgling contentedly. However, after a moment or two,

432

Michelle removed him from her left nipple, noticing as she did how red it was. The baby yelled for a second but soon quietened down as she lifted him to the right nipple, allowing him to close his mouth over that. He began sucking vigorously, his eyes darting back and forth as he accepted her milk.

'It's a pity *you* can't do this,' said Michelle, smiling.

Stuart rubbed his chest and shrugged.

'Sorry, love,' he said. 'Empty.'

They both chuckled.

Daniel continued to suck with ever increasing vigour.

'I'm sure he's getting some teeth,' Michelle observed, feeling the soreness beginning around her nipple.

'He's too young for that isn't he?' David asked, deciding not to bother with the tea. Instead he sat down on the edge of the bed beside his wife, watching as she nursed the baby. He remained there for a moment longer then got up and wandered along to the bathroom where he urinated gushingly.

Michelle held the baby to her breast, aware of a growing pain around her nipple.

The child had gripped the mammary in both tiny hands and was clinging on like a leech, his mouth still sucking hard. She was sure that he had some teeth, he must have. His jaws continued to move up and down, swallowing the milk greedily. Another minute or so and she'd move him back to the other nipple again, the right one was becoming painfully sore. Besides, he should have had enough by now.

She held him gently, frowning as she felt the pressure on her breast increase. His tiny fingers raked across the flesh leaving four red lines and she winced.

'I think you've had enough, young man,' she said, and prepared to transfer him back to the other nipple, if not to terminate the feed there and then. She lifted him gently.

He did not release her nipple.

'Daniel,' she said, softly, easing him away.

The child continued to suck.

Michelle took hold of one of his tiny hands and tried to pull him away but he wouldn't budge.

She felt a growing pain in her breast as he continued to suck.

'Daniel, that's enough,' she said, more urgently.

He seemed to be nuzzling against her with renewed vigour, pushing his head against the mammary, closing his jaws even more tightly over the protruding nub of flesh and muscle.

She let out a yelp of pain as she felt a sharp stab around her nipple. As if he were biting her. Using his teeth. Teeth which, by rights, he shouldn't have.

Michelle for some inexplicable reason felt suddenly worried. The child would not let go of her nipple and as she tried to pull him free she felt the skin stretching, most of it still held in his mouth.

The pain was growing.

'God,' she hissed as Stuart re-entered the room and looked at her.

He saw the baby pushing hard against her breast, saw the skin of that breast being pulled taut, saw the pain on Michelle's face.

Then he saw the blood.

It trickled from the baby's mouth, mingling with the overflowing milk to create a pink dribble which dripped onto the bed.

'What's wrong?' he said, worriedly, taking a step towards the bed.

Michelle didn't answer, she merely continued to tug at the baby who was now hanging on grimly, using both hands to anchor himself.

The pain spread across her chest until it felt as if her entire torso was ablaze and, finally, unable to bear it any longer, she pulled the child hard.

As she did, Daniel bit through her nipple, severing it.

Blood jetted from the swollen tissue, spraying the child and the bed, soaking into the sheets.

The baby swallowed the nipple with one gulp, blood and milk dribbling over its chin.

Michelle screamed and looked down at her torn breast, a flap of skin hanging over the lacerated mammary. Blood was pumping furiously from the wound and she hastily laid the baby down and tugged the sheet to her chest, pressing it against the wound which bled profusely.

Daniel lay contentedly on the bed, his eyes still as bright and alert.

'Oh Jesus,' gasped Stuart, moving towards her. 'I'll get an ambulance.'

He looked once more at his child, its face soaked in blood, still

434

chewing on a piece of skin which had come free with the nipple. Then he dashed for the phone.

'No,' Michelle called. 'Not the ambulance. Not yet.' She was pressing the sheet to her mutilated breast, trying to stem the flow of blood as best she could. 'You know who you've got to call.'

He hesitated a second longer then stabbed out the digits.

Behind him on the bed, the baby gurgled contentedly.

33

Stuart Lewis looked at his watch and then continued gazing out of the front window. Every few moments he would step back to take a drag of his cigarette but then anxiety would force him back to his vigil.

He checked his watch again.

5.46 a.m.

He had made the phone call more than twenty minutes ago.

'Come on, come on,' he whispered, agitatedly, his face pressed to the glass of the window again.

Finally the car swung round the corner and came to a halt outside the house. Stuart moved towards the front door and unlocked it, opening it as the occupant of the car clambered out.

Doctor Edward Curtis strode up the path and through the front door.

'Upstairs,' Stuart said, and the doctor followed the younger man as he bounded up the narrow flight, hurrying towards the bedroom where his wife waited.

As Curtis entered the bedroom he was struck by the strong smell of blood.

The sheet which Michelle Lewis held against her breast was soaked in the crimson fluid, some of it beginning to congeal on the material. There were spots of it on the wall and carpet. It looked as though she was wearing red gloves.

The child lay beside her, its shawl similarly dotted with crimson, its face and hands stained dark with its mother's blood.

It was the baby that Curtis approached first.

'How long ago did this happen?' he asked, unfastening the black bag which he carried.

Stuart told him.

'And you haven't called an ambulance?' Curtis wanted to know, smiling relievedly when Stuart shook his head.

Curtis reached into his bag and took out a syringe. He quickly took it from its plastic wrapping then pulled out a bottle full of almost colourless liquid. He upended it, jabbed the needle through the top and drew off 50ml then he gently took hold of the baby's arm, found a vein and ran the needle into it.

The child didn't murmur as Curtis pushed the plunger, expelling the liquid into its veins.

He waited a moment then withdrew the syringe, dropping it back into his bag. Only then did he turn to Michelle who was still holding the sheet to her chest in what looked like an exaggerated attempt at modesty.

'Let me look,' said Curtis and she lowered the blood spattered sheet.

Not only had the nipple been torn off but a piece of flesh as large as the palm of Curtis's hand had also been pulled from the breast. He could see muscles and vein networks exposed. Blood was still oozing from the wound, dribbling down Michelle's stomach.

Curtis reached into his bag once again, this time pulling out some gauze and bandages.

'I'll dress the wound as best I can,' he said. 'You'll need to go to the hospital, you've lost a lot of blood.'

Michelle nodded obediently as Curtis pressed a gauze pad to the place where her nipple used to be then hastily wrapped bandages around to keep it in place.

'Tell them whatever you have to,' he said. 'Whatever you can think of. The child will be fine now. But he's not to be left alone for a while.' The doctor looked at Stuart who nodded. 'He'll sleep now.'

Curtis got to his feet and headed for the door.

'Wait five minutes then call the ambulance,' he said. They heard his footfalls on the stairs, the sound of his car engine as he drove off.

Both of them looked into the cot where the baby lay, already beginning to drift off to sleep.

436

They smiled down at him then Michelle wet the tip of her finger and wiped some blood away from his mouth.

He was really such a beautiful child.

34

She had hesitated for a long time before finally deciding to call him.

It had been over a week since her father's funeral and she hadn't spoken to him since then, but now Sue Hacket sat beside the phone looking down at it as if expecting the digits to reach him without her having to touch them. She hadn't even been sure at first if she *wanted* to speak to him but she had found that loneliness is a truly contagious disease and Sue was finding it creeping into her life despite being surrounded by Julie and the family. She had tried rehearsing what she should say to her husband, even got as far as lifting the receiver once but then replaced it and resorted to pacing the floor of Julie's sitting room surrounded by the dozens of ornaments.

Julie was out shopping. Craig was at school and Mike at work. She was alone with only her thoughts for company.

Finally, almost reluctantly, she lifted the receiver and slowly pressed the numbers which would connect her with Hacket's school.

The connection was made, she heard the dial tone.

'Can I speak to John Hacket, please?' she asked when the phone was finally picked up.

The woman at the other end apologised but Mr Hacket had taken a week's holiday. She could leave a message if she wanted to, the secretary had his home number.

'No thanks,' said Sue and replaced the receiver, looking down at it for a moment before lifting it to her ear and jabbing out the digits of her home number.

Home. The word seemed curiously redundant.

The phone was answered almost immediately.

'Hello.'

She recognised his voice and, for a second, thought about putting the phone back down.

'Hello, John, it's me.'

'Sue? How are you?'

'I'm OK I rang the school, they said you were off for a week.'

'Yeah, I can't seem to concentrate. It's not fair on the kids if I'm not giving it a hundred per cent, besides I've got things to do around the house. I put it on the market, there's been three or four prospective buyers round already.'

'Any interest?'

'One couple seemed fairly keen until they found out what had happened here.' He was quiet for a moment. 'Some bloke came just *because* of what happened here, morbid bastard. I haven't heard anything from the others yet.' There was another awkward silence. 'You say you're all right, you sound tired.'

'I am. I haven't been sleeping too well.'

More silence.

Christ, it was excruciating, as if each was trying to think of something to say. They were like strangers.

'How's Julie and Mike?' he asked.

'They're not so bad.'

'And the boy?'

'He's all right too.' She didn't mention the incident in the car, having since tried to dismiss it from her mind.

'Good,' he said, wearily. 'So everyone's OK'

'Listen John, I had to speak to you. It's about you and me. I told you I couldn't come back to that house and I can't.'

'I understand that but things might not be that cut and dried. I mean, it's not just the house you're avoiding is it? It's me.'

She swallowed hard.

'I might *just* have managed to forgive you for the affair, John,' she said. 'But I'll *never* forgive you for what happened to Lisa. And, yes, I still blame you. I always will.'

'You phoned to tell me something I already knew?' he said, trying to control the irritation in his voice. 'How do you think *I* feel? I can't forgive *myself*, I don't need you to remind me all the time. It's me who's living in the house now. I'm closer to the memories. You're the one who ran away from them, Sue.'

'I didn't run away. If I hadn't got out I'd have gone crazy.'

'I know the feeling.'

There was another silence.

'John, the real reason I rang was to tell you that one of the schools down here in Hinkston has a vacancy for an assistant headmaster. Apparently there's a house included with the job.'

'Why Hinkston?'

'Because I don't want to live in London anymore, I told you that,' she snapped.

'And the two of us? If I got this job would you be willing to start again? A new environment, a new life perhaps?' He sounded hopeful.

'Maybe. We couldn't start from the beginning, John. Things would never be the same between us again.'

'We can try for Christ's sake,' he insisted. 'I still love you, Sue. I need you and I think you need me, whether you admit it or not.'

She sat in silence for a moment, knowing there was some truth to his words.

'It'll take time, John.'

'I don't care how long it takes.'

She gave him the address and number of the school.

'Let me know how it goes,' she told him.

'Maybe you could meet me when I come down for the interview.'

There was a long silence. For a moment he thought she'd gone.

'Yes, I will,' she said, finally.

'Sue, if you're not sleeping, love, it might be an idea to take something. Go and see a doctor. You've got to take care of yourself.'

'I was thinking of seeing Julie's doctor actually.'

Another long silence.

'I'd better go, John,' she said. 'Call me when you're coming down for the interview.'

'Sue, thanks for calling.'

'I'll see you soon.'

'Sue.'

'Yes?'

'I love you.'

She gripped the receiver tight for a second.

'See you soon,' she said, softly then put the phone down.

It was as if the conversation had drained her of strength. She sat back, looking down at the phone, feeling as if she'd just run a marathon. It was fully five minutes before she got to her feet and wandered into the kitchen. He was right, perhaps she should see a doctor. A few sleeping pills wouldn't hurt her, there was a small booklet lying on the kitchen table with a picture of a smiling cat and the legend 'Important People' embossed on it. Another of Julie's organisational aids. The address book contained numbers for everyone from the Gas board to the local vet. All in alphabetical order. Sue flicked through until she came to the 'D's'.

She found the name she sought almost immediately.

DOCTOR'S SURGERY.

And beneath it:

Doctor Edward Curtis.

35

It was a feeling Hacket thought he'd forgotten and he smiled as he drove, glancing out at the scenery which sped past him. The sun was high in the sky as if its emergence were purely to mirror his state of mind.

He hadn't felt this way for many months, years even. It was something like anticipation only it was more heightened, more acute. There was anxiety there too, naturally but, he actually felt reasonably happy and that particular emotion was one which had been intolerably absent from his life of late.

As he drew nearer to the outskirts of Hinkston and houses began to appear in greater abundance, he thought what his prospects were. If he could secure the job at the school and the house which Sue had told him went with it then he had a chance of rebuilding his marriage too. Hacket felt the surge of adrenalin once again and realised that it wasn't anticipation it was, in all senses of the cliché, a ray of hope.

He'd rung the school immediately after he'd finished speaking to Sue and had been surprised to find that they were prepared to interview him the following day. He'd expected a wait of a week at least but apparently they were anxious to fill the post, and consequently wanted to begin seeing applicants as soon as possible.

Hacket was also glad to be out of the house for a day. He hadn't felt like being surrounded by people, that was why he'd taken the week off work, but being imprisoned in the house, alone with just his thoughts, had proved almost as intolerable. The trip to Hinkston and the possibility of a new job had lifted his spirits a little. He'd even found it possible to face some music and had jammed a cassette into the machine as he drove. However, as he drove further into the town he switched the cassette off and contented himself with glancing around at the buildings which were beginning to form more regular patterns on either side of him.

As he paused at traffic lights, Hacket checked the location of the school on the piece of paper he'd written it down on. He wasn't far away now, he realised.

He felt nervous, though not about the interview. He knew his own capabilities, knew he was as able, if not more so, than most to fill the post but his anxiety grew from knowing that if he didn't get the job then his chance of rebuilding his marriage was also in jeopardy. He could stand to lose the job but not to lose Sue.

The lights changed and Hacket drove on. He guided the car through the town centre, looking around at what appeared to be a bustling community. There was an open market in the paved square, the awnings fluttering brightly in the light breeze. He could hear the shouts of traders as they vied for custom.

The school was on the other side of town, about five minutes' drive from the centre, and he finally spotted the iron railings which rose from the concrete like rusted javelins. The playground was empty but past a large red brick building he could see beyond to a playing field where a number of children were kicking a ball about. Hacket swung the Renault into the car park and switched off the engine. He glanced at his reflection in the mirror, running a hand through his hair, then

441

he climbed out and strode through the main doors of the school in search of the headmaster's office.

A young woman in her mid-twenties passed him and smiled and, for fleeting seconds, Hacket caught himself gazing at her shapely legs as she passed him.

A little like Nikki?

He sucked in an angry breath, mad with himself for even thinking about her, but her image would not fade from his mind as quickly as he would have liked. He walked on and finally came to a door marked: D. BROOKS. HEADMASTER

He knocked and walked in, finding himself in an outer office.

A tall woman smiled at him, trying to shovel the final piece of a Kit-Kat into her mouth, chewing quickly enough to ask him what he wanted. Hacket smiled and spared her the trouble.

'My name's John Hacket. I've got an appointment at ten about the deputy Head's job.'

She continued chewing furiously, nodding vigorously as she swallowed the pieces of biscuit.

'Excuse me,' she said, wiping chocolate from her lips. 'I'll tell Mr Brooks you're here.' She smiled again and knocked on the door behind her, walking in when called. Hacket was left alone in the outer office.

He glanced around at the diagram of the school which covered one wall, the paintings which adorned another. Each one had a small plaque beneath it which Hacket read. The paintings had been done by pupils, each one a prizewinner in a different age group.

One of the paintings showed an owl perched in a tree holding something small and bloodied in its claws. Hacket leaned closer, unable to make out the shape.

'If you'd like to come through, Mr Hacket,' the tall woman called, interrupting his inspection of the painting.

'Thank you,' said Hacket, taking a final look at the painting.

As he moved away from it he finally realised what the small bloodied shape was in the painting. He frowned.

In its talons, the beautifully painted owl held a torn and bleeding human eye.

442

The heat inside the office was stifling.

Hacket felt his skin prickling as he walked in, and he was aware of his cheeks colouring from the warmth.

The man who faced him across the wide desk, by contrast, was pale and, as he shook Hacket's hand, the younger man noticed how cold the others' touch was.

Donald Brooks was in his early fifties, his immaculate appearance spoilt only by a few flakes of dandruff on the collar of his grey suit. He was an imposing-looking individual despite his pallid appearance, and the eyes which looked out at Hacket from behind spectacles were an intense green. His handshake was firm, his smile friendly. He invited Hacket to sit down, noticing the scarlet tinges on the younger man's cheeks.

'Sorry about the heat in here,' Brooks said. 'I'm a little anaemic and I tend to feel the cold more than most.'

'I'd noticed,' Hacket said, smiling.

'My wife's always complaining about it at home,' Brooks went on. 'Even in the summer we have the central heating turned on.' He shrugged almost apologetically. He asked Hacket if he wanted a coffee and the tall woman in the outer office entered with one a moment or two later. He thanked her and she left the two men alone once more, allowing Brooks to flick through the two-page CV which Hacket had passed to him. The younger man sipped his coffee while Brooks nodded approvingly, reading the qualifications and commendations that Hacket had acquired over the last ten years.

'Very impressive, Mr Hacket,' he said, finally. 'Your qualifications are excellent and you have some very useful experience behind you. I see the school you teach at presently has over 900 pupils – that can't give you much opportunity for personal contact.'

'I'm afraid it doesn't. It's an occupational hazard I suppose, working in London schools. What's your pupil to teacher ratio here?'

'We average about twenty to a class, usually less. Most of the sixth-form classes have only three or four pupils.'

Hacket nodded approvingly and the two men talked for some time about the school, about Hacket's background in teaching and his desire for the present position.

'Are you married, Mr Hacket?' Brooks asked.

'Yes.'

'Any children?'

He hesitated a second, as if the word itself brought pain.

'No,' he said, sharply, reaching for his coffee and taking a sip, wincing when he found it was cold.

Stone cold. As cold as the grave.

As cold as Lisa.

'Have you had many applicants for the position?' Hacket asked, anxious to steer the conversation onto other things.

'You're the fourth,' Brooks told him. 'And, I must admit I'm impressed. When could you start if you were given the job?'

Hacket shrugged.

'Next week,' he said. 'There's details to finalise about selling our house in London, but a week should be plenty of time.'

'Excellent,' said Brooks. 'Then I think it's time I showed you around the school. You ought to see where you're going to be working.'

Hacket smiled broadly, got to his feet and shook the older man's hand, again feeling the coldness of his skin but this time he ignored that small detail. He followed the Headmaster out of the office, pausing again to look at the painting of the owl which hung in the annexe beyond.

'Quite a talented artist,' Hacket said, nodding towards the painting, glancing at the name on the plaque beneath.

Phillip Craven.

Brooks glanced at the painting then walked out of the annexe without speaking.

Hacket followed.

* * *

444

The tour of the school took longer than Hacket had anticipated. The facilities were extensive and impressive and he thought that the school must be one of the few State-funded seats of learning not to have been decimated by Government cut-backs in the past few years.

He and Brooks walked past the red brick building Hacket had seen when first arriving at the school and the teacher was informed that it was a gymnasium. A class of girls were playing hockey on the nearby pitch, a shrieking horde supervised by a mistress who had thighs like a Russian shot-putter and shoulders slightly broader than Hacket's. He grinned as he watched her hurtling up and down the pitch, whistle clamped in her mouth.

'You may be asked to take on some of the duties of the Games masters,' Brooks said. 'I noticed in your CV that you'd done that at your last school. Are you a sporty man, Mr Hacket?'

'I played rugby and football for my school when I was a kid. I wish I was as fit now as I was then. But I can manage. No heart attacks, I promise.' He smiled.

Brooks looked at him as if he didn't understand the joke, then he shivered and turned away from the hockey match and strode across the playground with Hacket beside him. The sun was still out but Brooks looked frozen. His skin had turned even more pale and he kept rubbing his hands together as if to restore the circulation.

'As you're aware, there is a house with the position,' he said. 'I'll show you around that too.'

It was a white-walled building hidden from the school grounds by a high privet hedge which was somewhat sparsely covered for the time of year. But it was enough to offer protection from any inquisitive eyes within the school. There were a couple of willow trees in the front garden which had been allowed to get a little out of hand. The grass was about six inches long and there were weeds poking through cracks in the path which led to the front door but it was nothing which couldn't be put right in a weekend, thought Hacket.

As for the house itself, it looked in good repair, all the slates were on the roof. At least the ones he could see. The paintwork was good for another six months at least. The only thing which did stand out was the newness of the front door. It hadn't yet been painted the same

445

dull fawn as the window frames and looked as if it had been affixed only days earlier.

Brooks fumbled in his pocket for the key and opened the door, ushering Hacket in.

The hall was narrow, leading to a flight of stairs carpeted with a rusty coloured shag-pile.

'How long has the house been empty?' Hacket wanted to know.

'About two weeks.' Brooks told him, pushing open the door to the sitting room.

There was no carpet on the floor in there and Hacket's feet echoed on the bare boards. There were, however, still some framed prints on the wall and a couple of armchairs.

They were covered by dust sheets.

'The teacher who lived here before,' Hacket began, glancing around the room. 'Why did he leave?'

Brooks rubbed his hands together again and shrugged, partly in answer to the question, mainly as a gesture to indicate how cold he was. He patted one of the radiators as he passed it as if hoping it would begin pouring forth some heat.

'It was very sudden,' he said, sharply and moved through into the dining room.

This room was also carpeted and Hacket wondered why just the sitting room should have been left bare.

There was more furniture, too, also covered by dust sheets.

'What was he like?' Hacket wanted to know.

'He did his job,' Brooks answered, as if that was enough.

'He left a lot of furniture behind. He *must* have left in a rush.'

They wandered through into the kitchen then back through the dining room to the hall and up the stairs to look into the three bedrooms.

'Did he have kids?' Hacket asked.

'He liked to keep his affairs private, Mr Hacket. I don't pry into the private lives of my staff,' said Brooks, stiffly.

'I only asked if he had kids,' Hacket said, somewhat bemused.

Brooks turned and headed for the stairs.

'Have you seen enough? I have to get back to work.'

'I understand,' Hacket said, shaking his head.

As they reached the front door once more Brooks locked it, pressing on the wood to ensure it was properly fastened.

'The teacher before you did what I believe is called a moonlight flit. I don't know *why*, Mr Hacket. I just hope you're more reliable.' He stalked off up the path, leaving Hacket standing on the front step.

'A moonlight flit, eh?' Hacket muttered to himself.

His thoughts were interrupted by the sound of a bell. The signal for lunch.

Within minutes, the playground was filled with children, the sound of their voices swelling the air.

Back in his office, Brooks pressed himself against the radiator, the colour gradually coming back to his cheeks. He stood there while Hacket thanked him for the tour of the school and the house then they said their goodbyes and Hacket left, weaving his way through the throng of children in the playground in order to get to his car. Only then did Brooks leave the radiator and move across to the window, watching as the teacher eased the car through the gates and onto the main road.

'I gave him the job,' said Brooks as the tall woman entered the office.

'Did he ask many questions?' she enquired.

Brooks nodded.

'He wanted to know about the teacher who was here before him, wanted to know why he left so suddenly.'

'What did you tell him,' the secretary asked.

'I didn't tell him the truth, if that's what you mean,' Brooks said, rubbing his hands together. 'I'm not *that* stupid.'

37

Hacket parked his own car behind Sue's Metro and then slid from behind the steering wheel. He glanced at the house, hesitating a moment before walking up the path to the front door. He rang the bell, feeling peculiarly nervous. Like a boy on his first date, afraid that no one will answer. He waited a moment then rang again.

The door swung open.

'Hello, John,' beamed Julie and kissed him gently on the cheek. 'How did it go?'

'Fine,' he said, stepping in past his sister-in-law. 'Is Sue here?'

'Go through into the kitchen,' Julie told him.

Sue was drying some dishes. She turned as Hacket entered the room, her smile rather thin.

He thought how beautiful she looked. It seemed like years since he'd seen her, not days. Even longer since he'd held her.

'I got the job,' he told her.

'That's great,' she said, her smile broadening a little.

Julie joined them, aware of the atmosphere. She filled the kettle and prepared three cups while Hacket sat down at the kitchen table. He told Sue about the school, about the job, the salary. The house.

She seemed pleased and even managed to laugh as he mentioned Brooks' obsession with the cold. They gazed at each other long and hard, Hacket searching for even a hint of emotion in her blue eyes. Some sign of love? Was that what he sought?

'Are you going back to London tonight?' Sue asked.

He nodded.

'I've got no choice. I'll have to arrange the move and there are people coming to view the house tomorrow. Why?'

She shook her head.

'Just curious.'

'If you two want to talk . . .' Julie said.

'No, don't be silly. You stay here,' Sue told her sister.

Hacket was a little disappointed but hid his feelings adequately.

'I'd like you to see the house next time I come down Sue,' he said.

'What did the headmaster say about the teacher who lived there before?' Julie asked.

Hacket grunted.

'Very little.'

Julie nodded almost imperceptibly and gazed down into her mug.

'Why?' Hacket asked, noting her expression.

'Perhaps I shouldn't say anything but I think he should have told you. Anyone from around here would have told you. It was all over the local papers at the time. Big news. The police never did find out why he did it?'

'Did what?' Sue wanted to know.

'One night, he must have gone crazy or something. He got a shotgun, killed his wife and his son and then stuck the barrel in his mouth and shot himself.'

38

Elaine Craven sat alone in the waiting room of the surgery.

Shafts of sunlight flowed through the wide windows illuminating the room, making it seem as if the white walls were glowing. Elaine glanced around her, smiling each time she caught the eye of the receptionist.

She was in her late thirties, dressed in a black skirt and a navy blouse, the left sleeve of which was rolled up to reveal a bandage which stretched from her wrist to her elbow. The limb was held stiffly across her chest and, each time she moved she felt a twinge of pain from the arm. Elaine glanced up at the wall clock above the receptionist's desk and noticed that she still had another five minutes before she was due in to see Curtis. She tried to move her left arm slowly in an effort to minimise the pain but it didn't work and she winced once again.

'What did you do to your arm?' asked the receptionist, noticing Elaine's obvious distress.

'A stupid accident,' she said, dismissively, and shrugged, but even that movement caused her pain.

The two women exchanged perfunctory conversation about the weather while they waited for Curtis to call Elaine in. Then, tiring of that particular topic the receptionist tried a different subject.

'How are your family? It's just the one boy you've got isn't it?'

Elaine nodded.

'Yes, Phillip. He's fine. My husband is fine. It's only me who goes around having stupid accidents.' She motioned towards the bandaged arm as if to remind the receptionist why she was here.

There was a loud beep from the console in front of the receptionist and she flicked a switch.

'Send Mrs Craven in, please,' said Curtis, his voice sounding robotic as it filtered through the intercom.

Elaine got to her feet and smiled at the receptionist once more as she passed through the door ahead of her marked 'Private'. It opened onto a short corridor which led down to another door. She knocked and entered.

Edward Curtis smiled as she entered his room. He invited her to sit down, his eyes drawn immediately to the heavy bandage on her arm.

'I hope your family are in better shape than you, Elaine,' he said, getting to his feet and walking around the desk to her. 'What have you been doing?'

'It was an accident,' she told him. 'It should never have happened.' She looked up at him and Curtis saw a flicker of something behind her eyes.

It looked like fear.

'Let me have a look,' he said, and she extended her arm until it was resting on his desk. With infinite care, Curtis began to unfasten the bandages, unravelling them as cautiously as he could, apologising when Elaine hissed with the pain. Finally he pulled the last piece free and exposed two large gauze pads which covered her forearm. He reached behind him, into a small tray on his desk, and retrieved a pair of tweezers. Then he took one corner of the first pad between the ends of the metal prongs and pulled gently.

'Good God,' he murmured, exposing the forearm more fully. 'How the hell did this happen?'

The skin which covered the forearm had been removed in several places. Not sliced or scraped but torn off.

The area around the first deep laceration was red and swollen and Curtis could see the first watery deposits of pus nestling beneath the torn flesh.

The second wound was even worse.

He pulled the gauze pad free and could not resist wincing himself at the damage which had been inflicted on the arm. Part of the flexor muscle closest to the ulna had been severed and the bone was showing clearly through the mass of twisted flesh and muscle. There was more pus forming on the extremities of the wound, this time thicker and more noxious. Some of it was already leaking into the savage gash.

He looked sternly at Elaine.

'When did it happen?' he said, harshly.

'Two nights ago,' she told him.

'Why didn't you call me?' he snarled. 'Was anyone else hurt?'

She shook her head, glancing down at the wounds which looked like dog bites, only made by some ravening animal unlike any ordinary pet. She gritted her teeth as he used sterile pads to clean the gashes.

'It was my fault, I know,' she said. 'I knew it was close to the time, I know I should have contacted you but he seemed all right.'

Curtis wiped away the pus, dropping the swab into his waste bin.

'The treatment must be kept up at regular intervals, you know that,' the doctor told her, repeating the procedure on the smaller gash. 'How *is* the boy?'

'Restless.' It was the only word she could think of.

'Bring him to me tomorrow, before this happens again.' He jabbed an accusatory finger at the two wounds.

Elaine nodded, watching as he re-dressed the torn forearm. When he was finished she got to her feet, pulled her coat carefully over her injured arm and turned towards the door.

'Tomorrow,' Curtis reminded her and she nodded, thanking him.

39

The sun was already bleeding to death as he left Hinkston. By the time he reached the outer suburbs of London the vivid crimson of the sky had given way to darkness.

Hacket was feeling a strange mixture of feelings. Anticipation, excitement and anxiety had all fused together inside his mind. Those three emotions were to do with the job and with the possibility of starting afresh with Sue but he also felt something else.

Suspicion? That wasn't the right word.

Unease seemed to better suit his mood.

Why had Brooks been so secretive about the previous occupant of the house? Granted, it wasn't the sort of thing which you told a man who was about to work for you, at least not in so many words. Hacket could understand how the headmaster had feared telling him about the double murder and suicide which had taken place inside the house. But why lie about it?

But, it wasn't Brooks' lies that bothered Hacket. It was the reason *why* the previous occupant had murdered his family then killed himself.

He pulled up at traffic lights, the thought tumbling around inside his head.

Pressure of work? That seemed a bit extreme.

Perhaps he didn't like her cooking, Hacket smiled grimly.

Maybe he'd had an affair and couldn't face her any longer.

A bit of a kindred spirit, eh?

Hacket tried to push the last consideration from his mind as the lights changed to green and he drove on.

As he drew deeper into the heart of the capital a curious but not altogether unexpected weariness began to close around him. Like some kind of cloying, unwelcome blanket, he had felt its folds slip from him as he'd left the city that morning, but now, as he drew closer to home he felt their invisible weight enfolding him again.

Perhaps it was the thought of returning to so many bad memories.

'. . . *But the night goes by so very slow* . . .' came from the car radio.

'. . . *and I hope that it won't end though. Alone.* .' Hacket switched it off.

He was less than five miles from home now and he glanced down at the dashboard clock.

8.38 p.m.

He yawned and drove on, slowing down as he came to a Zebra crossing. A woman pushing a pram piled high with boxes crossed first

452

then a young couple holding hands. Then, finally a tall, thin man who glanced at the car as he sauntered across.

In the light of the headlamps Hacket could pick out certain details of the individual.

The lank hair, the pale complexion, the sunken eyes.

There was something familiar about this man and Hacket felt his chest tighten, the hairs at the back of his neck rise.

It was then that he saw the dark birthmark on the side of the man's neck and, finally, he was in no doubt who the individual was.

Hacket gripped the steering wheel until his knuckles turned white, his eyes rivetted to the man.

To the man who had murdered his daughter.

Peter Walton sauntered past him.

40

Hacket was out of the car in seconds.

He hurled open the driver's door and scrambled out, pointing at Walton.

'You, stop,' he bellowed.

Taken aback by the shout, Walton didn't wait to find out who this madman was, he simply turned and ran up the street, bumping into people as he fled. He ran not even knowing why he ran, but he had seen the expression of pure hatred on Hacket's face and it had been enough to convince him that this man, whoever he was, was best avoided.

Hacket slammed his door and, ignoring the blaring horns of the cars behind him, ran after Walton.

Hacket didn't see the figure that followed *him*.

'Walton,' he roared as he pounded after the fugitive.

People on the pavement who saw him coming stepped aside, those who didn't were buffeted aside as the chase continued up the road to a junction.

Walton looked behind him and saw Hacket still hurtling after him. Without checking the traffic he ran into the road, a speeding Volvo narrowly avoiding him. A taxi coming the other way banged on his hooter as he also came close to hitting the running man. But Walton made the other side of the road safely and ran on, glancing over his shoulder to see that Hacket was still in pursuit.

The teacher also ran into the road without regard for the traffic.

A Capri slammed on its brakes and skidded to a halt just in front of him. Hacket leapt up onto the bonnet and slid off the other side while the driver yelled at him.

He hit the tarmac in time to avoid an oncoming mini which swerved, striking the pavement as it narrowly missed Hacket. He sucked in a deep breath and hurtled on, worried he might lose his quarry on the crowded street.

Up ahead, Walton dived to his left, into a cafe, pushing past the customers, bumping into a table and spilling the drinks that were there. One of the customers jumped up to challenge him but Walton merely pushed him aside and burst through the door which led to the kitchen.

Seconds later, Hacket entered the cafe, following his prey, also ducking through into the kitchen where he heard the cook yelling obscenities as he and Walton raced through and out the back door.

The cool air was a welcome change from the stifling heat of the kitchen but Hacket was already sweating profusely, the salty fluid running down the side of his face. However, he didn't slacken his pace.

Walton found himself in the alley which backed on to the café and he bolted down it as fast as he could, overturning dustbins in his wake. Anything to delay his pursuer, but Hacket merely hurdled the obstacles and ran on, desperate to catch his foe.

And when he did catch him? What then?

The thought faded as he stumbled over a box, almost falling. He shot out a hand to steady himself, tearing some skin from his palm on the brick wall of the alley.

Then suddenly, he and Walton were free of its confines, back on another street, amongst people again.

Walton slammed into a young lad, knocking him to the ground but he didn't stop, merely glanced round to see that Hacket was still after him. Walton saw a bus coming down the street and he ran into the road, running alongside it for a few yards before launching himself up onto the running platform.

He laughed as he saw Hacket running after the bus.

Up ahead, the traffic lights were about to change to red.

Stay on red, Hacket thought as he hurtled after the bus.

They did.

To Walton's horror the bus began to slow down and he looked ahead to see the glaring red light then back to see that Hacket was almost upon him.

Walton jumped from the bus, shaking loose of the conductor who tried to grab him. Then he jumped into the road and scurried back onto the pavement, the breath now searing in his lungs. His legs felt like lead weights and he didn't know how much longer he could run for.

Hacket was feeling the same. He could hardly get his breath but he ran on, his head spinning from lack of oxygen. Gulping in huge lungfuls of air in an effort to keep himself going. His heart was thudding against his ribs, threatening to burst but still he found more energy to continue the chase.

Walton looked up and saw what might be his sanctuary.

The neon sign for the Underground station glowed like a beacon in the darkness and he bolted across the road towards the entrance.

Hacket followed.

'Get out the fucking way,' shouted Walton, elbowing a passage through the gang of people emerging from the stairway. He battered his way through, slipping as he was five steps from the bottom. He toppled over, landing heavily on the dirty tiled floor.

Hacket ran on, taking the steps two at a time, ignoring the stench of stale urine and sweat which rose to greet him from the subterranean cavern.

Walton hauled himself upright and looked around, seeing the automatic barriers which led to the trains. He ran towards them, scrambling over, ignoring the protests of the man collecting tickets.

Hacket too vaulted the partition and hurtled after his quarry who was now heading for the escalator that led even deeper into the bowels of the earth.

Walton, scarcely able to walk now, staggered along on legs that felt like lumps of lead, struggling down the metal steps of the escalator, pushing past those who stood in his way.

Hacket followed, still unaware of the figure that pursued him.

He was panting madly, his throat dry and parched from sucking in breath, his muscles crying out for rest but he knew that if he could catch Walton on the platform he had him. There was nowhere for him to hide. No further he could run.

Hacket stumbled half-way down the escalator but steadied himself, seeing Walton reach the bottom and bolt to his right.

Over his own laboured breathing, Hacket could hear the rumble of an approaching train and a further realisation struck him.

Should Walton board a train before him then there was no way he'd catch the man.

The teacher forced what little reserves of strength he possessed into his screaming muscles and ran on.

There were about two dozen people on the platform, most of them moving forward as they heard the train drawing closer.

Hacket looked to his right and left, sweat now pouring from him.

There was no sign of Walton.

The train was emerging from the tunnel, its lights like the glowing eyes of some massive, fast-moving worm as it slid from the tunnel.

Hacket raced down the platform, looking frantically for Walton, glancing back over his shoulder as the train came to a halt and its doors slid open. Those already on the train watched with detachment as he ran back and forth up and down the platform, his face coated in sweat, his eyes bulging as he tried to get his breath.

Where the hell was Walton?

He heard the familiar whirring noise which came just prior to the doors shutting and, in that split second he saw the man he sought dive for the carriage at the far end of the train.

He got in just as the doors were sliding shut.

'No,' roared Hacket and leapt for the nearest door, jamming his hand into it, ignoring the pain, knowing it would force the doors to open fully once again. As they did he slipped inside.

Seconds later the train pulled away again, picking up speed as it entered the tunnel at the far end of the platform.

Hacket began making his way along the train towards the carriage where he knew Walton to be.

As he came to the door marked 'ONLY TO BE USED IN AN EMERGENCY' worried travellers watched him force the handle up and down until the door opened. He squeezed through, feeling the warm air inside the tunnel buffet him as the train sped along, threatening to shake him from his precarious perch. He struggled with the next door, anxious to get into the safety of the carriage, balanced on just the coupling which held the compartments together.

He almost had the door open when his foot slipped.

Hacket yelled in terror as he felt himself falling.

He shot out a hand and managed to grab the door handle which promptly twisted in his grasp.

The door flew open and he fell into the carriage, sprawling on the floor, watched by the other travellers but Hacket wasn't bothered by their stares. He dragged himself upright and struggled on, realising that they were only moments away from the next station. Once the train pulled in he could run along the platform to the carriage where Walton hid then he had him.

The train escaped the blackness and Hacket pressed himself to the sliding doors, ready to bolt out the minute they opened.

The train slowed down, came to a halt.

He was out in a flash, hurtling towards the front of the train.

Towards Walton.

His quarry, as if realising Hacket's plan, came flying from the foremost carriage, knocking a woman to the ground in his haste. He ran across the platform, through a narrow walkway and towards some stairs which led to a bridge across another track. Hacket followed, taking the stairs two at a time, his lungs now feeling as if someone had filled them with hot sand, his legs throbbing.

Walton looked round to see his pursuer was still there, still on his heels.

He jumped the last three steps, landing heavily on the concrete as Hacket ran on, now only yards from his quarry.

Walton turned to his right, onto another platform.

It may have been rancid ice cream, it may even have been a puddle of vomit left by one of the many drunks who frequented the

457

underground complex. But, whatever it was, Walton didn't see it.

His foot slid in the slimy mess and he skidded, stumbled. Then, with a despairing scream, he pitched forward, arms flailing in the air for interminable seconds.

He toppled off the edge of the platform, onto the rails.

Hacket dashed to the edge as he heard the loud crack and the hiss of thousands of volts as Walton's body was scorched by the incredible electrical charge. His flesh was turned black in seconds, the blood boiling in his veins, and his body jerked uncontrollably as the current continued to course through it.

Hacket reached the platform edge and looked down.

Walton's body resembled a spent match.

With a gasp, Hacket sank to his knees, eyes rivetted to the blackened corpse which lay across the lines.

The stench of seared flesh and ozone was overpowering, and for a moment he thought he was going to be sick, but the feeling passed and he knew only the terrible ache in his muscles and the pain in his chest.

Somewhere down the platform a woman was screaming but Hacket didn't seem to hear it.

He looked down once more at the body of Walton and smiled.

He was still unaware of the figure who watched *him*.

41

Edward Curtis pushed another log onto the open fire then sat back in the high-backed leather chair, watching the flames dancing in the grate.

His face was set in hard lines and he reached for the brandy glass on the table beside him, sipping it, not taking his eyes from the leaping flames. His mother used to tell him that you could see shapes in fire, but the only shape that Curtis could see was the outline of Elaine Craven's mutilated arm.

'I think it's getting out of control,' said Curtis, quietly.

'You're the only one who can do anything about it,' said the other occupant of the room, seated on the other side of the hearth. But the other figure's eyes were fixed not on the fire but on Curtis.

'There have been too many incidents lately,' Curtis said. 'The Kirkham girl at the hotel. The Lewis baby and now this business with Phillip Craven.'

'They knew the risks, Edward, you can't blame yourself.'

'Blame isn't the right word. I don't feel any guilt for what has happened, for what is going to happen. As you say, they knew the risks. But that doesn't stop me feeling a little helpless. There's still too much I don't know.'

'Are you saying you want to stop?' the other said, challengingly.

Curtis looked at the figure and shook his head.

'There's too much at stake to stop now. Besides, I've gone too far to stop.' He sipped his brandy. 'We both have.' He re-filled his own glass and then the glass of his companion.

'It's what they would have wanted,' the other said. 'We owe it to them to carry on.'

Curtis watched as the figure got up and crossed to the large bay window which opened out from the sitting room. Drink in hand the other pulled back one curtain and looked out over the lights of Hinkston which lay below.

'You make it sound like duty,' Curtis said. 'Saying we owe it to them.'

'Not duty, Edward. Love.' The figure swallowed a sizeable measure of the brandy. 'And something stronger.'

'Like what?' Curtis wanted to know.

The other figure did not look at him, merely kept on staring out at the lights of the town. The words were spoken softly.

'Like revenge.'

42

'What the bloody hell did you think you were doing?'

Detective Inspector Madden bellowed the words at Hacket who sat at the desk, his hands clasped around a paper cup full of black coffee.

'You're not a vigilante. This isn't New York,' Madden continued.

'Look, he fell . . .' Hacket began, but was cut short by the DI.

'Lucky for you he did. Also you should be thankful that there were plenty of witnesses on the platform to testify to that fact. We could have been forgiven for thinking you threw Walton on the line.'

The office inside Clapham police station was small, its confines filled with a thick haze of cigarette smoke. All three men were smoking. Hacket was sitting on a plastic chair in front of Madden's desk. The DI himself was pacing the floor agitatedly, and DS Spencer was leaning against the desk looking down at the teacher, a Marlboro jammed in one side of his mouth.

Hacket took a sip of the lukewarm coffee and winced.

'How long are you going to keep me here?' he asked.

'For as long as it takes,' Madden rasped.

'Takes for what?'

'As long as it takes for you to see sense. To keep your nose out of police business and stop acting like fucking Charles Bronson. Like I said to you you're not a vigilante and this isn't *Death Wish*.'

'I told you, Walton slipped. You know that. Why can't you just let me go?' Hacket asked.

'You're lucky we're not charging you,' Madden informed him.

Hacket spun round in his seat to look at the DI.

'Charging *me*?' he snapped, incredulously. 'With what?'

'Disturbing the peace. Causing an affray. Would you like me to carry on?'

'That bastard killed my daughter,' snarled Hacket getting to his feet. 'You couldn't do anything about it so I did.'

'You don't even know if Walton was the one who killed her,' Spencer interjected. 'There were two men involved in the murder.'

'Great. One down, one to go then.'

'I'm warning you, Hacket,' the DI said, sternly. 'You keep away from this case.' His tone softened slightly. 'I'm sorry, we're all sorry about what happened to your daughter but let the law take care of it.'

Hacket nodded.

'Let the law take care of it,' he echoed. 'And if you catch him, what then? He's not going to be punished is he? A few years in prison isn't enough for what he did to my little girl.'

'That's as maybe but he'll serve a *proper* sentence for his crime, proposed by a judge in a *proper* court of law. The Fearns family lost a daughter too didn't they? If you stop to remember that Hacket, two people died in your house that night. I haven't had any trouble from Mr Fearns wanting to be judge, jury and executioner.'

'If he can live knowing that his daughter's killer isn't going to suffer the way he should then that's up to him. I can't.'

'You've got no choice. I'm not *asking* you to keep your nose out of this case, Hacket, I'm *telling* you,' Madden snapped. 'The last thing I need is some self-styled avenger running around London. *We'll* take care of it.'

Hacket shook his head and took a final drag on his cigarette, grinding it out in an ashtray already overflowing with dead butts.

And what would you have done if it had been *your* child?' he said. 'Would you have accepted the judgement of a court?' His voice was heavy with sarcasm. 'Don't tell me you wouldn't have wanted to see the bastard suffer because I won't believe you.'

'And what if you'd caught up with Walton tonight?' asked Spencer. 'What would you have done? Killed him? That would have made you no better than him and you'd be in the cells now, under arrest.'

'Five minutes' satisfaction isn't worth ruining your life for,' Madden echoed. He took another drag on his cigarette then hooked a thumb in the direction of the door. 'Go on, go home before I change my mind and charge you with breach of the peace.'

Hacket paused at the door, turning to look at the two policemen.

'You know,' he said, smiling. 'I'm still pleased he's dead. I just wish he'd suffered more.' Hacket slammed the door behind him.

Madden dropped the cigarette on the floor and ground it out with his foot.

'Do you know the worst thing about all this, Spencer?' said the DI nodding in the direction that Hacket had gone. 'I agree with him.'

Spencer nodded slowly.

'Join the club.'

43

He stood outside the door for what seemed like an eternity. His eyes riveted to the doorbell, his hand wavering as he reached for it. Hacket wasn't sure if he was trying to summon up the courage to press it. Courage wasn't the word. Right now he didn't know what the word *was* and, what was more, he didn't give a fuck.

He pressed it and waited.

And waited.

He finally heard movement from the other side of the door.

'Who is it?'

He managed a thin smile as he heard the soft Irish lilt to the voice.

'It's Hacket.'

Silence.

'What do you want?' she finally said.

'I've got to talk to you,' he said.

Another silence then he heard the sound of a chain being slid free, of bolts being drawn back. The door opened.

Nikki Reeves stood before him in a long T-shirt which was so baggy it managed to hide the smooth contours of her body. Her eyes were bleary with sleep and she rubbed them as she looked at Hacket, blinking myopically.

'Do you know what time it is?' she asked. 'Nearly midnight.' She remained at the door, leaning against the frame.

'Can I come in?' he asked, and as he spoke she smelled the whisky on his breath.

'What's wrong, all the pubs shut and your supply of booze run out at home?'

He looked at her but didn't speak. She sighed and stepped aside, motioning him into the flat. He wandered through into the sitting room where he sat down on the sofa.

'Make yourself at home,' she said, sarcastically. Nikki sat down in the chair opposite him, the T-shirt riding up over her knees, exposing a greater expanse of her shapely legs.

Hacket gazed at them for a moment then looked at her face.

'You've got a bloody nerve coming here, John, after what's happened,' she said, sternly.

'I wanted to talk to you,' he said.

'I thought you'd said all you wanted to say over the phone.'

'I just thought you might like to know that your *little note* had the desired effect. My marriage came close to breaking up, I'm still not sure it'll last.

She merely shrugged.

'I told you not to use me like a doormat. I was hurt. I wanted to hit back at you and it was the only way I could think of.'

'You heard what happened to my daughter?'

'Yes. I'm very sorry about that.'

'Well your *little note* arrived the day of her funeral,' he rasped. 'It didn't take Sue long to figure out that I was with you when Lisa was murdered.'

'Have they caught the killer yet?' she asked, conversationally.

He merely smiled humourlessly.

'One of them is out of action, to coin a phrase,' he chuckled, glaring at her once again. 'What you did was unnecessary, Nikki. If you wanted to hurt someone then you could have had a go at me, not Sue. She didn't ask to be involved in this.'

'It's not my fault your daughter's dead, John. I told you I didn't mean to be vindictive. I'm sorry for what happened.'

'Sorry,' he grunted. 'Really? Well, you're right about one thing, it isn't your fault Lisa's dead, it's my fault. My fault for being here with you when I should have been at home with *her*.'

463

'And you came over here tonight to tell me that? What is this, confession time?'

He sat on the sofa looking at her, smelling the booze on his own breath as he exhaled.

'Do you want a coffee?' she asked, almost reluctantly. 'You look as if you need one.' She got to her feet and padded into the kitchen. Hacket waited a moment then got up and followed her.

'Sorry I called so late,' he said. 'I mean, you might have had someone here. I wouldn't have wanted to interrupt.'

'By "someone" I gather you mean another man?'

He shrugged.

'Why not? You're a good looking girl. I'm surprised there *isn't* anyone here.' There was a vaguely contemptuous tone to his voice which she wasn't slow to spot.

'Is that how you see me?' she asked. 'In and out of bed with any man I find?'

'It didn't take you long to sleep with me. Three dates it took, didn't it? Pretty fast going, Nikki.' He smiled, again without a trace of humour.

She made his coffee and shoved the mug into his hand.

'Drink that and go will you?' she snapped, walking back into the sitting room. He followed her once more.

'What did you hope to achieve by writing that letter to Sue? Just tell me that. Did you want to break up my marriage?'

'Just remember who started the affair, John,' she snarled. '*You* chased *me*, not the other way round. You knew the risks. We both did.'

'But you had to have your little bit of revenge, didn't you?' he said, bitterly.

'I don't like being treated like some kind of whore,' she rasped. 'You can't just pick me up, use me then throw me away when you feel like it.' She glared at him. 'Now drink your coffee and get out of here.'

Hacket put the mug down and got to his feet.

'Sue called you a tart and I defended you,' he said, shaking his head. 'I think she was right.'

'Get out, now.' She pushed him towards the door. 'Is that why you came here, tonight, John? For the same reason you wanted me in the first place? Because you still can't get what you want from your wife?'

Hacket spun round and lashed out, catching her with the back of his hand.

The blow was powerful enough to knock her off her feet and, as she fell to the floor, Hacket saw the ribbon of blood running from her bottom lip. She glared up at him then touched the bleeding cleft which was already beginning to swell up. She looked at the blood on her fingers and her eyes narrowed.

'Get out you fucker,' she hissed. 'Go on,' the last two words were shouted.

Hacket moved towards the door, pulled it open and looked back at her. She still sat on the floor, legs curled up beneath her as she dabbed at her bottom lip with the end of her long T-shirt. Blood blossomed on the material. He hesitated a moment longer then walked out, slamming the door behind him.

He rode the lift to the ground floor and walked out into the chill night air, standing beside his car for a moment, looking up at the window of Nikki's flat. Then he slid behind the wheel, twisted the key in the ignition and drove off, glimpsing the block of flats in his rear view mirror. Then he turned a corner and it was gone.

Out of sight, out of mind, he thought, wondering why that particular cliché had come into his head.

He wondered if it would be as easy to forget Nikki.

44

She knew she was going to be sick.

She knew it and, what was worse, she knew there was nothing she could do to stop herself. Amanda Riley gripped the edge of the sink, ducked low over the porcelain and vomited. As she stepped back, moaning, she almost over-balanced. It felt as if the floor was moving beneath her although she couldn't be sure if that apparent undulation was due to her own inebriation or the pounding of the music from downstairs.

She ran the taps, washing the mess from the sink, glancing at her own haggard reflection in the mirror. She groaned again as she caught sight of the apparition which stared back at her. Pale skinned, eyes black from too much smudged mascara. Her hair, so carefully prepared before the party, now hung limply around her face. There were stains on her red blouse and also on her tight white skirt. She shook her head but even that minor act of disapproval caused her to reel once more. She had no idea how much she'd drunk, or even what she'd drunk. The party had begun four or five hours ago, she thought, but now she wasn't even sure of the time. Amanda glanced at her watch but it seemed to dissolve before her eyes. Her drink-clouded vision refused to clear and she sat down heavily on the toilet seat, feeling the vomit beginning its upward journey for the second time that night. She clenched her teeth together and the feeling passed momentarily. It felt as if her head was spinning around on her neck like some bizarre kind of top. She gripped the edge of the toilet seat for fear of falling off.

Amanda was beginning to wish she had never agreed to come to the party. She didn't like loud music, she didn't know many of the other guests and, ordinarily, she didn't drink much. Perhaps someone had spiked her drink, she pondered, rubbing her stomach with one shaking hand. Whatever the answer was she knew she couldn't stand another night of this purgatory. She felt her stomach contract suddenly, struggling to her feet just in time to reach the sink. She hung over it, waiting for the inevitable but the spasms passed and she began to straighten up. Again she caught sight of her reflection. God, she thought. She looked about fifty instead of nineteen.

There was a bang on the bathroom door.

'Amanda.'

She barely recognised the voice.

'Amanda. Are you all right?'

She blinked hard, trying to clear not only her vision but her head too.

Outside the door, Tracy Grant exhaled wearily and banged once more. She was beginning to wish she hadn't invited Amanda. If she threw up on any of the carpets there would be hell to pay. If her parents discovered she'd had the party in the first place while they were away

466

for the weekend she'd be in big enough trouble but, if they came back to find puddles of puke everywhere then she may as well pack her bags and leave home. It would save them the bother of throwing her out. She banged again and repeated Amanda's name.

'Are you all right, I said?' she shouted, forced to raise her voice over the sound of the music thundering away downstairs.

There were a series of raucous cheers from below her and, despite her anger, she managed a smile as she heard the chugging rhythm of AC/DC's 'You shook me all Night long' and realised that her brother was more than likely engaged in his duckwalk dance.

Tracy heard the sound of a bolt being slid back and the door opened.

'You look awful,' she said as she saw Amanda swaying uncertainly before her.

'I *feel* awful,' the other girl told her. 'I'm going home.' She took a step forward, almost overbalancing.

Tracy grabbed her.

'Not in that state you're not,' she snapped. 'What have you been drinking anyway?'

Amanda could only shrug.

'I'll get Carl to drive you home,' Tracy told her. 'He's about the only one who's still sober.' She snaked an arm around Amanda's waist and the two of them struggled down the stairs. As they got to the hallway Amanda clenched her teeth together once more and put a hand to her mouth.

Tracy muttered something under her breath and dashed to the front door, pulling it open in time to allow Amanda to get her head out and retch violently into a rhododendron bush which Tracy's father had so carefully nurtured.

'You stay there,' said Tracy irritably and stalked off into the sitting room where the music was reaching ever more deafening proportions. Amanda gripped the door-frame as best she could, supporting herself while her stomach somersaulted, finding yet more fluid to expel should she lose control. A moment or two later Tracy returned with a tall youth in his early twenties, his face pitted around the chin from the ravages of acne. But, apart from that he had strong features and piercing green eyes which immediately focused on Amanda's backside and legs. He smiled appreciatively.

467

'Carl's going to drive you home,' Tracy announced.

'I don't want her throwing up in my car,' Carl Dennison said, suddenly realising the state of his intended passenger.

'Drive with the window open,' Tracy snapped, supporting Amanda with both arms as Carl scuttled along the path to his waiting Capri. He'd bought it off a friend about a week ago and the last thing he wanted was some boozed up bitch spewing up all over his mock-tiger-skin seats. Still, he thought as he looked more closely at his drunken passenger, she should be all right until he got her home. It was after midnight, the roads in Hinkston would be quiet. He could make it in less than twenty minutes if he put his foot down. Carl slid behind the wheel and started the engine, glancing across at Amanda who had already wound down the window and was leaning out, trying to suck in lungfuls of air. As the car vibrated the girl felt her stomach turning more forcefully and, only by a monumental effort did she manage to retain its contents.

Carl drove off, seeing Tracy in the rear-view mirror. She stood there for a moment then disappeared back inside the house.

Carl looked across at Amanda who was groaning quietly as he drove. The wind was whistling through the open window, blowing her hair away from her face. She had her eyes closed. He took his eye off the road momentarily to glance down at her legs. She'd kicked off her high heels and one leg was drawn up beneath her on the seat. Carl turned a corner, saw that the road was deserted and slowed down slightly.

As the needle on the speedometer dropped to below thirty he reached across with his left hand and touched her knee, feeling the soft material of her stocking beneath his fingers. He grinned.

Amanda moaned and slapped feebly at his hand but there was no strength in the rebuff, she was more concerned with holding down her drink.

Carl's hand slid higher, towards her thigh.

She mumbled something and drew her head back inside the car for a second, glancing wearily at him.

He withdrew his hand, aware of the erection which was beginning to uncoil inside his jeans, pushing painfully against the denim as it became harder.

As Amanda put her head back out of the window he let his hand slip back onto her thigh, but, this time, he pushed it higher, allowing his fingers to brush against the sleek material of her panties.

Again she tried to slap his hand away but this time he hooked two fingers into the top of her knickers, feeling her tightly curled pubic hairs. Amanda shook her head.

Carl smiled triumphantly and pulled his hand away just long enough to unzip his own jeans and pull out his erection. He grabbed her right hand and wrapped the limp fingers around his stiff shaft. What the hell, she was so pissed she wouldn't even remember what she'd done in the morning.

She pulled her hand away but he closed his own over it, forcing her back to his penis, guiding her, using her to masturbate him.

Amanda grunted in disapproval, not sure whether she was more disturbed by the vomit rising in her throat or the fact that she was an unwilling partner to Carl's approaching gratification. She turned in her seat, her hand still clasped around his shaft, his own fist wrapped around hers moving it rhythmically.

'Go on, do it,' he urged, his breathing now becoming more heavy. He was staring ahead at the empty road, aware of the sensations building in his groin.

Amanda finally lost her battle.

She leaned towards Carl and vomited into his lap.

He yelled in rage and disgust as his jeans, the car seat and his throbbing penis were all covered in the copious regurgitation.

He slammed on the brake and leant across, pushing open the car door, digging his elbow into Amanda's side, shoving her from the seat.

She fell heavily onto the grass verge at the roadside and Carl himself felt his stomach spinning as the stench of her vomit filled his nostrils. It covered him like a sticky yellow blanket.

He shouted something at her then drove off, leaving her lying on the damp grass.

Amanda tried to rise, tried to call him back but her protests dissolved into a flood of tears. She thought she was going to be sick again but the feeling passed. Finally she managed to rise, aware that her shoes were still in the car, now disappeared into the night. She felt the dampness soaking through her stockings as she walked.

She had no idea where she was, not even which part of Hinkston. There was a garage about a hundred yards down the road, the forecourt in darkness. But, beyond it there were houses. If she could reach one of those she could use a phone, call her parents. They'd be mad at her. Furious. But she didn't care. She just wanted to get home to bed, to drift off to sleep and shut out this terrible feeling once and for all. Amanda began to walk, her gait shambling, as if her legs would not obey her brain. Twice she stumbled, almost falling. The second time she fell against a hedge, the leafless twigs snagging her stockings and scratching her skin. She moaned, her head still spinning, her plight, it seemed, intensified by the chill night air. She felt as if her head had been stuffed with cotton wool.

She glanced towards the petrol station again and something caught her eye.

A figure moved on the forecourt.

Perhaps it was someone walking their dog. Someone who could help her. She tried to quicken her pace.

The figure stepped back into the shadows at the side of the main building and disappeared.

A second later she saw car headlights lancing through the blackness. The vehicle swung out of the forecourt turned and moved unhurriedly towards her.

It slowed down as it drew level with her then it stopped, the engine idling.

Amanda couldn't see the driver, he was hidden by the gloom inside the vehicle.

She staggered towards it, both surprised and relieved when the passenger side door was pushed open as if to welcome her.

'Help me please,' she slurred, fighting back the nausea as she stuck her head inside the car.

The stench in there almost cleared her head.

She jerked upright still unable to see the driver, appalled by the smell, aware that it was going to make her vomit.

She tried to step back but a hand shot forward and clamped across her mouth, forcing back both the seething hot bile and her scream.

The long, double-edged stiletto blade darted forward and buried itself in her right eye.

Amanda was dragged into the car, the door slammed behind her.

The car moved away, the driver indicating thoughtfully as he turned a corner. Only then did he speed up.

45

She heard the thunderous blows on the front door as he tried to batter his way in.

Sue Hacket stood in the hallway for long seconds, mesmerised by the incessant pounding, her eyes fixed on the door which seemed to bow inward an inch or two with each successive impact.

Another second and he would be through.

She thought about screaming but realised that it would do no good. The house stood at least thirty yards from its closest neighbour, even if they should hear her cry for help it was doubtful if they would reach her in time.

He was nearly through the door.

Perhaps they had heard the banging, perhaps the police were already on the way.

Perhaps . . .

Sue spun round and caught sight of the phone on the stand behind her.

The thunderous blows on the front door seemed to increase and her eyes widened in horror as she saw the first split appear in the wood. It zig-zagged across the paintwork like a crack in a sheet of ice.

If she could reach the phone. Call the police.

Would they arrive before he got in?

Before he reached her?

She had one hand on the phone when one panel of the door was smashed inwards.

Sue screamed, dropped the phone and hurtled up the stairs as fast as she could, stumbling on the fifth step. She whimpered under her breath, glancing around to see his hand reaching through the pulverised wood, feeling for the lock and chain which secured the door.

He freed it and kicked the door open.

Sue screamed again and hauled herself upright, running for the landing, towards the bedroom as she heard him career into the sitting room. Then out into the hall once more, his footfalls pounding on the stairs.

She slammed the bedroom door and stood with her back against it, her breath coming in gasps.

He would find her.

He didn't even need to hurry. There were only four rooms on the first floor of the house. He would be able to move at will from one to the other until he found her and then she knew what would happen.

Just like the woman who had lived in this house before her she would die.

Slaughtered like an animal by the man who supposedly loved her.

The last occupant of the house had been a schoolteacher just as the new occupant was. Only this new occupant was her own husband.

It was John Hacket who prowled the landing stealthily, the double-barrelled shotgun gripped in his bloodied hands.

She heard him kick open the door of the bathroom, then the other two bedrooms.

She heard the creak of the floorboards as he stood outside the room where she hid. There was only three inches of wood between her and her husband.

Her and the shotgun.

Sue crossed to the window and tried to open it but the old sash frame had been painted over and the emulsion secured it as if it had been nailed shut. Through the glass she could see the school beyond, its tall buildings rising into the night sky as if supporting the low clouds.

Hacket drove his foot against the door and the hinges groaned protestingly.

Sue spun round, knowing there was nowhere else to run. Knowing that this was the end.

She had just one comforting thought.

472

She would soon be with Lisa again.

Strange how, when death is near, the human mind clutches at even the most ridiculous notions to ease its fear.

Hacket roared with rage and drove his shoulder against the door.

It swung back, slamming into the wall and he stepped across the threshold, raising the shotgun to his shoulder, aiming at her head.

He was smiling.

Sue screamed.

Hacket fired and the scream was lost in a deafening crescendo of blazing lead as both barrels flamed.

The scream catapulted her from the nightmare.

She sat bolt upright in bed, perspiration covering her like a translucent shroud.

In the darkness of the bedroom she blinked, trying to readjust to the gloom, to push the nightmare from her mind, not sure for fleeting seconds what was real and what was a residue of the dream.

Like the figure which stood at the foot of her bed.

She blinked, expecting it to vanish.

It didn't.

Standing at the bottom of her bed, his eyes pinning her in an unblinking stare, stood six-year-old Craig Clayton. His body was quivering from head to foot.

46

Sue looked at the child through the darkness, barely able to make out his features, illuminated as they were by the thin shaft of light from the landing.

He seemed to be swaying gently back and forth at the bottom of the bed but, throughout the strange motions, his eyes never left her.

She pulled the sheet around her, aware of her nakedness and strangely uncomfortable beneath the unflinching stare of the boy.

'Craig?' she said, softly, as if trying to break his fixed concentration. To distract him from that piercing stare. He seemed almost trance-like.

She pulled her house-coat on hurriedly and swung herself out of bed, blinking hard to clear her vision.

As she approached him the door of her bedroom opened and Julie walked in.

Sue saw the look of shock on her sister's face as she looked at the boy and she motioned for Sue to stay back.

'I thought I heard him get up,' Julie said.

'When I woke up he was just standing there,' Sue explained.

'Come on, Craig,' Julie said, sternly, taking the boy by the shoulders as if to drag him forcibly from the room. 'You've disturbed your auntie now.'

'He didn't disturb me . . .' Sue began but then hurriedly closed her mouth as Julie shot her a withering glance.

'Craig, come on. Back to bed,' Julie snapped, pulling him with even greater urgency.

The boy wouldn't move. He shook loose from Julie's grip, his eyes never leaving Sue.

'Is he all right, Julie?' she asked, seeing the boy's expression darken.

Julie didn't answer, she merely gripped the boy by the shoulders and pulled.

He tore himself free of her hold, spun round and punched her in the side, his eyes blazing.

Sue looked on in shocked dismay.

'You'll have to help me,' Julie gasped, making another grab for the boy who was now facing his mother, his hands twisted into claws, as if ready to strike at her should she try to touch him again. Julie moved forward and Craig backed off, his back touching the wall. He glanced at the two women and Sue almost recoiled from what looked like pure hatred in those eyes.

'Mike, come here,' Julie shouted, rousing her husband.

She lunged forward and grabbed Craig, holding one of his wrists, but he gripped her hand, tugging at the skin on the back of it until his nails drew blood. Julie yelped in pain and withdrew her hand, the bloody furrows weeping red fluid onto the carpet. He looked at Sue as if daring her to approach him. She could see the first clear dribblings of sputum beginning to seep through his clenched teeth.

Mike Clayton entered the room, pushing past the two women, making straight for the boy, a look of determination on his face.

'Come on,' he snarled, grabbing Craig around the waist, lifting him into the air.

The boy writhed madly in his father's grip, trying to shake himself free, scratching at Mike's face.

'Get the doctor, now,' Mike hissed, struggling back through the door with the boy. 'Do it,' he snapped as Julie hesitated.

Sue, still bewildered by the tableau, followed Mike and his maddened son out onto the landing. Julie scuttled downstairs to the phone and frantically jabbed out the number, glancing behind her to see Mike carry the boy into his bedroom.

Watched by Sue, he threw the boy onto the bed then leapt on beside him, pinning the boy's arms to the mattress, using all his superior strength to prevent his son from moving.

The boy hawked loudly and spat into Mike's face.

Sue put a hand to her mouth, watching as the mucus dripped from Mike's cheek like a thick tear. But he didn't attempt to wipe it away, he seemed too concerned with restraining his son. The boy continued to twist and turn like an eel on a hot skillet.

'The doctor's coming,' shouted Julie, making her way back up the stairs, pushing past Sue, who could only look on in bewilderment.

'I hope to God he's quick,' Mike rasped. 'I can't hold him for much longer.'

Craig seemed to have found an energy and strength quite disproportionate to his age and size. A strength which took every ounce of his father's muscle to hold him down. Sue saw the veins standing out on Mike's forehead as he struggled to keep the boy pinned down.

Julie ushered her out of the room.

'There's nothing we can do until the doctor gets here,' she said, her face ashen.

'Whatever's wrong with him, Julie?' Sue asked, a note of fear in her voice. 'Is it some kind of epileptic fit?'

'Yes, that's right,' Julie said. 'A fit. He doesn't get them very often. I've never mentioned them to you. We thought he'd grow out of them.'

'But he's so strong.'

'He'll be all right when the doctor gets here,' Julie said, dismissing the observation.

Sue was about to speak again when she heard a deafening shout from the bedroom.

From Craig.

She felt the hairs on the back of her neck rise.

She felt suddenly afraid.

47

The needle came free and Curtis quickly wiped the puncture in the crook of Craig's arm with a swab, pressing the pad of cotton wool to the tiny hole for a second.

The boy winced and moaned slightly but Curtis merely pressed the palm of his right hand to the child's forehead. He could feel beads of perspiration there but at least the spasms had stopped. Craig let out an exhausted sigh and his whole body seemed to go limp. Curtis covered him with a sheet, watching the steady rise and fall of his chest.

Mike Clayton looked down at his son then glanced at the doctor who had slipped the hypodermic back into his bag.

'Will he be all right now, doctor?' Mike asked.

Curtis nodded slowly and headed for the door.

'We've heard things,' Mike continued, falteringly. 'Rumours. About the others.'

Curtis turned and looked at him, expressionless.

Mike swallowed hard, as if intimidated by the doctor's unfaltering stare.

'What's been happening to them?' Mike asked.

'I don't discuss other patients, Mr Clayton,' Curtis said, dismissively. 'Your sister-in-law, does she know about the boy?' He nodded in Craig's direction.

'No,' Mike said, hastily. 'She saw what happened tonight. We found him in her room.'

Curtis shot the other man a worried glance.

'Nothing had happened,' he reassured the doctor. 'Julie told her he suffered from epileptic fits. I think she believed it.'

'Good.'

He made for the landing, followed by Mike. They both descended the stairs, the doctor heading for the sitting room where Julie and Sue sat sipping cups of tea.

Julie stood up as Curtis entered but he motioned for her to sit once more.

'Is Craig all right?' she asked.

'He's fine. He's sleeping now.'

Julie looked relieved.

Curtis glanced at Sue and smiled and she returned the gesture, struck by the firmness of his features, the intensity of his eyes. Despite the late hour he looked perfectly groomed, as if he'd come from a dinner-dance instead of having been dragged from his bed by the emergency call. Julie performed a quick introduction and Curtis shook hands with Sue, gripping her hand in his own. She felt a pleasing mixture of strength and warmth there. She looked at him as he sat down, grateful for the cup of tea which Julie offered him. He seemed relaxed, almost at home in the sitting room. As if he'd visited it many times before.

'Do you live in Hinkston, Mrs Hacket?' Curtis asked.

Sue shook her head, unable to take her eyes from Curtis, her mind relaying facts back and forth as she tried to estimate his age.

'Not yet,' she said. 'We ... I have a house in London but I'll probably be living in Hinkston soon.'

'Any family of your own? I see you're married,' he smiled and nodded towards her wedding ring.

'No,' she said, quickly. For fleeting seconds it occurred to her to mention Lisa but the memory was painful enough locked away inside her mind without exposing it to conversation. She contented herself with a sip of her tea.

'If you don't mind me saying, Mrs Hacket, you look a little pale.' Curtis chuckled. 'An occupational hazard of being a doctor I'm afraid, I see everyone as a potential patient.'

Sue smiled too.

'I haven't been sleeping very well lately,' she told him.

'Well, if you do move to Hinkston then please feel free to come and see me. Your sister has the address of my surgery. Whereabouts in the town are you moving to?'

'My husband's a teacher. He's due to start work next week at the Junior school about half a mile from the town centre. You know the one? There's a house next to the school, it comes with the job.'

Curtis nodded slowly, his expression darkening slightly.

'I know the one,' he said, quietly. 'Well, the best of luck with your move.' He finished his tea quickly, as if the hospitality of the Clayton's was suddenly something he wished to be away from. He got to his feet and headed for the sitting room door.

'Don't forget, Mrs Hacket,' he said. 'Come and see me.'

'I will,' she assured him.

Julie and Mike followed him out into the hall.

'Thank you,' Julie said as he stepped out onto the front porch.

'Be careful,' Curtis said, looking at each of them in turn. 'Watch the boy closely for the next two or three days. Get in touch with me immediately if he suffers anything *like* a relapse. We were lucky this time.' He turned and strode off down the path towards his car, watched by the Claytons, who waited until he'd driven off before stepping back into their house and shutting the door.

Sue finished her tea then announced that she was going to bed. She left Julie and Mike sitting downstairs.

As she reached the landing she paused by the door to Craig's room. Hearing nothing she pushed the door slightly and peered in.

The boy was sleeping, his face peaceful. A marked contrast to the twisted mask which it had become only thirty minutes earlier. Sue closed the door and wandered across to her bedroom where she slipped off her house coat and climbed into bed.

As she lay there in the gloom she gazed up at the ceiling, waiting for sleep to come but knowing that it would not. She heard Curtis's voice inside her head.

'Come and see me'

She closed her eyes, seeing his face more clearly, remembering that mixture of warmth and strength in his grip. The penetrative stare.

Sue allowed one hand to slip beneath the quilt, to glide across her breast, the nipple already stiff and swollen. It was joined by her other hand which she pushed with exquisite slowness over her flat belly and into the tightly curled triangle of hair between her legs, her index finger probing more deeply until she found the bud of her clitoris. She began to stroke it gently, the moisture between her thighs increasing.

'Come and see me.'

She pushed one finger into her slippery cleft, her eyes closed now, the vision of Curtis' face filling her mind.

'Come and see me.'

48

He had killed Hacket's daughter and now he would kill Hacket.

Ronald Mills had decided on his course of action with ease. Ever since he'd seen Hacket pursue Peter Walton through the streets of London, ever since he'd seen his friend fall onto the tracks of the tube train. Mills had watched it all.

An eye for an eye, they called it. His mother had told him that came from the Bible. His mother had always quoted him lines from the Bible, and most of them he'd remembered. Like the one about suffer little children.

Mills chuckled.

God wanted little children to suffer did he? Well, if that was the case then God would love Ronald Mills. God would have looked down on him and Lisa Hacket that night and he would have smiled. He would have seen Mills clamp one hand across the little girl's mouth as he cut away her nightdress with the point of his knife. He would have watched it all. Watched as Mills climbed onto the bed beside her and unzipped his trousers.

Suffer little children.

Afterwards God would have watched as Mills cut the child repeatedly. He used the knife with almost surgical skill, pushing it easily through her flesh until the bed was soaked in blood, until she stopped writhing beneath him, until his penis was hard with lust again and he penetrated her warm but lifeless form for the second time that night.

Mills giggled again and inspected his hands. They were rough, calloused. The left one still bore the remnants of a tattoo but it hadn't taken properly and the skin had turned septic. In place of a snake coiled around a knife blade Mills sported a scab curled around a septic boil. He picked at the scab, pulling some pieces of hardened flesh off.

Mills and Walton had lived in the flat in Brixton for the last ten months. Neither of them had a job but they had made a living dealing in various illegal practices. Mills in particular had found a lucrative market in child pornography. He had become friendly with a couple of dealers and this little sideline had the added bonus of pandering to his own tastes too.

Walton had worked as a pusher around King's Cross, even done a little pimping.

It was on those proceeds that they'd bought the gun.

It was a .38 Smith and Wesson revolver and Mills gently stroked the four-inch barrel as he sat at the table occasionally glancing at the brown mess on his plate which, according to the box, was liver and onion. It certainly didn't look like the picture on the box. In fact, it looked as if someone had defecated on his plate. He prodded the cold food with the barrel of the pistol then wiped it on the makeshift table-cloth. Piled up on the other side of the table were some of the magazines he'd been intending to sell the following day. Every one featured photos of children, some as young as two years, engaged in various acts with both men *and* women. He had heard that one of his dealers could get hold of stuff which actually showed men and babies. Real, new born babies.

Mills smiled again, the stirring in his groin becoming more pronounced.

Suffer little children.

He picked up one of the magazines and leafed through it, his thick lips sliding back as he surveyed the pictures. Many were bad quality, grainy black and white shots taken by amateurs. Probably by those who participated, thought Mills, his erection now pressing uncomfortably against his trousers. But they served their purpose. He finished

480

looking through the magazine and dropped it back onto the pile, picking up the gun again, turning the empty cylinder, thumbing the hammer back then squeezing the trigger.

The metallic click echoed around the small flat.

It had been lonely since Walton's death. Mills didn't enjoy being alone. Apart from Walton he had no friends and he felt as if Hacket had taken from him the one person he really cared about.

He would make him suffer for that.

As he'd made his daughter suffer.

Suffer little children.

God would be watching him again. God was on his side.

He would kill Hacket and God would be pleased with him for upholding his word.

Mills raised the gun and sighted it, thumbing back the hammer again.

'An eye for an eye,' he said, smiling.

49

Birth, marriage and moving house.

Hacket was sure that was how the cliché went. They were the three most traumatic things in life. As he sat in the sitting room of the house, perched on one of the many packing cases that filled the place like an oversized child's building bricks he'd come to the conclusion that the former two paled into insignificance alongside the third. It had taken him more than three days to pack the cases, working for anything up to fifteen hours a day. Well, he had nothing else to do. It was better than sitting around in the old house with just memories for company. At least he didn't have to worry about selling the house in London before he could move into the one next to the school. No chain, no mortgage worries. The rent for the house was deducted from his salary every month. Once the house in London was sold the money would be straight profit. It was an enticing prospect.

The thought of the money together with the possibility of starting afresh should have left Hacket feeling elated but, as it was, he sat wearily on the packing case, holding a mug of tea and staring around the room his thoughts jumbled and confused.

He thought about Lisa.

About the deaths that had occurred in *this* house.

From one place of pain to another.

There was always pain.

And he thought about Sue.

He'd called her the previous night to let her know roughly what time he and the accumulated trophies of their life would be arriving but so far she had not turned up. He was beginning to wonder if she would. There was a phone box just across the street. Hacket glanced at his watch, decided to give it another fifteen minutes, then call her.

There was a knock on the door and the teacher jumped down from the box and hurried to the front door, a smile already beginning to form on his lips.

At last, now he wouldn't need to call her.

He felt his spirits lift as he fumbled with the catch.

Donald Brooks stood on the doorstep, immaculate as ever apart from the flakes of dandruff on his collar. The headmaster smiled at Hacket who just about managed to return the gesture, fighting to keep the disappointment from his face.

'Glad to see you arrived safely, Mr Hacket,' said Brooks. 'I won't come in. I just thought I'd say welcome and that I hope you'll be happy in your new home. You and your wife.'

'Thanks,' murmured Hacket, almost grudgingly.

'What does your wife think of the house?'

'She likes it.

'I won't disturb her, I'm sure she's busy unpacking. I'll go now. I look forward to seeing you on Monday morning.'

Hacket nodded and closed the door as the headmaster walked back up the path. The teacher sighed and wandered back into the sitting room. Perhaps he should phone Sue now. He glanced at his watch again. Give it another five minutes? He drummed agitatedly on the top of the nearest crate then the front door bell sounded again. This time he moved with less speed, pulling the door open wearily.

Sue smiled thinly as she saw his face.

'I was going to call you,' he beamed, stepping aside to allow her in.

She stepped over the threshold almost hesitantly, moving through into the sitting room, glancing around at the crates and packing cases.

'We'd better get started,' she said, rolling up the sleeves of her sweatshirt.

They worked in separate rooms, pulling the lids from the boxes and crates, unwrapping the contents as if they were Christmas presents. Sue worked in the kitchen while Hacket attended to the sitting room. He had ensured that the stereo was not left to the tender attentions of the removal men. He had transported that particular item himself on the back seat of the car. It had been the first thing he'd rigged up before unpacking and music filled the house as they worked.

Hacket had no idea of the time, surrounded by empty and half-empty packing cases, his ears filled with the music, his thoughts wandering aimlessly. He wiped his hands on his jeans and wandered across to the stereo, flipping the record before continuing his task.

Sue appeared in the doorway, her sweatshirt and jeans also covered by a thin film of dust. She had some dirt on one cheek and Hacket crossed to her to wipe it away. She smiled thinly but pulled away and completed the task herself.

'There's a cup of tea in the kitchen,' she told him and walked across the hall.

'. . . *But it was only fantasy. The wall was too high as you can see . . .*'

sang Roger Waters from behind him.

Hacket wiped his hands again and wandered into the kitchen. He sat down opposite Sue and picked up his mug of tea.

'I've just about finished in here,' she told him. 'I'll do upstairs next.'

'There's no rush,' he told her. 'We've got plenty of time.'

'I want to get it finished, John. I don't want the house looking like a bomb site for too long.'

He nodded.

'Do you remember the first place we ever moved in to?' Hacket asked, a thin smile on his face.

She raised her eyebrows.

'The flat. Trying to lug furniture up three flights of stairs past the snooker hall, wondering if the blokes inside were going to rob us as soon as we got settled in.' She almost laughed. Almost.

'Listening to them playing bloody snooker all night. It kept us awake at the beginning didn't it.'

'As I remember we didn't mind being kept awake.'

Hacket smiled.

'It was a nice place,' he said.

'Apart from the noise,' she added.

'And the damp.'

'And the cold.'

'Yeah, a great place.' He chuckled. 'It doesn't seem like six years since we left there.' He put down his tea. 'Unpacking today it made me think about the flat, about our first place. It could be like that again, Sue. This house is new. Things don't have to change.'

'They already have changed, John. *We've* changed. Circumstances have changed. It can never be the same between us.' There was an appalling finality in her voice. 'I still love you but a part of that love died with Lisa. Because her death could have been avoided.'

'I don't need reminding, Sue. Do you think there's a day goes by that I don't think about her? About what might have been? I made a mistake and I'm sorry. God knows I'm sorry. Sorry for the affair, sorry for Lisa's death, sorry for the way I hurt you and damaged our relationship. I know I can't put those things right and I don't expect you to forget. But if you could find a little bit of forgiveness, Sue . . .' He allowed the sentence to trail off.

She took a sip of her own tea and shivered slightly.

'I feel cold,' she said. 'Is the heating on?'

Hacket sighed wearily.

'I'll check it when I've finished my tea.'

She got to her feet and headed out of the kitchen. He heard her footfalls on the stairs.

'Shit,' he murmured, also getting to his feet. He wandered back into the sitting room to be greeted by the music once more.

484

He began opening another case, noticing that there were several photos laid on the top of the other items. Framed pictures. He unwrapped the first of them and found that it was a photo of Lisa. Hacket smiled and set it down beside him, reaching for the next one. It was Sue, dressed in a low-cut black dress, taken about a year ago at a party. She looked stunning.

The music behind him was building to a crescendo.

He took out the last photo.

A young couple on it happy and smiling.

Their wedding photo.

'... *When I was a child I caught a fleeting glimpse, out of the corner of my eye. I turned to look but it was gone, I cannot put my finger on it now* ...' Hacket frowned down at the picture. '... *The child has grown, the dream is gone* ...'

The glass had shattered, two long thin shards had cut deep into the picture.

50

She didn't know how long she'd been lying there listening to the slow, steady breathing of Hacket and the monotonously regular ticking of the clock. All Sue did know was that she was no closer to sleep now than when she'd first slid between the covers. It had been a tiring day, she had expected to be enveloped by sleep almost immediately, but it was not to be.

She lay still, hearing the house creak and groan as the timbers settled. After a moment or two of this she finally swung herself out of bed and crossed to the window, peering out into the darkness and the school beyond. She could just make out the shapes of the buildings in the gloom and she pressed her hands to the radiator, aware of a chill which had settled upon her. She had pulled on her house coat as she slipped out of bed, but the chill was present nonetheless.

Behind her, Hacket stirred, his hand reaching across for her. He opened his eyes slowly when he could not feel her next to him. The teacher sat up and saw his wife gazing out into the night.

'Sue,' he said, softly. 'What's wrong?'

'I can't sleep, as usual,' she told him, still continuing with her vigil.

'Come back to bed,' he urged.

She finally relented, sliding in beside him.

'John, it's cold in this house,' she said. 'I know the heating is on. It isn't that kind of cold. It's . . . well . . . as if there was some kind of atmosphere because of what happened here.'

Hacket sighed.

'I know what you think about things like that,' she went on, 'the eternal sceptic – but I can't help it. I felt like that in our house after Lisa . . . They say houses carry a residue of sorrow don't they?'

'Do they?' Hacket said, a note of irritation in his voice. 'It sounds like a line from a bad romantic novel. I can't feel anything, Sue, honestly.'

She shivered again.

'Relax,' Hacket said, sliding closer to her.

She flinched almost imperceptibly as she felt his arm glide across her stomach, around her waist. He pulled her to him. As their bodies pressed together she felt the beginnings of an erection beginning to press into her thigh. Hacket kissed her gently on the lips, his shaft growing stiffer.

Sue tried to move away but he held her more tightly, his hand now straying to her breast which he squeezed, thumbing the nipple.

'Not now, John,' she said, gripping his wrist.

But Hacket would not release her. He tightened his hold on her breast, kneading the flesh so hard that she almost cried out from the sudden pain.

'John, please,' she snapped, again trying to squirm away from him.

'I want you, Sue,' he said, raising himself up on one elbow. He straddled her, his erection pointing towards her face, his hands gripping her wrists, pinning her to the mattress. She struggled but could not move him.

'Get off me,' she shouted, angrily.

In one swift movement his hands had left her wrists and fastened around her throat.

Her eyes bulged as he began to squeeze, his thumbs digging into her flesh.

'I want you,' he breathed, squeezing more tightly.

She tried to swallow but couldn't. Her head felt as if it were swelling and, all the time, the pressure on her throat seemed to intensify. She looked up into his face, her eyes blurred with pain and fear. She felt her body beginning to spasm, the muscles contracting violently.

Sue tried to scream but his vice-like grip prevented that action.

She bucked beneath him, trying to dislodge him, already growing weak but, finally, with one last reserve of strength she brought her knee up into the small of his back.

The grip was released and, in that split second, she found the breath to scream.

Hacket twisted round in bed as he heard the scream.

He saw Sue sitting upright, massaging her throat, perspiration beaded on her forehead and upper lip.

'What's wrong?' he asked, shocked by her appearance. He put out a hand to touch her but she drew back, as if frightened of his touch.

Her breathing was harsh and rapid, her eyes bulging, glazed.

Only gradually did she regain her senses as the last vestiges of the dream faded.

It was then that she began to cry.

51

He felt the gun in his pocket.

As Ronald Mills stood looking at the 'FOR SALE' sign outside the house he gently traced his fingers over the .38.

There were no lights on in the house. Perhaps Hacket was in bed, he reasoned. After all, it was past midnight.

Mills walked past the house on the far side of the road, reached the bottom of the street crossed then walked back again.

Should he just knock on the front door? Wait until Hacket opened it and shoot him down on the doorstep? It would be simple but hazardous. Although he doubted that he would be caught. God had views about revenge too, Mills remembered.

Vengeance is mine saith the Lord.

He smiled as he remembered the quote from the Bible.

God would not allow him to be caught, after all, he practically had God's blessing for what he was about to do.

He glanced behind him, noting that the street was empty. Mills paused a moment then walked up to the front door of the house.

He didn't knock. Instead he pushed the letter-box open and peered through into the gloom beyond. He could see and hear nothing.

He moved along the front of the house to the bay window. Cupping a hand against the glass he looked through.

The sitting room was empty.

Something finally clicked inside Mills' rather dull mind and he glanced again at the 'FOR SALE' sign. He hurried around the side of the house, down the passageway which he remembered so well. He smiled as he thought of his last journey along this cramped stone corridor.

Smiled at the recollection of finding the child inside the house.

This time, however, it was not to be.

He peered through the rear windows only to have what he'd already surmised confirmed. The place was empty. Quiet as a grave. He smiled thinly, amused at his joke but angry that Hacket was not there. Mills scuttled back up the passageway, his hand touching the revolver in his pocket once again. He had intended to press the barrel to Hacket's neck or to his stomach, make him die slowly. Even shoot his eyes out. But now he had been cheated.

And so had God.

God wanted him to take revenge for the death of Walton. He knew that. He was only upholding God's law by killing Hacket. *His Will be done.*

Mills headed for the street, stopping beneath the sign again. This time, however, he pulled a piece of paper and a pencil from his coat pocket. Resting the paper in the palm of his broad hand he wrote: JEFFERSON ESTATE AGENTS, then the phone number.

Hacket may have left the house but he could be traced, thought Mills.

This wasn't over yet.

52

The sun was doing its best to force a path through the clouds and, every so often, a shaft of golden light would lance into the kitchen, bouncing off Hacket's knife as he ate.

Sue sat opposite him as he ate, chewing indifferently on a piece of toast. She dropped the bread and ran a hand through her hair.

Hacket saw how dark she was beneath the eyes.

'How are you feeling?' he asked.

'Tired,' she told him. 'I'm going to the doctor this morning, see if he can give me something to help me sleep.'

'Be careful,' he said, guardedly.

'Careful of what?' she asked.

'Doctors like to give out prescriptions for sleeping pills and drugs like that. It's easier than talking to the patient about their problems.'

'I'm not going to him to talk about my problems,' she said acidly.

'If you're not careful you'll need a shopping trolley to carry the tranquillisers and anti-depressants.'

'Have you got a better idea, John?' she snapped. 'It's all right for you. You start a new job today. I'm the one who's going to be stuck in a new house with nothing to think about but my problems.' She took a sip of her tea. 'I'm seeing the doctor and that's all there is to it.'

'All right, I'm sorry. I'm just suspicious of doctors, you know that.'

'Well this one is good. He's Julie's doctor. I met him the other evening.' She explained briefly about Curtis' visit to the Clayton's home, deciding not to expand on Craig's condition.

Hacket listened dutifully, nodding occasionally. When she'd finished he looked at his watch.

8.30 a.m.

'I'd better go,' he said, standing up.

'I'll finish tidying up the house when I get back,' Sue told him.

'There's no need. We can carry on tonight.'

'I need something to occupy me, John. Now, go on or you'll be late.' She brushed a hair from his collar, looking into his eyes briefly.

'Wish me luck,' he said, hopefully.

She smiled.

'You don't need it.'

He kissed her lightly on the lips and headed for the front door. She heard it close behind him then sat down at the kitchen table again, finishing her tea. She washed up, listening to the increasingly loud noise coming from the playground just beyond the tall hedge at the bottom of their garden. Then when nine o'clock came she heard the bell sound and the noise receded into silence again. Sue dried her hands and moved into the hall. There she found the number she wanted, lifted the receiver and pressed the digits.

It was answered almost immediately.

'Hello. Yes, I'd like to make an appointment for this morning please,' she said. 'I'd like to see Doctor Curtis.'

53

The match made a dull hissing sound as it was struck, the yellow flame billowing from its head.

Phillip Craven held it before him for a second, then slowly lowered it towards the boy spread-eagled across two desks.

The boy shook his head, staring up at Craven with pleading in his eyes, but the other lad was interested only in the match, which he now held close to the chest of his helpless companion.

Four children held Trevor Harvey down, making sure that he couldn't squirm away from the approaching flame as Craven waved it over his pale, white chest. He suddenly lowered it onto Trevor's left nipple and the boy shrieked loudly.

Craven and the others watched mesmerised as the delicate skin turned first pink then bright red under the fury of the heat. He held the match against Trevor's chest until it went out. Then he lit another.

And another.

He pressed both of them to Trevor's stomach this time, below his navel, watching as the skin rose in a red welt, already blistering.

Trevor didn't shout so loudly this time. He merely grunted and tried to pull away from the others who held him down.

'Oh come on, Harvey, scream for us,' said Craven, grinning.

The rest of the class, girls and boys, all the same age as Craven, looked on with the fascination most children of thirteen display toward the suffering of others. Most were glad they were not the one being burned but many looked on the whole tableau as a diverting exhibition and Craven as a master showman.

He lit three matches and pushed them towards Trevor's right eye.

The boy's eyelashes had actually begun to smoulder when a shout from outside the room caused him to withdraw the matches.

Another boy came dashing into the classroom, almost falling over in his haste to get behind his desk.

'He's coming,' he said, and the four holding Trevor also bolted for their own places leaving Trevor to ease himself off the desks. He swayed uncertainly for a minute then a rough push from Craven sent him crashing into a nearby chair. He sprawled on the floor amid the cheers and laughter of the other class members.

Hacket heard the rumpus as he strode up the corridor, finally finding the room he sought. He swept in, smiling, closing the door behind him.

'You are form 3A, yes?' he asked.

'Yes, sir,' they answered in unison.

Trevor sat hunched over his desk, his shirt still unbuttoned, his eye streaming from the effects of the match. Still, he thought, wistfully, it could have been much worse.

It could have been like it was last week.

Hacket introduced himself to the class, still smiling broadly, told

491

them where he was from, what they could expect from *him* and what he expected of *them*. Finally he walked to the centre of the room and, standing in front of the blackboard, looked around at the expectant faces.

'I want to get to know all of you so could you each stand up in turn and tell me your names, please? We'll see how many I can remember.' He rubbed his hands together theatrically. The gesture was greeted by good-natured laughter.

One by one the class obeyed and Hacket eyed each member. There were less than twenty of them, mostly sat in groups, apart from Trevor who sat alone at the front of the class, his head still bowed.

The list of names grew until there were just a couple left.

'Phillip Craven, sir.'

The boy sat down.

Hacket snapped his fingers, the name ringing bells of recognition in the back of his mind.

'The artist,' he said, smiling.

Craven looked bemused.

'I saw your painting in the annexe outside the headmaster's office. The one of the owl. It is you isn't it? There aren't *two* Phillip Cravens in the school?'

The rest of the class laughed, Craven turned scarlet and smiled.

'I was very impressed with the painting. A bit gory though, as I remember.'

'Life isn't always pretty, sir,' said Craven, his smile fading slightly.

'A philosopher too?' Hacket mused.

He looked at the last boy in the class. Trevor remained seated, his head still bowed.

'Your turn,' Hacket said.

The boy looked up at him but didn't move.

This one is either the comedian or the trouble-maker, Hacket thought. There was one in every class.

'Just stand up and tell me your name, please. It's quite simple.' He smiled.

'So is he, sir,' said Craven and the rest of the class laughed.

Hacket looked around at them and the noise died away.

Trevor rose slowly to his feet, his shirt undone, his hair untidy.

492

There were stains around his crotch and, even from a couple of feet away Hacket could smell the odour of stale urine. The boy was a mess.

'What's your name, son?' the teacher asked.

'Trevor Harvey, sir,' he mumbled.

Hacket didn't hear and Trevor repeated himself.

'He's the village idiot, sir,' Craven called and the class broke out into a chorus of laughs and jeers once more.

'That's enough, Craven.' Then, to Trevor: 'All right, sit down.'

As the boy did so his shirt billowed open and Hacket winced as he caught sight of the red and pink welts on his skin. Some were purple, where scabs had formed over wounds only to be scratched off once more. He saw bruises too, and some cuts.

'What happened to you?' Hacket asked, shocked by the boys appearance.

'Nothing, sir,' said Trevor, trying to button his shirt. But Hacket stopped him, inspecting a burn on his chest more closely.

'Who did this?'

Silence had descended like an invisible blanket, all eyes on the teacher and the boy.

'Trevor, tell me who did this to you,' Hacket said, quietly.

The teacher caught a slight movement out of his eye corner, just enough to see Craven hurl a large eraser. It struck Trevor in the face but he didn't react, merely sat down.

Hacket spun round and glared at Craven.

'What do you think you're doing, Craven?' he snarled, angered by the look of defiance on the boy's face. 'Do you know anything about Trevor's injuries?'

'Why should I, sir?' the boy said. 'He probably did them himself and he's too stupid to remember.'

Trevor was busily buttoning his shirt.

Hacket looked at both boys in turn, aware still of the slight smirk on Craven's face. He held the boys's stare, a little unsettled when the youth didn't look away.

'This isn't a very auspicious start to things is it, Craven?' he said.

'I'll try to do better next time, sir,' the boy said.

Hacket nodded slowly then glanced at Trevor once more.

'Are you OK? Do you want to visit the nurse, get those wounds looked at?'

Trevor shook his head, pushing some strands of hair from his face.

Hacket glanced around the class once more then picked up the chalk and began writing on the blackboard.

The bell was the signal for a mass exodus from the classroom. Hacket dismissed the children, watching as they trooped past him. Craven avoided eye-contact this time as he passed.

Trevor was the last to leave, wiping his nose with the back of his hand.

'Trevor, wait a minute,' Hacket called.

The boy hesitated but didn't turn.

'Listen to me,' the teacher said, quietly. 'Those marks on your body. If you want to tell me who did it, if you want to talk to me then you know where to find me. Do you understand?'

Trevor nodded and sniffed back some more mucus. Then he turned and headed for the door, closing it behind him.

Hacket exhaled deeply and wiped chalk dust from his hands.

As he looked up he saw Craven's face peering at him through the classroom window.

The boy was smiling.

54

Gravel crunched beneath the wheels of the Metro as Sue Hacket brought the car to a halt. She switched off the engine and looked up at the house which towered over her like some kind of ivy-covered giant. It certainly looked more imposing than the usual doctor's surgery, she thought, as she climbed out of the car. The leaded windows and the hanging baskets which adorned the oak front door made the place look more like a country hotel than a place of healing. She wondered how much it must be worth, set, as it was, in about half an acre of its own grounds. Separated by wide lawns and immaculate hedges from the main road which led into Hinkston. Private medicine obviously *did* have its advantages for those who practised it, she mused.

The large oak door opened easily when she pushed it and Sue stepped into what looked like a hallway. To her left was a dark wood door, to her left a white one marked 'SURGERY'. She walked in.

The waiting room was empty apart from the receptionist who smiled with genuine warmth, and not the practised response which Sue had seen so many times before in women of the same profession.

They exchanged pleasantries and Sue gave her name then was told that doctor Curtis would be able to see her in a minute or two. He, she was informed, would complete a form with her help in order to register her as a patient.

The door behind the receptionist opened and Curtis appeared.

He smiled at Sue and beckoned her through.

Once inside the surgery Curtis sat down behind his desk and invited Sue to take a seat opposite. She slipped off her jacket and draped it over the back of the chair.

Curtis smiled at her once more and, again, Sue was aware of the combination of strength and warmth which flowed from his gaze. She looked at him, not wanting to make it too obvious that she was taking in details of his appearance. As with their first meeting she was struck by the youthfulness of his features. His smile was reassuring. Inviting even. As he folded his hands across his lap she noted how powerful his hands were, his fingers long and slender, the backs of his hands covered by thick dark hair. There was more than the power of a healer in them she thought.

Sue felt strangely light-headed, as if being with Curtis were somehow intoxicating, his very presence a kind of drug.

An aphrodisiac?

She was aware that her nipples were beginning to stiffen. A welcome warmth began to spread between her legs as she continued to look at Curtis.

She tried to control the feelings, both puzzled and . . .

And what? Ashamed?

'Would you like a coffee while we talk?' asked Curtis.

'What about your other patients?' she asked.

'I don't have another appointment for an hour. That's one of the advantages I have over the National Health Service. I don't have twenty appointments an hour.' He smiled and buzzed through to the receptionist on the intercom.

'I'll just have to take some personal details if you don't mind,' Curtis informed her. 'Date of birth, medical history. That kind of thing.' He smiled that hypnotic smile once again and Sue answered his questions. The coffee arrived and the receptionist retreated back to the waiting room. Sue sipped from the bone china cup, watching as Curtis wrote on a pink sheet.

'If I recall, you were having trouble sleeping,' he said finally. 'Is that still the case?'

She nodded.

'Even when I do manage to get a few hours I seem to get woken up by nightmares,' she continued.

'What kind of nightmares?'

'The usual stupid things that make no sense in daylight,' she said, sipping her coffee as if anxious to avoid the subject.

'Have you any idea what's caused the disruption of sleep, Mrs Hacket?'

She put down her cup, avoiding his gaze for a moment.

'Trouble at home perhaps?' Curtis continued.

She took a deep breath, as if trying to summon up the courage to tell him.

'When we first met you asked if I had a family, any children and I said no. Well, I did have, *we* did have. A daughter. Lisa.' The words were coming with difficulty, as if she were learning some kind of new language. 'We used to live in London. A nice house. Respectable.' She smiled bitterly. 'Our daughter was murdered.'

It was said. Simple really.

'A few weeks later my father died of cancer, he'd been ill for months. The two things together were too much for me, especially with what happened to Lisa . . .' She found she could go no further.

'I'm very sorry,' Curtis murmured.

'Around the time of my daughter's murder, my husband was having an affair.' Again she chuckled but there was no humour in the sound. 'This sounds like a hard luck story doesn't it? Perhaps I should be telling an agony aunt instead of you.'

496

'A doctor should care for his patients' psychological welfare as well as their physical condition.'

'Everything seemed to happen at once. That was why I left London. If I'd stayed I'd have gone crazy.'

'That's understandable.'

Sue smiled at him, aware of how easily she was speaking. Secret thoughts which she had kept locked away were spilling out almost wantonly. And, as she spoke she felt a numbing weariness envelope her, as if talking about what she felt were draining her. It was like a criminal unburdening himself of guilt, glad to be given the chance to confess.

Was this what John had felt like when he'd confessed to the affair?

But it wasn't guilt she was purging herself of, it was an accumulation of misery.

She felt the tears forming in her eyes and pulled a tissue from the pocket of her jeans. A couple more deep breaths and she had regained her composure.

Curtis looked on silently, his eyes never leaving her then finally, sitting forward in his chair he leant towards Sue.

'Have you thought of having another child?' he asked.

'I can't,' she told him. 'I mean, I want one but, after Lisa was born there were complications. My fallopian tubes were infected. I can't have children.'

This time when she looked at him she made no attempt to wipe away the tears.

'You don't know how much I want another child,' Sue continued. 'Lisa could never be replaced, you understand that. But I think her death hit me harder because I knew I couldn't have another baby. It made things even more final.'

'And does your husband feel the same way? Would he have wanted more children?'

She smiled wearily.

'John always wanted another daughter. We used to laugh about it. You know, how men are supposed to want a son to carry on the family name. Not John. He wanted another girl.' She sniffed.

Curtis was already writing out a prescription.

'Sleeping pills,' he announced, handing it to her. 'Only a week's supply. They can become addictive. I could have given you tranquillisers but they only help you live with a problem they don't remove its cause.'

'Then how can I ever go back to normal?' she wanted to know. 'I know what my problem is. I want another child but I can't have one. It's an insoluble problem.'

'How badly do you want it?'

'I'd give anything,' she said, flatly. 'Anything.'

Curtis smiled benevolently.

'Promise me you'll come back in a few days, even if you feel better. Just to talk.'

She nodded.

'You've been a great help, Doctor. Talking about it helps.'

'So you'll come back?'

'Yes.'

She got to her feet and slipped on her jacket. Curtis showed her to the door and opened it for her. He shook her hand and she felt the warmth in his grasp. He smiled once more and then she was gone.

As Curtis closed the door and turned back into the surgery his smile vanished abruptly. He crossed to the door to the left of his desk which was already opening.

'You heard that?' he asked as the other occupant of the house entered the office. 'She said she'd give anything for another child. Anything.'

'Did you tell her?' the other wanted to know.

Curtis shook his head.

'She's got to be handled carefully but I think she's at the right stage emotionally. She seems particularly receptive.'

'When will you speak to her again?' the figure wanted to know.

Curtis heard the sound of Sue's car pulling away.

'Soon,' he murmured. 'Very soon.'

55

Hacket felt the air rasping in his lungs as he inhaled. He hadn't realised until now quite how unfit he really was. As he ran back and forth across the rugby field, following the play he could feel his heart thumping protestingly against his ribs. As a younger man he'd played both football and rugby for his school but that had been more than ten years ago. He might only be twenty-nine, but he felt as if he had the lungs of an eighty-year-old.

The mud-spattered boys who swarmed over the field with him did so with more urgency, as befitted their age. There were those, as there always were, who struggled to keep up, who were constant targets of abuse from their fitter, more athletic colleagues. They too plodded through the mud puffing and panting.

Hacket watched as a boy he knew as Lee Vernon received the ball and began to run with it.

He'd got less than twenty yards when Phillip Craven came hurtling at him.

Vernon tried to avoid the tackle but Craven caught him just above the waist, slamming his shoulder into the other boys solar plexus with something akin to relish. They both went down in a muddy heap and Craven rose quickly, smiling as he looked down at Vernon who had had the wind knocked from him. He lay in the mud wheezing, trying to suck back the air which had been blasted from him by Craven's crunching tackle.

Hacket ran across to the boy and helped him up, bending him over and patting his back in an attempt to re-fill his lungs. The boy gasped, coughed then began to breathe more easily but pain still showed on his face. Hacket asked him if he was all right and he nodded and trudged back into position.

The match re-started and this time it was Craven's turn to catch the ball. He gripped it tightly and ran, barging past a couple of half-hearted tackles, ignoring the boy who had run alongside him to support.

Two opponents came at him and Craven struck out a hand, catching one in the throat. The other was less fortunate.

Craven's hand connected with his nose with such force that the appendage seemed to burst. Blood spilled from both nostrils, pouring down the front of the boys shirt, staining it crimson. He moaned and fell forward into the mud while Craven ran on to score.

Hacket blew his whistle to halt the game, running across to the boy with the bleeding nose. It looked bad and the teacher could see that the boy was struggling to keep back tears. It might even be broken. There was certainly enough blood.

'Put your head forward,' Hacket instructed while a number of the other boys gathered around.

Streams of blood ran from the boy's nose and dripped into the mud between his legs. The sight of his own life-fluid draining away made him feel sick and he went a sickly white colour. Hacket thought he was going to faint, but the boy retained his grip on consciousness.

Craven trotted over, grinning.

'A hand-off is supposed to be with the *flat* of the hand, Craven,' he snapped. 'Not a fist. You do that again and you're in trouble.'

'It's not my fault if he can't take it, sir,' said the youth, defiantly.

'Are you all right, Parker?' Hacket asked the injured boy. He pulled a handkerchief from the pocket of his tracksuit and held it to the boy's nose. 'Go back to the school, see the nurse. You go with him,' the teacher said, pointing to another boy who seemed only too delighted to escort his companion off the field. At least it meant *he* was out of the action too.

Hacket watched them leave the field then re-started the game again.

The ball was lofted high into the air and it was Craven who caught it, running at speed towards the opposition. Hacket saw him pass two of them but a third, a powerfully built lad called Baker ducked low, beneath Craven's straight arm rebuff and gripped the other boy's legs. Hacket couldn't resist a slight smile as Craven went crashing to the ground, the ball flying from his grip.

'Good tackle, Baker,' shouted the teacher.

Craven tried to wrestle free of his captor, digging his boot into Baker's chest in the process. The other youth reacted angrily and, before Hacket could reach them, Baker had thrown a punch.

Craven jerked free and, instead of rolling away, he threw himself back at Baker, fastening his hands round his throat, bringing his face close to Baker's.

'Stop it,' bellowed Hacket, racing towards them, pushing past the children who had stopped to watch the fight.

Craven closed his teeth around the top of Baker's left ear and, as Hacket watched in horror, he bit through the fleshy appendage.

Baker screamed as the top of his ear was sheared off.

Blood spurted from it and ran down Craven's chin.

'Craven,' Hacket yelled, trying to reach the boy.

Baker continued to scream, looking up to see the portion of his ear still gripped in Craven's teeth.

He held it for a second then swallowed it.

'Jesus Christ,' murmured Hacket, finally reaching the struggling pair.

He hauled Craven to his feet, seeing the blood on the boy's face, the pieces of flesh between his teeth.

The grin on his face.

Baker had curled up into a ball, both hands clasped to his ear, or at least what remained of it. Blood was pouring down the side of his face, oozing through his fingers.

And he shrieked in pain.

'Go and get help,' Hacket roared at a boy close to him, still gripping on to Craven.

The boy ran off.

Another youth took one look at the bleeding mess which had once been Baker's ear and vomited.

Not only had the top half been severed, most of the remaining ear had been torn. The entire appendage was hanging, held to his head only by thin pieces of skin and muscle.

Hacket dragged Craven away.

Behind him, Baker continued to scream.

56

'Don't you think you're over-reacting a little, Mr Hacket?' said Donald Brooks, apparently more concerned that mud from the teacher's boots was dropping onto his office carpet.

'Over-reacting?' Hacket gaped. 'The boy is a lunatic,' he hissed, trying to control his temper. 'I saw what happened. If you don't believe me then go and look at Baker, he's in the medical room now waiting for the ambulance to arrive.'

Brooks raised a hand as if to silence the younger man.

'I didn't say I doubted you,' he said. 'But it was an accident.'

'Craven bit Baker's ear off. He swallowed it for God's sake. Are you trying to tell me that's normal?' Hacket snarled. 'What does he do for an encore, pull the heads of babies?'

'Now you *are* over-reacting,' Brooks told him, irritably. 'What do expect me to do with the boy? Call the police? Have him locked up? I've already called his mother, she's coming to pick him up. I've decided to suspend him for a couple of days until all this blows over.'

Hacket shook his head wearily and brushed a hand through his hair.

Brooks huddled closer to the radiator as if fearing that Hacket's presence in the room was somehow sucking the precious warmth from the air.

'Have there been incidents like this before involving Craven?' Hacket wanted to know.

'Nothing,' Brooks told him. 'The boy is a good worker, a highly intelligent child.'

Hacket was unimpressed. He walked to the door of the Headmasters office and peered out. Craven was sitting in the annexe, looking at his own painting. He was smiling unconcernedly.

The teacher glanced at the boy then closed the office door again.

'He seems to be the dominant one in his class,' Hacket said.

'Intelligent children usually are. I don't have to tell you that, Mr Hacket.'

'What about a boy called Trevor Harvey? Craven was picking on him this morning. Is there some kind of antagonism between them that I should know about?'

'Harvey is a little *slow*, for want of a better word. Again, you know that children like that are usually the butt of jokes. You can't accuse Craven of persecuting Harvey as well. You seem to have taken a dislike to this boy, Mr Hacket and it appears to be clouding your judgement.'

'It's got nothing to do with judgement. I'm not talking about character references, for Christ's sake, I'm telling you what I saw today. And I don't like it.'

The two men gazed at each other for a moment, their concentration broken by a knock on the office door. Brooks' secretary popped her head around the door and coughed rather theatrically.

'Mrs Craven is here,' she announced.

Brooks smiled and instructed the secretary to show the woman through.

She was dressed in a loose fitting tracksuit and trainers. Hacket saw that part of a bandage showed beneath the left sleeve of the tracksuit top. Her hair was long, jet black and tied in a pig-tail. She bustled into the room, smiling at Brooks then at Hacket. The headmaster greeted her then introduced her briefly to the younger man. Brooks offered her a seat but she declined.

'There's nothing wrong with Phillip is there?' she asked.

'There's been an accident, Mrs Craven,' said Brooks. 'Involving your son. A fight.'

'Is he hurt?' she asked, anxiously. 'I saw him sitting outside the room.'

'*He's* not hurt,' Hacket interrupted. 'But another boy is. Phillip injured him badly and I'm sure it was intentional.'

Brooks shot the younger man an angry glance.

'There was a slight fracas, Mr Hacket is right,' the headmaster said. 'We thought it best if Phillip stayed at home for a couple of days.'

'What happened?' Elaine Craven wanted to know.

Hacket told her.

She looked at him for a moment then turned to Brooks and smiled politely.

'I'll keep Phillip at home, if that's what you think is best. I hope the other lad is better soon.' Then she turned back to Hacket. 'I think you're a little too eager to blame my son for what happened.'

'I saw him do it, Mrs Craven.'

'He could have been provoked,' she said, defensively.

'Provoked into biting a boy's ear off?' Hacket shook his head.

She pulled up her sleeves and shrugged her shoulders, a gesture which signified defiance. Hacket caught sight of the heavy bandage which encased her left arm from wrist to elbow.

'I think it'd be best if I left now,' said Elaine. 'I'll take Phillip with me.' She turned and headed for the door, followed by the headmaster who waved Hacket back into the office. He waited there, listening to the mutterings coming from outside then he heard the door of the outer office close and, a second later, Brooks re-entered the room, making straight for the radiator. He pressed himself to it.

'Satisfied, Mr Hacket?' Brooks said. 'I believe you have a class to take.' He glanced at his watch. 'I trust there's nothing else you wish to discuss.'

'As a matter of fact there *is* something on my mind,' the teacher said. 'I'd like to know why you didn't tell me the truth about the previous occupant of my house.'

Brooks looked vague.

'The teacher who shot his wife and child then committed suicide,' Hacket continued.

'It's not something I like to talk about,' said Brooks rubbing his hands together.

'I had a right to know before myself and my wife moved in. Why did he do it?'

Brooks shrugged.

'You're asking me to give you answers I can't give now, Mr Hacket,' the headmaster said. 'Who am I to see into a man's mind? I had no idea he would do something like that. He may have been unbalanced. There were no outward signs. I'm a teacher not a psychiatrist.'

Hacket was silent for a moment, his gaze never leaving the headmaster.

'You should have told me,' he said finally.

'Would it have changed your mind about the job? Would you have decided not to live there if you'd known all the facts?'

Hacket shrugged.

'I don't know. It's a bit late for that now though isn't it? The main thing is, you should have told me.'

Brooks looked at his watch again.

'Your class, Mr Hacket,' he said, sliding his hands along the radiator.

Hacket hesitated a moment longer then turned and headed for the door.

Brooks turned his back and gazed out of the window. He could see Elaine Craven driving along the short driveway that led past his office.

Phillip sat in the back, a slight smile on his lips.

As Hacket passed through the annexe he paused for a second and looked at the painting of the owl on the wall.

The owl holding the eyeball.

Phillip Craven's painting.

Perhaps it would have been more appropriate if the owl had been holding an ear, he thought bitterly.

All around him bells sounded, signalling the beginning of another lesson.

Hacket looked at his watch.

1.30 p.m.

It was already turning into a long day.

57

As he pushed open the front door the smell of stew greeted him.

Hacket inhaled deeply, the mouth-watering aroma a most welcome one. He dropped his briefcase and sports-bag in the hall and wandered through into the kitchen.

Sue was standing by the cooker stirring the contents of a large saucepan.

'How did it go?' she asked, cheerily and Hacket was pleasantly surprised by the lightness of her tone. She was wearing a pink T-shirt and pair of faded, tight-fitting jeans. Both items of clothing served to highlight both the shapely curves of her figure and the fact that she wore nothing beneath the outer garments. She turned to Hacket and smiled.

He wondered if he'd walked into the wrong house.

It was as if time had somehow been reversed.

Her hair had been washed and, beneath the lights in the kitchen it seemed to glow. She wore just a hint of makeup on her eyes and her face looked as if it had been purged of any lines or shadows. She looked closer to twenty than twenty-five. And when she smiled at him he felt the breath catch in his throat.

It was like finding a long-lost possession again.

He moved towards her and kissed her, surprised when she stopped stirring the stew and, instead, snaked both arms around his neck, drawing him closer to her. Their lips brushed together and he felt her tongue flicking urgently against his teeth, pushing deeper to stir the moistness of his mouth. He responded fiercely, allowing one hand to fall to her bottom, squeezing its firmness. She ground herself against his groin, pulling away for breath, smiling as she felt his penis beginning to stiffen against her.

'The stew will burn,' she said, touching his lips with her index finger. Hacket backed off and sat down, a little bewildered.

Why the sudden change?

He looked at her and smiled.

'I asked how the day went?' she repeated.

He told her, deciding to skip details about Craven's antics on the rugby field. She listened intently, dishing up the dinner, sitting down opposite him as he spoke. Occasionally he would look up at her and, sometimes would find her gaze on him. Hacket's bewilderment at her change in attitude was rapidly overtaken by his joy and relief.

Was this the turning point?

'What about you?' he asked. 'What sort of day have you had?'

'I finished tidying up,' she told him. 'Things actually look respectable in the bedrooms now. I put your clothes away. There's just some stuff that needs to go up in the loft and that's about it.'

506

'And the doctor? How did *that* go?'

'Fine,' she told him, getting to her feet and scraping the remains of the stew into the waste-bin.

'Did he give you any pills?'

'Sleeping tablets. And don't worry, I won't get addicted.' She smiled.

Hacket looked at her for a moment then he reached out, pulling her to him. She didn't resist but instead allowed him to lift her onto his knee. She put her arms around his neck, feeling the strength in his grip as he held her. He wanted to speak, wanted to say something to her, to tell her how she'd changed. Tell her how much he loved the change. But the words wouldn't come. Hacket was worried that if he spoke to her about her change of mood then she would revert to the way she'd been before. He was both elated and frightened by this new face she was showing.

Face or mask?

She kissed him and he felt sure that it was with genuine warmth.

Had he been forgiven?

He doubted it but he didn't question, he merely enjoyed the moment, savoured the sensations he was feeling.

He wanted her badly.

When he felt her hand gliding across his groin he knew the feeling was reciprocated.

She stroked the inside of his thigh then trailed her fingers across his penis, squeezing it through the material of his trousers, coaxing its stiffness. She took one of his hands and raised it to her breast, anxious to let him feel her own excitement. He kneaded her breast gently, feeling her nipple stiffen and swell. She moaned softly and they kissed, deeply, wantonly. She slid from his lap onto the floor beside him, unzipping his trousers, easing his penis from the confines of the material. Then she leant forward and took the bulbous head in her mouth, slowly lowering her head until more of his stiff shaft disappeared into the warm orifice.

Hacket gasped as he felt her tongue lapping around his glans while, with her free hand, she gently rubbed his testicles. He unfastened his trousers and eased them down, not wanting to disturb her then, as she continued sucking he reached down and pulled at her T-shirt, easing it over her head.

507

She kneeled beside him, moving back slightly, allowing him to reach her breasts, to squeeze them in his eager hands, to tease the hard nipples between his thumb and forefinger.

She stood up and unzipped her jeans, wriggling out of them until she stood naked in front of him.

Hacket stood too, slipping out of his trousers and pants, allowing Sue to unbutton his shirt and tug it free.

Naked, they embraced and he felt her hand close around his shaft, urging him towards her slippery cleft, demanding that he penetrate her.

She moved back, her shoulder blades against the wall, raising herself up onto her toes as he took his place between her spread thighs.

His penis nudged the entrance of her vagina for a moment and she gasped as it rubbed her hardened clitoris then, with a grunt, he slid into her.

It was a pleasure he'd almost forgotten.

She raised one leg, snaking it around the back of his calves, allowing him deeper penetration, gripping his buttocks, unable to stand the torment any longer. He began to drive into her, long slow strokes which caused them both to gasp. Hacket bent his head to her breasts taking each nipple between his lips in turn, flicking his tongue over the hardened buds. Licking the mounds until they glistened with his saliva.

Sue looked into his eyes, her own eyes glazed as if she were in a trace, aware only of the thrusting of his penis and the sensations which were building between her legs.

She pressed her head against his shoulder as he increased the speed of his movements. Looking beyond him her eyes opened for a second.

'*Come and see me*'.

She knew that this was her husband who held her but she felt another.

'*Come and see me*'.

Curtis.

She mouthed his name as her ecstasy grew. Mouthed it but did not speak it.

And as the orgasm grew in intensity she closed her eyes, saw Curtis driving into her. Felt him bringing her to the brink.

She heard her name whispered but it seemed vague, muffled.

She cried out as she climaxed, reaching down to squeeze those swollen testicles.

Hacket felt her body trembling with the exploding pleasure, heard her moan her joy. Then, as her hand grasped him gently he too felt the beginnings of his orgasm. He thrust harder into her until he poured his thick fluid into her.

She groaned once more as she felt him come.

The image of Curtis filled her mind. It was *his* penis which throbbed inside her. *His* semen which filled her.

'*Come and see me*'.

Hacket slowly withdrew, his breath coming in gasps. Both of them were covered in perspiration but, even as he tried to pull away she gripped him hard, pulling his face close to hers, kissing him deeply.

Then she leant forward, licking his chest, lowering herself slowly, her tongue flicking over his belly until it reached his flaccid organ, now wet with secretions. She took it into her mouth, tasting herself on him. She licked, sucked, coaxed.

She demanded him again.

And Hacket responded, surprised at his own recuperative powers. He felt the stiffness beginning to return.

She led him, almost dragged him, towards the sitting-room and there they loved again. More slowly this time but with as much intensity.

Hacket felt as if the night had blurred into one long bout of glorious copulation.

Nothing else seemed to matter. He found reserves of strength he didn't know he had, spurred on by Sue's insatiability. She was tireless.

'I love you,' Hacket whispered as she lay with her head on his chest, licking the beads of perspiration from his flesh.

Her eyes were open, her breathing low. She didn't answer him.

All she could think of was Curtis.

And it began again.

58

It had all been so easy.

Much easier than he'd anticipated.

Ronald Mills sat at the table in the flat, smiling, looking down at the objects which lay before him.

At the .38 and its ammunition. The knife. The pad which bore the one word: HINKSTON.

Walton had always done most of the thinking when he'd been alive. Any deals to be worked out, they had been Walton's province. Any financial connivings, Walton had sorted them out, but now Walton was dead and Mills had to think for himself.

He spun the cylinder of the .38 then snapped it back into position, raising the gun so that he was squinting down the sight. He aimed at a dirty vase which stood on top of the sideboard and squeezed the trigger.

The metallic click sounded loud as the hammer slammed down on an empty chamber.

He put down the gun and picked up the knife, holding it almost lovingly in his hand. The hand which still festered from the tattoo. He grunted and picked a piece of the scab off, rolling it between his fingers for a moment before dropping it onto the floor. Then he reached for the sharpening stone, and began carefully drawing the blade back and forth across it, pausing every now and then to press his thumb to the edge.

After nearly five minutes of this task he pressed his thumb to the blade once more.

The knife split the skin effortlessly, opening the pad of Mills' thumb from the nail to the first joint.

He held it before him for a second, watching as the blood welled from the split and ran down his hand. Then he pushed the digit into his mouth, tasting the salty crimson fluid as it flooded onto his tongue. He sucked it as a child would suck on a nipple, coaxing more fluid from it.

Finally he lowered his hand, lowered the knife, his gaze drawn once more to the pad.

He had rung the estate agents and asked about Hacket's house. Said that he wanted to put in a bid for it. And they had believed him. Those fucking idiots who only cared about their commission, who only cared if they sold the house or not. They didn't care who bought it, who enquired, as long as there was the possibility of some money at the end of it all.

'Easier for a camel to pass through the eye of a needle than for a rich man to enter the kingdom of God,' chuckled Mills.

He didn't want money. He didn't care about money.

He wanted revenge.

He wanted Hacket.

The estate agent had tried to arrange a meeting with him, to show him round the house but Mills had hesitated. He had asked to speak to Hacket personally, he wondered if he would be willing to take a smaller offer.

The estate agent thought it might work.

Mills had smiled.

He had asked for a way of getting in touch with Hacket.

The estate agent had given him a phone number and an address in a place called Hinkston.

Ask and ye shall receive.

Mills looked at the word written on his pad then at the gun and the knife.

And at his bleeding thumb.

He knew where Hacket was, all he had to do was find him.

Slowly, Mills wiped his thumb across the pad, leaving a thick red stain.

It was just a matter of time.

Seek and ye shall find.

He began to laugh.

59

The frost crunched beneath his feet as he walked from the back door of the house.

Curtis made his way across the large lawn at the rear of the building, moving slowly, inhaling deeply. The early morning air smelt clean and unpolluted. When he exhaled his breath clouded before him. A watery sun was dragging its way up into the sky but, with dawn having broken scarcely fifteen minutes earlier it seemed to be finding the climb difficult. It wasn't yet strong enough to melt the frost.

The silence in the back garden, indeed all around the house, was almost total.

It was too early for any traffic to be either leaving or entering Hinkston, and the house was set sufficiently far back from the road to mask the sound even if some early morning traveller *was* passing.

The only sounds which Curtis heard as he made his way across the back garden were those of birds singing in the trees around him. Just two or three of them. A sparrow paused in its early morning song to peer quizzically at him as he passed beneath the branch where it sat.

Curtis drew closer to the bottom of the garden, towards the high, perfectly cropped privet hedge which towered a good nine feet.

There was a wrought iron gate set into it, supported on a wooden frame, the paint of which was blistered and peeling in places. Curtis opened the gate which squealed protestingly on its hinges as he walked through.

The area beyond the hedge was roughly twelve feet square. Surrounded by more hedges, these not quite as well cared for. They were neat but not immaculate. The grass which grew within the shaded square was that little bit longer than that of the lawns, not as neatly cropped. Weeds were poking through it in places. Curtis administered a swift mental rebuke as he surveyed the square because this was caused by *his* neglect. *He* was responsible for the care of this part of the garden.

The gardener wasn't allowed through the gate.

Curtis stood by the gate for a moment, looking around at the tall hedge, also covered by a thin coating of frost. The privet grew three feet taller than him here too. It sheltered the square perfectly.

He walked slowly towards the middle of it, towards the piece of stone which lay there.

The stone was cracked in places due to the ravages of the years and the weather. Moss had begun to grow on it here and there, infesting the cracks in the stone like gangrene infects a wound.

Curtis looked down at the name on the stone.

Below the name was a rose bowl, flecked with rust and, from this he took half a dozen dead stalks of flowers, gathering them up in one hand.

He replaced them with the fresh flowers which he held in his other hand, arranging them so that the red roses seemed to glow against the dull background of the stone.

They looked like a splash of blood on the grave.

Curtis straightened up, walked to one corner of the sheltered green square and dropped the dead flowers into the metal incinerator that stood there, then he brushed his hands together and returned to the graveside, gazing down once again at the name on the stone.

He stood there for what seemed like an eternity, his mind at peace, all thoughts banished. Again, the only sounds he heard were those of birds, his meditative state uninterrupted by nature's extraneous sounds.

Then he heard the footsteps beyond the gate.

Beyond the hedge.

Heavy footfalls which broke the blanket of frost.

Curtis turned his head towards the gate as the footsteps drew closer.

He heard the latch of the gate rattle, then the dull clank as it opened.

The figure walked through to join him.

Curtis turned back to the grave, hands clasped before him once more.

'I heard you leave the house,' said the figure, standing at his side.

'Sorry, I didn't want to disturb you.' the doctor said, softly, almost

513

reverently, as if to raise his voice would have been to defile the sanctity of this very private area.

The two of them stood silently for long moments, both gazing down at the stone.

And the name it bore.

'I've never thought this was right,' said Curtis nodding towards the grave. 'To lie here, even though it *is* our home.'

'Better here than with the others,' said the figure, defiantly.

Curtis nodded in agreement.

'Have you made up your mind what to do about the woman?' the other wanted to know.

'Mrs Hacket?'

'Yes.'

Curtis smiled thinly.

'Yes I have,' he said, his eyes still on the gravestone. 'She's due to visit me again today.' His smile broadened. 'I think the time has come.'

60

The woman was struggling with the books as she climbed the stairs, and Hacket could see what was going to happen.

As she reached the top step he saw the first of the heavy textbooks begin to topple from her hands. Five or six more followed it, landing with a thud on the floor. She muttered something under her breath and began retrieving them. Hacket scuttled up the stairs beside her and began picking up books too.

He glanced across at her as she shrugged and smiled.

She was very attractive. In her early twenties he guessed. Shoulder length brown hair and wide grey eyes. A nice figure too.

A little like Nikki?

He pushed the thought to the back of his mind, angry that it had even surfaced.

514

'You look as if you could do with some help carrying these,' he said, picking up half a dozen of the books himself.

'If you've got a fork-lift truck handy, it'd be most appreciated,' she told him, smiling. 'You're new here aren't you?'

He nodded.

'The new boy. Yes.' He extended his free hand, balancing the pile of books on the crook of his left arm. 'John Hacket.'

She took the offered hand and shook it.

'Josephine Milton,' she told him. 'But please call me Jo.'

She scooped up the rest of the books and they began climbing the stairs towards the second landing.

'What do you teach?' he asked.

'Biology. I dissect things,' she chuckled. 'What about you? English isn't it?'

'English *and* games,' he told her. 'I've got the strained muscles to prove it.'

She laughed.

'Of course, you took over from Ray Weller didn't you? I suppose you know the story?'

'About him killing his family then committing suicide. Yes.'

'Isn't it creepy living in a house where someone has died?'

'You get used to it,' said Hacket sharply. *Especially when you've lived in the house where your own daughter was butchered. It's a piece of cake.* 'How much did you know about Weller?'

She shrugged.

'Not much. Not enough to know why he should want to murder his family if that's what you mean. He was a nice guy. About your age, easy to talk to. He never struck me as a lunatic.' She raised her eyebrows. 'I haven't really been much help have I?'

Hacket smiled.

'It's probably not important,' he told her, pushing open a set of double doors to allow her through. Four classrooms led off from the landing they stood on.

'My little darlings are in there,' said Jo, nodding towards the door ahead of her. 'If you wouldn't mind just helping me in with these books.'

Hacket watched as she walked to the door and opened it, trying to

515

keep his eyes away from her shapely legs and tight buttocks but he lost the battle, content instead to admire them. She pushed open the door, expecting to be greeted by the usual cacophony of sound but there was only silence. The twelve girls in the class looked up as she entered.

All except one.

Emma Stokes remained at the bench, looking down at the white mouse which lay before her.

Its paws had been swiftly and effectively nailed to the bench, spread-eagling it.

Its stomach had been slit, the raw edges peeled back to reveal the network of intestines within.

It was these small tendrills of entrail which the girl was teasing from the ruptured belly of the mouse much as she might pull threads from a torn piece of material.

Hacket, close behind Jo, noticed with revulsion that the animal was still alive. Its head jerking back and forth, its small body quivering as the girl pulled ever longer lengths of intestine from it.

'What are you doing?' Jo snapped, dropping the books on the desk. She moved towards Emma who finally looked up from the eviscerated mouse and pinned the teacher in an unblinking stare. 'Give me that scalpel,' hissed Jo, holding out her hand to take the lethal blade from the girl who Hacket guessed was about twelve.

Emma hesitated.

'Give me that scalpel now,' Jo said, angrily, her attention flicking momentarily to the mouse.

Emma jabbed it towards Jo's outstretched hand.

The razor sharp blade cut effortlessly through the ball of her thumb and she hissed in pain as blood spurted from the cut.

She pulled the scalpel from the girl, dropping it onto her own desk. Hacket dragged a handkerchief from his pocket and passed it to Jo who pressed it against the wound, watching as blood soaked through the material.

'I'm all right, John,' Jo said. 'I can handle it now.'

He hesitated, looking first at the teacher's bleeding hand then at the girl who merely looked back indifferently at him.

He thought for a second he caught a hint of a smile at the corners of the girl's mouth. Not unlike that he'd seen on Craven's face.

516

The rest of the class remained silent.

Time seemed to have frozen.

Emma Stokes sat over the dying mouse, her face impassive.

Jo stood before her, blood soaking through the handkerchief.

Hacket hesitated a second longer then touched Jo's arm.

'Are you sure you're OK?' he murmured.

She nodded.

'You go. I'll take care of it.'

Hacket glanced around the class once again then walked out, closing the door behind him. He paused, peering through the small piece of meshed glass in the door, watching the tableau he'd left behind.

'Now Emma,' he heard Jo say. 'You tell me what you're playing at.'

He didn't wait to hear the answer.

He had a class of his own waiting for him.

61

'John, I want another child.'

At first Hacket thought he had misheard, or perhaps that his hearing was playing tricks with him. Lying on his back, pleasantly drained by their lovemaking, he heard Sue speak the words but it was as if they wouldn't register. She had her head resting on his chest, running one index finger up and down his belly, twisting the hairs around his navel.

The ticking of the clock beside the bed was the only noise in the room apart from their low breathing. No, he was sure now, he hadn't misheard.

'Sue,' he raised his head and began to speak but she looked up at him and pressed a finger to his lips to silence him.

'I know what you're going to say. I know what you're thinking,' she told him. 'But that's what I want. I *need* another child, John.'

Hacket exhaled deeply as she slid up the bed so that they lay face to face. He took her in his arms.

517

'Sue, it's impossible, you know that. After you had Lisa, after the infection, they told you there couldn't be any more children.'

'I know what they told me,' she said, a little more forcefully.

'Then why torture yourself like this?' he asked, softly. 'Why even think about it?' He stroked her hair softly then brushed her cheek with the back of his hand.

'I went to see Doctor Curtis again today,' she informed him, rolling onto her back.

Hacket propped himself up on one elbow, looking down at her.

'I told him how badly I wanted another child,' Sue continued.

'Did you tell him what the other doctors had said?' Hacket wanted to know.

'Yes I did. But it doesn't matter, John,' she said, smiling. 'He said that I *could* have another child. That there *was* a way.'

Hacket frowned.

'How?' he demanded. 'He has no right to tell you things like that, to raise your hopes.'

'I believe what he said and he says I can have another child.'

'It's not possible,' Hacket said, defiantly. 'I don't understand how he can tell you it is, not when half-a-dozen other doctors have said you can't. *You* know you can't. What makes you believe him?'

'Because I'm not the first. He's treated other women who were thought to be infertile, barren, not able to have children. Call it what you like. He's treated women in Hinkston and outside and those women have had babies.'

'Treated them how? He's a GP, Sue, not a surgeon. Your problem particularly is a surgical one. An *irreversible* surgical problem. How can he hope to treat a condition like yours?' There was a trace of anger in Hacket's voice.

'One of the women he treated was Julie,' she said, flatly.

'Your sister?' Hacket muttered, incredulously.

'She and Mike were told that they couldn't have children. But after Doctor Curtis had treated her she had Craig. You know how healthy *he* is.'

Hacket shook his head.

'He's offering us hope, John. Can't you see that?' she demanded.

'I don't know what I can see.' He stroked his chin thoughtfully.

518

'I want to try, John. I have to. I know another child could never replace Lisa, could never wipe out the memory of what happened but we have to at least try. Don't deny me that.'

Hacket saw the tears forming in her eye corners.

'What about you? Don't you want another child?' she wanted to know. 'What have we got to lose?'

He struggled for the words but none would come. The idea seemed simultaneously ridiculous and inviting. Another child, if it were possible might well bring them together again. It might go some way to helping them rebuild what they'd lost together.

But if it failed.

The pain would be unbearable.

So much pain.

'What have we got to lose?' she repeated.

The words hung in the air like stale smoke.

62

The petrol tank was full.

He'd have plenty of fuel to reach Hinkston *and* complete the return journey to London.

Ronald Mills glanced down at the fuel gauge and smiled. He'd anticipated having to fill up during the drive but he'd been lucky. The car he'd stolen had a full tank. He'd probably dump it in Hinkston.

Once he'd found Hacket.

Dump it then steal another to return to the capital.

The .38 was in the pocket of his jacket.

The knife jammed into his belt.

He drove with his lights on full beam, ignoring those drivers who flashed their headlamps at him when he dazzled them.

Fuck them.

There wasn't that much traffic leaving London, but streams of it moved through the night towards the capital.

A car overtook him but Mills hardly gave it a second glance. He was in no hurry. He had plenty of time.

He smiled to himself, glancing briefly down at the map on the passenger seat. He had ringed Hinkston with a large biro circle. The drive would take him about an hour he guessed.

There was no need to rush.

Ahead of him he saw the lights of a service station. The neon figure of a chef beckoned him from the road and he swung the car into the slip-road without checking the rear view mirror. The driver behind banged on his hooter as Mills cut across but he ignored the irate motorist and guided the car into the carpark of the service station.

A dog in the back of the vehicle he parked next to began to bark at him as he clambered from behind the steering wheel.

Mills stood looking at the animal for a moment, smiling as it barked and snarled, unable to reach him. Then he raised his hand as if to strike at the dog, driving it into an even greater paroxysm of anger. It threw itself against the glass in its efforts to reach him but Mills merely grinned and walked off, the dog's barks dying away behind him.

The service station restaurant was relatively quiet.

Half-a-dozen lorry drivers, a couple of families, one or two suited men. They were the only customers. None paid him any attention as he sat down and flicked through the menu, wiping the tomato sauce from one corner with his finger.

The waitress ambled over, stifled a yawn and asked him what he wanted.

He ordered then sat back in his seat, glancing around him.

One of the families sitting about twenty feet from him had two children. A boy and a girl. The girl was no more than eight, he assumed. Pretty. Long plaited hair.

Mills clasped his hands together, leant his elbows on the table top and fixed his stare on her.

She was sucking milkshake through a straw, swinging her legs beneath her seat.

Pretty.

He smiled thinly as he watched her, feeling the beginnings of an erection pressing against the material of his trousers. His gaze travelled from her face to her torso, then down to her legs, which were encased by woolen tights.

So easy to cut those tights away.

To feel her skin.

His erection grew more prominent and he slid one hand into his pocket, rubbing it.

'Here we are, sir.'

The voice startled him and he looked up to see that the waitress had returned with his order which she set down before him.

He took it without thanks, eating as if he was ravenous. She turned and walked away, glancing back at him as he shovelled food into his mouth, his eyes still straying back to the little girl every now and then.

When he'd finished he crossed to the pay desk, put down the exact amount and walked out.

Back inside the car he sat, watching the restaurant exit, watching for the little girl.

She and her family emerged ten or fifteen minutes after him and Mills watched them climb into a Volvo and drive off.

He looked down at the map, tracing his route with one index finger.

About thirty miles and he would be in Hinkston.

He started the engine.

The dog in the car next to him continued to bark.

63

Hacket smiled as he watched Sue cross to the front window and pull back the curtains, peering out into the night.

'Sue, he'll be here,' said the teacher. 'Don't worry.'

She looked back at him, shrugged and moved away from the window.

'You're like a kid on Christmas Eve, waiting for Santa to appear.'

They both laughed.

Hacket beckoned her to him and she sat beside him on the sofa, moving closer as he snaked one arm around her shoulder.

'I know how much this means to you,' he said, quietly. 'I feel the same way. If there is the possibility of us having another child then I'd be as happy as you.' He sighed. 'I just don't want you to raise your hopes.'

'Doctor Curtis wouldn't have told me about the treatment if he'd thought there'd be any doubt about its success, John,' she said, confidentially.

'What exactly *did* he tell you about the treatment?'

She shrugged.

'He didn't give any details, I suppose that's why he's coming to see us here, to explain it to both of us.'

Hacket was unimpressed.

Sue heard a car pull up and got to her feet again, crossing to the window. This time she saw Curtis walking up the front path. She felt that familiar shiver run through her as she watched him. He was dressed in a pair of dark trousers and a dark jacket.

She hurried to open the door, releasing the latch before he'd even knocked. Hacket heard them exchange greetings, then Curtis entered the living room.

Sue made the introductions and Hacket shook the doctor's hand, impressed by the firmness of the other man's grip.

Curtis declined Hacket's offer of a drink, settling instead for a cup of tea. The three of them finally sat down, Curtis aware that the eyes of the other two were on him.

'Well, I won't waste your time,' he said, smiling. 'Mr Hacket, I don't know if your wife has mentioned anything about our conversation the other day.'

'She said that you told her she might be able to have children again,' Hacket explained.

Curtis nodded and sipped his tea.

'That's right. She told me about your daughter. I'm very sorry.'

'Thanks,' snapped Hacket. 'Can you get to the point? Please satisfy my curiosity.'

Sue glared at her husband for a second, annoyed by his abruptness. Then she returned to looking at the doctor, enraptured both by his words and his appearance.

Christ, it was like some schoolgirl crush, she thought, barely suppressing a smile.

'My wife, as I'm sure you're aware, was told that she couldn't have any more children. Several doctors told her that,' Hacket continued.

'But you want another child?' Curtis said.

Hacket opened his mouth to speak but the doctor continued.

'*Both* of you?'

'Yes,' Hacket said, quietly, meeting the doctor's gaze.

'I've treated a number of women successfully over the past seventeen or eighteen years, Mr Hacket. They too had been told they couldn't have children, also by other experts.' There was a hint of sarcasm in the last word.

'Whatever it takes, we want another child,' Sue interjected.

Curtis smiled benignly at her, as a parent might smile at a child.

Hacket held up a hand, his eyes still on Curtis.

'Just a minute. Excuse my scepticism, doctor. It's not that I doubt your methods or your expertise but I'm concerned for my wife. If the treatment doesn't work then it could do her untold damage psychologically.'

'Don't talk about me as if I'm not here,' snapped Sue. 'I know the risks. I'm prepared to take them.'

'Please,' Curtis said. 'I didn't come here to start any arguments. I can see both points of view. If you'll just listen to what I've got to say.'

'I apologise for my husband, Doctor,' Sue said and, this time, it was Hacket's turn to feel the anger.

'You want to know about the treatment,' Curtis said.

Hacket nodded.

'I can't see how you can achieve anything without the use of surgery,' the teacher said.

'That is the advantage, Mr Hacket. The treatment can be completed at my own surgery. There is no need to involve a hospital or any other outsiders.'

'Why are you so anxious to exclude outside help? What's so special about this treatment?'

Curtis wasn't slow to pick up the note of challenge in Hacket's voice.

'Because it's *my* treatment, Mr Hacket. This is *my* project. I've done most of the work on it, I don't intend to let others start sticking their noses in where they're not wanted.'

'*Your* treatment. You've worked on this alone then?'

'Yes, for as long as I can remember. Ever since I qualified. It's been mine. My theories, my work. I've seen the results. I know it's successful. You can see the results for yourself, here in Hinkston. Some of them at your school.'

Hacket frowned.

'What do you mean?' he wanted to know.

'I said I'd treated a number of other women over the years. Some of the children they gave birth to are at the school where you teach.'

Hacket sat forward in his seat, his hands clasped together.

'Like who?'

'Phillip Craven. Emma Stokes.'

'Jesus,' murmured Hacket under his breath.

Craven. And he knew that other name too. *Emma.* What the hell had been her surname? *The girl who had been pulling the entrails from the mouse. The one who had slashed open Jo Milton's hand with a scalpel.*

'How old is the girl?' he asked.

'About twelve. A pretty girl. Long black hair,' said Curtis smiling.

Hacket nodded. It *was* her.

'Who else have you treated?' he wanted to know.

'A young couple, recently. Stuart and Michelle Lewis, they have a baby now. The Kirkhams, the couple who own The Bull in town, the hotel. They have a daughter, Paula, thanks to my work. And, as well as the Cravens' and the Stokes' families, there are a number of other children at your school whose mothers I treated. And of course there was Ray Weller.'

Hacket felt the colour draining from his cheeks.

'The man who lived here before us? The one who killed his wife and child then shot himself?'

Curtis nodded.

'A tragedy,' he said, wistfully, a faint smile on his lips. 'She really was such a beautiful child.'

Hacket felt the hairs at the back of his neck slowly rise.

64

'Why did he do it?' Hacket wanted to know. 'Why did Weller kill his family then himself?'

'I'm not a psychiatrist, Mr Hacket,' Curtis said, finishing his tea and setting the cup down. 'I thought you wanted to know about the possibility of your wife having another child, not about the misfortunes of this building's previous occupant.

Hacket looked coldly at the doctor for a moment then nodded.

'Yes, I do,' he said, wearily. 'We both do.'

'When could the treatment start?' Sue wanted to know.

'As soon as you agree to it.'

'You still haven't explained exactly what this treatment is,' Hacket reminded him.

'Well, without going into too much technical and biological detail, it involves an injection into the wall of the uterus,' said Curtis. 'It's as simple as that. There isn't necessarily any need for a local anaesthetic. The whole process is over in less than fifteen minutes.'

'But Sue's fallopian tubes were blocked, how can the egg travel from the ovaries?'

'It doesn't have to.'

Hacket frowned, his look of incredulity turning to one of near mocking. Curtis continued.

'A hormone is injected into the wall of the uterus, it stimulates growth. The foetus gestates in the womb as normal but the fallopian tubes become unnecessary.'

'So it's a kind of artificial insemination?' Hacket said, quietly.

'No. In the case of insemination, sperm is introduced directly into the ovaries. The egg grows there then travels along the fallopian tube to the womb where it grows naturally. As I said earlier, this process eliminates the need for that part of the cycle.'

Hacket shook his head.

'So how is the egg fertilised?'

'By your sperm, within the vagina, as in normal intercourse. The egg is already removed, again by drawing it off using a needle, then replaced in the uterus where it is *then* fertilised. Gestation is accelerated by the second injection which initiates growth.'

'What do you mean "accelerated"?' Hacket said, warily.

'The gestation period is shortened. The time varies according to the individual subject and how well they respond to the drug.'

'It's not possible,' Hacket murmured.

'On the contrary, Mr Hacket, it's not only possible but it works. You can see the examples for yourself. The Craven boy, Emma Stokes and the others I've mentioned to you.'

Silence descended as Hacket struggled to come to terms with what he'd heard and Curtis sat back almost smugly, glancing first at the teacher then at Sue who returned his smile warmly.

Hacket stroked his chin.

'I don't know what to say,' he muttered. 'If this process works then why haven't you done more with it? Brought it to the attention of the medical authorities? It could benefit women all over the country if it works.'

'You still continue to say "*if*", Mr Hacket,' the doctor observed. 'What will it take to convince you? Won't you believe it until you're holding your own child in your arms?'

Hacket swallowed hard.

'I suppose I'm frightened to believe it,' he said, quietly. 'It sounds too easy. *Too* simple. What are the risks to the child?'

'No more than in normal pregnancy.'

'I said I'm willing to take those risks, John,' Sue said, defiantly.

'Well I'm not sure *I* am,' Hacket said, flatly.

Curtis glared at the teacher for a moment.

'You still haven't told me enough.'

'It isn't only your decision,' Sue said, angrily. 'It's me who's got to carry the baby. I'm the one who's got to give birth. I told you, I *need* that child.'

Curtis got to his feet.

'I think it would be best if I left now,' he said, making for the door.

526

Sue hurried after him. Hacket sauntered to the door where he shook hands with Curtis once more.

A chill breeze blew in through the open front door and Hacket felt his skin rise into goose-pimples.

'Take your time and think about what I've said,' Curtis told them, but his eyes were on Hacket when he spoke. 'It's a chance to start again, Mr Hacket. Not many people get that.'

He said goodnight to Sue then turned and headed down the path to his waiting car.

Hacket stepped back inside the house, Sue stood on the step watching as the car disappeared into the night.

When she entered the sitting room, Hacket was sitting in front of the electric fire warming his hands.

'You were rude to him, John,' she said, irritably. 'Like he said, he's offering us another chance. We have to take it.'

Hacket inhaled, held the breath for a moment then let it out in a long sigh.

'Sue, it might be coincidence, maybe I'm overreacting but the kids he's treated ...' He struggled to find the words. 'There's something strange about them.'

'And what about Julie's son, Craig? Is he strange too?' she snapped, choosing to ignore the night Curtis had been called to the boy. 'It's not you that's overreacting, John, it's your imagination. Perhaps you've been a teacher too long, reading books too long. The name of this town is Hinkston not Midwich. These children aren't the children of the damned, they're not artificially created by some mad doctor.' She was angry, the anger mixed with scorn. 'They're the last hope for their parents. Just like Curtis is *our* last hope. She got to her feet and made for the door. 'I'm going to bed, John. If you want to sit up and think then fine, but just think about one thing. I'm having this child whether you want me to or not. And I won't let you stop me.'

65

Curtis drove slowly through the streets of Hinkston, only speeding up slightly when he reached the road that led towards his house.

The massive building was almost invisible in the gloom but for a couple of lights burning in one of the rooms on the first floor. However, as he drew nearer the outline of the house became visible against the black velvet backdrop of night.

The doctor swung his car into the driveway, brought it to a halt before the front door and switched off the engine. He sat for a moment, head bowed, then he swung himself out of the car, locked it and headed for the house.

His footsteps echoed on the polished wood of the hall floor as he entered and, as he made his way towards the sitting room he slowed his pace, glancing towards the stairs.

Listening for any sign of movement from above.

There was none.

The house was silent.

Curtis entered the sitting room, feeling the warmth from the dying embers of the open fire. They still glowed red in the grate and he moved across towards them, warming his hands close to the coals. In the red light which they cast it looked as though his face had been splashed with blood.

'What did she say?'

The voice came from behind him, from the high-backed leather chair which stood close to the fire. Curtis hadn't seen the figure sitting in it when he'd entered the room and the words startled him momentarily. He exhaled deeply, looking at his companion for a moment before once again turning his back and warming his hands.

'The woman is enthusiastic,' he said. 'She *has* been from the beginning. It's her husband who's resisting.'

Curtis got to his feet, crossed to the ornate drinks cabinet and poured himself a whiskey. He raised a glass, inviting the other occupant of the room to join him.

The figure nodded and Curtis handed him a drink.

'How much does he know?' the figure asked.

'He knows about Weller,' Curtis announced, then he swallowed a large measure of the whiskey.

'You expected him to, didn't you? A murder and a suicide in a small town like this are bound to be common knowledge.'

Curtis raised his eyebrows quizzically.

'Murders but not disappearances?' he mused.

'Hacket knows that Weller killed his family,' the figure said. 'What he mustn't find out is *why*.'

66

He stood beside the bed for what seemed like an eternity, watching the steady rise and fall of her chest as she slept.

Finally Hacket undressed and slipped into bed beside Sue. He lay back, one arm across his forehead, gazing at the ceiling, listening to Sue's shallow breathing.

Could what Curtis said really be true?

Was it even feasible?

Hacket exhaled deeply and rubbed his face.

He knew that the child was important to Sue. No, important was the wrong word. It had become an obsession. He wondered if he could stop her from undergoing Curtis' treatment now even if he wanted to.

But did he want to?

He knew the child meant everything to her and he also knew that it did offer their only chance of returning to anything like a normal existence. To be given the chance to start again. It was a chance which *he* dare not forego either.

But the risks.

529

Small compared to the joy which would come with the birth of the child.

What exactly was the treatment?

Curtis had described it. A form of artificial insemination. Only this was less clinical, less mechanical.

The foetus grows at an accelerated rate. Why?

Hacket sat up in bed and looked down at Sue. He reached across and gently pulled a strand of hair away from her mouth.

The thought of the child meant everything to her. He had no right to deprive her of that joy.

The children born because of Curtis' treatment were violent.

Only the ones you know about, he told himself. *Just two out of possibly dozens. It could be coincidence.*

It *had* to be coincidence.

'Oh God,' he murmured, irritably. The questions and queries could torment him forever if he thought about them. The only thing that mattered was that they had a glimmer of hope.

The chance of another child.

The risks . . .

'To hell with it,' he whispered to himself and swung out of bed.

It was then that the phone rang.

Hacket glanced down at the clock.

11.56 p.m.

He looked at Sue but the persistent drone of the phone didn't seem to have disturbed her.

It kept ringing.

Hacket got to his feet and padded down the stairs, shivering slightly from the cold as he reached for the receiver.

'Hello,' he said, quietly.

Nothing.

'Hello,' he repeated, wearily.

Silence.

Hacket put down the phone and shook his head.

Wrong number no doubt he thought as he turned and ascended the stairs once more.

He was half way up when the phone rang again.

530

'For Christ's sake,' he muttered and retraced his steps, snatching up the receiver once again.

'Yes,' he hissed.

No answer.

'Look, if this is a joke.'

His angry protestations were cut short.

'John Hacket?' said the voice at the other end of the line.

It was the teacher's turn to stand there in silence.

He didn't recognise the voice, hardly surprising, really, from the utterance of just two words.

'Is that John Hacket?' the voice repeated.

'Yes, who is this?'

Click.

The line went dead.

Hacket held the receiver away from his ear as if it were some kind of venomous reptile then, slowly, he replaced it. He stood looking at the phone for a moment, as if expecting it to ring again. When it didn't he made his way slowly back up to bed.

67

The smell reminded Sue of a hospital. The strong odour of disinfectant. A scent that was both reassuring and repulsive.

Sue thought of her father, lying alone in that hospital room, waiting to die. It was this smell which must have filled his nostrils for so long.

The memory came unexpectedly, all the more painful for that and she tried to push it from her mind. She sat in the waiting room of Curtis' surgery, nervously clasping and unclasping her hands, glancing alternately up at the wall-clock above the receptionist's desk and at the door which led through to the surgery.

She seemed to have been waiting hours, although she knew that barely five minutes had slipped by since she'd arrived and the receptionist had retreated into the surgery proper to tell Curtis of her arrival.

531

Sue wasn't sure what was making her more nervous, the thought of the treatment or the nagging doubt that it would fail.

She brushed the hair from her face, noticing as she did that her hand was shaking.

Hacket had wanted to come with her but she had assured him she would be fine alone. She trusted doctor Curtis. Felt safe in his hands.

'*Come and see me*'.

The door to the surgery opened and the receptionist ushered her through, finally leaving her alone in the office. Although it looked different from the other times she had visited. For one thing there was no sign of Curtis. Sue saw a door leading out of surgery and she heard footsteps approaching that door. A second later the doctor entered. He was wearing a white lab coat over his clothes but that was the only item of protective clothing in evidence. He greeted Sue warmly and invited her to follow him through the door which she did.

It opened onto the cellar.

The white-washed walls almost glowed so dazzling bright were they painted. In the centre of the room was a couch, covered by a white sheet and, beside it, a trolley which sported a dizzying array of surgical implements.

Sue swallowed hard as she saw them, and glanced anxiously at Curtis, who merely smiled and led her to the lower level.

It was unexpectedly warm down there and she could hear an almost monotonous drone of something which she guessed might be a generator. Access to it though was hidden by a series of screens which surrounded the couch.

'How are you feeling?' Curtis asked, smiling warmly, and Sue, once again, was captivated by his eyes. She felt as if she were drowning in them. Floating.

'A little nervous,' she confessed.

'Then the sooner we get started the better,' the doctor said. 'Are you warm enough? I want you to be comfortable. The procedure doesn't take more than about five minutes.' He touched her arm softly. 'And I'm sure you'll find it worthwhile.'

She smiled, relaxing visibly at his touch.

'If you could undress for me,' he said, quietly.

Sue nodded almost imperceptibly. The words were spoken slowly, almost tenderly. The words of a lover, not a physician. He handed her a white gown from another of the trolleys which she laid on the couch. Then she began unbuttoning her blouse, glancing at Curtis as she did, surprised that she didn't feel the slightest twinge of embarrassment.

Curtis turned his back as she pulled the blouse free of her jeans. He bent over the trolley, inspecting a number of syringes which were laid out, it appeared, in descending order of size. The largest was over eight inches long, the smallest no bigger than his index finger.

'Is your husband still opposed to this treatment?' Curtis wanted to know, his back still to her.

'He wasn't really opposed to it,' Sue informed him, unhooking her bra. 'He was worried because he didn't know all the details.'

'I told him as much as I could.'

'I know that.'

'Does it worry you?' Curtis asked, turning round.

Sue stood before him, naked from the waist up but she made no attempt to hide herself. Instead she stood facing the doctor, almost willing him to inspect her breasts, aware of the tightening and swelling of her nipples.

'I want a child,' she whispered, removing her shoes. 'I don't care what it takes.' As she spoke she began to unfasten the zip of her jeans, easing them down over her slender hips until she stood before him in just her panties.

The droning of the generator continued, a low hum which matched Sue's increasingly deep breathing.

As Curtis turned away from her for a second she was aware of the tingles running up and down her spine, of the growing excitement which was spreading through her body. As she prepared to remove her panties she felt the wetness between her legs.

Completely naked she swung herself up onto the couch.

Her breathing was coming in shallow gasps, her chest heaving almost expectantly.

'Slide your bottom forward to the edge of the couch and open your legs,' Curtis said, softly, laying one hand on her thigh to aid her in that simple manoeuvre. As he moved between her legs he could smell the musky odour of her sex. She shuffled around, gyrating her hips slightly, trying to slow the pace of her breathing.

'I'm going to give you a local anaesthetic,' he told her, quietly. 'Just relax.'

She eased her legs further apart, inviting him to move closer. Sue was gazing at the ceiling, she didn't see Curtis reach for one of the smaller syringes.

With infinite care he parted her outer labial lips, already swollen and red, slick with the moisture of her excitement. They had parted like the petals of a flower and he saw her stomach muscles contract as he gently moved the needle closer to her vagina.

The steel point slid easily into the tumescent flesh and Sue sucked in a deep breath as it penetrated her, holding that breath as Curtis pushed on the plunger, emptying the contents of the shaft into her. Then he withdrew the glistening needle carefully and laid it on the trolley.

'You might feel a little groggy,' he told her. 'If you do just let yourself fall asleep. There's nothing to worry about.'

She smiled.

'I know,' she whispered, closing her eyes, waiting for the next, deeper penetration.

'This time,' Curtis breathed and brought the largest of the syringes closer to her slippery cleft, pushing the needle inside until he felt it press against the spongy tissue of her endometrium. Sue arched her back slightly as the syringe was pushed deeper into her uterus and she felt fluid filling her. Felt a warmth spreading up from her thighs and across her belly. Her nipples ached, such was their stiffness, and she brushed one breast with her hand, suppressing a gasp as her fingers raked against the hard bud.

Curtis remained between her thighs, squeezing the last drops of fluid from the thick container, finally withdrawing it carefully.

Sue let out a long breath, her eyes flickering shut.

Curtis looked down at her and smiled.

'It's done,' he told her, watching as a smile spread across her face.

He reached for the gown and gently laid it over her.

'Rest for a little while,' the doctor said, standing over her until he saw that she was slipping off to sleep. Then he pulled off the rubber gloves he'd been wearing and tossed them into a nearby waste bin, washing his hands in the sink at one corner of the cellar.

He had his back to the door when it opened.

Curtis only heard the footsteps behind him, moving towards the couch.

Towards Sue.

He turned slowly to see the other figure standing over her.

They exchanged glances and Curtis merely nodded, a silent affirmation of what the other wondered. Like the mute answer to an unasked question.

The figure reached for the gown and pulled it up, inspecting Sue's body, gazing at her full rounded breasts, flat stomach and the small triangle of light hair between her legs. Legs which were still slightly parted.

Curtis, still drying his hands, joined the newcomer, who was still looking appreciatively at Sue's naked body.

'It won't be long now,' Curtis said, quietly.

The other nodded.

68

'That's about the tenth time you've checked your watch and we've only been out here for ten minutes,' Jo Milton said, smiling.

Hacket shrugged and dug his hands in his pockets as they walked.

'I promise not to look again,' he said, smiling.

All around them the sound of children playing, shouting, arguing, laughing and sometimes fighting merged into one endless cacophony of noise. Break-time, twenty minutes in which to unleash the furies built up during class, thought Hacket looking round at the children.

A group of boys were kicking a ball against a wall to his right. To his left three or four girls were standing around peering at a magazine. One of them looked at Hacket as he passed and smiled. The others dissolved into a chorus of giggles.

'Seems you've got an admirer,' said Jo, chuckling.

Hacket shrugged.

'Catch them young, that's my motto,' he told her. 'What about you, Jo? Any entanglements?'

'A boyfriend you mean?' She shook her head and sipped the tea she was carrying. 'Nothing serious.'

Hacket glanced at her, struck, as he had been at their first meeting, by her good looks. Her face was full but not fat, her pointed chin making her look much more thin-featured than she actually was. Her high cheek bones accentuated the look.

Was this how it had started with Nikki? A casual conversation?

Hacket tried to push the thoughts aside, but they persisted. Jo was very attractive indeed, and as she looked at him he found himself gazing deep into her eyes, stumbling through the clichés to find one that described them.

Inviting eyes?

He'd played this game before.

Come to bed eyes?

He forced himself to look away from her, glancing around the play-ground once again at the noisy throng of children.

'How long have you been married, John?' she asked.

'Five years,' he told her, again avoiding her eyes.

'Happy?'

'What makes you ask that?'

'It's an innocent enough question isn't it?' she said, defensively.

Well go on then, tell her, his mind prompted. *Tell her you're happily married. It's just that you wouldn't refuse if she was available would you?*

Or *would* you?

'Jo, can I ask you something,' he said. 'In your official capacity.' She smiled.

'That does sound grand, John. What is it?'

'Is it possible for a foetus to gestate inside the womb without having travelled along the fallopian tubes?'

'Is that a trick question?' she chuckled. 'What's the next one? Who won the FA cup last year?'

'I'm serious. You're a biologist.'

'I *teach* biology, there's a difference.'

'But is it possible?'

536

'Through certain forms of artificial insemination yes.'

'You mean that the egg is planted directly into the womb?'

She nodded.

'Is it fertilised first?' he wanted to know. 'I mean, the egg couldn't be placed in the womb then fertilised by normal means?'

'No,' she said, flatly. 'There are certain nutrients and proteins found in the ovaries and the fallopian tube which are essential to the development of the foetus.' She looked hard at him. 'If you don't mind me saying, John, this is a little *deep* for this time of the day isn't it? We're doing playground duty not "Mastermind".'

'Just humour me will you? What about the growth rate of the foetus, is there any way it could be speeded up? To cut the gestation period for instance?'

'Well, theoretically, yes.'

Hacket looked at her, stopped walking and gripped her arm.

'How?' he wanted to know.

Some of the children nearby saw him grab Jo's arm and turned to look but the two teachers moved on after a moment or two.

'How could it be done?' he repeated.

'Growth is regulated by the pituitary gland. Too little causes dwarfism, too much causes the opposite and disfiguring disease called acromegaly. The gland secretes the hormones that regulate growth.' She looked puzzled. 'I don't know what you're getting at, John.'

'Could the gestation period be altered by these pituitary hormones?' he wanted to know.

'Yes, but no one has ever done that.'

Hacket sucked in an almost painful breath.

'Why do you ask?' Jo persisted.

Hacket didn't answer.

All he was aware of were Curtis' words ringing in his ears.

'This is *my* project, Mr Hacket. *My* treatment.'

69

He pulled a piece of the scab from his hand, picking away at the crusted flesh until it came free.

His eyes, however, did not leave the playground.

So many children, thought Ronald Mills, smiling.

They ranged in age from eight up to about fifteen, he thought, watching as they cavorted noisily around in the school yard.

A tall privet hedge formed a boundary between the school field and the road on one side but Mills could see easily over this barrier as he walked along, glancing at the children as he did.

Groups of boys were playing football, girls were skipping or chasing each other or merely standing around talking.

Mills stopped as he caught sight of two young girls no more than nine years old. The first of them had gleaming blonde hair, so pure it looked almost silver. It reached to the middle of her back and, as she stood talking to her friend, she would occasionally toss the mane of hair with one hand. Her companion was slightly darker and a little taller.

Mills smiled as he gazed at them, feeling the first stirrings in his groin. He slipped one hand into his pocket, rubbing his stiffening penis.

Across the road from the school there was a row of houses, each one painted white with tedious uniformity. It was from the bedroom window of one of these houses that a woman watched Mills.

He stood staring at the children for a moment or two then moved on, looking behind him as he did so.

He saw the woman standing at the window.

She froze as she realised he'd seen her, attempting to duck back behind her curtain, but Mills merely stood gazing up at the window, as if challenging her to re-appear.

She didn't.

After a moment or two he moved on, glancing one last time at the two children in the field beyond.

It took him less than fifteen minutes to wander around the entire perimeter of the school and he came to the gates where he had begun his vigil earlier. There he lit up a cigarette and continued gazing into the playground.

He recognised Hacket immediately.

The teacher was with a woman, walking slowly, talking to her.

Mills sucked hard on his cigarette and watched Hacket with the same determined intent as a predator watching its prey.

He didn't know how long he stood there, but finally the sound of a bell disturbed his observations.

The children flooded towards the school buildings, Hacket and the woman were caught up in the flow and, in moments, they too were gone.

The playground was empty again.

Mills finished his cigarette then turned and headed back to his car.

He was smiling as he slid behind the wheel.

70

The house was in silence when he entered.

Hacket paused by the front door, listening for any noise from within but, upon hearing nothing, he gently closed the door and walked into the sitting room.

Sue was lying on the sofa, her eyes closed.

Hacket looked at her worriedly and immediately crossed to her, kneeling beside her, shaking her gently to rouse her. She opened her eyes, looked up at him and smiled.

'Are you OK?' he asked, softly.

She nodded and sat up, rubbing her temple.

'Just a bit of a headache,' she told him.

'How did it go this morning?' he wanted to know. 'With Curtis? I thought you might have phoned when you got back.'

'I didn't want to disturb you. Besides, there was nothing out of the ordinary. Everything was fine. I *feel* fine.'

'How long did it take?'

'I was back home within two hours. Doctor Curtis told me to take it easy so I did. I must have dropped off.' She began to rise. 'I'll get the dinner.'

'No, Sue, leave it. Just sit,' Hacket told her, crossing to the drinks cabinet. He poured himself a large whisky and Sue a Martini. Then he sat beside her on the sofa, easing one arm round her shoulders.

'What happened?' he wanted to know.

'It was simple, just like Curtis said it would be.' She told him what had happened. The injection. The period of sleep which followed. Hacket listened intently, sipping his drink occasionally.

'Did Curtis say anything more about the nature of the treatment? What it involved?'

'He told us about it the other evening, John,' she said, wearily.

'He didn't tell us everything,' Hacket protested.

'You're never satisfied are you?' she snapped. 'Why do you need to know so much? Surely the most important thing is that we can have another child.'

'I don't like the idea of you being used as a guinea pig.'

'Don't be ridiculous. You speak as if I'm the first he's treated. We know the treatment works.'

'Yes, we just don't know what the treatment *is*.'

She shook her head.

'I've been thinking about it,' Hacket continued. 'I was talking to one of the other teachers today.'

'About *this*?' Sue blurted, angrily. 'It's *our* business, John.'

'Calm down, Sue, I just needed to know a few things. I think I might know what Curtis is doing. What some parts of the treatment are. One of the biology teachers, Jo, she said . . .'

'*She*?' Sue interrupted. 'It's always a woman isn't it? You always seem to get on better with women, John. Is it easier to talk about your problems to a woman than another man?'

He knew where this was leading.

'She was better qualified to answer my questions,' he said, irritably.

540

'Well, a teacher is a step up from a secretary isn't it?' said Sue, acidly.

'For Christ's sake.'

'A little talk. Is that how it started before? With the other one?'

Hacket glared at her, his anger mixed with the guilt which still plagued him. He resented Sue for making him feel that guilt again. He got up and poured himself another drink, his back to her.

'Are we going to talk about this or not?' he asked.

'What? You mean about what your lady friend told you today? Or about our baby? Except you seem to be more interested in your little chat.'

Hacket turned slowly.

'I don't want to argue, Sue. Especially when we've nothing to argue about. I just want you to hear what I've got to say.'

She exhaled deeply.

'Go on.'

'The treatment which Curtis perfected, from what he told us, it sounds like some kind of growth drug. He said the foetus would develop at an increased rate. I think I know what he's doing. What he's using.'

Sue looked on impassively.

'The drug must contain some traces of pituitary secretion in order to cause that acceleration.'

'So what if it does?' she said, flatly.

'The baby could be affected by it. If the dose was wrong it could be too small, perhaps even deformed.'

'And your *friend* told you this, did she?' said Sue, her voice heavy with sarcasm.

'I mentioned it to her, she gave me her opinion,' he said.

'I don't care, John. I knew the risks, we both did. Do you honestly think that a man of Curtis' expertise is going to give me the wrong dose? He said himself he'd treated other women. He's not some mad scientist from a bloody horror film, he's a trained doctor and I don't care what your friend says. I'd trust Curtis with my life. Mine and our baby's.'

'Just try to see my point of view,' he asked. 'I love you. You're all I have since Lisa died. I don't want to lose you too.'

Sue got to her feet and headed for the hallway.

'If you don't want to lose me, then don't stand in my way,' she said. 'Let me have this baby.'

He heard her footsteps as she climbed the stairs.

Hacket waited another moment then poured himself some more whisky, downing the contents of the tumbler in one gulp.

He suddenly felt very alone.

71

Ronald Mills pulled the .38 from beneath the pillow and flipped out the cylinder, turning it slowly. Then he snapped it back into position and pushed the gun back out of sight.

Whenever he left the hotel he would take the gun with him, stuffed into the pocket of his jacket. The knife he would slide into his belt but now, he didn't intend leaving The Bull for the rest of the evening so he left the weapons beneath the pillow.

He crossed to the window which looked out onto the main street of Hinkston and peered down at the dozen or so people passing by. It was late, almost 10.30 p.m., the cinema down the street had emptied out about fifteen minutes earlier and the disco didn't open during the week, so the street was quiet.

Mills glanced across at the phone beside his bed.

There was a knock on the bedroom door and he opened it.

Paula Kirkham stood before him holding a tray.

She smiled broadly, shaking her head gently, allowing her long hair to cascade over her shoulders. She wore no bra beneath her T-shirt and Mills noticed that her nipples were straining against the material.

He stepped back to let her into the room, watching as she set the tray of food down on the bedside table.

'Will there be anything else?' she asked, smiling.

'No,' said Mills, holding the door open, as if to emphasise the fact that he wanted her out.

She looked most put out and wiggled past him, glancing briefly at him. He closed the door and she heard him lock it.

Paula hesitated outside the door, ear pressed close to it.

The man didn't seem attracted to her.

He'd been a guest at the hotel for the last five days, keeping himself to himself, ignoring the other guests and her own advances. She didn't think too much of him. Ugly bastard really.

But, he was single.

Alone.

He was a perfect choice.

Just like the man before him.

She struggled to remember his name.

Jennings, that was it. She smiled as she remembered.

The ones before Jennings she could *not* recall.

There had been too many.

She stood for a moment longer outside the door then slowly made her way along the corridor to her own room.

Mills heard her footsteps as she wandered away, only then did he turn his attention to the plate of food which she'd brought him. He nibbled at one of the sandwiches, his eyes flicking back and forth towards the phone every now and then. Finally he pushed the remains of the sandwich into his mouth and reached for the receiver.

Pulling the number from the pocket of his jacket he dialled.

And waited.

'Come on you fucker,' he murmured, listening to the purring at the other end.

The phone was finally picked up.

It was a woman's voice on the other end.

Mills sat listening to her, his breathing subdued, the smile spreading across his face.

'Who is this?' she asked.

He put the phone down.

Another five minutes and he called again.

This time he recognised Hacket's voice.

'Who's there?' the teacher snapped.

Mills sat on the edge of the bed, the phone held slightly away from his ear.

'Can you hear me?' Hacket rasped.

Mills put down the phone.

He chuckled, the grin slowly fading.

The game was nearly over.

Hacket's time had come.

Mills held the knife up before him.

And then there was the woman.

Paula Kirkham stood naked outside the door, her breathing low and rapid, like an animal in the heat.

She glared at the door as if trying to see through it to the man beyond.

To Ronald Mills.

She pressed herself close to the cold wood, feeling her nipples stiffen as she rubbed herself gently against the smooth paintwork, feeling the moistness between her legs.

Her mouth hung open, streamers of sputum dripping from it as she salivated madly.

She wiped her mouth with the back of her hand and smiled.

72

She heard movement on the landing.

Julie Clayton sat up, her ears alert for the slightest sound.

Footsteps on the carpet.

She swung herself out of bed, jabbing her husband as she did so.

Mike rolled onto his back and groaned, rubbing his eyes.

'What is it?' he croaked, seeing Julie pull on her dressing gown. He glanced at the clock and saw that it was almost 3.36 a.m. 'Shit.'

'Mike, hurry,' she said, moving towards the bedroom door.

The expression on her face told him how frightened she was. He hauled himself out of bed, following her out onto the landing.

She was approaching Craig's room, aware of the sounds coming from within.

'Oh God,' murmured Mike. 'Not again.'

Stuart Lewis stood over the baby, looking down, his eyes fixed to the blazing stare which seemed to pin him as surely as light draws a moth. He could not look away from his son.

The baby was gurgling loudly, rocking itself back and forth in its cot frenziedly, grasping at the sides with its tiny fingers.

Michelle joined him, reaching for the baby but Stuart put out an arm to hold her back.

'He needs me, Stuart,' she protested but her husband merely remained where he was, looking down at his child, watching as the boy suddenly stopped thrashing about and lay still, gazing up at his parents. His eyes flicking back and forth from one to the other.

Lewis shook his head slowly.

'It's not *us* he needs,' he said, quietly.

And she understood.

Elaine Craven picked up the phone immediately it rang. Despite the fact that it was so early in the morning she knew who it would be, and she was not wrong.

The voice at the other end belonged to Patricia Stokes.

It was her daughter, Emma, she said.

Elaine said she understood.

Patricia wasn't sure what to do.

Elaine tried to reassure her, touching her own bandaged arm as she spoke.

Upstairs she could hear the shouts and snarls.

She spoke calmly and slowly to Patricia who seemed to relax a little, the longer the conversation went on. Finally she said goodbye and returned to her own problem.

To her Emma.

Elaine waited by the phone a moment longer then she took a deep breath and made her way back up the stairs.

It had happened so quickly this time.

The shouting continued.

As she reached the landing she had to steady herself against the bannister, noticing that her hands were shaking.

She thought she had become used to it by now, but, somehow, the fear still remained.

73

She hadn't mentioned the pain to Hacket.

Hadn't thought it worth talking about the silent twinges which she felt around her vagina, especially during their lovemaking.

But now, as Sue Hacket reached for the can on the shelf before her, she sucked in a deep breath, reacting as if she had been punched. The pain was sudden and severe. She gripped the shopping trolley for a second, waiting for the discomfort to subside, which, thankfully, it did. A woman passed and glanced at her, noticing the look on Sue's face and, for a moment, Sue thought the woman was going to stop, but she merely smiled and carried on with her own shopping.

Sue dropped the can into her trolley and walked on, parading up and down each aisle, filling the trolley, trying to ignore the stabs of pain telling herself that they were lessening.

Curtis had said nothing about side-effects. Nothing about pain. If she still felt as bad when she reached home she would call him. Visit him if necessary.

However, as she reached the check-out the pains did indeed seem to be diminishing in severity. Sue ran a hand across her belly almost unconsciously as the woman ahead of her packed her groceries into a succession of carrier bags. Sue shuffled uncomfortably as she waited her turn, brushing a speck of dirt from the leg of her jeans.

She waited for the pain to return.

It didn't.

She began unloading her shopping onto the conveyor belt.

If she'd mentioned the pains to Hacket he would have panicked, she thought to herself. He would have started complaining about the treatment again. Why couldn't he just be happy in the knowledge that they were to have another child? Why all the questions and doubts?

She packed the groceries away then paid the cashier, using the trolley to transport the goods out to the car.

As she unlocked the back of the car the pain struck her once more.

A deep burning sensation between her legs and she gripped the trolley for a second until it subsided.

Sue put the groceries in the back of the car then turned to return the trolley.

The man seemed to loom from thin air.

He was carrying an armful of shopping which promptly fell from his grip as he collided with Sue.

'I'm sorry,' she said, dropping to her knees to help him gather up the spilled groceries.

Her own handbag had also fallen in the collision and she scrabbled to retrieve its spilled contents.

'It was my fault,' said the man, shoving tins back into the shopping bag. 'I wasn't looking where I was going.'

The combination of food and the contents of her handbag had rolled for several feet around the car, some beneath it, and it took about five minutes to pick up everything. Everything except a couple of squashed peaches which had fallen from the man's bag. He looked down at them and shrugged.

'I was eating too much fruit anyway,' he said, wistfully.

Sue smiled, the expression twisting slightly as she felt more pain.

'Are you OK?' the man asked, seeing her wince.

She nodded.

'Thank you, yes. I'll be fine.' She managed another smile. 'Sorry again about . . .' she motioned to his squashed fruit.

'No problem,' he told her, smiling as she climbed into the Metro and started the engine.

He was still smiling as she drove off.

He watched her turn a corner and disappear and, as she did he slid a hand into his pocket and pulled out the prize he'd taken from her handbag in all the confusion.

547

The purse looked small in his large fist.

Ronald Mills wondered how long it would be before she realised it was gone.

74

It was happening too fast.

It was as if someone had pressed the fast-forward button on life, and now events were moving at break-neck speed, faster than he could comprehend.

The ambulance, its siren blaring loudly, took the corner so fast it almost overturned.

Hacket gripped one edge of the stretcher to steady himself, with the other hand he held onto Sue's outstretched fingers. Her face was milk white, a thin sheen of perspiration covering her. She had her eyes closed tightly, her forehead wrinkling as each fresh spasm of pain racked her body.

'Isn't there anything you can give her?' Hacket asked the ambulanceman who rode in the back of the vehicle with them. But the uniformed man merely shook his head and looked on impassively.

'We're almost at the hospital,' he said, flatly, glancing at his watch.

Sue gripped Hacket's hand more tightly and he felt helpless to comfort her. All he could do was to wipe the sweat from her face with his handkerchief.

'It won't be long now,' he murmured. 'Hold on.'

Jesus, he felt so fucking useless. There was nothing he could do to ease her suffering. Nothing to stop the pain.

So much pain.

Her body stiffened then relaxed, as if someone were jabbing her with a cattle prod. The spasms became more frequent, more severe until finally she shouted aloud from the pain which raged inside her swollen belly.

Hacket pulled the sheet down and looked at her stomach. It was

548

bloated and, as he watched, he could see the skin gently undulating.

'How much further?' he rasped, glaring at the ambulanceman.

'Not far,' the man said, also glancing at Sue.

'John.' Her voice rose in volume, dissolving into a scream of pain.

Hacket saw the first droplets of blood dribble from between her legs and she stiffened, her body jerking every few seconds.

She began to breathe rapidly and loudly, holding Hacket's hand so tightly it seemed she would break his fingers.

'It's starting,' she gasped, raising her legs and opening them.

'Help her,' Hacket snarled at the uniformed man, his face pale as he saw a steady flow of crimson beginning to pump from Sue's distended vagina. The outer lips seemed to swell and open like a blossoming flower and the sheet beneath her was stained by her life fluid as the contractions became more savage.

The ambulanceman struggled towards the far end of the vehicle, almost overbalancing as it took another corner doing over fifty. He retrieved some oxygen and stuck the plastic mask over Sue's face, but she merely pushed it away, beyond help now, knowing that there was no turning back.

A searing pain filled her lower body and she felt an incredible pressure building between her legs.

Hacket held her hand, his eyes rivetted to her swollen vagina.

A moment later he saw something white appear between the folds of flesh. Something white and bulbous.

The baby's head.

Pieces of placenta were draped over the skull like bleeding streamers, some of which dangled from Sue's vagina as the child fought to free itself.

The head burst free.

Hacket sucked in a deep breath, watching as the torso began to emerge.

'Nearly finished,' he said. gripping Sue's hand even more tightly. 'Nearly . . .'

The words trailed away and he felt the bile rising in his throat, felt his eyes throbbing in their sockets.

The child had a large hump on its back, just below the nape of its neck.

A hump large enough . . .

Hacket shook his head in horrified disbelief as he saw the child emerge.

Sue was still contracting her muscles, as if anxious to expel the child from her body.

The ambulanceman looked on, his face also pale, his eyes wide.

The hump on the child's back wasn't skin and muscle.

It was bone.

Thick bone.

A second head.

The eyes had formed but where the mouth should have been was a gash. No lips, just a rent across the lower face. But the eyes were open, blinking away the blood and fragments of placenta which coated it.

And, in that brief instant before he finally surrendered to his revulsion and vomited, Hacket noticed that the obscene hole which passed for a mouth was curling up at either side.

The eyes fixed him in a blazing stare.

The second head was smiling at him.

He sat bolt upright in bed, his breath coming in gasps, his heart thudding madly against his ribs.

He turned to look at Sue, surprised to find her sitting up looking at him.

She was smiling.

75

Hacket wiped a hand across his face and sighed, the last vestiges of the nightmare gradually slipping away.

'Jesus,' he murmured. 'I had a bad dream. About you and the baby.'

She held his gaze for a moment then slowly leant across and kissed him, her tongue flicking against the hard edges of his tongue before sliding into the warm moistness beyond. Hacket responded, feeling her arms glide around his shoulders. He lay down beside her, raising one knee so that his thigh was rubbing against her vagina. She was already wet and he felt her moisture dampen his leg as he ground it against her, his own movements matched by her slow rhythmic thrusting. She moaned in his arms as he allowed one hand to find her right breast, teasing the nipple between his thumb and forefinger, then kissing the swollen bud for a moment before transferring his attention to her left breast.

Sue reached down and cupped his testicles, rubbing gently, grazing the base of his shaft with the nail of her index finger.

Hacket felt a familiar warmth beginning to spread around his groin.

Sue arched her back as he slid down the bed, his tongue flicking across her nipples while his probing fingers gently outlined the edges of her vaginal lips, parting them, spreading the tumescent flesh like the petals of a musky flower.

'Love me,' she murmured, her eyes closed.

Hacket felt her hands on his back. Felt her nails raking his skin.

'Jesus,' he hissed as she pulled her nails hard across his shoulder.

She raised the hand before her and saw the tiny pieces of his flesh hanging from her nails. She smiled down at him and Hacket looked into her eyes.

He could feel the grazes on his shoulder.

The tiny dribble of blood from the four places she had scraped him.

He slid back up the bed, kissing her breasts again, this time returning to her mouth. They kissed feverishly, his tongue plunging deep into her mouth.

She took his bottom lip between her teeth, sucking gently, then chewing.

She bit hard.

'Sue, for Christ's sake,' he hissed, drawing back. He put a finger to his lip and found that there was blood dribbling from it.

'Please, John, just love me,' she gasped, a note of pleading in her voice, 'Like you were doing before.'

Hacket hesitated a moment then slid down her body once more, blood from his cut lip staining her breasts and belly as his tongue flicked over the warm flesh. He probed inside her navel with his

551

tongue, slowing his pace as he drew nearer to the spot he sought. The tightly curled hair between her legs through which his fingers were already gliding. He withdrew one from her vagina, drawing a glistening trail across her belly with her own moisture. She gasped and pushed him further down towards her burning desire.

Hacket licked her belly again, tasting her wetness which he had smeared there.

The skin of her stomach rose a fraction beneath his tongue.

At first he thought it was a muscular contraction but, when it happened a second time he sat up, looking down at her belly.

'What's wrong?' she said, quietly. 'Don't stop now.'

Hacket rubbed the palm of his hand gently over her stomach.

He felt the movement beneath his palm.

Like . .

Like what?

Like the first movements of a growing child?

'It's impossible,' said Hacket, as if in answer to his own thoughts.

'John, what's wrong?' she wanted to know, watching as he moved away slightly, his eyes still on her stomach.

Was this another dream?

'I felt something,' he said. 'Like . .' He was struggling for the words, aware of how ridiculous it sounded. 'Like a baby moving.'

'Isn't it wonderful?' she beamed.

'Sue, it's not possible,' he snapped. 'Curtis treated you two days ago.'

'*Accelerated growth.*'

Hacket shook his head. No, this wasn't real. The foetus couldn't possibly have developed at such incredible speed. He had imagined it. Yes, that was the answer. He had imagined it.

Her stomach moved slightly again.

Sue pressed her fingers to the spot and smiled.

'Aren't you happy, John?' she said, smiling broadly. 'I am.'

'This isn't normal, Sue. I don't know what Curtis has done to you but it's not right . . .'

She cut him short.

'I'll tell you what he's done,' she snapped. 'He's given me what you never could give me. He's given me hope.'

552

'At least let another doctor examine you,' Hacket pleaded. 'There could be complications. Something could have gone wrong.'

'That's what you want isn't it?' she snarled. 'You want something to go wrong. You want me to lose this child don't you?'

'Don't be ridiculous, Sue. I'm worried about your health.'

'No you're not. You just don't want me to have another child. Well I'll make sure I don't lose this one. It was your fault Lisa died,' she hissed, hatred in her eyes. '*You* killed her.'

'Sue,' he said, his own anger building.

'If it hadn't been for you she'd still be here now.'

'Drop it,' he told her.

'If not for you and your whore.'

'I mean it,' he said, angrily. 'Shut up.'

'You killed our first child, I won't let you kill this one.'

'SHUT UP.'

He acted instinctively, not even realising what he was doing.

Hacket struck his wife a stinging back-hand blow across the face.

She fell back on the bed, glaring up at him.

Despite his anger he felt the remorse immediately.

'Oh God, I'm sorry,' he whispered, moving towards her.

'Get away,' she roared. 'Leave me alone. Leave me and my baby alone.'

Hacket looked at her. The blazing eyes, her hair coiled around her face and shoulders like damp reptilian tails. She looked like some modern-day Gorgon.

'What's happening to you, Sue?' he asked, quietly, his voice cracking. 'I'm losing you again and I don't want that.'

'Then stay out of my fucking way,' she snarled, getting to her feet. She tugged a sheet from the bed and wrapped it around her.

Hacket could only watch as she padded towards the door.

He heard her cross the landing then heard the door of the spare room slam shut.

Alone, he knelt on the bed, head bowed.

As if in prayer.

76

It was almost noon when she heard the knock on the front door.

Sue frowned and got to her feet, lowering the volume on the stereo as she passed.

It was too early for Hacket to be back for lunch. For one thing he hardly ever left the school during the lunch hour and, also, he had his key. He'd have no need to knock. She wasn't expecting Julie until later that afternoon.

She reached the front door and opened it.

The man who stood there looked vaguely familiar to her.

'Mrs Hacket?' he asked.

She nodded, somewhat tentatively.

'Yours I believe,' said the man and held out his hand.

Sue smiled as she saw her purse cradled in the palm of the visitor.

'You dropped it the other day when we bumped into each other,' said Ronald Mills, smiling. 'I'm afraid I looked through it in the hope of finding your address. I wanted to return it to you.'

'You're very kind,' said Sue, beaming. 'I thought I'd lost it.'

Mills shrugged, smiled even more broadly and handed her the purse.

As he did, Sue noticed the tattoo on his hand. The rough design, the discoloured flesh and the raw skin beneath where the scab had been picked away. He turned to leave but she stopped him.

'Look, I really am grateful. I don't know how to thank you,' she said. 'Would a cup of tea be enough? It doesn't seem like much of a reward, but . . .'

'That would be ample reward, Mrs Hacket,' said Mills, holding up a hand. 'Thank you.'

He followed her inside, his smile fading briefly as she turned her back on him.

The knife felt heavy jammed into his belt.

They exchanged pleasantries about the weather. He told her his name was Neville, that he was visiting relatives in Hinkston.

As he sipped his tea he glanced around the sitting room.

A photo of a little girl on the sideboard.

A little girl he recognised.

He felt the beginnings of an erection at the recollection of how close he had been to that girl. How close. How he'd held her.

He remembered using the knife on her.

The same knife which was now stuck in his belt.

'Your husband is out at work then?' he said, gazing at Sue.

'He's a teacher,' she said. 'He works in the school here,' she hooked a thumb in the direction of the building which backed onto their garden. 'That's why we moved here.'

'Your children must like it here,' he said, smiling, picking at the scab on his hand with his nail.

Sue smiled thinly.

'Your little girl, what's her name?' he asked.

'Lisa,' Sue said, quickly, then, trying to change the subject. 'Where abouts in Hinkston do your relatives live?'

'Lisa,' said Mills, ignoring her attempts to steer the conversation along different lines. 'How pretty. She's pretty too.' He got to his feet, crossed to the picture and picked it up. 'You don't mind do you?' he said, almost apologetically, regarding the photo carefully. 'Such a lovely child.'

With his back to Sue his smile faded once again.

So lovely.

'I can't thank you enough for bringing my purse back, Mr Neville,' Sue said, clearing her throat. 'I thought it had been stolen.'

'There are so many dishonest people in the world today, Mrs Hacket. You're lucky that it was me who found it. It could have been a criminal who picked it up.' He chuckled.

Sue found that his eyes were upon her once more, his stare unblinking.

'More tea?' she asked, anxious for the chance of a respite from those piercing eyes.

'Very kind,' he said, handing her the cup.

She took it and headed for the kitchen, aware of Mills behind her.

'You have a lovely house,' he said, stepping into the kitchen, watching as she poured him another cup of tea.

She thanked him.

'Lovely house. Lovely child.' He ran appraising eyes over her slim body. The tight jeans, the blouse which she always wore for housework, paint stained and threadbare in places. Her hair had been washed that morning and hung past her shoulders in soft waves. 'And you're lovely too if you don't mind me saying.'

She handed him his tea, beginning to feel a little uncomfortable. She sat down at the kitchen table.

Mills sat down opposite her, his eyes fixed upon her.

As he reached into his jacket pocket for his cigarettes his hand brushed the handle of the knife.

'You don't mind if I smoke do you?' he asked, lighting up. He offered her one and she declined, explaining about the baby. 'You are lucky. I love little children myself,' he said, grinning.

Sue shuffled uncomfortably in her seat, watching him as he sucked slowly on the cigarette. It seemed to take him an eternity to smoke it. Then, finally, he got to his feet and said he would have to go. Sue breathed an almost audible sigh of relief.

He followed her to the front door, standing behind her as she opened it.

She thanked him again and watched as he walked up the path, stopping half-way to smile courteously.

'Perhaps we'll see each other again,' he said. 'When we're shopping.' He chuckled.

Sue nodded, waved and shut the door.

She let out a deep breath, standing with her back to the door for a moment, listening for footsteps, almost as if she expected him to return.

He didn't.

She rebuked herself for feeling so uncomfortable in the man's presence, for being so jumpy.

Never mind, she told herself, he was gone now, *and* she had her purse back.

'Perhaps we'll see each other again,' she said, remembering his words. 'No chance,' she thought aloud.

It was then that the phone rang.

556

77

Doctor Edward Curtis glanced at the list of names written on the pad before him. He sighed as he ran his finger down the neatly written names. Finally he sat back in his chair, hands pressed together before him as if in some meditative gesture.

He was still sitting like that when the door opened and his receptionist popped her head round.

'Your next patient is here, Doctor,' she said.

Curtis nodded and sat forward, some kind of acknowledgement of the receptionist's presence. She retreated back to her own outer office and Curtis pushed the notepad bearing the names out of sight under a pile of papers.

He ran a hand through his hair and waited for the knock on his door.

It came a moment later and Sue Hacket walked in.

They exchanged greetings and she felt a peculiar pleasure from the fact that Curtis seemed genuinely pleased to see her.

He asked how she was feeling.

She mentioned the pains.

Always pain.

'I'd better check you over,' said the doctor, smiling. 'We can't be too cautious at this stage.' He motioned her towards the couch in the corner of his room and Sue paused beside it.

'Do you want me to undress?' she asked, her eyes never leaving his.

'Yes please,' he said, quietly.

She began unbuttoning her blouse.

Curtis, for his own part, turned to a tray of instruments covered by a sterile gauze sheet. As he lifted it up Sue saw two or three hypodermic needles lying there.

She pulled the blouse off and began unfastening her jeans, simultaneously kicking off her shoes.

'Did you tell your husband about the pains you were getting?' Curtis asked.

'No.'

'Why not?'

'He seems worried enough already, I didn't see the point in making things worse.' She pulled her jeans off and stood before him in just her bra and panties.

Curtis smiled at her and asked her to climb up onto the couch, which she duly did.

'Just relax,' he told her, his hands settling on her stomach. He began to knead the flesh gently, pressing occasionally, his fingers moving lower until he was brushing against the top of her knickers, stirring the silky strands of public hair which were in view.

'Show me where the pain was,' he said.

Sue took his hand and guided it between her legs, allowing him to rest against the warmth of her crotch. He pressed and stroked gently along her inner thighs and across her mound. She breathed deeply, her eyes closing. Keeping one hand on her warm vagina he took his stethoscope and pressed it to her belly.

Then moved it across. And down.

'Are you still getting pain,' he wanted to know.

'Only occasionally,' she breathed.

'The baby is fine, as far as I can tell. There's nothing to worry about,' he said, softly.

'When is it due?' she said. 'I know it's probably ages yet.'

'It needn't be,' Curtis said. 'If you want to accelerate the growth there is a way. If you're willing. It involves another injection though.'

'Do it,' she said, flatly. 'Now.'

Curtis smiled.

Sue hooked her thumbs into the sides of her panties and began to ease them over her hips, exposing her silky hairs and her vagina.

Curtis reached for the hypodermic, drew some fluid off from a bottle on the tray then eased the steel point past her outer lips.

She felt the steel penetrate her and it made her gasp. But there was little pain and, as he withdrew, she was smiling.

She dressed again slowly, almost reluctantly, then sat down opposite him at the desk.

'If you have any more trouble let me know,' Curtis said. 'Come and see me anytime.'

She thanked him and got to her feet, ready to leave.

'You don't know how much this means to me, doctor,' she said, pausing at the door. 'I don't know how I can ever thank you.'

Curtis smiled benignly.

Sue closed the door behind her and he heard her footsteps echoing away up the corridor.

His smile faded rapidly and he reached for the pad once more, his eyes skimming over the names he'd looked at a dozen times already that morning. The calls had all come in during a ninety-minute spell earlier that morning.

Calls from Elaine Craven. From Julie Clayton.

Stuart Lewis had rung. So too had Patricia Stokes.

All had been frightened.

Even the call from The Bull had sounded more urgent than usual. Could he come and see Paula, Mrs Kirkham had asked. It was very important.

Curtis knew it was important.

And he knew why.

He sighed as he re-read the list once more.

Had the time come again so soon?

78

Hacket prodded his dinner with his knife then looked across the table at Sue.

She was eating heartily, unaware of his stare.

'What else did Curtis say?'

Hacket finally broke the silence, dropping his cutlery on to the plate.

559

'He said the baby was fine,' Sue informed him. 'He said there was nothing to worry about.'

'And you believe him?'

She sighed.

'I have no reason to *disbelieve* him. John, I feel fine. I'm fine and the baby's fine. The only one who seems to have any problems is you.' She regarded him coldly for a second. 'He *did* say that the baby would be born earlier than we'd first thought.'

'How can that be possible?' he demanded.

Sue finished chewing the mouthful of food she had then put down her knife and fork.

'He gave me another injection,' she said, quietly.

'Jesus Christ. What of? More of his miracle fucking treatment? We don't know what's happening, Sue. Haven't you stopped to think about this? To think about what's happening to *you* as well as the baby?'

She didn't answer.

'You're changing, Sue,' he told her. 'Your attitude. Your temperament. Even your character, and it's all down to this fucking treatment.' He hissed the last few words through clenched teeth. 'You're blind to what it's doing to you. The only thing you can think about is that damned baby – you don't seem to care that Curtis could be doing you harm.'

'And all you seem to care about is yourself,' she countered. 'I thought you'd be pleased to think that we could have another child. You were the one who said you wanted to start afresh, a new beginning. And when that chance comes along all you do is criticise and complain.'

'I'm worried about you, can't you see that?'

'I can see your jealousy, John.'

'What the hell are you talking about.'

'You're jealous of Curtis.'

'Don't be so bloody ridiculous,' he snorted.

'It's *him* who gave me that hope. Is that what really hurts you? Is *that* why you're so opposed to this child?'

Hacket didn't answer. The muscles at the side of his jaw throbbed angrily and he pushed himself away from the table, getting to his feet.

'You don't understand do you?' he snapped, heading towards the sitting room.

560

Sue followed, watching him pour himself a large measure of whiskey. He downed most of it in one gulp and re-filled the glass.

'Are you going to get drunk now?' she asked.

'No. I'm going to have one more then I'm going to see Curtis,' he said, flatly.

The look on her face changed from anger to surprise.

'What for?' she wanted to know.

'I want to talk to him about a few things. Like what this treatment really is. What exactly he's been injecting into you and the other women he's treated. What is it that can make a child grow at five times its usual rate?'

'You can't just go barging into his house, John,' she said.

'Can't I?' he said, defiantly.

'This is because of that girl isn't it?' said Sue, acidly. 'That other teacher you spoke to. Until then you were as happy as I was about the possibility of having another child. But since you spoke to her you've changed your mind.'

'That's bloody stupid. It's got nothing to do with what she said.'

'Hasn't it?'

'You don't have to be a genius to figure out that things aren't quite right here. I don't like all the mystery surrounding what Curtis is doing.'

'There is no mystery.'

'He didn't tell us everything. He told us what he wanted us to know. Nothing more.'

Hacket finished his drink and slammed the glass down.

'Well, now I'm going to see what he's got to say.'

'No,' she hissed, blocking his path, her eyes narrowed in anger.

'Sue, get out of my way.'

She spread her arms so that he couldn't pass her.

'Come on,' Hacket said, quietly, a little unsettled by the look in her eye. 'You see what this is doing to *us* too. I told you, you're changing.'

'It's always me isn't it? Put the blame on me. As long as you don't have to face up to your own guilt. It's a wonder you didn't blame my father for Lisa's death. I mean, if I hadn't been out visiting him that night then you could have been with your bit on the side without

561

having to worry. I'd have been in the house. You'd have kept a clear conscience.'

'Get out the way, Sue,' he snapped, gripping one of her arms.

She spun round, her left hand clawing at his face, her nails raking his cheek.

Hacket hissed in pain as he felt his flesh tear.

She struck at him again but he managed to deflect the second blow, gripping her wrists, holding her at bay.

He was surprised by her strength.

'Get off me,' she yelled at him, trying to shake loose of his grip.

She kicked out, catching him a stinging blow on the shin and he winced in pain, pushing her backwards, bolting for the door. She was at him immediately, gripping a handful of his hair, tugging so hard that several strands came away from his scalp.

Again he swung round, this time managing to pin her arms behind her back. He lifted her bodily and carried her back into the sitting room.

As he was about to drop her onto the sofa she spat in his face.

Hacket looked at her, both surprised and horrified by the savagery of her reactions.

He pushed her away from him as if she had some kind of contagion.

Then, as she struggled to get up he sprinted for the front door, opened it and hurried up the path towards the waiting car.

'You stay away from him,' Sue shrieked from the door, watching as the car pulled away, its tail lights swallowed up in the darkness.

She was weeping madly, tears of rage pouring down her cheeks. She stepped away from the door and slammed it, walking through into the sitting room, her fury unabated.

She crossed to the window and looked out into the night then she turned and glanced at the clock on the mantelpiece.

9.46 p.m.

She looked to the phone.

Should she warn Curtis?

She was moving towards the receiver when the first stab of pain tore through her.

79

Ronald Mills looked at his watch.

9.54 p.m.

He picked a piece of meat from between his front teeth and spat it onto the carpet of the room then he crossed to the bed and pulled the .38 from beneath the pillow.

He sat on the edge of the bed, dug his hand in his jacket pocket and took out six bullets. He flipped the cylinder out then carefully loaded the pistol. That done, he snapped the cylinder back into place and spun it, holding the gun at arms length, peering down the sight.

Not that he would need to aim.

He intended getting close.

And then there was always the knife.

He wanted to be near to Hacket, and to the woman as well.

Wanted to see their pain, feel their agony.

Just like he had done with their child.

The thought of the act he had already committed and that he was about to commit caused the beginning of an erection which he savoured, smiling as he felt the stiffness growing.

Perhaps he would gag them in case their screams were heard, but that, he reasoned, would deprive him of one of the most pleasurable parts of the exercise. Hearing them beg for their lives.

He would take off the woman's breasts.

He had already decided that.

Cut deeply and sever them both.

He would make Hacket watch while he performed the act, slicing each mammary in turn. Then he would cut her. Five, six, seven. A dozen times. He wanted her to die slowly. He wanted Hacket to see it.

Then he would kill Hacket.

He would carve the man's eyes from their sockets.

'If thine eye offend thee, pluck it out,' he chuckled.

He looked again at his watch then he headed for the door, locking it behind him, feeling the gun in his pocket, the knife wedged into his belt.

The drive to the Hackets' house would take him about fifteen minutes.

It was 10.01.

80

The Renault skidded slightly on the road as Hacket spun the wheel and guided the vehicle into the driveway which led towards Curtis' house. The smoothness of tarmac was replaced by the loud crunching of gravel as Hacket drove on.

A powerful wind was gusting across the large open front garden bending a number of topiary animals to such extreme angles it seemed they would be uprooted.

Hacket heard the strong gusts hissing around the car but his attention was on the house itself.

The place seemed to be growing from the night itself. Only the dark outline showed that there was a building there at all, its frontage finally illuminated by the lights of Hacket's car.

There wasn't a light to be seen inside the house itself.

The teacher brought the car to a halt outside the front door, noticing immediately that Curtis' car was not in evidence. No lights. No car. *Nobody home?* He swung himself out of the Renault and crossed to the front door, the powerful wind buffeting him, blowing through his hair. He almost overbalanced, such was the force of the gusts. But, eventually he reached the large oak door and knocked hard, the sound dying away rapidly beneath the persistent howl of the wind.

There was no answer.

Hacket knocked again, harder this time.

Still no response.

He stepped back from the door and looked up at the windows. What little natural light there was reflected back off them and it reminded Hacket of staring into blind eyes. He looked around, wondering if there was access to the rear of the house.

To his right was a path which curved around one corner of the ivy-covered building. The teacher headed towards it. As he turned the corner the wind seemed to hit him with increased ferocity and he steadied himself against the wall of the house for a second before walking on. The path, sure enough, led to the back of the building but, as with the front, Hacket found it devoid of light.

Perhaps Curtis was out on a call, he reasoned. Well, if that was so he'd wait for him. He'd wait as long as he had to in order to speak to the other man, to find out what the hell he was up to, to find out what he'd been pumping into Sue.

Hacket found the back door and pummelled on it angrily as if expecting his outburst to elicit some kind of reaction.

He stepped back, passing along the path, peering into a couple of the windows close by. He could see nothing through the gloom. His frustration and anger growing he turned away from the house, glancing out over the similarly well-kept back garden. The rockery close by, the lawn which sloped down towards the high privet hedge.

Hacket frowned, narrowing his eyes in an effort to see through the gloom.

Down by the high privet hedge something moved.

He was sure of it.

Maybe the wind had disturbed one of the well-kept bushes down there, he thought at first. Maybe.

He took a couple of steps onto the lawn, his eyes fixed on the spot ahead of him where he was sure he'd seen the movement.

Whatever he'd seen before stirred again.

Hacket froze for a moment, not sure whether to advance or remain where he was. He swallowed hard, his initial anger now tempered slightly by the realisation that he was trespassing. If Curtis chose to, he could prosecute.

The doubts vanished from Hacket's mind as quickly as they'd come. What the hell did he care about trespassing? He had more important things to worry about than that. Besides, if Curtis had nothing to hide then he would not object to this visit.

Fuck him, thought Hacket, heading for the bottom of the garden and the area where he'd seen the movement.

As he drew closer to the high privet hedge he heard a high pitched squealing sound, carried to him on the blustery wind.

He squinted through the darkness once more and saw, a couple of feet ahead, a rusty metal gate set into the hedge.

It was a kind of entrance, he reasoned, the gate swinging wildly back and forth, flung helplessly by the wind.

Hacket paused as he reached the gate, gripping it in one hand to stop the maddening squeak of the hinges. He looked beyond into the area shielded by the high hedge.

Just a simple square of slightly overlong grass, a few flowers.

The flowers were scattered over the ground, tossed wantonly by the breeze.

He saw the piece of flat stone at the centre of the square.

Hacket let go of the gate, pulling it shut behind him as he moved towards the flat stone, finally glancing down at it. Even from so close it was difficult to read the words upon the marble. He knelt and fumbled in his pocket for his lighter. However, no sooner had he coaxed a flame from it than the wind blew it out. Cursing, Hacket leaned closer in an effort to read the words on the stone, realising, as he did, that it was a gravestone.

He ran his fingers across the stone, almost like a blind man, picking out each word carefully.

MARGARET LAWRENSON
BELOVED WIFE AND MOTHER
DIED JUNE 5TH 1965

Hacket frowned.

'Lawrenson,' he murmured. He didn't see the connection.

He was still pondering this anomaly when he heard the sound of a car approaching from the front of the house.

Hacket got to his feet and sprinted across the rear lawn towards the house.

The sound of the engine grew louder, tyres were crunching on the gravel drive.

The teacher pressed himself against the wall and peered round into the drive.

Doctor Edward Curtis brought his car to a halt outside the house, switched off the engine then swung himself out from behind the wheel.

Hacket watched. Waited.

Curtis glanced across at Hacket's car but seemed to pay it little heed, something which puzzled the teacher. Instead, the doctor crossed to the front door and unlocked it, then he returned to the car and fumbled with the bunch of keys, selecting one and pushing it into the lock of the boot.

Hacket watched, unaware that he himself was the target of other eyes.

The figure watched.

And waited.

81

'Bastard.'

She muttered the word under her breath, clutching her stomach with one hand, wincing with each fresh stab of pain. But it was not the pain to which she directed her anger. She glanced at the phone, wondering once again, if she should warn Curtis. Tell him that her husband was on his way. She looked at the clock. No, he'd have arrived at the house by now, surely.

Sue exhaled deeply, her mind turning over all the possible scenarios. A row. A fight even. She tried to push the thoughts from her mind.

Why was her husband so obsessed with the treatment she'd received? Why wasn't the gift of a child enough for him?

She felt another stab of pain. One which reached from her vagina to her naval and she sucked in a laboured breath, getting to her feet as if the movement would relieve the pressure on her belly.

The swelling there was only slight, as if she'd just eaten a heavy meal but it felt heavy. Sue felt bloated. Replete. As if the child she was carrying was growing not by the day but by the minute. Its progress to maturity accelerated beyond comprehension.

She walked across to the phone once more, her hand hovering over it for a moment.

Should she call Curtis?

She was still trying to decide when she heard the knock on the front door.

Sue froze for a moment, glancing down at the phone then at the door.

Could it be her husband? Had he finally seen the stupidity of his reactions? Perhaps their night would end in reconciliation instead of anger. She sucked in a deep breath and moved towards the door.

As she opened it she realised that if it had been her husband out there he would have used his key.

Ronald Mills stood on the doorstep, smiling.

Sue saw that he had a hand dug into his jacket pocket but, before she could speak he had pulled it free.

The .38 looked huge as it was pushed into her face.

'Don't scream,' snarled Mills. 'Just step back inside the house.'

She obeyed and he pushed her before him, stepping over the threshold.

The door swung shut behind them.

82

The boot of the car opened like a large metallic mouth and, as Hacket watched, Curtis leant forward and scooped something up from within.

Something large.

Something which he struggled to carry.

The object was about five feet long, perhaps larger, thought Hacket. Wrapped in a blanket.

Curtis stood still for a moment, the wind swirling around him, as he braced himself to carry his heavy load.

His large load.

Hacket squinted through the gloom once more.

It was big enough . . .

'Jesus Christ,' he murmured.

Big enough to be a man.

Curtis crossed to the front door of the house and entered, bumping one end of the object he carried against the frame as he entered. Hacket stepped back around the side of the house, pressing his back against the cold stone of the wall, sucking in deep breaths. He stayed there for long seconds then peered around into the drive once more. There was no sign of Curtis, he had not returned to shut the car boot, obviously more intent on depositing his cargo inside the house first.

Hacket realised what he must do.

He scurried towards the open front door and paused by the threshold, enveloped by darkness. Curtis had not bothered to turn on any lights when he'd entered.

From inside the house Hacket heard movement.

He entered, pulling the door closed but not shutting it, momentarily silencing the wild howling of the wind. He stood in the hallway, looking around in the gloom.

To his right there was a wide staircase which looked as if it had been plucked from some baronial mansion. It rose into even more impenetrable darkness.

To his left was a door.

It was slightly ajar.

Hacket advanced slowly towards it, hearing sounds from beyond. Another door being opened. The occasional bump.

He found himself in what he took to be Curtis' reception.

The door marked 'SURGERY' was open.

He moved through it, slowing his pace slightly as he came to the corridor which linked the doctor's office to the waiting-room. He moved slowly, trying to minimise the sound of his footfalls on the polished floor.

It was like being blind in the narrow passageway. No light to guide him.

569

It was then that he noticed the smell.

Hacket froze, his throat dry, aware of the pounding of his heart.

He recognised the smell.

Strong and coppery.

As he moved another step forward his foot slid in something wet and he almost overbalanced.

He stepped back, looking down at the spot which had caused him to slide.

He pulled the lighter from his pocket and flicked it on.

Illuminated by the sickly yellow flame was a puddle of blood about three inches across.

There were drops of it all along the corridor – they led to the door of Curtis's office.

Hacket flicked off the lighter and moved on, his initial anger now gradually turning to anxiety and something a little stronger.

Fear, perhaps

Why question it? he told himself. It *was* fear.

As he stood with his hand on the doorknob of the doctor's office he felt the hair at the back of his neck rise. He pushed the door gently.

It swung open to reveal yet more darkness.

And more blood.

It had dripped onto the carpet. Hacket could see it glistening in the natural light which flooded through the study window.

Outside the wind battered against the windows as if trying to gain entry, its banshee wail rising as Hacket glanced around the room, his gaze eventually coming to rest on yet another door.

It was like a maze inside the house.

He moved towards the last door and peered through it.

This time there was light beyond.

Beyond and below.

He realised that he was looking down into a cellar, lit from overhead by banks of powerful fluorescents.

Of Curtis there was no sign.

Only the drops of blood which spattered the stairs leading down into the cellar.

Hacket waited and watched, backing off slightly when he saw the doctor struggle into view, still carrying the blanket covered form. He finally laid it on a trolley and stepped back, wiping his hands on a paper towel which he then screwed up and tossed into a bin.

Hacket was mesmerised by the tableau before him, his eyes fixed on the blanket-swathed shape.

The wind continued to scream, its cries masking Hacket's low breathing.

If not for the wind he might have heard the heavy foot-falls on the wide staircase, descending slowly from above him.

83

She knew she was going to die.

It was just a matter of when.

But the inevitability of it made it no more acceptable and her fear grew by the second.

Sue Hacket sat on the chair in the classroom looking at her captor.

Ronald Mills glared back at her, the knife held in one hand, the .38 laying on a nearby desk-top.

She had been surprised at how easily he had gained access to the school, pushing her before him, expecting alarm bells to sound when the main door was eased open. But only silence had greeted her wish. There had been no bells. No panic.

No rescuers.

Mills had dragged her through the deserted school, up and down corridors, up a flight of stairs, finally pushing her into a classroom, hurling her towards a chair.

Then he had pulled some rope from his pocket and tied her to it, pulling so hard on the hemp that it had cut into her wrists and ankles. She could see blood running onto her feet when she glanced down. It looked black in the gloom of the classroom.

'I suppose you wonder who I am,' he said, speaking the first words since he'd brought her to this place.

She tried to swallow but her throat felt constricted.

'Well, don't you?' he hissed.

She nodded.

He moved towards her, the knife pointing at her face. He touched the point to her cheek, drawing it gently, almost lovingly, towards her eye.

She closed her eyes, gritting her teeth against the agony she knew must come next.

He pressed the point of the knife against the corner of her eye.

'Open,' he whispered.

She couldn't. Her eyes remained tightly shut, as if the thin flesh of her eyelids would protect her from the razor-sharp point of the blade.

'Open your eyes,' Mills snarled.

Sue opened them slowly, tears beginning to form, to trickle down her cheeks.

'That's better,' he said, smiling. 'I mean, don't you want to see the face of the man who killed your daughter?'

She felt her stomach contract and her body felt as if it had been wrapped in a freezing shroud.

She stared at him through tear-filled eyes, the knife still pressed against her cheek.

'Now we're going to sit and wait,' he told her, trailing the knife down towards her mouth where he ran the tip across her bottom lip. 'Sit and wait for your husband.'

84

Hacket took a step forward as he saw Curtis reach for the corner of the blanket. From his position at the top of the cellar steps, Hacket was hidden from the view of the doctor but still able to see what was happening. He looked on, his heart thudding against his ribs.

Curtis took hold of the blanket and pulled it free.

Hacket had to stifle a gasp.

Lying on the trolley was a man, he guessed in his mid-forties, dressed in a pair of trousers and a shirt, both of which were spattered with blood.

The long doubled edged stiletto blade still protruded from the dead man's right eye.

As Hacket watched, Curtis took hold of the blade and pulled, removing it from the eye with infinite care. He laid the knife on a table beside him, wiping some blood from it with a towel, then pulled off his own jacket and hung it on the back of a chair.

That simple task done he returned to the body and, using all his strength, turned the body over so that it was lying on its stomach.

Blood from the ruptured eye dribbled onto the trolley.

Curtis then pulled another, smaller, trolley towards him and Hacket could see the dozens of medical instruments laid out upon it. As he watched, the doctor reached for a scalpel; then he carefully pushed the hair away from the neck of the corpse and pressed the point of the scalpel to the nape of the neck, close to the base of the skull.

The razor-sharp blade cut effortlessly through flesh and muscle. More dark blood spilled from the incision.

Hacket gritted his teeth as he saw Curtis reach for a larger blade.

Hacket couldn't see but, from the vile sawing sounds which came from below he realised the blade had a serrated edge.

Curtis worked expertly with the tool, finally removing a piece of the occipital bone about two inches wide and three inches long. He discarded it into a metal tray close by.

Even from his high vantage point Hacket could see that the base of the victim's brain was exposed, and it took all the willpower he could muster to prevent himself vomiting. He gripped the door more tightly, hiding behind it, part of him wanting to run, to be away from this scene of butchery, the other telling, forcing him, to remain. Mesmerised by what he saw.

Using a pair of what reminded Hacket of pliers, Curtis cut through the spinal cord.

The snap of breaking bone echoed around the cellar like a gunshot and the head of the man on the table seemed to collapse forward now, unsupported by the brain stem.

573

Hacket watched as blood oozed from the open skull, some of it covering Curtis' hands as he worked, but he seemed oblivious to the crimson weepings.

He reached for a small pair of tweezers and another scalpel, pushing the twin prongs deep into the thick grey-pink tissue of the brain, seizing something within its bloodied folds.

Curtis smiled as he gently gripped the pituitary gland between the prongs of the tweezers. One swift nick and the gland came free. He held it before him like some kind of trophy, admiring the swollen, dripping gland for a second before dropping it into a jar filled with clear fluid.

Hacket could stand no more.

He spun round and bolted back through the doctor's office, his only thought now to be away from this place, to tell the police.

To tell his wife.

Sue. Sue. What had Curtis done to *her*?

Hacket slipped on the carpet, fell but dragged himself upright again, not caring if Curtis heard him. He crashed through the door and out into the corridor, heading for the reception then the hall beyond.

If he could reach his car.

He heard footsteps behind him, heard Curtis hurtling up the cellar steps.

Hacket wrenched open the door which led out into the hall, glancing back, convinced that he could outrun the doctor. He was half-smiling when he blundered into the hall.

He collided with the figure.

It stood before him, blocking his path, barring his way to the front door.

Hacket had but one reaction as he looked at the figure.

His eyes bulged madly in their sockets, he fell back and, as he did, he screamed until he thought his lungs would burst.

85

'I don't understand,' Sue Hacket said, quietly, tears spilling down her cheeks. 'Why are you doing this?'

Ronald Mills picked a piece of the scab from his left hand and rolled the hardened flesh between his thumb and forefinger.

'Why did you kill Lisa?' Sue persisted.

'Does it matter?' he asked, smiling, thinly. 'It's done now.' He moved closer to Sue, touching her shoulder, gripping it firmly for a second as if he were about to begin massaging it. Instead he pushed the knuckle of his index finger into the hollow beside her collar bone, digging hard until she winced in pain.

'She was pretty, your little girl,' Mills said. 'And so quiet too.'

Sue could not fight back the tears as he began to rub her neck, stroking his hand somewhat clumsily through her hair.

'When I went into her bedroom she didn't make a sound,' he continued. 'Not even when I climbed onto the bed beside her.

'Please,' Sue said, softly, not wanting to hear.

'I asked her what her name was and she told me. Lisa. Such a pretty name.' He began to tug on Sue's hair then allowed his free hand to slide down the front of her blouse towards her breasts.

'Stop it,' Sue sobbed.

'She started to make a noise when I got out the knife,' Mills said. 'I thought she was going to cry then. That was why I had to put my hand over her mouth.'

The tears were pouring down Sue's face, dripping from her chin, some falling onto the back of Mills probing hand. He gripped one of her breasts hard and squeezed until she groaned in pain.

'She tried to scream when I used the knife on her,' he said, softly, his erection now throbbing against the inside of his trousers. 'But I kept her quiet.' He smiled. 'I pushed the knife into her throat. You should have seen the way her eyes opened up. It was like there was some kind of spring inside her head. I pushed the knife in and she opened her eyes wider. The further I pushed the wider they got. I thought they were going to fall out of her head.

Sue was sobbing uncontrollably now, Mills' hand still roughly kneading her breasts.

'And when I fucked her,' he sighed, wistfully. 'She was so tight. So beautifully tight.'

'You're fucking mad,' Sue wailed, her exhortations dissolving into racking sobs.

'Am I?' he asked, stepping back slightly. 'Could a madman have done what I've done? Tracked you and your husband to this place, planned revenge the way I have done?'

Sue merely shook her head, her cheeks burning, her eyes blurred.

'I'm going to kill your fucking husband,' he told her. 'Do you know why?'

She continued to cry.

'Do you?' he roared at her.

'No,' she yelled back, her body shaking violently.

Mills took a step forward, the knife held before him. He pushed it beneath Sue's chin, pressing just hard enough to puncture the skin. A tiny dribble of blood ran down her neck.

'Because he killed my friend. The only friend I ever had. Your husband killed him. Made him fall under a train. And I saw it all. I saw what he did and now he's going to pay.'

'Haven't you done enough to us?' she sobbed.

Mills smiled crookedly.

He began unbuttoning Sue's blouse.

'Done enough?' he hissed, a slight smile on his face. 'I've only just started.'

86

Hacket was sure that his sanity had gone.

He was mad, that was the only answer.

A sane man would not have seen what he saw now.

He pushed himself back along the floor as the figure took a step towards him.

The teacher tried to pull himself upright but it seemed as if all the strength had drained from his body. He felt his bowels loosen, and the hair at the back of his neck stood up sharply. He shook his head slowly, wondering now if he was truly encountering madness.

The figure which faced him was not like those of a nightmare. No mind, however diseased, could conjure up an image like that which now confronted the teacher. No nightmare could be that bad.

It was fully six feet tall, about fifteen stone, perhaps more. A large man. *Man*? Hacket's tortured mind corrected itself. The monstrosity which stood before him was no man.

Supported on two legs the torso seemed much too broad, too heavy to be carried on even limbs as thick as those Hacket saw.

Its skin was pale, darkened only on the forearms by black hair. And there was power in those arms. Hacket could see each muscle clearly defined. Hands like ham-hocks swung from arms which looked a little too long, not quite simian but only a few steps removed. The torso seemed to widen as it reached the chest, and here, beneath the gauze-like shirt which the figure wore, Hacket could see several bulging growths. One on the right breast, another on the left shoulder.

It was the head which caused him to moan aloud as he stared at it.

Head?

Not one but two. Joined at the temple.

Four perfectly formed eyes fixed him in a freezing stare.

The mouths opened simultaneously and, had Hacket been in a position to reason, he may well have realised that the body was controlled by just one brain. The scalps were bald, graced only with fine whisps of gossamer like the hair of old men.

A growth the size of a fist swelled from the right cheek of the left head. Another from the other cranium. The flesh around the eyes was puffy, almost liquescent, as if it were filled with fluid waiting to burst. The growths looked like massive boils, replete with pus and ready to erupt.

The figure took another step towards Hacket who had managed to drag himself up onto his knees into what looked like an attitude of prayer.

He watched as the figure advanced, its piercing gaze never leaving him. His mind was still reeling, but somewhere inside the madness a note of reason told him that he was looking at a Siamese twin. Two bodies supported by just one pair of legs. Two entities in a single body.

The twin reached for him, one powerful hand lifting him to his feet.

'What do you want?'

The two mouths moved in perfect unison, the words not slurred and laboured but crisply spoken, eminently understandable. Coming from such a monstrous source it made them sound all the more incongruous.

Hacket could not reply. His entire body was shaking.

A door behind him opened but he was scarcely aware of it.

Curtis dashed into the hall, slowing his pace when he saw that the teacher had been stopped.

The doctor nodded and the twin hurled Hacket to one side.

He crashed heavily against the wall and lay there as Curtis stood over him.

'You're trespassing, Mr Hacket,' said Curtis, calmly. 'You realise that?'

'What the fuck is going on here, Curtis?' Hacket gasped, his gaze drawn once more to the other figure. 'What is *that*?'

The twin moved forward angrily but Curtis stepped in front of it.

'*That*, Mr Hacket,' the doctor said, angrily. 'Is my brother.'

Hacket laughed uncontrollably. Was this the beginning of madness, he wondered, his eyes beginning to fill with tears. This was the laughter of the insane.

Curtis looked on impassively.

Hacket wiped his eyes and glared up at the doctor.

'One of your fucking experiments don't you mean?' he snarled. 'The product of your treatment. The same treatment you gave to my wife. Is that what she'll give birth to?' He pointed at the twin.

'I ought to kill you now,' the figure said, quietly.

Hacket swallowed hard, stunned once more by the figure's voice.

'Kill me like you killed that poor bastard in your cellar?' he hissed, looking now at Curtis. 'Who is he? Why did you kill him?'

'Call him a donor,' said Curtis, smiling.

Hacket looked vague.

'I couldn't expect a man of your limited perceptions to understand, Mr Hacket. Perhaps I at least owe you the privilege of some kind of explanation. Although I doubt it will mean much to you.'

Curtis glanced at the twin. 'Bring him.'

Hacket rose, but as soon as he was on his feet the other figure grabbed him, one powerful arm snaking around his throat the other hand clamping onto the back of his head.

'If you try to struggle,' the figure said, softly. 'I'll break your neck.' As it pulled him backwards, Hacket felt the heavy growths on its chest rubbing against his back.

Curtis set off for the cellar, followed by Hacket and the twin.

'Time for you to learn, Mr Hacket,' said Curtis, smiling. 'You should feel honoured.'

'And when I *have* learned?' Hacket said, struggling to speak because of the pressure on his windpipe.

Curtis didn't answer.

They began to descend into the cellar.

87

The stench from the body made Hacket feel sick, but held as he was by the twin he could not pull away. Instead all he could do was gaze helplessly at the corpse, his eyes drawn to the gaping hole in the back of its skull, and also to the small gland which still floated in the jar of clear liquid.

'From death comes life,' said Curtis, smiling, gesturing first to the body then to the gland. 'To coin a cliché.'

'What are you talking about, Curtis?' asked Hacket, wearily.

'I'm talking about hope, Mr Hacket. Something which you and your wife didn't have until *I* came along.'

'What have you done to her?' Hacket rasped, trying to pull away but finding himself restrained by the powerful hands which held him.

'I've done what she wanted me to do. I've given her hope. Her and dozens of women like her over the years. Women who couldn't have children. Women who now, because of me, are mothers.' He lifted the jar. 'And all because of this.'

'What is it?'

'The pituitary gland. Source of the body's growth hormones. I'll try to keep this simple Mr Hacket, otherwise I'll end up sounding like some kind of mad doctor.' He smiled. 'They belong in bad horror films.'

'And you belong in prison you murdering bastard,' Hacket snarled. 'What about that poor fucker lying there? What about him? Where's *his* hope?'

'I said I'll keep this simple. I'll also keep it brief. My father began this work over forty years ago, on the directive of the British government. The project was called "Genesis". That name, I know, will mean nothing to you.' Curtis smiled. 'Except perhaps in its Biblical sense. The name was apt. Genesis describes the creation of life, and that was what Project Genesis was designed to do. My father perfected a fertility drug, refined from human pituitary glands. Given in the right doses it would cut the gestation period from nine months to three. In larger measures perhaps even to four weeks. And it worked.' The doctor's tone hardened. 'He did what *they* told him to do. The government, Churchill in particular, knew that the Germans would invade after Dunkirk. They also knew that there weren't enough men to combat an invasion. They needed my father and his work. Once the women had given birth the children would be regularly injected with the drug, their growth outside the womb would be as rapid as it had been while they were gestating. A child could grow into a man in less than two months.'

'You're mad and by the sound of it, so was your fucking father,' Hacket said.

The twin twisted his head sharply and Hacket felt excruciating pain in his neck and skull. He opened his mouth to scream but no sound would come.

'Another inch and I'll break your neck,' said the twin, leaning close to his ear, both mouths moving slowly.

Curtis held up a hand for the other to release the pressure and Hacket felt the force diminish somewhat. White stars danced before his eyes, and for a second he thought he was going to black out, but he kept a grip on consciousness, listening as Curtis continued.

'There was no madness, Hacket. Only supreme intelligence. But *they* couldn't see that. The men who had wanted his expertise were frightened by the success of his experiments. Some of the children were born deformed. Like my brother. Mentally they were perfect but their physical appearance was unacceptable.' He spoke the last word with sarcasm. 'They told my father to stop his work. He refused, so they had him murdered.' The knot of muscles at the side of the doctor's jaw throbbed angrily. 'My mother was left alone. She was pregnant at the time, carrying myself and my brother. She brought us up alone. Protected my brother, paid for me to go through Medical school. When the time was right she passed on our father's notes. I continued with his work. And, if people have had to die during the course of that work, then too bad. A few human lives are drops in the ocean. Besides, for every one that's died there's been another to take their place. A child where there would never have been one. Hope where there was only misery.'

'The grave in the back garden,' Hacket said, quietly. 'Who is it?'

'Our mother. Margaret Lawrenson. After we were born she gave us her maiden name. Curtis. Better for her to lie there than with others like those who had my father killed. The hypocrites and the doubters.'

'And she supported you? She knew what you were doing? Knew you were killing people?' Curtis asked.

'She knew that sacrifices had to be made if my father's work was to see true fruition. She believed, Hacket. Believed in *him*, believed in *me*.'

'And the children that were born by using your "*treatment*"? What happened to them?'

'All well. All thriving. There is one minor side-effect however. The introduction of so much growth hormone into their systems seems to stimulate other parts of their brains. Without regular treatment they revert to cannabilism.'

'And their parents *know* this?' Hacket gasped.

'Know it and accept it, Mr Hacket. How does the cliché go, love conquers all? Even the knowledge that your child may kill.' He smiled again.

'How come the police haven't found you by now?'

'If I told you that the wife of the local Inspector was one of my patients would that explain why?' Curtis smiled. 'They really do have the most beautiful young daughter. She's almost fifteen now.'

Hacket shook his head, his eyes screwed up tight.

'You *are* mad,' he murmured. 'This whole thing is insane. Weller thought so too, didn't he? The man who lived at the house before me. He knew didn't he?'

'Very astute, Mr Hacket. Unfortunately Weller wasn't prepared to live the kind of life necessary to protect his son. He was ungrateful. And he was a fool. He's better off dead. I gave him what he wanted and he destroyed it.'

'I won't let that happen to my wife. I'll stop her having that child.'

Curtis shook his head and sighed.

'I'm afraid you have no choice, Mr Hacket,' he said, his tone darkening. 'Besides, it's far too late to stop it now.'

88

The pains were growing worse.

Each fresh contraction caused Sue Hacket to wince. It felt as if someone were pulling her intestines out through her navel with red hot tongs. The burning sensation had spread to her vagina too and she shifted as best she could on the chair in order to try and alleviate the growing pain.

Ronald Mills walked up and down the darkened classroom agitatedly, glancing alternately out of the window then at his watch. He swore under his breath then strode across the room towards Sue.

'Where is he?' he hissed. 'Where's your fucking husband?'

She gritted her teeth as a fresh wave of pain swept through her.

'I don't know,' she grunted.

'Lying cunt,' he snarled and lashed out at her.

The blow with the back of his hand caught her across the left cheek. A blow so powerful it almost knocked her over.

'Where is he?' Mills repeated.

'I don't know,' Sue wailed, helplessly, the pain from her lower abdomen eclipsing that from her cheek. She tasted blood in her mouth as she licked her tongue across her bottom lip.

Mills gripped the knife before him, pressing it to her chest, prodding her bare breasts with the tip. He brushed it against her left nipple which stiffened with the cold touch of the steel. Mills grinned, feeling the first stirrings of an erection. How easy it would be to cut that fleshy bud off, he thought. The idea excited him even more. No. He wanted Hacket to see it. Wanted him to see his own wife in agony, bleeding. He wanted to hear her pray for death.

And then it would be Hacket's turn.

Mills had waited a long time for the moment and he intended savouring it.

583

He watched as Sue doubled over, a fresh jolt of pain filling her. Mills grabbed a handful of her hair and wrenched her upright, so that he was staring into her face. Tears were flooding down her cheeks once more.

'I want to know where your husband is,' hissed Mills.

'And I told you I don't know,' Sue sobbed. 'Why don't you believe me?'

Mills took the knife and carefully slashed the waistband of her skirt, tugging aside the material, leaving her in just her panties. Then he slid the blade under the elastic at the side and pulled them from her.

She continued to cry, now exposed to his leering stare.

'I don't think I can wait any longer,' said Mills, smiling, running approving eyes over her naked body. He could feel the erection pressing almost painfully against the inside of his trousers.

'I think I'll have to start without him.'

89

Hacket knew he had to break free but the task seemed impossible.

The pressure on his neck and throat reminded him of that.

Curtis regarded the teacher silently for a moment.

'What did you hope to gain by coming here tonight?' he said, finally. 'If it was the truth you wanted, then at least now you know it.'

Hacket's arms dropped to his sides, he didn't struggle against the pressure on his neck, merely stood there, half leaning, half-supported by the immense strength of the twin.

'And now I know?' he asked. 'Are you going to kill me?'

'What choice do I have?' Curtis snapped. 'I offered you something more precious than you could have imagined, you *and* your wife, but you couldn't be content with that.'

'How many more people will you have to kill, Curtis, to carry on this fucking insanity?'

'As many as it takes. It's people like *you* who are mad, not me,'

Curtis said, jabbing an accusatory finger at the teacher. 'What I do I do for the good of others. As I said to you, sacrifices have to be made.'

'Very noble,' Hacket chided, his hand brushing against the twin's leg. 'What about the families of the people you kill, do you ever think about what they must feel? You cause pain, Curtis. It's all you're any good for.'

So much pain.

Curtis glanced at the twin and nodded.

Hacket felt the pressure tighten on his neck.

It was then that he reached back and fastened his hands on the twin's testicles, squeezing as tightly as he could, gripping them in a vice-like hold which made the twin shriek in pain.

Hacket gritted his teeth and squeezed harder, pushing backwards.

The twin screamed again and the two of them fell to the ground.

Hacket felt the pressure on his neck released.

He struggled to his feet, turning swiftly to drive a powerful kick into the groin of his fallen captor. He turned back to face Curtis who had lurched towards him, his hand clasping the stiletto blade.

The doctor lunged at Hacket and the teacher shouted in pain as the blade sliced through his shirt, cutting into his forearm. Blood burst from the wound and Hacket jumped back, avoiding the twin's large hand as it grabbed for him. The monstrosity was raising itself up, trying to block his path.

Hacket lashed out again, kicking it in the chest this time but the impact had little effect.

Curtis struck at him once more, the blade carving through his shirt at the back this time.

Hacket screamed in pain as he felt the blade scrape his shoulder blade. The wound opened like a mouth, spilling more blood onto the already damp material of his shirt. He fell forward, crashing into a tray of instruments. Scalpels, forceps and syringes were sent skittering across the floor of the cellar and Hacket gripped one of the scalpels, turning to face the twin as it bore down on him.

He struck out wildly but the blow was effective.

The twin shrieked as the razor sharp blade cut through its calf. It staggered for a second, blood pouring from the wound, some of it spattering Hacket, who was now trying to reach the cellar steps.

He dragged himself to his feet and slashed at the twin once more.

Both mouths opened simultaneously to shout their pain as the blade sliced effortlessly through an outstretched hand. The palm was laid open to the bone, the thumb nearly severed.

Hacket edged backwards, Curtis and the twin advancing on him, blood from his own wounds dripping on to the floor. His left arm was beginning to go numb where Curtis had cut him, but he gripped the scalpel in his right hand, glancing from one attacker to the other, waiting for the inevitable rush.

Before it could come he took his chance and turned, running as fast as he could for the stairs.

He had reached the fifth one when the twin caught him.

Hacket felt a huge hand grab his arm, jerking him back but, as he fell he brought the scalpel around, driving it deep into the side of his attacker.

More blood spurted from the wound and onto Hacket, who again struggled free, looking up to see Curtis preparing to strike.

The stiletto blade hurtled down, nicking Hacket's cheek. He felt warm fluid running down his face and knew that the cut was deep. As he sucked in a breath he could feel the cold air hissing through the wound.

Curtis pressed his advantage but Hacket ducked beneath the next swipe, striking upwards, catching the doctor in the thigh, burying the scalpel so deep he felt it scratch against Curtis' femur.

The blade remained embedded, quivering there as Curtis dropped his own knife and tried to pull the scalpel free.

From the amount of blood jetting from the wound he thought for one fearful second that his femoral artery had been severed. For fleeting moments he forgot all about Hacket, intent only on ripping the blade from his leg. It finally came free and Curtis screamed in pain.

Hacket, his throat now filling with blood from his slashed cheek, scrambled up the steps and managed to reach the cellar door. He tore it open and crashed through, feeling sick, his head spinning.

The twin, bleeding from the wound in its side, followed.

Curtis remained at the foot of the steps, using his handkerchief to stem the flow of blood from his thigh.

586

Hacket staggered on through the house, knowing his only hope was to reach his car, to get out of this house, away from this madness.

He blundered through the waiting room and out into the hall.

The twin followed.

Hacket ran for the front door and tugged on it.

It was locked.

He beat frantically against it, as if trying to smash his way free.

The twin reached the hall a second later.

Hacket turned to face it, watching as those two mouths turned upwards simultaneously in a grin of triumph.

'You should have stayed away,' the twin told him, clutching its injured side.

Hacket stood close to the door, the scalpel held before him, his breath coming in gasps, hissing through the savage gash in his right cheek.

As the twin advanced slowly, Hacket glanced to his left and saw another door.

He suddenly turned and bolted for it, crashing through into what, he guessed, was the sitting room.

The twin followed, shouting something after him.

There was a large bay window in the room and Hacket knew what he must do. There was no time for thought, no choice.

He ran towards the window and launched himself at it.

He screamed as he leapt at it, covering his face with his arms, hitting the glass like some kind of human projectile.

The window exploded outwards, huge shards of glass bursting into the cold night air.

Hacket hit the driveway outside with a sickening thump, dazed both by the impact and by the collision against the glass. He was close to unconsciousness, but the cold wind rapidly revived him and restored his senses. He rolled over in time to see the twin clambering through the remains of the window.

Hacket felt for the scalpel but he'd dropped it.

The twin was practically free of the window, ignoring the jagged pieces of glass which scratched it.

Hacket got to his feet and ran for his car, dragging open the door, jamming the key into the ignition.

587

The twin was pulling its bulk clear now, about to drop down onto the driveway.

Hacket twisted the key.

Nothing.

He gripped it harder and turned again.

The engine roared once then faded as his foot slipped off the accelerator.

The twin was lumbering towards him now, blood spilling not only from its hand and side but also from both of the mouths.

Hacket turned the ignition key again, the twin now less than twenty yards from him.

The engine roared into life.

Fifteen yards.

Hacket jammed the car into gear.

Ten yards.

The twin roared in defiance and ran at the car.

The Renault shot forward as if fired from a cannon.

It slammed into the twin, the impact so great that the figure was catapulted into the air, slamming down on the roof of the car before flying off. It crashed to the ground behind the Renault.

Hacket saw it in the rear-view mirror and reversed at top speed.

The second impact knocked the twin flat, the rear wheels running over the huge head.

It seemed to burst under the weight and pressure.

A vile flux of blood and brains exploded from the riven skull, some of the seething mixture flying up around the car as the back wheels spun impotently on the gravel drive for a second, then Hacket jammed the car into first and swung it around, heading for the main road.

Had he looked in the rear-view mirror he would have seen Curtis emerge from the house to see his dead brother then to bellow something after the fleeing car.

As it was, Hacket gripped the wheel as tightly as he could and pressed his foot down on the accelerator.

The car skidded violently as it reached the main road but the teacher kept control of it, guiding it towards Hinkston.

He seemed to forget his pain, even the horror of what he'd just experienced. It was all pushed to the back of his mind.

For now, all he could think of was his wife.

And the monstrosity she might be carrying inside her.

He drove on.

90

12.08 a.m.

Hacket brought the car to a halt outside his house and glanced at the clock on the dashboard.

He swallowed, fighting back the nausea as he tasted blood. As he swung himself out of the car the wound in his back began to throb mightily, an accompaniment to the pain he was feeling from his gashed forearm. But fighting the pain as best he could he hurried to the front door and selected the appropriate key.

The house was silent as he walked in.

No TV.

Not even any lights.

Maybe Sue was in bed, he reasoned.

Hacket made his way up the stairs, his breath coming in gasps.

Half way up he called her name.

No answer.

As he reached the landing he stood against one wall, feeling a wave of pain wash over him, and for a second he thought he was going to faint; but the feeling passed and he moved into the bedroom, calling her name again.

The room was empty.

Hacket didn't even bother checking the other rooms, he hurried back downstairs, slapping on lights as he went, calling her name once again.

It was in the hallway he saw the blood.

There was more on the kitchen door.

He pushed it open.

The back door was open, banging gently against the frame as each fresh gust of wind blew it. The table and two of the chairs had been overturned. The room was a wreck.

He whispered her name under his breath, his eyes finally alighting on the piece of paper propped up on the draining board beside the sink.

He strode across and snatched it up, examining the large, almost child-like, letters. As he read the words he felt his body beginning to quiver.

COME TO THE SCOOL

COME AND GET YOUR

FUCKING WIFE

91

Why hadn't the alarm gone off?

It was a curious thought, but one which nevertheless occurred to Hacket as he paused by the main door of the school, peering through the glass into the gloom beyond.

He could see smashed glass inside where his wife's kidnapper had broken in, but the alarm obviously hadn't gone off. He must have disabled it first, the teacher reasoned, pushing the door tentatively, wincing as it creaked slightly on its hinges. He slipped inside and stood in the entryway, ears alert for the slightest movement. The silence was chokingly oppressive. Like the darkness through which he moved, the solitude seemed almost palpable, holding him back from his quest.

Sue was in the building somewhere, along with the man who had abducted her. At least Hacket assumed it was a man. Just who it could be he didn't know. All he wanted to know was that she was alive. The questions could come later.

He gripped the carving knife he'd taken from the kitchen and made his way down the corridor to his left, peering into each darkened classroom in turn.

There was no sign of her.

He paused for a moment, aware of the burning pain coming from his wounds. But then he pressed on, checking the next corridor.

It was also empty.

Sandwiched between the two was the library.

Hacket pushed open one door and stepped inside, glancing around, squinting through the blackness.

He passed through the library quietly, as if preserving the usual reverence for a room normally silent. There was no sign of Sue in there either.

He wandered back up the corridor towards the dining room.

As he wandered around it the questions began to fill his mind.

Why had she been taken?

When?

By whom?

For what purpose?

Hacket leant against a door frame and sucked in a weary breath. There were so many questions. His head was spinning.

Was she still alive?

Was the child still alive? . . .

The child . . .

He shuddered as he thought about it, about what had happened at Curtis' house.

A noise from above him interrupted the whirlwind of questions spinning around in his head.

He pushed open the double doors which led through into the assembly hall. Hacket hurried across the varnished floor towards another set of double doors.

Beyond these were the stairs that led up to the first floor of the school.

He heard the sound again and slowed his pace, gripping the carving knife more tightly.

Hacket ascended slowly, eyes fixed ahead of him. He stumbled as he reached the half-way point, cursing when pain from the wound in his forearm shot through him. He turned a corner, trying to control his harsh breathing and the thudding of his heart.

He reached the top of the stairs and pushed the next set of double doors.

Four rooms faced him.

He checked them one by one.

Through the window in the door of the third room he saw Sue.

She was naked, tied to a chair, a gag stuffed unceremoniously into her mouth.

Hacket tried the door and, to his delight found it was unlocked.

He blundered in, tears filling his eyes.

She looked up and saw him but the look was not one of relief but one of horror.

Her eyes bulged and she shook her head.

'It's all right,' he whispered as he crossed to her.

She continued to shake her head, nodding towards him.

Towards him?

Her eyes were not on him but on something behind him.

As he reached for the gag he heard a metallic click.

The sound of a hammer being thumbed back.

'I've been waiting.'

Hacket spun round as he heard the voice.

'Drop the fucking knife.'

Hacket obeyed, watching as Ronald Mills stepped from the shadows, the .38 aimed at the teacher's head.

92

'Get over there,' Mills snapped, motioning to the desk opposite Sue.

Hacket did as he was told, his eyes on the large man who held the pistol on him.

Sue moaned beneath the gag as another particularly powerful stab of pain lanced through her.

'Who are you?' Hacket wanted to know, watching as Mills moved towards Sue.

The big man removed her gag, pulling it free roughly.

'Tell him who I am,' he snapped, the gun still aimed at Hacket.

Sue hesitated, her words choked away by sobs.

'Tell him,' rasped Mills, pulling her hair.

'You bastard,' snapped Hacket and took a step forward but Mills levelled the pistol at arms length, drawing a bead on a point between the teacher's eyes.

'Tell him who I am,' Mills repeated. 'Tell him what I did.'

'He killed Lisa,' Sue sobbed, tears running down her cheeks.

'Oh Christ,' murmured Hacket, his voice low.

'Does the name Peter Walton ring a bell?' Mills said. Hacket didn't, couldn't answer.

'I'm talking to you, cunt,' Mills snarled. 'Peter Walton. Do you remember him? What happened to him?'

Hacket exhaled deeply, the feelings of frustration, helplessness and fear filling him in equal proportions.

'He was killed. Fell under a train,' Hacket whispered.

'No. You murdered him. I saw you. I saw you chasing him. Saw you push him.'

'He slipped. I didn't touch him.'

'You wanted to.'

'Fucking right,' snarled Hacket. 'And if I could I'd have put you under that fucking train with him, you animal.'

Mills tugged hard on Sue's hair, the gun still aimed at Hacket.

'You better shut your fucking mouth, Hacket,' he rasped.

'What are you trying to do to us? It's me you want. Let my wife go.'

'Fuck you. If she suffers, *you* suffer. You'll get your turn, don't worry but I want you to see *her* die first. Just like I had to watch you kill Walton. He was the only friend I ever had. The only person I ever trusted or cared about. Who cared about *me*.' He shouted the last sentence. 'And you murdered him.'

'The police will come,' Hacket said, desperate for any idea which might save them. 'You'll be caught, perhaps even killed.'

'What do *I* care? At least you'll have died before me.'

'Just tell me one thing,' Hacket said. 'Why did you kill Lisa?'

'She was there. If it hadn't been her it would have been another girl. We broke in to rob you. Finding her was just a bonus.' He grinned broadly and, with his free hand, began unfastening his trousers. 'Now you watch me, Hacket.'

She looked imploringly at her husband, realising that he was as helpless as she to stop this madman. If he rushed Mills then he would either shoot Sue or the teacher himself. There was a chance he might just wound Hacket but, from such close range, Sue was as good as dead. Hacket could do nothing but watch as the big man tugged the rope from Sue's legs. He saw the red welts where the hemp had cut into her flesh.

'Open your legs,' Mills told her, unfastening his trousers to reveal a large erection.

Hacket understood.

'She's pregnant for God's sake,' he yelled.

'Shut up, fucker,' roared Mills, moving towards Sue. He grabbed her ankles and pulled her forward. He had to bend at the knees to manoeuvre his penis towards her vagina, all the time keeping the gun pointed at Hacket, who sucked in a painful breath.

Sue screamed as Mills drove into her, his shaft penetrating her deeply.

He began to thrust back and forth.

Sue felt him inside her and she sobbed helplessly, looking at the moon face before her but then she felt more contractions, a movement deep within her belly. Movement which seemed to transfer itself to her vagina.

Hacket looked on helplessly, clenching his fists until the muscles ached.

Dear God, just for one second . . .

Just one clear run at Mills.

Sue moaned aloud.

'I think she's enjoying it,' said Mills, still thrusting hard into her. He grinned again but the smile suddenly dissolved into a look of surprise.

Hacket looked more closely at him.

No, not surprise.

It was pain.

Mills thrust deeply once or twice more then tried to pull away.

But he couldn't.

Pain began to grow around his penis, spreading across his groin.

Sue had stopped crying.

She was smiling now as she watched the pain on the rapist's face.

He tried again to pull away and this time he screamed in agony.

His penis felt as if it were being squeezed inside her vagina. As if her inner muscles were contracting, closing like a fleshy vice. But the pain was sharper than that.

Mills pushed against Sue as the pain grew more intense.

Hacket looked on, mesmerised.

Sue merely continued to smile.

Mills shrieked uncontrollably as he felt the grip inside her vagina increase. As if he was being held by small hands.

The hands of a baby.

He felt pain unlike anything he'd ever experienced. An excruciating agony which almost caused him to faint.

Blood began to pump from Sue's vagina but it was not *her* blood. Mills was frantic now, desperate to be away from her, from that grip which was mutilating him. His knees buckled and he began to fall.

He fell backwards.

The scream which he uttered was like nothing Hacket had ever heard before. A bellow of absolute suffering torn from the depths of his soul.

As Mills fell onto his back Hacket could see that where the big man's penis had once been there was now only a spurting stump of shredded flesh. The big man put his hands into the wound as if trying to stem the flow of blood and recover his mutilated manhood.

He screamed and screamed, the sound echoing around the classroom, drumming inside Hacket's head as blood spurted from the savage wound. The teacher felt his own vomit clawing its way up from his stomach as he staggered towards his wife, stepping past the writhing shape of Mills but, as he drew closer, Hacket saw the final act of horror and, this time, he could not control himself.

The lips of Sue's vagina slid open and the torn off shaft of Mills' penis was pushed out to drop onto the floor amidst the puddle of blood which had formed there. Like a child spitting out a distasteful piece of food, the vaginal opening yawned wide to expel the remnants of Mills' manhood.

Hacket swayed then turned to one side and vomited until there was nothing left in his stomach.

Sue continued to smile, gazing down at Mills who was still screaming, his yells becoming fainter as the loss of blood gradually sapped his strength and his life gushed away through his fingers.

Hacket freed her, wrapping her in his shirt which he hurriedly pulled off.

Bloodied and dazed they stumbled past Mills.

'We have to get the police,' Hacket gasped, wiping his mouth with the back of his hand.

Mills' screams had degenerated into low burblings as they staggered out of the room.

Hacket didn't know how long it took a man to bleed to death.

They supported each other down the stairs and out of the school, heading back towards their house, sucking in the cold night air, as if wishing it could wash away the stench of blood and death from their nostrils.

Hacket shivered but he realised that it was not all a product of the cold wind.

Sue, bloodied and barely conscious, looked at him and smiled.

Hacket felt the hairs at the back of his neck rise.

They reached the house and blundered through the back door, Hacket slamming it behind them. Then they struggled through into the sitting room, the teacher slapping on lights as they went.

He froze.

Sitting in one of the armchairs, the stiletto blade held in his hand, was Doctor Edward Curtis.

596

93

For long seconds Hacket couldn't speak, his eyes remained fixed on Curtis.

'My brother is dead, as you may have guessed,' the doctor finally said, his face emotionless.

'It has to end, Curtis,' Hacket said, leaning against the door frame to support himself.

'I agree with you,' the doctor echoed, rising to his feet, the knife held before him.

Sue looked first at her husband then at Curtis.

Then she felt the pain. So powerful she yelled in response to it.

'You've done this to her,' Hacket screamed. 'God knows what she's carrying. Something like your . . . brother? Help her. Abort the baby. Now.'

'No,' Sue moaned, her face twisted into a mask of pain. 'Don't let it die.' She looked imploringly at Curtis. 'Please.'

'Kill it, Curtis,' Hacket snarled. 'It's unnatural.'

Curtis took a step towards Sue, dropping the knife on the sofa.

'I need it,' she said. 'Help it live.' She gripped Curtis' hand and pulled him closer to her.

Hacket stepped forward, pushing the doctor away, slamming him up against the wall, hands clasped around his throat. There was a look of hatred in his eyes. Hatred and something else.

Madness perhaps?

Curtis struggled against Hacket's grip, supported by his hands but dying because of them. His head felt as if it were beginning to swell, and he was fighting for his breath as Hacket dug his thumbs deeper into the doctor's windpipe, lifting him off his feet with the ferocity of his attack.

'You've done this to her,' snarled Hacket, exerting yet more strength on Curtis' throat. 'I'll kill you.' He bellowed the words into the other man's face.

Hacket felt the pain in his lower back first.

Like a punch in the kidneys.

Then it came again. Harder this time and he felt the coldness now. The third time he realised.

Sue drove the stiletto blade into his back, severing his spinal cord.

He lost his grip on Curtis then dropped to his knees.

As he did she brought the knife down again.

This time it powered into his neck, severing the carotid artery. A huge fountain of blood erupted from the wound, spattering Sue and spraying the wall of the sitting room crimson as surely as if it had been splashed with red paint. Hacket turned and looked at her, tears in his eyes, then he fell forward, his body jerking slightly.

Blood filled his mouth and he blinked hard as his vision began to cloud both with pain and tears.

How long would it take a man to bleed to death?

He would have the answer soon.

Curtis looked down at him, massaging his throat, scarcely able to speak.

Sue continued to sob, the knife still in her hands, crimson dripping from its point like thick teardrops.

'Why did you want to kill it, John?' she sobbed. 'Why?'

Hacket tried to speak but the only sound he could make was a liquid gurgle. Blood spilled over his lips, he felt it run from his nostrils. He reached out towards her, wanting to touch her hand, knowing he was dying. Along with the pain there was fear too.

'The child will live, Hacket,' Curtis said, rubbing his bruised throat.

'My child,' Hacket gurgled, but the effort of speaking only brought fresh pain and a massive heaving within his body. He began to shiver.

Curtis smiled down at him.

'No,' he said softly. 'Not *your* child. *My brother's.*'

Even through her tears Sue was smiling too.

John Hacket closed his eyes.

Some wounds never heal. Some pain is never soothed.

Anon

Hatred shouldn't be forgotten. It should be nurtured.
And self-hatred is the bloom which responds best.

Anon

I have looked into the mirror of madness and seen my own reflection . . .

May 16, 1988

TWISTED SOULS

Shaun Hutson

Imagine your worst fear. A fear that eats away at you – a fear of death, of illness, of needles, of fire. Even of feelings themselves.

In London, Emma Tate's life is collapsing around her: her job is in jeopardy, her parents have been killed in a crash that she blamed herself for and her husband's business is failing.

Seeking some kind of respite, Emma, her husband and two of their friends hope to find some temporary peace in a country house. But Roxton is a place of strange secrets. What was the reason for the closure of the mine that had been the life-blood of the town? What riddles are hidden in the stained glass of the church? What mysterious force is at large?

Emma's desire to uncover these secrets will lead her and her companions into a nightmare from which there will be no waking and to a meeting with their own most twisted and vile desires . . .

DYING WORDS

Shaun Hutson

Can it be true that God demands a terrible price of those He has gifted with great creativity? Giacomo Cassano, little known mentor of Dante, thought so. He held other beliefs too – beliefs that the Church found so abhorrent they had him blinded and his tongue cut out to silence his blasphemy forever.

Bestselling biographer Megan Hunter's new book about Cassano looks set to be as successful as her previous biographies of Caravaggio and Dante. But as she embarks on a publicity tour, Megan finds her book attracting attention for the wrong reasons when her editor is found horrifically murdered. It is a classic locked-room mystery. The only evidence is the destroyed remains of Megan Hunter's Cassano biography and the latest blockbuster by John Paxton. But there is nothing to link the two authors. Nothing but another murder. And another.

And a secret beyond the belief of even Cassano himself …